An
Albert
Payson
Terhune
Reader

Volume II

The stories in this collection are works of fiction. All names, characters, places and scenes described herein are the results of the author's imagination and genius. Any resemblance to actual persons, living or dead, is purely coincidental. And a good part wishful thinking.

These stories were published at a time when political correctness had not yet caused serious cultural and moral decay. Certain ideas, terms and social conventions found herein are no longer considered acceptable (some for rational reasons, others not). A mentally healthy reader (the kind for whom this book was lovingly compiled) will understand that, and not give the matter further thought.

The text in this book is version 1.0. Anyone finding errors, please send them to the e-mail below. You will be aknowledged (anonymously or by name, as you wish) in a subsequent version.

An Albert Payson Terhune Reader Volume II
ISBN: 978-1-945307-07-2

Book compilation and design by Rodney Schroeter.

The Silver Creek Press
PO Box 334
Random Lake WI 53075-0334

rschroeter@silentreels.com

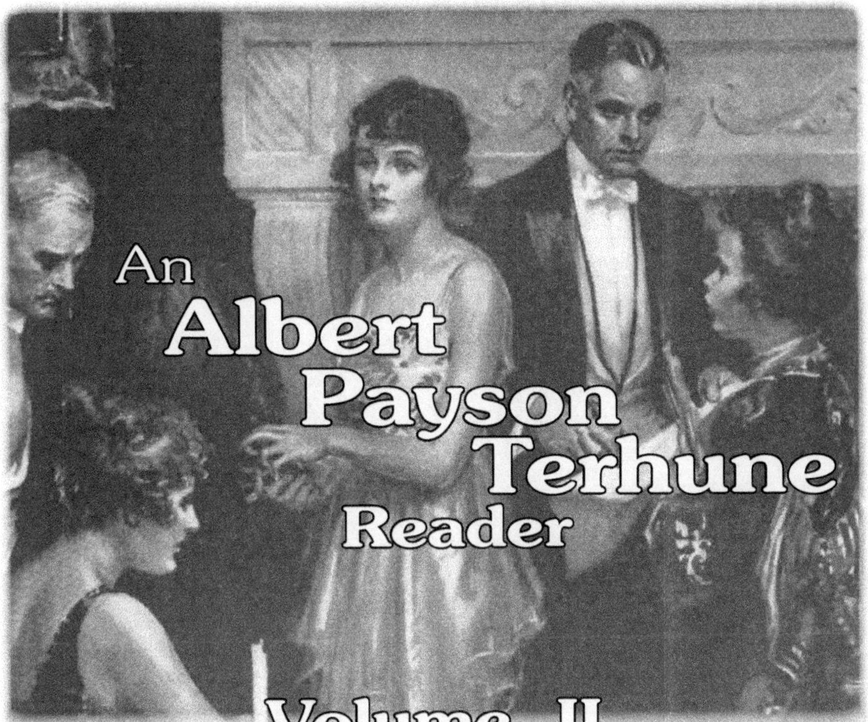

An Albert Payson Terhune Reader

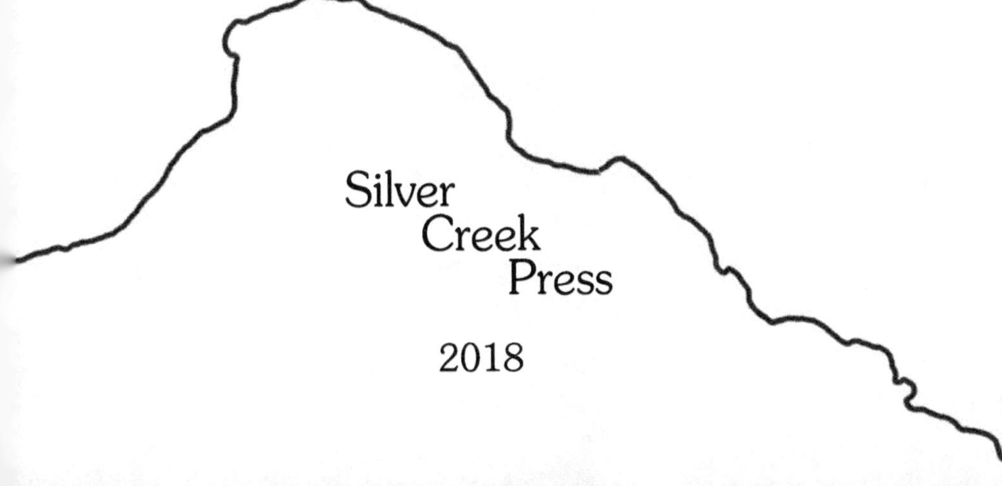

Volume II

With the original illustrations from the source publications

Compiled by Rodney Schroeter
Introduction by Anthony Tollin

Silver
Creek
Press

2018

Table

of

Contents

Albert Payson Terhune as a young man
Photo courtesy of Sanctum Archives.

Albert Payson Terhune—
More Than Just "The *Dog* Man"

By Anthony Tollin

More than seventy-five years after his passing, Albert Payson Terhune remains *the* brand name in canine fiction. The popularity of Terhune's dog stories changed America's perception of their loyal companions and encouraged our modern obsession with man's best friend.

Terhune's best-remembered book, *Lad: a Dog,* has never been out of print in the century since it was first published in April 1919. Debuting at a time when dog stories were anathema to book publishers, the book re-established the sub-genre and forever branded its author as "the *dog* man."

Terhune strongly resented that typecasting, and how interviewers invariably only wanted to question him about his dog stories. "Terhune the *dog* man!" he bellowed. "Every time I am introduced to someone my introducer invariably says—'You know, Terhune the *dog* man!' I'll bet if I could prove I wrote the 23rd Psalm, I should still be known as Terhune the *dog* man!" His wife Anice gently interjected, "Probably the *shepherd* dog man."

Albert Payson Terhune had good reason to feel pigeonholed. He'd been a successful writer for nearly two decades before he wrote the first of his famous Lad tales. His debut book, *Syria from the Saddle,* had been published in 1896 (chronicling a trip through the Holy Land that also provided the background for "The 'Tip' of the Rocket" in *Adventure).* The busy wordsmith averaged between $12,000 and $30,000 annually between 1910 and 1916 (when he wrote the first of his classic canine stories). The unprecedented popularity of his dog stories would soon boost his magazine compensation from $200 to $2,000 and even $2,500 per story, and his annual income to $90,000.

During the Golden Age of Magazines, Terhune appeared in most of the major fiction periodicals, including *The Saturday Evening Post, Argosy, All-Story Magazine, The Cavalier, Cosmopolitan, Red Book* and *Blue Book.* His stories were regularly accompanied by art from America's top illustrators, including Dean Cornwell, Robert Graef, William Oberhardt, Harvey Dunn, Paul Bransom, J. Allen St. John, and even cartoonist Fontaine Fox. Many of these illustrations are reprinted for the first time here (and in our companion books, *An Albert Payson Terhune Reader,* Volumes I and III*).*

Terhune maintained a busy freelance career throughout his 21 years as a newsman and editor at Joseph Pulitzer's *New York World,* and his journalism work provided the background for "The Beat that Failed," his 1900 story for *Lippincott's Magazine,* and its 1914 reworking as "An Inside Scoop" for Street & Smith's *Popular Magazine.* Aware that Terhune had fought as a boxer during his college years, the *Evening World's* sports editor assigned Bert to go three rounds each against six of the sport's greatest fighters, including Bob Fitzsimmons, Jim Jeffries, Kid McCoy and former heavyweight champion Jim Corbett (who proclaimed Terhune "the best amateur boxer in the country"). Terhune's experiences in the ring provided the background for numerous boxing tales, including his 1919 *Saturday Evening Post* story, "The Laugh."

Many of this book's stories are set in the world of high society, a community that Albert Payson Terhune was familiar with and welcome in. His family had been prominent since colonial days, and his great-grandfather, Lieutenant Abraham Terhune, had served as General George Washington's bodyguard during the Revolutionary War (and is prominently featured in Emanuel Leutze's famous painting, "Washington Crossing the Delaware"). Bert's wife Anice also possessed an impressive pedigree that included the prominent Morris and Stockton families, including Richard Stockton, a signer of the Declaration of Independence. Bert and Anice's lavish parties and extravagant Manhattan lifestyle mandated that he maintain a lucrative freelance writing career in addition to his newspaper job.

Bert had grown up in fashionable society. His father was a noted clergyman, while his mother, under her "Marion Harland" pen name, was one of America's best-selling authors. At their Sunnybank summer home, the Terhunes regularly hobnobbed with such famous guests as author Louisa May Alcott, poets James Russell Lowell and Bayard Taylor, newspaper publisher Horace Greeley, actors Edwin

Booth and Lawrence Barrett, generals Ulysses S. Grant and Philip Henry Sheridan and statesmen James G. Blaine and Ezra Cornell.

As a member of the Adventurers Club and the Explorers Club, Terhune regularly socialized with Theodore Roosevelt, Rough Riders commander Leonard Wood and famous explorers such as Vilhjalmur Stefansson. Bert also belonged to the Players Club and the Lambs theatrical organizations, along with his childhood friends, Hollywood producer Cecil B. De Mille and playwright William De Mille.

In the latter years of the 19th century, tattoos became a fad among members of European aristocracy and London and New York high society, with celebrities including Winston Churchill's mother, American actress Jennie Jerome, acquiring discrete permanent artwork. In 1897, the *New York World* claimed that 75 percent of America's high society women sported tattoos, and the fad continued into the suffragette era. It's likely that the newspaper article (and others like it in subsequent decades) inspired the high society tattooing party chronicled in Terhune's 1919 *Cosmopolitan* story, "Branded."

Working in a variety of genres, Terhune wrote suspenseful tales such as "She and the Monster" for Munsey's *Argosy* and crime tales including "The Watcher in the Hall" and "The Montclair Flurry" for Street & Smith's *Top Notch,* along with "When Man Meets Man," a manhunt tale featuring the Royal Canadian Mounted Police. The busy author also occasionally indulged in sympathetic social commentary in stories like "The Girl Who Couldn't Go Wrong" for *Smart Set* and "The Welcher" in *Blue Book.*

Terhune formed a close professional relationship with Ray Long, the editor of the Chicago-based *Red Book, Blue Book* and *Green Book* magazines, writing romantic misadventures including "The Tale of the Taxi-Meter," "The Man Who Went Wrong," "The Greater Radiance" and theatrical tales like "The Songbird." Long would invite Bert to write the first of his famous Lad tales in 1915, and continued to purchase Terhune's fiction and articles after Long became America's top-paid editor when he was recruited by William Randolph Hearst to oversee the Hearst Magazines, where he edited *Cosmopolitan, Harper's Bazaar, Good Housekeeping* and many other popular periodicals.

As the son of bestselling author "Marion Harland" (a.k.a. Mary Hawes Terhune), Bert was well aware of the talents and abilities of womankind, and documented their groundbreaking achievements in his books *Superwomen* (1916) and *Wonder Women in History* (1918). His stories for *Green Book* such as "Pretty Baby" and "The Dented Halo" showcase women challenging society's expectations, pushing boundaries to establish careers and new lives in the big city.

Strange as it may seem, Albert Payson Terhune occasionally reworked popular themes from his earlier sentimental tear-jerkers in his famous dog stories. Several of the tales in this collection involve infidelity and the resulting emotional pain of the rejected party. Sunnybank Lad was placed in a similar position in his debut story "His Mate" when his beloved Lady rejects her lovesick canine beau for an elegant visiting show collie. A Canadian Mountie's struggles against a harsh environment in "When Man Meets Man" parallel Lad's epic attempt to return to his Sunnybank home in "Lost," while "The Day of Battle," perhaps Terhune's finest dog story, benefits from Bert's earlier experience writing boxing stories and pounding out action-packed pulp thrillers for *Argosy, All-Story Magazine, Popular Magazine* and *Top Notch.*

Albert Payson Terhune's tales featuring his beloved Sunnybank collies Lad, Wolf, Bruce, Treve and Gray Dawn propelled him to his greatest fame and made him a national institution, but the 27 previously uncollected stories in this volume demonstrate that the author was always far more than just "the *dog* man."

Anthony Tollin co-authored The Shadow Scrapbook *with Walter B. Gibson, who wrote most of the original Shadow novels. He is the editor-publisher of Sanctum Books' trade paperback reprints of the classic Doc Savage and The Shadow pulp novels. The longtime DC Comics professional and popular culture historian collaborated on books, recordings or broadcasts with Walter Cronkite and humorists Stan Freberg and Bob Hope. As a breeder and trainer of champion dachshunds, Tollin regularly exercised his dogs at the Terhune Sunnybank Memorial Park (formerly Terhune's Sunnybank estate). A lifelong canine enthusiast, he owns a significant portion of Albert Payson Terhune's personal dog reference library and professional research archives.*

A mustached Albert Payson Terhune (second from right)
in the *New York Evening World* newsroom, early in his journalism career.

Terhune works on a magazine story.
Note the copy of *Blue Book,* of which only the spine is visible.

The Beat that Failed

The "Rocky Mountain Show and Parliament of Rough Riders"—
or rather a delegation therefrom—were coming to be photographed
for the "Sunday Planet."

That, of course, was no concern of the evening edition of the
"Planet" nor of its staff, the Sunday and evening departments being
eight floors apart and under separate management.

Still, when Robbie Kennedy, the diminutive head office-boy of
the "evening," announced in a shrill treble that the hall leading to the
tower elevator was "chuck full of heathens," a general exodus towards
the aforesaid hall-way followed his inspiring words.

The few members of the staff who did not join in the rush had
the best of all reasons for remaining: the paper was to go to press in
twenty-five minutes, and the biggest "story" of the month had just
come in.

The City Editor and the Managing Editor were consulting as to
another end of the story; a copy-reader was building a spread head,
counting up the letters thereof on his fingers; and a hot, dusty reporter,
who had not stopped to remove hat or overcoat, was turning out copy
at a rate of two pages a minute.

A boy snatched up each scribbled sheet ere the writer could howl
"Copy!" and rushed it over to the copy-reader, who paused long enough
in his task of counting letters for a "head" to glance at it, make a dash
here and there with a blue pencil, and give it to another boy, who shot
it upstairs through a wheezy pneumatic tube to the composing-room.

A second reporter was writing, with scarcely less haste, the history
of the case whereof this particular story was the climax. He stopped
from time to time to drive into a pile of "obituary" envelopes at his
side.

The work went on to an accompaniment of telephone bells, whirring tickers, and clicking telegraph instruments. Not that any one noted this Babel.

The Managing Editor glanced at the clock.

"We'll beat the town on this," he said. "We ought to get on the street ten minutes ahead of the 'Globe.'"

The City Editor puffed away at his cigar, but said nothing. He seldom wasted words.

"The story's all up," called the copy-reader.

Then he went out to look at the "Parliament of Rough Riders" in the hall.

Meanwhile the youthful reporter whom the Sunday Editor had detailed to show the Rough Riders over the building had piloted the entire half-hundred to the composing-room. There the copy-reader found them.

Amid the forest of tracks, linotype machines, type-setting apparatus, and sweating compositors stood the conglomerate mass of visitors.

In one group were ten Cossacks,—thin, wiry little bronzed men with long beards and bad eyes, clad in saffron tunics and gray caps. In another alley of machines were a galaxy of German Uhlans, cuirassiers, Irish lancers, collarless and unkempt cow-boys, a stray alleged Arab or so, and Orapezo, the great Mexican lasso expert.

Compositors, office-boys, and loungers paid the passing tribute of a glance to this kaleidoscope of nations, but kept their widest stares and weirdest comments for a larger, more fantastic throng that stood, distrustfully, near the elevator shaft.

This last group consisted of some twenty Indians boasting various degrees of ugliness. Their high feather war-bonnets loomed up above the composing-room machinery; their profusely illustrated faces peered from behind valve and bar.

Coldly incurious, their eyes swept the unfamiliar scene; with a mask of profound indifference, they listened to the half-breed interpreter's translated explanation of the way a paper was printed.

Robbie Kennedy and his fellow office-boys (regardless of the fact that howls of "Copy!" were wafted up from the city-room) stood gazing in open-mouthed awe at the savages.

"I bet that big feller—the one next to Dutch soldier with the tin bonnet—is a Terror of the Plains," commented Robbie.

"He ain't, either," contradicted an associate runner of copy. "See? He's only got half as many feathers as the Injun behind him."

"What's that got to do with it?" sneered Robbie. "A lot you know about it!"

"I do so know," retorted the other, who had a splendid fund of ignorance on the subject of Dagoes in general and Indians in particular, "they grow ten new feathers for every man they kill—slay, I mean."

"Get onto the kid that biggest one's got with him," interposed Robbie, unable to combat this point in natural history.

The "kid" in question was an amber-colored pappoose, perhaps two feet high. She was Utsayantha, only daughter of the Sioux war-chief, Howling Wolf.

This baby, alone of all the troupe of Indians, gazed with keen delight at the sea of strange faces and the funny black machines. From time to time a fear lest these machines were of the biting variety would take possession of her, and she grasped with both arms her warlike sire's beaded buckskin knee.

"Oh, how pretty! Look! She's the first Indian child I ever saw!"

A slender, girlish figure appeared among the crowd, who cheerfully made way for her as she knelt beside the little yellow savage.

The girl was Kate Westervelt, youngest and prettiest of women-reporters.

"Won't you come to me?" she asked pleadingly of the solemn-eyed Utsayantha.

The baby did not, of course, understand a word; but with outstretched hands and a gleeful little squeal she ran into Miss Westervelt's arms.

"Are you her father?" asked the girl of the lordly Chief.

Howling Wolf deigned no reply, principally because he could not understand; but he strongly disapproved of any white squaw handling his beloved first-born.

"Can't I take her down to my desk?" went on Miss Westervelt. "I've some candy down there that she can have, and I want to show her to the Managing Editor. Maybe there's a special story in it."

The half-breed interpreter overheard the girl's words, and thinking to conciliate a paper that owned so many inexplicable machines, he interposed:

"Sure, miss. He's ignorant, old Howlin' Wolf is. He don't understand. Take the pappoose down with you if you like. I'll explain to its father."

With a word of thanks Miss Westervelt, carrying the baby in her arms, made for the winding stairs that led down to the city-room.

Howling Wolf, with a throaty sound like the growl of an angry dog, took a step to stop her. The interpreter checked him, and in a few words explained that the child was safe and that Howling Wolf must not interfere.

The father, a pethetic look of doubting misery in his stolid face, stood still, gazing into the crowd at the spot where he had seen Utsayantha disappear.

Downstairs in the city-room Miss Westervelt was proudly exhibiting her capture to a ring of office friends.

The baby, enthroned on the girl's roll-top desk, sat delightedly sucking away at a bonbon and sturdily refusing to speak a language she had never before heard.

Miss Westervelt, in her anxiety for the special story, naturally forgot there might be a time limit to her little guest's visit.

In the composing-room a scarlet-haired "Make-up Editor" was fuming and swearing at the "gang of freaks that blew in there at the busiest time of the day and distracted everybody's attention."

A few remarks of this sort led the reporter-escort to hint to his charges that they would better clear out.

Accordingly, they filed into the great elevator, the Cossacks going on the first down trip, the Indians last.

As the elevator came up for the noble red men, the interpreter gave an order, and the feathered, hand-painted savages filed timidly into the car.

No one noticed that they were one man short; none heeded a single tall, forbidding figure that stood statue-like against a stereotyping-machine, waiting in vain for his missing child.

What was in Howling Wolf's heart as the last of his fellow-countrymen entered the car and sank out of sight, leaving him alone among a swarm of wretched pale-faces, no one can tell.

What he looked was another matter.

His usually wooden face was an open book. The first word expressed on it was Trouble; then Grief; and, last of all, Fury.

"What's the old jay waitin' for?" asked a compositor.

No one knew. Such as remembered the pappoose's abduction fancied the child was with the rest of the troupe, and had no idea she belonged to this increasingly angry Chief.

"Now then," said the Make-up Editor briskly, "run along with your tribe. We're busy up here, and you're only in the way."

Howling Wolf looked stolidly down on the man and remarked,—

"Utsayantha!"

"I don't understand your lingo," retorted the irate Editor, "and I want you to get out."

"Utsayantha!" repeated the Chief, this time in a deeper voice.

"Yes, yes, I daresay it's all true, only I don't understand. Clear out, or I'll send for a policeman."

It began to dawn on Howling Wolf that perhaps he had not made the case sufficiently clear to this excitable person. So he began to explain the situation, speaking with studied self-control and in excellent Sioux dialect.

"Talks like a dinner-bell, don't he?" commented Robbie Kennedy in admiring awe.

"He's givin' us an oration. Maybe tellin' how many men he's slewn," added the office-boy who had advanced the theory concerning feathers.

A grin from the compositors and loungers followed this speculation.

This was too much for Howling Wolf. Not content with stealing his precious child (perhaps roasting her alive), they were actually laughing at her stricken father.

Striding forward, and thrusting the crowd contemptuously from his path, the Chief passed through the alleys of machinery, tables, and cases, his keen eye looking everywhere for the hiding-place of his daughter.

Coming at length into an open space, he halted.

He had stopped beside an oddly shaped table, topped by carved metal.

There was that in his look and manner which made two men who were busy at the table move quickly out of reach.

The Make-up Editor set up a yell and rushed towards the post they deserted.

This structure—probably an altar to the demons who inhabited the great black machines—was evidently a sacred spot among the pale-faces; and here Howling Wolf made his stand.

In an instant he was surrounded by a mob of excited shirt-sleeved men.

The "table" against which he was leaning happened to be a "truck," and on that truck lay a page-form just locked. The two men scared away by the Indian had been about to remove the form to the stereo-typer's heating-table, whence it was to go downstairs to the press-room, there to serve for the printing of a page of the waiting edition.

The paper was due on the street in fifteen minutes, and that particular page-form chanced to bear in double-leaded type under a "scare" double-column head the story which, according to the Managing Editor's prophecy, was to "beat the town."

Hence the horror of all concerned when this decidedly belligerent savage took up his stand before the truck bearing that form.

"What are you men waiting for?" shouted the Make-up Editor. "Hustle that form over to the heating-table, or we'll delay the edition. That Indian can't hurt you."

Now the "Planet" boasts the best lot of compositors in New York, yet just then none of them seemed anxious to obey orders.

Howling Wolf glanced rapidly about him. He saw the consternation caused by his presence at that truck and resolved to stay there. He even had a lingering idea of carrying it away as hostage for his lost child.

A plan occurred to him:

Why not offer to give up possession of this mysterious table on condition that the pale-faces restore the child?

He made the offer in his most persuasive Sioux dialect.

"Rush him, boys!" ordered the foreman; and the men gathered for the onslaught.

Now, though Howling Wolf's knowledge of English was less than limited, his knowledge of fighting left little to be desired.

He had crouched in the rank grass at Sitting Bull's side, twenty years before, when a certain long-haired notoriety-seeking General had ridden to his death beyond the woods of Little Big Horn. It was Howling Wolf who had counselled Sitting Bull to the strategic trick which emptied so many government saddles that summer day in 1876; and he had, with his own hand, struck down the foremost United States cavalryman.

After such a record, why should he fear a gang of unarmed men of peace?

His quick eye noted the gathering rush; and a second later the advancing compositors found themselves looking into the muzzles of two Smith & Wesson revolvers.

These were the weapons which Howling Wolf and his fellow-Indians discharged daily at the old-fashioned stage-coach in the "Attack on the Overland Stage."

This attack was a "star" feature of the Rough Riders' Show. For the purpose each Indian wore at his belt two revolvers. They were, of course, loaded with blank-cartridges, and Howling Wolf knew it.

He had the best reason in the world for this knowledge; for had he not, when first engaged by the Show, attempted one day, in a drink-inspired moment of playfulness, to murder Red Cloud, a brother chief, with these same weapons? Had he not fired fourteen shots at that worthy savage before finding that the cartridges were harmless? Had he not been the laughing-stock of the whole tribe in consequence of his silly failure?

But he doubted whether these new pale-face foes had the same knowledge concerning the revolvers.

When a man is looking into one end of a pistol and an enraged Indian is manipulating the other end, he seldom stops to conjecture whether the weapon is loaded with blanks or ball.

Hence the compositors recoiled in a heap.

The Make-up Editor did a war-dance before them, to the Chief's secret admiration.

"The paper ought to be on the street in five minutes!" screamed the Editor. "The 'Globe' 'll beat us out of our boots. It was the biggest story we've had this year, too; and the 'Globe' 'll have it all in this edition. Here!"—hauling out of his pocket a wad of bills—"here! you dissolute old heathen, help yourself to these and let us get at that form!"

As he spoke, he advanced on the Chief.

Bang!

One of Howling Wolf's 44-calibre pistols had spoken, and the echoes reverberated through the great, low-ceiled room.

The pistol was fired point-blank. It sent the Make-up Editor reeling back, his red beard and eyebrows singed, and his lungs choked with powder-smoke.

"I'm hit," moaned the Editor, and collapsed.

This was the signal for a general break.

One man started for the police, but decided to climb up behind a linotype machine instead. The rest sought any shelter that came to hand and held a council of war.

Lurid messages and queries as to the cause of delay floated up through the tube from the press-room, where all was at a stand-still pending the arrival of the missing page.

"Rush him from behind!"

"Get a policeman!"

"Throw a lead cut at him!"

Thus advised a score of voices, whose owners were modestly concealed behind trucks or machines.

Robbie Kennedy had a strong impulse to step forward and harangue the Chief, like the hero of Wild West dime novels. He had even framed a speech beginning, "Hail to our wigwam, dusky brother," when a glance from the Chief again sent his canary-colored head ducking behind the truck.

A new figure appeared on the scene. It was the Managing Editor. In one hand he clutched a copy of the "Globe." Its first page bore the great story with which the "Planet" had hoped to beat the town.

"Mr. Halpin!" thundered the Managing Editor to his make-up associate. "Why have we not gone to press? We should have had the paper on the street twenty minutes ago. We're beaten again by the 'Globe,' and beaten through the fault of the composing-room. What was the matter? and,—good Lord, man! what are you doing behind that truck?"

"I'm shot," muttered the make-up man incoherently.

"Half-shot, you mean," sneered his superior. Then, as his eye swept the room, he howled:

"What is the row? Are you all crazy, or are you playing hide-and-seek?"

And, indeed, the spectacle of all the composing-room's staid habitués crouching behind various shelters was unusual enough to excite any new-comer.

Robbie Kennedy's treble floated across from behind a truck, mingled with a horde of half-uttered explanations from the other Indian-hunters,—

"Please, Mr. Frothingham, there's an Indian Chief, and he won't let us work."

The Managing Editor stepped forward. The cases that had shut off Howling Wolf from his view were passed, and the two Chiefs, white and red, stood face to face.

Howling Wolf fired a salute with both revolvers, and the Managing Editor, never stopping to ask questions, joined Robbie behind the truck.

But Howling Wolf had acted on the defensive long enough. These men were cowards. It would be pleasant to frighten them further.

With a yell, the Indian began firing a perfect salvo at everyone in general, accompanying the volleys with some ghost-dance steps and snatches of a Sioux war-song.

"Say!" yelled the embattled Managing Editor, "there's an Indian kid downstairs. Miss Westervelt's getting her sketched. Maybe the kid can act as interpreter and find out what the old chap wants. Where's the regular interpreter?"

"All the Indians went down in the elevator except this one, and the interpreter went with them. They drove away long ago," replied a compositor.

"Someone go down and get the pappoose from the city-room," ordered the Managing Editor.

A reporter who chanced to be nearest the stairs and farthest from Howling Wolf made a break for the former, hopping wildly in air as he heard a pistol-shot behind him. On the way downstairs, a thought struck him. He remembered now that he had seen Miss Westervelt take the pappoose with her. He recalled too that the baby had been standing beside this very Chief; and the situation was clear to him before he reached the desk where Miss Westervelt, an artist, a reporter, and two office-boys were standing admiringly about the edition-delaying Utsayantha.

"Miss Westervelt!" shouted the reporter, "hurry, please! Old Mr. Afraid-of-his-Squaw, or whatever he calls himself, is running amuck upstairs because he can't find his kid. He's delayed the edition nearly an hour and let the 'Globe' beat us on that big story. He's shooting people now."

Snatching up the baby, who wept lustily at this sudden removal from a sphere of admiration and candy, the reporter galloped upstairs with her.

As he reached the composing-room he was sent reeling back to the stairway by a mighty blow. When he had found his balance, he beheld Howling Wolf, the recovered Utsayanta in his arms, shouldering his way back to the elevator shaft.

Among civilized nations, when a lost child is returned, the first act of the heart-wracked parent is to spank it.

Savages are human, after all.

As Howling Wolf passed along the alleys of machinery, bearing Utsayantha, a sound as of violent applause arose, mingled with the bitter wails of the recovered baby.

As father and child reached the shaft, the elevator door was flung back and the half-breed interpreter, pale under his brown skin, appeared in company with the manager of the "Rocky Mountain Show and Parliament of Rough Riders."

"Here's your lost sheep," remarked the Managing Editor, indicating the bellicose Howling Wolf, "and, incidentally, your Show's going to have the biggest suit on its hands that ever happened."

From far below came a faint "thud! thud! thud!" The paper was going to press—an hour and ten minutes late!

Sometimes a trader smuggles a supply of fire-water into the Indian Reservation; not enough to inspire the braves to the noble art of cutting settler's throats, but just sufficient to set boastful tongues a-wagging.

At such times a venerable man—a war-chief of the Sioux Nation, by the way—arises from his seat at the camp-fire and holds his credulous hearers breathless by a certain oft-repeated tale.

He tells of a strange house in a land towards the Rising Sun, where, amid a host of black, iron demons, he, Howling Wolf the Terrible, once held a pale-face army at bay, and saved his first-born from being burned at the stake and fed to those strange-smelling iron monsters.

In the "land towards the Rising Sun" there is an irritable Make-up Editor who knocked down a new reporter last week.

The reporter had innocently asked the Make-up Editor how he supposed it felt to be shot.

The Seal of Silence

DENTON was to sail for Europe the following morning.

He had announced that his last evening in America would be entirely taken up with packing. With that excuse he had refused divers invitations to farewell suppers.

Yet half-a-dozen men from the office, happening around unexpectedly at the "Tarascon" apartment-house to wish him bon-voyage, found his rooms in order and his trunks all packed, and found Denton himself seated reading in the apartment's one remaining chair.

He received his unannounced visitors civilly enough, and explained that his packing had taken less time than he had expected, which accounted for his present idleness.

The men seated themselves wherever they could find room, whether on trunks, tables, or strapped boxes.

The talk turned in a few minutes to Barret's newest story.

While his six companions listened envyingly, the writer outlined the plot of this story of his.

"It's almost identical with a short story of Balzac's," commented Denton when the recital was finished.

"I never read a line of Balzac's," returned Barret stiffly. "If there's any resemblance, it's accidental. If I—"

He was interrupted by a swift, rustling sound outside the door. Now, the "Tarascon" is a bachelor apartment-house, and the rustle of skirts there is a sound uncommon enough to make men pause to listen. The knob was quickly turned, and the door opened and shut again before the men could catch their breath.

Leaning against the closed door and facing them stood a girl. She was dressed with elaborate plainness, but bore the word "thorough-bred" stamped on every feature of her flushed, frightened face, on every curve of her slender, trembling figure.

She stood there aghast at sight of the six men. They returned her stare in a dazed fashion. Then her eyes met Barret's and she went pale as death.

Denton, attracted by the sudden silence, glanced up, taking the cigar from his lips as he did so.

"Oh," he said indifferently, "you've come about the wash? That's all right. Your mother called for it an hour ago. I paid her. Goodnight."

Then, without a word, she left the room.

Barret, since his first glimpse of her, had sat, open-mouthed, staring into her face. Now he turned slowly and looked at Denton.

The latter met his gaze carelessly and resumed the subject they had been discussing when the girl's sudden entrance had checked them.

"Yes," he said, "that story of yours, Barret, is a dead steal from Balzac. You make a mistake in not reading Balzac. He is the greatest author of the century, bar none. Did any of you men ever read his story, 'The Seal of Silence'?"

"Balzac never wrote a story by that name," objected Carter. "I've read every line he ever wrote."

Barret again opened his lips to speak; but Denton, in the same careless voice, cut in ahead of him:

"I never saw the story in any of his collected works. I ran across it by chance, years ago, in an old magazine. Perhaps the title was changed in translation. That visit of my washerwoman's daughter reminded me of it."

"What had Miss—the—the washerwoman's daughter to do with it?" asked Barret in a stifled voice.

"Only that it happened to be so much like a scene in 'The Seal of Silence.' Here's the idea of Balzac's story: A young Parisian named Duval is about to sail for America. He loves Eugénie Farâche, the daughter of a wealthy Countess. Duval is a poor hack-writer, and no match for a rich girl. But they become secretly engaged. The old Countess learns of the engagement and forbids Duval the house. He is about to sail for America, as I said. He may be absent for years. He and Eugénie may never meet again. He has no chance to see her once more at her home. So the lovers decide on a step that neither would have dared in cold blood. The scheme is this: The night before Duval sails, Eugénie is to slip away from home with her maid (whom they have bribed) under pretext of going to visit an old school-friend. She is to come un-observed to Duval's rooms (her maid coming along to play propriety) and bid him farewell. A sentimental, foolish plan, if you like. But lovers who are to be parted for years are apt to be foolish and sentimental. You see, she loved him, Barret. She loved him with all her heart.

"The interview would last barely five minutes, and then she would return home. Surely it was a slight sacrifice to make for the man who was going to lose her—perhaps forever."

"Where does the washerwoman element come in?" asked Van Loo, who began to feel bored.

"I'm coming to that. Now, as Duval sat waiting for her, in came a lot of men he knew to wish him good-luck on his voyage,—just as you chaps came here to-night. Among them, Barret, was a man she knew. His name was Belfontaine. He was an old friend of hers, and a constant visitor at the Countess's house. He knew nothing, of course, of Eugenie's engagement to Duval."

"Well?" asked Barret in the same stifled voice.

"Well," resumed Denton, lighting another cigar, "the men were loafing around Duval's room, talking, when suddenly in came Eu-génie. She had left her maid in the hall and had come in alone—to confront a roomful of men. She just stood still a second, panting with terror. She saw Belfontaine and knew he recognized her. If he once let out the secret of her presence there she was disgraced forever. The visit was innocence itself; but the whole world would condemn her unheard."

"How did she get out of it? What did Bel—what's-his-name—do?"

"Before Belfontaine could say a word, Duval used almost the same words I did to that washerwoman's girl to-night. He asked if she had come for the wash, or some such question, and sent her away, leaving the other men to believe she was really some working-girl."

"And Belfontaine?" asked Van Loo.

Denton laughed.

"Why," he said, "that's the very point of the whole story; and that's just where this miserable memory of mine fails me. I don't remember what Belfontaine did. You see, Eugenie's safety, her whole future, hung on Belfontaine. All the other men present were strangers to her. But Belfontaine was a different proposition. Why, Barret, the poor girl's life lay in the hollow of his hand. He could blast her reputation and bring shame on an honored family. Her parents were friends of his. Would he curse her and her family for all time by telling that she came by stealth to a man's rooms? Would he do such a thing as that? What could he gain by it? If some good angel could have shown him the truth about her visit, even as—as the story shows it, wouldn't he be the lowest cur on earth to betray her secret?"

Denton's voice had lost its habitual carelessness and there was a ring of genuine appeal in it.

"I'll tell you what Belfontaine did," suddenly announced Barret.

"What! Do you—"

"Yes. I remember the story perfectly now. I must have read it in the same magazine that Denton did. I suppose, Denton, the magazine may have been lying about your rooms somewhere and I picked it up."

"No doubt, no doubt!" assented his host eagerly. "And I—"

"What did the man do?" broke in Van Loo.

Barret sat silent a moment before continuing. His face was very white, and there were in it lines that had not shown earlier in the evening. He was looking out of the high window, across the city.

"You forgot one point in the 'Seal of Silence,' Denton," he began at last, his eyes wandering over the distant river-lights as he spoke. "Or perhaps you never grasped the point at all: Belfontaine loved Eugénie."

Denton started, then tried to cover his confusion with a laugh.

"He loved her," went on Barret. "They had been friends all their lives, and from childhood he had worshipped her. She knew nothing of his love. He had tried to succeed in life with the wild hope of winning her. Then came that horrible evening when he met her face to face at Duval's rooms. He knew nothing, at first, of her motive for coming there. All he knew was that his idol and his life-hopes lay crushed in the dust. Then Duval found a means of telling him the whole truth, and he—"

"And he—" echoed Denton.

"Say," broke in Carter, "this is a fake story from first to last. I've read Balzac's works from beginning to end, and he never wrote a story on such lines. The plot, the style, the handling, are utterly unlike Balzac. I believe it's a story Denton made up, and that he told it to us by way of 'trying it on the dog' before sending it to a magazine. And I believe Barrett knows it's a fake too, and is just trying to help Denton out."

"Pardon me," remarked Barret, "but I happen to know it is not a 'fake,' as you call it."

"Well, then," said Carter triumphantly as the men rose to go, "how do you reconcile your knowledge of the story with what you said half an hour ago about never having read anything of Balzac's?"

Laughing to think how easily he had detected the fraud and routed his foe, Carter shook hands with Denton and left the room without waiting for Barret's reply. The others trooped out after him, Barret going last of all.

Barret turned as he reached the door-way. For a moment he and Denton stood face to face.

"Duval was a cad—a miserable, contemptible cad, Denton," he said slowly, "to permit a girl he loved to take such a terrible risk."

Denton bowed his head in silence. Then he stretched out his hand appealingly towards the departing guest.

"But Belfontaine—what did Belfontaine do?" he implored.

Barret ignored the proffered hand.

"Belfontaine?" he replied. "Why, he kept silence. What else should he do? But, of course, it was hard for a cur like Duval to understand that. Good-night, Denton. Bon-voyage!"

She and the Monster

"Why do they call it a 'monster?'" she asked.

"I don't know," confessed Wolfe, "unless maybe because it *is* one."

"It's more like a monster than that reason is like humor," she admitted judicially.

Then, somehow, they fell silent and continued their survey of the creature.

In a big, hinged, blanket-lined box it lay; its two and a half feet of dull, black and yellow length coiled stiffly amid the blanket folds; the blunt-nosed head inert, the lidless eyes dim and glassy. The box's under lid bore a scrawled legend: *"Gila Monster. Habitat Southern Arizona."*

"Is it dangerous?" queried Miss Frayne, after a pause. "I seem to have read somewhere—"

"Not just now," said Wolfe. "There's a big difference between the blistering sands of Arizona, and blizzard-swept New York. The thing's torpid at present, and likely to remain so till it thaws out."

"And yet you just lighted the fire? In five minutes the room will be—"

"In five minutes the Gila monster will be safely boxed again," explained Wolfe, dropping the lid over the motionless reptile's blanket nest. "There! Now do you feel safer?"

"I'm afraid I didn't have a single thrill of fear to revel in," she returned. "Really, do you think it was worth while to drag me up two long flights of stairs to this ice-cold study of yours just to stare at—?"

"But it isn't going to be ice-cold any longer," he protested. "I've just lighted the fire, and—"

"Wilful waste!" she reproved, "if it was lighted on my account. For I'm going down again now to wait for Helen."

"Why not wait here?" he pleaded. "See, it's getting beautifully warm, now the door's shut and the fire blazing. And you shall have my biggest leather chair. The children will tell Helen you're here as soon as she comes in. Honestly, you'll find this is the comfortablest place in our whole blizzard-buffeted house. *Please* stay!"

"I wait here under protest," said Miss Frayne, whisking a few stray cigar ashes from the big chair and resigning herself to its soft leathern depths. "I still consider I was lured up to your study under false pretenses. Here I have braved a blizzard and a subzero temperature to come all the way across the street to see your beloved sister, only to find she has ventured out to market. All I got for my heroism is a view of an extremely ugly black and yellow lizard that you miscall a 'monster' and—"

"Not to mention my sister's two very delighted children and her still more overjoyed brother. Surely, we ought to be counted in, if only after the monster."

"Oh, the children, of course. They're dears. But you hustled me away from them, up two whole flights of stairs, to—"

"Yes," he sighed in contrition, "the same two offending flights you mentioned before. I'm sorry I couldn't induce Helen to give me a study on the ground floor, or else provide an elevator. I'm sure if she had dreamed you'd honor my poor quarters—"

"I shouldn't have honored them but for the promise to show me a real live monster."

"And haven't I kept my word? It isn't my fault he's no livelier. I'm sorry you don't like him. I've had such a lot of bother with the measly brute, I rather hoped to be repaid for some of it by giving you a little amusement."

"If you don't like him why did you get him?"

"*I* get him? On the level, Marjorie, do I look like the idiot who would buy that sort of a pet? Don't rub it in."

"But if he isn't yours—?"

"He's Dick Baldwin's. You've heard me speak of Dick. He lives just outside of Hackensack. Keeps what he calls an 'Ophidiarium'—I guess that's Latin for a 'snakery.' He's got all breeds of weird serpents and other reptiles, and pays fearsome prices for them. He sent out to Arizona for this Gila monster. It reached New York yesterday and he was shipping it out to his place when he happened to tell the trainmen about it.

"They swore the thing shouldn't go in the baggage-car, and the station hands wouldn't have it in the trunk-room. So he brought the box here to me and threw it on my mercy till the roads are open enough for him to take it out to Hackensack in his motor. That's how I come to be temporary guardian of a veritable monster."

"I don't see why Helen allows such a thing in the house!"

"She doesn't. She doesn't know. That's why I keep it up here. No one knows. I didn't mean any one should. But I sacrificed my secret as a bait to give me a half hour with you without the children butting in to—"

"A gruesome sort of bait!" she commented. "I'm going now."

"Oh! *please* don't. Let's—let's think up a name for the poor thing! Great idea. What shall we call it? How would Cephas do?"

"Cephas!" she echoed in high scorn. "Who ever heard of a Gila monster—?"

"Called Cephas?" he finished. "I never heard of one that was called anything else. It struck me as a neat, innocuous, scriptural name—but if you can improve on it—"

"What I was going to say," she corrected with dignity, "was that no one ever heard of such idiocy as giving a Gila monster any name at all. I—"

"Then let's set the custom!" he urged eagerly. "Now if you don't like Cephas, how would Claude do? Or May Blossom or Gregory? There now! *Gregory* seems to me an uncommonly good name. Rugged, yet with a certain Old-World stateliness. Shall it be Gregory? I'm sure any self-respecting monster would be proud of such—"

"Roy Wolfe!" she laughed vexedly, "were you ever sane in your life?"

"Always," he replied with solemn protest, "till I lost my head over you. Since then—"

"Don't!" she ordered.

"Why not? It isn't news to you. If you don't like to hear me say it, that's no fault of mine. I've said it so often—only more so—that you ought to be getting used to it by this time. Aren't you getting just a *little* tired of giving me the same unkind answer?"

"Must we go over all that again? If you were different—if you weren't content to be an idler living on other people's brains—if you would act and think for yourself—"

"I'd rather act and think for you, Marjorie. There might be some inspiration in that. But—"

"Learn to do it for yourself, first. When you do, I—"

"When I do, I can look for a different answer? Is that true?—*Marjorie!*"

"When you do—when—" She paused in confusion; then, rising and glancing about as if for means of escape, stood suddenly stock-still, her fresh young face paling, her dark eyes dilated.

For the lid of the forgotten box near the fireplace had stirred. It lifted a few inches. A blunt nose, then an evil, black and yellow head were thrust forth.

Wolfe, in dropping the lid, had neglected to note that a tiny corner of blanket prevented the lock from catching.

Now, following the direction of Miss Frayne's wild gaze, he was just in time to see the long, thick body slide from the box to the polished floor. The fire-warmth had done its work. The monster was thoroughly awake.

Wolfe took an involuntary step toward the creature. With a breathy, hissing sound, it wheeled with awkward haste to face him. He halted, irresolute. "The bite is deadly poison," he mused aloud. "I don't care to risk picking the thing up and putting it back. And it cost Dick a lot. I don't like to kill it. Better get out, Marjorie. I'll find some way to catch the thing."

But as it chanced, the chair where Miss Frayne had been sitting was at the far end of the room from the door. As she started, in a shrinking détour, to leave the study, the swish of her skirt caught the monster's attention. Apparently mistaking the motion for a challenge, it rushed at her; ugly jaws wide-stretched, the short legs clawing desperately for firmer foothold on the polished boards.

The unlooked-for attack robbed the girl of all power of flight. Fascinated, she stood watching the clumsy yet swift onrush.

Wolfe, barely in time, picked her up with a sweep of his arm and lifted her to the broad surface of his study table. He himself joined her there with highly ungraceful haste, just as the serrated fangs, striking at his ankle, tore a clean-cut little semicircle from the bottom of his left trouser-leg.

"Rather close call!" he observed ruefully, eying the mutilated garment. "Bite's deadly, too, as I think I mentioned."

"What—what *are* we to do?" gasped Miss Frayne, as the monster, with a quick succession of little snaps and hisses, lumbered furiously about the table-feet, seeking means of getting at them.

"I'm afraid," remarked Wolfe, looking down at their assailant, "I'm afraid Gregory hasn't awakened in a very sweet temper. He seems almost peevish."

"But what are we to *do?*" she repeated.

"Do? I'm afraid we must rob Dick Baldwin of his fine specimen of Gila monster—habitat southern Arizona. In fact, unless we care to sit perched up here all day, Gregory must be wafted forthwith to the happy Gila grounds. He's getting livelier and livelier, the warmer he grows."

The man was balancing a heavy paperweight in his hand as he spoke. Now, with all his force, he hurled it at the biting, hissing thing sidling along just below them.

The sharp corner of the projectile drove a deep dent into the hard floor, scarce an inch from the monster's head.

"A clean miss!" grumbled Wolfe. "Gregory is an elusive little pet! He ducked as prettily as Jim Corbett. And I don't seem to have improved his temper much. See, he's trying to jump at us. They're furious jumpers, for all they're so awkward, I've heard. But he can't get enough foothold. Floor's too slippery. Here goes for the inkstand! Better luck this time."

Poising the broad, cut-glass receptacle, he threw it, deluging himself, the table, and the floor with the flying ink. But though this time a corner of the missile grazed the monster's neck, no further effect was wrought than to lash their foe to a fresh access of murderous rage.

"What a deceptive object an inkstand is!" commented Wolfe, sopping his handkerchief across his spattered face and raiment. "That one didn't look as if it held a gill. Yet I've at least half a gallon of ink on me, to say nothing of the floor. Poor Helen! How pleased she'll be when she sees that floor!

"Just look at Gregory! There's actually foam on his jaws. He has a most unfortunate disposition. I hope his temper wasn't guaranteed gentle when Dick bought him. Now for— By Jove! There isn't another blessed thing on this table heavy enough to crush a mouse. If I could get across to the fireplace where the poker is! Perhaps I could make a dash for it and—"

"*No!*" cried the girl, clutching his arm. "You *mustn't!* He would be there before you. You see how terribly fast he moves."

"But there might be a chance—"

"Roy," she panted, tightening her hold, "if you think I'm going to be left alone on this table—with that awful beast prowling around the foot of it—"

"All right!" he said in beautiful resignation. "As long as you'll hold on to my arm like that, I promise to stay. But I own I'm disappointed in Gregory. Maybe our treatment, though, hasn't brought out all that is best in his nature. He—Look! He's trying to jump again. This table used to seem almost too high for comfort—but now it seems to be getting lower and lower every minute. I'm glad the floor is so slippery. I wish we could think how to pacify him. Oh, Gregory, 'in our hours of ease, uncertain, coy, and hard to—' Shall I try him with a blotting pad? I might scare him, or—"

"No! Let him alone. It would only make him angrier. Oh, *what* a position!"

"I'm sorry the table isn't comfortable," he answered. "If I'd have had any idea you'd ever choose it for a roosting-place, I'd have had it nicely upholstered. Let's play we're pirates adrift on a raft and that Gregory's a shark. It'll make the time pass quicker till some one comes to—"

"Till some one comes?" she repeated. "Roy, do you know what that means? It means that horrible thing will attack anybody that happens to enter."

"So it does," he replied. "And I was just going to sing out for help, too, on the chance that my voice might carry as far as the ground floor. There's no one else up in this part of the house. Say, Marjorie," he went on in sudden despondency, "I'm beginning to see something. When you were down upon me for not 'acting and thinking for myself,' I thought you were wrong. Now I see you weren't. Any fellow with a man's-size brain and the power to help those he cared for, could figure a way out of this nasty scrape. *I can't.*"

"Don't talk of that now!" she pleaded. "You've behaved *splendidly.* I never thought you were so brave and so—"

"So inky?" he supplemented, surreptitiously rubbing blots of the black fluid from his forehead. "Well, I am! And a pretty mess my idiocy has got us both into. Can you ever forgive my—?"

"Oh!" she interrupted, "he almost reached the edge of the table that jump. I suppose next time—"

"He isn't going to reach *you,*" the man reassured her. "So don't worry your pretty head about that. Oh, Gregory, Gregory! What a misspent, undisciplined youth yours must have been! If only you'd learned self-control or read Dr. Watts's—"

A rattling of the door-knob cut short his apostrophe. Untrained little fingers without were wrestling with the handle.

"Uncle Roy!" announced a clear treble, through the keyhole, "I'm coming in. It's lomesome down-stairs and—"

"Keep out! Go away!" croaked Wolfe, a great horror sanding his throat at sound of his baby nephew's voice.

The monster, drawn by this new diversion, twisted away from the table and faced the door, ready to meet the newest antagonist. Rising high on its stumpy forelegs, the foam-flecked jaws snapping like castanets, it awaited the child's appearance.

"Back!" vociferated Roy, and Marjorie echoed his shout with a scream of frantic warning.

The only reply was a gurgling laugh from beyond the door. The baby fingers had at last mastered the secret of the knob. The handle turned and the door creaked open.

Roy, at first call of the child's voice, had sought to leap to the floor. But the convulsive grip of both Marjorie Frayne's white hands about his arm could not be shaken off.

Then came his inspiration. Scrambling to his knees as the knob turned, he snatched up with his free hand the heavy desk chair from beside the table. With one supreme effort he whirled it aloft and sent it smashing—through the broad double window just beyond.

In rushed the blizzard driven by a sixty-mile gale, filling the room with a blast of zero air that flung the slowly opening door wide and sent an icy draft whizzing through the whole house.

And, at first breath of that bitter chill, the monster, standing full in the path of the wind, collapsed into a motionless, senseless, wooden lump. The spawn of red-hot sands and burning sun could not for one instant withstand the ice touch of the North. As Roy, with his rare flash of inspiration, had hoped, the danger was all at once ended. The dreaded Gila monster was as powerless now for evil as the broken inkstand itself.

The baby stood in shivering wonder on the threshold, watching his uncle lift from the table a very limp and trembling girl. Her clasped hands had somehow shifted from his arm to a still less conventional position that necessitated the encircling of their attendant arms about his neck.

Roy's pale, ink-stained face was very close to Marjorie's own, and he was whispering:

"Did I 'act and think for myself,' for once, sweetheart?"

"Oh, you did! Indeed you *did!*" sobbed Marjorie.

And in the ensuing confusion which arose several of the ink-streaks were carelessly transferred from Roy's lips to her own.

"As a matter of fact," continued Wolfe, when he remembered to speak again, "I did nothing of the sort. Any one else would have had sense enough to brain Gregory with that chair ten minutes earlier. But *I* don't care, if *you* don't. Good old Greg!"

The Bridegroom's Dilemma

"IF I had a little more sense, I'd be half-witted!"

Harry Shaler made this confession for the benefit of all whom it might concern, and halted in consternation, midway between the hotel-doors and the office-desk.

Though at least a dozen people were within ear-shot, only one of them understood the young American's announcement of his mental status; for the simple reason that only one—Mrs. Harry Shaler —could understand English.

Mrs. Harry was a dainty, pink-and-gold fluff of humanity—very appealing, very inexperienced, very much in love with the big young New Yorker whose wife she had been for eight whole days.

"What is it, dear?" she queried now, as her husband's sudden halt brought her own progress to a stop.

The hotel *commissionnaire,* loaded down with their luggage, came to anchor alongside.

"I forgot it," he answered ruefully—"clean forgot to stop at Munro's Bank, as we planned, on the way from the station, and draw that thousand francs on our letter of credit."

"Well, what of that? You can go around there later."

"But I ought to have the money now. I've exactly two francs left. And I don't know anything about Paris hotels. At home, in God's country, they don't make you pay in advance if you have luggage. But it may be different over here. Suppose they ask us to pay when I register? And I with just two silver francs to show them."

"But what are we to do?" she cried, her big eyes widening with alarm at the mental picture of their disgrace in being turned out of the gaudy hostelry.

"Let me think a second," he replied. "Here, I have it! Simplest thing on earth. Madge, you wait here—in that little reception-room. I'll chase over to the bank, draw a thousand francs, and be back again in no time at all.

"How clever of you!" she exclaimed. "You always know just what to do in every crisis. I—I think that's one reason I fell in love with you. You always make me feel so safe. If you were any other man on earth I'd be frightened to death waiting alone here in a strange city, in a hotel I never heard of before, in a country where neither of us knows one word of the natives' language. But with you—"

She paused, unconsciously affected by the stern array of solitude she had conjured up.

"Perhaps," she ventured—"perhaps I'd better go to the bank with you instead of staying here all by myself."

"Nonsense," he laughed, "you're tired from the long railroad trip. Stay and rest in the reception-room. I'll be back before you know it."

Signaling the *commissionnaire* to pile the luggage in a corner of the foyer, Shaler led his wife to the reception-room, installed her in the coziest chair, glanced around to see no one was covertly on the watch, then kissed her good-by, and hurried off on his quest.

"Drive me to No. 7 Rue Scribe!" he ordered a waiting cabman.

The *cocher's* face remained blank.

"No. 7 Rue Scribe!" repeated Shaler, speaking very loudly, as is the reasonless custom of most people in addressing foreigners. Then, to make it plainer, he added: "Munro's Bank."

"*Munro et Fils, Rue Scribe, Sept!*" cried the *cocher,* catching the idea. "*Mais oui, m'sieu! Toute de suite!*" Shaler climbed into the dilapidated *fiacre,* and the lean horse set off at a lumbering, whip-punctuated gallop, for this was before the days of taxis. Shaler leaned back among the musty cushions to enjoy this glimpse of the wonderful pleasure city. All his life he had longed to visit Paris.

When he and Madge became engaged, he had learned it was her own dream as well. They had planned from the very first to spend their month's honeymoon there.

They had planned, too, to fit themselves for the trip by studying French together during the all-too-brief engagement evenings. But those evenings had been filled somehow with so much pleasanter employment that the study course had been shelved.

However, one could always find plenty of interpreters. So the failure to waste golden time in poring over French grammars troubled them little.

On the evening of their wedding-day they had boarded *La Lorraine*. Early this morning they had landed at Cherbourg. And now—at last—Paris. The life dream was fulfilled.

II

THE *fiacre* drew up with a jolt in front of a gray stone building. Shaler glanced at the name over the entrance, jumped out, and reached into his pocket. He had with vast difficulty mastered the intricacies of French currency, but he did not know enough of the language to ask the amount of his fare nor to understand the driver's reply had he done so. So he handed the cabman his two francs, and stood on the curb awaiting his change.

The driver, however; merely pocketed the couple of coins, shouted, "*Merci, m'sieu!*" whipped up his horse, and clattered away.

"Custom of the country, I suppose," soliloquized Shaler. "What a queer feeling to be penniless in a foreign land."

He slapped his waistcoat pocket complacently, to gain reassurance from the familiar pressure of his letter of credit. Then, all at once, the smile on his lips froze into a panic-stricken grimace. Instead of touching the little leather case, his blow had broken two cigars. The letter of credit case was not there!

That morning, on leaving the boat, he had sought to honor France by donning a brand-new white waistcoat. The gray tweed vest that went with his traveling suit was now carelessly rolled up in one of the two suit-cases. And in the discarded garment's breast pocket reposed the letter of credit.

"I'm not a born fool," he told himself. "Till I fell in love I was sane enough to build up and hold a fair law practise. But, being married, and crossing the Atlantic for the first time—and coming to Paris—all seem to have turned my head. Now, I *must* be sane for a minute, and do some rapid and real thinking."

He could not go to the cashier of Munro's and demand money on an unproduced letter of credit. No, the only thing to do was to go back to his hotel, get the letter, and bring it here. Or—

A better idea struck him. He ran up the steps, entered the bank and approached a man who stood behind one of the windows. The official was evidently an American.

"I have a letter of credit on your bank," said Shaler. "No, I don't want to draw on it just now. I merely want to ask a question. In Paris hotels are guests who have luggage required to pay in advance?"

"Certainly not," was the reply.

"Thank you," said Shaler, much relieved, and he hurried out into the street.

"All that bother for nothing," he chuckled. "I'll call a cab, drive to the hotel, make the hotel people pay the cabby, and let the silly letter of credit wait till to-morrow. Then, when we're rested, Madge and I can drive around here together, in the morning, and get what money we want. If we need any cash this evening the hotel people will surely advance us some. We've enough luggage to inspire all sorts of confidence. But I'll have to keep my wits about me after this or I'll get into a really serious scrape before I'm through."

He looked up and down the Rue Scribe. A hawk-eyed cabman, scenting prey, bore down upon him.

"Where to, *monsieur?*" queried the driver in very fair English.

"To—to—to my hotel," muttered Shaler, a sudden sinking sensation at the bottom of his heart.

"Assuredly, *monsieur,*" rejoined the driver politely. "But *what* hotel?"

"I—I don't know," groaned the American.

It was all so horribly impossible, yet so disgustingly natural. The name of his hotel had quite slipped his memory; save that it had several syllables, and perhaps an apostrophe and an accent or two, he could recall naught of it. One Paris hotel's nomenclature was like another's to Shaler. He had heard of the Grand, the Ritz, the Chatham, but he knew the name of his chosen stopping place was longer and less easy to pronounce than any of these. What could it be?

"Will you tell me the names of some of them?" he asked feebly.

The cabby, with rapid-fire speed, rattled off a list of titles. Shaler's raised hand checked him.

"Never mind," protested the New Yorker. "I wouldn't recognize them from their French pronunciation, anyhow. I have forgotten the name of my hotel. But"—brightening a little—"it was about fifteen minutes' drive from here, I think."

"*Monsieur,*" said the cabman with growing suspicion, "there are fully forty hotels within that radius. Within two minutes' ride from here is the Café de la Paix—the 'center of the universe.' Hotels by the hundred radiate off from that spot. I fear—"

"Never mind," broke in Shaler. "Drive me to a dozen or so of them. I shall recognize mine when I see it. It is on a side street, just off a long avenue. And a tall man in gold-braided livery stands in front of it."

"*Monsieur* has accurately described no less than fifty hotels of Paris," remarked the cabman, his lids narrowing. "Does *monsieur* wish me to drive him to all of them?"

"Yes," shouted Shaler, in desperation, "to the whole lot. I don't care if it takes ten hours. Let's start at once."

For suddenly there had risen before his mind a vision of a fluffy, trustful little figure sitting alone in a reception-room, frightened at her own isolation, wondering what unknown ruffians might have captured her absent husband. Madge was so little, so helpless—

"We'll go the rounds of every hotel in Paris if necessary," he repeated aloud.

"By all means," sneered the now thoroughly skeptical cabman; "but as the journey is likely to be long I must venture to ask monsieur for a franc or so of fare in advance. Believe me, I am desolated to—"

With a growl of utter desperation Harry Shaler turned away and started aimlessly off down the street. Without a sou to his name, with no idea where or how to go, he began his hopeless quest on foot.

Following a sense of general direction, he presently found himself in the Place de l'Opéra, and thence was swallowed up by the rush and gay bustle of the Boulevard des Capucines. The names on the corners would at any other time have filled him with delight, as fulfilments of early dreams. But now he was too busy exploring each of the network side streets to pay heed to the scene about him.

Through the gathering dusk he pushed on until he reached the glare and broad spaces of the Place de la Concorde. Before him sloped the Champs Elyseé upward toward the far off arch. To the right rose the gray columns of the Madeleine.

To the left ran the Seine. Sight of the water gave him a prick of memory. He had crossed a river that day. Was it while he was in the train, in the bus or in the cab? He thought it must have been in one of the two latter. His hotel was probably somewhere on the opposite side of the Seine.

He crossed the Pout Neuf and struck straight ahead into another Paris, the tortuous, queer old Paris of the Latin Quarter. Did ever another youth penetrate the frontiers of Bohemia with so perplexed and heavy a heart? Into the Rue de Dragon he wandered, searching everywhere for a facade like that of his lost hotel.

He passed a rickety building whose door panel bore the painting of a green-and-gold dragon. A man issuing from the doorway collided violently with him.

"*Mille pardons, monsieur,*" began the newcomer.

Then, as a ray of light from the passageway lantern struck across the American's face, the stranger cried incredulously:

"Harry Shaler! By all that's impossible! What wind blew you to the Quartier?"

Shaler had already recognized the other as Mark Vane, a Columbia classmate who, two years earlier, had come to Paris to study art. He could have fallen on the student's neck. The Unknown City had at last raised up for him a friend in need.

"I'm here with my wife—" he began excitedly.

"Your wife?" echoed Vane. "How long ago did that happen? I never heard—"

"Oh," returned Shaler, with an attempt at lightness, "man and boy, I've been married nearly nine days. I—"

"And where are you stopping?"

"I don't know. I—"

"Don't know. Where is Mrs.—"

"I don't know. I've lost her. She's at our hotel, I suppose, or else—"

"What hotel?"

"I don't know. You see—"

"I see the water wagon has lost a promising recruit, or else the *Maison des Fous* (insane asylum) has gained one. Which is it?"

Briefly, and as clearly as possible, Shaler explained his plight. Vane heard him with a fast-growing emotion of some sort, that at the climax found vent in a howl of laughter.

"I'm glad you can enjoy it so much," growled Shaler. "Nice joke, isn't it? My poor little wife sitting alone for hours in a strange hotel, crying over the husband whom she always relied on to shield her from trouble? Half crazy with fear about me, poor, helpless baby that she is. Fine joke."

"I'm sorry, old man," apologized Vane, with due contrition. "I was a cad to laugh. But, honestly, you aren't in nearly so bad a fix as you say. It didn't occur to you, I suppose, to go somewhere and telephone the different hotels, or—"

"I'm not quite devoid of horse sense," snapped Shaler. "Of course it occurred to me. Only two little details prevented me. One is, I don't know a word of French, and—"

"That's all right. I'll do the telephoning."

"And the other obstacle," pursued Shaler, "is that I haven't a cent in my pocket. I suppose telephoning, in Paris, isn't on the free list? "

"Whew!" whistled Vane. "That's a horse of another color. I wish I could help you out. You see, my remittance was due last week. It hasn't come. That's why I went up to those Dragon ateliers just now—to try to borrow five francs. But I couldn't raise a single coin there. I'm richer than you, for I've got four big copper sous clinging in my pocket. But they are all that are left from the watch and pin I pawned Tuesday. I'm flat dead broke. Say! Have you tried to pawn anything?"

"How could I? I kept my eyes open for pawn-shops, but I didn't see one."

"No? They aren't very common on the Boulevard or around the Opéra or the Place de la Concorde. But there's a bunch of them within a block of here. Come along."

Ten minutes later Shaler was shoving fifty francs into the pocket that had recently held a very costly watch. Vane was at a telephone, running his finger along the list of hotels. Calling up the first, he asked in French:

"Is there an American lady there, whose husband has left her alone and is supposed to be wandering somewhere about the city?"

"Yes," came the instant answer.

"Good!" cried Vane. "We've found her, Harry, the very first call. "What is her name?" he asked the hotel clerk.

"Which one?" was the reply. "There are no less than seven American ladies here whose husbands have left them alone, and—"

Vane slammed down the receiver with a groan.

"No use!" he declared. "You say you didn't register?"

"No," replied Shaler; "not yet."

"We needn't ask them to examine the register for names, then," interrupted Vane, turning again to the instrument. "Now for the next hotel!"

For a solid hour the various hotels of Paris were interrogated. Then, as a last resort, the office of the police prefect was called up.

No, nothing had been reported concerning a frantic American woman pleading for her husband's rescue from the terrors of a great city.

As the two friends faced each other in despair, after this final hope had failed, Vane exclaimed:

"Man, you're white as a sheet! When did you eat last? "

"I had a cup of coffee on the steamer early this morning," replied Shaler weakly. "But never mind how I look! We've got to scour Paris all night if—"

"We've got to get you some decent food," retorted Vane, "or we'll have you in the hospital. This worry and the faintness have knocked you out. Wait," as the other sought to interrupt; "*I'm* in command now, and you'll do as I say. Come across to the pawn-shop. Leave your rings and scarf-pin there and get fifty francs more. Then we'll take a cab to some good restaurant in the heart of the hotel district, get a hurry-up dinner, and start out on a thorough round of every hotel. It'll be only a matter of a couple of hours or so, at most, before we locate Mrs. Shaler, at that rate."

"Go loafing around in cabs and eating dinners while my poor little wife is suffering agonies of fear!" stormed Shaler. "What sort of cur do you think I am? We'll start on our round of the hotels this very instant. Heaven grant the precious child may not have grown so nervous about me as to venture out alone—without any money—into the streets—to look for me! We—"

He staggered slightly from sheer fatigue. Vane caught him by the arm.

"We won't get far if you go keeling over like that," he exclaimed. "You'll do as I say. There's a green-light cab. It'll take us across the river and over to the center of the universe in ten minutes. At the St. Simon de la Plage they have enough American custom to know how to serve a good dinner in a rush. We'll go there, get a square meal, and then start on our hunt. Buck up! It'll be all right!"

A little later the cab disgorged the Americans in front of a lighted building. Shaler, sunk in an apathy of despair, followed his friend and commander blindly into the foyer, mechanically handed his hat and overcoat to an attendant, and suffered Vane to lead him across a corridor to the dining-room.

With equal apathy he sank into a chair and dropped his head on his breast. The lights, the voices, the white napery, and the glitter of silver annoyed him unreasonably. He shut his eyes and fell to conjuring up pictures of a tear-stained, horror-blanched little face set in a halo of fluffy curls.

"Take a brace!" whispered Vane. "Don't look as if you were going to be hanged. Want to see the menu? Don't fidget. Our waiter'll be here in a second. He's spending an unconscionably long time taking that order at the next table. I can't blame him, though. By Jove! She's a stunner. As dainty as a bit of Sèvres. Take a look. It'll do you good."

"Shut up!" commanded Stealer. "Why should I want to stare at a Paris beauty when all my heart and mind are—"

"But she's looking at you," persisted Vane. "Lord! How those gorgeous eyes of hers are dancing! And not one glance for me. Just for *you,* you unappreciative—"

With a grunt of disgust, Shaler sought to cut short his friend's jarring rhapsodies by turning mechanically in the direction Vane indicated. Idly he looked, then, galvanized, he glared with bulging eyes and fallen jaw.

"*Madge!*" he gurgled.

Clad in her flimsiest evening gown, her bright face unmarred by tears or pallor, Madge Shaler was sitting expectantly at the adjoining table. Harry, doubtful lest his eyes had tricked him, lurched across to where she awaited him.

"You never even looked my way!" she pouted in mock anger. "And I wore my prettiest dress just to please you; I was going to come over to your table in another minute to find out why—"

"Madge," he panted, "what does it all mean? You aren't lost—or frightened—or—"

"Lost?" she repeated. "Why, I've been here all afternoon—ever since you left me. I waited an hour for you to come back. Then I supposed you were so taken up in seeing the city that you'd forgotten how lonely I'd be. So I registered for us, had the trunks taken to a lovely little suite of rooms, unpacked, and took a nap. At dinner-time I came down and—"

"You weren't frightened? "

"Why should I be frightened?" she asked in genuine wonder. "You are so strong, so wise, dear! I knew no harm could have come to you. So—"

"So, while your 'strong, wise' husband has been capering hysterically all over Paris in search of you," supplemented Shaler, "my helpless, fluffy little wife has been taking care of herself like a veteran globe-trotter!"

"Sweetheart," whispered Madge, with the air of imparting a great secret, "let me tell you something. There is no woman on earth—however masculine and independent she may be—who doesn't in her heart like to be petted and taken care of and guarded. And there isn't a woman in the world—however fluffy and helpless she may seem—who can't, at a pinch, take just as good care of her own comfort as if she had a 'strong, wise' husband at her elbow to do it for her."

And, in the face of such sublime wisdom, all Harry Shaler could do was to mutter savagely:

"If I could lay hands on the paretic who invented that simile about the 'sturdy oak and the clinging vine,' I'd break his measly neck! Madge," he added aloud, "there's my old friend Mark Vane. I'm going to ask him over. The poor fellow's dead broke. Mustn't it be terrible to find oneself penniless in a foreign land?"

A Jersey Knight Errant

"WILL you go on a knight-errant quest for me?" asked the one girl.

I drew myself up and tried to look as much as possible like a paladin of old. (This is no light task when one weighs two hundred pounds, has scarlet hair, and is only five feet three. Yet I made shift to appear as knightly as might be.)

"Command me, lady fair," I entreated. "Shall I singe the beardless King of Spain's beard? Or hold Brooklyn Bridge in right heroic fashion against all Long Island? Or do you want me to be utterly daredevilish and tell some girl her hat is unbecoming?"

"Don't be absurd!" exhorted the one girl. "I said a 'quest'; not 'suicide.' Will you do something for me?"

"*Something?* Anything! Speak on! Your word is law."

The one girl let her big eyes rove from my rotund figure, over the velvety stretch of lawn at the fire-blue lake beyond.

"It is very beautiful," she murmured.

"If my quest leads me to search for a lovelier," I returned, gazing solemnly at her, "I decline it as hopeless. There's not another face—"

"I was speaking of the landscape," she reproved. "It is *so* lovely! And the one thing needed to make it perfect was—"

"I came by the first train after I got your mother's invitation," I pleaded.

"Was a peacock," she ended.

Vanity slumped six points. I repeated dully:

"A peacock?"

"Yes," she went on. "In all the pictures of English country-seats there is always a magnificent peacock in the middle distance. I've wanted one for so long. Think how he would add to the picturesqueness of—"

"Say," I broke in, "I don't know whether they carry a line of peacocks down at the village general store, or whether I'll have to chase to the city for one. But if *that's* my 'quest,' I'll engage to have a husky specimen of the bird of vanity here inside of three days. When is the next train for town?"

"You're an *awfully* good fellow, Bobbie," said the one girl. "I honestly believe you'd give up your week-end here and go back to the city this broiling Saturday afternoon to find one for me. I—"

"Of course I would. And I *will*. Isn't that the quest?"

"Not entirely. Listen: Ever since father bought this place I've teased him to get me a peacock. And last week he consented. The bird came yesterday by express."

"Oh!" I growled in dire disappointment.

"He is gorgeous!" she declared in ecstasy. "A mass of blue-and-gold gorgeousness. I've named him Rhadamés. After the hero of 'Aïda,' you know. Father wanted to call him Simon Peter, to take down his vanity. We had quite a family quarrel over it. We compromised at last on—Rhadamés."

I had an experience with such "compromises" on the part of the one girl. And I nodded sympathetic assent.

"He came yesterday," she continued. "The coachman locked him in the disused chicken-house until the bird could get used to the place and wouldn't run away. Just before you came, half an hour ago, I went to the chicken-house to look at him. A panel of the rickety paling was gone. And so was Rhadamés."

"Flew the coop?"

"Exactly. I've looked all over the grounds for him, but I can't find him anywhere."

"And you want me to scour the neighborhood and bring him back to you?" I hazarded.

"Oh, if only you *would!*" she cried. "I know it's horrid of me to send you out in the heat when you're all tired from your train journey; but the coachman's driven to the village, and father isn't back from town yet. And Rhadamés is so beautiful and—and valuable—I'm afraid some one will steal him. For instance, there's old Homer Griswold, the man with the farm just over the hill. He grabs everything that strays onto his land and—"

"Say no more," I declaimed, jamming on my straw hat and striding off the veranda into the sunshine. "Your knight errant herewith departs on his quest. Prythee, lady fair, hie thee to the window of thy bower on the castle battlements, and there make ready to weave a rosy wreath to reward me on my triumphant return. Fare thee well! What ho, minions! My snow-white palfrey and my Sunday armor! "

II.

I DEFY the most ardent nature-lover to cull one atom of joy from tramping dusty roads and sneaking through barbed-wire fences to peer into equally dusty and more breathless bits of woodland, in search of a wandering peacock, the while the midsummer sun is rolling up a thermometric record of ninety in the shade.

That is what I did for the two solid, torrid hours. I did not enjoy it. Far fainer would I have set ashen lance in rest and braved mere death in the lists against some doughty knight.

I have seldom seen, or even imagined, so few peacocks in so large a space of territory. Not a sight nor sound of any such elusive fowl did I secure.

Once I heard something rustling through a copse. I chased it for a full half mile of tangled undergrowth; falling over logs, tripped by briers, rent by brambles—only to find I had been pursuing a mongrel dog.

Again, I ran after a large, half-seen fowl, across a field of waist-high waving wheat—and discovered my quarry was a stray rooster.

The sun was nearing the horizon. Dusty, parched of throat, perspiring of face, my collar wilted, my clothes torn, I halted in my quest. Pompford had always seemed to me one of New Jersey's fairest spots. Now I *loathed* it.

Even the thought of the one girl could spur me to no further futile efforts. I turned miserably toward her home—a failure! A quarter mile or so from my destination I passed a ramshackle farmstead. It was the abode of one Homer Griswold, the local "meanest man in this 'ere place." There is one in every rural community, you know. And as I plodded by the unpainted house and toward the rickety cluster of barns, ricks, etc., I recalled what the one girl had said about the worthy Griswold:

"He grabs everything that strays onto his land."

What more possible than that he might have annexed the erring Simon Peter Rhadamés? As the thought struck me, a loud, raucous screech shattered the country stillness.

It was like the blare of a cracked army-trumpet. And it came from somewhere in that bunch of unpainted farm buildings.

Now, I know little enough about peacocks. But nobody who has ever heard one of them screech needs to be taught again the nature of the cry.

My quest was to be rewarded. My Sherlockian instincts were correct. Yonder, in the barn or farmyard in front of us, the stolen Rhadamés was incarcerated.

At a bound I had cleared the crazy fence and the intervening space of grass, and was plunging through the half open door of the barn.

On the instant the screech was repeated, just ahead of me. Through the barn I dashed, and out into the farmyard behind it. There, preening his gaudy plumage on a fence, looking down with aristocratic scorn at the humbler fowls below—there stood the most magnificent peacock my eyes had ever beheld.

His neck and chest shone with burnished blue-green. The crest on his absurdly small head gleamed like a crown. His wonderful tail was spread like a Chinese emperor's fan, all aglow with a thousand shimmering hues.

I crossed the barn-yard in two jumps, scattering an indignant colony of chickens to right and left. With outstretched arms I hurled myself at the peacock.

In stately dignity he eluded me and hopped to the top of a corn-crib. I stood below, and called coaxingly:

"Rhadamés! Here, Rhadamés, Rhadamés, *Rhadamés!* Come down before I insult you by calling you 'Simon Peter'!"

He replied with a trumpet note. I climbed cautiously up the side of the rickety crib. As I reached out a tentative hand, the bird flapped his clipped wings and flew.

Quick as he was, I was quicker. I grabbed for him as he rose in the air.

My hand closed about a mass of feathers. The bird was caught; or, rather, part of him was caught. For, with a truly demoniac yell he fluttered to the roof of the barn, leaving in my clutch a great handful of gorgeous yard-long tail-feathers.

Tailless, yet free, he reached the barn roof-tree. Aghast, I sat on the corn-crib, gazing at the mass of marvelous feathers I held.

"I'm afraid I haven't caught quite enough of him," I sighed.

And, carefully pocketing the tail-feathers, I began to climb laboriously from the corn-crib's summit, up the slippery, sagging roof of the barn.

From the roof-tree Simon Peter Rhadamés watched my approach, with his head on one side, his golden eyes glaring down at my sprawling, wriggling two hundred pounds of abbreviated bulk.

He had lost much of his grandeur, and the absence of three feet of tail gave him a curiously lopsided appearance. Vaguely, I felt he would no longer seem quite so beautiful to the one girl.

Yet, even though I must restore him to her in two sections, I was all the more resolved she should have all of him there was, and I continued my writhing ascent.

A rough voice hailed me in rage from the barn-yard below. Glancing over my shoulder, I beheld a shirt-sleeved, gray-whiskered giant shaking his fists at me. A white bulldog at his side flashed a horrible dental display.

But I was not minded to quit the race with the goal so near. Neither understanding nor heeding old Griswold's protests, I climbed upward.

"That Excelsior chap in the poem had nothing on me," I panted to myself. "I can settle with the old thief down below there after I catch Simon Peter Rhadamés. Possession is nine points of the law. But—I wonder how many points an angry bulldog scores?"

The decayed barn-roof was sagging and creaking perilously under my weight, but I was near my quarry.

Almost within arm's reach was Rhadamés. He was already crouching to speed away on another clipped-wing flight. I wriggled forward once more. The bird flapped upward. As he took flight, my right arm shot out. It was nip-and-tuck. But I won.

My fingers reached one of his legs. The squawking, flapping, panic-stricken bird was mine. *All* of him.

In triumph I tightened my grip on his leg, half rose to my feet, and—

There was a ripping, rending, tearing sound that mingled right harmoniously with Rhadamés's shrieks, and with the howls of the farmer below.

The barn roof gently collapsed under me—about ten square feet of it. And, peacock in hand, I drifted downward.

They say—in the science books—that a falling body travels sixteen feet the first second; from which I infer that my downward flight lasted just five-eighths of a second. At the end of which time I found my descent stopped by a broad beam about nine feet above the hay-littered floor of the barn. Below me, as I balanced precariously on the dusty timber, lay the wreckage of shingles.

Above, the late afternoon sun poured in through the impromptu window my body's flight had inserted in the roof.

I managed to right myself by an effort worthy of a circus equilibrist. I sat astride the wide beam, my fall checked, and that abominable peacock still safe in my grasp. I had not even spilled the tail-feathers from my pocket.

The quest was accomplished. I had won!

Just how I was to get to the ground and—past the farmer and his dog—home again, I had not time to figure out.

For, barely had I established my balance on the beam, and assured myself that no bones were broken, when on the floor below me appeared Griswold. Gamboling at his side was the big bulldog, doing a veritable dance of delight at prospect of meeting me.

"Waal," drawled the farmer in the cheery tones of a sick bear, "I guess I've got ye now, all right! Come down."

"I cannot bring myself to accept invitations from total strangers," I retorted coldly.

"Come down here, I tell ye!" roared Griswold, reaching for a ladder that lay in a corner, "or I'll come up after ye."

"That *might* be better," I agreed. "It will be amusing to upset the ladder just as you get close to the top."

He stopped, laid down the ladder, grunted in perplexity, and ran his gnarled fingers through his beard. I took advantage of his indecision to speak a few thoughtfully chosen words.

"Mr. Homer Griswold," I began, "I have in my hand—and in my pocket—a peacock, variously known as 'Rhadamés' and as 'Simon Peter.' What's in a name? I fared forth to-day to find him. I did so. If he chanced to be on your barn, it was no fault of mine. Nor was it my fault that you let your barn roof fall into such disrepair that part of it refused to stay where it belonged. I catch you red-handed in possession of the aforesaid Simon Peter—pronounced Rhadamés. If you want to avoid a lawsuit, kindly remove your dog and let me go on my way in peace."

"Waal, of all the— Avoid a lawsoot, hey? *Avoid* it? Say, you red-headed hipperpotamus, lawsoots is meat and drink to me. An' I guess I've got the right end of the biggest one I've ever had. You trespassed on my premises. You've broke into my buildings. You've sp'iled my barn, an' you've tried to carry off a peacock valued at—"

"Prythee, peace!" I commanded. "Seek not to enmesh the real issue in a maze of words. I came here to get this peacock. I got him. Unless you want to go to jail, let me pass. O denizen of Pompford-loveliest-village-of-the-plain, enchain thy faithful hound, that I and this bird of vanity may depart in safety. Hasten, good yokel!"

"I don't speak them furren languages," he returned. "An' I don't need to. I'm a plain American citizen, an' I know my rights. I've caught ye breakin' the law an' damagin' my prop'ty. Are you comin' down, or ain't ye?"

"Are you going to tie up that dog first?"

"Not much, I ain't."

"Then," I decided, "be it never so humble, there's no place like this beam. Here I stay until—"

"Just as you please," he agreed suddenly. "Here, Rover! Watch him! *Watch* him, I say!"

The dog increased tenfold his eagerness to be near me.

"Thar!" announced Griswold. "Rover don't never stir away from anything I tell him to watch. He'll stay right here till doomsday. An' if ye try to git down, he'll be waitin' for you. Stay where ye be, if it soots yer. I'm off to git Constable Bartholf an' a posse. Ye'll sleep to-night in the calaboose, freshie! Ye'll stay where ye be till I bring 'em here. An' what they see for themselves then will be evidence enough. *Watch him, Rover!*"

He stamped out, leaving me a prisoner of hopelessness, a fugitive from injustice. What was to be done? Clearly I could not wait here until a posse of rustic Jersey constabulary should dislodge me and drag me off to the local lockup.

I had come to Pompford to spend the week-end with the one girl's family. And now I was like enough to spend it in jail. For in cooler moments, I could see that I had perhaps overstepped the rigid letter of the law by climbing a stranger's barn.

Even though the theft of the peacock could readily enough be proved on Griswold, I was liable to arrest for trespass. The one girl would never let me hear the last of it.

No, I could not stay there, tamely awaiting the arrival of Griswold and the law. Equally clearly, I could not descend and risk sudden death at the hands—teeth, I mean—of a large and very temperamental bulldog.

I glared at the offending, struggling peacock. He responded with an ear-splitting scream. The bulldog renewed his dance, to a deep-growled accompaniment.

I sat alone, aloft, unloved.

I have been happier. Several times.

Then I shook off my lethargy. I was ever a man of action. And now, if ever, was the time to act. But how?

I glanced about me, like a good general studying the battle-ground. And the survey brought no fruits.

I looked down winsomely on the dog. I chirped at him, and lyingly addressed him as "Good old doggie!" He retorted with a perfectly earth-shaking growl. No. Diplomacy would not suffice.

The peacock's struggles not only wholly engaged one of my hands, but endangered my balance. I took off my long tie and bound the bird's legs together with it.

I had a momentary thought of tossing Rhadamés down to the dog. Perhaps the brute might devour the bird, and then sink into a slumber of repletion, during which I could steal away unnoticed.

This was true strategy. But I would not do it. Not for naught had I been endowed with red hair and a square jaw.

I had fared forth on a peacock quest for the one girl. And I would return home with that peacock or not at all. So I tied him to my belt, and did some more thinking.

And, as I meditated, I recalled a story I had read years ago, of a man who circumvented an angry bulldog. My more or less fertile brain at last hit on a variation of that plan.

With me, to *think* was always to *do.* Or misdo, as the case might be.

Gingerly I took off my coat. Then I lay face downward at full length along the beam, Rhadamés squawking lustily at my belt the while.

My maneuvers stirred the bulldog into new activity. He leaped upward, snarling again and again in a crazy effort to reach me.

Gripping the beam, equestrian fashion, with my knees, I got a firm hold on one of the sleeves of my discarded coat. Then I dangled the garment insultingly over the dog.

While I shook the coat in tantalizing fashion, I shouted jeeringly at the animal. The double affront was more than any self-respecting bulldog could stand.

He sprang at the dangling sleeve of the coat. Adroitly I twitched it out of his reach.

Again I lowered it. This time, half dazed with fury, he launched himself, openmouthed, at the offending cloth.

His mighty jaws met in the sleeve, several feet in air, caught their grip and held it like grim death. The weight of the dog's body, as he swung from one end of the coat while I clutched the other, almost hurled me from my perch on the beam.

But I kept my balance. Without letting the dog's feet touch ground, I swung the coat to and fro like a pendulum. To its sleeve hung the dog, resisting all my seeming efforts to shake him loose.

He had clamped his powerful jaws upon the cloth, and was not to be jerked free of it by any puny attempts of mine.

Wider and wider grew the swing of the pendulum. Tighter grew the dog's jaw-grip. Then, bracing myself harder, I gave a final swing-ing heave that brought dog, coat, and all upward till they touched the beam, not a yard from my face.

The dog, feeling the broad, solid beam under his feet, scrambled madly for a foothold, found it, dropped the coat, and rushed along the beam toward me.

But I was not there.

The instant I had seen the brute's feet touch the beam, I had let myself downward to the full sweep of my arms and had dropped awkwardly but safely to the hay-piled floor below.

There I scrambled to my feet, made sure the squawking peacock was still flapping secure at my belt, and looked upward.

Crouching on the beam, nine feet above ground, snarled the dog. But never yet was there a bulldog, be he never so brave, that dare launch himself downward to earth from such a height.

He capered along the beam, howling in an impotent rage that touched my heart.

I have sometimes wondered what old Griswold must have thought when, on his return, he found me gone and his faithful watchdog occupying my place on the beam. On less foundation, in ancient times, have tales of witchcraft been evolved.

III.

COATLESS, disheveled, yet triumphant, with the peacock tucked under my arm, I walked through the glory of the beautiful sunset to the house of the one girl. She was on the lawn.

So were her father and mother. So was the other man. They were gazing admiringly at something that their intervening bodies shut off for the moment from my view. I stole upon them silently, and then cried, exultant:

"See, the conquering hero comes! Behold Rhadamés! Here is part of him under my arm, and the rest is in my pocket. The Jersey knight errant has fulfilled his quest, O lady fair! I—"

My jubilant tones trailed away into a gasp. The others had turned as I spoke.

And then it was that I saw the object they had been admiring.

On the lawn in front of them strutted and posed a gorgeous peacock.

"The coachman," began the only girl, at first sound of my voice, "had put him in the stable because the chicken-house wasn't strong enough. He was there all the time! I'm so sorry I sent you— Why, Bobbie Ballard," she continued, catching full sight of me, "what's the matter with you? And what have you got there?"

I let my prize flutter to earth. With a farewell squawk, he made off in the direction of the Griswold farm.

"Why," went on the only girl, "that is old Mr. Griswold's peacock! The very apple of his eye. He—"

I stalked to the house. At the door I turned and said majestically:

"The days of knight errantry have fled forever. I think I will lie down for a while. Before I go to jail, you know."

A week later I paid a bill, itemized as follows:

```
    R. Ballard to H. Griswold, Dr.
To 1 broaken roof ...................................$55.79
To 1 Trespsing ......................................... 50.10
To 1 Ill-treetment of a inosent dog....... 25.25
To 1 borowing a pecock........................ 10.
To 1 Loss of said pecox tale ...................  30.05
Total. ...................................................$171.19
Please remit.
```

Yes, I "remitted." And cheerfully. I was too happy to care. Although, on the same day I had the delight of "remitting" $250 more.

For an engagement ring.

The Watcher in the Hall

Chapter I.
The Job Hunter.

THE Matterhorn Apartment House was disgorging an angry and excited swarm of occupants.

First came the man who was clutching a fur coat. He darted through the doorway, cleared the low flight of front steps at a leap, and struck the ground with a thud that seemed likely to jar him to pieces.

But he recovered his balance on the instant, turned sharply to the right, and ran at top speed toward the avenue, a half block away.

Next, close at his heels, emerged from the apartment house a shirt-sleeved janitor, greasy of face, a monkey wrench clutched in one hand.

Then, in quick succession, flashed forth two elevator men, a tele-phone-switchboard operator, and a male tenant or two. Last of all, a rather overdressed woman emerged from the doorway, and stood on the steps, where she screamed lustily.

The janitor was built for endurance, rather than for speed, so, though he vigorously pursued the man with the fur coat, he was quickly outstripped by the long-legged telephone operator.

The latter, taking the lead among the pursuers, bore down like a young whirlwind upon the coat bearer.

The fugitive, hearing the beat of steps growing uncomfortably close behind him, halted so suddenly as to almost upset his balance, whirled, and faced the oncoming group of runners.

As he turned, his free hand sought his hip pocket, flew forth again, and pointed toward his would-be captors. And in the clenched fist he leveled at them he grasped something—something that glittered blue in the morning sunlight. The men ceased their onrush with an abruptness that was ludicrous.

There is something about the little, blue-gray muzzle of a pistol that is highly disconcerting. And the pasty-faced man who menaced the crowd seemed as much in earnest as is the proverbial cornered rat in a drain.

The lanky operator pulled up a bare two yards from the pistol mouth, and glanced back for reassurance toward his clustered followers.

"Stop, thief!" he yelled.

As the thief had not only stopped, but had stopped his pursuers as well, the command seemed a trifle unnecessary.

But it seemed to tide over a strained situation. So the operator repeated it; and the cry was caught up by the others.

Meantime, the thief stood, gripping the pilfered coat to his breast with one arm, while with the other he held the revolver threateningly pointed at one after another of his overwary opponents.

Up and down the sunny, quiet street there was no visible sign of a much needed policeman. In fact, the only other person on the block was a compactly built, plainly dressed young man, who had just turned the corner from the avenue, a few yards ahead, and was walking in leisurely fashion in the direction of the Matterhorn.

The newcomer noted the chattering, shouting knot of men, and the fellow who held them at bay, and he quickened his steps. Hearing some one hurrying close behind him, the thief whirled again, preparing with uplifted weapon to bluff this latest adversary, or, if possible, to dodge past him and make a new break for liberty.

The thief turned with lightning swiftness, his extended pistol arm moving, as he moved, like the bar of a semaphore. But the compact young man was quite as quick.

As the flying pistol arm whizzed about toward him—before the thief could gain balance to level the weapon—the newcomer jumped forward and struck.

He did not clench his fist, after the manner of story heroes, and lay the miscreant at his feet with one mighty blow. A man can shoot almost as effectively from the ground as in any other posture, and the felling of the thief would probably have started a fusillade.

Instead, the compact young man did a far cleverer, if less dramatic, thing. With open palm, striking hard, and with an agility the eye could scarcely follow, he slapped the other's hand with the force of a horse's kick.

The pistol flew from its owner's grip as if it were endowed with wings, and fell unheeded into the middle of the street; then the newcomer sprang forward, just as the thief ducked nimbly and sought to dash past him, the skirts of the stolen fur coat blown wide by the sudden maneuver.

The thief still gripped the garment by its collar, and the stocky young chap, seizing the flowing skirts deftly as the bullfighter wields his red cape, flung it over the thief's head and shoulders.

The great folds of soft fur enveloped the fellow like a shroud, shutting out the light, confusing his sense of direction, half stifling him.

The stranger flung his arms about the queerly muffled form, balking the other's efforts to wriggle from under the heavy garment, cramping his struggles, and rendering useless his hands and arms.

With a sharp twist, the newcomer swung his victim around, swathing the cloak tightly about him from the waist up.

Then, propelling the half-smothered, ridiculously helpless victim before him, the young captor calmly forced a way through the gathering crowd, ran his man forward blindly until the apartment-house steps were reached, and there shoved him into the grasp of two policemen whom the woman's screams had at length drawn to the scene.

"Hold on a moment!" he protested, as the patrolmen seized eagerly upon their easily acquired prey. "Don't handle him roughly—*yet*. You may harm this pretty fur coat. Wait till I unwind it from him."

With a careful turn or two, he disengaged the all-enveloping fur from the prisoner's shoulders and head, caught the coat by the collar, and gently shook out its wrinkles.

"That was a neat trick, all right!" commented one of the officers. "Trussed him up like a roasting chicken."

"Say, young fellow," put in the second policeman, pulling out a notebook as he and his comrade finished handcuffing the writhing thief, "what's your name and address? We may have to call you for witness."

"I hope not," answered the victor. "I was glad to be of use in getting back this cloak, for it seems to be of value. But I have no time to waste on witness duty. I expect to be pretty busy."

"We'll have to get your name and address, just the same," insisted the patrolman.

"My name is Arthur Bixby," was the rather impatient answer.

"Address?"

Bixby hesitated; then replied:

"This apartment house."

"You don't live here!" broke in the janitor.

"No, but I expect to from now on."

"But," said the janitor, "all the apartments are taken, and I haven't heard of any one moving out. And," he continued, "the leases forbid tenants to take boarders. So, unless you belong to the family of some of the tenants you—"

"I don't!" laughed Bixby. "I expect to belong to your own official family, janitor. I'm to be the new hall-man!"

Chapter II.
Mr. Crain.

For a moment the janitor stared, surprised, at the unexpected announcement.

"What's that?" he exclaimed at last. "Are you stringing me? You've got more the ways of a college chap, or a swell clerk, or—"

"I'll try to make my ways fit yours," returned Bixby. "In the meantime, what am I to do with this coat?"

"It belongs to Mrs. Frere," interposed the lanky telephone operator. "She—"

But the lady whose screams had brought the two policemen was already volubly explaining her case to those blue-clad arms of the law.

"Yes," she exclaimed, "of course I'll lodge a complaint! What a question to ask! You see, I was just starting out, when I remembered I'd left my hand bag upstairs. I laid my coat across that chair in the entrance hall there, near the front door, while I went back to get one of the elevator men to go up for my bag."

"And," spoke up a plump, red-headed elevator man, who seemed momentarily about to burst through his tight livery, "she hadn't but just turned her back, when that crook, who was passing, jumps up the steps, sneaks into the hall, sudden like, yanks the coat off'n the chair, an' starts to make a getaway. Mr. Trabb—that's the janitor, here—was just coming out from jacking up the elevator. Him and me both sees him at the same time. So do the others. So we starts a nice little Marathon, and—"

"We'll take him to the station now, ma'am," interrupted one of the policemen. "You can step around later and make the complaint. It's lucky for you that we got here so quick."

"Yes, ain't it?" chimed in the irrepressible elevator man. "If you'd got here five minutes later, Bixby would 'a' had to lug the guy around to the station by himself. And he could 'a' done it, I bet, just as easy as he caught him all by himself. Why, he—"

"Shut up, Carrots!" ordered the janitor.

The police were ostensibly and ostentatiously deaf to the irreverent Carrots' slur on their prowess. Mrs. Frere had already hurried indoors to impart the news of the adventure to her family.

Just then a tall, stout man, middle-aged, and dressed with scrupulous neatness, came out of the house.

"What is the matter with the elevator, Trabb?" he demanded sharply of the janitor. "I rang for five minutes, and then had to walk down. Is—"

He got no further. His gaze fell upon the policemen standing before him on the steps.

Bixby, idly glancing at him, saw the man's florid face grow a shade paler, and saw his pale-gray eyes contract like those of a cornered animal.

The expression was but momentary. Again, in a fraction of a second, the man's countenance regained its normal indifferent calm.

"I'm sorry, Mr. Crain," the janitor was saying. "You see, we just caught a sneak thief, and every one was so excited nobody thought to tend the elevator. It shan't happen again. I'm sorry you had to walk down."

Mr. Crain nodded carelessly, and prepared to resume his descent of the steps. The next stride brought him almost face to face with the captured thief.

Again, Bixby, still watching him narrowly, thought he saw a swift, almost imperceptible, change cross the calm, florid visage, as his eyes chanced to meet those of the thief.

Then Mr. Crain strolled slowly up the street toward the avenue, as though dismissing the whole sordid incident from his mind.

"If I were a betting man," mused Bixby to himself, "I'd wager a small fortune he has reason to fear the law. And that he knows that sneak thief, too. It may be interesting to study him,"

Chapter III.
The New Hallman.

"Now, then," remarked the janitor, as the policemen and their prisoner moved away, "what was that talk of yours about coming here to work? I've heard nothing about it. And the Bruce Estate generally trusts me to hire my own men."

For answer, Bixby pulled a letter from his pocket and handed it to Trabb. The envelope bore the imprint:

BRUCE ESTATE
Apartments and Houses. Suburban Cottages
Office: Blank Street and Broadway

The janitor, at sight of the imprint, took the envelope with much the same air that a field marshal may have received one of Napoleon's dispatches, opened it slowly, and read, with moving lips, the half dozen typewritten lines.

"H'm!" he commented. "This says you're to have the job of hallman here, at thirty dollars a moth. Signed by Colonel Bruce himself, too. Is he a patron of yours?"

"No," laughed Bixby. "I'm not lucky enough to have a 'patron.' If I had, he'd probably give me something better than a hallman's berth. I went into the Bruce Estate offices, and asked for a job. Colonel Bruce happened to be there, and saw me himself. He liked my credentials, and I must have answered his questions pretty satisfactorily, for he dictated that note to you and sent me on here."

"Gee!" commented Carrots. "You're in great luck, all right, all right! If *I* was to get next to Colonel Bruce just once, I'd touch him for a raise, and I'd sing him such a spiel about my good points that he'd think I was worth—"

"Cut that out, Carrots!" ordered the janitor. "And chase back to your elevator. The bells there are ringing like a—"

"A Swiss bell-ringer troupe," suggested Carrots. "All right—I'm on my way."

"Colonel Bruce," announced the janitor pompously, "is the head of the whole Bruce Estate. Maybe you didn't know that, young man? He owns no less than forty apartment houses in this city alone. You were lucky in getting a job through him. I hope you will try to deserve it, and make good."

"I will try, sir," agreed Bixby meekly.

"How about *me?*" spoke up the lanky telephone operator wrathfully.

"Well," replied the janitor nervously, "*how* about you, Marks?"

"When the hallman job fell vacant, last week," snapped Marks, "you promised it to *me*. You said you had pull enough at the office to get it for me. Where do I come in?"

"I can't go back on Colonel Bruce's own orders, can I?" protested Trabb.

"You promised!" insisted Marks stubbornly.

"Be sensible, can't you?" wheedled the janitor. "What can *I* do? Besides, a telephone operator, at eight dollars a week, is better off than a hallman, at thirty dollars a month."

"Like blazes he is!" contradicted Marks hotly. "A hallman wears a uniform, and has no wear and tear on his own clothes. He gets tips all the time. He's in on the 'tipping ring,' too, and can hold up the elevator men for a rake-off. Who ever tips a telephone operator? Eh? Not once in a blue moon. A measly slice of the general tip at Christmas time. That's all. And now—"

"I'm sorry," said Bixby. "I didn't know I was barring somebody else out of the job."

"Don't you worry about Marks," interposed the janitor. "He's always kicking. Talk about tips! Why, from Mr. Crain alone, Marks gets more tips than all the other employees put together."

"Who says I do?" flared Marks, his pasty face reddening. "What have I got to do with Mr. Crain, or—"

"I don't know," returned the janitor, "and I've been wondering; but I do know he tips you, for I've seen him do it when he didn't know I was in the hall."

"Spying, eh?" said Marks disagreeably.

"That'll do for you!" shouted the janitor, taking refuge in gusty anger. "I don't want any back talk from my s'bord'nates. You've got an easy berth, Joe Marks; and yet you're always grouching. How about *me*—with only twenty-five dollars a month, and—"

"And your rent and gas and whole basement apartment to yourself," sneered Marks, "and big tips from the tenants, and a chance to do lots of odd 'neighborhood jobs' on the side. To say nothing of rake-offs for plumbers' supplies, and coal, and a dozen other things. Oh, it's too bad about *you*, Trabb!"

"I warned you not to give me any more back talk!" thundered the janitor. "If you want to keep your job you'd—"

"Oh, I'll keep it, fast enough," retorted Marks, turning back toward his angrily buzzing switchboard. "I know too much about your lines of graft for you to fire me."

He was gone before Trabb could frame a fitting retort. The janitor scowled after him, then turned to Arthur Bixby.

"Pay no attention to Marks, young man," he said. "I'm too easy with all that bunch, and they impose on my good nature something terrible. And don't you go believing what he said about graft," he added nervously. "There's no chance for graft here. And if there was I wouldn't take it. I'd fire Marks for hinting such a thing, only I can't bear to see a poor fellow thrown out of work. If ever Colonel Bruce should be here on one of his inspections, and should ask you—"

"He won't," answered Bixby. "And now shall I get to work?"

"Come on, and I'll dig out the last two hallmen's uniforms, to see if they'll either of them fit you. You'll work from nine a.m. till eight p.m., with half an hour for lunch and for dinner, and every other Sunday off. In the evenings, the elevator man that's on duty does hallman work, too. You're to keep the pavement and steps and front hall dusted off, and the hall furniture and brass work cleaned up, and take charge of the elevator men and operators, and tend door, and—"

"Hold on!" suggested Bixby. "Suppose we wait till I'm in uniform, and tell me things more gradually. It's a bit confusing to have them fired at one like this. I'm liable to forget some of them."

To himself he added, as he followed the janitor to the storeroom:

"I think this should prove rather interesting. I wonder why that man Crain is afraid of the police, and how such an ultrarespectable-looking man should happen to know a sneak thief? And," he added, as they passed the telephone switchboard, "I wonder why Marks was so indignant when the janitor spoke of his 'pull' with Crain?"

Chapter IV.
Learning The Ropes.

Arthur Bixby had for some days merged his individuality in a somewhat ill-fitting dark-green livery, with thin red stripes down the legs and on the collar and cuffs. On one side of the collar, too, was a tarnished gilt inscription, "Matterhorn"; on the other, "Hallman."

He found his duties not overdifficult when he had succeeded in systematizing them. The hours, however, were long, and there were stretches of time when there was practically nothing to do.

To sit in a silent hall, to converse with elevator men or switchboard operators, to keep an eye on the negative duties of his own department—all this bored him to extinction.

So he explored the building when he could find time, asked innumerable questions, sought the "why and wherefore" of the thousand details relating to apartment-house routine.

To an outsider, there are a myriad unknown things in the most simply conducted flat or apartment building. The system is usually kept as much out of sight from the public as are the engines of an ocean greyhound from the promenade-deck passengers.

And it was this complicated system that Arthur Bixby set himself to acquire, throwing himself into the task with the zest that a zealous student might bring to the study of a new and fascinating language.

In spite of a few snubs from Trabb and Marks, the young man made real progress in his odd research. He never needed to ask the same question a second time, but showed an instinctive grasp of the subject.

He mastered the intricacies of the great steam-heat furnace in the sub-cellar, knew to a pound what coal it needed, and how the supply could best be graded to suit the weather.

He quickly learned the secret of the telephone switchboard—that utter mystery to most outsiders—and was soon able to manipulate the twenty-five plugs and keys of its cribbage-board surface with the ease of a veteran.

He found out how to "size up" visitors to the apartment house; to differentiate between legitimate callers and the sprucest-looking canvassers.

He at once set about studying the elevator and its workings. He incidentally won the devotion of both elevator men by declaring that each of them should keep his own tips—instead of pooling them, as before, and paying tribute to hallman or janitor.

Deep he delved into everything, from the dumb-waiter service to the intricate rules governing the alternate use of the roof clothesline.

He found out, among other things, that apartment-house life is a world in itself. There were twenty-five families in the Matterhorn. Each had its own affairs, which it doubtless considered private, but which, after the gossip of elevator men and telephone operators had thrashed them out, were about as private as a glass case's interior.

The elevator and switchboard men, having many scattered moments of spare time on their hands, were wont to gather in the lower hall and piece out each other's store of gossip.

They knew, to a nicety, how much food, and of what sort, every family ordered; what people were living above their means, and which were saving.

They knew what callers the various young girls received, how often each swain called, and how late he stayed.

They knew every detail of the latest fierce quarrel of the couple on the "top flour, south." This quarrel, begun in the elevator—and faithfully reported by Carrots—had had its culmination, hours later, over the telephone, and had been told by Marks. The intervening scenes were supplied by the couple's maid, who confided it to the night elevator man.

In fact, the maids, who were usually of a talkative sort, managed to fill up any gaps in the house employees' knowledge of their tenants' affairs.

Between telephone, elevator, and servants, there were few facts that did not reach the unofficial council of workers below stairs.

"It's queer," Carrots once observed, when Bixby had commented on this. "These guys who live in apartments, not only here, but all over town, think they're close-mouthed as a bunch of Little Necks. They put on all kinds of 'dog,' and they go sailing in and out past us as if they had a mortgage on the earth. And all the time we know more about 'em than their own kin ever know. Gee! If I was to hand out some of the telephone talk I hear—"

"It seems to be pretty generally handed out," observed Bixby.

"Oh, among ourselves and the servant goils!" answered Carrots.

"I don't like it," said Bixby. "It doesn't seem honorable."

"Who said it did? But if folks is going to spiel all about their private biz over the phone, or in the elevator, or before their maids, or talk loud about it just when one of us is happening to go past their doors—what can they expect? I read a dandy bunch of stuff in a noospaper once, called 'Dumbwaiter Di'logues.' I liked it a whole lot, just because it was true.

"But when I heard some folks outside, once, laugh about it, I saw all at once that it was meant to be funny. Folks thought it was a joke. I guess if those folks had stood at the foot of a dumb-waiter shaft as often as us chaps do, they'd 'a' found it was straight talk, and not a ha-ha song. There's just one feller in the whole bunch whose number I can't get."

"What do you mean?"

"I mean Crain. None of us knows anything about him. And that makes me think there's something funny going on. When a man lives a year in a house like this, and the help know nothing about him—it don't look right. How do you dope him up, Artie?"

Chapter V.
A Matter Of Dislike.

Before Bixby could answer the elevator man's question, the bell rang, and Carrots, straightening his collar, slipped into the car, and slammed shut the gilded gate.

Bixby was moving down the hall when the telephone switchboard buzzed. Marks was out at lunch. So Bixby sat down in the operator's chair, and fastened the steel ear cap over his head.

The call came from a second-floor apartment—Crain's. Bixby opened the switch. Crain's voice sounded through the receiver:

"Give me one hundred and six—"

A truck loaded with iron rails went past the open front door at that moment, filling the air with a deafening racket. The last part of the number demanded by Crain was utterly lost.

"Will you please repeat that, Mr. Crain?" said Arthur. "There was so much noise down here I couldn't catch what you said."

"That isn't Marks' voice!" called Crain sharply. "Who are *you?*"

"I am Bixby—the hallman."

"I want Marks."

"He is out at lunch, sir. Shall I send him to you when he comes back?"

"Send him to me?" echoed Crain, in a lofty scorn that seemed to hold, nevertheless, a trace of nervousness. "No, of course not! Why should you? What could I want to see a switchboard operator for, stupid?"

"You said just now you wanted him," returned Bixby, slightly irritated, as well as puzzled.

"I meant I wanted him on the wire," was the answer.

"I'll tell him to call you up," said Arthur.

"Oh, you thick-headed young fool!" roared Crain. "I want him to connect me with some one on the phone. That's all. Why should I want him to call me up? I don't even know him by sight."

"I am in charge of the switchboard in his absence," said Bixby. "I'll get you whatever number you wish."

"No, you won't!" growled Crain, and left the telephone.

"Why not?" muttered Bixby to himself, as he left the switchboard. "What can he have to say that is so private as to keep every one but Marks from giving him the connection? Especially as he says he doesn't even know Marks by sight. Why should he trust him, then, rather than the rest of us? It's a queer game."

His perplexed reverie was cut short by a tall, slender girl, who had entered the house and come down the hall. She was carrying a heavy suit case.

Bixby ran forward to relieve her of her burden. As he did so, their eyes chanced to meet. He saw a daintily aristocratic little head, crowned by a pile of soft, rust-colored hair; a flushed little flower face, and two big, deep-brown eyes, that were regarding him with frankly bewildered interest.

For an instant the two stood thus. Then Bixby, suit case in hand, turned toward the elevator.

"Aren't you—" she began impulsively.

Then, at a glance at the back of his ill-made livery, as he plodded on ahead of her, she finished in a more sedate key:

"Aren't you a new hallman?"

"Yes'm," mumbled Bixby, as he moved on.

"I thought so. I didn't remember seeing you before I went away."

"No'm," answered Bixby dully.

He had reached the elevator, and stood punching the electric button, his back still toward her.

The girl's fresh young presence seemed to him to fill the dim hall with spring sunshine. Yet he did not turn again to look at her. Apartment-house employees sometimes are taught not to stare.

Almost at once, the car descended, and Carrots flung back its door. The girl nodded pleasantly at the elevator man. Carrots responded with an expansive grin of welcome.

She entered the car, and it went up, leaving Bixby gaping after it in the hallway that all at once seemed darker and gloomier than usual.

"Some class to *her!*" remarked Carrots, when the car came down again. "That's Miss Lois Raynor. Been spending the winter with old Mrs. Frere. The old lady's her aunt. The girl went away on a visit last month. Just got back."

"Yes?" answered Bixby indifferently.

"You old owl!" scoffed Carrots. "Every feller in the house walks with his head turned over his shoulder at her as long as she's in sight. And you just grunt 'Yes?' as if it was a pot rassler I was talking about. You ought to go lay down somewhere till you wake up—specially since she took the trouble to ask about you."

"Eh?" queried Arthur suddenly. "What's that?"

"Waked up at last, haven't you? Another minute, and you'd 'a' fell out of bed. Yes, she asked about you. She said: 'I see we've got a new hall-man!' "

"Oh!"

"Now, don't go looking like the dollar you'd found was only a doughnut," admonished Carrots. "She said some more. She says: 'What's his name?' I told her. Then she asks: 'Where did he come from, do you know?' "

"What did you say?" demanded Bixby, in unwonted fervor.

"All het up, ain't you?" grinned Carrots. "I didn't want to let on you was just a greenhorn, that'd hardly got broke in yet. She might 'a' lost int'rest in you. So I just says—"

"Well?"

"I says: 'He come here, miss, straight from the St. Crœsus, where he'd been head elevator man for three years.' 'Are you sure?' asks she, kind of doubtful like. So it was up to me to cinch the yarn. I says: "Course I'm sure. I ought to be—he's my own cousin. I got him the job here.' "

"Carrots!" said Bixby, with something like a sigh of relief. "If you had lived in olden times, you would have made Ananias weep on the shoulder of Baron Munchausen."

"Munchausen?" echoed Carrots doubtfully. "That's a new one on me. He must 'a' run on some of the Western tracks. There's no horse here in the East of that name."

Marks slouched in from lunch, and Bixby left the switchboard. Just then a buzz sounded on the telephone. Marks picked up the receiver, and growled:

"Well?"

There was a pause. Then he said:

"All right, ma'am."

Turning from the board, he went on: "Mrs. Beaujolais is sending in a howl for some one to go up to the roof and show her new maid about the clotheslines. The girl's up there, she says, with a basket of clothes, and doesn't know which lines are hers."

"I'll go up," said Bixby. "Take me to the top, Carrots."

The telephone sounded again, and Marks once more put on the receiver. As the car started, Bixby heard him say, in a servile, eager tone, far different from his ordinary surly voice:

"Yes, Mr. Crain."

Chapter VI.
A Run-In With Crain.

It was fifteen minutes before the new maid could be taught in full the mysteries of roof clotheslines, and which of them she might or might not use. Then Bixby ran down the scuttle stairs to the top of the elevator shaft. The car was descending with some callers who had just left a top-floor apartment.

Sooner than wait for the elevator's return, Arthur started downstairs on foot, expecting to meet Carrots on the return "up trip."

Down he went, traversing the various white-stone flights that wound about the square elevator shaft. The canvas-soled house shoes that he always wore when on duty made practically no sound as his light, athletic tread struck the stone steps.

And so he moved on until he was descending the flight leading from the third to the second floor. There, as he was rounding the corner of the shaft, he saw a door in front of him open.

A man slipped silently out, closing the door behind him, and ran swiftly down the short flight to the ground floor.

So furtive were his motions that Bixby, unseen from the protecting shaft corner, eyed the flying figure keenly. He had but a momentary glimpse before the other vanished below. But that glimpse was quite enough for him to identify—Marks!

Bixby halted in amaze. What was Marks doing in one of the apartments? Why had he slunk out of it so stealthily, so fast?

Arthur glanced at the door Marks had just closed behind him. It was that of Crain's flat. He recalled Crain's recent words: "I don't even know him by sight," and "What could I want to see a switchboard operator up here for?"

Surely both declarations were odd enough, in face of what Bixby had just seen. Nor could he at all understand. Then came to him the unwelcome fear lest Marks had stolen into the apartment in its occupant's absence, and had looted its valuables.

He had often heard of apartment-house thieves. In fact, Trabb had told him of a Matterhorn elevator man who had been discharged only a few months earlier for that very fault.

Marks was not of pleasing personality. His shifty eyes and sharp face were not of a kind to inspire trust. If he had seen Crain go out a few minutes earlier, perhaps, and had run unnoticed upstairs to—

Bixby resolved to make sure. Going to the apartment, he rang the bell. If it were not answered, his suspicions would be confirmed.

For Crain lived alone, keeping no servant, getting his meals at a near-by hotel, receiving practically no visitors, and living in all ways like a recluse. Therefore, if he were now out—

But he was not. Almost on the very instant of the ring, the door swung open, and Crain's heavy body blocked the threshold.

On sight of Bixby, the big man glowered. He looked the uniformed figure up and down in cold surprise; then asked:

"Well, what do *you* want?"

"The day switchboard operator came out of here a moment ago," began Arthur, in some confusion, "and I—"

"He did not!" rasped Crain.

"The switchboard man—Marks," went on Bixby, thinking Crain misunderstood. "He came out of your apartment just now. And—"

"He did *not!*" reiterated Crain, in the same emotionless, hard voice. "No one has come into this apartment or left it all morning."

"You are mistaken. I saw—"

"You saw nothing. I have been here all morning. No one could have come in or gone out without my knowledge."

"I see," said Bixby. "Marks came and went *with* your knowledge, then. That was all I wanted to know. I was afraid he had—"

"Look here!" demanded Crain. "What do you mean by hanging around the door of my apartment and spying on me like this? Eh? What do you mean by it? I shall report you, and have you dismissed."

Bixby was turning away, too angry to trust himself to speak, when Crain caught him by the arm.

"Answer my question!" he ordered. "What do you mean by hanging about the hall in front of my apartment, and trying to spy upon me?"

"The halls of this house, Mr. Crain," said Bixby, swallowing a crazy desire to drive his fist into the plump, scarlet face that glared down bullying into his, "are public to all of us. As hall-man, I am in charge of them, as well as of the hall employees. And when a man who is supposed to be on duty at the switchboard downstairs is found sneaking like a thief out of an apartment, it is my duty to make inquiries. And I shall not be discharged for doing that duty."

"We shall see about that!" retorted Crain. "If the agent of this building chooses to keep an impertinent, spying hallman and to lose a sixty-dollar-a-month tenant, he can do so. But I shall give him that choice."

"Listen, Mr. Crain," replied Bixby, with ominous quiet: "That is the third time you have called me a spy. Let it be the last. Otherwise, the hallman will not be discharged for impertinence, but for thrashing the sixty-dollar-a-month tenant. Is that quite clear?"

"Do you know," blustered Crain, "I could have you sent to jail for making such a threat?"

"Oh, no, you couldn't," corrected Bixby easily. "That would involve summoning a policeman. And I fancy you dislike policemen almost as much as you dislike impertinent hallmen."

"What do you mean by that?" thundered Crain, his red face showing mottled spots of ashy white. "How dare you—"

But Arthur had turned on his heel and started downstairs. Reaching the ground floor, he walked straight to the switchboard.

"Marks," he demanded, "what were you doing in Mr. Crain's apartment five minutes ago?"

Marks' jaw dropped, and his dull eyes stuck out.

"Wh-what's that?" he sputtered.

"I say," repeated Bixby, "what were you doing just now in the Crain apartment?"

"Who—me?" answered Marks, recovering some of his shaken self-control. "I—I don't know what you mean. You're crazy! I've never been in the Crain apartment in my life. What would I be doing there?"

"That's what I want to know," said Arthur.

"You're nutty!" declared Marks. "I've been sticking close to this switchboard ever since I came back from lunch. If you don't believe me, ask Carrots."

"You can't prove anything, either way, by me," spoke up Carrots. "I'm just back from lugging old Mother Davis' carpetbag to the car for her. She give me a whole nickel for a tip," he added, "and she told me not to spend it foolish. I promised I wouldn't. I said I'd put it with a two-cent stamp I'd saved up, and buy a seagoing aeroplane with it."

"What were you doing up there, Marks?" insisted Bixby.

"I tell you I was never there in my life," growled Marks, who had turned momentarily to the telephone in answer to a call from one of the apartments. "If you don't believe me, we'll go up right now and ask Mr. Crain."

"Carrots," observed Bixby, with seeming irrelevance, "I told you a while ago you had Ananias and Munchausen beaten. I take it back. That record belongs to Marks."

Chapter VII.
Fire!

Marks sprang up with a snarl. But a wild shriek from somewhere in the upper part of the house broke in upon his reply.

The scream was repeated. Another feminine voice caught it up. And through the house rang the cry of "Fire!"

An acrid whiff of smoke swirled down the shaft.

"Gee!" yelled Carrots. "Me for the alarm box!"

And he bolted out of the front doorway at top speed. Marks, in confusion, was running hither and thither. The janitor, appearing from the lower regions, added his quota to the inefficient turmoil.

But Bixby had not waited. Even as Carrots ran for the front door, Arthur sprang into the elevator, and threw over the lever.

Up went the car. The cries above grew steadily nearer as it rose. And the reek of smoke, so faintly perceptible from the entrance hall, waxed sharper.

At the fourth floor the smoke was swirling in thick waves, and almost blinded Arthur. Dimly he saw that the landing was full of excited women.

The door leading to Mrs. Frere's apartment stood wide open. Out through the doorway poured a dense volume of gray smoke.

At sight of Bixby, Mrs. Frere and several other women from adjoining flats on the same floor set up a louder cry.

"Help!" screamed Mrs. Frere. "Oh, don't leave us here to burn!"

Out of the babel came Lois Raynor's clear young voice, calm and authoritative; yet with a tinge of impatience.

"Don't, auntie!" she pleaded. "None of us are in danger. We could go down by the stairway perfectly well. As it is, we can all take the elevator, and—"

But the others evidently felt this was no time for mere sanity to prevail. As Bixby stepped out of the car, they flung themselves bodily at him.

Out of the clamor of simultaneous exclamation and explanations—and through later knowledge—Arthur gleaned the following facts:

Mrs. Frere's maid had been sponging a dress with naphtha. The daylight being somewhat faint in her room, the maid had struck a match to light the gas. In another moment the place had been ablaze.

The maid, her dress flaming, had rushed, with a screech, into the near-by drawing-room, where she had managed to convey the fire in an instant to the flimsy curtains, and thence to the painted woodwork.

Lois had thrown the frantic servant to the floor, and had rolled a thick rug about her, extinguishing the burning dress.

But by that time the flame and smoke had driven them all pell-mell to the outer hallway.

"And my dispatch box!" wailed Mrs. Frere, above the rest of the noise. "With all my bonds, and jewelry, and *everything* in it! I left it in my—"

She had barely half completed the words when Lois, who stood nearest the open door, turned, and, with arms shielding her lowered head, ran back into the apartment.

A bare half minute had passed since Bixby had stepped from the car. During that time he had busied himself to his utmost power in the task of unclasping a hysterical and badly burned servant's embrace from about his neck, and in transferring to the floor a portly woman from the next flat, who had chosen his unwilling arms as the receptacle for a fainting fit.

Now, at sight of Lois' foolhardy act, he let the fainting woman slip to the floor, shook free from the crazed maid, and dashed for the door.

Mrs. Frere, who was unaware of her niece's departure, clutched futilely at him as he sped past her.

"Oh, hallman!" she whimpered, "take us down! Don't leave us here like this!"

Arthur deftly slipped out of his livery jacket, left the garment in her grasp, and hurled himself through the smoke wall into the apartment.

Cries from other floors reached him, and the sound of many running feet. Instinctively he closed the door behind him, to shut out the back draft, and to shut in the smoke.

Once Lois should be safe, he planned to close any open windows, as well, to confine the blaze as much as possible to that one apartment until the firemen should arrive.

Down the hall he groped his way. The smoke buffeted him, clogging his lungs, choking him, torturing his throat, burning his eyes almost to utter blindness.

Momentarily the smoke and the heat grew more terrific. He could make no progress. His ignorance as to which room Lois Raynor had sought to reach still further baffled him.

Down he dropped on all fours, wriggling along, chest to the floor.

Smoke always rises, except when beaten downward by some strong air current, and, in case of fire, safety lies near to the ground.

Now, with his anguished face a bare six inches above the hall carpet, Arthur found breathing again possible. Not easy, but possible. Also, he could see, very dimly, a little distance ahead of him, along the floor. And he could wriggle forward.

He shouted aloud—twice, three times—calling Miss Raynor by name. To force the cry through his smoke-parched throat was agony. As he drew in his breath after each call, the smoke rushed stingingly into his aching lungs.

He listened. But no answer came to his strangled shouts. And fiercely, yet hopelessly, he pushed on.

He knew not in which of the various rooms that opened upon either side of the hallway, Lois might be. He could no more see into these rooms than if he were blindfolded. And she did not answer his frantically croaked shouts.

To explore the place, room by room, was equally impossible. At the maddeningly slow rate of speed with which he was forced to crawl, the apartment would be a roaring furnace before he could half complete so tedious a search.

So—doggedly, despairingly, almost mechanically—he writhed onward, holding his mouth close to the dusty hall carpet, and breathing as seldom as possible.

His outstretched hand touched something that thrilled his dazed brain back to keen activity. For his fingers had closed about the hem of a skirt.

Raising his eyes, he saw dimly, just ahead of him, in the threshold of a bedroom, the body of a woman. It was Lois Raynor. She was lying motionless, her loosened grasp still holding to her breast a bulky metal dispatch box.

Bixby understood. She had known in what room Mrs. Frere kept the box hidden, had made her way thither through the murk and heat, had found the box, and had started back with it. Then, overcome by the smoke, she had fallen—senseless.

Bixby called on his strained forces for a mighty effort. Reaching Lois' side, he lifted her bodily across his shoulders.

In moments of stress, some minor detail often catches the attention. So Bixby now noted that as he lifted the slender, unconscious body, the dispatch box was also lifted. A second glance showed him that she had buckled the box's strap handle to the heavy gold bracelet she wore.

There was no time to waste now in disengaging the heavy case, and, handicapped by the extra weight of metal, Arthur started to return by the way he had come toward the apartment door.

He still clung close to the floor, taking advantage of every whiff of breathable air. The girl's weight, which would ordinarily have been as nothing to so powerful a man, became, in these cramped conditions, a veritable incubus. Yet he fought his way onward.

Here it was that Arthur Bixby's past thirst for information about the house stood him in good stead. He had studied the printed diagram of every apartment, and knew just where each room lay, and its relation toward the street, court, and air shafts.

The fire escapes, he remembered, on this side of the house, ran down past the kitchen windows. And the kitchen was one room behind him, to the right. Turning awkwardly about in the narrow space, he writhed forward as might a football player from under a mass of opponents.

He reached the kitchen door, raised his hand, running his fingers along the jamb until he found the knob.

This he turned, pushed open the door, and dragged Lois inside. The kitchen, though full of smoke and rapidly waxing hotter, was less unbearable of atmosphere than had been the hall.

Bixby knew the way to the window. After what seemed an eternity, he reached it. Laying down his burden with a gentleness that was instinctive, he held his breath, closed his eyes, and rose to his feet.

Fumbling eagerly, he found the window catch, turned it, and threw the sash open. A breath of blessed fresh air rushed in and fanned his fiery, hot face.

The contact with outer air, in that brief instant before the smoke could dispute his possession of it, served as a tonic to the worn-out youth.

Stooping, he lifted Lois in his arms, and stepped with her out upon the fire-escape balcony. He had presence of mind to pause and shut the window behind him, temporarily barring in the smoke. Then, exhausted, gasping, half choked, he sank down on the grilled balcony.

In all his eventful young life, he had never known so wondrously grateful a sense of utter relief as was now his. Crouched in the angle of the fire-escape landing, the senseless girl supported across his knees, he sat inhaling deep breaths of the clean, untainted spring air, feeling life return to his pain-dulled brain, and strength to his overstrained muscles.

Below, he could hear the clang and whistle of fire engines, the tramping and shouts of firemen. From the open windows just ahead of him he could see smoke belching forth from the apartment he had just quitted.

He knew the house was practically fireproof, that unless the flames spread, by means of open windows, from one floor to another, the blazing apartment might burn itself out without spreading the conflagration beyond its own confines, the more especially as the firemen had come so quickly.

Hence, all immediate danger was over. It only remained now for him to bring Lois to her senses again, and to help her down the fire escape into the first apartment whose open kitchen window might offer them ingress.

But, as it happened, that apparently simple feat proved somewhat more complicated and interesting than Arthur Bixby could foresee.

Chapter VIII.
Darkness!

As Bixby leaned over Lois, prepared to apply such few means of restoration as he knew, the girl opened her eyes. She drew a long breath. Then her vague, puzzled gaze fell on Bixby.

Long and inquiringly, she looked up into the blackened, fire-blistered face, with its singed brows and lashes. Then, still half unconscious, she murmured, more to herself than to him:

"Was not your hair once a good deal—longer? And didn't you wear a mustache and glasses? And—wasn't your face tanned?"

The rambling, seemingly senseless queries from the half-awakened girl were barely audible. Arthur replied, his throat still rough and sore, his words almost incoherently hoarse:

"I'm Bixby, the hallman, ma'am. Are you feelin' better?"

She stirred again, glancing amazedly about her. Then weakly she got to her feet, with his help, and stood balancing herself, with one hand gripping the fire-escape rail.

"I—I remember now," she said, still dazedly. "I—I went back for the dispatch box. It—"

She paused, noticing for the first time the box still hanging from her wrist.

"I remember feeling choked and dizzy," she went on. "And then—what happened?"

"And then, ma'am," croaked Bixby, "we got out here where the air's easier to breathe. Are you strong enough to climb down to the next floor?"

Once more she looked up at him in lingering doubt. But his

scorched face, its close-cropped hair, his coatless livery, and the gruff diction wherewith he spoke—seemed to decide the question that was on her lips.

"Yes," she made quiet answer, "I think I am strong enough. Shall we start?"

"Give me the dispatch box first," he suggested. "That is, if you're willin' to trust me with it. You'll climb easier without that weight hangin' to your arm."

Without a word, she unbuckled the strap from her bracelet, and handed the box to him. He fastened the strap to his own wrist, then motioned her to precede him down the ladder.

"Go careful," he warned. "Don't look down, or it may make you dizzy. If you get to feelin' faint, stop an' shut your eyes, an' hang on. I'll come around t'other side of the ladder, there, an' catch you."

She had already started the descent. Now she paused.

"Ain't feelin' dizzy already, are you, miss?" he asked.

"No," she returned, "I am not. I was just wondering how it is that you speak like an educated man when I overhear you giving orders to the other employees, and yet, just now, you talk like—"

"'Scuse me, miss," he interposed; "but I think you'd better do your wonderin' after we get safe to ground. There ain't much time to waste. I hear the firemen inside the apartment, an' the smoke at the winders is changin' to steam. The hose is at work. We don't want to get a duckin' when the stream hits a winder."

She moved meekly downward, and in another few steps were on the landing outside the third-story apartment's kitchen. There Bixby, sliding down the ladder, joined her.

"We'll go right in here," said he, "an' through to the elevator shaft. I don't b'lieve the fire's got out into the hall so as to stop the car runnin'."

He tried the kitchen window. It was locked. The apartment's occupant had evidently joined the excited throng in the outer hallways, for a loud rapping on the glass brought no response.

Bixby, realizing at last the futility of trying to attract attention in so deserted a section of the house, swung back the heavy dispatch box, and prepared to win entrance by smashing a pane. But Lois Raynor checked him.

"Don't!" she said. "You might cut your hand with the flying glass.

Let us go down to the second story. The kitchen window there may be unfastened; and, if worst comes to worst, we can break that."

As she spoke, she began the descent. Bixby followed her. On the second-story landing of the fire escape they paused again.

The ladder ran but a yard or two below this bar-floored landing, leaving a sheer ten-foot drop to the courtyard-below. No great feat for a young and athletic man, possibly; but out of the question for a girl.

Bixby turned to the kitchen window. It was locked, and the shade was pulled down, doubtless to render the room's interior invisible from windows across the court.

Indeed, from several of these opposite windows, even now, people were interestedly watching the adventures of the two young people on the fire escape, and suggestions that they did not heed or even hear were called across to them.

Bixby tapped on the windowpane, waited a moment for a reply, tapped again, and then swung back his dispatch box for a smashing blow.

But instinctive dislike to destroying any of the house property changed his purpose. Unfastening the dispatch box and handing it to Lois, he felt in his pocket for his knife. He opened the longest, thinnest blade, then pushed the palm of his hand against the window's lower sash.

He had already heard the sash rattle to his knock, and knew it must be loose. He was right. By pressing on the glass, he forced a narrow opening between the upper and lower sashes.

Through this aperture he ran his knife blade, moving it until it found the window fastening. A moment of steady pressure of the blade against the fastening, and the latter slipped to one side with a click.

Closing and pocketing the knife, Bixby raised the now unlocked window. Reaching in, he gave the lowered shade a jerk that sent it whizzing automatically up into its top roll.

The way was clear. He stepped down from the fire escape into the kitchen, and turned to help Lois in. The girl at that moment chanced to turn her head in response to a new shout of advice from some tenant across the court.

Bixby opened his lips to speak, but before the words could come, something descended with a crash upon his skull from behind. He saw, through a blaze of lights, a hand jerk down the window and the shade.

Then a great blackness rushed up about him, and he pitched to the floor.

Chapter IX.
"What Happened?"

With an aching head and stiff joints, Arthur Bixby came slowly to himself. He was lying on a long bench in the cubby-hole at the back of the entrance hall, where the employees usually sat and rested and chatted during their moments of leisure.

Above him leaned Carrots and Marks. The former had loosened Arthur's collar, and was fanning him vigorously with a ragged feather duster. "He's comin' to," said Marks. "The poor, delicate chap must have gotten a breath of smoke, and keeled over. It's too bad we haven't a nurse for such a delicate little chap!"

"That'll be just about all from you, friend Marks!" growled Carrots. "I guess we don't want nothin' from you but silence. And mighty little of that! If you're going to knock a feller that's just coming back from Knock-out Land, you'd better chase yourself back to your switchboard, and tell yourself stories into the receiver."

"It's pleasanter than to tell things to a blockhead like you," retorted Marks.

"If I can't be any more use to him—"

"Any more use?" mocked Carrots. "A sweet lot of use you've been! I had to carry him here and do all the working over him. You've just stood by and made a noise like a paper of pinheads. Chase!"

Marks slouched back to the switchboard, that had begun purring angrily. Bixby lifted his head. A pang of anguish swept through it, and he lay back again, nauseated, weak, dizzy.

"Take a nip of this," urged Carrots, producing from his lunch basket a bottle of cold, black coffee.

He held it to Bixby's parched lips. Arthur drank deep of it.

"That's the stuff!" remarked Carrots cheerily. "Black coffee's just as fine a bracer as booze is, any day, if folks only knew it. And it tastes better, too!"

The bitter, strong liquid quieted Bixby's sensation of illness as by magic. It cleared his racked head, too, and brought a tinge of color into his pallid cheeks.

And, with returning senses, came memory. He half started up.

"The fire!" he muttered.

"You're way behind the times," said Carrots. "It's out. The last fire-man faded away five minutes ago. It sure was a torrid little flare-up while it lasted. But they kept it in the one apartment, and as soon as they'd swatted it with the hose a few minutes it lay down and quit. But what—"

"Miss Raynor?" broke in Bixby, a new and startling scroll of recollection coming into action.

"Miss Raynor?" echoed Carrots, in frank amaze. "Say, Artie, if you've been in dreamland all this while, how'd you know about her?"

"I don't know. What happened? Is she safe? Tell me!"

"Safe? She sure is! If she was any safer, she'd have a call to get nervous about herself. She went back after the old dame's strong box. She couldn't get out of the door, so she made a break for the fire escape, and she clumb down to the second story. A couple of firemen saw her standing there, cool as a cucumber, and they set up a ladder and carried her down the rest of the way. Trabb saw 'em do it. It was him that told me. Gee, but I'd 'a' give a week's pay to 'a' rescued a queen like that."

Bixby lay back, his eyes shut. Full memory had returned to him. He recalled how Lois had stood on the second-story fire-escape landing, waiting for him to open the kitchen window. He had opened it, then had held out his hand to help her into the room.

He remembered that she had been standing at the moment with her back to the window, having turned to hear what a tenant across the court was bawling at her. Then had come that fearful blow on the head, a faint subconscious perception of some one slamming shut the window and pulling down the shade with a simultaneous gesture.

Then had come utter unconsciousness.

And now he pieced out the happenings as best he could. He had entered one of the second-floor kitchens, but so eager had he been to help Lois into the room that he had not looked around, and had taken absolutely no note of his surroundings.

The tenant of that apartment had probably come into the kitchen just then, and had seen a seeming marauder in the act of helping a possible accomplice into the room.

The tenant had undoubtedly struck Arthur down from behind; then, without noticing that the person on the fire escape was a well-dressed young girl, and not a sneak thief, had closed and locked the window, and hauled down the shade.

What must Lois have thought, when, turning, she found Bixby gone, and the window barred against her? The thought turned Arthur cold.

But now a new wonder filled him. If he had been knocked senseless in a second-floor kitchen, how came he to be lying now in the cubby-hole under the ground-floor stairs? Had his assailant, discovering the mistake, summoned the other employees to carry him away? The idea seemed probable.

Bixby opened his eyes again. Carrots was eying him with a keen curiosity.

"Say, Artie," suggested the elevator boy, "I don't want to feed you with fool questions while you're still feeling groggy, but when you get your brain all back on the job, maybe you'll tell me."

"Tell you what?"

"How you come to be there?"

"I got in through the kitchen window, and—"

"Holy Jehoshaphat!" cried Carrots. "Your belfry's chuckful of little songbirds. Got into an elevator through the kitchen window, hey? I've been running elevators ever since I stopped being a bell hop, but I never yet saw one with a kitchen window to it. You're batty!"

Chapter X.
A Clew.

Bixby stared at Carrots in amazement for a moment.

"One of us is batty, all right," he agreed faintly. "What's all this talk about elevators?"

"You don't remember?"

"I remember running the car up to the fourth floor, when the cry of fire was started; but—"

"That's right. The dames bear you out in that. And the cook up there—her that started the blaze by trying to find out if naphtha had spunk enough to burn—she told me how you stopped the car at the fourth floor, and got out, and how they all made a grab for you."

"Yes—yes! I remember."

"Well, she says you shook loose from 'em, and that was the last she saw of you. I got back from turning in the alarm about then, and I hiked upstairs to take charge of my car. I shoved all the scared women into it, and down we came. Gee, but they sure did squawk like a whole New Jersey poultry show!"

"Go on!" urged Bixby. "What happened next?"

"When I'd left 'em here at the bottom, I started up again, to see if there was anybody left on that floor. But the wind was sucking the smoke down the shaft so thick that I couldn't breathe. So I left the car at the second floor, and I started up on foot, because the smoke wasn't so thick on the stairways as it was in the shaft. Then the firemen got here and ran their hose up the stairs, and—"

"But what has all this rigamarole to do with my being in an elevator? I didn't get into it again."

"You didn't, hey? You sure did!"

"What do you mean?"

"After the hose began to work, I came back to get my car and take it down. I got to the second floor. No car there, and the shaft door was shut. Then I heard a thumping and banging down here, and I ran down. Here was the old elevator, with the power turned on. It would hit the bumpers, and then bound up into the air a foot or so, and hammer down on 'em again."

"Well?"

"Well, I got the door open and watched my chance, and slid into the car and shut off the power. That was when I saw you."

"Me?"

"Lying in a tumbled-up heap in the bottom of the car."

"No?"

"Yes! And yes a couple of times more—and then some. There you were, all knocked out and crumpled, on the elevator floor. I figure that you got into the car at the second flight, and started her down, and then keeled over. It's lucky I found you when I did, or the old elevator would have knocked its own machinery to smithereens in another half minute—and the jouncing wasn't doing you any good, either."

Bixby sat bolt upright. The motion sent pains through his bruised head, and made his brain swim. But he was too excited to heed his own sorry state.

"Carrots!" he gasped. "Do you mean to tell me you found me lying senseless, alone, in the bottom of the elevator?"

"I have been telling you, steady, for the last five minutes," retorted Carrots testily. "Now maybe you'll be so obliging as to come back with a story of how it happened."

Bixby sat dazed, incredulous. His dulled eye fell upon his own clenched fists as they lay idle in his lap. The fingers were convulsively closed through no volition of Arthur's. They had thus clenched at the moment of his unconsciousness. And, as often happens in the case of suspended animation, they had remained so, the nerve centers not yet having responded to the will.

The nails and knuckles were cut and bleeding from their recent grip of the floor.

With difficulty, Arthur unclenched his battered fists. As he did so, something fell from one of them and fluttered to the ground at his feet. He picked it up.

Chapter XI.
In The Park.

As soon as he was able to move, Bixby left the Matterhorn, and limped home. He was too weak, too used up, to continue the day's work. But a half day's rest did much to recuperate him.

Late that evening, he was returning from the doctor's, whither he had gone to have his head examined—and to find it was none the worse, save for a bruise, for the rap it had sustained—and he struck through Central Park as a short cut to his home.

The evening was dark, and there were few people abroad in the big pleasure ground.

The bypath along which Bixby walked was lighted only by gas lamps set at long intervals. By making a wrong turning, Bixby found himself with an extra quarter mile to traverse.

He found, also, that he had overestimated his recuperative powers, for his sore head began to throb again abominably. He sat down on a bench to rest until the pain should lessen.

The bench he had chosen at random was in the middle of the space between two lamps. Thus it and himself were practically in complete shadow.

One lamp was set at a curve in the path some distance to his right. As Bixby sat slowly mastering the ache and fatigue, the sound of measured steps came from beyond this curve.

Two men rounded the curve a moment later, walking in his direction. They were deep in low-voiced conversation.

Bixby glanced carelessly at them. Then something familiar in the gait and bearing of one of the two set him to looking more intently.

They neared the lamp. For one instant, before the shadow it cast from their hat brims blotted out their faces from view, Bixby had a comprehensive glimpse at both men.

The glow from the gas jet struck full on their faces. Then they passed on, and were merely silhouetted blackly against the radius of light.

Arthur, in that fleeting space of time, had recognized them both. One was Crain. The other—though Bixby could scarce believe his own eyes—was the sneak thief whose capture had marked Arthur's introduction to the Matterhorn.

Crain was talking in a low, authoritative voice; the other, almost humbly, breaking in from time to time. If either noted the lounging figure on the bench in the dark, he no doubt seemed one of the many homeless ones of the big city.

As he had been already sitting there when they came in sight, they must have known he could not have come to the spot to spy upon them. Hence, Bixby was not observed with any attention.

As the two came within earshot, Arthur sat staring dumbly,

amazedly at them. He caught Crain's voice, in the very middle of a sentence. The big man was saying:

"—lucky to have been able to get you out so soon. Why did you do such a crazy thing?"

"I didn't mean to, boss; honest, I didn't!" pleaded the thief. "I was coming for your orders about the Trenton deal, an' I saw the coat on the chair, an' it looked so easy, I—"

"Not so loud!" sternly cautioned the big man. "It was a mad, useless thing to do. That is what I get for employing a man who can't keep from stealing. I've warned you before. If you ever steal another thing, if ever I learn—"

They passed out of hearing. Bixby stared after them until they came to the next lamp and moved beyond it into the darkness.

What was the meaning of it all? Arthur could not guess, rack his wits as he would. Of course, from their talk, it was evident that Crain was the other's employer; that he had come to the Matterhorn for some sort of instructions from Crain; that, seeing the fur coat, he had stolen it, and that Crain, exerting some political pull, had managed to get his jail sentence shortened.

That much was obvious. But what sort of employment could the portly, sprucely dressed recluse have for such a man? What "orders" had the thief come for?

Why were the two now choosing such an isolated spot for their chat? A drizzling rain had begun to fall. It was the last sort of night one would choose for a pleasure stroll in the park.

The stranger was a thief. Was Crain the leader of an organized gang of thieves? The idea was preposterous, for there had been a note of undoubted sincerity in the big man's voice just now as he had expressed his contempt for stealing.

Crain had even threatened some penalty if ever he should again hear of his employee stealing. Surely those were not the sentiments and threats of a man who headed a gang of thieves!

He had been in fervent earnest, too, when he spoke so. There could be no question of that. The mystery grew more and more absolute as Bixby pondered over it.

Arthur, his weariness and headache forgotten, walked across to the lamppost. There he drew something from his pocket. It was the object he had found clutched in his fist when he had regained consciousness that morning. At first glance, there was little enough that was dramatic or spectacular about the thing. It was a small, clipped oblong of paper, in form like a dry-goods "sample."

The paper was blank on both sides. No word of lettering was on it. Yet, somehow, in appearance and to the touch, it differed from ordinary paper such as Bixby had hitherto seen.

For a minute or two, Arthur turned it over and over. Then he came to a sudden resolution.

Leaving the park by the shortest route, he hailed a passing taxicab—a luxury he could ill afford on his meager wages. He gave an address to the chauffeur, then settled against the padded cushions.

Chapter XI.
Discharged!

Bixby reported for duty at the Matterhorn an hour late next morning.

"Trabb wants to see you," said Marks, as Arthur emerged from the cubby-hole where he had been changing from his street clothes into his livery. "He'll be up here in a minute. He's been asking all morning why you hadn't showed up."

There was a subdued joy in Marks' manner as he made the announcement, and from this Arthur foresaw little profit to himself in the forthcoming interview with the janitor. He walked back to where Carrots was sitting glumly in the idle elevator. The red-haired elevator man welcomed Bixby with gloom.

"Say, Artie!" he broke out, yet not loud enough for Marks to hear. "Trabb is sore on you for something. Crain went down to the basement this morning, and they had a powwow. And after that Trabb telephoned the Bruce Estate offices. I don't know what about. He used the switchboard himself, and chased the rest of us out of hearing. Even since then—that's half an hour ago—he's been asking for you. Don't bother to go down there to his flat. He'll be up here again in a minute or two, he says. You'll see him soon enough without going on a hunt for trouble. Save your legs."

"All right," agreed Bixby, sitting down beside the elevator man. "Don't look so glum about it."

"Glum? I'm about as merry as a pair of yellow shoes at a funeral. It's been a rotten day so far. I started out with a scrap with Marks."

"That's surely no novelty."

"No; but this was a queer kind of scrap. I don't see even yet how it happened. We started a little game of 'bill poker,' and—"

"I've told you fellows not to play that. Here it's only two days after pay day, and I bet you've lost most of your month's salary. Besides, I won't have gambling here."

"I know that," grinned Carrots, "but you weren't here, Artie, so it seemed a good time for a game."

"Bill poker," be it known to the uninitiated, is a game rather much in vogue among a class of youths who have time and a few spare bills on their hands.

Every dollar bill has a serial number. The players match their respective bills, for some small stake. The figures in the serial number are counted as are the cards in a poker hand. Thus, "99323" counts as "two pairs"; "87877" as a "full house," et cetera.

"We had ten cents bet on each hand," went on Carrots. "Each of us pulls out a bill. The number on Marks' was X19625307. Not even a single 'pair' in that measly number, you see. So I thought I had him beat, sure. I squints down at my bill. What d'you s'pose its number was?"

"How should I know?" asked Arthur indifferently.

"It was X19625307," announced Carrots.

"But you said that was the number on Marks'."

"So it was. And on mine, too."

"You must have misread it," protested Bixby. "Two bills wouldn't have exactly the same serial number."

"I know they wouldn't," assented Carrots. "But they did."

"You're mistaken. The government—"

"Oh, I know all about the gov'ment. But it's so—those two bills had just the same number on 'em."

"I never heard of such—"

"Well, mine was an old, battered bill, and Marks' was a crisp, crackly, new bill that Crain had slipped him as a tip when he opened the front door for him. It ain't Marks' job to open the doors, neither, and he knows it. But you wasn't here. My bill was older'n his, so I claimed the stake, because the number on mine must 'a' been put there before the number was put on his, so it takes prec'dence. See? But he wouldn't have it so. That's how the scrap—"

Bixby was not listening. With knitted brows, he was staring straight in front of him.

"Carrots!" he broke out excitedly, interrupting the other's tale of grievance. "I—"

Just then Trabb appeared. The janitor beckoned Arthur grimly into a corner.

"I'm sorry, Bixby," said he, "but I've got to fire you."

"What?"

"I've got to do it," went on Trabb, "and I hate to, for you're a lively, decent chap, and you work hard."

"Then, why—"

"Mr. Crain lodged a complaint against you this morning. He came down to my flat, and said you'd been sassy to him, and threatened to beat him up. He said either you'd have to go, or else he'd get out. And he told me to put it up to the agent."

"But surely the agent—"

"I called up the Bruce Estate offices. Colonel Bruce's own son was there, and I was switched onto his phone. I told him about it, and made it as light for you as I could, but there was nothing doing."

"Colonel Bruce's son?" queried Bixby. "But it was the colonel himself who gave me the job. If I appeal to him, perhaps—"

"No use. His son's a smart fellow, and the old man gives him his head in all the routine ways. I've had him on the wire once or twice before, and every—"

"And he says I've got to go?"

"Yes," replied the janitor, "unless—"

He hesitated.

"Unless what?" asked Bixby.

"Oh, it's nothing a chap of your spirit would ever do. He says you've got to get out, unless—unless you'll go up to Crain's apartment and eat dirt."

"Apologize to Crain?"

"Yep! And if Crain accepts the apology you can stay, but if he won't—What's the use? You'll never do it."

"You're wrong! I'm going up there just as quickly as I can."

Chapter XII.
In Strange Quarters.

Bixby turned away from the wondering Trabb, and walked up the single flight of stairs to Crain's apartment.

He did not ring. Instead, he drew out a bunch of janitorial duplicate keys, and unlocked the door. Then, closing it quietly behind him, he went in.

His canvas-soled shoes were noiseless on the hall floor. He passed on through the passageway to the drawing-room. A heavy curtain hung before this door. He pushed it aside, and entered.

Bixby found himself in a room furnished as surely never was any other "drawing-room." At first glance, it resembled a cross between a laboratory and a job-printing office.

A sharp odor of acids filled the air. On a central table, under a group of powerful arc lights, was a table half covered with a slab of dull, grayish stone. Around it were a litter of engraving tools, a neat pile of oblong "plates," two powerful microscopes, and several other implements whose nature and use Bixby did not know.

In a corner stood a small press of complicated mechanism. Cabinets lined one side of the wall.

Arthur got no farther in his swift examination. For at that moment, Crain emerged from an adjoining room rubbing his chemical-stained fingers with a piece of medicated sponge.

At sight of Bixby, he halted, thunderstruck, his mouth open, his pale eyes staring.

Arthur faced him with an air of respectful attention.

"Mr. Crain," said he, "I came up here to—"

"How—how did you get in here?" gasped Crain, finding his voice, though somewhat unsteadily. "How dare—"

"I was ordered," said Bixby, "to come up here, on penalty of discharge, to beg your pardon for—"

"How did you get in?" roared Crain. "Get out of here!"

"To beg your pardon," calmly resumed Bixby, "for being impertinent to you, and for threatening to thrash you. I hereby apologize for both those faults."

"It's a lie!" panted Crain. "You sneaked in here to—"

"I came in this time," gently retorted Arthur, "by the front door, not by the kitchen window. For that reason, I shall go out on my own feet, and not trouble you—as I did yesterday—to carry me out to the elevator and throw me aboard it, and turn the lever to start the car downward. You should be grateful to me for saving you so much bother."

"You were conscious all the time!" murmured Crain, under his breath. "Yet I could have sworn—"

"I was quite senseless," Bixby assured him. "I merely pieced together the happenings. I did not enter your flat yesterday to spy on you. You must have guessed that later, when you heard about the young lady who was shut out of your fire-escape balcony. I was trying to help her in at the window, and—"

"But to-day—" began Crain excitedly.

"To-day," replied Bixby, relapsing into his former meek respect, "to-day I am here to apologize to you, in the hope of saving my job. If you doubt that, call up the Bruce Estate offices. My instructions come direct from there."

Crain looked doubtful. Then he glanced furtively about him. With a vain, but mighty, effort at civility, he said:

"I dabble a bit in chemistry for a living. I am experimenting chemist for a wholesale drug firm downtown. I use my apartment as a laboratory. The agents might not like to have me put it to such use. That is why I don't like employees to come in here. They might report it to the agents, and—"

"I assure you, I shall not," said Bixby, "and I cannot see why they should object, even if I did. I don't suppose you use dangerous chemicals?"

"Of course not! I—"

"And this?" queried Bixby innocently, laying his hand on the engraver's stone. "I suppose this is a block of some solid chemical that you take samples from?"

"Exactly!" approved Crain. "You are quite right. It is sulphuric acid in its congealed form."

"Really?" marveled Bixby. "I didn't know 'H 25SO4' was even in that form."

He had named the technical formula for sulphuric acid as though speaking without considering his words. The effect on Crain's forced geniality was electrical. This seemingly stupid hall-man had glibly rattled off a chemical formula that none but a man who had studied chemistry would know.

"Will you kindly accept my apology?" begged Arthur, reverting to the former theme. "I don't want to lose my job. I need the money."

Crain looked at him long and strangely. At last he said:

"Yes. I'll let you off this time. Now go back to your work."

"Thank you, sir!" exclaimed Bixby gratefully. "Good day."

Instead of turning away from Crain, he backed out of the room, keeping his eye on his host. He fancied that a shade of disappointment crossed Crain's face at this simple maneuver.

As he reached the curtain, Arthur carelessly drew out the bit of paper he had found in his hands after recovering consciousness the day before.

"This belongs to you," he observed, carelessly tossing it on a chair. "I took it by mistake yesterday. Properly treated with the 'chemicals' that you're so fond of dabbling in, it will probably become worth its weight in gold."

The seemingly meaningless words made Crain start back as if he had been struck in the face. Bixby coolly walked out of the apartment and back to his work.

Chapter XIII.
Marks Plays Informer.

It was an hour later that Marks, who had been temporarily absent from the switchboard, without leave, walked into the main hall of the Matterhorn. A stranger was with him. The two walked back to the cubby-hole, ignoring Bixby and Carrots.

The latter hailed Marks, who made no reply, but passed on with the other man.

"What's he up to now, I wonder?" said Carrots. "He's acting queer. Just after you came down from Crain's apartment, some one from up above called Marks on the phone. He sneaked upstairs, and was gone a while. Then he came back, and went to the cubbyhole. I heard him monkeying around in the lockers. He went out after that, and now he comes back with a chap that looks—"

"I came to help auntie search the burned-out apartment," said Lois Raynor, who had come down the hall as the two men were talking. "Is she here yet?"

"No'm," answered Carrots, as Bixby turned away. "Not yet."

"She has the key," remarked Lois, seating herself in a hall chair. "I'll have to wait for her."

"Gee!" whispered Carrots, a moment later, glancing at an automobile that had stopped at the front door. "There's Colonel Bruce! Making one of his inspection tours, I s'pose. He's got three other men with him."

Bixby, in his capacity as hallman, had already run forward to hold open the door for the visitors. They all four trooped in, the white-bearded colonel leading the way.

"Take these gentlemen up to their floor," he ordered Carrots.

Then, glancing at Bixby, he went on: "You are the hallman I gave a letter to last month, aren't you?"

"Yes, sir," replied Bixby.

"Do you like the place?" continued the colonel, nodding pleasantly, as he spoke, to Trabb, who was hurrying forward.

"Yes, sir," replied Bixby, "very much, thank you."

The colonel's three companions had gone up in the elevator without waiting for him. Carrots now brought the car back to the ground floor, just as Marks and the stranger emerged from the cubby-hole.

The colonel made as though to step into the car. Then he paused, and said to Bixby:

"I want you to take a message to my chauffeur out there. Tell him—"

The stranger with Marks interfered.

"Get some one else to carry your message," said he roughly. "This man's got to come along with me."

The colonel, unused to having his orders disputed in his own apartment house, eyed the stranger coldly.

"Who are you?" he asked. "And by what right—"

"I'm a plain-clothes man from the station around the corner," was the reply. "This man," indicating the startled Bixby, "will have to go there with me."

"On what charge?" demanded the colonel, in surprise.

Marks, swelling with malicious self-importance, cut in:

"I was going through the lockers a while ago, sir, looking for something in my coat there. I got my hand into the coat pocket of Bixby's street clothes by mistake. I found a wad of fiber paper, such as money is printed on, and a couple of half-finished counterfeit one-dollar bills."

"What's that?" admonished the colonel. "Be careful what you say. This is a serious charge."

"That's what I thought, sir," answered Marks. "I've been reading in the papers lately how the city has been flooded with a lot of counterfeit dollar bills, that were made so cleverly they could hardly be detected. I'd read how the secret-service men were scouring the town for the man who makes them and the accomplices who help him put them into circulation."

"Yes, so I have read. But—"

"So I thought it my duty to go around to the nearest police station to tell what I had found. They sent this man back with me. I showed him Bixby's coat, and he found the things in the pocket, just as I said."

"It's a lie!" yelled Carrots belligerently. "A dirty lie! Artie Bixby's as white a man as ever happened. And you're a cur! If there was phony stuff in his pocket, you put it there."

"Shut up, Carrots!" ordered Trabb. "Colonel, I've suspicioned all along that Bixby was somehow crooked. I never liked him, or trusted him, either. Now that he's caught with the goods—"

He paused, and turned, as did they all, at the sound of shuffling feet on the stone stairway that wound about the elevator shaft. Down the stairs came four men. Three were the visitors who had entered the house in company with the colonel.

Among them, handcuffed, his florid face gray and haggard, moved Crain.

Chapter XIV.
A Boomerang.

"It's all right, Dowling," called one of the three captors to the plain-clothes man, who stood beside Bixby. "We got him, and we've grabbed enough evidence in his apartment to convict an archbishop. You needn't keep up the farce any longer. It's too late now for your man to warn his boss. Take him."

The plain-clothes man grinned. With a quick gesture, he caught Marks by the shoulder.

"You're my pris'ner, young man," he announced.

"What? What's that?" shrieked Marks, in mortal terror.

"We got wind of this from the Federal authorities this morning," said the plain-clothes man, "so when you came around to the station, the captain telephoned, and got orders. He sent me to pretend to arrest Bixby and to keep you from warning Crain, in case you happened to suspicion anything. You're a dandy informer, but your information works backward."

"What—what are you pinching him for?" gasped Carrots.

"As an accomplice of one of the cleverest bill counterfeiters in the business," returned the plain-clothes man.

"Don't—don't Bixby get run in, too?" asked Trabb dazedly.

"Not this time," returned Colonel Bruce. "At least, not as a counterfeiter. But," he continued gravely, "perhaps we might lodge a charge of false impersonation against him."

"I always knew there was something crooked about him," reiterated the janitor, in triumph.

"There is," pursued the colonel. "He came here under false pretenses. He called himself Arthur Bixby, and claimed to be a hall-man. Both statements are false."

"Good!" chuckled the janitor. "Trust me for sizing up a crook!"

"He's a white man!" broke in Carrots. "And any one lies who says he isn't!"

"He is not Arthur Bixby," resumed the colonel, "and he is not a hallman. He is Clyde Bruce, my son. And he is vice president of the Bruce Estates Company. He came here to the Matterhorn to study the inner workings of apartment houses, because one day he will own all of mine; and while here, he stumbled on this counterfeiting affair, and notified me. He was at my office this morning. In fact, it was he who gave you permission, over the telephone, to discharge 'Bixby' unless he apologized to Crain."

The janitor was staring blankly. Carrots roared with glee at Trabb's panic-stricken face.

"Trust you for sizing up a crook, Trabb!" he squealed. "Oh, this is the best ever!"

"Carrots," said Bixby, in lofty reproof, "you are discharged for being impudent to good, wise Mr. Trabb, and because I want you in my own office, on a job that is worth just about four of this."

Bixby moved away, to avoid Carrots' effusive thanks. As he did so, he caught sight of Lois Raynor, who had sat, an excited, unnoticed spectator, through the whole scene. He hurried across to her, with outstretched hands.

"Lois!" he whispered eagerly. "Can you forgive me for deceiving you so? I had to, or—"

"Deceiving me?" she laughed, a soft blush mounting to her very brow. "You silly boy! Don't you suppose I knew you all the time?"

The Montclair Flurry

Chapter I.
A $350,000 Gift.

"YES," grumbled old Pruett, trying to look loftily contemptuous—and only succeeding in giving the impression of having a very bad toothache—"yes, that's what it cost. I wouldn't believe it when they told me. I didn't think there was that much money coined. But I read it afterward in the Newark *Star*. And what you read in print is bound to be true."

Pruett glowered out into the pretty park which was rapidly filling with people who streamed in from Orange Road and the cross streets; and moved toward the new art-gallery wing of Montclair's Carnegie Library.

In the dusty cubby-hole of a basement room of the library, which served him alike for workshop and sleeping apartment, Pruett was tinkering with a broken picture frame and growling his grievances to two highly amused younger men who had lounged in the doorway.

"So you really saw it in print?" remarked one of the men. "Of course, that settles it. It must be true."

"Yes," asserted Pruett, "you can make mighty sure of that, Mr. Seymour. What's in print has got to be true. I know, because I was on duty with the White House bodyguards when Mr. Lincoln ordered it. That was nigh on fifty years ago; but I guess no newspaper is going to dare disobey Abraham Lincoln's orders, for all that."

"So President Lincoln made the newspapers truthful, did he?" laughed Seymour.

"He sure did. Forbade any war news to be printed by any of 'em till it could be proved. I was there. That's why I knew it must be so when the Newark *Star* said the picture was worth three hundred and fifty thousand dollars. But think of paying all that good money for a square of canvas and a few daubs of paint, when you can get a lovely chromo for a half dollar. I saw one down on Bloomfield Avenue, in a window, marked down to thirty-eight cents. It was called 'Learnin' Millie to Swim'; and it—"

He intercepted a wink between the two younger men, and at once flared up.

"Whatcher grinning at?" he demanded.

"Oh, nothing," said Seymour hastily; "only I couldn't understand how such an unimportant thing as the presentation of a three-hundred-and-fifty-thousand-dollar Murillo to the Montclair Art Gallery should have found mention in a newspaper."

"Well, it did," snapped the old man. "If you don't believe it, here's another piece in to-day's Montclair *Guardian*. Listen."

He fished a folded newspaper from his pocket, and, tracing the lines with one knobby forefinger, began laboriously to read aloud:

"The famous Murillo portrait, known as 'The Woman with the Lilies,' purchased in Madrid by the Honorable L. Z. Seymour for $350,000 and presented by him to the new art gallery of this city, will be placed on exhibition for the first time this afternoon, when the formal ceremonies of unveiling and presentation will take place. The—"

"My father," said Seymour gravely, "will be tickled to death to know he's got his name in print at last. Hey, Caspar?"

His companion nodded with equal gravity, adding:

"It isn't every man who can get his name in print for a paltry sum like that. But isn't it almost time for us to be getting upstairs? If we want good seats for the ceremony, we ought to—"

The door opened, and a plump, rather fussy-looking man bustled in. It was Alstyne, curator of the gallery.

"Hello, Sandy!" he greeted young Seymour. "How are you, Price? Pruett, I'm glad to have found you at last. I've been looking everywhere for you. I've special duty for you tonight."

"Work! Work! Always work!" grunted Pruett. "When they gave me this job because I was a Civil War veteran, they told me it was a snug, easy berth for my old age. But it's more like a berth in a cattle car. What's the new work, Mr. Alstyne?"

"The Murillo is to be left at the gallery to-night for the first time," replied Alstyne, paying no heed to the plaint of overwork. "And, of course, we are all a little nervous for fear it may be stolen. Ever since the theft of the Mona Lisa from the Louvre in Paris, every art-gallery curator in the world has gone in fear of picture thieves. This Murillo of ours is priceless, so I should—"

"Three hundred and fifty thousand dollars," corrected Pruett carefully.

"So," continued Alstyne, "I should like you to stay in the art gallery or in the adjoining corridor to-night. You can move a cot up there if you like. To-morrow, the patent door-and-window fastenings will be here. But to-night—"

"Oh," said Pruett, "is that all? Sure. It'll take a good, slick thief to sneak away anything when I'm on guard. I remember once when I was on sentry duty, back in sixty-two—"

"As soon as the gallery is closed for the evening," went on Alstyne, "you will consider yourself on duty there till I come to relieve you in the morning.

"Come on," he added to the others; "the ceremonies will begin in a few minutes. Coming, Pruett?"

"Me?" snarled the old janitor, in a sudden gust of temper. "Not me, sir. I'll have no part nor parcel in anything so silly."

"Silly!" echoed Alstyne, in horror.

"Yes, *silly!*" reiterated Pruett. "What else is it to spend three hundred and fifty thousand good round dollars on a measly picture by a 'dead one' when this country's clamoring for more old soldiers' homes, and when Ireland needs home rule, and when I'm only earning forty dollars a month? Answer me that! I say it's crim'nal, and silly, too. And I'll have no part in it. I won't even clap my eye on the picture, for fear I'd want to put a foot through it when I think of all the soft money that it cost."

"That will do, Pruett," said Alstyne pompously. "You presume on your long services to be impertinent. What can an ignorant man like yourself understand about art?"

"I can understand that a fool and his money are soon parted by a picture that *I* wouldn't give eight cents for!" retorted Pruett.

Alstyne waved the two younger men from the room, and followed them hastily, as if he feared to listen longer to such blasphemies against art. But, once outside and mounting the stairway to the upper floors, his pompous manner underwent a sudden change. Laying his hand on the arm of one of them, he said nervously:

"Sandy, your father is a good deal worried. So am I. So are we all."

"What's up?" demanded Seymour. "Has the Murillo turned out to be a fake? Or is there more trouble with the customs people over it?"

"No. But—did you ever hear or read of Walt Whitson?"

"Must be in one of the bush leagues," hazarded Seymour, amused by the curator's air of tragic mystery.

"No," corrected Caspar Price solemnly. "If I remember rightly, he's a new 'white hope.'"

The curator glared doubtfully from one to the other. Their sporting vocabulary was unintelligible to him. But he dimly suspected they were joking, so he answered with added solemnity:

"Whitson is one of the cleverest picture thieves on earth. You may, perhaps, remember his share in the famous Gainsborough portrait robbery. He was seen in the Louvre not two hours before the Mona Lisa was missed. He has been concerned in the theft of fully a dozen old masters. Yet he has done his work with such diabolical cleverness that never once has the law been able to hold him. He has been arrested again and again. And he always gets off on some technicality."

"Wise old Whitson," commented Seymour. "You talk of him as though he was the original Bogey Man, Mr. Alstyne."

"This is not a matter for jest, gentlemen," said the curator, "as perhaps you will agree when I point something out to you."

They had reached the upper floor of the art-gallery wing by this time. Alstyne, with the air of the "first conspirator" in an old-time melodrama, led the two younger men to a hallway window whence they could look directly down into the gallery itself. The walls were hung with paintings. The floor space in front of an improvised dais was covered with rows of camp stools. Most of these seats were already full, and people were still pouring in through the rear doors.

On the platform sat several local dignitaries. On the wall just behind them hung a framed picture, covered by a sheet, awaiting the moment for unveiling.

"There!" whispered Alstyne, pointing dramatically. "There in the second row from the front, to the left, just under the 'Moonlight Scene at White Lake'; that man with the scar on his forehead."

"Well?" queried Price.

"That man," declaimed Alstyne hoarsely, "is Walt Whitson!"

Chapter II.
The Picture Thief.

"Well?" asked Seymour, "what of it?"

"Don't you understand?" fumed Alstyne. "There is Walt Whitson, most daring picture thief in America. And *there,* not twenty feet away from him, is the three-hundred-and-fifty-thousand-dollar Murillo; one of the most valuable paintings extant."

"Go to it, Whitson, old scout!" chuckled Price.

Alstyne glared as though the young man had struck him.

"Mr. Price," he said, in cold rebuke, "the Honorable L. Z. Seymour, donor of this wondrous Murillo, is the foremost director of the Montclair Art Gallery. His son here, Mr. Alexander Seymour, is therefore a privileged person as far as I am concerned. Were it not that you are Sandy's most intimate friend, I should order you to leave the building for saying so outrageous a thing as you have just said."

"Keep the sand out of your gear box, Alstyne," soothed Seymour. "Price meant no harm. He only wanted to show you how foolish you are to be nervous. There's Whitson, you say. And there's the Murillo. But there are also a thousand other people packed in all around Whitson. He can't very well grab the picture and run, can he? What are you so scared about?"

Alstyne gazed in hopeless wrath from one to the other.

"The fact that Whitson is here at all," said he, as though trying to teach a lesson to some unwontedly dull pupil, "shows he has his eye on the Murillo. And when so clever a thief once gets after a picture—"

"If it worries you," suggested Price, "why not have him arrested? There are two policemen at the back of the room."

"Arrest him?" snorted Alstyne. "On what charge? Of being at the presentation ceremonies? Of possible intent to steal? We have no proof. He would sue us for false arrest, as he did those in London who arrested him in the Royal Academy rooms."

"Then," observed Price, "since he can't get the picture and you can't arrest him, what's the use of all this high-tragedy business?"

But Alstyne was not to be calmed.

"It is all very well for you to sneer," he returned. You are a penniless, irresponsible college boy, who knows nothing of the cares that surround a man in my position. I tell you, that man's presence spells danger. But I also tell you, young man, that, clever as Whitson is, he'll find himself balked if he puts his brain against mine. You see that Murillo? There it shall hang in safety, at that very spot, for all Mr. Walt Whitson's cunning. I stake my reputation on that! If it is a duel of wits between him and me, he will learn he has met his match in Simon O. Alstyne. Watch and see, young man."

The presentation ceremonies were over. The world-famous Murillo portrait, "The Woman with the Lilies," had been duly and eloquently presented to the city of Montclair. Its history and merits had been wordily set forth.

The covering sheet had been dramatically drawn aside, disclosing to the initiated a masterpiece of ripened coloring, construction, and technic. To "low-browed" outsiders, the painting gave an impression of a somewhat muddy-faced woman in a stiff brocade dress, sniffing at a handful of stiff yellow lilies, against an even muddier background— and all at a cost of $350,000.

The ceremonies over, the audience filed out, only a few favored persons being allowed to remain for a longer, closer view of the picture.

At Alstyne's orders, the two policemen had kept a keen eye on Whitson. But there was apparently no need of the espionage, for the celebrated thief was one of the first to leave the gallery.

Alstyne personally, and with a mysterious manner that drew all eyes to him, followed the thief down Orange Road, and continued his role of amateur sleuth until he saw Whitson board a New York train at the Lackawanna station.

Then, satisfied that he had at least momentarily staved off the danger, the curator returned through the dusk for a farewell inspection of the gallery before going home to a well-earned night's rest.

The gallery was vacant by this time, except for old Pruett. He had carried into it his work table, which, with an oil lamp on it, he installed near the door. Beside him were several picture frames somewhat in need of gilding and of other repair.

"Might as well keep myself awake by working a bit," he said, as Alstyne hustled in. "Here's these picture frames you pointed out to me yesterday to be shined up. I've brought 'em all over here instead of taking 'em to my shop downstairs, and I'll give 'em their first coat of gilding to-night."

"Be careful not to let any of the gilding get spattered on the picture themselves," warned Alstyne.

"Look here, Mr. Alstyne," protested the janitor, "I've been gilding every frame that needed it ever since this gallery started, and I never yet got a drop of gilt on the pictures. I'm no bungler. Leave that to me."

By the dim light cast through the gallery by one oil lamp, Alstyne peered through the gloom. There, in the shadow at the far end of the long room just above the dais, he could distinguish the faint outlines of the Murillo—the square frame, the half-invisible face of the painting itself. He turned back to Pruett, who was running a gilding brush along his thumb.

"Pruett," said the curator impressively, "a grave and great trust is imposed upon you this night."

"Sure, everybody's always imposing on me," muttered Pruett. "I—"

"Pruett," resumed Mr. Alstyne, waving a pudgy hand toward the Murillo, "yonder is *art*. Three hundred and fifty thousand dollars' worth of art. And, for to-night, you are its sole custodian. On you and on your vigilance may depend its safety. I do not wish to alarm you, Pruett, but—"

"Alarm me?" sniffed the old man in high scorn. "I like that! Wasn't I in the trenches of Petersburg, and wasn't my regiment—me in the front rank at that—right spang in front of Pickett's charge at Gettysburg? Alarm me, hey? Why, I—"

"Please don't interrupt me, Pruett," resumed Mr. Alstyne. "I say I do not wish to alarm you. But it is only fair that you should know a desperate thief is planning to steal the Murillo. My vigilance has scared him off, for the time. But he is likely to make another attempt. So be vigilant!"

"Oh, beans!" growled Pruett. "A body would think there'd been enough speechifying here to-day."

"These windows," went on Alstyne, "are secured by bars. The only entrance through the gallery is by means of the double doors just behind you. By your leave, Pruett, I think I will lock these doors when I go out. Do you mind?"

"Not so long as you go out first," was the enigmatic answer.

Alstyne stared in haughty doubt at the old man. But Pruett was already back at his task of gilding one of the battered frames.

The curator said with all his former impressiveness:

"Remember, Pruett!"

Then he went out, closing and locking the great doors behind him and pocketing the key. Having thus left treasure house securely fastened, and a trusty, if crusty, watchman inside, Mr. Alstyne went home with a carefree mind.

"I fancy Mr. Walt Whitson is pretty well checkmated," he said to himself.

At almost the same moment, Whitson, who had remained on the New York train only as far as Glen Ridge, alighted once more at the Montclair station.

Chapter III.
The Wrong Hat.

Alexander Seymour was strolling homeward along Orange Road. He had been spending the evening on Upper Mountain Avenue at the house of the One Girl. So had several other young men.

As Seymour had deemed it his solemn duty to "sit out" all the other callers, he had not left the girl's home until after eleven o'clock. Now he was walking abstractedly toward his own domicile, his head buzzing with a dozen clever things he had meant to say during the evening and had thought of too late.

So absorbed was he in this most fascinating mental pastime that only the stubbing of his toe against an inequality in the sidewalk pavement brought him back to a sense of his whereabouts.

He found that he was within a block or so of home, and was almost directly in front of the library. In fact, he was just passing under that portion of the building known as the "Art-gallery Wing."

This fact caused him no stir of interest, and he was about to plunge back into his pleasant reveries of "retroactive" wit, when a gust of autumn wind, sweeping sharply about the corner of the street, smote him in the face.

Seymour's hat had been carelessly tilted backward from his forehead. The puff of breeze now snatched it from his head and sent it bowling merrily along the strip of lawn which divided the gallery wing from the street.

The hat, under impetus of the breeze and moved by the perversity that seems to lurk in runaway headgear, bounced across the lawn, and rolled into the paved passageway between the wing and the main library building.

As in most residence streets of Montclair at so late an hour on a windy night, practically no one was abroad. Seymour satisfied himself that he was alone on the street, and that his annoying little mishap had passed unseen; for no one likes to be watched in the pursuit of a wind-blown hat. So, turning in from the thoroughfare and crossing the patch of lawn, he went after his lost headgear.

The mouth of the passage was pitch dark. Seymour could not tell whether his hat had rolled down the path ten feet or fifty. He did not care to step on and wreck a five-dollar derby in the darkness. So, at the alley's narrow entrance, he struck a match.

The wind, whistling down the chute-like aperture, put out the flame before the man could see a yard in front of him. Then a second and a third match were tried with the same sorry results. After which Seymour gave up the effort to illumine the dark way before him.

Instead, he groped along at snail's pace, touching his outstretched hands on either side of the wall, and carefully shuffling sideways with his feet, to come in touch with the elusive hat.

It was not a graceful mode of progress, and he was heartily glad that no one could observe it.

After working his way in this fashion for perhaps ten yards, Seymour's right foot collided gently with something rather yielding. He stooped down. There was his hat lodged snugly in an angle formed by the jutting of a water pipe on the gallery side of the wall.

Grateful at not having had to spend more time on so ridiculous a quest, he turned and retraced his steps more hastily, holding the recovered derby in one hand, while with the other he used the wall as a sort of vertical support.

He reached the street, and paused directly under the nearest electric light to brush off his hat. But, though the powerful white rays from the light above him beat down sharply on the derby, Seymour could find in it no dent. Nor was its glossy black surface marred by so much as a single grain of dust.

Seymour stared at his hat in wonder. It had rolled across a dusty lawn. It had bounced down a stone path whose thick-strewn dust particles had whitened the seeker's shoes. Yet it was as clean as if it had just left the hatbox.

"Must be a new kind of dust-proof lid," commented Seymour to himself. "I thought I'd have to brush it for a good half hour to get it clean again; but it looks almost cleaner than it did when I put it on after dinner to-night."

He placed the hat on his head and set forth again, homeward. But at the first step he halted in perplexity, took off the derby, readjusted it to his scalp, then yanked it once more free from his head, and glared at it.

Alexander Seymour was as careful about the fit of his hats as he was about the set of his well-made coat. And he was the despair of every hatter; for it was always necessary to try at least a dozen hats on him before he could find one that he thought fitted him comfortably and becomingly.

And the hat he had just recovered from the dark passage was a full half size too small. One touch of it to his head had assured him of this. Now scanning the derby more closely under the light, he noted other differences. The brim was wider, and had more of a roll to it than had his. He turned the hat upside down. The maker's name too, was different.

"This isn't my hat!" he exclaimed disgustedly. "What other poor unfortunate could have had his derby blow into that Cave of the Winds? It's queer that the same thing should have happened to two people. But it's queerer still that he didn't bother to go after it. Derbies must be cheap where he comes from."

Still holding the strange hat, Seymour turned back. He reëntered the narrow passageway, and repeated his former maneuver of slowly shuffling along in an effort to feel for his lost derby with his feet. But he did not begin this until he had reached the water-pipe abutment. For he knew it could not be in the first part of the path, as he had already traversed that in vain.

About six feet beyond the pipe his toe touched the missing derby. He picked it up, and, a hat in each hand, returned to the street. Under the electric light, he glanced at the two hats.

The derby he had last found was undoubtedly his own. But its top was dented in by the bumps it had received. And it was gray with dust, just as a hat might be expected to look that had rolled along forty feet of dusty alleyway.

"Two hats blew in there," mused Seymour. "One of them comes out spotless; the other looks like a stage tramp's. That's not natural. The dust that soiled one should have soiled the other."

He stood for a moment with furrowed forehead, puzzling over the phenomenon. Then, almost incoherently, he began muttering his deductions half aloud.

"That first hat," he mumbled, "never rolled all the way. It was carried to the foot of the water pipe and laid there carefully. Why?"

Another period of silent wrestling with the problem. Then:

"When the gallery wing was built, Price and I climbed that water pipe—for a stunt. And I remember we laid our hats at the foot of it, to keep them out of our way while we climbed. And that's what some one else has done," he went on more excitedly. "Those dinky iron ornaments make the pipe easy for any supple chap to swarm up. Some one's there now. Why? I'm going to find out."

Chapter IV.
The Man In The Dark.

Seymour hurried back toward the alley's mouth. Reaching it, he laid both hats on the grass. Then, on second thought, he took off his coat and laid it beside them; for the puzzle was piecing itself together in his mind with greater and greater completeness.

He was familiar with every inch of the building, of which his father was the chief director and benefactor. He remembered that the water pipe, with its ornamental black-iron fastenings, ran straight up from gutter to roof, passing midway between two of the broad-silled art-gallery windows on the second floor.

Any man who had taken careful observations of the spot, and who was sufficiently light and agile, could climb with almost no peril to the level of the gallery, and could there find foothold on one of the sills. It would then be merely a matter of sawing through the iron grille that protected the window, cutting with a diamond or a glass cutter the plate glass just above the inside fastening, and stepping into the room which held a Murillo portrait valued at three hundred and fifty thousand dollars.

The bait was surely tempting enough to draw any thief who might know of its whereabouts. And the task of breaking through the barriers that guarded the treasure was simple enough to be within the understanding of any second-rate cracksman.

Seymour wondered that Alstyne's many fussy precautions for the Murillo's safety had not included this very strong possibility. Then he remembered the curator's order to Pruett to spend the night on guard in the gallery; and he realized that Alstyne might have a few gleams of human intelligence after all.

Still, Seymour knew that poor old rheumatic Pruett—probably unarmed—would be the flimsiest sort of opponent to a determined and desperate robber. The mental vision of the old man's plight in such a conflict caused Seymour to quicken his pace down the pitch-black pathway to a breakneck run.

He did not consider the wiser course of summoning help. The idea did not even cross his mind. Secure in his prowess as a college athlete, and without physical fear, he tingled with anticipation of the possible adventure.

Reaching the rain pipe, he felt for the iron fastenings, and prepared to begin his ascent. As he did so, he recalled, for the first time, Alstyne's melodramatic identification of Whitson that afternoon. He understood now why the notorious picture thief had attended the presentation ceremonies. Under cover of listening to the speeches, Whitson could readily have made a study of the Murillo's exact position, the fastenings of the nearest window, and the best mode of attack upon the outer grille. He had doubtless already made an examination as to the best means for reaching the window from the outside.

Up the rain pipe Seymour began to climb. He gripped the ironwork, and strained his eyes upward through the almost impenetrable gloom, trying to detect the outlines of a human figure above him against the paler gray of the cloudy sky. But he could see nothing.

He had mounted barely four or five feet when something struck him full in the face—something light, hard, cold, that had evidently dropped from above. The object rebounded from his stinging forehead, and fell with a tinkle to the stones below.

"A file," muttered Seymour to himself. "A light file or saw with a watch-spring attachment, such as is used for cutting bars. I saw one at the police station when they caught the Caldwell housebreaker last year. It must have slipped from his hand as he was cutting away at the grille."

And now the water pipe and its fastenings began to shake under his grasp. Some one was apparently descending it in haste. And, again peering upward, Seymour had a momentary glimpse of a vaguely silhouetted form against the background of sky climbing down the pipe with the agility of a monkey.

"Coming down for the file he dropped," guessed Seymour. "Well, he'll find me waiting for him."

Noiselessly Seymour let himself down to the ground, and took one step back from the pipe. He was not a second too soon. Scarce had he braced himself against the farther wall, when the sound of feet striking the walk proved the other man had reached earth.

The thief paused an instant, and seemed fumbling in his clothes for something. Then the blinding white streak of a pocket flash light split the darkness like a sword.

The man had drawn out the light, and was turning its rays downward, that they might play upon the walk at his feet. There, in the small disk of radiance, lay such a file as Seymour had once before seen—the file that had struck his face in falling.

The thief stooped to pick it up. The reflected glow was barely strong enough for Seymour to make out the shadowy outlines of the fellow's form as he stooped. His first impulse was to launch himself upon the robber, catching him unprepared. But a keen, perhaps foolish, sense of fair play made him change his plan. Instead, crouching for a spring, he said coolly:

"Hands up!"

In the wink of an eye, the flash light was extinguished, leaving the passageway in utter blackness.

Seymour heard the man bound forward like a deer toward the entrance of the alley farthest from the street.

And Seymour, with all the speed and accuracy of a trained football tackle, dashed after the fugitive. Before the latter had traversed half the distance to the open space beyond the passageway, Seymour was upon him.

The thief wheeled like lightning as he felt Seymour's outstretched hand touch him, and the two grappled.

No word was spoken, no sound uttered save the quick intake of breath as the two men came together with a shock.

Chapter V.
The Fight in the Passageway.

It is not easy to fight in pitch darkness. No man who has not done so can realize how awkward and semi-helpless a combatant can become, temporarily deprived of eyesight's aid. Moreover, in the passageway where Seymour and his unseen foe battled, there was barely a space of three feet between the two high side walls.

This left room for no footwork, no retreat, no swinging. It was a question of brute force, unhelped by sight or science, and crippled by narrow boundaries.

From one wall to the other the struggling men caromed, striking at each other blindly. Sometimes Seymour could feel his clenched fist strike yielding flesh. Again his knuckles would crash against the brickwork of the wall, numbing his arm almost to the shoulder.

The men clinched, tore loose, and pummeled fiercely at each other, then ran once more into a clinch.

Again and again this was repeated. Neither could guess at what damage he might be inflicting. Not a word, not a cry came from either. The only sounds were the rain of blows, the gasping of labored breath, the dully echoing thud of feet on the paving stones of the walk.

Now a blow from the thief caught Seymour glancingly across the temple, driving his whole head back against the wall with a force that made the blackness alive with whizzing stars.

Before Seymour could rally, the man was at his throat—strong, lean fingers feeling for his windpipe.

Shaking off the sensation of numbness, Seymour beat fiercely at the invisible face behind the gripping hands, showering one wild, short-arm blow after another upon it.

Some of the blows went wild; but enough landed to jar loose the thief's throat grip, and to send him reeling back against the opposite wall.

Swift to follow up his advantage, Seymour rushed at his man, seizing him in the terrible underhold that means a broken back for its victim unless it can be broken before its full force can be exerted.

Wildly, dumbly, the robber struggled to break that iron hold. But the muscles that had carried Seymour to many a hard-fought football victory and the clean life he had led now combined to aid him.

He clung to his enemy like grim death. His hands were locked behind the small of the other's back, just above the hips. His chin was buried in the hollow between the thief's neck and shoulder.

With this leverage, he was slowly, inexorably putting forth every atom of his wiry, clean strength.

No mortal power could long withstand such a pressure. Nor could the thief's frantic struggle loosen or break the hold by even the fraction of an inch. All at once the robber changed his tactics. Plunging one hand into his pocket, he drew forth the heavy flash lamp that he had slipped there at Seymour's order of "Hands up!"

Now, before his opponent could guess his purpose, the thief, with one last remaining rally of strength, brought down the lamp with all his might upon Seymour's left temple.

It was a fearful blow, and in a vulnerable spot.

Seymour's iron grip grew loose. He sank slowly to his knees. Still vaguely fighting for consciousness, he felt the thief tear loose from his weakened hold.

Seymour feebly caught the man about the legs; but the other wrenched free, and struck again at his head.

There was a momentary glare of light. Seymour, drifting into unconsciousness, dimly wondered if it were caused by the same "stars" he had seen before, or whether the thief, before making good his escape, had turned the flash light on in a desire to see his fallen enemy.

Then everything went black.

A few minutes later, Seymour felt his senses returning. He was lying propped up against the wall at the street opening of the passageway.

A man was leaning over him. Still half dazed, Seymour thought it was his late opponent, and he feebly started up to grapple with the newcomer. But, instead, he reeled back against the wall, and stood there, swaying dizzily, kept from falling by the man who still held one of his shoulders.

Then, by the electric light, Seymour recognized Caspar Price. And the latter was hatless, and his face was bleeding.

"What—what on earth are you doing here?" gasped Seymour.

"Getting you out of trouble, as usual," answered Price cheerfully. "What happened to you, anyhow?"

In a few broken words, Seymour told of his adventure, and finished by commanding:

"Go back there, and see if he's still hiding in the passageway."

"There is no one in the passageway," muttered Price, as if talking to a sick child. "Do you suppose a thief would stay there looking for more trouble? He knows you'll probably raise the whole town after what's happened."

"I shall!" panted Seymour. "We'll catch him if he's still in Montclair."

"Certainly," agreed Price. "And in the meantime you can be sure he understands that. And he's putting all the distance he can between himself and this place."

"But," demanded Seymour, his faculties gradually returning, "how on earth did you happen to find me?"

"I went to your house," explained Price. "I got a telegram half an hour ago from my father. He is ill out in Denver, and he wants me. I am starting on the earliest train to-morrow morning. I don't know when I'll get back. So I came to say good-by. You weren't home. I guessed easily enough where you'd be calling. So I thought I'd stroll up toward her house and meet you on the way back. Just as I got over to that corner there, I saw you."

"Saw me?"

"Yes. You were turning into that alley."

"With a couple of hats in my hand?"

"Yes. I wondered what was the joke. I waited a few minutes. You didn't come out, so I went in to look for you. I found you lying in a crumpled heap on the ground, and I dragged you out here. That's all."

"You didn't see any one else?"

"Not a soul. I didn't even see you till I stumbled over you."

"But—your face is bleeding!" cried Seymour, noting for the first time his friend's hatless, disheveled condition.

"Is it? I guess it was my fall that did it."

"What fall?"

"I ran into that confounded water pipe in the darkness. I bumped my face against it, and then lost my balance, and bumped my face and the rest of me on the flagstones. It was just after I got up that I stumbled across you. Say! I must look pretty badly by the queer way you're staring at me."

For Seymour—a sudden, hideous thought rousing him utterly from his recent lethargy—was glaring at his friend in open-mouthed horror, his eyes dilating with a sudden and growing suspicion.

Chapter VI.
Suspicion.

For a full half minute Alexander Seymour stood staring at his friend; keenly, almost fiercely, noting every detail of the bruised face, the hatless head, with its tumbled hair, the disheveled and dusty clothes.

"Well," said Price, apparently a trifle ill at ease at the close scrutiny, "do you like my looks?"

"No," answered Seymour dazedly, "I don't."

A station hack, returning from taking some one to the midnight train, rattled past, going down Orange Road. Seymour hailed it.

"I must get to police headquarters at once," said he, clambering aboard, "and have a special officer here inside of five minutes. There's no time to waste. Good-by, Price. I hope you'll find your father better. Police headquarters, driver, in a hurry!"

He spoke rapidly, almost like one reciting a hard lesson. As he finished, the driver whipped up his tired horse. So much in haste was Seymour that he did not appear to notice Price's hand outstretched to him in farewell.

Leaving his amazed friend standing in the middle of the street, Seymour clattered off in the rattletrap hack. But as the driver turned the first corner, the young man leaned forward.

"I've changed my mind about going to the police," said he. "Take me home instead. Seymour's house, Myrtle Avenue. Quick, please!"

He sank back in the musty-smelling seat, and set his still-aching head to work on the tangle.

"Price!" he whispered to himself. "Price, of all men. I'd have sworn to his honesty. He's the closest friend I've got on earth. I'd never have believed it but for my own eyes' evidence. I knew he was hard up and he always laughs at honesty. But—"

He winced as a jolt of the carriage set his bruised shoulder to throbbing.

"It can't be any other way," he went on miserably. "His face and knuckles were bruised, and his body was dusty where we'd rolled in our fight. His hat was gone, too. And to think he invented such a flimsy story to account for it. He must have turned the flash light on me and seen who it was as I lay senseless. Then he dragged me out to the street, and I came to myself before he could get away. So he trumped up the first story he could think of. Oh, I'd have staked my life on Price's squareness. What can I do? I *can't* give him away."

But his plan of action was already roughly mapped out. Indeed, it had been so when he gave the driver the order to take him to police headquarters. The command to go to the police, and his statement that an officer would be at the art gallery inside of five minutes, were intended as warnings to Price not to attempt again the theft of the Murillo in his absence. For he knew the man would never dare to do so with only five minutes in which to work.

Now, the rest of Seymour's project shaped itself. Reaching home, he paid the driver. Then, when the hack was gone, he ran upstairs to his room, stuffed one or two articles into his pockets, then set off swiftly and silently toward the art gallery.

His head still ached and his muscles were sore. But he had been mauled far worse in many a football game, and had continued to play on as vigorously as ever until the final sound of the referee's whistle.

Youth, perfect health, and fine athletic condition were already rallying to his aid.

He did not approach the gallery wing by way of Orange Road, but went to the rear in a wide detour, and, crossing a lawn, entered the dark passageway from the end farthest from that by which he had gone into it earlier in the night.

Seymour felt his way along cautiously in the darkness. Soon his foot touched something. He stooped and felt it. It was a derby hat, crushed almost out of recognition. A few feet farther on, he came upon the second hat, in similar condition. Derbies are not improved by being fought over and rolled on.

Useless for further wear as the hats were, Seymour carried them both along with him until he came to the base of the water pipe. Then he laid them down and kicked off his shoes, which he carefully laid beside the broken derbies.

Next, slowly and skillfully, he mounted the water pipe by means of the iron fastenings. Up he climbed, his bruises now and then causing him to wince as they struck against some projection.

At length he had reached the art-gallery floor. He lifted his head above the sill. In the great room a lamp was burning.

Still more cautiously, Seymour stepped to one of the two sills that were within reach of the pipe. His stockinged feet planted firmly on the broad stone coping and one hand gripping the heavy iron grille, he peered in.

At one end of the room, near the locked doors, sat old Pruett. His back was to the window, and he was still at work gilding the frames that were piled about him.

On the table in front of the old man burned a kerosene lamp, whose weak rays cast only a dim, ghostly light over the farther portions of the big gallery.

Seymour next turned his gaze to the opposite end of the room where the Murillo had that afternoon been hanging.

As he gazed, he breathed a long sigh of relief. Faint as was the lamplight, he could, nevertheless, make out the shape of the frame, and could see that it still held its picture.

"I was in time, after all," he muttered.

Next, he drew from his pocket a flash lamp he had just brought from his own room. Another look at Pruett's back reassured him, and he turned on the light. He examined every detail of the iron grille—its bars, its hinges, its fastenings. All were intact.

Then, creeping back to the rain pipe, he crossed to the second window, and repeated his inspection. As in the case of the first, the grille was still firm. But a closer scrutiny showed that one of its fastenings was sawed almost half through from the outside. The thief had evidently reached this point in his midnight labors when the slipping of the file from his hand had caused him to descend to earth in search of it.

Satisfied as to the results of his examination, Seymour pocketed the flash lamp, worked his way back to the rain pipe, and thence to the ground.

He was about to depart for home, when it suddenly occurred to him that it was barely possible the thief might still be lurking somewhere near by, and, seeing that no policeman arrived, might make a second attempt to scale the rain pipe and file his way through to the treasure.

"I'll stay on guard," mused Seymour, "till daybreak, anyhow. Then if no one has come, I can get home without being seen. In the meantime"—drawing from his hip pocket a revolver he had brought from his room—"in the meantime, if any robber *should* come, I won't need to rely on my fists alone."

So, leaning against the foot of the rain pipe, the only spot whence an ascent to the gallery windows could possibly be made, Seymour began his long vigil.

"Whitson or Price?" he asked himself a dozen times as he crouched there. "Whitson or Price? Or both?" And each time his logic answered against all the anguished protests of his heart:

"Price! Your best friend!"

Chapter VII.
A Strange Discovery.

Mr. Alstyne that night enjoyed the slumbers that are supposed to be reserved for the just. Had not the institution, of which he had the blissful honor to be curator, secured one of the finest old masters in all America?

Had not he, that same curator, recognized Whitson, the notorious picture thief, at the presentation; and had he not assured himself that that wily scoundrel had actually left Montclair? Had he not still further made certain of the picture's safety by placing honest old Pruett on guard over it for the night, and by locking him into the gallery with it?

Who, therefore, had better right than worthy Mr. Alstyne to sleep the deep, sweet sleep of duty nobly performed? And he slept it, straight on until sunrise.

The first rays of the morning sun, pouring into his room, aroused the curator from happy dreams of having charge of a whole gallery full of $350,000 Murillos.

He woke and stretched himself lazily. It was good to feel so thoroughly comfortable. Then gradually it dawned upon him that, while he himself was at ease in a soft, warm bed, poor old Pruett was still locked in a drafty, unheated picture gallery.

The thought disturbed Mr. Alstyne. A little remorseful at having kept a rheumatic old man up all night, he scrambled out of bed, dressed himself with unwonted haste, and hurried around to the library building to release the captive watchman.

Mr. Alstyne entered the gallery wing by means of the key he always carried. Then he toiled up the stairs to the door of the gallery. He unlocked this, and tried to open it. It resisted his efforts.

"Pruett!" he bellowed, in quick fear.

"All right, all right," grumbled the old man from the far side of the door. "Don't be shouting your head off. Since you thought it made things safe by locking me in from the outside, I thought I'd make things even safer by barring myself in from the inside. Hold on a second till I slip the bolt."

He did so, and the doors swung open.

Mr. Alstyne looked past the tired watchman, the littered table, and the heap of half-gilded frames to the far end of the room. There, above the dais, the picture hung.

Mr. Alstyne sighed happily.

"Pruett!" he said, with ponderous graciousness, "you are a worthy—a *most* worthy man."

"I've suspected I was for the past half a century," grunted Pruett; "but you've just found it out all of a sudden."

In disgust, the old man gathered up several of the frames and started down to his basement workshop with them.

"They'll need another coat of gilt," said he; "but I'll have to wait till they dry. I'll be up for the rest presently."

"Quite right," approved Mr. Alstyne. "Waste no time. The president passes through Montclair next Tuesday, and I think we may be able to prevail on him to stop off for a view of our Murillo. When he comes, I want everything to be shipshape here. No ugly gaps on the walls where pictures have been taken down to have their frames gilded and have not been returned. You will remember, won't you, Pruett, just where you took each picture from? And you will be certain to hang each back in its exact place?"

"Aw, haven't I done it for years?" growled Pruett, as he disappeared with his load. "And am I likely to get flustered and make a break about it just because a president happens to be coming to look at 'em? Me, that's seen and hobnobbed with Abraham Lincoln himself?"

His peevish voice trailed off down the stairs. Mr. Alstyne seated himself in the chair Pruett had just vacated, and looked beamingly around the gallery that was the pride of his life. His nearsighted little eyes twinkled as they swept along the ranks of pictures on the long walls. He felt like a general reviewing a peerless army.

Presently the old watchman came limping rheumatically back for the second load of frames.

"Pruett," observed Mr. Alstyne, "yours was indeed a high privilege—to pass a whole night in the presence of so wondrous an art work as our Murillo. I can fancy how, in the intervals of your labors, you paused and gazed at it for inspiration."

"Not me," grumbled Pruett. "I waste no time gazing and gawping at a foolish waste of money. I'd rather look at a piece of corned beef. I'd be seeing something then that was nearer worth the money it cost. Why, for that much cash, the city could have bought—"

"That will do, Pruett!" interrupted Alstyne coldly.

He surveyed the old janitor with a pitying contempt. That any man could be so ignorant as to sneer at the Murillo filled him with a yearning to convert the mocker.

A thought occurred to Mr. Alstyne. Pruett scorned "The Woman with the Lilies." Probably that was because the old man had never looked at it. Once having beheld its beauty, he must assuredly fall victim to its charms.

And a wild thought entered the curator's brain. Without exceeding his own authority, he would force Pruett to look upon the Murillo. To look—and to remain to worship.

"Pruett," he said craftily, "it seems to me the Murillo is hanging a little crookedly. Just step across there, will you, and straighten it."

Pruett stumped down the room to the dais, grumbling as he went.

"Looks straight to me," he remarked. "I can't see as it hangs crooked. I—"

He checked his speech, and, after standing for a moment directly in front of the picture, broke into a cackle of laughter.

"Pruett," gasped Mr. Alstyne, in horrified rebuke, "how dare—"

"Oh! Oh! Oh!" roared the old janitor amid cracked squeals of laughter, "Oh, me! Oh, my! A fine lot them old heathens knew about women and lilies! If they took that for a lady and lilies, they'd take me and my broom for a cherub and a harp! 'Tis a dandy-looking woman, all right, all right. With *whiskers!*"

Alstyne had involuntarily started across the room in horror to check such blasphemies against high art.

But the severe rebuke died unspoken on his lips. Ten feet away from the dais he halted, staring as if smitten by apoplexy.

For, at that point, his nearsighted eyes had been able for the first time that morning to focus themselves or the painting. And, at what those eyes now beheld, Mr. Alstyne's knees smote together.

He sank weakly down upon the edge of the dais, and stared goggle-eyed, hoping that the frightful apparition which met his gaze would prove to be merely a crazy ocular delusion.

But the longer he looked, the clearer the spectacle became. And all the time, at his elbow, old Pruett was rocking back and forth in unholy laughter.

"A woman with lilies!" cackled the janitor. "With *lilies;* yes, and with a pipe. And—and with them whiskers!"

Chapter VIII.
The Lost Murillo.

Mr. Alstyne had been prepared to behold the portrait of a rather simpering and absurdly slender maiden in white draperies, bending over a sheaf of lilies, and with a dim background of forest behind her.

What he actually saw was this:

A hideously painted picture in oils of a Gloucester fisherman in a sou'wester hat, his tanned face fringed with bristling chin beard, and an old clay pipe in his half-toothless mouth, with a background of bumpy, solid-looking sea.

The picture, as a picture, did not amaze Alstyne as much as it would have done had he not been so familiar with every painting in the gallery.

He recognized it at a glance. It had been presented to the Montclair Art Gallery by an eccentric merchant who did *genre* painting as a pastime, and did it horribly.

The picture would have been rejected without thanks had it not been accompanied by a fat donation to the art fund. In view of this, it had been allowed to hang in a remote corner of the gallery, where, the directors fondly hoped, few people would notice it.

But now it was occupying the place of high honor reserved for the priceless Murillo!

His first spasm of dumb horror passed, Mr. Alstyne ran shakily to the dim spot in an obscure angle of the gallery where the Gloucester-fisherman picture usually hung. It occurred to his dazed brain that perhaps old Pruett by mistake had shifted the positions of the two paintings.

But there was a gap on the wall where the fisherman picture belonged.

Round and round the whole gallery, like a plump, elderly rat in a cage, ran Mr. Alstyne. He peered at every picture on every wall.

The Murillo was not among them. It was gone! Indubitably gone! With a bleat of hopeless rage, he bore down upon the hapless Pruett.

"Where is it?" bawled Mr. Alstyne. "What have you done with it, you doddering old scoundrel? Speak, or I'll tear the truth from you!"

"I may be old," retorted Pruett, trying to sneer, "but when it comes to 'doddering'—whatever that means—you've got me beat a block. I'm going to look up that word 'doddering' in the library dictionary. If it means what I think it means, I'm going to hunt you up and—"

But Mr. Alstyne was not listening.

"Where is it?" he screeched, waving his pudgy hands threateningly at the janitor. "Where is it, I say?"

"Where's what?" yelled Pruett, as angry as he and far more perplexed. "Where's what? What on earth are you jabbering about? What have you lost now?"

"The Murillo! The wonderful Murillo! The—"

"You ain't lost it," replied Pruett more gently, as it dawned upon him that the curator's mind might suddenly have become muddled. "There it is. Right there, where it's been all night."

He pointed at the Gloucester fisherman as he spoke.

"That—that—" sputtered Mr. Alstyne.

"That's it," went on Pruett cheerfully. "Only those old-time dagos must have had queer ideas what women and lilies looked like. Or else maybe the women in them days wore whiskers and smoked pipes. I remember now I saw a bearded lady once at—"

"Be still, can't you?" wailed Mr. Alstyne. "Our Murillo has been stolen! Our priceless Murillo!"

"Are you daft, man?" exclaimed Pruett. "Can't you see it there?"

"That is the fisherman picture painted and donated by Mr. Pembroke!" fumed Alstyne. "You know that as well as I do. It has hung in the gallery for over a year."

"D'you s'pose I've nothing better to do than to spend my time rubbering at these pictures?" demanded Pruett. "I know one of 'em from another. All I know is when their frames needs mending or gilding, and then you take 'em down and I fix 'em and put 'em back. That's all I know about 'em. One picture looks like another to me. Only some is uglier."

"Don't you understand?" cried Mr. Alstyne, breaking in on the janitor's profound art criticism. "Our Murillo is stolen."

"Is it?" answered Pruett phlegmatically. "Well, I'll just be carrying the rest of them frames downstairs."

"Hold on! You were in here all night?"

"Sure I was. Didn't you just unlock the door?"

"Of course, of course. And no one could have gotten in by a duplicate key, for you had the door bolted on the inside, too. No one could have gotten in that way, even if you had been asleep."

"Asleep? Me? I never slept a wink. D'you s'pose I could have got the first coat of gilt on all them frames you piled up in the corner for me if I'd wasted time sleeping?"

"You were here all night—awake all night—on guard all night—and yet you didn't see the theft?"

"There wasn't any theft, I tell you. Not a thing was taken out of this gallery all night, and no one but me was in here. That's why I say you're daffy when you talk about the picture being pinched. If it was here yesterday, it's here to-day."

"It was here yesterday! I saw it. A thousand people saw it. Art critics examined it closely through lenses, and declared it was undoubtedly genuine. The last thing before I went home last night, I saw it was hanging in its place. And now it is stolen!"

"Mr. Alstyne," said Pruett, in disgust, "you talk fine and loud, but what you say don't make sense. Nothing's been taken out of here during the night. You saw yourself that the doors was locked, and—"

"The robber may have put a ladder to one of the windows and crept in while you were asleep!" cried Mr. Alstyne, trotting off to examine one window after another.

"I'm telling you I wasn't asleep!" declared Pruett. "And as for any one getting by the windows, they'd have had to cut their way through the iron grilles and the panes of glass besides. There ain't a pane of glass cut. And there's not a window fastening undone."

Mr. Alstyne was going from window to window and hurriedly verifying this assertion.

He found each window intact and locked; nor did any of the grilles appear to have been tampered with.

The excitement, the unwonted exercise, and the closeness of the room made Mr. Alstyne giddy. In search of fresh air, he unlocked and threw open one window.

The morning air was as a tonic to his hot face. To enjoy it the more thoroughly, he unlatched the iron grille and pushed it back. Then he leaned far out. His glance, straying downward, was caught by a strange sight.

On the paved walk of the passageway just below lay a man, dead or fast asleep. His head rested against the base of the rain pipe. In one hand was a revolver, in the other was a flash lamp. In front of him on the ground lay two battered derby hats.

"Pruett," shouted Mr. Alstyne, in wonder, "come here! Quick!"

At sound of the cry, the sleeper on the ground was awakened.

Stumbling to his feet, he took a hasty glance around, snatched up the two hats, and made off at a run before the nearsighted Mr. Alstyne could get a glimpse of his face or identify the vaguely familiar aspect of his disheveled figure.

"Stop thief!" screamed Mr. Alstyne, in a voice of thunder. "Stop thief! Help!"

Chapter IX.
The Mystery.

It is not often that Montclair or any other town of its size—except in case of a wholesale tragedy—can claim columns of first-page space in the great metropolitan newspapers. Yet, the day after the Murillo's loss, every New York paper carried a long story on the mystery. In fact, it was the mystery, as much as the actual theft, that caused newspaper interest.

A Murillo valued at $350,000—one of the most valuable paintings in America, and therefore a matter for national pride—had vanished from a locked and guarded art gallery, under circumstances which not even the shrewdest and most imaginative news-gatherer could explain.

The papers told how the portrait had been on view and had been seen by hundreds of people; how, immediately after the unveiling, a watchman had been placed on duty in the gallery and the doors and windows locked; how, next morning, the doors and windows were still fastened, the watchman awake and on guard and the Murillo gone!

Reporters and detectives hunted the gallery. They inspected every inch of the building. They examined and cross-examined old Pruett and Alstyne until the nerves of both those overwrought persons were in tatters.

An enterprising reporter made a discovery that tended to thicken the whole mystery. He found that an attempt had been made to saw through one of the window grilles' iron bars from the outside. The bar was sawed half through, and the freshness of the cut showed the thing had been done recently. But further scrutiny showed no more tampering, and the grille was still as solid as a wall.

One reporter evolved a theory that Pruett was in league with the thief; that the latter had entered the gallery on the night of the theft, being admitted by the watchman, and had walked off with the picture. Pruett, then, according to this brilliant theory, had relocked and bolted the door, had hung another picture in the place of the Murillo, and had calmly awaited the discovery.

When the same clever reporter came to the gallery for more news, Pruett chased him off the premises with a garden hose. The theory died a natural and easy death. No one after five minutes' talk with the surly, eccentric old janitor could believe a word of it.

And yet there was no other possible solution. Even this one was disproved when it was learned that the gallery doors had been locked by Alstyne from the outside. Pruett could not, therefore, by any possibility, have let himself out of the room in order to let any one else into the building, for he had no key to the gallery proper.

Mr. Alstyne's story of having seen a man asleep at the foot of the rain pipe, holding in his hands a revolver and a flash lamp, and with two smashed derby hats in front of him, was laughed at as absurd; the more so when the curator added the statement that the man in his flight had carefully carried away both the worthless hats.

Friends kindly suggested that Mr. Alstyne had suffered a hallucination through sheer excitement. Enemies accounted less leniently for the supposed vision.

The mystery remained at a deadlock. Art stores, outgoing ships, the rooms of well-known receivers of stolen goods, all were scoured in vain. Big rewards were offered.

Of course, the stolen Murillo could not be offered publicly for sale. But many a rich picture collector, the papers said, would doubtless be glad to pay the thief many thousands of dollars for the masterpiece, for the sake of secretly possessing so wondrous a treasure.

The only person who derived the slightest pleasure or gain from the whole affair was the merchant artist who had perpetrated the Gloucester-fisherman picture. To his unbounded joy, he saw his work of art reproduced in no less than four New York papers in connection with the tale of the robbery.

As for Pruett and Mr. Alstyne, they lost weight and acquired age in a truly pitiable fashion under the grueling of police and press.

But to return to Seymour on the morning of the robbery. Awakened by Mr. Alstyne's hello from the window above him, he had started up guiltily to find he had fallen asleep at his self-assigned post of duty. He had sense enough to realize that his presence there might well call for questioning, so he departed at full speed, taking with him the two hats, one of which had his initials inside the crown.

He did not wish to leave his hat as evidence of his vigil, and he had no time to learn, at a glance, which of the two wrecked derbies was his own.

When he had gained the safety of the street, he picked out his hat, and was about to throw away the other when a thought occurred to him.

"If it's got any marks by which Price could be identified," he mused, "I'd best get it out of the way."

So he carried it home.

The hour was still so early that in the better residence district almost no one was astir. By back ways Seymour reached his home unobserved, and repaired to his own room. There a bath and a change of clothes removed all the more glaring traces of his night's adventure.

He went down to breakfast, leaving the examination of the hats and the painful reflections on Price's conduct until a later time, and faced the family's outburst of mingled horror and raillery. "You're in a fine condition to appear at table!" exclaimed the elder Seymour.

"I'm sorry, sir," said the son meekly, "but I got into a friendly scrimmage last night, and it got more strenuous than we expected."

The explanation sounded lame, indeed, but Seymour could not relate the facts and betray his friend.

Further discussion, however, was saved by Mr. Alstyne's bursting into the house with the news of the Murillo's loss.

Seymour, junior, sat silent amid the babel of excited comment that surged around him.

He was dazed. The thing was unbelievable. He had made certain that no one had broken into the gallery by way of the windows. And yet—

As soon as he could, he slipped away to his own room. His brain was in a whirl. And he needed, just now, to think very clearly and wisely.

The Murillo was stolen. And he had caught Price, practically red-handed, in the effort to break into the gallery.

Had Price found some other way to get in afterward, or had he stolen the picture during the time Seymour lay senseless, hidden it, and then revived his victim?

Neither answer to the miserable riddle satisfied him. Nor could he see in which way lay his duty.

"What on earth am I to do?" he demanded wrathfully of his haggard reflection in the glass. "Caspar Price is my best friend. How can I go to the police, and say: 'He is a thief?' Again, suppose I'm wrong in thinking he stole the picture. I'd be in a position of falsely accusing my chum of theft. But, if he did steal it, have I any right to keep silent—to rob the gallery directors and the city of their one chance of tracing the picture? Oh, was ever an unlucky man in such a situation before? If only I could find out if Price really took it!"

And on the moment there flashed across him a solution of his dilemma. He jumped to his feet, all weariness forgotten, and dashed across the room to a tall wardrobe that stood in one corner.

"This will decide!" he muttered.

Chapter X.
Guilty Or Not Guilty?

From the wardrobe, after much fumbling among various garments, Seymour drew forth a golf cap. It was a cap Price had worn one afternoon when he had come to Seymour's home to dress for a dinner party which both were to attend. He had left the cap and the tennis flannels he had been wearing, and had meant some day to call for them. During the interim they had remained in the wardrobe.

Seymour now hauled out the cap and laid it on his desk alongside the derby he had found at the foot of the water pipe. Then he took from a drawer a tape measure, and carefully measured the inner circumference of the cap's sweatband.

Making note of the measure, he next applied the tape line to the battered derby's sweatband. Comparing the two measurements, his face cleared as by magic.

"Great!" he exclaimed, in utter relief. "It proves I was wrong. Lucky I thought of measuring them. The hat is a whole size smaller than the cap. The same man couldn't have worn both. And the cap is Price's. Good old Price! I ought to be kicked for having dared to suspect him. He's always been the squarest man I know."

Then his brow knitted once more. If not Price, then who? He knew now that Price was telling the truth when he said he had seen Seymour enter the passageway, and that in following him, he had received his own bruises and cuts by falls. Price was innocent, of course.

But who was the man with whom Seymour had fought in the darkness of the passage—the man whose hat now lay on his desk? Was it Whitson? Probably. But if so, how had Whitson managed to steal the Murillo?

Seymour had interrupted the thief before he could saw his way into the gallery window. According to Price's story—now proven true—Price had entered the alleyway only a minute or two behind Seymour. Hence the picture could not have been stolen, as Seymour had imagined, during his own temporary unconsciousness. There would not have been time.

Nor could the thief have mounted the pipe later in the night. For, even though Seymour had at last dozed, no one, he was certain, could have passed over his body to the pipe without awakening him.

The Murillo was stolen. That, at least, was sure. It had been taken in the night while he was on guard at the foot of the wall and Pruett watching inside the gallery itself. The thing seemed wholly impossible. But, none the less, it was true; undeniably true.

And Seymour, in the midst of his indignation, found scope for a thrill of admiration at Whitson's phenomenal cleverness. The man was assuredly a peerless genius in his own way.

The fact that Price was exculpated relieved Seymour's own mind so entirely that he could not feel the rage he showed at Whitson's crime.

He was sorry, ashamed that he had for a moment suspected so old and tried a friend as Price. He recalled with disgust his frigid demeanor toward his chum when they parted the night before. He resolved to sit down at once and write the whole silly story to Price, confessing his groundless suspicions and begging pardon.

But he did not know how to address such a letter. Price had said he was starting at dawn for Denver to see his father, who was ill. But Denver is a large city, and a letter with no more exact address could scarcely reach a mere transient there.

While Seymour hesitated, a servant knocked at his door, and handed him a special-delivery letter that had just arrived.

It was addressed to Seymour in Price's sprawling handwriting, and was postmarked "New York, 5 a. m." Seymore tore open the envelope, wondering vaguely what matter of importance could have led his chum to pause in the hurry of departure and write to him. And this is what he said:

> DEAR OLD SANDY: Just a scribbled line, while I'm waiting for my train, to square myself with you. You seemed queer when we said good-by to-night, and you glared at me like a melodrama villain.
>
> I've been wondering why, ever since. And I suppose you must have found out about taking the picture away—the Murillo—and that you are sore on me for it. I'm sorry, old man. But the temptation was on strong, as you'll admit. I'll bet, if the idea had come to you, you'd have done it yourself.
>
> I wanted to let you in on it, but I was afraid you wouldn't agree, since your father's interested in the picture and all that. Besides, I wanted you to be able to say you didn't know anything about it, in case there should happen to be any fuss raised.
>
> I'll be back in a month or so, at most, and we can talk it over. In the meantime I'm sorry if you didn't like it. If I'd had any idea it would peeve you, I'd never have done it.
>
> Ever yours, CASPAR.

Seymour read and reread this remarkable letter at least six times. Then he got up and paced the room dizzily, at last for still another perusal.

His mind was in a jumble. Price was the thief, after all! And, so far from realizing the enormity of his crime and the peril he ran, he had written a full confession in this weird letter, and had treated the affair as though it were nothing more culpable than one of the boyish pranks he had always delighted in playing.

"The man's crazy," gasped Seymour, "or he was born without a shred of normal sense! Here he steals a priceless masterpiece, and then writes: 'I'm sorry if you didn't like it!' He seems surprised that such an atrocious act should 'peeve' me, and says I'd have done it myself if I'd been in his place. What on earth can he be thinking about to write like that? A letter like that, found by the police, would convict him in any court in the land. Oh, he's stark mad!"

Then, in looking up from a final perusal of the note, Seymour's eyes fell upon the derby and the cap that were still lying on the desk. Again he measured them. Again the figures showed conclusively that the two could not possibly have been worn by the same man.

If Price had stolen the Murillo, as he confessed, whose was the hat Seymour had found? Were Price and Whitson in league? If so, with which of them had he fought in the black gloom of the passageway?

If this derby before him were Whitson's, what had become of Price's hat? For Price had been bareheaded, and it had been too cold a night for a man to wander voluntarily about the streets without a hat.

The harder Seymour thought, the more absolutely puzzled and baffled he became. What had Price done with the Murillo? He had been empty-handed when he and Seymour had talked together. And a $350,000 picture is not the sort of thing to be hidden carelessly in a corner until one can come back for it.

"What ought I to do?" mused Seymour, in desperation. "If I give this letter to father or Alstyne, Price will be arrested. I can't write to Price or go to him, for I don't know where to find him. He says he's guilty, but something tells me he isn't. And that same 'something' is going to be strong enough to keep me from disgracing my chum and smashing his whole future until I can see him face to face and find out the whole truth."

Swayed by this illogical impulse, acting wholly against reason, Seymour tore the letter into countless bits.

"I suppose," he told himself dully, "that now I'm an accessory to the robbery."

Chapter XI.
The Miracle.

The days spread out into weeks, as days have a way of doing, and police and press were still at sea regarding the lost Murillo. Then came the day for the monthly meeting of the directors of the Montclair Art Gallery.

These meetings were usually held in the board room on the ground floor, but this time the arriving directors were met at the threshold of that room by a fuming and apologetic curator and an unwontedly surly janitor.

"What's up?" queried Seymour, who had come as representative of his father, who was detained in New York on business.

"A fixture in the board room got out of order," answered Mr. Alstyne pettishly; "and when Pruett and I came there to prepare the room for the meeting, we were almost overcome by escaping gas. We opened all the windows, and in time the odor will dissipate. But just now the smell of gas is dreadful, and it is too cold for us to sit there with the windows up. What can we do?"

"As there are fully a dozen rooms in the building where we can meet just as well as in there," said Seymour dryly, "I wouldn't get softening of the brain over the affair if I were you. It is 'closed day' for the art gallery. Why not hold our meeting up there?"

The suggestion was favorably received, and the directors trooped upstairs, led by Mr. Alstyne, who solemnly unlocked and flung open the gallery doors for the distinguished officials.

In filed the directors, Mr. Alstyne bringing up the rear. They drew up camp chairs and benches around an onyx table that had been bought in Tuscany by a traveling Montclair man and donated to the gallery.

The chairman, taking his seat at the head of this table, was about to call the meeting to order, when Mr. Alstyne sought to "improve the occasion."

"I am sure," sighed the curator, "that it must be as melancholy, for all of you as it is for me to come into this room. I used to spend every spare hour in here. But now, except when my duties demand it, I never set foot in the place. The memory of our terrible loss is so much more poignant to me when I am in here, where once—"

His prosy speech ended abruptly in a wordless gurgle. As he had spoken of the loss the gallery had sustained, his eyes strayed by habit to the spot on the wall where once the Murillo had hung. And what he saw struck the power of speech from him as though he were suddenly palsied.

He could only point wordlessly, his round face the color of chalk.

The gurgle, the man's blank stare, his trembling gesture, drew every one's attention to him. And, following the direction indicated by his shaking arm, the directors involuntarily turned and gazed at the section of wall to which Mr. Alstyne was pointing.

A gasp of amazement burst from the onlookers.

There, in its old place of honor on the wall, hung the stolen Murillo!

The directors stared a moment, petrified. Then, as one man, they surged forward to verify at closer quarters the evidence of their own eyes.

There could be no shadow of doubt. In the full light of the afternoon sun, the $350,000 "Woman with the Lilies" met their dumfounded stare.

The original Murillo, past all doubt. Not a copy, but the wondrous, priceless picture itself. Restored as miraculously as it had disappeared.

For a minute or so no one could speak. Then everybody began talking, or rather chattering, at once. And around the Murillo a veritable Babel raged.

Mr. Alstyne alone could not find voice. For once in his pompous, garrulous life astonishment held him gasping and tongue-tied. He was face to face with the apparently impossible, and it stunned him.

Seymour was little less affected. For weeks he had fought a ceaseless battle between duty and friendship. And this—this miracle—decided it.

"It *couldn't* have been Price!" he kept saying over and over to himself; "for Price is in Denver, and the picture—"

"I was in this room four hours ago," sputtered Mr. Alstyne, finding incoherent speech at last, "and that wall space was vacant. The Murillo was not there. I locked the door when I went out, and you saw me unlock it again when we came in just now. No one else could have got in."

"Have you the only key to the gallery?" asked Seymour.

"No," answered Mr. Alstyne, adding: "At first I had the only key to the gallery proper. Now the janitor has one."

"The janitor?" exclaimed Seymour. "Pruett!"

He shouted this name down the stairway, and a surly reply came from below. But before the rheumatic old man had even started to mount the stairs, some one else gained the top of the landing and swung airily into the room.

It was Price.

"Hello, Sandy!" hailed the newcomer, meeting his friend at the threshold. "I just got back half an hour ago. I dropped in at your house, and they said you were here. Pruett told me to come right up. I seem to be butting in on some sort of a meeting?"

"Mr. Price," exclaimed Alstyne dramatically, "there's the Murillo!"

Price glanced carelessly at the great picture.

"Well," he said inquiringly, "I see it? What about it?"

"It is there!" declaimed Mr. Alstyne. "There, where it used to hang."

"Well," repeated Price, evidently puzzled, "where else would it be?"

"Do you mean to say," thundered Mr. Alstyne, "that you have not read of the robbery?"

"What robbery?" queried Price "I've been away for a week or two, you know. And I never read the newspapers, anyhow. You know that, Sandy," he added, turning to Seymour for confirmation. "Besides, my father was ill and I scarcely had a chance to hear much news. What robbery are you talking about?"

Old Pruett limped into the room at that instant. Instead of answering Price, Mr. Alstyne wheeled on the janitor in a new frenzy of dramatic fervor.

"Pruett!" he cried. "Look! Do you see that picture?"

"Sure I see it," grunted Pruett, uninterested. "Anything the matter with it?"

"Matter with it?" babbled Alstyne. "How do you suppose it came to be there?"

"I don't 'suppose' anything," retorted Pruett. "I know just how it happens to be there."

"You *know?*" echoed Mr. Alstyne dazedly. "You know? How?"

"Why shouldn't I know?" demanded Pruett. "I hung it there myself not two hours ago."

Mr. Alstyne threw up both hands in muddled helplessness. He was once more bereft of speech. Pruett, looking around the circle of directors, saw every eye focused upon himself in wondering question. Under the battery of that multiple gaze he spoke.

"What's the game?" he asked defiantly. "I ain't made a mistake, have I? That was the only place where there was a hook to hang the picture."

His words were as Greek to the directors.

"Say—say that over again, Pruett!" faltered Mr. Alstyne, both pudgy hands clutching at his whirling head. "Maybe it will make sense the second time."

"I say," resumed Pruett, bewilderment at the other men's strange aspect stirring him to sullen wrath, "I say I hung it on that hook because it was the only hook in the room that didn't have a picture on it. If you want it somewhere else, say so, and I'll put a hook there for it. There's no call to glare at me like that. Even s'posing I've hung it in the wrong place, it's easy remedied. What's the matter with you all?"

Seymour had drawn Price aside. For a few moments they had been talking in quick undertones. Now Seymour came forward into the excited, mystified group.

"I think I can clear up this jumble," said he. "Pruett, that picture over there—the one you hung to-day—was that one of the paintings whose frames you've been regilding?"

"Yes," snapped Pruett; "and three times as long its frame took to gild as did any of the rest. The wood just soaked up gilding. But I kept at it till it took a decent-looking shine. That's why I didn't get it done sooner."

"But," fumed Mr. Alstyne, "I don't—this can't—"

"One moment, please," interrupted Seymour, checking the eager curator. "Pruett, was this one of the batch of framed pictures you began to gild on the night the Murillo disappeared?"

"Sure. And the way that old frame soaked the gilding—"

"Gentlemen," interrupted Seymour, turning to the directors, "the mystery which has baffled the whole world is no mystery at all. I can explain it to you, with Mr. Price's leave, in a few words."

A murmur of keen interest urged him on.

"On the day of the presentation ceremonies," continued Seymour, "you may remember that several pictures which needed gilding were taken from their hooks and placed in one corner near the door for Pruett to take away.

"As the last of the crowd filed out, it occurred to Mr. Price that it would be a good joke on Mr. Alstyne to take the Murillo from the wall and place it among that lot of pictures on the floor, putting in its place one of the pictures that had been left there for regilding. He did this in the moment after the guests went out and before Mr. Alstyne returned to the room."

Alstyne started up, purple with fury. Seymour waved him back to his seat, and went on:

"Mr. Price thought, of course, that both Mr. Alstyne and Pruett would at once detect the change, and would restore the Murillo to its place. But it seems Mr. Alstyne did not look closely at the Murillo. And, as its frame and that of the Gloucester-fisherman picture are of about the same size, he mistook one for the other in the dim light. Pruett, too, did not notice, as he never had seen the Murillo. And, as there are in this gallery no less than seven portraits of women with lilies, he naturally did not associate this one, afterward, with the Murillo. To-day, he returned it to the gallery. That is all."

"Pardon me," spoke up Price above the clamor that followed on Seymour's words, "that is *not* all!"

And he told briefly, yet vividly, the story of Seymour's encounter with the man, who was undoubtedly Whitson, in the passageway, and of Seymour's night-long vigil.

"He saved your picture for you, gentlemen," finished Price, "though he is too modest to say so himself. For my part, all I can do is to ask your pardon for an abominable piece of freshness for which I am heartily ashamed."

"Ashamed?" croaked old Pruett. "The man who ought to be ashamed is the guy who charged three hundred and fifty thousand dollars for a bit of three-by-three canvas, when down at the Newark Art Store you can get one, double the size, for eighty-nine cents. Those old masters sure gave short measure on their pictures!"

The Girl Who Couldn't Go Wrong

RAEGAN told it to me. For a short, happy space in his mottled career, Raegan had been a settlement worker. But someone in charge was so base as to accuse him of a greater interest in the working than in the settlement. And he had departed—with a grievance and several more negotiable mementoes.

It was during the "Minimum Wage for Working Girls" legislation that I ran across Raegan. What or whom he was doing at the Capital I never clearly knew. I had a fine idea for an epigram which, if I could whittle it into scintillant, mordant keenness, I intended to embody somewhere in my wage story.

It was to the effect that the same low pay scale which keeps girls from being respectable keeps men from being anything else.

I rather fancied this statement of a double standard in the relation of poverty to goodness. And, in the first glow of inspiration, I repeated it to Raegan. Of course he did not grasp the idea. And when I put it in more and simpler words he flatly contradicted me. The fact that my pretty catch phrase could be proven untrue pleased me immensely. For it proved the thing an epigram.

I told Raegan so. But, perhaps thinking I was arguing the case, he undertook at some length to prove me wrong. Then, by way of illustration, he told me the following tale—gleaned during his brief, bright settlement experience. I do not vouch for it. Nor do I wholly know what it proves. But this I do know: it proves *something*. That is not an effort to be funny, but the statement of a solemn certainty. And wiser folk than I are at liberty to find the proof.

No (began Raegan), you're dead wrong when you spring that

puzzle picture speech about girls finding it hard to live up to their Elsie books just because they're broke. Often as not, they find it harder to do anything different. Being broke is the very thing that keeps them in line. And Maudie Kirk's case cinches that.

There're two halves to Maudie's story. The first half reads like all the dreary, Heaven-Will-Protect-the-Woiking-Goil wheezes ever ground out. The second half isn't quite like anything else I've happened to run across.

Maudie came to New York from one of the "small time" towns that have names like a Roman general and populations like a road company Roman mob. I don't remember just what line of honest endeavor her father had chased. But there's no doubt he *was* honest. For he died, leaving a bedridden widow and Maudie and—after the M.D. and M.A. (why, Mortuary Assistant, of course) had taken theirs—about a hundred dollars.

That meant the bell had rung for Maudie to listen to the factory whistle. And, being a dutiful kid, she listened. There was no chance, up in her own bailiwick. So she hearkened to the call of the city. There were jobs to be had in New York. And a girl could live here on almost nothing, if she knew the right sort of food and clothes—and let them alone.

And she could send all her spare savings up-State to pay board for Mother, who was deposited at Uncle Barney's, on the Pompton road, at three fifty a week. Some money, in those parts, I'm told!

So Maudie came to New York. She was no fluff skulled Maid of Yaphank, to be lured or otherwise pleasurably excited by the hidden perils of the Big City. Not she. She knew what to steer clear of and why to steer clear of it. She was a good girl, clear down to her number six soles. And level-headed. And equipped with an 1840 New England conscience. Why, on form alone, you could have backed Maudie to go around the track six times without leaning over the rail once to crop any infield grass.

"I know what the city is," she told her mother, as she finished brailing the telescope bag and double-reefed the ancestral umbrella. "And I know the traps it holds for fools. I know, too, that a good, sensible, self-respecting girl can always make her way anywhere. So don't worry your precious old self about me."

Good talk, what?

So to New York came Maudie. And what's more, she got a job—after a while. It was in the basement (plus two) of a department store. The section that never is intruded on by Customers, Daylight or Real Air. And they paid her $5.50, as a starter. Just for pottering around pretty steadily from eight to six thirty, with very near twenty whole minutes off for lunch—sometimes.

Part of the while she was able to send home the three fifty a week for Mother's board. And part of the time she did it, anyway, by working overtime. You see, it was one of those generous stores that allow their girls overtime pay, except at the busy season.

Well, for a couple of months or so Maudie was pretty near as happy and carefree as a blind mule on a treadmill. Then there was a cut-down. And the bulk of the new girls were let out. Maudie was among the bulk. And by this time she'd trained off a whole lot of loose flesh that she didn't need.

But, bless you, even when her first landlady locked the door on her and lost the key, Maudie was as plucky as ever. And just as dead sure as ever that a good, self-respecting girl could win her way along the straight road—even if there were a few stray bumps therein, to keep the liver from getting torpid.

Next, after a kind of long stage wait, she got her chance in a steam laundry, at six per. No overtime. But she scalded her face and arms pretty badly one day in a steam escape. And by the time she got back from the hospital the laundry people had decided she was a hoodoo, and wouldn't take her on again.

Through the Y. W. C. A. (where she used to get weekly thrills by listening to those startling lectures on "Child Widows of India," and "How to Tell the Wild Flowers from the Birds") she annexed a nice general-housework job in a family of nine that kept boarders. The mistress was the grandniece, by marriage, of Simon Legree. She paid Maudie fourteen dollars a month and kept her from taking on fat. But Maudie fainted one day, when there was company. And she was fired. You see, they wanted a strong girl.

Did she lose her faith in that splendid Self-Respect wheeze? She did not. She still shut her eyes and her ears to the Easiest Way and stopped eating for a while; and then landed a fine position in a sweatshop.

She lasted for nearly five months. Then the girls "walked out," she at their head. One of the papers called her a Joan of Arc and printed a snapshot of her. The other girls got back. Maudie didn't.

Being a member of the Arc family isn't on the free list.

Then came a spell when there was no work. At least none for Maudie. The day that the last member of the Dollar Family quitted lodging with her a letter came from Uncle Barney. It said, among a lot of other demonstrative things, that Mother's board money must be paid up in full or the old lady must get out.

There was a poorhouse handy, went on Uncle Barney, with his inimitable dry wit, and he wouldn't grudge giving Mother a free drive there. He enclosed the doctor's bill for $98.60. And at the bottom the big-hearted old family physician had scrawled a line to the effect that he'd pay no more calls till a full settlement was forthcoming. Uncle Barney's love letter wound up by mentioning that Mother was some worse.

The letter got to Maudie Kirk on Christmas evening, early.

She read it all through a couple of times. Then she read again what the doctor had to say. After that, she crossed her room (one step did it) to the looking glass. The glass showed back about the sorriest-looking hall-bedroom in the City of Hallrooms. The landlady had been soft-hearted, because Christmas was near, and she had told Maudie she needn't get out till New Year's.

Well, over to the glass went Maudie. It was a flawed glass at that. But it served her all right as an audience. She looked into it. And she began to speak, out loud, to the girl there.

"I've given it a fair trial," she said. "I came here strong in my faith that self-respect and willingness to work would carry a woman safe to success. I've slaved like a dog. And I've starved. I've given Decency all the chance it could want. I've lived as Mother would have wanted me to live. And I've suffered as she couldn't understand, if I told her. And what's come of it?

"I can't get work. I can't get food. I can't get the money that will keep Mother out of the poorhouse. I can't get any of those things honestly and decently. If I was the only one concerned, I wouldn't care. But Mother is going to have a home and a doctor's services.

"She's going to have them. And I'm going to get them for her. I've

read a lot about a girl not needing to go crooked just because she's poor. And it's a lie. A silly lie. I've tried the heaven path. And it's bumped me into a stone wall. Here's where I go to hell!"

And just as carefully and as honestly as she had toiled heavenward, she set out to trip the Short-Cut, Down-Grade route. She planned it all out. But she overlooked one bet. She'd been too busy orating at herself in the glass to pay any sort of notice to what that same glass had to say in come-back. If she had, she might—or she mightn't—have noticed a few things:

First, that ten months of systematic starving had taken everything off her body but the bones; and had tried to square itself by making those twice as large. Second, that the eyes had gone hollow. Not with dark, fancy shadows, but with a burnt-hole-in-a-blanket effect.

Likewise her face was greasy and so was her hair. Hers was mouse-colored hair at best, and it had got thin and stringy and it was strained back. The only dress she had left was grease-spotted and shiny and darned. It had never been anything that Worth or Paquin would have thrown a fit over. And now it had lost whatever it had started with. Her shoes, too—well, never mind her shoes. And she had no gloves. Her hat, by the way, wasn't much the better for about forty rains that had landed on it since she had hocked the family umbrella.

Yes, sir, that was the general blue print front elevation of the damsel that had set out to go wrong. But off she started. She had pluck.

She sneaked out of her boarding house, and hit Broadway about eight o'clock. There's apt to be several people around at that hour of the evening. 'Specially Christmas night.

Maudie was resolved on her Hades trip, all right. But she didn't quite know the road. So up Broadway she started. She'd always scuttled along the streets like a scared little hen, with her eyes fixed, purely, on her feet, ever since she had struck New York. But tonight she acted up real brazen. She walked slow along the Big Blonde Path, eyes high, manner heroic and her heart hammering up in her poor thin throat.

From Thirtieth Street to Fiftieth she strolled. Then back again as far as Fortieth. Nothing happened. Just nothing at all. She couldn't understand. She'd heard about girls who walked Broadway. She'd just walked it. And she might as well have been stepping down to the store from Uncle Barney's house.

Something was wrong, somewhere. She couldn't guess what, till she saw a squab just in front of her drift dreamily alongside a fat man who looked as if his name belonged on a Rhine Wine List, and say something to him as she passed. Maudie could only catch the word "dear." It sounded rather free-and-easy for a total stranger. But it seemed to be the thing to do.

So up to a dapper little fur-coated man sidled Maudie. She tried to say "Dear," too. But the word stuck. The man looked at her, kind of cross. Then he grunted:

"This is Panhandleville all right. Fifth touch in six blocks. Oh, well, it's Christmas!"

And he flipped her a dime. Maudie gathered it up. Dimes had a market value, even if souls hadn't. Then she stood looking after him, all choked and white. He'd taken her for a beggar. Not for a Seductive Delilah at all. But just for a Christmas Night beggar.

Next time there was no chance for any mistake like that. She said "Dear," to the red-faced clubman who lurched toward her out of a side canyon. She said it right out loud. Pretty near hollered it. He stopped dead short with his mouth open. Maudie backed away a bit. She didn't know what was the next thing to say. Besides, he reeked of booze. But she got fresh hold of her courage and said "Dear" again. She said it the way McGraw coaches the runner on third.

The man let out a roar of laughter.

"Oh, if the boys could see!" he sniggered, hopeless-like. "And they'll never believe me! On Broadway, too!"

He hailed a taxi and rolled aboard it, still roaring. Maudie took a kind of bashful step toward the taxi. But he howled to the meter brigand to put on double speed, and slammed the door.

The next man told her to go get a new face. The next said the Scarecrows' Home ought to keep earlier closing hours.

And so on, all the way down the line. It was raining, too. Once a cop saw her at work and he laughed himself sick. You see, the happy Christmas spirit was abroad.

The only job that is supposed to pay the amateur better than the professional followed the example of all the other jobs Maudie Kirk had looked for. Gee, but it must have been tough for a girl, with Maudie's conscience, to cut loose and turn her back on all she held holy—and then be refused the chance of profit by it. As if when old Faust offered to swap his soul, the red basso devil had carolled, "Nothing doing!"

A night's sleep gave her some new courage. And she made up her mind to try again. Women of That Kind wore ropes of gems and rode in limousines and had the sort of flat they call "Bijou"—whatever that means. Maudie had read so. Also, the wicked city was swarming with men who were eager to prey on defenseless womanhood. She'd read that, too. So she couldn't see where she'd failed.

She hadn't read—because nobody's yet had sense or nerve enough to write it—that the average plain working girl has about as many temptations in New York as she has on a desert island. And that at best—or worst—such a girl's unlawful earnings wouldn't keep her in carfare. But where's the living girl who doesn't snuggle to her heart the belief that she could rake in a fortune if only she chose to be wicked? And, after all, Glass is as precious as Diamonds—until one tries to sell it.

Maudie planned a new angle of attack. There is a famous "Red-Haired Siren" whose lures captivate Wall Street and who is by now richer than John D.

Poor Maudie had heard about her. Everybody has heard about her. Except perhaps Wall Street.

The Street was screaming next day over a story that nobody really believed. A story about a thin, ragged-looking wreck of a woman— most likely batty—who had managed to get past the sleepy door guard into old Cyrus Q. Spillaker's private office and had stammeringly hailed the old geezer as "Dear"—just before the whole working office staff had industriously run her out.

Well, it took Maudie Kirk just two days to learn—she was no fool—that she could no more go to hell than she could to Mars. Morally, she was a goner. For she'd said good-bye to Goodness and Decency and Conscience. Said goodbye to them, out loud, in front of her looking glass. But she'd never since had a chance to make that farewell anything but a solo. And she knew now that she never could.

That was about dusk, two days after Christmas.

A couple of hours later, a tug captain off East Twenty-sixth Street boathooked a bunch of sleazy clothes that had just hopped off the dock with a starved woman inside of them.

Maudie couldn't even score a success as a drowner. The captain lugged her to Bellevue, and pretty soon she came around and began to eat. She had a few months' arrears of food to make up. And she sure did her best at it.

You know young Galahad Templar? Sure you do. He runs the Settlement. He has all the cash that's fit to coin. And he spends it on the Uplift of his fellow man and woman. Fits up the Settlement gallery with pre-cubist pictures to elevate their souls, and has long-haired woplets from the Metropolitan and Carnegie Hall come down once a week to show them how Tschaikowsky really ought to be rendered. It's a big help to East Siders with rabbit families, I can tell you. Why, lots of them can tell a Corot from a Greuze and the "Largo" from Raff's "Spring Song."

Well, Templar happened to be on his monthly philanthropic butt-in at Bellevue when Maudie Kirk was brought there. He got interested in as much of her story as she could tell him between eats (we got the whole of it from her later at the Settlement), and he pulled wires to have her ambulanced over to his Settlement House.

Say, it was a miracle what a few weeks of rest and real food and warm clothes and a few dozen baths and shampoos did to that girl's appearance. And when she was all well again and plump and kind of pretty and winsome, Templar paid her mother's bills and found her a fine easy fifteen-a-week job in the office of one of his chums. She'd got a fair start at last, poor kid!

Did she hang onto *that* job? I'm sorry you had to ask such a question. And I'm pained, something terrible, to say she didn't. Templar was so proud of his work of reformation that he—well, last time I heard of them, he'd gotten her a nice comfortable little morganatic flat uptown, somewhere, near the park. The sort of flat they call "Bijou"— whatever that means.

Chapter I.
Where Cold Is King.

A RAMBLING huddle of snow-streaked black relieved the endless white of the waste. And from this huddle, across the gathering night, shot warm rays of yellow-red light. Fort Simpson's wonted ugliness was transformed to rare beauty for Lieutenant Barry Hegan as his worn-out horse turned in that evening at the barracks' gate and halted in the half-swept space before the door of the officer's quarters.

To a denizen of the real world—the world of moderate temperatures, of modern houses, of amusements, of well-dressed men and women—the returning lieutenant of his majesty's Royal Northwest Mounted Police would just then have borne rather the aspect of an arctic scarecrow than of a trim and stalwart young commissioned officer of constabulary. But to the orderly who came forward with a salute to lead away his horse, the lieutenant was merely a superior officer and quite correctly garbed—for a man who had been riding thirty miles in subzero weather on special-inspection detail.

Hegan—a shapeless, faceless ball of fur, leather, and wool—rolled off his tired horse, stamped heavily to restore the circulation to his half-numbed legs; beat his swathed arms across his chest for the same purpose, and made his way into the warm glow of the mess room. He paused a second, before opening the door, to glance at the spirit thermometer that hung on the outer lintel, and whose tube was visible by reason of a shaft of light from an adjacent window.

"Fifty-one below!" he read, half aloud. "And it'll drop another nine degrees before morning. That means no one should be abroad alone," he added to a man who had crossed the yard, and who was mounting the steps behind him. "It means, too, that if a drop of water were to be tossed into the air it would—"

"Turn to a pellet of hail before it touched ground?" queried the other, a civilian guest at the fort and new to the far North.

"Not at all," said Hegan. "It would crackle like a toy torpedo and burst into a million fragments. That's what'd happen."

"If it's a joke—" hesitated the newcomer.

"Friend," quietly reproved Hegan, "during weather like this, in the North, nothing is a joke. Here is where Mother Nature drops her smile. I'll give you another tip. I see you pack a new, shiny, useless pistol with you. In this kind of weather never draw it out of a warm pocket and fire it. If you do, something is liable to happen right suddenly to the hand that does the firing."

Hegan had fumbled for the doorknob with his formless fur mittens, found it, and opened the door. The two entered, closing it swiftly behind them. Several men in undress uniform were lounging about the big room. They looked up and nodded to Hegan as he stamped in. Returning their careless greetings, Hegan crossed to a cloak room at the far end of the hall, to shed his voluminous outer garb. A little wall mirror with a flawed glass reflected his image as he passed. Whimsically he paused before the glass an instant, to note the odd picture it showed him.

Then he unbuckled clumsily his huge fur mittens, and pulled off the thick, fur-lined gloves beneath them. Next he loosened and threw back from his head the fur-and-wool hood of his parka, or greatcoat, revealing on his head, face, and neck a covering of knitted wool that resembled nothing so much as a fat stocking with a lateral slit halfway down its expanse. This slit had served as an eye opening for the wearer. And a few inches below it were two great lumps of ice—his frozen breath, which had penetrated through the wool and congealed on the outside. Boots, outer socks, and thick overalls were then doffed. And the erstwhile bearlike creature stood up, shapely and powerfully graceful in his uniform of a lieutenant in the Royal Mounted.

His outer garments laid aside, Hegan strolled back into the mess room. Too well versed in the ways of the North to yield to the temptation of going at once up to the roaring open fireplace, he took a seat far from the radius of pleasant heat, and fell to chafing one cold-numbed hand against the other.

There were more officers than usual in the room. The commanding officer of the district happened to be at Fort Simpson with his staff, as were also several commissioned officers from Fort Mackenzie. Hegan answered in civil monosyllables the friendly remarks made to him as he joined the lounging half dozen men in the mess room. He was tired and cold, and he wanted to rest and let the gentle warmth of the wood fire seep through his chilled body before joining in the general talk. His companions well understood his mood, and the flow of talk went on around him.

A comfortable drowsiness came over Hegan as he relaxed his weary body and felt himself grow warm again after so many hours of exposure to the Barren Grounds cold. He had dropped half asleep when he chanced to catch a few words of a story a grizzled captain was telling.

"Just over the divide," he heard the captain say. "That was three days ago. He was afoot, and headed in the general direction of the Great Slave Lake. Afoot, mind you. With tattered clothes, feet almost bare, and only one blanket—a torn one. No pack, and no gun."

"It was suicide!" broke out one hearer. "The man was crazy. Why didn't you bring him in?"

"We tried to. But a snow flurry came up, and he gave us the slip. He was fifty yards away when we saw him. We yelled, but he broke into a stumbling run, as if he was afraid of us. Just then up came the flurry. When it passed we couldn't find a sign of him."

"In the Barren Grounds; in January," mused Hegan, with a shiver. "A man with one blanket and no pack or gun. It isn't possible. It was a snow trick on your eyes."

"No," vehemently denied the captain. "Two of my men saw him, too. Maybe a run-out from some mining camp, or a prospector. Whoever he was, he's dead before this, for he was making southeast; not in the direction of any fort or post."

Chapter II.
A Desperate Exploit.

HEGAN shrugged his shoulders, and dropped out of the conversation, mildly resentful that so absurd a story should have roused him from an incipient nap. He did not know whether the narrator had been deceived by snow strabismus into mistaking a bowlder for a man, or whether the captain were telling a purposely tall story for the benefit of the young civilian—who, however, ignorant of the North, seemed bored by it.

Hegan's four years of service in the Northwest had taught him enough of the Barren Grounds winter rigors to make him sure that no man, clad and equipped as the captain had described the traveler to be, could reasonably hope to win his way to safety across the "Land of the Little Sticks" in an arctic January. He saw no point in so unimaginative a joke as the falsehood appeared to be. And again he lapsed into drowsy indolence.

It was good to lounge thus in a warm mess room, among good fellows, with a hot supper in immediate prospect, after a day in the bitter open, where the wind had alternately buffeted and stabbed him and the cold had gnawed to his very bones. Such an evening as this, and in so congenial a company, was one of the few compensations that starred Hegan's winters in the sunless white North.

He was an efficient and gallant officer, as even the most misanthropic of his superiors admitted; and he loved his chosen profession. Yet in midwinter its discomforts and its long periods of dull inaction palled. It was one thing to fare forth in light uniform on a prancing horse through the civilized towns of the Northwest on a bright summer day, and quite another to fight zero in the desolate wastes of the Barren Grounds—the Mackenzie Valley region north of British Columbia, where his troop was quartered.

Yet the winter days here at Fort Simpson held one flawless joy. Elise Dufour, the post trader's daughter, was here; and Elise and the Irish police lieutenant had been engaged for nearly six months. Hegan was planning to cross to her father's house, as soon as supper should be over, for his regular evening call. And, now that he was at last warmed and rested, he grew impatient at the delay in supper's announcement. His impatience began to be shared, for more practical reasons, by the other waiting officers. One of them spoke of it.

"Waiting for the chief," was another's explanation. "He's still closeted with those two whiskered foreigners that drifted in from Dawson this afternoon. He—"

An orderly came into the mess room, singled out Hegan, and in machinelike monotone informed him that the colonel desired his immediate presence in the latter's office.

"That means a wigging," cheerfully prophesied a grizzled captain. "The chief means to find out why Barry spends all his spare evenings over at the post trader's instead of staying here to help out our quartet with his bass."

"More likely he wants him to start east to-morrow with some papers for headquarters," suggested another. "Fine weather for traveling," he added, with a grin.

"I think," said Hegan, as he left the room, "that the chief more likely wants the benefit of a really sensible man's conversation for a few minutes after listening to you chaps chatter for three meals a day."

He made his way to the office across the hall. There sat a lean man, leather-faced, white-haired, with eyes like Yukon ice, and a hard but not unkindly mouth. On the other side of the table from him were two men whom Barry Hegan had not seen before. They were thickset, bearded, and clad in close-fitting dark-green uniforms.

"Lieutenant Hegan," said the colonel, with a formality under which lurked a decided friendliness for this favorite subaltern of his, "you are familiar with the entire Mackenzie River region?"

"Yes, sir," replied Hegan.

"Gentlemen," said the colonel, speaking in French as he turned to address his two guests, "Lieutenant Hegan is the man above all others for such a difficult task as this. He tracked two Indian murderers last year from the Great Slave to Dawson, and brought them in single-handed. He has the true scout instinct, and is fearless and resourceful."

Both the foreigners rose and bowed to the lieutenant, who returned the bows with a military salute, then stood once more at attention, facing his commander.

"Barry," said the colonel, dropping into English and a manner more fatherly than military, as was often his custom with Hegan, "Barry, you're still engaged to Miss Dufour, aren't you?"

Hegan flushed, and cast a covert glance at the strangers.

"Don't worry," interposed the colonel. "They don't speak or understand any English. Nothing but French and Russian."

"Russian?" repeated Hegan.

"Yes. They are government emissaries from St. Petersburg. I'll come to that presently. You are still engaged, aren't you?"

"Yes, sir."

"When do you expect to marry?"

"As soon as I can get my troop, sir. One can marry on a captain's pay, not on a lieutenant's."

"Very wise. But promotions in the Royal Mounted don't follow on engagements—unfortunately. Promotion at best is slow."

"Deucedly slow, sir," admitted Barry.

"Your record is good," went on the colonel. "Were one distinguished—let us say spectacular—exploit added to it, I think I could safely promise that your captaincy would follow within a month."

Barry's eyes brightened. He longed to demand leave to set out at once upon the most hair-raising, desperate exploit on record. But he merely bowed understanding. The wise old colonel read his face like a printed page.

"I am saying all this," he went on, "because I am going to detail you on special duty that will be arduous and dangerous. I do not want it to seem thankless as well. I am going to ask you to find a needle in a haystack. I want you to find a man who is supposed to be somewhere between Dawson and the Great Slave Lake. That is the closest direction I can give you. The chances against your success are a thousand to one. But I believe the chances of any other man in my command of finding him would be barely one in ten thousand. That is why I am sending you. The weather is dangerous, so is the man you are to look for."

"Yes, sir," said Barry quietly as the colonel paused.

Hegan was not thinking of the thousands of square miles of trackless white waste to be scoured on this seemingly hopeless errand. He was thinking only how a pair of dark-brown eyes would glow when he could flash before their fond gaze a captain's commission.

"I will outline the case to you briefly," went on the colonel. "These officials will give you such details as you may wish. You have heard, perhaps, of Verkhoyvansk?"

"Somewhere in Siberia, isn't it, sir?"

"The northwest penal colony there. Being so isolated and difficult to leave, it is less heavily guarded than most of the Russian prison settlements. It has been the boast of the Russian government that no captive has ever escaped from Verkhoyvansk. It is no longer their boast. A captive *has* escaped. And, to restore the grisly prestige of Verkhoyvansk, he must be brought back. So Russian police agents have been scouring the world for him. These two have traced him to the Barren Grounds."

Barry showed his amazement. "Why, isn't the thing impossible, sir? How could any man get here from—"

"This is not 'any man.' Apparently he is a man in a million—strong as an ox, with unbelievable endurance and a mind to match. He eluded one guard, stunned another, and got to Bering Straits. There he thrashed a boatload of Chuchi Indians that tried to win the standing reward by capturing him. There were three of the Indians, it seems— puny little fellows. He routed them, took their skin canoe, and crossed the Straits among the ice cakes. That alone is a feat not one man in a hundred could manage.

"He worked his way down to St. Michael, and got a job as fireman on a Yukon steamer that took him to Dawson. Then, over a spur of the Canadian Rockies he came, and so southeastward into the Barren Grounds, scarcely a day ahead of the police agents who were after him. These are the agents. Of course, they lost all track of him. As they don't know the country, they came here for help. They have extradition papers duly countersigned by our government, and the authorities have sent special instructions for us to offer the Russians every aid in our power."

"And I am to find him for them, sir?" asked Barry, his enthusiasm ebbing.

The tale of the convict's daring escape had stirred him. Hegan had heard of the horrors of Siberian prisons. It irked him to think of himself as the means of sending back to Verkhoyvansk a man who had escaped. Yet, over and above all, Barry was an officer in the Canadian Mounted Northwest Police. And to him his colonel's order was supreme law, so he merely repeated:

"And I am to find him, sir?"

"If you can."

"May I ask a few questions of these agents, sir?"

At the colonel's nod, he turned to the Russians. "Please describe this man you seek," he said in French.

One of the agents, for reply, handed him a printed slip, wherein the fugitive's description was printed in parallel columns of Russian, French, Italian, German, Spanish, and English. Barry pocketed the slip, to study at his leisure.

"He was alone?" he asked in French.

"Yes," replied one of the agents in the same language. "Alone, and with almost no equipment. Were it merely his life we seek we might sit here in comfort, knowing he must die of exposure within a day or two at most in this death land. But that is not sufficient. We must take him back alive. Alive, in order to teach the lesson to others. He must meet his punishment, after we get him safe back to Verkhoyvansk. Thus shall he be a warning to others. Were we to return merely with news of his death, it would be thought he had eluded us, and that we invented the story that he is dead. He must go back a living witness that none may hope to escape from Verkhoyvansk."

"I see," said Hegan coldly. Then, to his colonel, in English: "I think I understand your wishes, sir. I am to find this man, and bring him here alive."

"Quite so," answered the colonel. "And if you can do it, as I said, I think I can promise that you will receive your captaincy. And you will merit it, if ever a man did. When can you start?"

"By the time my orderly can get my equipment ready and my horse saddled, I shall have had time for a bite of hot supper. I can start in half an hour."

"Half an hour!" echoed the colonel. "On a night like this? Morning will be time enough. It may be warmer by then."

"Morning, sir, by your permission, will be a loss of ten hours. When one is searching haystacks for needles, it is well to remember that the longer one waits the deeper the needle may burrow or settle. With your permission, sir, I'll start in half an hour."

"What force do you want?"

"I'd rather go alone."

"In weather like this it is not safe."

"I understood you to say, sir, that this was not precisely a picnic jaunt as it stands; and 'safety' means delay. I will stand a better chance of getting my man if I go alone and at once."

"As you wish," grunted the colonel, his tanned brow furrowing.

"I commend your spirit," put in the second police agent, and, to the surprise of the colonel and Barry, he spoke in flawless English.

After saluting his commander, Hegan turned on his heel, and left the room. Calling a direction to his orderly, he sought out the grizzled captain whose mess-room story of having seen an ill-clad, unequipped man on foot had roused Hegan from semi-slumber. Giving no reasons for his curiosity, he proceeded to pump that astonished but gratified raconteur in a series of volleylike questions, until he had learned every detail of the fugitive's probable direction, his speed of travel, and his appearance.

Chapter III.
The Man From Siberia.

FOR three days, Barry Hegan followed the trail. For three days, through the arctic winter's gloom he worked southeastward, pressing on through the wilderness as fast as he dared urge his sturdy pony on what might prove a long-distance hike. At night he took but scant rest, hobbling his mount—heavily blanketed and further protected by such moss or evergreens as could be found—in the lee of bowlder or snow hill, and scooping out for himself alongside a snow bed and place for his fire.

It was primitive camping, and comfortless. The night's simple tasks were made onerous by the bitter cold. Hegan found it no easy matter after leading or riding his pony for hours through deep feather drift, to dig down to hardpan for bed and blaze, and to find material for a fire; to melt snow in his tiny kettle, and to cut with cold-stiffened fingers the strips of bacon for his frying pan.

Once, having built his fire imprudently near a shelving rock, he was awakened an hour after he had fallen asleep by an avalanche of heat-loosened snow from the rocks that utterly banked his blaze and rendered it necessary for him—if he would avoid freezing—to go through the whole tedious snow-digging, fuel-gathering process once more. Again, a starved wolf pack scented him out, and he was forced to rise at midnight to drive away the marauders from his panic-stricken pony, and to shoot two of them in order to satisfy the hunger of the rest, and thus save his mount from further peril. But of all his hardships that boring, gnawing cold was worst; and next to that the snow pain in his throbbing, bloodshot eyes. All this, however, he recognized as part of the day's work for a man in the Royal Mounted. And he hung like grim death to his purpose of tracking down the Russian convict.

His task, apart from its terrible hardships, was far simpler than his colonel had fancied. He went to work with careful method. Recalling the spot where the captain had seen the ragged refugee, and the statement that the man was making southeast toward the Great Slave, Hegan had struck off from Fort Simpson at a radius that might reasonably be expected to cut the fugitive's trail. And, after casting about for a day like a dog on the scent, he found it. He was much helped by the fact that no snow had fallen for several days. The convict, probably ignorant of trail blinding, had apparently made no effort to hide his tracks. And in more than one spot these tracks were marked with blood, as from an ice-cut foot.

Stronger hourly grew the spoor as the hardy arctic pony gained on the exhausted pedestrian. At last, one noon Hegan knew the end of the chase was at hand. The tracks were fresh. The loose snow still crumbled around their edges.

In front rose a ridge of rocky hill—icy, precipitous, practically inaccessible—cutting the flat landscape transversely in front of Hegan. In one spot—toward which the staggering footmarks had plowed through the drift—the ridge was split by a steep gorge which formed the only visible pass to the far side. The wind sweeping through this gorge had brushed it clean of snow. Its sides and twisting path were smooth with ice. Toward this gap Hegan headed his sure-footed pony.

He loosened his carbine in his saddle holster, and pulled his outer mittens from his hands. The weather had greatly moderated during the preceding twenty-four hours. Hegan, from long experience at temperature guessing, knew the thermometer could now register but little below zero, and that his carbine and his hands were in no present danger from the cold.

Up the twisting, glassy incline started the shaggy pony. As it neared the turn, Hegan half drew his carbine from its holster. He was not minded to be ambushed, in case his quarry had seen him approaching, and had chosen this difficult spot for a last stand against the law. The pony was scarce ten feet from the curve when suddenly it stopped dead short, planting all four feet together, and stood thus, trembling, ears forward, nostrils dilated.

Before Hegan could urge his mount forward, or get off to investigate, the narrow space in front of him was blocked by a figure huge, hairy, hideous. Around the curve in the pass had shambled a great Rocky Mountain grizzly. Startled in some way from its winter nap, it had issued from its lair furious and homicidal. At sight of horse and rider, the bear rose on its hind legs. And the pony followed bruin's example. So suddenly and violently did his mount rear that Hegan had neither time to prevent the move nor even to get his carbine clear of its holster.

The pony's hind shoes slipped on the glare of ice. Back tumbled the scared mount, striking its head against a rock and falling stunned on its side, pinioning its rider's left leg under its flanks. The impact sent the carbine flying ten feet up the path.

The bear, seemingly taking the fall for a hostile move, came forward in a rush toward the prostrate man. Hegan writhed vainly to tear himself from under the fallen horse. There was no time to waste. Already the bear was upon him, its giant bulk towering above his head, its steel claws bared and menacing.

Hegan, giving up his efforts to free himself, drew from his belt the hunting knife he carried on long trails. Still pinioned to earth, and his every motion cramped, he struck upward with all the force and accuracy he could muster, at the shaggy bulk above him. A sweep of one claw-armed forepaw smote the knife from the man's hand with the strength of a steel hammer and rent Hegan's heavy sleeve coverings.

In the same instant, as the paw swung aloft for a clean blow at the defenseless, struggling victim, the rocky sides of the pass echoed and reechoed deafeningly to the roar of a shot. The bear, with a tired little grunt, lurched sideways and collapsed slowly to the icy ground. There it lay moveless; nor did a second shot, ripping through the enormous carcass, cause so much as a nervous quiver. The first bullet, through the heart, had ended bruin's life—and saved Barry Hegan's.

The lieutenant lifted himself on his elbow, and stared dazedly about him. At the turn of the pass, scarce ten feet away, stood a man. In his hands was a carbine which Barry at a glance knew for his own. Yes, and he knew the man who held it—knew him from the Russians' printed description slip, and from what the grizzled captain at Fort Simpson had said of him.

The rescuer was of great height, with massive breadth of shoulder and depth of chest. Tangled flaxen hair fell unkempt about his eyes and neck, and a matted yellow beard covered the lower half of his face. He was frightfully emaciated, and as white as a corpse. His haggard blue eyes looked out through sunken hollows. His clothes were in tatters. Through a gap in one torn shoe oozed blood.

For a second or more the two men looked at each other without words. Alone in the dead world of a Northland winter, naked soul spoke to naked soul.

The momentary spell was broken by a convulsive movement from Hegan's pony. The tough little horse was recovering from its head's stunning rap against the outjutting rock at the side of the pass. The pony snorted, rolled to one side, freeing the weight from Hegan's leg, and scrambled awkwardly to its feet, where it stood, stupid, dizzy, sides heaving, head sunk.

Hegan rose from the ground. An agonizing pain in his ankle told of a serious wrench or sprain, and sent a wave of physical nausea over him. Sick with pain and reaction, he nevertheless made shift to limp across to where the convict stood.

Chapter IV.
Short-Lived Relief.

THE stranger, still holding the carbine, made no effort to raise the weapon against the man he had saved. Barry, by a mighty effort, forced back the flood of gratitude that swelled up in his heart, and forced himself to speak and act like a well-constructed automaton—a tiny but perfect cog in that matchlessly disciplined organization, his majesty's Royal Canadian Northwest Mounted Police. Laying a hand on the carbine, he said formally in French:

"You are my prisoner. You know who—or, rather, what—I am, I suppose?"

"Yes," returned the convict, in halting French. "I understand. And I know who you are. You are of the Mounted Police. I have seen pictures of them. I recognized you as you crossed the plain down there. I was waiting here, in the curve of the pass, with a rock in my hand, to kill you if need be; to stop your hunt of me, at all costs."

"Yet," muttered Hegan, taken aback by the man's admission, "yet later you saved me from death."

The convict shrugged his shoulders. "We were men," he replied simply, "alone here in the wastes. The bear would have killed you. Even a policeman is better than a bear, I suppose. So I picked up your carbine—"

"I find it hard to follow your French," interposed Hegan, who caught with difficulty the drift of the other's halting, ill-accented words. "You speak no English, I suppose."

"Why shouldn't I?" returned the convict in English, his wan face brightening. "I was born in Des Moines, and I lived there until I was thirty."

"What?" gasped Hegan in wonder, "You're an American? They said you were a Russian convict. I—"

"And I supposed you were foreign, too, from your speaking to me in French. No, I am American. My name is Alan Brower."

Hegan released his hold on the carbine, and laughed aloud in sheer relief. "You've lifted a mighty big load from my mind, old man," he exclaimed, "even though I've been following the wrong fellow for three days, and have lost my chance of a captaincy by losing him. Just see what a rotten fix I thought I was in: You saved me from being killed—and I won't try to thank you in words, for there aren't any to cover such a service. You saved my life, and I thought I was bound by my oath to my government to arrest you and take you back a prisoner. Would ever any other living man have been in such a vile position as that? To send back to prison a man to whom I owed my life. Lord, but I'm glad, clear through, that you're an American! Here I've been tracking you for days on the idea that you were an escaped convict from Verkhoyvansk. But what on earth are you doing here in the Barren Grounds with no horse, no dogs, and no equipment? You must let me give—"

"What am I doing?" echoed Brower drearily. "I am trying to get back to Des Moines, or to any point, of civilization where Uncle Sam rules—somewhere that I can hide safely until Russia stops hunting me."

"Russia!" gasped Hegan. "Then you *are*—"

"I am the man you have been looking for. I am a fugitive from Verkhoyvansk. Now arrest me, and have done with it. I can't go any farther. I'm played out. It would have been a matter of only a day or two longer at most before the wolves got me. I ate my last strip of bacon rind two days ago. My shoes are about gone, so is my strength. The cold gets nearer to my heart every hour. I didn't think any man could live against the cold as long as I have."

He still held the carbine. Hegan, resting his weight on his uninjured foot, stood staring at him. At last, shaking off the bewilderment and heartache that gripped him, Barry limped forward.

"I have to arrest you," he said dully. "You are armed and I am not. If you choose to defend yourself I can't prevent you. If you shoot me, my horse and provisions are yours. But I have to arrest you, for all that, if I can, and to take you back to the fort where the Russian police agents are waiting for you. You are my prisoner."

He reached for the man as he spoke, seizing the carbine. Brower made no move to resist or even to maintain his hold on the weapon. Limply he released the carbine.

"I told you I was played out," said he. "I might fight; I might win, but it would only postpone the end."

Hegan, puzzled at the other's lack of resistance, put the carbine under his own arm, and laid a hand on Brower's shoulder.

"Come," he said. "What you need first of all is a square meal. We will camp here at the foot of the rocks. A dinner and a sleep will put you in better shape for our journey. I can spare you an extra pair of wool oversocks and a blanket."

He set to work preparing a fire, scarce watching his prisoner. He knew from what he saw of Brower, as well as by the latter's admission, that the fugitive was on the verge of utter physical breakdown. Indeed, as Barry realized, no man with less than a giant's endurance could so long have continued the flight across the Barren Grounds. And now that surrender had come, Brower's body and whole nervous system were in a state of semicollapse. He would be as easy to guard, for the present, as a two-year-old child.

Chapter V.
An Accepted Parole.

BARRY HEGAN'S heart was heavy within him. He felt crushed beneath a shame that well-nigh annihilated his self-respect. In vain he reminded himself of his sworn duty, of his oath to the government, of the captaincy whereof this exploit was to be the reward. Through all his reasoning and sane self-justification blazed forth one stark, undeniable fact: This man had saved him from a horrible death. And, in reward, he was dragging back his rescuer to the living grave of a Russian penal colony. Hegan could not act differently. He knew that. Yet he was sick with the shame of what he must do. For the first time in his years of service he hated his profession.

Sullenly he bustled about the new-lit fire, melting snow for coffee, and heating the skillet bottom for its coat of bacon fat. Brower, huddled in his blanket on the far side of the blaze, sat doubled, his arms wrapped about his ankles and his head on his knees, more like a bundle of rage and matted hair and fleshless bones than a living man. The vital spark seemed to have been suddenly snuffed out, the long-enduring energy snapped.

Neither man spoke until the meal was ready. Then Hegan heaped a tin platter with food, and filled a big tin cup with smoking black coffee. Placing the food and drink beside Brower, he touched the bowed head lightly, to rouse the convict from his apathy, and said:

"Eat. You will feel better."

Brower wearily raised his head. The pungent odor of the coffee assailed his nostrils, stirring within him a dormant and long-unsated hunger. He fell greedily upon the rude fare his captor had prepared, eating more like a famished dog than a civilized man. When he had drained the cup and cleaned the last crumb from the platter, he leaned to the fire's warmth with a sigh of physical contentment. Hegan drew out his cigar case and passed it across to his prisoner. It contained but two cigars, and these Barry had been saving against some supreme moment of the hunt when they would serve to comfort or sustain him. It did him good to see the delight wherewith Alan Brower seized one of them.

"Tobacco!" exclaimed the prisoner. "And a cigar at that! I had forgotten there was such a thing in all this Hades that we call the world!"

He lighted the cigar by means of a sputtering wood splinter, and lay back at full length.

"You are good to me," he said simply.

"I am not," roughly denied Hegan. "You saved me from death, and I'm showing my appreciation by lugging you back to prison."

"Don't take it so hard," said the American. "I understand. You can't help it. It's the only thing you can do. Those things you are so courteously hiding under your blanket roll are a pair of handcuffs, aren't they? Go ahead and put them on me if you like. I can't expect you to accept my parole; and without a parole I'd probably try another break for liberty as soon as a little of my strength came back."

"It's none of my business," said Hegan uncomfortably. "And officially I've no right to ask it. But I've been wondering for the past hour how an American—and an American of your sort—happened to be in a Siberian penal colony. Of course—"

"Oh, there isn't any mystery about it. I could tell you in a mouthful of words, if you want to know. There is nothing unusual or new in the story. It has happened, with variations, a hundred times."

He spoke with a dreary hopelessness that went to Hegan's heart.

Barry listened eagerly, as the disjointed, emotionless sentences came from the worn-out man across the fire from him. Brower showed no excitement in sketching his case. His weary tone was all but impersonal.

"I was in Moscow," he began, "on business for the firm. I sat in a cafe one night. A girl came in, selling flowers. A sharp corner of her flower tray caught in the gold braid on the uniform of an officer sitting near me—tore it. He swore at her and hit her in the mouth. I lost my head and thrashed him. Yes; I surely gave him the thrashing of his life. They can't take that away from me. I was arrested. It seems he was one of the grand dukes—Lord's anointed, and all that kind of thing, you know. And I'd thrashed him—pounded him to a pulp, thank Heaven, before they could haul me away!"

"Good for you!" exclaimed Hegan, in impulsive approval. "But, at worst, wasn't that just a case of assault and battery?"

"You don't understand, or else you don't know Russia. It wasn't just an affair of licking a drunken beast that had struck a woman. I'd thrashed a grand duke, the sacred cousin of the still more sacred czar. I, an insignificant foreigner, had laid impious hands on royalty, and in Russia."

"I see. But—"

"They jailed me. After a while I got word to our ambassador. But they were ready for such a move. By that time they'd framed a nihilist charge against me—handmade evidence, letter-perfect witnesses, and all. That was enough. The testimony was too strong, even for Uncle Sam's representatives over there. I was promised by my friends that the case would be probed to the bottom, and they'd work day and night to prove I was innocent, and get me out. That's all the good it did. I was sent to Verkhoyvansk. When I couldn't stand it any longer, and there was no sign of help from my friends, I got away. There's the story. You won't believe it, of course. There never yet was a convict anywhere who didn't swear he was the innocent victim of a conspiracy. So I don't expect you to swallow my story. But you wanted to hear it, and I owed you something for the bully dinner and the cigar."

For the moment Hegan made no reply. He sat, tugging at his cutty pipe and looking into the fire. At last he said, half to himself:

"I do believe you, Brower. Lawyers look for evidence; but here in the North we learn to read men instead of testimony. I believe you.

And, believing, I've got to take you back. There are times when an oath of duty hangs around one's neck like a millstone. Get an hour's sleep if you can. For we must be on our way back. And—and I'll take your parole not to try to escape—if you care to give it."

"I give it," answered Brower.

Their hands met in a short, hard grip. Hegan tossed the handcuffs back into his blanket roll.

Chapter VI.
One Surprise—And Another.

THE northern night had settled down in a blaze of borealis glow as captor and captive reached Fort Simpson. The warmer weather had held during their return journey. Hegan's ankle was still painful; but Brower's flagging strength in large measure had come back to him under the influence of three days of square meals. They had returned to the fort by a shorter way than the somewhat circuitous route of the chase, and this fact had atoned, in time, for their necessarily slower speed of travel.

Hegan, leaving the tired pony with an orderly, escorted the prisoner straight to the colonel's office. At the door leading from anteroom to office he paused and motioned Brower to a seat.

"Wait here a moment, old man," he said. "I must speak to the chief alone, first."

As Hegan entered the office the commanding officer raised his head from a deskful of official-looking documents. Recognizing his visitor, he jumped to his feet and hurried forward, his lips parted in an eager question. But Barry, closing the door behind him, made no move to respond to the cordial greeting. Drawing himself to attention, he saluted, saying at the same time in a dry, formal voice:

"I have the honor to report, sir, that I have captured the escaped convict after whom you sent me, and have brought him here to Fort Simpson in obedience to your command."

"You have—"

"And I have the honor, sir," pursued Barry, "to tender to you herewith my resignation as a commissioned officer in the Royal Mounted. I shall take the necessary steps at once to confirm this verbal resignation."

"Resignation!" cried the colonel. "Has the cold turned your mind, man? I told you success in this expedition would mean a captaincy for you. And it shall, even though—"

"Pardon me," said Hegan. "It shall not. In pursuance of my duty I have captured an innocent man. An American, too; not a Russian. I have made myself the means of sending this brave white chap back to the Siberian Hades he had escaped from. I've done all this because I am an officer and because my duty and my oath demanded it. But I'm a man, too. That's why I'm leaving the service here and now. And that's why, sir, I intend to move heaven and earth to get Alan Brower his freedom, even to attempting a rescue on the way between here and Dawson. I realize, sir, that I am liable to arrest for that threat. But when I've told you my story, and Brower's, I doubt if you'll take that course."

Briefly, yet vividly, Hegan sketched the pursuit, the saving of his life, the capture; and he repeated the story Brower had told him. From the first impetuous words of his subaltern's speech, the colonel made no reply, no attempt to interrupt. Returning to his desk he reseated himself and listened, thus, with masklike face, to the statement of the younger man. For several seconds after the conclusion of the recital, the commanding officer did not speak. Then he said quietly:

"And for the privilege of making a fool of yourself you are ready to throw over your career, to put off still farther your marriage, to run foul of the law that you have so long and so zealously upheld? You have weighed the cost?"

"I have, sir," replied Hegan, his indignation simmering down to calm, stern resolve. "I have considered it from every angle. It isn't a question of what I want to do, but of what a white man in the circumstances must do."

Long and keenly the commanding officer eyed the lieutenant. Then irrelevantly he asked: "Where is Brower?"

"In the anteroom—waiting for the Russian police agents to take charge of him."

"I'm afraid," objected the colonel, "that he will tire of waiting. They started back for Dawson this morning."

"Thinking I could not catch their man?"

"Hoping—at the last—that you couldn't. This morning word came to them from St. Petersburg. Friends of Brower had stirred up not only enough influence in Russia to reopen the case, but to clear him. His pardon has just been signed by the czar; and the bloodhounds have been called back to the kennel."

"Then," cried Hegan, in incredulous joy, "then Brower is—"

"Is to be a guest at our mess, if he will, till we can arrange for him to return to Des Moines. Where are you going, Hegan?"

"To tell him! He'll be—"

"He'll be told. But will it be by Barry Hegan, ex-police officer; or Captain Barry Hegan, of the Royal Mounted?"

Hegan paused. For the first time he realized what he had thrown away, and how useless a sacrifice he had made in prematurely discarding his beloved career for the friend who no longer needed that sacrifice.

"Hegan," said the colonel, one of his rare smiles lighting the leathern old face, "as I sat dozing here in the twilight, I dreamed that one of my most promising officers came to me, howling like an angry timber wolf, and trying to resign his commission. But it was only a silly dream, such as we old men often have. I'm awake now, and I know it never really happened. By expediting matters a little in the right quarters, Hegan, I think I can promise you'll receive that captaincy within a month at latest. I mention this in case you care to set the date for your wedding. I'd like to add that, while you're something of a hothead, you are a great deal of a man. Now, bring Brower in here."

An Inside Scoop

By Albert Payson Terhune

THE city editor puffed away at his cigar in silence. He seldom wasted words.

"The story's all up," called the copy reader. Then he went out to look at the "Parliament of Roughriders" in the hall, who had come to be photographed for the Sunday *Planet*.

Meanwhile the youthful reporter whom the Sunday editor had detailed to show the Roughriders over the building had piloted the entire half hundred to the composing room. There the copy reader found them.

Amid the forest of trucks, linotype machines, typesetting apparatus, and sweating compositors stood the conglomerate mass of visitors. In one group were ten Cossacks—thin, supple, wiry little bronzed men with long beards and beady eyes, clad in saffron tunics and gray caps. In another alley of machines were a galaxy of German Uhlans, cuirassiers, Irish lancers, collarless and unkempt cowboys, a stray alleged Arab or so, and Orapezo, the great Mexican lasso expert. Compositors, office boys, and loungers paid the passing tribute of a glance to this kaleidoscope of nations, but kept their widest stares and weirdest comments for a larger, more fantastic throng that stood, distrustfully, near the elevator shaft. This last group consisted of some twenty Indians boasting various degrees of ugliness. Their high feather war bonnets loomed up above the composing-room machinery, their profusely illustrated faces peered from behind valve and bar. Coldly incurious, their eyes swept the unfamiliar scene; with a mask of profound indifference, they listened to the half-breed interpreter's translated explanation of the way a paper was printed.

Robbie Kennedy and his fellow office boys, regardless of the fact that howls of "Copy!" were wafted up from the city room, stood gazing in open-mouthed awe at the savages.

"I bet that big feller—the one next to the Dutch soldier with the tin bonnet—is a Terror of the Plains," commented Robbie.

"He ain't, either," contradicted an associate runner of copy. "See? He's only got half as many feathers as the Injun behind him."

"What's that got to do with it?" sneered Robbie. "A lot you know about it!"

"I do so know," retorted the other, who had a splendid fund of ignorance on the subject of Indians; "they grow ten new feathers for every man they kill—slay, I mean."

"Get onto the kid that biggest one's got with him," interposed Robbie, unable to combat this point in natural history.

The "kid" in question was an amber-colored papoose, perhaps two feet high. She was Utsayantha, only daughter of the Sioux war chief, Howling Wolf. This baby, alone of all the troupe of Indians, gazed with keen delight at the sea of strange faces and the funny black machines. From time to time a fear lest these machines were of the biting variety would take possession of her, and she grasped with both arms her warlike sire's beaded buckskin knee.

"Oh, how pretty! Look! She's the first Indian child I ever saw!" A slender, girlish figure appeared among the crowd, who cheerfully made way for her as she knelt beside the little yellow savage. The girl was Kate Westervelt, youngest and prettiest of the women reporters. "Won't you come to me?" she asked pleadingly of the solemn-eyed Utsayantha.

The baby did not, of course, understand a word, but with outstretched hands and a gleeful little squeal she ran into Miss Westervelt's arms.

"Are you her father?" asked the girl of the lordly chief.

Howling Wolf deigned no reply, principally because he could not understand; but he strongly disapproved of any white squaw handling his beloved first-born.

"Can't I take her down to my desk?" went on Miss Westervelt. "I've some candy down there that she can have, and I want to show her to the managing editor. Maybe there's a special story in it."

The half-breed interpreter overheard the girl's words, and, thinking to conciliate a paper that owned so many inexplicable machines, he interposed: "Sure, miss. He's ignorant, old Howlin' Wolf is. He don't understand. Take the papoose down with you, if you like. I'll explain to its father."

With a word of thanks, Miss Westervelt, carrying the baby in her arms, made for the winding stairs that led down to the city room. But Howling Wolf, with a throaty sound like the growl of an angry dog, took a step to stop her. The interpreter checked him, and in a few words explained that the child was safe and that Howling Wolf must not interfere. The father, a pathetic look of doubting misery on his stolid face, stood still, gazing into the crowd at the spot where he had seen Utsayantha disappear.

Downstairs in the city room Miss Westervelt was proudly exhibiting her capture to a ring of office friends. The baby, enthroned on the girl's roll-top desk, sat delightedly sucking away at a bonbon and sturdily refusing to speak a language she had never before heard. Miss Westervelt, in her anxiety for the special story, naturally forgot there might be a time limit to her little guest's visit.

In the composing room a scarlet-haired "make-up editor" was fuming at the "gang of freaks that blew in there at the busiest time of the day and distracted everybody's attention." A few remarks of this sort led the reporter escort to hint to his charges that they would better clear out. Accordingly, they filed into the great elevator, the Cossacks going on the first down trip, the Indians last.

As the elevator came up for the noble red men, the interpreter gave an order, and the feathered, beaded, hand-painted savages filed timidly into the car. No one noticed that they were one man short, none heeded a single tall, stalwart, forbidding figure that stood statue-like against a stereotyping machine, waiting in vain for his missing child.

II.

WHAT was in Howling Wolf's heart as the last of his fellow countrymen entered the car and sank out of sight, leaving him alone among a swarm of wretched palefaces, no one can tell. What he looked was another matter. His usually wooden face was an open book. The first word expressed on it was trouble; then grief; and, last of all, fury.

"What's the old jay waitin' for?" asked a compositor.

No one knew. Such as remembered the papoose's abduction fancied the child was with the rest of the troupe, and had no idea she belonged to this increasingly angry chief.

"Now, then," said the make-up editor briskly, "run along with your tribe. We're busy up here, and you're only in the way."

Howling Wolf looked stolidly down on the man and remarked: "Utsayantha!"

"I don't understand your lingo," retorted the irate editor, "and I want you to get out."

"Utsayantha!" repeated the chief, this time in a deeper voice.

"Yes, yes, I dare say it's all true, only I don't understand. Clear out, or I'll send for a policeman."

It began to dawn on Howling Wolf that perhaps he had not made the case sufficiently clear to this excitable person. So he began to explain the situation, speaking with studied self-control and in excellent Sioux dialect.

"Talks like a dinner bell, don't he?" commented Robbie Kennedy in admiring awe.

"He's givin' us an oration. Maybe tellin' how many men he's slewn," added the office boy, who had advanced the theory concerning feathers.

A grin from the compositors and loungers followed this speculation.

This was too much for Howling Wolf. Not content with stealing his precious child, perhaps roasting her alive, they were actually laughing at her stricken father! Striding forward, and thrusting the crowd contemptuously from his path, the chief passed through the alleys of machinery, tables, and cases, his keen eye looking every-where for the hiding place of his daughter. Coming at length to an open space, he halted beside an oddly shaped table, topped by carved metal. There was that in his look and manner which made two men who were busy at the table move quickly out of reach.

The make-up editor set up a yell and rushed toward the post they deserted. This structure—probably an altar to the demons who inhabited the great black machines—was evidently a sacred spot among the palefaces, and here Howling Wolf made his stand. In an instant he was surrounded by a mob of excited, shirt-sleeved men.

The "table" against which he was leaning happened to be a "truck," and on that truck lay a page form just locked. The two men scared away by the Indian had been about to remove the form to the stereotyper's heating table, whence it was to go downstairs to the pressroom, there to serve for the printing of a page of the waiting edition. The paper was due on the street in fifteen minutes, and that particular page form chanced to bear in double-leaded type under a "scare" double-column head the story which, according to the managing editor's prophecy, was to "beat the town." Hence the horror of all concerned when this decidedly belligerent savage took up his stand before the truck bearing that form.

"What are you men waiting for?" shouted the make-up editor. "Hustle that form over to the heating table, or we'll delay the edition. That Indian can't hurt you."

Now the *Planet* boasts the best lot of compositors in New York, yet just then none of them seemed anxious to obey orders.

Howling Wolf glanced rapidly about him. He saw the consterna-tion caused by his presence at that truck and resolved to stay there. He even had a lingering idea of carrying it away as hostage for his lost child. A plan occurred to him: Why not offer to give up possession of this mysterious table on condition that the palefaces restore his child? He made the offer in his most persuasive Sioux dialect.

"Rush him, boys!" ordered the foreman; and the men gathered for the onslaught.

III.

NOW, though Howling Wolf's knowledge of English was less than limited, his knowledge of fighting left little to be desired. He had crouched in the rank grass at Sitting Bull's side, twenty years before, when a certain general had ridden to his death beyond the woods of Little Big Horn. It was Howling Wolf who had counseled Sitting Bull to the strategic trick which emptied so many government saddles that summer day in 1876; and he had, with his own hand, struck down the foremost United States cavalryman. After such a record, why should he fear a gang of unarmed men of peace?

His quick eye noted the gathering rush, and a second later the advancing compositors found themselves looking into the muzzles of two revolvers, the weapons which Howling Wolf and his fellow Indians discharged daily at the old-fashioned stagecoach in the "Attack on the Overland Stage." This attack was a "star" feature of the Roughriders' Show. For the purpose each Indian wore at his belt two revolvers. They were, of course, loaded with blank cartridges, and Howling Wolf knew it. He had the best reason in the world for this knowledge; for had he not, when first engaged by the show, attempted one day, in a drink-inspired moment of playfulness, to murder Red Cloud, a brother chief, with these same weapons? Had he not fired fourteen shots at that worthy savage before finding that the cartridges were harmless? Had he not been the laughingstock of the whole tribe in consequence of his silly failure? But he doubted whether these new paleface foes had the same knowledge concerning the revolvers.

When a man is looking into one end of a pistol and an enraged Indian is manipulating the other end, he seldom stops to conjecture whether the weapon is loaded with blanks or ball. Hence the compositors recoiled in a heap. The make-up editor did a war dance before them, to the chief's open contempt.

"The paper ought to be on the street in five minutes!" declared the editor. "The *Meteor'll* beat us out of our boots. It was the biggest story we've had this year, too; and the *Meteor'll* have it all in this edition. Here!"—hauling out of his pocket a wad of bills—"here! you dissolute old heathen, help yourself to these and let us get at that form!"

As he spoke, he advanced on the chief.

One of Howling Wolf's forty-four caliber pistols spoke, and the echoes reverberated through the great, low-celled room. The pistol was fired point-blank. It sent the make-up editor reeling back, his red beard and eyebrows singed, and his lungs choked with powder smoke.

"I'm hit," moaned the editor, and collapsed.

This was the signal for a general break. One man started for the police, but decided to climb up behind a linotype machine instead. The rest sought any shelter that came to hand and held a council of war. Lurid messages and queries as to the cause of delay floated up through the tube from the press-room, where all was at a standstill, pending the arrival of the missing page.

"Rush him from behind!"

"Get a policeman!"

"Throw a lead cut at him!"

Thus advised a score of voices, whose owners were modestly concealed behind trucks or machines.

Robbie Kennedy had a strong impulse to step forward and harangue the chief, like the hero of Wild West dime novels. He had even framed a speech beginning, "Hail to our wigwam, dusky brother," when a glance from the chief again sent his canary-colored head ducking behind the truck.

A new figure appeared on the scene. It was the managing editor. In one hand he clutched a copy of the *Meteor*. Its first page bore the great story with which the *Planet* had hoped to beat the town.

"Mr. Halpin!" thundered the managing editor to his make-up associate. "Why have we not gone to press? We should have had the paper on the street twenty minutes ago. We're beaten again by the *Meteor*, and beaten through the fault of the composing room. What was the matter? and—good Lord, man! what are you doing behind that truck?"

"I'm shot," muttered the make-up man incoherently.

"Half shot, you mean," sneered his superior. Then, as his eye swept the room, he howled: "What is the row? Are you all crazy, or are you playing hide and seek?"

And, indeed, the spectacle of all the composing room's staid habi-tués crouching behind various shelters was unusual enough to excite any newcomer.

Robbie Kennedy's treble floated across from behind a truck, mingled with a horde of half-uttered explanations from the other Indian hunters: "Please, Mr. Frothingham, there's an Indian chief, and he won't let us work."

The managing editor stepped forward. The cases that had shut off Howling Wolf from his view were passed, and the two chiefs, white and red, stood face to face.

IV.

HOWLING WOLF fired a salute with both revolvers, and the managing editor, never stopping to ask questions, joined Robbie behind the truck. But Howling Wolf had acted on the defensive long enough. These men were cowards. It would be pleasant to frighten them further. With a yell, the Indian began firing at every one in general, accompanying the volleys with some ghost-dance steps and snatches of a Sioux war song.

"Say!" yelled the embattled managing editor, "there's an Indian kid downstairs. Miss Westervelt's getting her sketched. Maybe the kid can act as interpreter and find out what the old chap wants. Where's the regular interpreter?"

"All the Indians went down in the elevator except this one, and the interpreter went with them. They drove away long ago," replied a compositor.

"Some one go down and get the papoose from the city room," ordered the managing editor.

A reporter who chanced to be nearest the stairs and farthest from Howling Wolf made a break for the former, hopping wildly in air as he heard a pistol shot behind him. On the way downstairs, a thought struck him. He remembered now that he had seen Miss Westervelt take the papoose with her. He recalled, too, that the baby had been standing beside this very chief; and the situation was clear to him before he reached the desk where Miss Westervelt, an artist, a reporter, and two office boys were standing admiringly about the edition-delaying Utsayantha.

"Miss Westervelt!" shouted the reporter, "hurry, please! Old Mr. Afraid of his Squaw, or whatever he calls himself, is running amuck upstairs because he can't find his kid. He's delayed the edition nearly an hour and let the *Meteor* beat us on that big story. He's shooting people now."

Snatching up the baby, who wept lustily at this sudden removal from a sphere of admiration and candy, the reporter galloped upstairs with her. As he reached the composing room he was sent reeling back to the stairway by a mighty blow. When he had found his balance, he beheld Howling Wolf, with the recovered Utsayantha in his arms, shouldering his way back to the elevator shaft.

Among supposedly civilized nations, when a lost child is returned, the first act of the heart-racked parent is to spank it. In the present instance, the noble red man displayed that touch of nature which makes the whole world kin. Savages are human, after all. As Howling Wolf passed along the alleys of machinery, bearing Utsayantha, a sound as of violent applause arose, mingled with the bitter wails of the recovered baby.

As father and child reached the shaft, the elevator door was flung back and the half-breed interpreter, pale under his brown skin, appeared in company with the manager of the "Rocky Mountain Show and Parliament of Roughriders."

"Here's your lost sheep," remarked the managing editor, indicating the bellicose Howling Wolf, "and, incidentally, your show's going to have the biggest suit on its hands that ever happened."

From far below came a faint "thud! thud! thud!" The paper was going to press—an hour and ten minutes late!

Sometimes a trader smuggles a supply of fire water into the Indian reservation; not enough to inspire the braves to the noble art of cutting settlers' throats, but just sufficient to set boastful tongues a-wagging. At such times a venerable man—a war chief of the Sioux nation, by the way—arises from his seat at the camp fire and holds his credulous hearers breathless by a certain oft-repeated tale. He tells of a strange house in a land toward the rising sun, where, amid a host of black iron demons, he, Howling Wolf, the Terrible, once held a paleface army at bay, and saved his first-born from being burned at the stake and fed to those strange-smelling iron monsters.

In the "land toward the rising sun" there is an irritable make-up editor who one day knocked down a new reporter. The reporter had innocently asked the make-up editor how he supposed it felt to be shot.

The Tale of the Taxi-Meter

DURAND had left the dinner early—which was odd, since it was given in his honor—or, rather, as a good-by. For he was to take the ten-o'clock boat next morning for France, to be gone for perhaps a year.

He was an artist—one of the best black-and-white men on this side of the Atlantic. Now—whether from whim or for the sweet uses of advertisement—he was going to Paris at the zenith of his fame, to study color, under Matisse. Hence the little farewell dinner.

Durand had made a tolerably well-turned speech in reply to a formal toast by Craddock, his chum. Then formality had departed. And, shortly thereafter, Durand had departed too—on excuse of letters and of much unfinished packing.

The party had lagged, after the exit of its only excuse. And presently Craddock and three other men had drifted away from it.

The evening was young, as stag evenings go. And Craddock said he was going to drop around on Durand for a last chat and to give him a hand with his packing. The three others—Jermyn, a painter, Kellogg, a composer, and Bryce, who ran a curb brokerage concern—promptly invited themselves along. They had arrived at a state of mind, during

the dinner, which made all things seem possible and most things highly desirable.

Craddock was sorry he had made known his intent. Durand was his dearest friend—though one was an artist and the other a bank's vice-president—and he was sorely grieved over his chum's proposed absence. He wanted that last chat without a noisy trio of accompaniment.

The four callers turned in, off the avenue, at Nineteenth Street, and stopped in front of a stable that was sandwiched between two garishly lofty apartment houses. The front of the stable had been left unchanged and unbeautified by Durand when he had bought the two-story building, ripped out the interior and converted it into a five-room abode for himself.

Taking up all the front of the ground floor and extending two-thirds of the way to the rear, was Durand's studio. The front door opened directly upon it. The studio itself was as bare as it was big. Unadorned, mercilessly light, more sparsely furnished than a carpenter shop, it was a work-room, not a scented, dusty-draperied place to give teas.

There was no instant response, tonight, to the visitors' summons, although light filtered through the shades of the high windows. Craddock rapped twice with the black iron knocker. Then Jermyn and Kellogg and Bryce took turns playing a joyous tattoo on it.

"He isn't home yet," decided Craddock, raising his voice to be heard above the hammering of the knocker. "He told me he sent off his Jap this afternoon. And—"

"Then let's camp on the step till the wanderer floats home," suggested Jermyn. "It'll be a nice surprise for him. Besides. I want to be here to chide him tenderly for saying he had to go home and pack, and then not showing up."

"Don't let's bother to wait," suggested Craddock. "He may—"

But a chorus of dissent silenced him. The three—who had drunk just enough to make them obstinately jolly—were already sitting in a huddled row on the steps and were feeling for their cigarette cases.

"*J'y suis; j'y reste!*" announced Jermyn, who prided himself on the fund of French he did not possess. "And I'd just as soon stay on till morning, if the supply of cigarettes holds out. Will stick around for an hour or so, anyhow."

He burst happily into a song addressed to one "Jenny," whom he tunefully exhorted to wait till the clouds rolled by. Kellogg and Bryce chimed in with horrible close-harmony. At the end of the first bar, the door flew open. Durand stood there, neither his pose nor his face suggesting very hearty welcome.

Craddock noticed that the artist had changed his dinner coat for a velvet house-jacket, but that otherwise he was still dressed as he had been all evening—an attire not wholly suited to the work of trunk-packing.

THE three other visitors, ignoring their host's incipient scowl, fell upon him with effusive friendliness, like a welcoming litter of puppies, and by sheer weight bore him back, ahead of them, into the studio. Craddock followed more leisurely, just in time to hear Durand explain that he had fallen into a doze over a half-packed trunk in an upper room, and therefore had not known of his guests' presence until the frightful sound of their singing had awakened him.

The three disposed themselves gleefully through the big, bare room, and Kellogg, seating himself at the piano, suggested:

"Let's celebrate this last sad occasion by music—fringed with drinks. Especially drinks."

He looked suggestively toward the kitchenette which also served Durand as a wine-cellar, and began to pound out the classic strains of "Something Seems Tingling."

"Music fringed with drinks!" assented Jermyn in cordial approbation.

"You boys have had almost enough drinks to keep you from dying of thirst till you get home," said Craddock, noting the annoyance on their host's thin face.

"Durand's tired. And he's got packing to do. Let's clear out."

"That's right," agreed Bryce. "Durand's tired—so tired he went to sleep over his packing. Poor old Durand! A drink'll do him worlds of good."

"Like blazes he went to sleep!" dissented Jermyn. "When a chap goes to sleep, his hair gets all mussy. Look at Durand's hair. He's brushed it since he got back here. Just the same," he added, judicially, "a drink *would* do him good."

Kellogg, at the piano, had ceased playing the "High Jinks" melody. And he began now to improvise an air, on his own account. He sang, in a hopefully rasping voice:

> Oh, I had a little hen and she had a wooden leg,
> And every day she laid a little wooden egg—
> She's the finest little chicken I've got around the farm;
> And—and—and another little drink wouldn't do us any harm!

"I made up that tune!" he finished, beaming on Durand. "I'm going to include it in my 'Songs Without Music.' Which leads me to touch delicately on the subject of a drink. Listen: Here's a Gregorian chant, that I made up. At least, I haven't made it up yet. But I will, as I go along. Just try this on the family comb:

> We've said good-by, in Scotch and Bourbon too,
> In booze that's elderly and fizz that's new.
> But ere you sidestep for the Gallic shore,
> Suppose we say good-by—'bout twelve times more.

"Say," he continued, smitten by a brilliant thought, and whirling around on the piano stool, "Craddock makes a dandy cocktail. Turn him loose in your kitchenette. How about it?"

Craddock glanced again at Durand. The artist's face was pallid. There was a furrow between his eyes. Sweat beaded on his forehead. He looked like a man who is nervous or sick or frightened—or all three. Craddock took the situation into his own hands.

"Listen, you Indians!" he exhorted. "If I go in there and build you just one round of drinks, will you get out directly afterward?"

There was a chorus of protest. But Craddock was firm.

"One drink apiece," he repeated, "and then go. Otherwise no drinks at all. Choose which it is to he."

Grumblingly, yet optimistically, they at last consented to the single drink followed by instant departure. Craddock's cocktails were famous. And they knew him well enough to be certain he would mix none unless they agreed to his terms. Durand brightened visibly.

"There are enough ingredients left in the kitchenette for one round, I think," he said, adding in a whisper to Craddock: "Thanks, old man! Rush the mixing as fast as you can, won't you?"

Craddock nodded, and made his way through the swing door at the studio's rear, to the little room beyond. Somewhat to his surprise, the host did not follow him, but crossed the studio, toward a passage-way on the wall of which was a telephone.

Kellogg, still at the piano, struck into tango music. Bryce, his feet inspired by the jingle of the tune, caught Durand around the waist before the artist could reach the passage-way, and essayed to dance with him. And at that moment there was a light rap at the door-knocker.

So fine was the tap that Kellogg, hammering at the piano, did not hear it. Bryce was noisily entreating Durand to dance, and his voice, together with the piano's rhythmic rattle, drowned the low sound of the knock. Jermyn, lounging in the front of the room, alone heard it. He jumped up and flung the door wide, hospitably admitting the newcomer.

The draft from the open door struck Kellogg in the back. He turned to learn the cause, and his hands fell from the keys. At cessation of the music, Bryce glowered at Kellogg. Then, seeing the pianist's eyes fixed on the doorway, he turned, as did Durand, to discover the cause.

There stood a woman.

She was tall, statuesquely full of figure, as dark as a Spaniard. Over her evening dress hung a flame-colored wrap, open in front, showing a perfect neck and upper bust.

Wide-eyed, flushed, trembling a little, she stood there, trying for an instant to accustom her night-blurred vision to the glare of light. In that brief instant of hesitation, Jermyn instinctively shut the door behind her. Then, like Kellogg and Bryce, he stared dumbly and in dire embarrassment from her to Durand.

The latter, his face white as chalk, smiled pleasantly at the woman and took a step forward.

"Good evening," he said, his voice careless, yet tinged with civil regret. "I'm sorry, but I find I'm too tired to draw, to-night. It was a shame to bring you here on a fool's errand. I'll mail you your check, for the pose, in the morning. Shall I call a taxi for you?"

"Thank you," she answered, with equal unconcern, "but I won't trouble you. I have one, outside."

Durand reached for the door-knob as she turned to go. With a nervous haste that belied his calm tones, he pulled open the door for her, saying:

"It was a shame to bring you here for nothing. But I can finish the sketch, I think, without another sitting. And—"

"Hold on!" intervened Jermyn, slipping between the hurriedly departing woman and the door.

On learning the newcomer was a model, his embarrassment had fled and his instinct as a painter flared up.

"Hold on!" he repeated. "What is your name and where do you live?"

He put out one hand toward the woman's bare arm, to stay her. She shrank away as in a panic.

"I am Hildred Jermyn," went on the painter incisively. "I'm at the Sherwood. Wait and have a drink with us. I want to talk with you. You're the perfect 'Juno' type I've been looking for. I want you to pose for Boadicea in my panel of—"

He got no further. With a single comprehensive movement, Durand had brushed aside his outstretched arm and had gently drawn the frightened model out. Beyond, sounded the *chug-chug* of a taxi-cab. Durand escorted the woman to the curb, shutting the studio door behind him, in Jermyn's astonished face.

"Well, I'll be—" began Jermyn, angrily.

He was interrupted by the swinging open of the kitchenette's door. Craddock came in, bearing on a tray the five promised cocktails.

"Just enough left in the bottles to make these," announced Craddock, as he set down the tray. "Not a tablespoonful over. And I made them in record time, too. Drink up and let's go. Why, where's Durand gone? And,"—with a glance at the three perturbed faces—"what's the matter? Have—?"

"You missed it!" chuckled Bryce; "you missed it, Craddock, my son. You missed the whole show. Juno's been here. Or was it Boadicea, Jermyn? Anyhow, she was a winner. And Durand was so afraid Jermyn would get a chance to paint her that he nearly pinched off the poor fellow's fingers in the door."

"The dog in the manger!" fumed Jermyn, wrathfully. "Here I've been chasing around for weeks, hunting just that type for my Boadicea. And Durand's too jealous to give me a chance to paint her. He's going away for a year, too, so *he* can't use her for a model. Yes, 'dog in the manger'—that's what he is. And I'll tell him so, when he gets back."

Craddock looked blankly from one to another of the trio.

"Is it a joke?" he asked. "I don't get the idea."

Kellogg spoke up.

"Not a joke," he denied, "—a visitation. I looked around from the piano and there she was, in the doorway. The original Wonder Woman. Seems she's a model that Durand had a date to draw. And he told her he was too tired to work, and he packed her off. He's out there, now, stowing her into a taxi—and taking his time doing it. Jermyn butted in, to make a date to paint her. But Durand shut him off by slamming the door on him. That's why Jermyn's so wrathy. He—"

Durand reopened the front door with a pass-key and stepped in. The dead pallor was gone from his face, Craddock noted, and the crease from between his brows; and his hand was steady again. But he was breathing hard, and in his eyes there was a great fatigue, as of reaction.

"Why did you hustle her off like that?" demanded Jermyn. "You did her out of fifty dollars in model fees. Where does she live?"

"Oh, come on and have a drink," interrupted Craddock, as Durand's lips parted in an impatient answer. "Remember, you all promised to get out after one round."

FIVE minutes later, the front door closed on the exuberant trio. Craddock had been for departing with them, but Durand had whispered to him to wait. So, on some excuse, he lagged behind, half promising to join the others later, at the Astor grill.

"What was wrong, old man?" he asked, solicitously, turning on Durand the moment they were alone together. "When we came in, I mean. You looked as if you'd seen a ghost—or more as if you were expecting to see one."

"I was," returned Durand, curtly. "And I did."

"Don't blame me for those half-drunk wild men trailing in here," went on Craddock, after a briefly futile effort to grasp the sense of his friend's answer. "I happened to tell them I was going to stop at your house on my way home, and they wished themselves on me. I couldn't get rid of them. It's lucky you're single. They'd have broken in just the same on a man's wife and family. They're a jolly lot, but they aren't fellows I'd let come within a half mile of my own house or meet any woman I'm responsible for."

"No," responded Durand vaguely.

He was not listening. He had seated himself on a carved chest at one side of the grate fire and was staring moodily at the smoldering coals. Craddock crossed to where he sat and put a hand on his shoulder.

"What is it?" he asked, clumsily, man-fashion. "Can I help? Or are you just blue at going away?"

Durand did not answer at once. He sat, a-sprawl, his chin in his cupped hands, his elbows on his knees, still studying the white-flaking embers. At last, he said:

"I asked you to wait, after I got rid of the others, because I wanted to—to—"

He broke off his muttered sentence, and looked curiously, almost angrily, up at his friend.

"Well?" he asked, his tone sharp and challenging.

"Well?" repeated Craddock, in mild surprise.

"You had gone out to mix the cocktails. Did you get back before she went away? I want to know. That's why I asked you to wait. Did you?"

"Why, no," answered the puzzled Craddock. "When I got back, the men were still goggling at the shut door. But the model had gone."

Durand shot a look of sudden inquiry at the other; then, reassured, he nodded in glum relief.

"I'm glad," he said presently. "I was afraid you'd caught a glimpse of her. It didn't matter about the others. They travel in a different stratum. It was a thousand to one that none of them had set eyes on her before or ever will again. But you may know her. At least, she knows several people that you know. I've heard her speak of them. And if you'd seen her, to-night,—even if you'd never met her before—there's an off chance you might see her again sometime at one of the houses you and your wife visit. I wouldn't want you to misjudge her."

"Misjudge her?" laughed Craddock in genuine amusement. "Misjudge a model? My dear boy, it's you who are doing the misjudging. We travel in a tolerably broad-minded set, Phyllis and I. But it's a set that doesn't include artists' models. We wouldn't be very likely to run across your Junoesque friend—your 'Wonder Woman,' as Kellogg called her. And even if we did, what's the disgrace in her coming here in the evening to pose? Any model is—"

"She isn't a model."

Craddock whistled softly.

"Clever man!" he commented. "You got away with it to perfection. And,"—with sudden inspiration—"you were expecting her? That's why you broke away from the dinner—and why you got so nervous when we trooped in on you?"

Durand nodded.

"So?" commented Craddock. "No wonder you looked as you did! A woman coming to say good-by to you at your studio, and four men arriving just ahead of her. Why did you let us in?"

"I didn't, till I heard Kellogg say he was going to sit on my steps for an hour. I knew the sight of you people out there would drive her away. I knew, too, that *you* might recognize her as an acquaintance, or might remember her if you should see her again. So I let you in, hoping—"

"Hoping you could get rid of us before she came? I see. I did my best for you."

"You did, indeed. Thanks."

THERE was another brief silence.

Craddock drew a chair to the fire, sat down and lighted a cigar.

"Smoke?" he said, offering his case to Durand.

The latter shook his head.

"Thanks," said Durand, again; then: "I'm glad you didn't see her."

"It wouldn't have made any difference. I'm not a moralist. In fact, my wife tells me I haven't a moral to my back. Not that she knows, except from the theories I've aired. I've played square, with *her*. But that's because I've never been able, in all these nine years, to fall out of love with her. But, in theory, I'm too civilized and too comfortably modern to believe in such bugaboos as morality. Virtue is a bogy that was set up, centuries ago, by the weak, as a revenge on the strong. We've outlasted it."

"You're lucky to be able to feel that way about it," returned Durand. "I wish I could. I can't. It's the New England blood, I suppose. It doesn't make my conscience strong enough to keep me puritanical or to stop my doing a thousand things I ought not to do. But it's just strong enough to make me miserable and ashamed, while I'm doing them, and to rob me of most of the pleasure of it all."

Craddock grinned appreciation at the ludicrous dilemma, so earnestly voiced. Durand went on, speaking low and in detached phrases, his tired eyes fixed on the last gleams of the fire:

"This woman, to-night, for instance. Care to hear about it?"

"Only what you won't feel sorry afterward that you told me," said Craddock.

"I'm not a cur!" rebuked Durand. "I don't tell things, about women, that I'll have cause to feel sorry for, afterward. In fact, you've never before heard me talk about an affair with any woman."

"Don't get riled," soothed Craddock, amusedly. "I didn't mean to jar you. And you know it. Late at night, when a man's looking into a fire, he's apt to blab things he wishes afterward he hadn't. That was all I meant. Blaze away. She came here to say good-by?"

"Yes."

"H'm! She was taking chances, big chances. Anyone might have seen her coming or going. And she might have happened on some acquaintance here."

"I—I tried to guard against all that. I thought I had."

"But you hadn't. It was a nasty risk. She must care a lot. Or else, she doesn't care very much about—other things."

"You are wrong," snapped Durand. "She is good."

"My mistake. I'm sorry. You care, too?"

"Care?" echoed Durand, speaking as if to himself rather than to Craddock. "I care more than everything else in life put together."

"I'm sorry for that," said Craddock in real concern. "It's foolish for a man to let himself care that way about any woman who doesn't legally belong to him. It blinds him—at just the time he ought to see clearest."

"I care," went on Durand, unheeding, and still addressing the dying fire rather than his friend, "I care so much that I've forgotten how to care about anything else."

"Yet you're going away."

"That is why I am going."

Craddock gaped, in cross bewilderment.

"Say it again," he urged. "I must have misunderstood. You care more for this woman than for everything else—and that is why you are turning your back on her for a whole year? Man, it doesn't make sense."

"No," sighed Durand, "it only makes honor."

"I don't—"

"She is married," added Durand, as though explaining everything.

"WELL?" queried Craddock, honestly perplexed. "What then? You and she love each other, don't you?"

"Too much for me to stay on here. She is married. I used to know her parents. They were kind to me. I've even met her husband once or twice. How can I do anything that would make me afraid to shake hands with him, if I should happen to meet him again?"

"Lord!" exclaimed Craddock. "This isn't just the New England conscience talking. It's the blood of all the Puritans and the Pilgrim Fathers and Anthony Comstock and Sir Galahad rolled into one! Wake up, man! You're living in the twentieth century. And in New York, too. Not in Plymouth, in 1620. I don't agree with some of my French friends, that husbands were made to be fooled. But if you love a woman and she loves you, and only some unloved husband stands between—"

The telephone in the passage-way buzzed. Durand went to answer the call, closing the door behind him. Presently he came back.

"She got home safely," he reported. "But she is terribly wrought up. By the way, I was just starting to telephone a warning to her, on the chance she hadn't left home yet, when that sot of a Bryce caught hold of me and tried to make me dance. It was while you were out mixing the cocktails."

HE sat down again. Craddock rose to go.

"Don't hurry," protested Durand, "unless I bore you. It does me good—in a mawkishly maudlin way, I suppose—to be able to talk to you about this affair. It's the biggest thing that

ever came into my life. And sometimes it has been hard to keep it all to myself."

"Talk on," adjured Craddock. "It's refreshing to find a sweet bud of innocence, like yourself, in this wicked world. There, there! I didn't mean to get your back up by joking about it. And you know I'm interested."

"Yes," repeated Durand, absently, "I know you're interested. You're always interested. And your advice is always good. I've proved my faith in your advice by following it, more than once... I love her. I've known it always. But *she* never knew it till a month ago. I hadn't meant to speak. But I—"

"Yes; I know. It always happens that way. Go on."

"I found that she cared, too. She had cared for a long time. We made up our minds we mustn't see each other again. But—we did."

"Naturally. And then—?"

"No. There wasn't any 'and then.' But we were both afraid there might be."

"Afraid?"

"She is good."

"Oh! I'd forgotten, for the moment. So—"

"So I decided our only safety was for me to go away. That's why I'm starting, in the morning, for Paris."

Craddock was eyeing him with the frank interest a botanist might feel for some totally new specimen. Durand continued, unnoticing, his gaze again on the coals.

"But I *had* to see her once more—alone, with no one to interrupt, no one to spy on us—before I went. I felt—and so did she—that this was our right, since we were both giving up everything else. At her own home, there was no certainty of privacy. So she promised to come here, this evening, just for five minutes, to say good-by to me—to let me kiss her glorious eyes and—"

"Five minutes," mused Craddock. "It was surely little enough to ask of Fate or of the gods or even of Mrs. Grundy. Yet even that was denied you. And your beautiful farewell scene was turned into a ghastly, dangerous farce. Hard luck! Virtue may be its own reward. But it's also its *only* reward. So you're turning your back on all the sunshine and exiling yourself—just for a principle?"

"My ancestors, I believe, had a trick of dying for principles. It would be easier, too, than to—"

"Than to run away from happiness? It would. And quite as sane. Listen, old friend: In this measly world of ours, there's mighty little happiness, except the kind we buy or work for. And there's still less love. And when both happiness and love are tossed into a man's lap, he's about as sensible, in running away from them, as a starving beggar would be in tearing up a thousand-dollar bill he found. Both these things have come to *you*, by gift of luck, things that most men would risk their souls for. What right have you to throw them away?"

"What right have I to steal them?"

"Steal?"

"I told you she has a husband. I've never yet robbed any man, that I know of. And I fail to see how I'd be any less a thief in stealing another man's wife than in stealing his watch. Maybe I'm wrong, but—"

"You are. If a man left his watch exposed to the reach of every passer-by, if he neglected or misunderstood its uses, so that it ceased to be of any personal service to him—would he really have a right to kick if it were lost? Besides, the cases aren't alike. A man doesn't buy a wife—at least, not openly. He wins her love and marries her. To my mind, the marriage lasts, and she belongs to him, just as long as he takes the trouble to *hold* her love, and no longer."

"You're—you're wrong—horribly wrong!" panted Durand in torture. "My decency tells me that. And yet—oh, I—"

"And yet your common sense tells you I'm right. Here! I suggest a compromise: You love this woman enough to marry her?"

"Why, of course," answered Durand, simply, and in surprise at the question. "Of course I do."

"Then it's perfectly plain sailing. And without a jar to that Puritan conscience of yours. (Which same conscience, by the way, was born of the sturdy old Puritans' fear of consequences and of the treatment that wrong-doers used to receive at the hands of their fellow-Puritans.) Here's the idea: Let her fake a quarrel with her husband and leave his house in a rage and take the next train for Reno or for some other divorce-mill colony. In a few months the whole thing will be settled without a breath of scandal. Then you can run out and marry her. Perfectly simple. Everyone satisfied. No crime, no breach of morality, no regrets."

"But—but her husband?" muttered Durand, a-quiver with excitement and with the new-born hope that had stolen into his face. "Her husband?"

"He will come out of it better than he had any right to expect. No one will laugh at him as the man whose wife was stolen. He won't be under the painful annoyance of shooting or suing anyone. His wife won't have eloped. She will merely have quarreled with him—perhaps over some other woman, so far as the public can tell—and separated from him; and, in due time, he will marry somebody else. It happens every day."

"But he may love her."

"A dozen men may court the same debutante. Do any of these men hold back because eleven other men love her?"

"You're right. Oh, you're *right!* And yet—"

"It's certain she doesn't love *him,* or she wouldn't be in love with you. Probably she never loved him enough to set the river afire."

"She never did. She told me so. He had money and her parents hadn't. They coaxed her into the match."

"Same old story. It was her parents that did him the real wrong, the one unforgivable wrong. Parents do. They sold him their daughter's body without her soul, and let him think he was getting the whole thing. It was as crooked a deal as to sell, for a perfect watch, a watch-case that has no works in it. He was rich, eh?"

"Yes. He was about the richest man she knew. They made her set her cap for him and—"

"And a fool and his money are soon courted. Well, he's already been swindled. You can't rob him of what he never had. Your skirts are clear. So is your Plymouth Rock conscience. You won't even have the remorse of feeling you won her away from him."

"You're—you're—*right!*" said Durand again, almost in a whisper, his hands tight clenched, his eyes aglow.

"It's a way I've got," laughed Craddock. "I came here to-night when you were on the brink of what you thought was the Great Renunciation. I think I've proved to you that you were only on the brink of the Sublime Idiocy. Haven't I?"

Durand's "Yes" was almost inaudible. But his transfigured visage fairly shouted affirmation.

"Now start in unpacking those silly trunks of yours," resumed Craddock, taking full charge. "And, in the morning, have a talk with this 'Wonder Woman.' If she cares as much as you think she does, she'll be on her way to Reno before the end of the week. I speak to be your best man. And the one supreme wish I can give you and your 'Wonder Woman' is that you may be a tenth as happy as Phyllis and I have been. By the way," he broke off with the air of a scared schoolboy, "for Heaven's sake, never tell Phyllis—or let your future wife tell her—that I advised you in this. Phyllis has all the morals that I haven't. She'd never understand. And I'd get blue blazes. And,"—his gaiety returning—"I herewith order you both to dine with us the first evening after you come back from your honeymoon. We'll send the invitation to 'Mrs. Carl Durand, 999 West Nineteenth Street.' Doesn't that sound good? I suppose you'll keep the studio?"

He got up, stretched, and looked across the dead fire at the artist, with a smile of real affection. He was fonder of Durand than of any other man he knew. From boyhood they had been chums. To-night, he had found his friend writhing in a self-dug Pit of Despair. He had, by his own keener judgment and greater knowledge of life, lifted Durand from the depths, and set his feet firmly on the road to Happiness. And Craddock was heartily pleased with himself.

"It is *Faust* and *Mephistopheles,* in modern dress," he said lightly, as he and Durand paused for an instant at the front door. "Only, this time, *Mephisto* is preaching sanity, not sin." And Durand, a line from Goethe flashing into his brain, involuntarily quoted *Faust's* bitter heart-cry:

> How doth he seem to cast a hellish light o'er what but now appeared so beautiful!

"It does credit to your memory," commented Craddock, "but I fail to catch the connection. What's the point?"

"There isn't any," replied Durand with a little shiver. "I don't know what put the ranting old quotation into my mind. Thanks for all you've made me see, to-night, Crad. And the best proof of my gratitude is that I'm going to do as you advise. Good-night."

"Good luck!"

Craddock, on the doorstep, glanced at his watch, and lighted a fresh cigar. The match-flare flashed back from the fresh-gilded numbers on the transom.

"'Nine-ninety-nine West Nineteenth,'" mused Craddock quizzically. "If there's anything in the gambler's idea of repetition, this address ought to bring a lot of luck."

TWENTY minutes later, Craddock turned into his own street and up the steps of his big and very ugly house. As he was drawing out his latch-key, a hail from below and behind him caused the home-comer to turn around.

A taxicab stood, chugging, at the curb. Its chauffeur had jumped to the sidewalk and was clumping hastily toward Craddock.

"Hey!" called the man, for the second time. "Do you live here?"

"Yes," announced Craddock; "what do you want?"

"I want my fare. That's what I want."

"Your fare?"

"I thought the dame was comin' out again, when she run in there without paying me. That's why I didn't stop her, and that's why I've waited. But I'm gettin' sleepy and it's late. Ask her is she comin' back, will you? If she ain't, let her send out the fare, so I can go to bed. She was all shaky when she went in. Maybe she was so shook up in her mind that she forgot about me. She looked it, all right. Jog her mem'ry, will you, boss?"

"How much is your fare?" asked Craddock.

"Four-thirty, just. An' I—"

"Four dollars and thirty cents? Why, that's—"

"It's all this waitin' that's made it pile up so high. That an' for takin' her from here to 999 West Nineteent' an' back, an'—"

Craddock pushed a five-dollar bill into the chauffeur's hand, and with dizzy brain and faltering feet made his way once more up the steps.

He let himself into the house, walked blindly, like a man in a nightmare, into his library, closed the doors behind him, switched off the lights and collapsed into the nearest chair.

And as he sat there, in the black darkness, for the first time in his life he *saw*. He saw his own soul—laughing at him.

The Man Who Went Wrong

THIS is the story of Mason Clyde, who began life as a reasonably white man and suddenly became a cur. One has the testimony of everybody who knew him that he was once a more than fairly decent chap, and the still more forceful testimony of his wife and her confidantes that a single light attack of illness changed him from what he was to what he became.

Now Balzac and a host of lesser mental vivisectionists swear that the character of a full grown man cannot change—that gold is always gold and that dross is always dross; that the fires may purify the gold and burn away the dross, but that no flame of reformation was ever yet hot enough to change dross into pure gold. Wherefore, except in old-fashioned plays, the true villain never reforms. Nor does the thoroughbred become a mongrel.

All of this dry philosophy is quite correct. Yet—there was Mason Clyde.

Clyde and his wife had been married for about eight years. They lived comfortably enough—that is, they lived as do most people whose income is sixty dollars a week and whose gross weekly expenditures range somewhere between fifty-nine dollars, and fifty-nine dollars and ninety-nine cents. There was enough, but not enough and to spare.

MY story begins just after the week's illness that left Clyde absurdly dazed and shaky. On the first day he was allowed to leave the house he went out for a ten-minute walk; and he returned three hours later extremely drunk.

Mrs. Clyde met him at the door with eager solicitude for his long absence. She also met the unwonted reek of liquor and an angrily growled request not to make a silly fool of herself by worrying over his condition.

Hilda Clyde shrank back as though her husband had struck her or sworn at her. Never before in their eight married years had he spoken to her like this. And never before, in her recollection, had he been the worse for liquor.

She was prepared, after the first qualm of disgust, to accept his contrite apologies for both lapses.

But no contrite apology was forthcoming. When, next morning at breakfast, she strove to break in upon an unwonted grouch of Clyde's by hinting at such amends, he blazed forth:

"What have I got to be sorry about? That I told you not to make a fool of yourself? It's a pity some one didn't give you that advice when you were young enough for it to do you some good."

"Mason!" she exclaimed.

"If you want me to say I'm sorry," he went on, speaking out of one corner of an unpleasantly sneering mouth, "if you want me to say I'm sorry for breaking away from this dreary old tomb of a flat and from the boredom of listening to your endless drivel, and having an hour or two of fun at a jollier place—why, I'm not going to say it. For, I'm not sorry. I'm only sorry I've lacked the nerve to do it sooner."

She stared at him, her eyes wide and wet.

"I—I don't know you, this morning," she managed to say at last. "You—you aren't like yourself, not one bit like yourself, Mason. How can you say such things to me? I thought you loved staying at home with me. I've made the flat as pretty and homelike as I knew how. I—"

"It's a pity you didn't 'know how,' better, then," he retorted. "As a leader of the Suffrage Cause or as a discoverer of the Fifth Dimension you might perhaps score a hit. But as a wife and homemaker, I don't mind telling you, you leave a lot to be desired. Sometimes, it's seemed to me I'd explode if I didn't have some sort of let up from the horrible grind of it all: after the office day, always to have to trot back here to some greasy meal and to a dead-and-alive evening around the lamp; or to a show, or to some other place, where I had to do just the things *you* wanted to do and to talk to you and to no one else. Lord! But I've longed to get an hour away from this office-to-house and house-to-office treadmill, with one woman to bore me to death all the time and no prospect of any let-up!"

SHE fought back the tears at his snarled tirade, then said gently: "You aren't well, yet. You don't mean the horribly unkind things you're saying. Let's try to forget them. Sha'n't we, dear?"

"Yes," he snapped. "By all means. Let's forget them. Let's forget them and go on with the stifling old slavery, now that I've at last screwed my courage up to make the break! Not much, we won't! We're going to have a new deal. I mean to get some fun out of life."

"But—but you used to say what good times you had here in our home, evenings, and in going around to places with me. You said I was your chum. 'The dandiest chum a man ever had,' you told me once."

"I've told you a lot of things in my day," he answered. "Some of them were true. But one gets tired, after a time, of even the 'dandiest chum'—just as I've no doubt you've gotten tired of me, even if you won't confess it to yourself."

"I haven't! I—"

"What's the use?" he protested, crossly. "We aren't honeymooners any longer. We've been married for eight interminable years. Why should we keep up the fool fiction that there's nothing in life for either one of us but the other? Lots of married couples take account of stock when they've been married a few years, and decide they'll get on better if they ease up the fetters a bit, and give each other more leeway. It's time *we* did the same thing."

"Mason! Oh, you're so different—so—!"

"Don't let's get hysterical. When people have traveled a long time they're always sure to have piled up a lot of 'excess luggage.' And they make room in the trunks for things that are better worth while, by getting rid of that excess."

"What has that to do with—?"

"It has everything to do with it. You and I have a pile of excess luggage: in the form of sentimentality that's getting threadbare; in the shape of our eight-year-old tradition that we can't have jolly times except when we're with each other; that this bum flat which we miscall a 'home' is the most desirable place on earth; that I'm tied to your apron strings by a goo-goo adoration and can't stir anywhere without you. It's time we got rid of all that and looked Life in the face and told each other the truth."

"The truth? Why, Mason, I've always—"

"Yes. The truth. Look at me! I'm not a sighing swain that you worship. Why pretend I am? Why not admit I'm middle-aged and not an Adonis and that my figure is—well, 'not lost but gone before;' and that you simply regard me as a good sort of meal-ticket and side partner?"

"How dare you say such things? I never gave you reason to—"

PARTLY because of his coarse brutality, partly from indignation at his word-picture of herself, she was crying now.

"So," he resumed, "let's start a new and happier deal. I mean to get some joy out of life, before I'm too old. I'm going to spend my evenings where and how I please, and with whom I please. You can do the same, for all of me. If you take it decently, we'll get on very well. If you like it—well, there's nothing to keep you here."

"You're—you've tired of me?"

"Frankly, yes—as you are of me. Only, being a man, I'm honest enough to say so. Being a woman, you will lie about the way you feel, even to yourself, for the fun of being a martyr."

She tried to speak, and could not. She pushed back her chair, got up hastily from the breakfast table and started toward the door.

"Wait!" he ordered, roughly. "I'm going to be away this evening. But if you think you'll be lonely, you can ask anyone you care to, to dine with you."

"I don't want to," she said, her face averted, her voice muffled.

"Any of my friends will be glad to waste an evening here, for my sake, if I ask them," he continued. "Suppose I ring up Derrick Wayne, or—"

"No!"

The monosyllable was not muffled, like its predecessors, but was sharp and decisive. And she turned to face him.

"No?" he echoed. "Suit yourself. But Derrick's a good chap. I'm sorry if you don't like him. A good chap—and he's the only close friend of mine who's rich. So I don't like to lose him. He's always good for a loan. That's about all he *is* good for. But that's enough."

"Do you mean to say," she demanded, incredulous, "that you keep on friendly terms with Mr. Wayne just because of the money he has?"

"What better reason could there be? I've never borrowed from him yet. But I always know I can. And, besides, he comes in handy. Why, when I was sick, didn't he drop around nearly every day and bring me fruit and cigars and—"

"Oh, it *is* the illness that makes you talk so!" she declared. "You're another man. You're not yourself."

"I'm a saner, honester, pluckier self than I've been. And I mean to be a happier self, too. And, speaking of happiness, I wish you'd do your tiny share toward it by having less appetite-killing things to eat. You're supposed to pride yourself on your wonderful housekeeping—as most people pride themselves on what they haven't got. So, suppose you live up to it, for a change. This breakfast, for instance, is—"

But she had gone.

HE did not jump up and run after her, in eager remorse, and beg her forgiveness—as he had done after the fewer-than-rare quarrels that had starred their placid eight years together. Instead, he left the house without so much as going to say good-by to her.

Nor, that evening, did he come home to dinner.

It was well past one in the morning when he reached the flat. His wife, lying tense and wakeful in her own room, heard him stumble noisily along the hall, swearing with great fluency when in the dark he collided with a door-jamb.

In the morning, he gave no explanation and she asked none. Their breakfast was eaten in silence, except for his exclamation of distaste as he pushed aside an *omelet aux fines herbes* which Hilda, remembering it was his favorite morning dish, had herself prepared for him.

Then he went to the office. That night he did not come home at all—returning only in time, next morning, for a bath and a change of linen, before going to work.

And so, for dreary weeks, affairs dragged on. Few were the evenings Clyde spent in the flat. Fewer were the evenings when he came home without liquor-reek and thickness of tongue. At last, despite the woman's stout resistance of the impulse, she grew almost to loathe him. She dreaded his homecoming more than his absences—the meals she must sit through with him, more than the solitary and memory-haunted repasts without him.

ONCE he related, with chuckling amusement, a chance nocturnal meeting with his friend Derrick Wayne and the latter's futile attempts to induce him to sober up and go home. "He's a measly Puritan," said Clyde, "—a sniveling saint, as far as booze and women go. He was shocked at the shape I was in and worse shocked at the place I told him I was on my way to. I guess I mislaid my temper for a minute. I know I told him, for once, what I think of his sanctimonious ways and his butting in on my amusements. I've lost him, for good, I suppose. A white man couldn't very well stomach a lot of the things I said to him. Well, it's no great loss at that. I only wish I'd had the sense to get a loan before I killed the gander that laid the golden advice."

Money was becoming a problem, nowadays, in the household. Clyde no longer brought home his pay envelope for division between Hilda and himself. Nor, after one disastrous attempt, did she risk a tornado of rage by suggesting that he do so.

At last there came a day when she sought no longer to beg or to protest, a day when her heart died within her, when she felt that at last love was slain. It was when she chanced upon a photograph on the floor where it had fallen from Clyde's cast-off coat, the evening before—a woman's photograph, with a love-phrase scrawled on its back.

Clyde, meeting her eyes as he nodded to her, on coming in late that afternoon, could not have failed to read the truth. A child could not have misread the look wherewith she returned his sulky gaze. The air, all at once, seemed unbreathable to her, now that he had returned. Without an excuse, she put on hat and coat and left the flat. She wanted to be by herself, out in the open, to think.

And there, in the twilight chill and dimness, she fought her battle—fought it and won—or lost. For to her came the calm and certain knowledge, bit by bit, that she could not hate Clyde, that whatever he had done or become, she must stand by him, must win him back if she could; win him back to decency and—to herself.

Weak with reaction, she turned home, to begin at once, if might be, her seemingly hopeless task. Praying silently, passionately, for help, she went. She let herself into the flat with her latchkey. Through the half-drawn curtains of the living-room, as she opened the front door of the apartment, she could see Clyde.

He was sitting at a table, writing. Several sheets lay, scattered, in front of him; and he was halfway through another.

AT SOUND of her step in the hall, as she came toward him, Hilda saw the man jump up, a look of scared guilt on his face, and claw the several sheets of paper into a wad. He glanced at the grate. But the fire was not lighted. Then, drawing the waste-basket toward him, from under the table, he made as though to tear the pages.

But Hilda was already in the room, and keenly watching him. There was no disguising the embarrassment in his every look and move. He muttered something, in an incoherent growl; and in dire confusion he thrust the crumpled paper-wad into the side pocket of his coat.

"Why do you do that?" she asked coldly, disgust at his ratlike secretiveness checking for the moment her new born impulse to come to a better understanding with him. "I was not going to ask impudent questions about your correspondence. I never do."

"It—it wasn't correspondence," he muttered, uneasily. Then, manlike, masking his confusion with a show of anger:

"If you've got to know things that are none of your business, I've been figuring up the household expenses for the past six months, and comparing them with the six months before. And I find," he blustered savagely, "that we're living at twenty per cent more outlay and about fifty per cent less well, than we did a year ago. You've got a positive genius for spending more money and getting poorer results for it, every day of your life. It's got to stop. And it's *going* to stop."

She flared up at once in defense of her powers of economy.

"You are mistaken!" she declared, hotly. "We live as well as ever we did, in spite of the rise in prices. And we don't spend a penny more on the bills than we did three years ago—not a penny more."

"Think not, eh? Well, the figures prove otherwise."

"I don't 'think.' I know. Let me see the figures, and I'll find where you've made the mistake."

"I haven't made any mistakes in them. I leave that to *you.*"

"Let me see them," she insisted, holding out her hand for the paper. But he made no move to take it from his pocket.

"I'm going out," he said, "and—"

"I want to see those figures. I can show you where they are wrong, if they say we spend more than we used to."

"Well, you're not going to see them."

"I have a right to."

"Yes? And maybe get a chance to juggle them? No, thanks. I've proved what I wanted to, in them."

"You've made a charge of incompetence against me, as a house-wife. I have a right to see the so-called proof of that charge, Mason. I have a *right* to. Wont you be honest enough to—"

"'Honest?'" he jeered. "How about the honesty of squandering my cash as you do, and getting such rank bad results from it, eh? Don't let's start the subject of 'honesty.'"

"We *shall* start it! And we shall prove you're wrong. I have stood about all I mean to, Mason. When you accuse me of being incompetent and dishonest, I demand to see your proofs. And I warn you I'm going to see them. Those figures belong to me as much as to you. I am going to see them."

HE HAD turned his back on her as she talked. Going out into the hall, he took his overcoat from the rack. She followed closely.

"Show me those figures!" she commanded again.

He did not answer, but began to struggle into his overcoat. One sleeve was refractory, its lining being ripped, and he tussled crossly to shake it into place, yanking the coat and his own body sharply to and fro. The ball of paper he had thrust into his gaping sack-coat pocket bounced out and fell to the floor, during one supreme heave of his ludicrously violent battle with the ripped sleeve-lining.

Hilda picked up the fallen paper. She did not do it surreptitiously; yet, so immersed was he in wriggling his arm into the jammed sleeve and in swearing at her carelessness in not having mended the rip, that he did not see. Nor did she call his attention to her victory. She told herself, as she had told him, that she had a right to study the figures. And she crushed the ball of paper in her hand.

Then, as on second thought she half-decided to tell him, and to ask him to come back and go over the figures with her, he reached for his hat and grunted:

"I'm off. So long. By the way,"—pulling a wad of bills from his trousers pocket and dropping it on the hall table,—"here's some cash I won last night. Keep it safe for me till I get back. It's more than I like to carry at night. I've counted it, so I'll know if you take any."

The coarse insult froze her impulse to confess. She stood aside to let him go out.

As he passed her, he leaned down and brushed his lips carelessly against her cheek. The caress savored rather of mockery than of affection. The laugh that went with it made her wince. Before she could speak, the front door had jarred shut behind him, and she heard his dragging step on the stairs.

HILDA CLYDE went back into the living-room, sat down beside the lamp and smoothed open the crushed sheets of paper. They were covered with penciled scribblings. Instead of a row of figures, a line of writing on the top of the first page seemed to leap upward to meet her. A wave of almost physical sickness racking her whole slender body, she perused the line once more; then, with set jaw, she forced herself to go on with the entire miserable scrawl. This is what she read:

"Sweetheart—my own, *own* sweetheart:

"You're never going to see this letter. And perhaps I am foolish to write it. But it's good-by—the only good-by I can give you. And it will be a comfort to say what I've longed to say—even if it's only on paper, and even though you'll never see it. For I'm going to tear it up as soon as it's written. I *must,* you see. If I let you know, then all the hell of these past weeks would have gone for nothing. And they've cost me too much torture for me to rob you of their good.

"Before I go, I'm going to try to kiss you—just once—if I can do it without making you suspect. Do you know, my sweetheart, it is more than five weeks—five weeks yesterday morning—since I kissed you? It seems five centuries.

"There's another thing I must try to do as naturally as I can before I go: I must leave the money with you. The money you'll need for the last expenses and before the insurance comes in. It's all yours, what there is of it. I've saved it. You thought I was squandering it, didn't you? I was saving it. Because it *had* to be saved for—for what is coming. We hadn't enough laid by.

"Shall I go back to the beginning of this whole nightmare, dear? It started, the last day I was sick. Derrick Wayne came to see me. After he'd gone out of the room there was something I remembered I wanted him to do for me downtown.

"I was lying on the couch, with a bathrobe on. I got up and went out into the hall—in my stocking feet, to catch him before he left the flat. I suppose I must have moved pretty softly, for neither of you heard me. You were at the door, letting him out. As I got halfway down the hall, from my room, I heard what he said and what you answered. Do you remember what it was? But of course you do, even though it was evidently in the very middle of a talk you and he were having.

"I caught just this much: Wayne said: *'But he won't die. He may live for years.'* And you answered him: *'It's the only honorable thing to do. Be patient.'* Then I heard him sigh: *'You're right. You're always right. But it means everything to me. More than life, more than heaven itself.'* You said: *'Do you suppose it means nothing to anyone else? Be patient. It will all come out right some day. Don't stop loving—'*

"I DIDN'T wait to hear any more. I went back to my room. At first, I couldn't think very clearly. It was the way, I've read, soldiers feel just after they are hit—all numb and dead and indistinct, with no pain.

"I pretended to be asleep when you came back into the room. I wanted to think, to understand. And by and by I was able to. I pieced it all together. No one could help doing it. It was horribly easy.

"You and Wayne loved each other. And somehow—I know it must have been by accident—you both had found out your love was returned. For you are too honorable, and so is he, to avow such a thing, purposely. Then had come my illness. And down in your hearts you had hoped that might be the solution. But I was getting well. As Wayne had just said: *'But he won't die.'*

"And you had both turned your backs on happiness and on love; to take up Duty once more and to wait until you should be free to go to each other. I understood.

"Will you think even less of me than I've lately taught you to, if I tell you that for a few minutes I was burningly furious at you both? I couldn't help it. You see, I had always loved you so, my glorious wife. I had been so divinely happy with you. And I had tried so hard to make you happy. It had never occurred to me that I might not have succeeded; or that perhaps I wasn't all the world to you just as you were—and *are*—to me.

"It had been such a wonderful time for me—these eight perfect years. You were all I asked God to give me, either here or Hereafter. You're so beautiful, so dear, so all-satisfying to every side of me.

"And our life together had been so inexpressibly sweet. Our dear home-evenings, the dandy little sprees at theaters, and all that sort of thing. You were always the ideal chum—just as you were always the ideal sweetheart.

"And—oh, it was a death-blow to know the love was all on one side and that you'd stopped loving me and had come to care for some one else and that you stuck by me only from duty! Can you blame me for resenting it, at the very first?

"Then I got myself in control; and all at once I knew that nothing else mattered in comparison with making you happy. If the only way for you to be happy was for you to be with Wayne, why—there was just one thing for me to do. All that was left was to plan how to do it best.

"I knew I was safe in leaving you to Derrick Wayne's care. He's the truest, best, cleanest man, I ever knew. And he has plenty of money to grant every wish you could have. You'll be happy with Wayne.

"But I know you so well—every detail of your marvelous character—that I knew if I should die under ordinary conditions, you'd be remorse-stricken. You would always remember how I'd loved you. You would idealize me. You would remember that you'd fallen in love with another man while I had still been alive. And you would blame yourself cruelly for it all.

"You would think—wrongly, of course—that you had no right to happiness, under such circumstances. You would want to atone for your imagined infidelity to me, by denying yourself the right of marrying the man you really care for. You know you would, you overscrupulous little sweetheart of mine, with your rock-bound New England conscience.

"You might even carry remorse to the point of martyrdom and refuse to marry Wayne, at all. At the very least, you would go through fires of unhappiness and self torture; and my memory would always give you a twinge of sorrow.

"SO I had to think of some way to prevent all that, by killing your respect for me—even as I had unknowingly let your love die—and making you look on me as a beast who is better out of the world than in it, a beast whose death even the kindest-hearted woman cannot honestly regret. That would remove the very last barrier between you and Wayne.

"All night long I worked out plan after plan, till at last I hit on the right one.

"Oh, my darling, my darling, you'll never know how hideously hard it has been for me to be such a cur. To tell you I was sick of being with you, was like sacrilege. To speak slurringly, as I did so often, of your dear beauty and your adorableness, was like murdering the God of Love…

"Do you know how much I've drunk, this past five weeks? I'm not certain myself. But I bought a half-pint flask of whisky, that first day. And it's still more than a third full. Always, just before I came home, I'd steep my mustache in it. If I'd wanted to drink, I should have done it, I suppose. But I've never learned to like liquor.

"The effect was the same, though. It's easy to play drunkard for the benefit of a woman who knows so little about the real article.

"Do you know where I've been, these evenings when I've gone out? In the Park. And twice I spent the night there. I'm going there now, for a while—for the last time—when I've finished this good-by that you'll never see. I am going there to wait—until it is late enough. Life's so much bigger than the people who live it!

"Do you remember the bench just back of the Falconer statue? Of course you do. Neither of us will ever be able to forget that bench; or how we stopped there and sat down, that day nearly nine years ago when we were out for a walk together; and how all at once I found myself daring to tell you I loved you and asking you to marry me. Dear, *dear* old bench!

"WELL, I've sat there every evening and all evening—sat there till I thought it must be the hour when a man might be expected to come back from an orgy. It was dreary and cold and dark and sometimes rainy. But I had memories for company.

"And, as I've told you, I spent two whole nights there. Once on my way to the park I happened to meet Wayne. And an inspiration came to me to make certain *he* wouldn't have any remorse either, about having loved the wife of his friend. For I like him—never mind where I told him I was going. I'll never forget his utter disgust. It stung me more sharply than I had thought such things could.

"Then yesterday, I made one more move in the sorry game. I bought the photograph of a professional beauty. I don't know her name. I forgot to ask. I picked out the one with the fewest clothes and the toughest face. And, with my left hand, to disguise the script, I wrote on the back: *'To my very dearest, very newest lover. With all my love. Gladys.'* I don't know, at all, whether that's the sort of thing such women write on photographs they give men. But *you* don't know, either. So it served. I've never been honored by such a gift.

"Then this morning I hung up one of my coats by the sleeve, as if I'd hung it that way when I was drunk. And I turned a pocket inside out and strewed the picture and some letters on the floor directly under it.

"When I came home to-night I saw by your eyes you'd found the photograph there. And I saw something else in those dear eyes of yours. Something I'd never seen before. The kindliness was gone— the kindliness that had replaced the sweet old love—and so were the bewilderment and the pain and the pleading that have stabbed me so, this past few weeks. I saw my task was over. There was nothing in your eyes but contempt for me.

"The time has come. The work is finished. You loathe me. You will have no remorse, now—only relief.

"And I am going out into the Dark. (I used to hope—yes, and to pray, too, every night—that when the end should come, God in His mercy might let us go out of the world together, you and I, holding each other's hands very tightly. It wouldn't have been darkness then. It would have been Heaven, wife of my heart.)

"DEAR, do you realize how easily—how ridiculously easily—you have come to believe that I could change in a single day from a man who adored you into a brute that nobody could love? I did it very badly—much too suddenly. I see that, now. Yet it convinced you—as fully as the most consummate and long-drawn-out acting could have done.

"I wonder if anyone could be convinced of a man's reform, one-tenth as quickly and readily as of his degeneration.

"You've gone somewhere, out of the house. And I must go, to-night. It is so lonely here without you, even when you're away for just a little while. And oh, my whole soul cries out to tell you I'm not so vile and so damnable as I've taught you to think. That is why, as much as for the other senselessly sentimental reasons, I've sat down to write this before I go.

"When you get back, I'm going. I want so much to stay for one little hour, near you, before the end. But I am such a coward and such a miserably bad actor, I know I'd say or do something to betray myself. I *couldn't* keep it up, when I know it would be the last time I was to see you.

"So I am going, when you return. I'm going out to the bench, until it is late enough for me to have gotten hopelessly drunk: then I am going to pour the rest of that flask of whisky over my mustache and coat, to make redolent of the fumes of it. After that, I am going to reel into the nearest subway station and stand swaying on the lower edge of the platform, where several people can see me and notice how drunk I am.

"As the first train comes whizzing in, I'm going to lose my balance. There will be plenty of witnesses. And the smell of liquor will help. It will be an accident. No one ever suspects a drunken man of doing such things on purpose. There'll be no trouble collecting my insurance, either.

"You'd be the very last person who would suspect my death wasn't accidental. It will be a shock to you. I'd avert that, if I could. But I can't. It will be a shock. But where there is no heartache, one soon gets over a shock.

"And now, good-by, my darling. You have made my life glowingly happy. And it is sweet to know that at the last I can do one great deed for *your* happiness, too.

"I don't think it is wicked, this thing I am going to do. If a man is blessed for laying down his life for his friend, he can't very well be cursed for laying down his life for—"

HERE the writing stopped abruptly, in the very middle of a page.

Hilda Clyde sat, staring blankly at the sheet that trembled between her fingers, staring as though she expected more words to appear on its surface. Then, of a sudden, she cried out. Her cry rang and echoed through the stillness of the room, reverberating, piercing to the farthest corners of the apartment.

She sprang up, her hands clenched on her breast, caught at her throat as in a spasm of mortal pain; then she ran hatless from the flat and outside.

Night had fallen, windy and raw, with a whipping rain that soaked the woman's light dress and drenched her to the skin. On she ran, eyes staring, lips parted, jostling blindly against the few passers-by.

A man, lounging along under an umbrella, noticed her as she sped past him under a street lamp. He caught her by the arm and said ingratiatingly:

"What's the hurry, little girl? Stop awhile, won't you, and—"

With a sudden snakelike dart of the head, she buried her teeth in the detaining fat hand. The man jumped back with a yowl of pain and surprise. And Hilda ran on, straining every nerve and every sinew in her flight.

She reached an entrance to the Park, and staggered onward, taking short cuts over lawns and through copses of shrubbery, colliding with trees, in the semi-darkness, once falling heavily.

Her skirt was torn in a dozen places and was foul with mud. Her lace waist was rent to ribbons by prickly shrubs. Her breath and her strength were fast going. Yet she pressed on.

And after a nightmare-like lifetime of flight she came to a rain-washed statue. Huddled on a bench behind it sat a man.

Hilda threw herself bodily upon him, clasping him to her breast in fierce yearning, crushing his cold lips and his wet cheeks with hot kisses, staining them with hotter tears.

"Oh, my *boy!*" she sobbed, frantically. "My own splendid, crazy boy! Come home with me! Come home to me. You're all so wrong, so insanely *wrong!* Derrick's engaged to Molly Mercer. It's a dead secret. She made us both promise not to tell. Her father won't allow it. He says they shall never marry as long as he is alive. And Molly was weak enough to promise not to. Derrick was telling me—"

"Hey, youse!" bellowed a voice from the path in front of them; and a waterproofed policeman loomed on their view. "Break away, there!

Break away, before I run you both in. This is a city park. It ain't no spoon-foundry."

"No!" yelled Mason Clyde, as new, vibrant life surged maddeningly through him. "You're wrong, Officer. It isn't either one. It's Paradise. That's what it is! It's *Paradise!*"

Clarissa-Out-of-a-Book

THE twisting country road lay dust-pallid, with pulsing heat-waves rising against its skyline. Floury dust lay an inch deep on it, sending up little swirling dust-devils when a stray whiff of breeze touched it. The wayside grass and leaves were powdered gray. The bushes were a-droop from the month's drouth.

Drayton, chugging along in his small runabout, had been breathing dust-powder for the past hour. He had been viewing the whole world through a stinging dust-haze, a haze that made his eyes smart, that pringled his nostrils, that sanded his thirsty throat.

Such wind as the moderate speed of his car managed to drive against his face was hot and dry. His tongue was parched. His head ached from the heat. And he had another full half-hour's ride before he could hope to reach the inn at Sparta Junction where he was spending his vacation.

For the last hour or more he had been keeping a dust-bleared lookout on either side of the way for one of those purling and silvery roadside springs which are found in crystal profusion in summer fiction, and which in real life—fortunately for those who would avoid typhoid—are a decided rarity.

Drayton had found no icy spring whereat he might quench his teasing thirst. But now, at a new twist of the road, on the outskirts of a village, he saw the next best thing. Above a four-foot rough-cast wall rose the boughs of an orchard. And among the leaves of one tree, not twenty yards beyond the wall, shone big yellow harvest apples—dozens of them, golden spheres, palpably ripe: a sight to maker a thirsting man forget that trespass is a misdemeanor and that theft is a felony.

Drayton brought his runabout to a jarring halt in the roadside brass, close to the wall. Then, from the seat, he stepped directly across to the wall-top and paused to scout the scene.

A glance showed him a rectangular space, perhaps four acres in area, bounded on three sides by stone wall and filled with more or less orderly lines of ancient apple trees. At the far end, half invisible through the foliage, he could catch the outlines of a rambling white house with green blinds, and with a white picket fence beyond. The orchard, so far as a casual survey could tell him, seemed vacant of human or animal life. And the leafy boughs might be counted on to shut him off from observation from any of the house's back windows.

Whereat, Drayton dropped to the ground inside the enclosure and made for the near-by harvest-apple tree. The ground beneath the spread of gnarled limbs was strewn with fallen apples. Stuffing one into each of his side pockets and munching thirstily at a third, Drayton turned to retrace his way. He took a half-score steps and then halted, the partly eaten apple tumbling forgotten from his hand.

Directly before him, on the sward in an angle of the wall, sat a girl—a girl such as came oftener into the vision of Romney or of Sir Joshua than into that of any observer since those beloved portraitists' days.

She was small and slender—almost fragile, scarce greater in stature than a well-grown child of thirteen. She was clad in flowered muslin, billowy in cut, low in neck and with elbow sleeves. A soft white fichu and filmy lace elbow-length mitts modified these brevities. The voluminous and multi-flowered skirt was spread on the grass far to either side. From its hem peeped one small foot in a French-kid sandal slipper.

The girl's fair hair was piled high above her little head, in a mode

that went out with the first Empire. A tall tortoise-shell comb topped it. Her brow was broad, and the eyebrows were level. The eyes—which

just now were surveying the amazed Drayton with no faintest hint of embarrassment—were blue and almost too big for the daintily featured face.

In one half-mittened hand she held an apple—an apple wherein a single semicircle of toothmarks showed. In her other hand was a book, battered of binding and yellowed of leaf, a bound volume of *The Gentleman's Magazine* for 1764. In her lap, completely filling it, reposed a large gray cat with a scarlet bow about its furry neck.

Drayton stared. The girl with her wide, fearless blue eyes, and the cat with its sleepy yellow orbs, stared back at him, though according to tradition the girl should have sprung to her feet with a little startled cry on his sudden advent, and the cat should have scuttled hysterically up the trunk of the nearest tree.

His arrival had interrupted a peaceful hour in this picturesque nook. Yet neither occupant of the niche showed the faintest annoyance. To Drayton it seemed that they were willing to suspend judgment until they should hear his side of the story.

JUST beyond the wall, on a commonplace and modern village road, his commonplace and ultra-modern gasoline runabout was waiting. And at a single bound, he had come from all that sort of thing, into a veritable bit of the eighteenth century. Like one who goes from glaring electric light into soft candle-gleam, he was inclined to blink bewilderedly.

The girl looked not a day over twenty-one. Yet, to judge by her costume, she must be nearer one hundred and fifty. Oh, it was sheer nonsense! Drayton roused himself from the spell, enough to rub the dusty back of one hand impatiently across his eyes. Whereat, the dream-girl did not melt away, after the approved method of dream-women. Instead, she spoke.

"La, sir!" she said (and her voice was sweet and thin and mincing like that of a Sheridan ingenue), "la, sir! I trust we have not alarmed you?"

"I—I—" began Drayton, brilliantly.

Then he paused. And she spoke again, this time in a tone and diction more suited to present-day needs.

"You are very welcome to the apples I saw you take," she went on. "We don't enforce our 'Trespass' signs, except with tramps. Please don't look so much as if you thought you were going to be scolded."

With the girl's momentary descent to the language of his own century, Drayton's tongue-tied diffidence died.

"I owe you a very humble apology, I'm afraid," he began. "It was rude of me to come charging into your orchard sanctuary like this, and to steal your apples. I was dead with thirst, and they looked so cool and good. I—"

"Take more," she adjured him. "Take as many as you like. And," she added in a careless graciousness the sincerity and impersonality of which he could not doubt, "you look hot and tired. It's cool here by the wall. Wont you sit down and rest for a few minutes before you go? Bring some apples over here with you."

THERE was no hint of coquetry, of familiarity, of boldness, in the girl's invitation, or in her manner. There was nothing beyond a dissociated, wholly sexless friendliness. It was such an invitation as one man or one child might have bestowed on another. The blue eyes met his frankly, in pleasant welcome; and she shifted the wide-flung hem of her skirt a little to make room for him in the wall-niche beside her.

"Thank you, very much," Drayton heard himself saying in a voice he tried to make matter-of-fact. "It is the hottest day of the year, I think. And this is the only cool place I've found. But I'm interrupting your reading?" he suggested, with a second glance at the time-smeared volume.

"No," she denied, "I have read it all through, twice. I have read most of them through twice. I wish there were more."

"More?"

"More books. There are only two shelves. They belonged to Grandfather. Father used to love to read them, just as I do. They are all old—very old, older than this dress."

Catching the bewilderment in his look, she explained:

"This isn't really my dress, you know. People don't wear such clothes nowadays. I wish they did. I found it in the cedar chest in the south attic. They belonged to my father's grandmother, the shoes and mitts and fichu and comb and all. We have a picture of her wearing them. So I knew the way all the things should be put on. I often dress up like this and come out here to sit. It's lots of fun."

"And so bring back the sweet old Colonial days, by putting on Colonial dress and sitting out in this Old World corner and reading Old World books! It is a delightful idea!"

"Yes," she assented, as if glad that he caught the spirit of her idea. "And making up Old World plays and living in them too. I like it so much better than the nowadays life. Don't you?"

"I always shall, after this," he promised on impulse.

She nodded grave approval.

"I can talk as they did, too," she told him, tapping the frayed cover of *The Gentleman's Magazine* with one mittened hand. "And I love to. I was thinking that way, when I spoke to you first."

A GLINT of fun lighted the great eyes, and with mincing voice she continued:

"Sir, I fain would offer you a dish of Chinese tea, to cheer and solace you. For I see full well you are not in spirits, and I fear me the heat hath proven an overshrewd companion for you this day. But my revered aunt is from home, and it were not meet I entertain gentlefolk in the drawing-room in her absence. Therefore I crave your indulgence for not bidding you to come within."

Drayton rose to his feet, bowed low and sweeping the ground with his cap, made answer:

"Gramercy for thy sweet courtesy, O most amiable of thy sex. But put thyself not out to be at pains for mine entertainment. While I would full fain meet thy lady aunt and sip tea with her, yet I am right content to rest me for a space e'en as I am."

The speech cost him no little effort. And he was repaid by her delighted laugh. But at once her face grew painfully grave again as she replied:

"You are prodigious civil, sir, I protest. May I make bold to ask how so courtly a gentleman styles himself? of what name and lineage may you be?—if I give no offense in the asking?"

"My sponsors in baptism," he returned in like vein, "gave me the name of Hugh Drayton. I be a scrivener by occupation."

"A fair name and a fair calling," she deigned to approve. "I be Mistress Clarissa Harlowe, vastly at your service."

"Clarissa Harlowe?" echoed Drayton, forgetting his role. "Why, *Clarissa Harlowe* was the heroine of old Richardson's book—"

"'Twas ever a favorite of my sire," she answered, in stately explanation. "I doubt not that 'twas he that had me christened 'Clarissa,' my given name being 'Harlowe.' "

"Clarissa Harlowe!" he repeated whimsically, the name seeming to fit her and her costume to a charm.

"And this," Clarissa resumed, laying a mittened hand on the furry head of the recumbent gray cat, "this is my chief counselor and confidant. Master Hugh Drayton, I crave leave to present Peter Grimm, my cat. Saw ye ever so softly gray a coat as his?"

"'Tis assuredly soft," he agreed, passing his hand down the cat's back. "But I trust his grayness is premature and—ouch!"

This very unclassical interjection was caused by the cat, which suddenly nipped with needle-like teeth the hand of the stranger who ventured such liberties with his coat. A long red claw-scratch on the offending hand added further testimony to Peter Grimm's resentment of familiarity on so short acquaintance.

"Oh!" exclaimed the girl, dropping into the present century, with a look of real concern. "I do hope he didn't hurt you much."

"Not at all!" lied Drayton, putting his hand behind him. "It was my own fault. I was trespassing on his fur."

"He is very temperamental, Peter Grimm is," explained Clarissa. "I think it's partly the liver."

"He's bilious? I never knew that cats—"

"The liver we feed him," she corrected. "Every night of his life he has exactly one quarter of a pound of liver. It keeps his coat glossy and it keeps him from getting mange; and it isn't enough to keep him from being a gorgeous mouser. You *are* a gorgeous mouser, aren't you, Peter Grimm?" she broke off, turning to the temperamental cat for confirmation.

But Peter Grimm had once more curled himself up in a heap in her lap and refused to testify. Clarissa continued:

"He's the best mouser in all this neighborhood. He's famous for it. And he's much the prettiest cat around here, too. I think it's the liver. He's had his quarter-pound of it every single evening since he was six months old. He's never been allowed to miss it once."

"You spoke of your aunt," said Drayton, who was more interested in the cat's young mistress. "Would you mind very much if I should ask her permission to come and see you? I—"

A shade of sadness flitted across the girl's face.

"It wouldn't be any use," she said. "She wouldn't like it, I'm sure. But—I'm here every clear afternoon after lunch. Won't you come over the wall again some time soon—to-morrow perhaps? And we'll play once more that we're people out of a book—just as we did a few minutes ago. Please come. Won't you?"

HUGH DRAYTON was halfway back to his inn before his super-muddled thoughts cleared enough to be set forth in anything like logical sequence. And even then there was scant logic in what they told him.

On the face of it he had met a woman who, without introduction, had spoken to him, had invited him to sit beside her, had talked and jested with him as with a time-proven friend, and had wound up the shocking performance by asking him to call on her, clandestinely, the next afternoon. All of which was not in the least what Drayton cared for.

On the other hand, the impersonal friendliness, the fearless frankness, the stark absence of anything but sexless comradeship for a congenial soul—all these weighed far more heavily with the man (to his own surprise) than did the uncouth facts.

He was not one atom in love with this puzzling girl-out-of-a-book. He knew that. But there was something so out of the ordinary, so elusive, so elfin about her; that he could not drive her from his mind.

At last he decided she was a young woman who had, for some reason, singularly little knowledge of the outer world and its trammels. And he decided that he, a denizen of that same outer world, would be taking a despicable advantage of her sweet ignorance should he keep up the chance acquaintance. He would not go back to the orchard..... Yet the next afternoon found him swinging over the four-foot wall and dropping down on the orchard grass beyond!

At the same moment a distant flutter of white caught his eye. Through the leafage he saw her. She was just emerging from the far-off house. And as he watched, she picked her way daintily along the path through the trees, toward him.

The sense of unreality again encompassed Drayton as he looked at the slender figure in its hundred-and-fifty-year-old dress, its tortoise-shell comb holding the high-piled fair hair in place, the heelless French-kid sandals, the silk mitts.

As she caught sight of the man, she quickened her pace. Coming nearer, she held out both her hands to him in a gesture that was more childlike than womanly in its eager appeal.

"I'm so glad you came!" she exclaimed. "I was afraid you wouldn't or else that you had come and gone again. I couldn't get out here any sooner. I've been having such a horrid time!"

She spoke breathlessly. Looking closely, Drayton saw signs of tears.

"Can I help?" he asked, without releasing the hands that had so appealingly met his own.

"Oh *will* you?" she cried eagerly. "I so hoped you'd offer. *Will* you?"

"You know I will," he assured her.

"Thank you!" she breathed, in deep relief. "I'll never forget it. It's— it's about Peter Grimm."

"Oh!"

"It's about Peter Grimm," she repeated. "He's going to be locked up. And—and starved."

Drayton did not answer. He was wrestling with flat chagrin. A damsel in distress—a damsel he had vowed to succor—and her only grief was over a miserable "temperamental" cat!

"Mr. Hixson—he's our postmaster, you know," she was saying, "—his post office is overrun with rats. They ate up eleven dollars worth of stamps last night, for the glue on the backs of them—the back of the stamps. And he came and borrowed Peter Grimm, because Peter Grimm's the best mouser around here. It was just an hour or so ago. And I didn't know anything about it. I sent down his quarter-pound of liver as soon as I found it out, and I wrote Mr. Hixson to be *sure* to give it to him for supper. And—he sent the liver back and said only hungry cats are any good as mousers, and if Peter Grimm had any liver he wouldn't be so anxious to eat rats. And he's going to keep Peter Grimm all night. All *night!* He's never been away from home since he was born. And he's never gone without his liver, since—"

"But," broke in Drayton, seeking to stay the torrent of childlike explanation, "what can I do? I'm awfully sorry about the cat, of course, but what—"

"Why, I've been thinking it all out. And a man's got to do it. *I* can't."

"Do what? Thrash the erring postmaster, or storm the prison and rescue the temperamental Peter Grimm, or—?"

"No," she replied, with very evident reluctance at having to veto such alluring offers. "No, I'm afraid not. It's a duller, commonsensible favor I want to ask of you."

" 'Unto the half of my kingdom,' " he quoted, resigning himself to her whim and mildly stirred by curiosity. "What shall it be?"

AN ant was crawling along one of Clarissa's innumerable flowered flounces. She shook the skirt to dislodge the insect. An almost imperceptible breath of lavender came to the man's nostrils. It seemed the complement of the yellowish lace on her sleeves and girdle. Again Drayton was back a hundred and fifty years; the modern world seemed very far away. He brushed the odd fantasy from his mind and tried to pay heed to what Clarissa was saying.

For she had begun to speak again, not in the archaic diction she loved, but with a directness worthy of Napoleon.

"The post office," she began, "is just to the right of the general store. It's only half a mile down the road. You must have passed it on the way here. It's only one big room and it's painted gray. There are three windows. They are locked at night, of course. But the locks don't amount to anything. Once I heard Mr. Hixson say anyone could run a knife-blade between the sashes. He says he's going to have patent locks put on—when he gets around to it."

From the beaded reticule at her girdle she drew forth a small oblong package and held it out to Drayton. Mechanically he took it. Through the several thicknesses of paper it had a moistly chilly feeling.

"The windows are nearly five feet from the ground," she resumed. "And the lock is much too high for me to reach. That's how I happened to think of getting *you* to do it."

"Do what?"

"Open the back window and—"

"Break into a post office? What under heaven! Why, Miss Harlowe, it's a Federal offense."

"Break into the post office?" she echoed. "Of course not. What would be the sense of that? How silly of you! The post office closes at six, every evening. So does the store. By nine, that part of the village hasn't a soul around it. No one would see you. All you have to do is to open the window, toss the liver down into the room, shut the window and come away. It's very simple. A baby could do it—if he was tall enough."

"The—the liver?"

"In that package. It's Peter Grimm's supper. I couldn't sleep if I thought of him starving all night."

Her mittened hand was on his arm; her big eyes were looking up at him, in perfect trust and gratitude. Drayton made one futile effort at sanity.

"But you said the post office is full of rats," he argued. "Peter Grimm will have a hearty supper on them. Why bother about the liver?"

"He doesn't like rats. He kills them, but he doesn't care for them after that, except when he's fearfully hungry. And—and I know I shouldn't sleep a wink—and you promised, you know."

With a groan, Drayton bade farewell to common sense. He could no more have resisted that appeal than he could have refused the gift of a doll to a child.

"Mistress Clarissa," quoth he, "I deem myself right favored of the gods, to do this quest as your gallant knight. The dragon shall be duly slain—fed, I mean."

She swept him a low courtesy.

"I vow 'tis monstrous polite of you, Sir Hugh," she declared, "and minstrels yet unborn shall chant the tale of your prowess. You have lifted the vapors of dread from my heart. Fare forth to your devoirs, and when you return conqueror, you shall wear my scarf in your helmet, for guerdon."

"Full blithely do I hie me forth," he pledged himself. "And lady, I pray you be at the casement of your bower between the ninth and tenth hour this night. For as I gallop back past here from my quest, my palfrey shall—shall honk four times to let you know I have fulfilled your wish."

NEVERTHELESS, as Drayton set out on his idiotic errand that night, he felt anything but blithe. The commission seemed to him utterly ridiculous and unworthy a grown man. More than once he was minded to throw the package of liver in a ditch and turn back to the inn. Yet he had promised. And the little woman had trusted him to keep his word.

Leaving his runabout a hundred yards away, and switching off its lights, he walked along the unlighted village street to the post-office building and made his way to the rear of it.

Opening the packet of liver and laying it on the high sill, he took out his knife and, reaching upward, passed its largest blade between the upper and lower sashes. He had to work wholly by sense of touch, for here under the trees the night was pitch black.

Presently, his groping knife-blade found the catch. A single pressure, and the catch slid back. A sharp push, and the lower half of the window was raised. With his hand free, Drayton felt for the liver. His fingers closed over it. And then, simultaneously, several things happened.

Something soft, but violently propelled through the darkness, smote Drayton squarely in the face. The force of the impact, as he was still standing on tiptoe, nearly upset him. He reeled backward two steps to regain his balance.

As he did so, a dazzling dagger of light from an electric torch pierced his eyes, and a voice from that same darkness observed:

"Up with your hands, young man. Up with 'em! *Way* up! Now then, Mr. Titus, I'll trouble you to go through him for concealed weapons and such. It's all safe. I've got him covered."

"What's—what's all this?" demanded Hugh.

"I warn you," came the preternaturally solemn voice from behind the light: "Anything you say is liable to be used against you. Now, whatcher got to say?"

"Nothing on him that I can find, Tim," reported Mr. Titus, a dapper, nervous little man, "except a penknife and a piece of raw meat."

"Raw meat!" triumphantly echoed the light-holder. "That's the man, all right. Same one that smashed into the post office up at Zion. Don't you remember how they found the postmaster's watchdog, up there, dead next morning? Poisoned meat! Same here, too. Lucky for

Hixson he don't keep a dog. Hands *up*. I told you twice!" he snapped in last-warning tones.

"Look here!" cried Drayton. "Who in blazes do you take me for? I'm—"

"I take you for a slick gentleman that Uncle Sam's so anxious to clap hands on that there's a seven-hundred-and-fifty-dollar reward out for him. A feller who's been making a round of up-State post offices and borrowing stamps and money and so on, out of 'em. I've been watching this post office every night for a week on the chance that maybe you might—"

"I'm Hugh Drayton. I'm a newspaper man. I'm spending my vacation over at the Hilislope Inn, at—"

"I ain't overmuch versed in burglar-etiquette," responded the man behind the light with elephantine irony, "but if it's the thing to make introductions at times like this, why, I'm Timothy Laher, marshal of this village. And the gentleman who's just relieved you of your weapon and the poisoned meat is Mr. Titus, who teaches the school here. I happened to meet him, passing by, and I—"

"Poisoned meat!" snarled Drayton. "You idiot! Here! Call up the Hillslope Inn if you doubt that I'm all right."

"I guess the lock-up's good enough inn for you to-night, friend."

"I came here," protested Drayton, realizing the futility of his story, "to bring this liver to Miss Harlowe's cat, that's locked in the post office. I hate to bring her name into this, but it seems the only way to avoid a lot of trouble and publicity for both of us. Mr. Hixson wanted the cat to catch some of the rats in there. She was afraid the cat might be hungry. So she asked me to bring some liver to—"

"Sure it wasn't a dish of ice cream?" interposed the marshal.

"No cat in there," reported the schoolmaster, who had lighted a match and peered in through the opened window. Nothing alive in there at all."

"Miss Harlowe—"

"Who's Miss Harlowe?" demanded the Marshal.

"Miss Clarissa Harlowe," returned Drayton, "is the young lady who lives at that big white house, half a mile above here, on this same road—the house with the big orchard behind it and the gray stone wall all around."

"And you say a Miss Harlowe lives there?" asked the marshal. "Sure that's the house?"

"Of course I'm sure. She lives there with her aunt."

"And what might Auntie's name be?"

"I—I don't know."

"Well, *I* do. Mrs. Henry Bliss lives there. I happen to know because

I married her sister. The only flaw in your story is that she hasn't a niece, and that there's no young lady living there, nor ever has been. Hands up! 'Twon't do you no good to grab your head like that, unless you can shake a better lie out of it next time."

"Mr. Laher," stammered Drayton, with one last mighty effort at making possibility out of the impossible, "I've a ten-dollar bill in my pocket. Wait!"—forestalling a virtuous retort. "I'm not bribing you. I'm offering it as a reward, if you'll take me up to Mrs. Henry Bliss' home before you lodge me in the lockup. Put the handcuffs on me if you're afraid of a trick."

TEN minutes later, the marshal and the schoolmaster on either side of him, Drayton stood on the threshold of the rambling white house in whose orchard he had met his impossible dream-woman. At the marshal's summons a tall and angular woman of fifty had come to the door, and she stood now, listening to Laher's report and glaring in cold indignation at the handcuffed malefactor.

It was not at her bony and rugged face that Drayton was looking as the marshal declaimed. His eyes were fixed in rapt incredulity at the height of her ankles—gingham shrouded ankles against which a large gray cat was effusively rubbing its arched back.

Peter Grimm! So much of the affair, then, was not a dream.

Peeping shyly around Mrs. Bliss' arm was a lank-haired, pencil-legged child of perhaps thirteen, her eyes round with excitement as she stared at the prisoner. A "hired girl"—not a "maid"—filled the interstices on the other side, wiping red hands on a dirty blue apron, and gaping like a Japanese goldfish at the three men. The lamplight from behind revealed the sextet sketchily.

"I never knew anyone called Harlowe," coldly announced Mrs. Bliss, as Laher's recital ended. "And there is no young lady staying here. And I haven't a niece to my name. And you know it, Tim Laher."

"Yes, yes," agreed the marshal, "I knew it. So did everybody. But this crook, here, didn't. If he had, he'd of picked out some other house to put the story onto."

"But," said the woman judicially, "there's one part of his yarn that's true, and I can't think how he came to find it out. The cat—"

"It's—it's *all* true!" wailed a voice that made Drayton jump from his doze of hopeless apathy. "It's *all* true!"

It was the lank-haired, pencil-legged child who spoke. And now Drayton recalled that for the past five minutes she had been trying to interrupt. "It's all true!" she repeated. "And it's all my fault! Oh, Mr. Drayton, I'm so sorry! Honestly, I am! Honestly!"

"Gertie, be still!" snapped Mrs. Bliss. "Run along to your room. Now, about that cat, Tim: I really did send—"

"It's my fault, Mamma," insisted the child, holding her ground. "I sent him with the liver to feed Peter Grimm."

"*You* sent him. He said—"

"And when Peter Grimm came home a few minutes ago, I supposed he'd let him out. I was waiting at the window upstairs, as he told me to, to hear his motor-horn—"

Drayton remembered the soft impact in his face as he had opened the post-office window. The Return of Peter Grimm was explained. But he scarce noted the fact. He was staring agape at the child, the over-big blue eyes, the lean, small-featured face, the corn-colored hair, the childish simplicity and directness that would be elfin charm in a grown woman.

"I—I met him in the orchard," Gertie was sobbing, "when I was playing 'Old Times,' in those things of Great-grandma's that you said I could have. He was ever so nice, and he knows how to talk book-language just as I like to, and—"

"You said," put in Laher, whirling on Drayton, with a last clutch at the chance that he had made a capture, "you said it was a 'young lady'—Mrs. Bliss' niece—named 'Harlowe.' "

"I—I told him that," said Gertie, bravely fighting back her tears. "It was part of our game—all except being a young lady. I never told him any such a story. Why, he'd have known better, just by looking at me—"

"Yes," muttered Drayton, confusedly, as one waking from a dream, "I—I would. But I didn't."

"And now that I have gotten you into such a terrible scrape," faltered Gertie, "I suppose you'll never, never come to see me again?"

"Oh, yes, I will," promised Drayton, touched, as before, by the almost infant-like appeal in her face and voice. "Indeed, I will. In—in just about seven years."

The Greater Radiance

KEITH MINOT was an artist. He illustrated magazine stories when fate threw such work in his way. And he painted covers for magazines—painted them, and sometimes sold them.

Ruth, his wife, had for a time served him as model. And a good model she was—pretty, well formed and naturally graceful, and with an infinite patience for maintaining rackingly hard poses.

Never until after her marriage to Keith had she posed. She hated it, but she knew it saved her husband fifty cents an hour; and half-dollars were rare visitants in the Minot family in those first days. Wherefore she never told Keith she disliked the dreary task.

For hours she would sit in a flaring picture-hat and Colonial gown, against a multichrome background, posing for a cover design. Or, clad in white muslin and with a bonnet swung from her wrist by a ribbon, she would stand, glancing coquettishly upward at the studio manni-kin, serving as model for the illustration of some magazine story.

The smile would freeze on her lips, and her cramped body would send shooting-pain warnings to her aching brain, as she posed there while Keith worked, erased, measured—muttering annoyance or grunting approval.

Then, from the dear little Indiana town where they had been born and married, the two Minots had come to New York—because Keith said New York was the Mecca of his craft. He wanted to be "on the ground." Fear of the roaring civic wilderness had well nigh swallowed up Ruth's sick pain at leaving the home town she loved.

In New York they lived, toiled, slept and hoped—and occasionally ate—all in a suite comprising a somewhat stuffy studio and kitchenette. Being "on the ground" was no synonym for "on the ground floor," as Keith Minot speedily learned. Life resolved itself into a blend of grinding labor, interspersed by tedious pilgrimages from one art editor to another. And the net profits meant a bare—a very, very bare—livelihood.

Indeed, if Keith had not found he could scribble short stories, of a sort, and illustrate them in a way that mildly tickled the fancy of one weekly periodical's editor, the wolf and the door must long since have formed a merger. As it was, grim poverty eased itself, gradually, under the strain of tireless work, into semi-cozy penury.

It was at this point that Trouble came rapping at the door. That is not a figure of speech, but a literal fact. Trouble rapped very demurely. And Ruth let it in—much as she might have let in a process server or a typhoid germ.

SHE answered the knock at the studio door. And on the mat stood Trouble—dressed in the sleazy ghost of the fashion after next, crowned by a glory of fire-colored hair and rejoicing in the ready-made *poseuse* name of Editha Lauteret.

Ruth did not at all realize that Miss Editha Lauteret (once known to her parents as Emma Higgs) was Trouble. But Ruth had lived in a New York atelier long enough to see that the visitor belonged to the flying squadron of work-questing models of the obscurer sort, who drift from studio to studio even as the obscurer men who employ them drift from editor to editor.

But Ruth recognized something more. She noted the flaming hair and the head-poise. And she saw its poster or magazine value to Keith. Also Miss Editha Lauteret might well have stepped bodily from the blurred galley-sheets of one of the infrequent stories which Minot had just been commissioned to illustrate. The girl was the exact type called for by the author. Only that day Keith had bemoaned the difficulty of transposing placid Ruth into the willowy siren he was seeking to draw.

Wherefore Ruth invited Editha to come in and to wait for Keith's return from his round of the offices. The model obeyed. She was meek, almost deprecating, in her bearing toward the wife. She accepted a cup of tea with the air of a stage villager at the gallant young squire's lawn party.

Presently Keith Minot came home—tired, blue, despairful, his portfolio as plump as when he had set out. He lounged into the studio, dropped the shabby portfolio in a chair, tried to smile reassuringly at Ruth as she came to greet him—then stopped short, staring in open wonder at the model who stood in a swirl of sunlight in the center of the bare room.

Ten minutes later he was at work sketching her head. Four days later he sold the sketch as a cover design for $225—his record price.

DURING the next three months Keith made more money than during the past two years. His work on the story, for the pictures of which Editha posed, so pleased the editor as to elicit two more orders. Another magazine-cover and two posters (both with a flame-haired, transparent-skinned girl of pre-Rafaelite contour—or lack of contour—as their central figure) were sold as readily; and they brought fresh openings.

Trouble was beginning operations by paying big dividends to the Minot family.

And more dividends came as byproducts of Editha's daily presence in the studio. During rests and at lunch, now that her first diffidence had worn off, she was forever chattering. And Keith coined her chatter into minted gold. For, finding he dabbled in story-writing, the model would devise, offhand, the quaintest plots imaginable, and retail them for his benefit. A full half-dozen of these, Keith worked into short stories, fantastically illustrated and couched in the odd diction that was the girl's mother tongue. He found quick market for them, all from editors who had curtly but very firmly rejected his own unaided efforts.

With growing wonder and with still faster growing delight, he sketched and listened to the flame-haired girl. With a dull ache that slowly crept into her heart and which she strove in vain to banish, Ruth Minot watched the change that came over her husband and her home.

She was helpless. She told herself she was disloyal and that she ought to rejoice in Keith's new prosperity. But ever between her and happiness rose the girl with the dead-white face, the fire-hair, the gutter-cleverness and uncanny imagination.

Ruth thrust behind her the jealousy for which she loathed herself. She resolved not to sulk or to show Keith she was unhappy, but to try to win her own battle. She had read of women doing that. It was a feat for which she found herself oddly ill prepared. For a heaviness and an almost unconquerable lassitude had of late come over her. Clear thinking had grown to be an effort. Yet gallantly she set herself to the ordeal.

The first blow of the conflict was struck one morning as Editha, swathed in a dark blue robe, sat on the rickety throne, her glowing hair smoothly parted and lying in long braids at either side of her little head. Keith, in his shirt-sleeves, a cigarette in one corner of his mouth, was busily marking a two-by-three canvas with sure charcoal strokes. Ruth had just come in from an hour's splashy labor in the kitchenette, and paused behind him.

"What is it going to be, dear?" she asked.

Keith frowned, unconsciously, at the interruption. But he forced his knit eyebrows to unwrinkle again as he made answer, pleasantly enough:

"I'm starting in on it at last. The fit is on me. We've got money enough ahead. And I can afford to."

"Starting in on what?"

"My Madonna."

RUTH said nothing, but the girl on the throne saw her dull-hued face grow a shade more leaden in color and the soft lips tighten. For two years—ever since his marriage—Keith had dreamed aloud of the Madonna that was to be his life-work—the work he was to begin as soon as he could afford to toil for fame instead of for chuck-steak and potatoes. Not a sketch, this, but a fulfilled vision in oils—something that was to show the whole world what an American painter could achieve.

"But—but Keith," presently ventured Ruth. "You—I thought—we always said, you know—that I was to be your model for the Madonna.

Don't you remember?"

Keith Minot laid down his charcoal for an instant and glanced from his tired-faced wife to the radiant occupant of the throne.

"I know," he said guiltily; "I haven't forgotten. But I may not have time again, little girl, for a long while, to start my Madonna. And you've had so little exercise lately, and you've kept so close to the house, that all your color is gone, and even the light seems to have seeped out of your eyes. I can't paint you as a Madonna until you get in better health. Why don't you take long walks in the Park, or 'bus rides up the Drive, or do something else that will keep you more in the open air—so you'll get back some of your old-time color and liveliness? To-day, for instance—it's such a fine, bracing morning. Why not go for a good brisk tramp around the Reservoir? It'll start the blood back in your cheeks."

"I'd rather not, if you don't mind," she said, dully. "I don't feel like it. I'll stay here—if I'm not in your way."

"Why, of course you're not," he said, with quick—far too quick—reassurance. "What a silly idea!"

Ruth gathered up her sewing and settled herself in a chair near the door. For the moment her eyes were too misted to see the stitches. She winked back the tears; and she welcomed a battle-rage that awoke in her heart.

THIS flaring-haired, transparent-skinned model, with the thin snake-body and the daily bolder little eyes and tip-tilted nose, was no Madonna. And so Keith would discover as soon as his picture should begin to take shape. Faustine, perhaps — even Laïs — but never, *never* the Mother of God! He would learn that for himself before the painting was half done. Then would come Ruth's own turn. Meanwhile—

"Say, Keith!" hailed Editha, who had taken advantage of the interruption to stand up and stretch herself after the manner of a waking panther. "How would this go for a story? Girl comes to New York to conquer the good old town and catch an easy millionaire or two and wear ropes of pearls—real pearls. Tries the Great White Way, gets crazy about the life and all, but can't make enough out of it to support her bedridden old mother and has to start a respectable dressmaking shop to earn a living—has to turn good or starve, and it breaks her heart. How about it? With vignettes of—"

Keith's loud laugh broke in on the recital.

"Great!" he roared. "Corking! The *Fifth Avenue Magazine's* editor will eat it alive. It's just the cynical, sane, anti-drivel stuff he loves. Editha, you're an inspiration! That's what you are! A veritable inspiration. I'll get at the story this evening, as soon as the light goes bad. About twenty-five hundred words, hey?"

Chuckling delightedly, he picked up the charcoal again, and Editha fell back into her pose. Ruth, forcing herself into the firing-line, spoke up, her voice a shade high and shrill from the stir of battle.

"Keith," she said, *"I've* been thinking up plots for you too—in the night, sometimes, when the noise of the 'L' won't let me get to sleep. I have one or two beautiful ideas. For instance—"

She checked herself, fancying she heard a smothered snicker from the direction of the model-throne. Then she felt she must have been mistaken, and bravely went on:

"Here's one of them: A man and a girl meet at the same seaside hotel. He hates women and she hates men. They tell each other so. And they agree to have a flirtation with each other because it will be so perfectly safe for them both. And then, at the end of the summer, when they come to say good-by, they find they're really in love."

Again there was a stifled sound from the throne. Keith cleared his throat and said very kindly:

"Yes, dear. That would be very nice. Perhaps, some time, I could write it."

"I was sure you could!" cried Ruth, in her triumph failing wholly to note his stark dearth of enthusiasm. "And you could get such pretty moonlight-and-sea effects into the pictures. But I have two more ideas every bit as good."

"Really?" asked Editha, with ponderous solemnity. "What on earth could be as good as the one about the man and girl at the seaside?"

KEITH frowned. But satire was ever lost on Ruth; and she hurried on:

"I got this second idea from something one of those newspaper men we met at Guffanti's told me. But I've twisted it around into an original form. The scene is in a newspaper office, and a murder has just been committed and everyone is terribly excited. And the star reporter tries to find out who committed the murder, and he can't. And no one else can. Then a new reporter, they call them 'Cubs,' Mr. Chalmers says,—a new reporter that everyone looks down on, discovers a clue; and he brings the murderer to justice and gets a 'beat' for his paper. You know, a 'beat' is—"

"Yes," said Keith absently, as he sketched in a difficult bit of detail, "I know. That's—that's a good idea for a story. Thanks."

"And," she went on, "here's the third one: This one can be funny and have clever dialogue in it. A man and a girl meet on a train, and she has lost her ticket and he pays her fare, and they get acquainted, and they fall in love with each other. And when they get to the end of the journey, they find they're both going to the very same house-party and that he is her brother's college chum."

"Lord!" groaned Keith.

"What's the matter? Don't—don't you like it?" she asked in sudden chagrin.

"Why, yes. Of course. Yes, of course I do. I was swearing over the way this detail dodges me. It's a great story, Ruth. Thanks. I'll—"

He slammed the charcoal down on the hardwood floor, where it broke and scattered into a dozen black smudges.

"Rest!" he ordered Editha. "My nerves have gone bad, and every line I draw is worse than the one before it. Yet fifteen minutes ago I had the whole thing in my mind and at my fingers' ends. I'm going out to do a mile or so in five-an-hour time and see if I can jog my brain into shape again."

"Would you like me to come along?" asked his wife.

"Not this time," he said. "You couldn't keep up with me."

HE snatched his hat from the table and swung out of the room. Ruth, too accustomed to his vagaries to be ruffled, picked up her sewing once more.

A pleased little smile played about her colorless lips. She felt she had scored a point. Editha had given Keith the plot for one story,—a very improper and pointless story, it seemed to Ruth, while *she* had supplied him with three really clever ideas—in a row.

The knowledge did much to soften the blow of his change of

models for the Madonna. And now, while she was still in the vein, she must try to think up more plots—if possible, just as good, or almost as good, as those she had just told him.

He fell to pummeling her tired brain, and began tediously to evolve an up-to-date story of the European war.

Editha Lauteret, meantime, had left the throne, exhumed a cigarette from somewhere beneath her blue draperies, lighted it and curled herself on the couch in the corner. Blowing smoke in two tiny columns from her nostrils, she was surveying the wife between speculatively half-shut eyelids.

A cool and softly insolent voice broke in on the wife's inspiration.

"Mrs. Minot," Editha was saying, "I hate to seem unkind, and I don't want to start anything, but honest, it's time you and me had a little talk."

"Yes?" queried Ruth abstractedly, her mind dragging itself back to the woman who lounged so lazily and so confidently in front of her.

"When I came here, back in March," went on Editha, "Keith was on his last legs. He was making just about enough to starve on. Now he's pulling down something like four hundred dollars a month."

"He has been very fortunate these past few months," agreed Ruth, who found it vaguely distasteful to discuss her husband with his model. "But you are mistaken in saying he was starving when you first came here. We were making nearly one hundred dollars a month then—almost every month. There was a time, before that, of course, when he—"

"When he was eating snow," finished Editha. "I know. And he was lucky it was winter time when there was plenty of good, nourishing snow to eat. But that isn't what I'm getting at. Here's the point: Keith is clearing up pretty near five times as much as he was a few months back. And he's due to double that inside of a year—what with his drawing and the color work and his side-line of story-writing. He's a comer."

"HE is very fortunate," repeated Ruth placidly. "He has fought the great city. And he has won."

"Yes," said Editha, her smooth voice grating ever so slightly, "he's won. He's got his start. He's got one hand through the crack in the door. He'll always make some kind of a decent living now if he keeps plugging away. But are you content to have him just make a decent living?"

"What do you mean?" asked Ruth, disturbed at the girl's tone.

"You've said he's 'fortunate.' You've said it twice. You've said he was bound to succeed. Well, who made him 'fortunate?' Who made him succeed? Tell me that?"

"Why," said Ruth, shyly, "he's—he's always said I was his 'inspiration.' Ever since we were engaged, he's said it—till to-day. But I thought that was just because he loved me. I didn't suppose *you* had noticed—"

"Noticed?" flared the girl, stung to gutter-wrath. "Noticed *what?* That you are hanging to his neck like a bag of wet dough, weighting him down and tiring him out and tangling up his feet? Sure I've noticed it. I'm not wall-eyed. I've noticed that he was half starved and stumbling along at day-labor pay so long as *you* were his 'inspiration,' as you call it. I noticed, too, that from the minute *I* came here he's been like another man. Inspiration, huh? Maybe it was you who were the 'inspiration' that got him two hundred and twenty-five dollars for a cover design? Maybe it was *you* who gave him the ideas for those hot little stories the *Fifth Avenue Magazine's* editor is so daffy over? Maybe it's you who are going to 'inspire' that Madonna of his to make New York sit up on its hind legs and gawp? Maybe—"

"What are you saying?" babbled Ruth, aghast. "What do you mean? I—"

"That's just it," stormed the model. "You never do understand. You kept him broke and kept him a sixth-rater from the day you put your brand on him. 'Inspiration?' You're the kind of 'inspiration' that's made of lead and putty. Why, you can't even see how you're holding him back. Take to-day, f'r instance. Why d'you suppose he bolted out of here just now, when ten minutes earlier he was all on fire to get to work on his big picture? It was because you drove him dippy with that fool jabber of yours about plots for stories. Plots! Why, the only one of 'em that didn't have snow-colored whiskers on it was too silly to use in a bughouse literary monthly. That's how *you* help him. You queer his ideas and pour dishwater all over his enthusiasm; and you'll end up by making him a screeching idiot. No man—nor horse, neither— can carry more than just so much weight without crumpling up. And every ounce of *you* is overweight for Keith Minot."

RUTH had gotten to her feet. Flinching as from fist-blows, she cowered away from the pelting blast of the girl's furious tirade. In all her gentle life no one had spoken roughly to her. She had never imagined such invective as this. And it stupefied her, benumbing every faculty. Her newly apathetic brain and body could not be brought to cope with the amazing attack.

She tried to speak. But she could not think what to say. And her throat, besides, was suddenly constricted past all utterance. She blinked dumbly, hopelessly, feeling as if she were in a nightmare. And the model raged on:

"I didn't mean to put it as raw as all this. But it had to be said. And something more's got to be said, too: You claim to love Keith Minot a lot. Well, do you love him enough to let him go? To let him wiggle out from under the dead weight and climb up to where he belongs? Do you? Are you going to keep him down, or are you going to let him take the good luck that's waiting for him? I've done more for Keith in three months than ever you did in all your life. And it isn't a patch on what I *can* do. I wasn't much of a success till I tied up with him. And he wasn't any kind of a success at all till he tied up with *me.* But together we're a team that'll travel the whole distance. Are you going to lie in front of us to trip us up, or are you going to be a good sport and roll to one side? One thing more: I—I care for him. And he's the first man. You can believe that or you needn't. And he cares for me, too."

"He—he doesn't!" croaked poor Ruth, her throat sanded with horror.

"He does. Oh, he hasn't said so. Maybe he doesn't even know it yet. But *I* know it. I can see how his face gets bright and interested when I come here. I can see the keen way he listens to everything I say, and then the kind-father way he listens to *your* blitherings. I inspire him. He knows I do. He says so. You heard him, to-day. Well—what are you going to do?"

"I love him," faltered Ruth, her brain awhirl and refusing to think clearly, clinging to her life's one supreme Fact.

"I suppose you do. But does that mean you love him enough to let him go free, or only enough to keep strangling him with your weight around his neck?"

"I—he loves me. He loves me dearly. *I* know that, even if you don't. He's told me so a million times. I—oh, I didn't think God ever made anyone so horrible as you are! I can't answer you. I don't know what to say to you at all. I ought to tell you to go away. I ought to tell Keith about it. I—"

"Rot!"

"He has always loved me. If he hadn't, he wouldn't have married me. He wouldn't come to me with all his troubles and his happiness the way he's always done. Even if I can't pose for his Madonna and give him the plots of nasty stories for a nasty magazine—"

"Are you going to be square enough to let him go, or aren't you?"

"No!" declared Ruth in a spasm of almost hysterical excitement. "I'm not. Never, never, *never!*"

"Because you love him so!" sneered Editha. "Because you'd rather have him starve with you than get famous with another woman! Wonderful love!"

"No—not because I love him, but because he loves me!"

"Loves *you*. The way a man, maybe, would think he loved a dog that's too old to be any more use, or an old coat he's gotten used to, or—"

"No!" cried Ruth, erect and for the first time looking into the model's blazing little eyes. "Not in any of those ways, but as a man loves a woman who is going to be his son's mother!"

EDITHA took an involuntary step backward. The glare ebbed out of her eyes. Her dead white face lost some of its rage-distortion.

"That's it, eh?" she mumbled.

"Yes! Are you content? Are you answered now?"

"Answered? No!" returned the girl, rallying to the assault. "It only means he has one more overweight to drag along. No wonder he's so cranky sometimes—looking forward, like that, to—"

"He's not 'looking forward.' He doesn't know. We've wanted it so much—we've prayed for it every day of our lives! And I didn't want to take his mind off his work, just as he is beginning to win, by telling him yet. I didn't dare interrupt his progress with such happiness till his success should be a little more assured. It would be a joy that might set him to dreaming instead of slaving. *That* is how he loves me. And that is how he loves—our son! Have you any cheap fame to offset what I am blithely risking my life to offer? If not—"

The studio door opened. Keith Minot came in, laughing and excited.

"I have the idea, Editha!" he exclaimed, beginning to speak before he had crossed the threshold. "I have it! It came to me all in a flash just now. We won't pose you for the Madonna at all. I've got something worth fifty of that. Listen: A half-length of you, with your gorgeous hair unbound and a flood of white sunlight beating down on it. Light from above, you see. And your face upraised and your hair swirling all around it and about your bare shoulders and catching the full glare of the sunlight on it. Get the notion? I'm going to call it 'Radiance!' We'll start right away. Put on a—"

He checked himself, noting the model's strained attitude.

"What's up?" he demanded. "Feeling ill or anything?"

His eye traveled to Ruth, standing in the very focus of the merciless north light. Her face was strangely flushed, and something glowed behind her dark eyes, something that seemed to transfigure her. Her hands were clasped across her breast, whether in appeal or in exaltation. Her mystic gaze—unfathomable with the Secret of the Ages—was fixed upon him—not upon his eyes, but upon the soul of him.

FOR a long minute he stood there, held by the unearthly glow that seemed to come from within her, glorifying her eyes and illuming the cheeks that had been so pale. The slumping, leaden-complexioned housewife of an hour agone had vanished. In her place stood a woman whom Keith did not know. His whole artist nature was astir.

"The Madonna!" he murmured, half aloud. "The *Madonna!*"

"Yes," scoffed Editha, making a plucky fight, yet her courage ebbing as she saw the glint of reverence that crept into his gaze. "It's the Madonna, all right—and everything that generally goes with the picture."

"Ruth?" whispered the man, scarce daring to trust his own voice.

He held out his arms, as to a saint. And slowly, very slowly, the Vision moved into their trembling circle.

Editha Lauteret looked for a moment at the two who were so

divinely unconscious of her presence. Then she spat the cigarette from between her lips, kicked aside the blue robe, jammed her hat down on her flaming hair and viciously drove its pins into place.

Neither husband nor wife heard her go, though she went with head high and heels clicking. She was a game little loser, this meteor child of the gutter and the studios.

THE Academy picture that laid the foundation-stone for Keith Minot's fame was not called "The Madonna," after all. He named it "The Greater Radiance"—to humor his pretty wife's whim, one of the papers said.

From the "Tip" of the Rocket

"I'M GLAD you're as cross as you know how to be," observed Maia.

Perhaps the man did not hear. Certainly he did not heed. He sat looking blankly to westward, over the roofs of the city.

"Because," explained Maia brilliantly, "then you can't be any crosser than you are."

Even this perfect feminine logic did not shake the man into a reply. Maia Garth tried to crush him with a single look, but her glare was wasted. He did not see. He did not see anything but the line of black Palisades to the westward—black against an only less black sky.

Maia poked daintily with a waxed-paper straw at a fugitive cherry that lurked elusive amid the ice fields at the bottom of her long glass. Then she looked—despairingly, this time—at the man; and, noting his fixity of look, let her own gaze follow his.

Out over the heat-baked roofs, dull and misty, broken by rect-angles of smoky, furnace-like glare from the intersecting streets she gazed; then over the dimmer void that was the North River, to the inky wall of rock, its crest picked out here and there with diamond points of blue-white electric lights, that stood out so primly against the starless sky behind.

The spectacle did not inspire Maia. Indeed, it vaguely depressed her. And, coupled with her escort's fixed abstraction, it tended to bring on a fit of blues.

To shake off the cloud, she turned eastward and leaned over so that she could see above the parapet of the roof-garden into whose far corner their table was wedged. Here, forsooth, was a spectacle of life to drive away the most persistent blues from any one who dwelt upon the outer crust of his own soul.

Below snapped and sparked joy! Real, hand-made joy. A form of joy that it took an aged and otherwise sane Dutch city three centuries to evolve.

The hot night air was vibrant with light and sound. A swirl of color blended and tinged the sky, from the hundred different hues cast by Gargantuan electric signs—signs that seemed to hang unstained in midair, in the dark murk of the Summer evening.

And in this white street itself and in its cross currents loafed and panted and sweltered the pleasure chasers, for few are adrift on Broadway at nine o'clock of an August night for anything but amusement—amusement that is fresh and optimistic; amusement that has grown stale unto boredom; noisy or apathetic or shop-worn amusement. Yet the lights, the crowds, the racket, all merged into one rather stirring note by the time they reached the altitude of roof-garden parapet.

At any rate, Maia found it a vast improvement on watching a glum-faced man eying a glum-faced line of Palisades. And thus cheered, she tried to galvanize Moylan Kiel back to life again.

"I can't just now think," she mused aloud, "of a jollier way to spend an hour in Summer than in the corner of a roof-garden, looking from a seltzer-lemonade glass that is empty to a man whose expression makes the glass seem brim full by contrast."

"H'm!" murmured Kiel abstractedly.

"Perhaps so," she agreed meekly. "That's one way of looking at it, of course. Moylan, are you thinking of staying cranky much longer? I only ask because the Fraynes are over there at the fourth table. And if you could set a time limit on your sulkiness, I could go across and sit with them till then. Or—"

Kiel came out of his abstraction with a start. Some of her words, or else a sudden realizing of her displeasure and of his own remissness, seemed to revive him.

"That is Grantwood over there," he announced, with a general gesture toward the Palisade crest. "Somewhere along there; just a little to the north, I think."

"Wonderful!" she sighed in stark rapture. "This is worth sitting up for! Grantwood! Oh, *think* of it! I'll just step over and tell the Fraynes. They'd love to know."

Kiel shifted his eyes from the west and looked doubtfully at her. He had not clearly understood. Her effort at irony had quite escaped him. Now he tried to rally his flagging attention.

"I—I beg your pardon," he faltered confusedly, "I—"

"It's about time," she announced, sarcasm shifting in a breath to indignation, as she caught the note of semi-penitence. "When you asked me to come here with you this evening, I was foolish enough to be a little glad. Then you brought me to this hole-in-a-corner table. And since you ordered I don't think you've spoken twenty words."

"I'm sorry. You see—"

"I don't see. If you wanted to get on a housetop and glower in dead silence at New Jersey, why did you bring me along to watch you do it? There are more exciting ways for a girl to spend the evening. Moylan!" she broke off sharply; for his troubled eyes had left her face and were once more fixed broodingly on the Palisades.

This time her exclamation brought him permanently to himself.

"I'm sorry," he said again simply. "I really am. It was rotten of me. Will—will you let me tell you about it? I didn't want to—yet. I wanted it for a surprise. That's why I asked you to come here. But if it was going to happen, it would have happened by now, I think. It's quarter past nine. And nine was the time he said—"

"If you'll put it into English," she interposed with labored patience, "perhaps I can understand part of it. Start at the subject before last. What about Grantwood? And then, passing lightly to the next cage, who is 'he'?"

"Grantwood," said Kiel, "is one of the dozen or so suburbs that fringe the top of the Palisades. Judge Gregg lives there."

"And it's out of friendship for your old chief that you stare at the Palisades he lives on? Loyal friend!"

"No," returned Kiel. "It's to see what he means to do."

"Oh," exclaimed Maia. "Certainly! If only you had a night glass and watched long enough you might even see him wind the clock and put out the cat."

"No," he corrected, "I might see him make my career, or set me adrift."

SHE looked at him keenly, and at the stolid earnestness in his face, her own lost its banter and annoyance. Leaning forward, she touched ever so lightly the tanned fists clenched together on the table top.

"Tell me," she said softly.

"They want him to go back to Damascus," answered Kiel. "You know how popular he was with the natives and the Turkish Government while we were there, he and I. I was only a kid at the time—the youngest vice-consul in the East, they said. But I was old enough to appreciate all that Judge Gregg was doing for Uncle Sam over there, and how he stood head and shoulders above the rest of the diplomatic bunch."

"You've told me. But I thought he came back to his law practise here because be was sick and tired of the East. Why should he go again?"

" 'Once you've 'eard the East a-callin', " chanted Kiel, villainously off key, " 'you won't 'eed nothin' else.' "

"But—"

"The Government wants him to go back. The Syrians in New York have heard about it, and they heard he was undecided. So they went over there tonight—a big delegation of them—to wait on him; to make orations and pleas and other Oriental arguments to urge him to accept."

"But you don't think he will, do you?" asked Maia in real concern. "Why, Moylan, if he does, what will become of the plan to take you into partnership? You've built so on that plan, and—"

"I've built on it," he returned grimly, "a lot more than you can realize. Perhaps a lot more than you can care. As one of the hungry army of young lawyers in this overlawyered city I'm barely able to keep my head above water. Another ounce of weight would sink me. And—and I've been longing lately to take on a good deal more than an extra ounce. It's meant everything to me. I hadn't any right to say so. I haven't, yet, till I'm perfectly certain the Judge won't accept."

His tone sent a faint red to her throat and forehead, and her breath came a little faster. But, as he paused, she did not reply.

"The Judge solved it all when he offered me the partnership the other day," went on Kiel. "As his partner my future was assured. He made the offer conditional on his refusing the Damascus job; but I gathered that he didn't mean to take it. It's always hard to tell just what good old Gregg will do. His training in law, and in diplomacy too, has made him pretty secretive. If he takes me into partnership I'm made. If he goes to Syria I'm going, too."

"No!"

The negation broke involuntarily through Maia Garth's paling lips; and at the word a light crept into the man's eyes.

"I hope I won't have to," said he. "I'm not going as his vice-consul, as I went before. There's no future in that. I'm going to make money. I know how it can be done over there—in a hurry, too. A single stake. And the winning end of that stake is fortune. A chap tried it while I was at Damascus."

"And he won the fortune."

"No," hesitated Kiel. "He blundered. And he won—the other thing. But I sha'n't. I figured out the whole business, long ago, just as a matter of curiosity. And I hit on a way to do it in safety, perfect safety."

"What do you mean?"

"I'm sick of plodding along on nothing a week and of working ten hours a day to get it. I manage to get bread, a roof and cheap clothes. That is all. If this partnership scheme falls through, I mean to win enough at a single throw to put me on 'Easy Street'—enough to give me the one thing in life I want."

"But what is this 'single throw'? What is the venture that you say is safe for you, but that seems to have cost some one else his life?"

She spoke with growing uneasiness. For the first time he withdrew his gaze wholly from the dark west and looked steadily at her.

"The *Shem-es-Nabi*," he made answer, half whispering the words.

"If you are beginning to talk Arabic again," she said vexedly, "just stop to remember that all of us haven't had your advantage of being the son of a missionary and of spending our childhood in Syria. A few of us are more at home with our own language."

"The '*Shem-es-Nabi*' " he explained, too eager to be rebuffed by the interruption, "is literally, 'The Sun of the Prophet.' It was Mohammed's signet-ring."

"Oh!"

"It was the ring that Mohammed took from the dead hand of the Negus of Abyssinia, who was slain in battle by the Moslem hordes, back in the seventh century. It was supposed to be a talisman of vast power. The Negus had looted it from a Parsee shrine. On the jade stone of the ring is carved a rising sun. And there are hieroglyphs under it."

"What about it?"

"It is one of the 'Six Treasures of the Moslem Faith.' The Islamites look on it with a veneration that couldn't make you understand. It is kept under guard at the *Serail* in Damascus, and it is on view only three times a year. It will next be shown four weeks from today. And if Judge Gregg upsets my hopes by going to the East again, I'm going to take it, that day."

"Are you crazy?"

"Not yet."

"But how—"

"A silver-gilt reproduction of the *Shem-es-Nabi* was made by the Sultan's orders, years ago, and given to Judge Gregg as a special mark of honor. Only a fair copy, but good enough to deceive a casual onlooker—especially in the dim light of the *Serail*. The Judge gave it to me as a memento when we left Damascus. I have it at home. It would be easy for a man who was quick with his hands to substitute it for the real treasure and to get out of the city before the exchange could be found out."

"The exchange? The theft, you mean! If I didn't know you were joking—"

"How would it be theft? Whose ring is it? Mohammed stole it from the dead Negus and the Negus first stole it from a Parsee temple, to which it had probably been brought as a votive offering by the general or the sheik who stole it from its original sun-worshiping owner. One can't well steal what is already stolen and whose rightful ownership was buried in obscurity nearly a thousand years ago. The ring is as much mine, or yours, or anybody's, as it is the Turkish Government's."

"That's sophistry."

"That's sense. But we don't need to argue it. For I'm perfectly sure now that there'll be no need to go for it. But if there were—well, the Sultan's people would pay enough for the ring's return to keep me comfortable forever. And then a while longer."

"You'd probably be caught."

"No, I know the country too well. I'd have framed up my line of escape. And when I got back here I'd treat with Turkey at long range."

"It's horrible! And however much you gloss it over it *wouldn't* be honest. I'm glad you don't have to do it. But why do you say there'll be no need to go? A few minutes ago you were afraid Judge Gregg might—"

"The delegation must have finished its addresses and its pleas half an hour ago. And he has refused."

"What makes you think so?"

"I know the Syrian customs. And I know from Krikorian, their chairman, that they've brought along the usual big box of fireworks. If the Judge's answer were 'yes,' then—a hundred dollars' worth of fireworks in ten minutes; and three hours' lawn-cleaning for the Judge's gardener tomorrow morning. That's why I watched the Palisades so closely, till long after nine o'clock."

"Oh, I see! And I thought you were sulking. I'm sorry I—"

"Sulking? Worse than that. It meant everything to me; the loss of everything I'd been longing for; the need to go out to Damascus on my great venture. Do you wonder I couldn't see or hear anything else, till the danger grew less?"

"But why didn't you tell me beforehand? Then we could have watched together."

"Because I was afraid to. Because I was afraid I wouldn't be able to tell you without telling you something else—something I'm going to tell you, whether you want to hear it or not, the moment I'm certain there's no chance of his accepting. Do you mind if I leave you for a minute? Its a certainty by this time that he's refused. But I want to call him up and clinch it. Till then I've no right to say—"

A LITTLE gasp from the girl broke in on his speech. Her face had whitened and her eyes all at once had grown larger.

Moylan Kiel saw that she had shifted in her chair and was staring westward. He whirled back to his neglected post of vigil in time to see a red rocket burst high in air above the Palisades, just to the north, showering the black night with sparks and jets of falling scarlet flame.

Man and girl looked at each other in tense silence for a full minute; while a second rocket, then a third and a fourth, cut huge hairy arcs in the dull Jersey sky and strewed the lower air with their varicolored stars.

Then Moylan Kiel rose just a little unsteadily to his feet and held out his hand.

"Do you mind," he asked quietly, "if we go home now? There's a French liner sailing at dawn. And I've a bit of packing to do."

"A French liner?" she echoed vaguely.

"To Havre," he explained, as if laying out a tour for some one in whom he felt no interest. "Then across by land to Marseilles. I'll just catch a messagerie boat, there for Port Said. Three days at most from there to Damascus. Perhaps two, if I can make the right—"

"Damascus! Moylan, you're *not*—"

"Please don't," he begged her very gently. "Shall we go now?"

Dumb from plenitude of speech rather than from its dearth, she followed him to the elevator. A backward glance showed her the western skyline, at one point, fairly snapping with fireworks that danced and whizzed and sputtered, and otherwise profaned the solemn night of Summer.

She said no word, nor did Kiel, as they chugged uptown in a wheezing taxicab through the sick heat and smells of the streets. But, the door of the Garth apartment reached, and the motor-brigand dismissed, Maia spoke her mind. She spoke it briefly and in a low tone, but very much to the point.

She told the sullenly listening Kiel just what a criminally reckless and recklessly criminal exploit he was planning. She proved clearly that no man in his senses would set forth on such an errand, and that no one who was not at heart dishonest could so much as give the scheme a second thought.

She said he would break her heart with worry. Also that she should not give him a second thought nor would she care what might befall so evil a man. She told him that the taking of the *Shem-es-Nabi* would be wicked theft that no wretched legal sophistry could condone, and that a man who could do such a thing and make any girl so miserably unhappy by going into danger was not worthy her bothering over.

She did not play the virago, nor did she cry. She was a brave little girl. Her voice shook, it is true, and she spoke very fast— in fact, some of her words and even sentences had to be guessed, and Moylan guessed them with fearful correctness.

One thing, however, she did not leave to his imagination nor to the chances of guesswork. At the end of her little speech, and when a bad cold began to impede her diction, she said slowly and distinctly that if Kiel should persist in his wildly sinful intent he need never, *never* come to see her—or try to communicate with her upon his return. The acquaintance would end, here and *now*.

To which he retorted that if he did not go the acquaintance must end anyhow, since he had reached the point where it could no longer be mere acquaintance, and as finances would never, under present conditions, reach the stage where it could be anything stronger.

With which grumbled morsel of repartee he kissed her, before she could prevent him, and then strode tragically and rapidly away before she could rebuke him—a double unfairness that was perhaps the cause of her sleepless and somewhat lacrimose night.

At daybreak Maia called up Kiel's rooms. She had framed a new and absolutely irrefutable set of arguments against his going to Syria, but she had no chance to deliver them. For, after a century's wait, Central reported with blithe optimism—

"909090 Gram'cy don't seem to answer."

Then Maia called up Judge Gregg, whom she had never met.

The telephone toll from New York to Grantwood-on-the-Palisades is ten cents for five minutes. Maia's total bill was ninety cents. And at that she continued the talk, an hour later, in the Judge's Nassau Street office. And many times thereafter.

II

"LA ILLAHA ILLA 'LLAH!" smugly intoned an Imam, in pious and questioning salutation of the somewhat foreign-looking devotee in native garb who lounged past him out of the *Serail* at Damascus, just four weeks later.

And the man who the Imam had at first thought might be an outlander infidel utterly disarmed suspicion by whining unctuously in flawless Syrian Arabic—

"Sâïdna Ma'moud rasôul Allâh!"

With which speech Moylan Kiel slouched forth from the Government building with the *Shem-es-Nabi* safely reposing in the breast of his *abieh*.

He went at snail's pace until he rounded the corner. Then, tucking up his robe, he ran at top speed through twisty streets and foul alleyways until he reached the native house where he lodged.

Safe in his stone-floored room there, he drew forth the ring and laid it on a tabouret near the one small barred window. The light was better than in the *Serail* treasure room, but not brilliant. So far as Kiel could see by it, the *Shem-es-Nabi* was not greatly different, on close examination, from the imitation he had so deftly substituted for it.

The band of gold was old and badly worn, so badly that its row of hieroglyphs was well-nigh effaced. There was a crack across the jade stone, splitting transversely the rude carving of a rising sun.

From its general aspect, Kiel judged that an antiquary might have given ten dollars for the ring, as it stood. Scarcely more. Yet this was one of Islam's Six Treasures—the relic supposedly endowed with magic powers, which the Prophet himself had handed down as an all-prized heirloom to those of the Faith who should come after him. For more than twelve hundred years it had been guarded with adoring reverence, none of Islam's sons for a moment questioning its potency.

For a treasure so jealously watched over, its theft had been absurdly easy.

Kiel had reached Damascus but a day or two before the thrice-a-year exhibition of the Relics, at the *Serail*. There, vouched for by a local muezzin—whose total lack of previous acquaintance with the foreigner was easily bridged by a judicious use of *bakshish*—he had entered the treasure chamber with a line of devotees.

As he passed the guarded little shrine he had stumbled awkwardly over the hem of his robe, had lurched forward and had caught at the shrine to save himself from falling. Then as two soldiers and a priest had sprung at him he had recovered his balance, salaaming low. And as soon as possible he had withdrawn from the room and from the building, having neatly palmed the ring and left in its place the substitute presented to him by Judge Gregg.

Now that the first and worst peril was past, his wits rose to the next step. Within an hour or two the room at the *Serail* would be closed. The ring and the other treasures would be put back in their proper resting places. Then, infallibly, the guardian of the *Shem-es-Nabi* would discover the fraud, and the alarm would flash throughout all the Moslem world.

Fanatic zeal would wing the search, and that search would be of a sort not lightly eluded. Yes, and if it were not successfully eluded, there would be consequences that Moylan Kiel did not care to contemplate. There is no legal death penalty in Turkish dominions, but criminals sometimes disappear, and when they do they are seldom found again, even in sections.

Clearly, there was no time to be lost in getting out of the Ottoman Empire. The shortest way to the coast from Damascus is by way of Beirut. Next to that, a journey southward to Jerusalem and Jaffa, or a trip over the mountains westward to Tyre or Sidon, or some other coast town where ships touch.

Wherefore, as Kiel had already forecasted, every one of those ports would be watched with a vigilance that would make the all-seeing Eye of Mormonism seem strabismic. The customs folk, with an array of police-spy helpers, would infallibly search to the skin every departing native or tourist.

And Kiel had laid his plans accordingly. Having wasted a bare half minute in the inspection of his booty, he wrapped the ring in a dirty amulet case such as desert travelers wear, and strapped it firmly beneath the bend of his left knee. He covered this strap with a ragged cloth on which were traces of dried blood. It was a typical Syrian bandage—one that would have brought tears of horror to the eyes of a first-year medical student.

Then, arranging his small hoard of money in a turban and putting it on his head, he wrapped his other belongings in a big bundle, slung it over his shoulder and, with a serviceable old-fashioned army pistol stuck prominently in his belt, sallied forth.

Through an alley he wound his way. Thence to the bazaar section, with its rattan-woven roofs of brown, through which the East's yellow light filters coolly down upon the shop-lined byways. The bazaars were crowded, for the heat of the day was passing, and Kiel was forced to slacken his pace more than once as the foot-crowds were jostled aside to permit the passing of some laden camel or string of donkeys, or a rich man's horse.

The bazaars were left behind, after an interminable time, and he swung out into the clearer passage of "The Street That Is Called Straight"—the oldest street, with a name, on earth.

In time this merged into walled orchards and then into open spaces where scavenger dogs and black-winged gray crows squabbled over carrion.

A final turn brought Kiel into a field where a swarm of men were loafing idly about a dozen busy natives who were engaged in arranging loads upon the backs of as many kneeling camels.

This was Kiel's first stopping-place, and he drifted unobserved into the throng of onlookers.

"*Ohé!*" a gorilla-faced man in a once-white caftan and a green turban was squalling. "*Ohé,* Mulai, brother of ten thousand infidels! How can the leader camel move without a breaking back when you load her with three hundred pounds on the left side and with but two hundred on the right? Is her back as unbalanced as your swinish brain, O descendant of the donkey folk?"

He bustled off to where a mangy dun camel was kneeling, and to a fat giant near the beast's head he shouted furiously:

"*Imshi,* Child of Gehenna! Be off to the gutters where you belong. Where learned you to load a caravan camel? How think you the brute will rest at night when on neither side, as he kneels, the load touches the ground? Shall we be dragging after us a worn-out saddle-galled camel before the third day? Halil, show this fool of many thumbs how to adjust the load."

From camel to camel the caravan owner moved, now nodding with an approving grunt, now shrieking imprecations whose utterances seemed to threaten him with apoplexy. To his men—as to all Oriental porters—this tirade was a daily affair, and they took it with true Eastern apathy.

AS THE owner paused a moment on his tour, Kiel approached him.

"O Brother of Giants," said Moylan ceremoniously, "may you lie where rose leaves shall fall upon your tomb!"

"May you live to scatter them there!" surlily vouchsafed the owner.

Not that he had the remotest wish of the sort nor even a rudimentary desire to be civil. But the Oriental etiquette, which demands that a conversation open with a compliment, also demands that the initial compliment be capped by one more florid, and this foreign-looking stranger looked too prosperous for the caravan owner to kick.

"You start for Bagdad?" queried Kiel.

"Yes," returned the owner more interestedly. "Have you freight? My journey is thirty-five days, to the hour. I have one camel—by the grace of Allah and to your own blessed fortune—that is not laden. Five hundred pounds she can bear. And my price for safe delivery of her cargo will be but—"

"I have no freight."

The owner, in disgust, turned back to his work of supervision. He had no time and less inclination for answering idle queries.

"But I wish to go as a passenger," announced Kiel, loudly enough for all around him to hear, and speaking with a studied nervousness. "I am in haste to reach Bagdad. Can you let me ride with you and spare me food?"

"No!" snarled the owner.

"*Bismillah*," carelessly returned Moylan, and walked off.

The owner let him go a few steps. Then, finding he showed no sign of coming back, ran after him.

"One hundred *medjidie*," he said.

"Robbery!" wailed Kiel.

"The miles of the journey are long, O Effendi!" explained the native.

"But the feet of my brother's camels are swift as the wings of the day," replied Kiel, in true Eastern bargain tone, "and they are in grace like to the sacred beast that bore the Prophet—on whom be peace—from Medina. I am stricken and poor. I do not own a hundred *medjidie*."

"Eighty-nine," countered the camel-man, now in his element as a trafficker.

"*Inshallah!* Is my purse so red with gold? I am poor. What says the blest Koran? 'He that hearkeneth not unto the cry of the True Believer who is needy—' "

"Eighty," retorted the other.

"It is sheer theft!" moaned Kiel right loudly. "But my need is great. I accept!"

The camel-man had great ado to keep from bursting into tears. He had asked a hundred *medjidie* for a passage worth thirty. And he had hoped by judicious bargaining to get his customer to pay forty. Now, starting at a hundred, he had been taken up when he got to eighty. And he cursed his stars that he had not in the first place demanded from the spendthrift fool five hundred.

The listening crowd, too, murmured loudly in wonder at such a bargain. Tongues were certain to wag in the bazaars on the morrow anent the man whose need for instant departure from Damascus was so great that he paid almost treble the regulation passage money for the privilege.

"Eighty *medjidie*," the discomfited owner at last found breath to acknowledge, adding as a clever afterthought:

"Half in advance. The rest at the oasis of—"

A commotion from the rear of the crowd drew all eyes away from the chaffering. The hero of the place had just come into the Square of Caravans. He was a huge negro, clad in spotless white; a kinky beard and shaven upper lip distinguishing him from the other blacks scattered through the throng.

His reception by the idlers reminded Kiel strongly of the entrance of Escamillo, the Toreador, in "Carmen."

This black giant was a local hero, the demigod of loafers and camel-men alike. Even the arrogant little caravan owner deigned to smile pleasantly at him, for the newcomer was the great Ben Nassar

Raad, mail-carrier between Damascus and Bagdad. Where the ordinary plodding caravan took from five to six weeks to make the tedious journey across the Syrian Desert, Raad on his Bisharin racing camel covered the distance in ten brief days—a feat that called forth the wondering admiration of all Syria.

To him sand-storm, Bedouin raid, perils of thirst, of sickness, of sunstroke, were matters for easy scorn. Was he not the fearless Raad whom no less a personage than the Pasha himself was wont to salute in the bazaar?

Kiel grudgingly paid down his forty *medjidie* advance money to the caravan owner, finding and counting out each piece with a separate groan. As he finished the operation his glance momentarily crossed that of Raad—Raad whose pet he had been as a child, in the mission house at Nabous—Raad, with whom he had passed an important hour the previous day—Raad, who at this minute had in his money-belt three hundred *medjidie* which Kiel had turned over to him twenty-four hours earlier.

The negro's gaze traveled carelessly past Kiel, and the redoubtable mail-carrier continued on his way to the corner of the field where his two camels were cared for by a black attendant.

Between these two camels and those of the caravan there was as much difference as between a Percheron and a thoroughbred race horse. Gray-white in hue, they were clean of limb, graceful as fawns, unbelievably swift.

One was for Raad's use; the other was to traverse the desert journey, alongside, in case of accident or emergency. He rode each on alternate trips.

Both now were well rested from the last jaunt from Bagdad. Their spongy feet were free from abrasions. Their humps were high and pendulous. At a pinch, and if not meantime supplied with water, both were able to travel a hundred leagues, across desert sands, in five days.

But at the end of such a forced ride their humps would be little larger than a man's two fists, and they would be as savage as sick bears. And, after stopping for water, they would be loggy and slow for the next two days.

"The mail-carrier starts when we do?" Kiel asked the caravan owner.

"Not he!" sneered the latter. "He is too proud to start with common folk. And he starts after star-shine, that he may make his first twelve hours in the cool. Mount your camel, Effendi. We start. *Mleh!*"

His cry of "Mleh!" was taken up by his men. Kiel jumped to his kneeling mount. Grunting and bubbling, the twelve heavy-laden draft camels scrambled to their feet and, of their own accord, took their proper alignment for the march.

It was not Moylan Kiel's first, nor hundredth, experience in the unlovely art of camel riding. He understood the knack of getting into the divan-like, high-pommeled saddle and, once there, how to dispose of the painful excess of leg length that such a position always develops.

He did not even feel the almost universal qualm that assails amateur riders when a camel rises pitchingly to its feet and strikes its gait—a gait not unlike the motion on a ship deck in a choppy sea.

Off moved the twelve-beast caravan in triple alignment, four deep, sixty feet between ranks, out of the Square of the Caravans and outward toward the barely visible strip of sand that lay like a yellow sword-blade, a day's journey to the northeast. Kiel settled himself, as nearly comfortable as an outlander may, on his huge saddle. He caught the rough, sagging motion and swayed his body, native fash-ion, to it. He was the only rider. The natives at this early stage of the journey chose to plod afoot beside their ungainly charges. Later, when the desert sands should begin to burn the feet and the desert suns to play unholy tricks with the eyes, they would be clamoring for their turn to climb atop the more lightly burdened of the brutes.

The owner, first removing from his feet a pair of vehemently scarlet slippers and slinging them over his shoulder for safety, took his place at the head of the caravan. A tiny gray bell-donkey pattered sturdily at his side—the donkey that is the mascot, the real guide, the highly important leader of every Syrian caravan.

Camels may bolt, may sulk, may go *musth,* may exhibit in any fifty ways an artistic temperament that would make a prima donna seem stolid by comparison—indeed, they usually do. At such times all human power over them sinks into obscurity compared to the control exerted by that one sober little gray donkey. The tinkle of its bell is more potent than the frenzied howls of all the professional drivers in

Islamlik.

Kiel remembered, from his vice-consular days, the case of a quasi-humorous American who had been haled to the Damascus Serail, on the grave accusation of *lese-majeste,* for propounding to his Syrian dragoman the conundrum—

"Why is the Ottoman Empire like a string of camels?"

The answer, "Because it is led by a donkey," had been taken by the dragoman as of doubtful compliment to the Sultan. He had so reported it, and Judge Gregg had needed all the influence of the consulate to clear the ribald one.

Kiel, familiar with the surrounding country, knew to an inch where the caravan would rest for the night. He knew, too, that the present jolting would be of short duration, since, whether a caravan starts at dawn or at dusk, its first day's journey is precisely forty furlongs—no more nor less—and it has been so from the birth of history, for what cause no living man knows, any more than it is known why the universal speed of all camel caravans is gaged to the second at sixteen furlongs an hour.

Wherefore, by Kiel's calculations, the night's rest would occur a hundred yards beyond the Tomb of Assad, five miles from the Square of the Caravans, and the halt would be called in just two and one-half hours from the time of starting. It was to prevent a premature halt that the start had been delayed until after the late afternoon call to prayer.

The forecast was wholly correct, as forecasts involving Eastern customs—but not Eastern temperaments—are more than reasonably certain to be. Just beyond the tomb the camels were made to kneel, and there, still laden, they were left for the night, while fires were lighted and food prepared.

His labors and his vocal efforts momentarily ended, the caravan owner looked about for his passenger, with whom he had decided, during the five-mile walk, to have a most interesting and profitable conversation.

He was barely in time to see Kiel walking slowly away from the firelight radius out into the starry darkness, to southward, his bundle over his back. That a man should needlessly carry any burden was beyond the grasp of the owner's Oriental mind, and he inferred that Kiel, stretching his legs after the ride, had feared to leave his bundle behind lest it be looted.

The incident gave the Syrian a desirable peg whereon to hang his carefully prepared talk.

"*OHÉ*, Effendi!" he hailed Moylan.

The latter moved on without turning. The pursuer's short legs were put to their best to catch up the passenger two hundred yards away from camp.

"What does this mean?" raged the caravan owner, in a rage not wholly made to order, when at length he ranged alongside his quarry. "Why do you carry your luggage when you stray? My men are honest. I am their master—I, Imbarak the Honest."

"Well," laughed Kiel, glancing about him and then laying down his bundle in the narrow camel track that links Damascus with Bagdad, "what then, O Imbarak the Honest? May I not do as I will with mine own?"

"Your own?" scoffed Imbarak. "'Tis the catchword of every thief."

"Thief?"

"No man pays triple passage money unless he is in flight," summed up Imbarak; "no man guards a bundle unless it be precious. You are a thief. You have stolen that which is of value and puts the black fear into your heart. You are in flight."

"Well?" repeated Kiel amiably. "What then, my little man?"

The calmness of the accused rudely shook Imbarak's convictions that he was a thief. For do not thieves—Syrian thieves—on accusation, ever beat their breasts and cry aloud upon Allah to witness their innocence?

Yet of one thing Imbarak was right certain—Kiel must have had some powerful reason for leaving Damascus in haste, to have made him pay so exorbitant a price. And, whatever the reason might be, its very existence sufficed Imbarak the Honest.

"When I took you as my passenger," said he, "I consented to a low fare, since you besought me in the name of Allah the Merciful and because you vowed you were poor. You are not poor. And you are a thief. Therefore I will take you no step beyond this."

"No? Then I must walk back to Damascus to await the next caravan, and meantime to lay information before the Cadi against one Imbarak the Honest, who hath robbed me of forty *medjidie* in passage-money."

"You dare not go before the Cadi. For I, too, shall return, at your side, and I shall tell why I refuse to let you bring ill fortune to honest folk by remaining on the march with us. On suspicion you will be searched and—"

"Exactly. How much?"

Here was a man with a soul too gross for the bliss of bargaining, and with a sigh of joys foregone, Imbarak the Honest replied—

"Nine hundred *medjidie*."

"Oh, Offspring of the Gadarenes," observed Kiel, "if I possessed nine hundred *medjidie* I would not be traveling with outcasts upon lame and mange-stricken camels, owned by a pickpocket of the bazaars."

To be termed a pickpocket and to hear his men referred to as outcasts was a mere every-day pleasantry that ruffled Imbarak the Honest not at all, but a slur on one's camels is as mortal an insult as is an affront to one's religion. And at the expressions "lame and mange-stricken" Imbarak figuratively and literally soared high in air, and he came down bodily upon Kiel, ugly curved belt-knife in fist.

Kiel took the assault as philosophically as a move in a chess-game. It was, in fact, a move he himself had prepared, and he was quite ready for it.

Imbarak struck downward—a move in Syrian knife-fighting that means merely a wound or a scratch, as differentiated from the gruesome up-thrust and its subsequent wrench of the crooked blade.

Kiel neatly blocked the blow with his bundle—which received thereby a mortal wound in its vitals—and with his right fist caught the Honest Imbarak flush on the left point of the chin.

The caravan man was transformed into a limp huddle of twitching clothes.

"He ought to be good for at least five minutes," mused Kiel, as he hurried cityward along the camel track, "unless I've forgotten how to put steam into a right lead."

A hundred yards farther on he stopped, as a soft quadruple *pad-pad-pad* of spongy feet broke on his ear. Two camels, huge in the gloom, rose ever larger, in his path.

"Raad!" called Moylan softly.

"It was well played, Howaji!" laughed the negro as he made the led camel kneel to receive its new burden. "Yet it is worth my commission if it be found out. Here are the swathing-cloths. Wrap them as I taught you, else you will be shaken to a jelly before the ten days be past. Now, mount and ride. We can reach Bagdad and you can leave it, full ten days ahead of the hue and cry."

III

MAIA GARTH had made it clear—very painfully clear—that Kiel's venture in quest of the *Shem-es-Nabi* would mark the end of his acquaintance with her. She had told him so, many times and from different angles, that August night when he left her at the door of her apartment. She had expressly forbidden him to hold any further communication with her on his return from the East.

For which excellent reasons, Moylan went to the Garth apartment direct from the ship. He arrived at a barbarously early hour and had the good fortune to find her at home and momentarily devoid of visible relatives. It was not an average condition, and he took hope.

She received him as if he had called barely a day before, instead of after a lapse of more than two months; nor did a shade of expression show she noted how thin and how brown he had grown, and that a queer hunted look was still lurking at the back of his eyes.

"Well?" was her cryptic greeting.

"I have it," was his, as he drew forth the *Shem-es-Nabi.*

"So I see," she answered, scarcely glancing at it, "but you've forgotten something."

"I—I don't—"

"That I don't care to number thieves among my friends."

"It *isn't* theft!" he burst forth. "I explained that—"

"I don't want to discuss it. Will you go now, please?"

He looked at her and he saw she was far worse than angry. She was entirely herself—cool, unruffled, pleasantly firm. He read no possible change of verdict in her clear eyes.

"As you like," he said, feeling all at once very sick and old. "I got this thing, and I risked my life to get it. Then I dodged the knife of a camel-man to keep it. Then I made a ten-day trip that was a hospital-furnace nightmare, fringed with two Bedouin chases, a touch of sunstroke and a day of sand blindness. I've spent every dollar I had on earth—all for this measly relic, and for what it meant to me. And now it—it means nothing."

"Nothing at all," she assented sweetly.

"Good-by!" he muttered, trying to find the door.

"It *is* good-by," she agreed. "I'm sorry, but it is."

He paused, looked at the ring in his palm, then again at her.

"You've made your choice," she reminded him, in an access of tact.

"Yes!" he growled. "I've made it. Just this minute. If it weren't for this thing, you'd let me—"

"Isn't it too late to think of that?"

"No. I'll send it back. I'll—have it sent to the *Serail* at Damascus, if you'll—"

"Are you in earnest?"

"Do I look like a merry jester?"

"It means all that to you?"

"What's the use of rubbing it in? You know what it means, even though I've no right now, to tell you, and probably never shall have. Let it go at that. I can keep on coming here sometimes if I send this ring back?"

"Yes."

He looked again at the ring, then looked only at her and tried to forget that he had ever dreamed and ventured.

"You'd have saved time and money," she went on unkindly, "by believing me when I said the same thing last August."

"I thought—I thought when you saw what I had done, and—and knew it meant wealth—"

"I tried to catch you by cable; but—"

"I didn't use my own name. It was safer not to."

"I see. And how will you get the ring back?"

"I'll send it to Judge Gregg. He must be there by now. He'll manage the diplomatic part of the business."

There was another miserable pause. Then Maia twisted the subject.

"There's an Italian colony on the Palisades just south of Grantwood," she observed irrelevantly.

He looked at her in tired perplexity, but made no comment on the wondrous news. She continued:

"It seems they had a fiesta of some sort out there—a Saint's Day, or something—last August. Bands and—and fireworks."

"Fireworks?"

The word woke uncomfortable memories.

"Yes. Rockets and things. A lot of them. At night, you know."

And at last a gleam of intelligence dawned in Moylan's deadened brain.

"Rockets?" he babbled feebly. "Not the night when we—?"

"Yes."

"But Judge Gregg—"

"Judge Gregg is still waiting impatiently for a man he wants as a law partner."

"Oh!"

"He is a dear," pursued Maia enthusiastically. "I like him. We've become pretty well acquainted these last two months, he and I."

"He—"

"He talks so interestingly about the East. For instance he told me a secret—a terribly *secret* secret—the Sultan told him. Want to hear it?"

Moylan was too busy digesting facts to reply. But she took his assent for granted.

"THE Sultan told him," said she, "that the *Shem-es-Nabi* has been locked in the treasure vaults under Yildiz Kiosk for three hundred years. An imitation of it is on view at Damascus. Or, rather, a series of imitations. For they are stolen at the rate of three a year. So a big supply is kept on hand. The Sultan gave one to Judge Gregg. Every now and then a story is carefully circulated that some one has been killed for stealing the ring."

"The—the—"

"You didn't steal anything. You just traveled across the world to change one copy of a ring for another. Wasn't it funny? And—Oh, you bad, *poor* boy! Don't look like that! How thin you are, and how brown; and—oh, it's a *shame, dear!*"

The Welcher

THE snow had changed to rain, and dissatisfied with the change, had tried to turn back to its first form. The result was sleet.

In Cleveland's double-spaced residence section, this sleet would do pretty things to shrubbery and to bare tree-arms, by giving them crystalline suits of mail. In Cleveland's workaday regions the sleet found no pretty branches to adorn, but far from being discouraged, it proceeded to clothe the pavements with glass. And the streets became a horror for walkers.

There was no real need of this added attraction to make life miserable for those who must be abroad. The early December dusk had long since set in. The air was both sharp and sodden. Yellow mist hung thick, and through it crawled the frozen rain. Horses were slipping; motor-cars were skidding; people on foot were scrambling crablike over the slithery glare, on their way home from work.

This brings us to Eve Soral, who slipped and lost her balance oftener than did most of the home-going parade—which was odd, for the girl was young and looked vigorous as well as graceful. At length both her feet started in the same direction and at the same time, through no volition of hers. And only her instinctive clutch at a grilled railing saved her from a nasty fall.

She clung dazedly, for a second, to the icy iron scroll of the railing, breathing heavily from the shock and from fatigue. Then to her nostrils came a gush of hot, odor-laden air from the grating at her feet. The odor went to her brain and set her nostrils aquiver. She looked up and took stock of her surroundings.

She was standing in front of one of the larger, gayer restaurants, on a busy corner. The rail to which she clung ran between the front windows and the sidewalk; the grating gave sensory proof of the kitchen's presence; the scent of cooking foods rose thick through the soggy air. To Eve it was at once fragrant and intoxicating.

She paused before resuming her slippery pilgrimage and stared longingly through a gap between the yellow silk draw-curtains of the window in front of her. The long opening was scarce an inch wide, but it gave Eve Soral a Cubist impression of white cloth and pink table-shades and soft warmth and repletion and—and *food!*

She looked from the gap to the silk of the curtain. Thanks to the stronger outside lights, the window thus became a sort of mirror—shadowy and uncertain, but still a mirror. In it she could get a sketchy glimpse of a girl, dressed not only neatly but with an approach to something like style—a girl tall and well made, if a trifle lean, a girl with good features and rebellious dark eyes, a girl decidedly pretty.

This mirrored survey of herself was an old story to Eve. Just at present she was far more interested in that tantalizing inch-wide view of the paradise within. And she shifted her position to get a better view.

JUST then a figure separated itself from the haze of passers-by in the mirror's background and took a hesitant step toward her; then it came quite close to where she stood, and curiosity made Eve turn.

Facing her was a stocky, big-shouldered man, perhaps forty years old. He was swathed in a fur-lined coat. A soft hat was jammed low on his head to guard his face from the slap of the sleet. The face itself did not impress Eve pleasantly. It was swarthy, thick-jawed, black-mustached—the type of face that used to be associated with melodrama villains, and that is quite as frequently found in real life on peaceable delicatessen-dealers or architects or steam-laundry proprietors.

The stranger was staring at the girl in frank interest, his heavy-lidded eyes taking in the various points of her figure and features with an appraisal she found vaguely offensive. She made as though to turn back to her survey of the window. Then, realizing that she must look absurd peering at a sheet of curtained plate glass, she hesitated and took an uncertain step onward. She slipped and again caught at the iron railing.

Before she could touch it, the man had deftly caught her elbow and was holding her steady. She could not well resent the act of courtesy. But she could and did resent the words that went with it.

"It's not safe for anybody to be walking, a brute of a night like this," the man was saying. "Better let me get a taxi for you."

She drew her elbow away from his light clasp.

"No, thank you," she said frigidly—with an involuntary mental vision of the seven pennies that nestled in the bottom of her hand-bag and formed her whole present capital.

"It's a rotten night," continued the man, taking no heed of her rebuff. "I was just dropping in here for dinner, to try to forget the weather. I hate to eat alone. You wouldn't care to join me, I suppose?"

Eve started back a little and glared at him in surprised contempt. They would have made an excellent tableau of "The High-Souled Maiden and the Love-Pirate." But, in real life, the curtain has an exasperating way of failing to fall at the moment of climax.

And just then a fresh gust of food-aroma swirled up through the grating. It mounted to Eve's senses like heady wine. She checked her onward step and looked back, over her shoulder, at the man, irresolute.

"I hate to eat alone," he repeated, "and I'm famishing hungry. They have good things in here,—mighty good things,—if one knows what to order. And I know what to order. Won't you take dinner with me—please?"

"Yes," said Eve suddenly, "I'll be very glad to, if you care to have me."

AND then things seemed to grow misty and to whirl foolishly around her. She had not eaten in thirty hours. From many miles away she heard the man's cheery thanks for her acceptance. She felt his hand on the sleeve of her thin jacket. He was guiding her into a long, wide room—a room that was lusciously warm and softly lighted—where sat many people and where waiters moved as softly and rapidly as black-and-white ghosts.

Then they were at a table, far down the room and in a shallow alcove, and a waiter was helping her off with her jacket. She was faintly grateful that the waist beneath it—her last—was still presentable.

She looked about her, taking mechanical note of details. Her glance fell on two college boys a few tables distant. A double porterhouse steak, smothered in mushrooms, had just been set down between them. The steak was a full two inches thick; it must have weighed two pounds. The mushrooms were heaped high; and gold-brown gravy filled the bottom of the dish.

Eve heard the man opposite her dictating an order to the waiter—an order that seemed to include such useless and non-filling things as caviar and grapefruit cocktail and—

Eve broke in with an apologetic laugh upon his careful marshaling of dishes.

"Would you mind so very much," she pleaded, "if I broke all sorts of rules of politeness and had just exactly what I like, for dinner?"

"Why, of course not," answered the man, though visibly chagrined at the interruption of what was to him a sacred ceremonial. "Go ahead. Order anything you like. I ought to have asked you, anyway, what you'd—"

"You see," she explained lamely, "I get so tired of eating the same things all the time—the things everybody orders for dinner. Just for once—just for the lark of it—I'd like to order something different. You don't mind?"

"Not a bit," he assured her, with overdone joviality. "Go as far as you like. What'll it be? Nightingales' tongues, garnished with Senators' brains stewed in sauterne, or—?"

"It'll be—*that*," she interrupted, pointing toward the steak one of the two boys was beginning to carve.

Up went the man's bushy brows, ever so little. And from under the brows he glanced swiftly at her. But before she could meet his gaze his heavy face was expressionless once more.

"Certainly," he agreed. "Double porterhouse, rare, with mushrooms. Or shall it be onions?"

"You're making fun of me!" she accused vexedly.

"Not a bit," he protested, "not a bit. I never met but three girls in all my life who knew how to order a dinner. Two of them died of indigestion, and the third one married a man who couldn't afford to buy her anything better than corn-beef and pie. I knew a girl who used to live on milk-and-vichy. And I've known fifty whose idea of a banquet was lobster salad and ice-cream. So no freak menus can scare me."

He gave her order—then looked questioningly from her to the wine-card. She caught the wordless query.

"No, thanks," she replied, smiling deprecatingly.

"No?" he said. "The wine-cellar here isn't bad. And they've a wizard of a drink-mixer out there..... Just as you like."

He gave his own order and then devoted himself to somewhat ponderous efforts to entertain his guest until the food should arrive. He talked well, in a sketchy way, and Eve tried to rouse herself from her hunger-inertia to meet him with more than monosyllables. Dully she felt his manner toward her had changed. But in what way, she was too exhausted to understand. Also there was a new look in his eyes—a look of mild perplexity, she thought.

But Eve had scant attention to give to any details except that she was ravenous and that food was in prospect. She tried to visualize the glories of the coming steak. But the effort was too much for her.

AFTER a century of waiting, the dinner arrived. "I had no idea I was hungry," the girl heard herself saying, in a tone that would not have deceived a deaf-mute. "But this steak looks delicious. I actually believe the cold weather has given me an appetite."

"Same here," chimed in the man. "I'm half starved. Say, let's make a bargain. Let's neither of us say a word for ten minutes, till we've taken off the razor edge of our appetite. We'll have plenty of time, afterward, for talking."

He bent over his plate. For some minutes he devoted himself solemnly and industriously to his task of food-stoking. He did not once look up—or if he did, Eve did not catch him at it.

The girl was too hungry to note the oddity of his suggestion that they eat the first part of their dinner in silence. To her, it seemed a heaven-sent inspiration. She tried to eat with a semblance of daintiness, but more than once she found she was fairly wolfing her meal. When at last it dawned upon her that she could eat no more, there was alarmingly little of the huge steak left. She looked guiltily across at the man. But, head down, he was still busily eating—or seeming to eat. She was grateful for his gluttony, even while it disgusted her.

Eve's fatigue was gone. So were the numbness of body and brain, the sick despondency, the desperation, that had gripped her. With the recuperation of healthy youth, she was once more strong and alert—wholly her best self. And with other returning powers, came the power to fear. And all at once Eve was mightily afraid. She was afraid of what she had done; she was afraid of what onlookers must think; most of all, she was afraid of this massive beast of a man who sat across the narrow table from her. She was no unsophisticated child. She knew perfectly well what the man had implied when he invited her—a pretty and loitering girl—to dine with him. She had known it all along; but when hunger is king, there is no peril his victims will not risk to get out of his clutches. Eve Soral had taken that risk, in the belief that her quick wit would show her some way of escaping.

And now her revived brain came to the rescue of her fear-shaken body; even as she ate the last few morsels of food, she was covertly looking about her. The restaurant was in the shape of an L, the apex of its angle being the arch that connected its two rooms. Into the shorter and wider room Eve and her escort had come; and in this room they were still sitting. Through the arch, Eve could see a little way into the other room. As she looked, she saw people advancing down the second room toward the arch, from some point beyond her line of vision, and taking seats at tables. That must mean the other room also opened on a street. She remembered that the restaurant was on a corner. The second room's entrance-door was of course on the side street. And with this bit of strategic knowledge, her inspiration was born.

THE man looked up from his plate.

Eve noticed two trivial things: first, that for all his assiduous eating, much of his food remained untouched; second, that the pearl scarfpin he wore was either worth less than one dollar or more than five hundred.

"Well," he remarked comfortably, "our ten minutes must be up by this time. Hope I haven't kept you waiting. While he's getting the dessert order, suppose I send a messenger boy for seats to some show? What do you like best? Tired-business-man-musical-comedy that's too light to understand? Or problem-drama stuff that's too heavy? They're all alike to me. So take your choice."

"Why—why, either one—will be ever so nice," she faltered. "Whichever you like best. I'll be glad to—Oh!" she broke off, catching her coat from the chair-back as she started to her feet, "there's Molly Mercer, in the next room. I haven't seen her for an age—not since she got married. Will you excuse me, just a second? I want to speak to her."

Her strategic position was perfect. She was facing the longer room beyond the arch. The man's broad back was toward it. He did not even turn as she pointed.

"You'll excuse me, won't you?" she repeated. "You—you can order the dessert while I'm gone."

"All right," he nodded assent. "And if your friends would like to go along with us to the show, I'll get a box. We can shake them, later."

"Thank you," she said, sick with fear.

Coat on arm, she made for the arch. Once out of the man's sight, in the second room, she looked eagerly for the door opening on the side street. There it was—but at the end of a long vista of tables.

Down the room Eve made her nervous way, toward the door and to safety.

But the tables were many. The aisles were narrow and tortuous. Waiters got in her way. She had to stand aside to let parties of newcomers pass. To her frightened mind, she seemed to waste a century or more in getting to the room's far end.

At last the goal was reached. She stood at the double portal that led to freedom. A uniformed boy swung wide the door to let her pass out. She slipped through the opening like a pursued rabbit into its warren. And on the threshold she collided with some one who stood there waiting. It was the man who had been her host at the unfinished dinner!

EVE gaped at the man in abject horror, speechless, dumfounded.

"You lost your way," he said very quietly, taking hold of her arm as he spoke. "I was afraid you might. Lots of people do. So I came around to meet you and steer you safe into port."

Too dazed to resist, too starkly confused to make answer, she unresistingly suffered him to lead her along the interminable length of room, through the arch and to their own table.

"Sit down," he said.

She obeyed. He seated himself opposite her. She felt absurdly helpless—as defenseless as a schoolchild sent to the principal's office for punishment. Her intelligence told her that the gate of her prison was open, that she was free to walk out at any moment, that he dare not detain her by force, that at worst she had but to call for help and he would be sent to a police-station cell for annoying her.

She knew all these things, but she took advantage of none of them. She just sat there, blinking sulky defiance, her first senseless dread slowly warming into a very normal and wholesome wrath. For a few seconds the man did not speak. Then he said, with no trace of emotion in his heavy voice:

"Do you happen to know what a *welcher* is?"

"No!" she snapped, wondering just how offensive the new word's meaning might be.

"A *welcher*," he defined, seeming to search clumsily for the correct phrasing, "a *welcher* is a person who enters into a bargain and refuses to pay, a person who bets and loses and then won't make good, a person who sets a price, receives the goods and then—"

"I don't understand how this—" she began, but he contradicted gently:

"I think you understand—because all those definitions of a *welcher* also describe *you*. It is not pleasant to be called a welcher. Why are you one?"

"I'm not!" she blazed, anger now at full tide and sweeping fear before it. "I'm not! I never did a dishonest thing in all my life. How dare you say I—"

"Never did a dishonest thing?" he repeated quizzically. "Not even when you sponged on me for a dinner and then tried to sneak, as soon as you were fed up. Was that honest? You knew well enough—"

"I knew you—what you were trying to do!" flared the girl, "and I escaped from the horrible trap. I—"

"No, you didn't," he denied good-naturedly. "You only tried to. You didn't escape. And I didn't set any trap, either. You came in here of your own accord. You say, yourself, you knew what I was trying to do. So you—"

"So I let you fool yourself into thinking you could. It served you right. Men who try to—to do such things deserve to be tricked."

"My young friend," put in the man philosophically, "all the money and all the fascination and all the trickery on earth won't influence a woman—if she doesn't want them to. If you weren't—"

"You beast!"

"Well then," demanded the man, "if you weren't—willing to come with me, please tell me why you pretended to be."

"Because I was starving. That's why. Because I was starving!" she exclaimed passionately, indignation sending an avalanche of speech to her lips. "Because I hadn't had anything to eat since yesterday noon; because the smell of the food made me crazy. I had to eat. I *had* to! When you came sidling up to me in that odious way, and asked me to dinner, I saw how I could keep from famishing. I owed nothing to a man who would do such a thing. And I made up my mind I'd fool you. I knew I could take care of myself afterward. I—I was starving. I—"

"That's a different thing," he said gravely. "It puts a new angle on the case. But if you'd told me you were hungry and asked me for—"

"You'd have tossed me a dime and gone on your way thinking you'd done a wonderful piece of generosity. And I had to eat—"

"So you became an object of charity? If that's what you are, leave word with the waiter to give you all you want to eat and a package of food to carry home. I'll pay for it now, and get out. You can finish your meal without any more annoyance from me. I'm very glad to help—"

"Do you take me for a pauper?" she shrilled, more furious at the supposition than at his earlier idea of her.

"I'm afraid that's the very kindest thing I can think about you," he returned, unruffled. "You must be rottenly poor, or else—"

But a new torrent of angry denial burst in on his surmise.

"Well, I'm not!" she snarled, catlike. "My parents are able to take care of me. *Well* able to. And what's more, they're anxious to. There isn't a week that one of them doesn't write to beg me not to keep on with my career, and to come back home. They're lonesome without me. And Father has enough to keep all three of us. He—"

SHE checked herself, a little ashamed of her babyish domestic revelations. The man was looking at her, a half-smile wrinkling his broad face. He seemed mischievously amused. She pushed back her chair.

"I'm going now!" she declared. "Good night," he said civilly.

He made no move to detain her. Puzzled, she hesitated a moment. The desire for the Last Word overcame her.

"I suppose you want me to thank you," she said in elaborate sarcasm, "for the dinner you've given me."

"No," he returned judicially, "I don't know that I do. You see, you've eaten only part of it. And besides, I ought to feel honored that a young lady with a Career and a plutocrat father should condescend to eat with a poor everyday mutt like me. It's up to *me* to thank *you*. I don't meet an heiress in disguise, every day."

"I never said I was an heiress," she made tart reply. "And I don't care to have my father made fun of."

"Who am I," he rejoined in deep humility, "to dare make fun of our moneyed classes? I leave that to the muck-rake newspapers. I've a cringing reverence for the idle rich. Your father—"

"I never said my father was rich. He isn't. He has the house and about two thousand dollars a year from the business. He's in Hay and Feed," she added, blundering on as the words she hadn't meant to say popped out in place of the scorching ones her angry brain was coining. "And he—"

"And he lets his only child go around cadging meals from strangers? Or doesn't he know? And by the way," he continued, forestalling a hot interruption, "you spoke about a career: may I ask what it is? It's none of my business,—as you were about to say,— but I'm curious. It must be something pretty wonderful if it made you leave a home where you were comfortable and where your parents are lonely for you; and if it's fascinating enough to make you want to stay here in Cleveland without anything to eat. What sort of career is it? Music or the stage or art or—?"

"I—I took a course in millinery and a course in stenography, too," she defended herself awkwardly, in a queer eagerness to speak to some one of her vicissitudes. "And I've held good jobs in both, since I came here last year. I've got dandy references. If the hard times hadn't shut so many thousand people out of work, this fall, I'd be holding a good job still—either at a typewriter or in a shop. But everywhere, they tell me, 'We're firing, not hiring.' I was on my way back to my room after ten hours of job-hunting, when I met you. And I—"

"I see," he assented. "I see. Too bad! It's a common story, this year. But—I asked you about your career. What is it—if you don't mind telling?"

"I just told you," she said in perplexity. "I came to Cleveland to make a living, and—"

"And," he broke in with ostentatious amaze, "and *that's* what you call your career?"

"What else should I call it?" she demanded.

"Well," he drawled, "personally, I should call it your graft."

"I—"

"Don't go up in the air," he admonished. "*Graft* is the word I used. I used it because I couldn't think of a better word to describe a girl who leaves her well-to-do parents to a lonely old age, and comes to the city to earn money she doesn't need, by grabbing jobs away from girls who need those jobs to keep their families and themselves from starving. If that isn't graft, I don't know what is."

"You have the same old-fashioned, silly ideas my parents and most back-numbers have," she scoffed. "You can't understand the change that has come to women, these past twenty years. You—"

"Oh yes, I can," he chuckled. "A whole lot of that 'change' has come to them from me, from time to time,—in amounts from a nickel to a thousand dollars,—including the check for tonight's dinner."

BUT she was too excited to heed the sneer. In the zeal of talking about herself and in the battle-joy of finding a target at which to launch her pet theories, she had lost not only her earlier fear but her later blind rage. Here was a man of the outworn, old-fogey type, who needed convincing—a man who stuck to the asinine doctrine that a woman's place is in the home, and who was daring to question her right to a career.

I think no truly independent modern woman will wonder at Eve Soral for forgetting her grievance and flying to the defense of her holy principles. Even so ignoble an opponent as this fleshy and fleshly man was worth while convincing.

"What was my life?" she orated, "my life at home? I was a fifth wheel in the family machine. I helped Mother about the house. I sang to Father in the evenings; I taught a class in Sunday-school; I sewed and mended and embroidered; I had my place in a small town's society. That was all—absolutely *all!* It was stifling. I was wasting my youth, my life, my prospects! And all the whole world was calling to me to come and join in its glorious work—to help prove woman's industrial independence, to enroll myself with my fellow women who were proving their equality and—"

"I think," interposed the man, half-apologetically, "I *think* you read all that last part in a book—or heard it in a speech. It somehow has a kind of familiar creak. And folks don't talk that way in real life— at least, not off the platform. So—let's see—you got tired of the home town, and you made the old people's life a hell by your sulking and fretting and nagging, till they let you go and gave you the money to start out with. That's generally the first step in a girl's independence."

"I'm going to pay them back every cent of it!" she said indignantly. "Every cent of it! I told them so. I wont be dependent on anyone. And as for fretting and sulking—"

"So you came here to Cleveland," he resumed ponderously, "after you'd studied millinery and stenography. And you got a job—two good jobs—one after another—in both lines, I think you said. Let me tell you something about those jobs. On the same days you got them, two other girls went out looking for work. They were just as well equipped for labor as you were. They had no cash. One of them was a country girl who had come to Cleveland because she had a bed-ridden mother to support and couldn't make a living nearer home. The other girl was an orphan from the slums here, with a bunch of younger sisters and brothers who had to look to her for bread and a roof."

"But—"

"THOSE two girls couldn't get work," he meandered on, "because you had their jobs. Let's say the country girl's sick mother went to the poorhouse and died there for lack of the comforts her daughter's wages would have given her. The other girl—well, the Children's Society probably looked after her kid brothers and sisters. And she herself—well, if she's not in Lake Erie, she's most likely making a living of some kind, by now. But it's ten to one it's a kind of living she would not care to have her dead parents know about. So you've done that much, anyhow, my friend, for woman's industrial independence. I congratulate you."

"You're talking nonsense—crazy nonsense," she cried, fighting back a shudder at the crude word-picture. "What right have you to say—?"

"*Is* it nonsense?" he urged. "Haven't you lived in Cleveland long enough to know that there are at least a dozen applicants for every good job? (And you say both of your jobs were good.) Most of the applicants need those jobs to keep bare life in themselves and in the people who depend on them. Was I so very far wrong in guessing that you put a rather murderous crimp in the fortunes of two families, when you got those two jobs and shoved back the two girls who would have had steady work if it hadn't been for you?"

"In the business world—" she babbled, racking her memory for a quotation she could not recall.

"In the business world," he supplemented, "it's 'Wolf eat wolf.' But I never yet heard of a four-legged wolf that would leave a comfortable feast of its own, in order to snatch a half-gnawed bone from some starving fellow-wolf. It remained for industrially independent women to show wolves the full possibilities of wolfhood."

"I don't want to argue with you," she said. "It's your sort of men who kept women in shackles for six thousand years. You can't hope to understand—"

"To understand that men have made business such a wide field in the past few years that they had to call women into the business world, because there weren't enough men to fill all the new jobs at low enough wages to bring profits? Oh, I understand that, all right. And I take off my hat to the girl who must work to keep from starving or to keep some one else from starving. She tackles her job gallantly, as a rule, and she's a big factor in the industrial world. She's going to be a bigger and bigger factor, as the years go on. She's made more progress in twenty years than men made in two centuries."

"Then why do you sneer at *me* for—"

"I'm speaking of the girl who has to work—not the girl who robs her of a chance to, by stealing her job."

"I didn't steal—"

"You stole more than that. You stole money from your parents—don't get excited: you did. You took money from them and used it against their wishes to fit yourself to rob them of your society. Because they were unselfish—as parents have a habit of being—and let you have your own way, don't imagine you've robbed them any the less. That brings up your present total of robbery to five victims—the two girls you spoke of, your two parents, and—worst robbery of all—yourself."

"Myself?"

"Yes, you're the unluckiest victim of the lot, you poor welching little failure. You had a good home and parents that loved you enough to work to take care of you all your life. (You had all that; so you don't realize what a treasure it was.) You had everything a million girls crave and can't get—home, peace, safety, prospects, social position and love. And you robbed yourself of them all. For it *was* robbery. If you'd thrown away those things in the hope of being a great singer or writer or artist or something else that would have made the world better and happier for your sacrifice, there might have been some little excuse for you; but you threw away the very biggest gifts God can give—in order to be a milliner's assistant or a stenographer. What in blue blazes have either of those jobs to offer, that can make up to you for what you lost?"

"I wanted to—"

"To be independent, like a man. Just as the Æsop hen wanted to crow. For three thousand years the world has been laughing at that hen and at the man who sold his birthright for a mess of pottage. But, on the level, they were both of them a million times less silly than you are."

SHE tried to be angry again. She tried to feel grossly insulted at his brutal scolding. She tried to think of some crushing Feminist arguments to silence him. But to her own self-disgust she found herself feeling ridiculously like a naughty little girl whose teacher is pointing out her myriad faults.

"I don't want to try any sob-stuff maudlin sentiment," rumbled on the man, "because it isn't in my line. And it wouldn't do any good. But maybe there's a side to this that you haven't bothered to think much about. Most young folks don't. I take it your parents are getting old. They must have worked pretty hard, and denied themselves a good many things—if your father has been able to pay for a house and to work up a two-thousand-dollar-a-year business in a country town. You're the only child they've got. They spent a lot of cash on you, soon and late. And at the start, your mother threw dice with Death for the privilege of bringing you into the world. Yes, they staked a lot on you.

I know you didn't ask them to put you on earth or to bring you up. But they did it, for all that. And it seems they did a billion times more than the contract called for. You've welched with *them*, too."

"I haven't. I—"

"No? Didn't you let them think you came here to make good? You haven't made good. You've sunk to street-woman tricks to get a square meal. Pretty soon, at this rate, with no job, you'd have to go a step further to get food and clothes and a room—not because you haven't any better way of living, but because you're too stubborn to go back home where you belong. Isn't that welching?"

"I tried to make good," she half-sobbed. "I did my best. I did indeed. And I've tried to get work. I try every day and I try all day. I've pawned everything I have—even my trunk—except the clothes I'm wearing and this little ring of Grandma's. I'd have pawned these, too, and gotten a cheaper suit, but appearances count for so much in a work-hunt. If a girl looks prosperous and well-groomed—"

"She is more apt to catch the fancy of some cur who may hire her? A sweet use to put your grandmother's ring to, isn't it? You seem to be welching on Granny too. She'd be pleased, wouldn't she? Just as your parents would be pleased to see you sitting here now with a man whose name you don't know."

"My parents—"

"YOU said, awhile back, that you wanted to be independent or earn your own way—or something like that. You earned your own way, at home, a lot more than you've ever earned it since then. That's something most young girls are too all-fired wise to understand. In a family that can support her, a daughter 'earns her way' by just being alive. You told me about helping your mother with the work. Did you suppose there wasn't any payment to her, for all she'd done for you, when you were working alongside of her and being jolly company for her and making the house a nice place for her to stay in while your father was away? And then you spoke about singing to the old man in the evenings. I guess the evenings are kind of long and lonesome, nowadays, when he comes home dead tired from the store, and sits around wishing his girl were there singing the old songs to him and saying things to make him laugh and forget how tired he is. And—"

"Stop!" she begged.

"I don't much wonder that they write to you, every few days, hinting how nice it would be for you to come back home. *They* seem to think you were earning your way pretty well when you were helping make their old age happy. There's a billion girls who could have a 'career' in millinery or shorthand. And there's just one girl on God's earth who can have the 'career' of making those two old folks' lives bright for them. It's bad enough when parents waste all their love and their cash on a daughter and then leave her chase off and marry some guy. Yet that's part of nature; and no one has a right to kick. But when a girl throws over her home—when she doesn't have to—to take shorthand dictation or to sew blue canary feathers on a purple hat! Say, on the level, now that you think it over, don't you feel just a little less like Industry's Joan of Arc and a bit more like a heartless idiot?"

"Yes," she said, her swimming eyes at last meeting his and her voice queerly shaky, "I do. I don't know just why, but I do. No one else was ever brute enough to talk to me as you have. I didn't know there were men who talked so, to women. It's horrible, and I think I hate you. But—but it's true."

"Good!" he vouchsafed. "And now we've settled that, let's get down to business."

"To—to—what?"

"To business. All the lectures that ever happened don't change a woman's mind. And I owe you something for being civil and listening to me. Here's my proposition: I can get you a city job as stenographer. If you're any good at all, you can hold it forever—and then some. The pay will be about twelve or fourteen dollars. There isn't a fortune in it, but it'll save your face, when you write home. And it'll keep you from rubbering in at eat-shop windows like the beggar-kids on a Christmas card. How about it?"

"I—I—"

"Don't get me wrong," he admonished. "The job isn't in my own office. And there's no come-back, no obligation. You don't have to see me again. Here's twenty dollars. It'll get some of your things out of hock and keep you going till the next pay-day. (If ever you feel like paying it back, I sha'n't stop you.) So the heaven-sent career can go right on careering. And if—"

"WAIT, please!" she said, her hands fumbling as she worked the ring from her finger and laid it on the table in front of him. It was a circlet of chased, antique gold, gripping a topaz. Its pawnshop value was probably five dollars.

"What's the idea?" he asked, looking appraisingly at the ring and gauging, to a penny, its value.

"It's—it's collateral," she explained haltingly. "I'm not a welcher—or a grafter, either. At least, I'm not going to be. I'll take the twenty dollars—as a loan. When I've paid it back, you can give me my ring again. If anything should happen to me, you can sell the ring for a lot more than twenty dollars, I'm sure. And now that we've put it on a business basis,"—as the man nodded and stuck the ring in his waist-coat pocket,—"I—I want to thank you, and to—"

"Forget it!" he said gruffly. "I'll give you a card to the right man, and I'll 'phone him besides. He'll fix you up with a stenographer job. Let's—"

"I wont need it, thanks," she interrupted in a very small but very determined voice. "I'm going to—I've made up my mind to—to take up my career where I left it off."

"But this job is—"

"I'm speaking of my *real* career. I'm going home."

"Home? But—"

"To-night—on the next train. There's one in about an hour, I think; there's nothing at my room worth getting. This twenty dollars will be more than enough for my ticket, because I sha'n't need return-fare. I'm not coming back. And,"—her last shred of armor crumbling,—"and I'm so glad! But—I wish I didn't hate you so."

"That's all right," he said pleasantly. "A woman always hates a man who yanks her out of a slough, by the hair, and sets her safely on the highroad again. Just as a man never quite forgives a woman for daring to 'reform' him. But I'll walk to the station with you, if you don't mind. I'd like to see as much as possible of the first girl I ever knew who was immodest enough to change her mind in public."

The Songbird

HE had never heard her sing—did not hear her until nearly a month after they were married.

They met, the first day out, on a New-York-to-Naples voyage. She was going to Italy for her voice, and he was going thither for his firm. They saw nothing of each other after they landed at Naples, because she went directly to Rome to begin her three-month course of lessons, and he went directly to Tuscany and Lombardy to interest merchants in his firm's new cash-register.

But they met on the return voyage. A shaft broke—and so the homebound trip lasted nineteen days. And the night before the two sighted the Statue of Liberty, they became engaged. For love-making purposes, nineteen days on shipboard is as good—or as bad—as a month at a summer hotel or a year in a big city.

She went from the boat to her uncle's little camp in the hinterland of the Adirondacks. And she arranged that he should be invited to the camp for his vacation.

At his vacation's end, they were married; and she went along on one of his Western business trips, by way of honeymoon. Thus it chanced that he did not hear her sing until they were settled in their own flat.

Now, in a sense, there was nothing remarkable about this fact; but viewed in another light it was very remarkable indeed. For both of them adored music; indeed, it was this mutual music-love that had first attracted them to each other. He was an opera-fan, a concert-zealot, a recital-fanatic. To him, a golden contralto voice was the most wonderful thing on earth. Schumann-Heink, Louise

Homer and Gilderoy Scott were his goddesses—not that he had met any of the three, but they all were of the type of contralto that tears out a man's heart and then puts it back in place again, glorified. The knowledge that Ruth Morton had a pure contralto voice first drew Dick Herron to her. And the rest had followed in due course.

Yet he had never heard her sing. On shipboard the weather had been more suitable to deck than to a cabin in which the piano had been surrounded by couchfuls of seasick women. At the primal Adirondack camp there was no musical instrument at all. Ruth's uncle loathed music. And on the wedding tour, their stopping-places were pianoless hotel-suites.

But the very first article of furniture moved into the Herron's new-leased flat was Ruth's adored baby-grand piano. Dick saw it, the moment he came home from the office that first evening. And straightway he forgot the jumbled and half-complete state of the rest of the flat's furnishings. The piano was there. That was enough. Now they could follow the plan they had arranged weeks earlier.

They had mapped it all out. After dinner he was to get into house-coat and slippers and sprawl comfortably in a big leather chair. And she was to go to the piano and sing for him. They had even laid out the program. It was to begin with the two wonderful contralto arias from Saint-Saëns' "Samson and Delilah," to be followed by "Mon Fils" and then by "Exaltation" and "The Snow-white Gull."

This was the sort of thing Dick Herron had dreamed of—to loaf back at ease in his own home, and to be sung to, not only by a contralto, but by a contralto he loved. And Ruth had been dreaming of it too. She told him that she had always felt her singing would be really inspired if she could but sing to some one she loved.

Wherefore, as anyone can see, this was a genuine Occasion—the fulfillment of a dual life-longing.

RUTH sat down at the piano, got up, readjusted the stool's height, sat down again—and with a firm, sympathetic touch began the piano prelude of Delilah's wonder-lyric, *"Mon cœur s'ouvre à ta voix."* And Dick—her modern Samson—leaned back with half-shut eyes to enjoy the gloriously passionate song of wooing. His wife's touch of the keys in the brief prelude showed her artistry as a musician.

Then she began to sing. From her deep chest and up through the creamy column of her throat poured the opulent volume of sound.

Dick Herron's half-shut eyes opened wide. The new-lighted cigar fell unnoticed from his suddenly nerveless fingers into his lap, where—still unnoticed—it proceeded very industriously to burn a ragged and undarnable hole in a pair of eleven-dollar trousers.

Dick could not have moved; he could not have spoken, he could not have *thought,* consecutively, had his very life depended on it. He could just sit there spell-gripped and gape helplessly at this adored bride of his, who was singing out her very soul to him in one of the most seductive love-arias ever written. She was singing the aria that his enchantresses Schumann-Heink and Homer and Gilderoy Scott had so endeared to him. And she was singing it as not one or all of the three had ever sung it.

Nay, she was singing it as never before had any living or dead contralto even tried to sing it. In brief, she was squalling the golden aria in the most grotesquely appalling and hideous fashion that human ingenuity could imagine.

Discords, dissonances, perpetual variance from the pitch, a horrible flatting that varied from a halftone to a note and a half from the key, a positive genius for never once striking the right note—these were the chief characteristics of Ruth's interpretation of the heaven-born melody. To add to the awfulness of it all, her accompaniment (she played with the music before her) was perfect in its correctness and was musicianly to a degree. And her vocal tones were velvet in richness and glorious in their vibrant strength. She sang with rare feeling and expression; her tempo was faultless; but—so far as the tune went—she might have been singing a Swahili war-chant.

DICK, listening open-mouthed to the massacre of melody, was too aghast to think consecutively. One broken thought after another raced through his bemused brain. At first he half believed this was some sort of abominable joke his wife was trying to play on him. Then he realized that a devout music-lover (as she undoubtedly was) would no sooner mangle so beautiful a song than an art-devotee would paint purple whiskers on the Mona Lisa.

No, it was not a joke. One glance at the singer's rapt face confirmed that. Then what, in the name of David's sacred lyre, *was* the matter?

Ruth was a trained singer. For three years in New York, and later for three months in Rome, she had taken lessons from high-priced masters. She had even studied opera roles with a possible view to the stage. Her New York teacher had written to her, not two weeks earlier,—Dick had seen the letter,—begging her to renew her lessons and declaring that so unusual a contralto voice as hers was too precious to waste on private life. Dick had read, too, a letter from her Italian maestro, ardently praising her voice and entreating her to come back to him for at least a year's course in grand-opera coaching. These men were famous teachers. Yet now their pet pupil was singing with a fervid tunelessness that would have shamed a back-fence tomcat. What was the answer?

There was no answer at all, that Dick Herron's muddled intellect could evolve. But one thing was certain: she was tremendously in earnest. And there could be no shadow of doubt that she believed she was singing divinely. He knew her well enough to be sure of that. And through the horror and almost physical pain of listening to the ungodly noise, Herron was aware of a great surge of pity. He felt as he might had a loving child spent its month's allowance on a diamond for him—a diamond that proved to be a worthless fragment of broken glass.

When, after the second verse, she came again to the line: "List, oh list, to my fond wooing!" she smiled alluringly at him and partly held out her arms, after the manner of Louise Homer. The gesture and her expression of face and of voice were adorable—and the sound that accompanied them was indescribably awful. It reminded him of a vilely cynical statuary group he had seen in the *"Sala Particolare"* of the Naples Museum.

Yet, being a hero, he returned the smile and hammered his stricken face-muscles into a semblance of delighted approval. After a century—perhaps after an æon—of torture, the song ended. And Ruth came over to where Dick sat.

SHE stood in front of him, silent, aglow, to hear his praise. He rose without a word—he could not speak, just yet—and put his arms about her. She looked up lovingly into his troubled face.

"Thank you, dear," she said very softly. "That is the way I hoped you would take it. Silence and such an expression as yours mean a million times more than any applause. I was singing straight to your heart. And now I know I reached it. Oh, I was so afraid you mightn't like my voice. One or two people don't."

He tried to look indignantly surprised. And he succeeded so well that she continued:

"They don't. Honestly, they don't. Several people don't—Dad, for instance. He doesn't know a thing about music, of course—not a thing. But he positively hates my singing. And my chum at school,—Rhoda Brainard,—she hated it too. And one or two other people. And I got so, for a while, that I wouldn't sing for people any more. It seemed like casting pearls before swine. That isn't conceited of me, is it? For really my voice is a divine gift, and the credit for it isn't due to *me*."

Again the man tried to speak. But still the right words would not come.

"I told my teacher about some people not caring to hear me sing," she pursued, "—Otto Wyckoff, my teacher here in New York, you know. And he just laughed. He told me he has met no fewer than twenty people who detest Caruso's singing. And he says two or three box-holders used to make a point of staying away on the nights when Melba was to sing. He says everybody likes a mediocre voice, but that there are always a few people who can't appreciate really fine vocal music—just as everybody likes potatoes and lots of peoples can't appreciate mushrooms or truffles or caviare. It comforted me so much to hear him say all that. And it explained everything so clearly to me. He himself went wild over my voice. So did Signor Barratti, in Rome. And nearly everybody praises it. But I was so afraid *you* might be one of the few who wouldn't enjoy it. And *your* praise meant more to me than everyone's else put together. Wasn't it silly of me to be afraid?"

He forced some sound or other from his queerly contracted throat. It was a sound almost as discordant as a sample of her own singing. But it managed in a general way to imply assent and reassurance. And it quite satisfied her.

Leaving him, she crossed again to the piano. And again a prelude began. Now it was the prelude to "Exaltation"—a song that always thrilled Dick. And now she was singing—yes, just as before, if not worse.

And so through the whole sweet program that she and Dick had so delightedly mapped out and whose rendition was so terrible. Before the end Dick had not only rallied enough of his discord-scattered wits to voice a magnificently lying approval but to shape the course he must pursue.

ONE of two things was evident: Either he had suddenly been stricken with melodic insanity and did not know one note from another, or else this dear girl of his was the most atrociously bad singer on the Western Hemisphere. He did not think he had all at once lost his sense of sound-relation, for the piano-notes still struck him as true. It was equally hard to believe that a three-year musical education had left Ruth so hopelessly tuneless as she seemed to him. Her voice was glorious; that was undeniable. But she used it as a five-year-old idiot child might strum on a priceless Stradivarius violin. In other words, the singing was all the more horrible because it emanated from a golden voice.

The whole thing was a mystery. Dick Herron did not like mysteries; and therefore, the next morning before going to the office, he set out to solve this particular one.

Professor Wyckoff had a studio and two other rooms in the "music side" of the Carnegie Building. This morning, in one of his inner rooms, he had just finished shaving and was donning his velvet coat and Windsor tie, when the imperative purring of an electric button brought him to the outer door of his suite.

On the threshold stood a well-dressed man, somewhat athletic of build and just now very determined of aspect.

"Mr. Wyckoff?" asked the visitor curtly.

"Professor Wyckoff," blandly returned the host. "Yes."

He was appraising this youth. The newcomer did not look soulful enough to be a prospective pupil, and he had not the unmistakable bearing of a collector or a canvasser. His tense incisiveness vaguely jarred upon the *maestro's* artistic soul.

"My name is Herron," announced the caller, stalking unbidden into the softly lighted studio and leaving the worried musician to patter nervously after him, "—Richard Herron. I am here in behalf of my wife. She was Miss Ruth Morton."

"Ah!" exclaimed Wyckoff.

NOW he understood. Miss Morton had given up her highly expensive lessons in order to be married. He had heard that. And now, of course, she was sending this brusque husband of hers to arrange for the lessons' renewal. Professor Wyckoff fairly exuded cordiality. "It is a delight!" he murmured, "I assure you I—"

"The pleasure is all yours," snapped Dick, glowering at him with strong distaste. "I'm here to ask you a few questions. I'd like straight answers to them. I won't take up much of your time."

"If you are speaking about my plans for Miss Morton to study for grand opera, under my guidance," gushed Wyckoff. "I shall be glad and honored to help her. I can—"

"I'm not," interrupted Dick. "I want to ask you about her voice."

"It is a marvelous voice," declared the teacher. "And—"

"It is," grimly assented Herron. "It is a marvelous voice. There are magnificent tones in it. And she has beautiful expression and understanding and feeling. But—her *singing* is not like anyone's else."

"Quite true! Quite true!" enthused Wyckoff. "Her singing is remarkable. It—"

"It is, indeed," said Dick. "It would cause remark, even in a boiler-factory. Do all your pupils sing as my wife sings?"

"Alas, no!" sighed the professor in regret. "If only they did—"

"If only they did, the Board of Health would shut up your studio as a public nuisance. Drop bluffing, man, and talk turkey. Unless you're deaf or a congenital fool, you know as well as I do that my wife can't turn a tune. She can't sing any more than a cow. She has a glorious voice, and plenty of feeling and temperament behind it, but that's all the good it does her. What's wrong?"

"I—I don't understand, sir!" exclaimed Wyckoff in fine

astonishment.

"No?" sneered Dick. "Then I'll have to put on the screws. You've just offered to help my wife study for grand opera. You made the same suggestion to her. If you don't give me straight answers, I propose to go into court and swear to the offer you made. She can swear to it too. Then I will let her sing to the jury. And if they don't jail you for fraud, it will be because they've all gone insane from the noise. The papers will enjoy the story too. Now will you speak up?"

WYCKOFF stared in terror at this brute of a visitor. He realized the man was in earnest. He saw, too, that ruin was uncomfortably near.

"If you'll tell me the truth," added Dick, "I wont prosecute. Take your choice."

Wyckoff promptly if tearfully took his choice. Dick's curt questions elicited the ensuing facts:

Ruth Herron was totally and unconsciously tone-deaf.

She could play the piano by note—as can any deaf person. But without her notes she could not tell one musical sound from another. She was gifted with every quality of a perfect musician, except only the all-necessary quality of "ear." The black and white keys guided her piano-playing. But as there are, unluckily, no black and white keys in the human throat, her singing was wholly tuneless.

Such an affliction Du Maurier described in "Trilby." Such an affliction is far more common in real life than anyone but an aurist or a musician realizes. Tone-deafness in no way affects the ordinary hearing. It merely makes its victim unaware that she is singing off the pitch. Sometimes—as in the case of Ruth—a person thus cursed can even detect musical defects in others and not in herself. It is a freak malady that is supposed—like ordinary deafness—to come from any of a half-dozen different causes. Sometimes it is inherent, sometimes not.

All this Professor Otto Wyckoff explained more or less technically. He had several such pupils, he said.

Pressed by Dick as to why he had not told Ruth, at the outset, that she could never hope to sing, he reluctantly hinted that her money was as good as any other applicant's—also that her three half-hour lessons a week, at eight dollars per lesson, had helped materially in driving the wolf from the studio door. The same thrifty incentive, he opined, had moved his Italian colleague, Signor Barratti—to whom he had sent her for three months.

"What harm?" pleaded Wyckoff as Dick fought strenuously against a yearning to kick him. "If I say to a pupil, 'You can never hope to sing,' will she believe me? *No!* She will go to the next teacher—and so on, until she finds one who will lie to her and take her money. Then why not I? It happens oftener than outsiders know. The pupil is taught all I can teach her. She is made happy by my praise. Her friends either are too polite to tell her her singing is bad, or else they think it must be good because she is taking high-priced lessons. When at last she thinks she is ready for opera or for the concert-stage, she believes it is the manager's cruelty and stupidity that keep her from getting the chance she wants. The managers tell her she cannot sing. She knows better. And she is a martyr to prejudice—which makes her happy. Women love to be martyrs. So, you see, I do no harm to anyone. Everyone is satisfied. And really, some of my pupils have had great careers. For example, there was—"

But Dick, fearing the kick-temptation might overcome him, stamped out of the studio.

ONE thing was clear: Herron had not the courage, or the heartlessness, to tell Ruth that her singing was abominable. He could not do it. Her joy at his supposed rapturous approval of her vocalism was pathetic. She took to singing as she moved about the flat. And nervous people, above and under them, began to hammer on the walls. Dick felt as though he were in a daytime nightmare. Nearly every evening, now, she would go to the piano as soon as dinner was over. And a half-hour of torment would follow. She had also resumed her practicing. The family next door complained to the janitor—who truculently waylaid Dick in the downstairs hall—and whom a ten-dollar tip reduced to doubting complacency and to a reluctant vow of protection.

And through it all he was a million times sorrier for Ruth than for himself. He loved her with all his heart. She adored him, and she lived only for his happiness. She was so innocently vain of her singing, and so proud of the pleasure he said it gave him. He could not break her heart by destroying this poor delusion of hers. So he set his teeth and bore it. And thus three cacophonous months screeched along.

THEN came surcease. Ruth went out, one slushy winter day, with fur-laden shoulders and silk-clad ankles; and she came back with a nasty cold that settled in her throat. Of course, singing was quite out of the question, even when the hoarseness grew better. She must wait for nearly a month before trying to sing again. For, as she ruefully explained to her sympathizing husband, a voice may be forever ruined by singing too soon after a cold.

Dick was half tempted to ask her, in that case, to sing at once. But he swore at himself as an unworthy beast for harboring such a thought. And he bought her the long-desired vocal score of "La Bohème"—in limp leather covers—by way of penance.

Two days later he was sent West to sing the song of the cash-register siren to a Denver capitalist. Long and hopelessly Dick's firm had sought to interest this Denver man in their new type of cash-register. His influence and his money would mean fresh life to their slightly sagging enterprise. As a last resort Dick was sent out to see him.

The capitalist was Waller K. Gurnee, a silver king who liked to dabble in profitable new ventures. But Dick found it singularly hard to interest the old fellow in this particular enterprise, and he clawed about furtively for some common ground whereon they two could meet.

He found this common ground during the very first hour. He found it when he asked Gurnee to go to some show with him that evening. Gurnee refused the invitation with the air of a Puritan declining a ticket to a Sunday dog-fight. The Chicago Opera Company, he said, was in town, and Gilderoy Scott was to sing a "guest-performance" that night in "Samson and Delilah." Gurnee added the information that he would not miss a treat like that for all the so-called "shows" between Frisco and Rahway.

THAT night they sat side by side, spellbound, at the opera.

Then they adjourned to Gurnee's bachelor-quarters, where till two A.M. they alternately thrummed opera-music from memory and wrangled over rival singers and composers. They parted as intimate friends—to lunch together next noon and to sit rapturously together through an "Aäida" matinée.

Three days later Gurnee (somewhat interested at last in the new cash-register and infinitely more interested in his new music-loving chum) started east with Dick to look over the proposition in person.

Dick was elated. Yet he was too experienced a salesman—and fisherman too—not to realize that it is one thing to hook a big fish and quite another thing to land him.

If this Gurnee deal should go through, it meant the doubling of Dick Herron's salary. If the deal, at this late stage, should slump, then Dick's would be the blame and the punishment for the failure. Wherefore he played his prize right warily.

Gurnee, during the journey, railed against the sameness of dining-car meals. He went on to complain of a bachelor's miserable fate in having only restaurant meals, at best, and of missing the subtle charm of home-cookery. Loudly he declared that he would rather eat home-cooked chuck-steak and potatoes than the most elaborate hotel-banquet Brillat-Savarin ever devised.

This was Dick's cue. He was proud—and justly proud—of his wife's skill as a housekeeper. He now boasted modestly of it, and ended by asking Gurnee to take potluck with them at a family dinner the next night. Gurnee eagerly accepted.

Through Dick's joy—enhancing it, while he was ashamed of the disloyal thought—ran a throb of delight that Ruth could not possibly sing for their guest. Had her voice still been in commission, he knew he would not have dared invite Gurnee to the flat. The music-mad Westerner would have fled in panic terror from such sounds as she produced in singing. For the success of his enterprise Dick felt that it would be as wise to kick Gurnee in the face as to let Ruth sing for him.

But the month of enforced songlessness was not more than half gone. And without hurting her feelings, Dick could avoid asking her to sing. Whereat he rejoiced.

RUTH was looking her very prettiest when Waller K. Gurnee was ushered into the dainty little living-room of the flat at seven next evening. Gurnee's look of appraisal quickly changed to one of real approval. Before he had been there three minutes, he announced fervidly:

"This is a *home!*"

The little dinner itself was simple and delicious and well served. Ruth made herself very charming to the elderly guest. Gurnee expanded into perfect contentment. Dick, furtively watching him, felt his own hopes soar to the stars. The fish was hooked!

After dinner, while the three were at coffee in the living-room, a call from the office drew Dick to the telephone at the opposite end of the flat. One of the partners had called him up on a matter of routine business; and it was a full ten minutes before he could get back to his guest.

(In ten minutes, battles have been won or lost, fortunes have piled up or collapsed, city-wide conflagrations have gotten beyond control, tall ships have sunk with all on board, kings have been crowned or assassinated—and hooked fish have torn free.)

As Dick returned to the living-room, he halted on the threshold, limp and sick with horror at what he saw.

Ruth was standing at the piano, turning over the vocal score of "Samson and Delilah." Gurnee, at her side, was beaming with delight.

"Say, Herron!" boomed the capitalist as he caught sight of Dick. "Why in blue blazes didn't you ever tell me your wife was a great contralto? That wasn't fair, old man. You came near robbing me of a wonderful treat."

"I—she—my wife has a bad cold!" stammered poor Dick, his face ghastly. "She—she has a glorious voice. I love to—to hear her sing. Everybody does. But she can't sing with such a cold. It might ruin her voice forever. That's why I didn't tell you. I—I was afraid you might ask—"

"Oh, my cold is all right now," Ruth reassured Gurnee, whose face had grown long with disappointment at Dick's words. "It is entirely gone. It wont hurt me to sing. I'd be very glad to. See, here is the *"Mon cœur s'ouvre à ta voix"* aria. That was what you asked for, wasn't it, Mr. Gurnee?"

"You bet it was!" declared Gurnee as he settled back in an easy-chair with a grunt of sheer happiness. "I could listen to it all night."

"*Ruth!*" began Herron in despair.

THEN he checked himself. And a wholesome indignation surged through him. This lovely girl-wife of his had done her level best to make his guest's evening happy. In offering to sing for him, she was seeking to give him pleasure. If the man did not like her pitiful singing, he could get out and stay out.

Again a great gush of pity and loyalty toward Ruth surged up in Herron. He felt as might a mother whose crippled child essays to dance. And glowering at the smugly expectant Gurnee, he braced himself for the ordeal.

Then Ruth threw back her bare shoulders and began to sing.

Dick Herron's jaw dropped, even as at his first hearing of her voice. Far more than that, amazement gripped and held him spellbound. He even forgot to glare at Waller K. Gurnee. From the girl's full throat and into the hushed room issued a flood of heaven-born melody. Her voice sank from velvety high notes to glorious organ-tones and soared again. All the passion and beauty of the Saint-Saens melody swept through her marvelous interpretation. And true as compass to star was her voice to the pitch.

Seldom, off the grand-opera stage, had such contralto singing been heard. It was golden; it was hypnotic; it was—why, it was unbelievable!

Soon—all too soon—the divine aria sank into silence. For an instant longer the trance of incredulity still enwrapped Dick Herron. He glanced blinkingly across at Gurnee. Tears were rolling unchecked down the Westerner's rugged cheeks, tears of pure art-loving ecstasy.

Neither man applauded. Neither man stirred. Ruth turned from the piano in wistful appeal to her husband.

Dick could not speak. He got unsteadily to his feet, walked over to her and,—oblivious of Gurnee's presence, bent down and kissed her. He felt like a man in a wonder-dream from which presently he must awake. Then Gurnee found voice:

"Oh, tremendous! God-given!" sputtered the Westerner brokenly, "More! *More* of it, won't you—*please?*"

IT was after Ruth had sung herself almost hoarse and Gurnee had at last torn himself away from the most rapturous music-evening of his life. Herron and his wife were alone together. And still Dick did not know what to say nor how to say it.

"He seemed to like my singing," ventured Ruth.

"*Like* it?" repeated Dick. "I should think he did. *Like* isn't the word. We went crazy over it—both of us. What—why—"

"I think I sing even better, since my operation," she said.

"Operation?" he echoed. "What operation?"

"Oh, I didn't mean to tell!" she exclaimed. "I forgot. I didn't tell you before you went West, because I was afraid it would worry you."

"*What* operation?" he demanded.

"When I went to Dr. Colfax about my cold," she confessed, "he looked over my breathing-apparatus and my nostrils and my ears, and all my head and throat. And he found I had a sort of—of 'adhesion,' I think he called it—somewhere in the eustachian tubes, on each side. And he advised me to have it attended to, because some day it might thicken and make me deaf. So I did. It was a very simple operation. It hardly hurt at all. And I had to stay indoors only two days. And—"

"Why didn't you tell me?" he asked in keen concern.

"You would only have worried. And it wasn't a bit serious. But the funny part of it is that it seemed to do something queer to my hearing or else to my voice. For when I began practicing again, a few days ago, I found I made the most dreadful sounds! I'm glad you weren't here to listen to them. It almost drove me crazy to hear them. It was *awful,* Dick! I suppose the operation had changed the connection between my hearing and my voice. (Dr. Colfax warned me that it does, sometimes. He says people have been cured of tone-deafness, for instance, that way.) So I had to adjust myself all over again to the scale. It was easy enough, of course. But for a day or two I was afraid my singing would never again be what it had been. Wasn't it lucky that didn't happen when Mr. Gurnee was here?"

"Yes," he admitted dazedly, "it—it was lucky. It was—it was—yes, dear, it was—*lucky!*"

NEXT morning Dick encountered the janitor in the lower hall. "Say, Mr. Herron," confided the guardian of the furnace. "The agent ought to pay you a commission. That fam'ly on the floor below you has just decided to stay on here for another year. They say they wouldn't move away from that voice of your wife's—not if they had to pay twice the rent. And they was the folks that was kicking worst about it, a month back. Funny, ain't it?"

"Yes," assented Dick, "it is funny. Have a cigar. Have *three* cigars."

The Rabbit Man

HE was named Hector Dangerfield. And the name was as completely wasted on him as a Winter Garden show on a blind man.

No, he did not have gloomily smoldering eyes set deep in a chiseled face beneath a crown of crisp, black curls. His voice did not have an organ-note to it that stirred women's souls. His shoulders were not massive. And his form in no way suggested the graceful power of a panther's.

To summarize: he was Hector Dangerfield in name only.

His hair was wispily yellow. His eyes were pale blue and large. His front teeth were many and prominent. His curving nose had a funny way of quivering, when he was perturbed. His body was angular—long rather than tall—and gangling.

Less because of his eyes and nose than from his mental attitude toward life, a fellow in the office had dubbed him "the Rabbit Man." And the name stuck.

The Rabbit Man was thirty-eight years old. He was drawing a salary of forty dollars a week as cashier in the brokerage office of John Brewster, at 999 Wall Street.

Forty dollars a week is grossly inadequate pay for the cashier of such a firm. Everybody knew that, from Brewster himself down to the new office boy—at least, everybody knew it except the Rabbit Man.

When Hector had been brusquely notified, three months earlier, that he was to be promoted from his twenty-five-dollar job as chief clerk, to the cashier's coop left vacant by old Hinkle's defalcation, he had wept tears of real joy and had chokingly promised Brewster to dedicate his whole future life to the firm's welfare. And he had ever since been busy trying to prove his gratitude for the glittering promotion.

Had it not been for that lachrymosely grateful pledge of lifelong service, John Brewster would probably have offered him an almost suitable salary to go with the new post, for the Rabbit Man was a splendid worker. But even while Hector was blurting his thanks, Brewster did a bit of lightning calculation—not in figures, but in human nature. And he added the tidings that Dangerfield's weekly wage would henceforth be forty dollars.

This news served only to add to the Rabbit Man's delirium of joy. Forty dollars means a sixty per cent increase over twenty-five dollars. What it means, otherwise, in an era of forty-nine-cent butter and fifty-four-cent eggs no householder needs to be told.

HECTOR DANGERFIELD, on the day of his raise, went home to his wife with the glorious story. He did not "run every step of the way," as good-news-bearers do in stories—because he lived on 149th Street, and the subway moves faster than a man can run—sometimes.

But in toiling up the four flights of stairs that led to his flat, he used very creditable speed. And he burst into the living-room of his flat with a really excellent imitation of a whirlwind.

There he found his wife playing a particularly atrocious game of solitaire known as double Canfield—at which she was cheating herself, with brazen dishonesty.

One need not be a Hector Dangerfield in looks and prowess, as well as in name, to win the hearts of some women. Look about you at the drearily stupid and ugly and lifeless and non-magnetic and impecunious and even disgusting men of your acquaintance. Practically all of them have managed to marry. And some of them have won glorious wives. Is it any miracle, then, that long before he was thirty-eight the Rabbit Man had been able to annex a bride?

She was a drab-haired, flat-faced little woman who affected brown clothes and common-sense shoes. About her breath ever clung a faint aroma of cold tea—about her sallow skin a similar hint of cold cream.

Sadie Dangerfield was a good soul, and sweet and simple, withal. And she loved her rabbitical spouse. Yes, and she revered him too, as the most wonderful man on earth. Hector could audit tradesmen's bills and compute interest on their savings-bank account, with a swift accuracy that fairly took away her breath.

When he announced that he was now cashier of the sterling brokerage house of John Brewster, she eyed him in dumb amaze. When he went on to say that his salary would henceforth be forty dollars a week, Sadie uttered a little birdlike screech and proceeded to dissolve in tears of pure bliss.

That evening they had round- (instead of chuck-) steak and scallions for dinner; afterward they went to a fifteen- (not ten-) cent movie, and wound up their Monte Cristo evening by a supper at a restaurant.

The celebration-spree ended, they joyously took up the burden of their new and exalted life. For days they felt absurdly rich. That extra fifteen dollars, weekly, in Hector's pay-envelope seemed at first to represent a needless weight of wealth.

BIT by bit, however,—indeed, with sickening rapidity, they adapted themselves to their swollen fortunes. And presently, to their dismay, they found themselves facing the same fiscal pinch as before, at the close of each month.

A raise of salary lasts, usually, about two weeks—so far as its actual effects are concerned. One has lived in tolerable comfort on a certain sum; that sum is increased; by all logic, one can live on the same sum and in the same style as before, and put the extra money in the bank. This, as a rule, one fatuously plans to do. But presently, with no conscious addition to the price of livelihood, the whole amount goes for the purchase of the very same livelihood as did the former salary. And there is nothing left over.

There is no answer to the sorry riddle. It is just one of the grim mysteries of life. The "high cost of living" has nothing at all to with it, as everybody can testify who remembers the same phenomenon, away back in the days of lower prices.

So, with the Rabbit Man and his adoring wife, the miracle of added wealth soon simmered down to the daily grind of keeping out of debt. More than once, on rent-day, Sadie found herself wistfully regretting the dollar and eighty-five cents that had so needlessly been squandered in a single night on celebrating that raise of Hector's.

At the office, in his brass-grill hutch by the east window, the Rabbit Man was proving himself a splendidly efficient cashier. Being totally without imagination, he had a genius for figures. This same dearth of imagination barred him from maudlin ambition and from the temptation to take Wall Street plunges with the firm's funds.

During the hours he was on duty, money ceased to be money to him. It became merely a set of valueless counters in an intricate game he was paid to play. He did not even indulge in the immemorial cashier's grouch over the fact that though thousands of dollars passed weekly through his fingers, only forty dollars of the whole huge sum was allowed to stick to them.

John Brewster had risen to his present estate chiefly because of his unerring estimate of men. He had read Hector Dangerfield as though the Rabbit Man were eighteen-point type. And he knew he could trust the colorless cashier with his very soul.

For this reason the examination of Hector's accounts was purely perfunctory. And the cashier was the only man in the place, except Brewster himself, who had access to the safe and vault.

The Rabbit Man, with meek joy, noted these proofs of his master's approval. He even dared to hope, in optimistic moments, that he might be allowed to hold his present job, at his present pay, until he should be at least seventy years old. Such things had happened. The prospect thrilled Hector. And more and more he strove to render himself worthy of it.

ORDINARILY the John Brewster offices were as drab and unimaginative as was the Rabbit Man himself. But there were rare and bewildering exceptions. These exceptions invariably took the form of Mona Brewster, wife of Hector's employer.

Mrs. Brewster, once a month or so, used to gladden the dull brokerage firm by a visit. Her passage from the outer door to the glass-enclosed private office of her husband was like a bird of paradise's flight through a jungle-mist. Conservative women were wont to speak charitably of Mrs. Brewster's toilets, as "extreme." To the Rabbit Man, they were kaleidoscopic visions of loveliness. Sometimes they were of flaming scarlet, slashed with black, and with a huge picture-hat to match. Sometimes, in summer, they were dazzlingly white, gay with gold braid and crowned by a snowy lace hat.

Seldom did Mrs. Brewster wear the same dress twice to the office. Never did she deign to appear in a costume that would not have drawn a goodly share of attention away from a political parade or a full-speed ambulance. She always walked with a swinging rapidity which did little to detract from the notice her clothes brought her. Her facial coloring was vivid—and it was her own. She had glorious eyes, too, and a bewitching collection of dimples and a quick smile that was sunlight.

In any place her advent would have created a stir. In the Brewster brokerage house, nothing but office discipline prevented a total suspension of work while she was there. Of all the efficient little band of workers, in those gloomy offices, John Brewster alone seemed unimpressed by her glory. Brewster, indeed, displayed positive signs of crankiness when Mona honored him with a call. How much of this peevish ungraciousness was due to the husband's reluctance to part with the checks she invariably bore away with her, and how much to a distaste for cyclonic interruptions during business hours, Brewster alone knew.

ONE day, a year earlier, the Rabbit Man had chanced to be in the private office when the boss' wife came in. Brewster had not introduced the subordinate to Mona, but had dismissed him from the room with a grunt. Ever since then, however, Mona had nodded carelessly to the Rabbit Man when she had passed his desk in the outer office.

A week after his installation as cashier; Hector went to the private office in response to a summons from Brewster. While he was listening to some routine orders, Mona came breezing in at top speed, clad in a wondrous lavender creation that was topped by a hat that looked as might a multicolored wastebasket which had gone to heaven.

The Rabbit Man humbly returned her nod—and edged crablike toward the door. But Brewster halted him.

"Hey, Dangerfield!" snapped his chief. "Hold on a second. This is my wife. When she brings you checks made out to 'M. K. Brewster,' cash 'em.—Dangerfield's our new cashier," he added gruntingly to his wife—and ended the odd introduction by jerking one thumb toward the door and saying to Hector:

"That's all, this morning."

The Rabbit Man was halted at the threshold as he departed. Mona Brewster, with a very decided light of interest in her big eyes, had stretched out her gloved hand, exclaiming:

"So you're cashier now, Mr. Dangerfield? I'm ever so glad! I hated old Hinkle. He was so stuffy and grouchy and—"

"That's *all,* 'smorning, Dangerfield!" interposed Brewster's snarl by way of second dismissal.

And Hector dared not stay longer than to touch in limp response the warmly firm little hand outstretched so cordially to him.

He went back to his hutch with a step that was almost springy. Just as the first glow of his new position had begun to ebb, here was a new proof of the esteem wherein his high office was held. As chief clerk, he had won the barest of nods from the boss' wife. Now, thanks to his cashiership—his hand still tingled from her warm clasp.

Nor did the acquaintance end there. Not a week later Mrs. Brewster brought him a check to cash. And she lingered at his window for fully three minutes, in a brilliant and almost intimate chat with him. The intimacy (and indeed the whole conversation save a few mumbled monosyllables and foolish grins) was all on her side. The brilliancy was supplied by Hector, later on, as he coined apt replies he might have made to her various remarks if he had thought of them in time.

The Rabbit Man's imagination had begun to work.

THAT same imagination—or an intuition, which was just as good—warned him that Sadie would be no happier if he should tell her of his acquaintance with the boss' flamboyantly lovely wife. So he did not mention the matter at home. It was his first secret from Sadie.

After Mona's second check-accompanied visit to the gilt-grilled hutch, the new chief clerk undertook to rally Hector on the interest taken in him by the fair caller.

"Gee, but you're running strong, Rabbit!" quoth the chief clerk in elephantine pleasantry. "Look out, son, or you'll have the old man jealous of you. Oh, I saw the way she gave you the eye! There's a hen on the nest, dead sure!"

But Hector, who had ever prided himself on his powers of quick repartee, answered with an instant and scintillant cleverness that amazed even himself. He said:

"Is *that* so?"

Just like that. It was a harsh thing to say to a friend. Hector realized it. But the fresh chief clerk needed a set-down.

Followed more interviews through the cage-window, and then more. Hector wondered at himself for the queer little thrill that went through him at sight of the woman—at the dizziness in his head and the clamminess of his hands while she talked with him.

His imagination was not only awake; it was beginning to smolder at the edges. He took to going without lunch, once a week, and carrying home on that day a bunch of carnations to Sadie. The gift always delighted his brown little wife, and it had an oddly soothing effect on his own newly troublous conscience.

Then came the afternoon when the office-boy slouched grinningly over to the hutch with word that a lady wanted to talk to Dangerfield in the 'phone booth.

Patteringly and fast the Rabbit Man scurried across to the booth. In all his work-life he had only twice before been summoned to a telephone by a woman. Both of those times Sadie had been at the far end of the wire—once to tell him his mother, out in Kansas, was dead, and once to notify him that sneak-thieves had rifled the flat while she was marketing. And so a call from a woman on the 'phone was at once associated in Hector's mind with disaster.

"Hello!" he called nervously into the receiver. "What's wrong?"

"Oh, is that you, Mr. Dangerfield?" came the reply in a voice he had grown to associate with picture-hats and Morny sachets. "I want to ask a favor of you."

The Rabbit Man turned to make sure the booth door was tightly closed. Then he said breathlessly:

"Anything—anything, Mrs. Brewster."

"How dear of you!" she cooed. "I'm in such a lot of trouble! I wonder if you could manage to drop in here on your way uptown this afternoon?"

"Drop—drop in *where?*" babbled Hector.

"At our apartment," she said, "—the Alhambra, you know. I want so much to see you. About what time can you be here?"

She seemed to take it for granted he was coming—which, after all, was probably the surest way of getting him. His growing imagination had not yet reached the size or age of permitting Hector to fancy his employer's wife was inviting him to her apartment for a personal call. He supposed she wished to see him on a matter of business—perhaps to teach her how to balance her private checking account, as once she had laughingly asked him to.

AT ten minutes past five the Rabbit Man entered an apartment-house foyer that looked like a cross between the nave of a cathedral and the Metropolitan lobby. He was borne upward by an openly supercilious elevator-boy and was deposited outside a mahogany door labeled APARTMENT 65. And presently he found himself ushered into a softly lighted room the very aspect of which made him pause and blink.

The room resembled a Belasco triumph of scenic art and lighting. Through a pinkish haze of veiled lamps, the languorous beauty of it stirred Hector to the soul. He realized, for the first time in his life, that the 149th Street apartment (on which Sadie had spent so much loving care and on which he himself had so gladly squandered more cash than he could afford) was trashy and garish and shoddy—also that it often smelled of dead dinners, dinners wherein cabbage or onions had played prominent rôles.

From a couch at the far end of the room lithely arose Mona Brewster. She came toward him, a wondrously gracious smile of welcome on her vivid face, both her hands held out in eager greeting.

What she said—what he sputtered in slack-jawed reply—he never clearly remembered. He came to himself—a little bit—to find he was sitting on the end of the couch, whither Mona had wafted him, and that she was sitting beside him, so near that the Morny sachet filled his quivering nostrils and the nameless charm of the woman fairly grappled his bemused brain.

And she was talking—he had a vague memory that she had apologized ever so prettily for bothering him to call—and was thanking him for being there. Then, out of the mist, he caught coherent words, such as these:

"And one can talk so much more freely here than at the office. I'm all alone to-day, you know, except for the servants. Mr. Brewster won't be back from Chicago till day after to-morrow."

"I know," said Hector, his rabbit-nose twitching, his rabbit-eyes fixed on her in helpless fascination.

"At the office," she said, "I always have a dreadful feeling as if every word I speak can be heard by everyone. The people there all stare at me so queerly. I wonder why."

She seemed to expect an answer. "Maybe because you're the boss' wife," he hazarded.

Then something—perhaps the tiny contraction of her brows—told him his explanation was unfortunate. So, with an access of heroism, he continued:

"But I guess a good deal more likely it's because you're so pretty."

HER eyes glowed with a strangely happy light. For the briefest instant her warm white hand was laid in his clenched fist. Then she laughed.

"You will make me vain, Mr. Dangerfield," she said almost bashfully.

"Why?" he demanded, bold as a lion. "It's true."

"I am in such a predicament," she said then, changing the subject, her eyes still caressing him. "And I want your advice. Will you help me?"

"Why, of course I will!" he exclaimed.

"When Mr. Brewster went away yesterday, to the Bankers' Convention out in Chicago," she continued, "I forgot—and he forgot too—about my dance tomorrow night. He won't be back till the next day. And I don't like to telegraph or 'phone him about it, because he says he hates to be annoyed by what he calls trifles, when he is away on business. So you're the only person I can turn to for help."

"Help you?" echoed Hector, incredulous at his own good fortune. "Why, sure, Mrs. Brewster. Any way I can."

"My dance is for to-morrow night," explained Mona. "And nearly all my jewelry is in the vault at the office. I have it kept there, because I've a morbid horror of burglars. Well, after telling me to be sure to wear it all, my absentminded husband calmly runs off to Chicago and forgets to take it out of the vault for me."

"Mr. Brewster had a lot of things to remember, when he went away," said Hector. "You can't hardly blame him for—"

"But I *do* blame him," she declared gayly. "Here he tells me to load myself down with jewelry to impress some guests whose husbands he wants to stand well with, and then he goes away, leaving all the jewelry locked in the vault. He told me, once, if ever I wanted anything of mine out of the vault while he was away, to ask *you*—because you have the combination. But I know what responsibility and extra work it will mean for you. So I hate to ask—"

"Why should you hate to ask me?" he queried. "Why, I'll be ever so glad to. And as for responsibility and extra work, why, that's foolishness! The extra work will be to take you down to the vault, open the door for you and close it after you leave. As for the responsibility, I don't quite see where that comes in at all."

"No," she hastened to assent, "neither do I, now you put it that way. And I'll be a million times obliged to you. It's perfectly splendid of you, Mr. Dangerfield. What time does the office open?"

"In the morning? At nine. But I'm generally there half an hour earlier."

"Are you the first one down?"

"No. The chief clerk is due a little after eight."

"Then," she suggested, "if I should get there—and if I could trouble *you* to get there—at about a quarter to eight, I could take the jewelry up to Tiffany's and have it gone over, during the day, and delivered here to me in time for the dance. Some of the settings are old and need looking after. Would it be a horrible lot of trouble to you to meet me there at a quarter of eight? I'm sure Mr. Brewster will appreciate—"

"We can leave Mr. Brewster right out of this, if you don't mind," said Hector with a gallant air worthy of his name. "I'm doing this as a personal favor to *you,* not as part of my job. And I don't mind telling you I'm tickled to death at being able to help you. I'll be waiting at the office for you, at seven-forty-five."

"You're a dear!" she cried in sudden fervor.

Before the utterly dumfounded man could guess her intent, she had thrown both arms around his neck and kissed him on the mouth!

Then, laughing with almost hysteric gayety, she sprang to her feet and ran to the door. Holding it open, and laughing tenderly up into his face, she said:

"Your dinner will be stone cold. I'm a little beast to have kept you here so long. But—but oh, it was *good* to see you!"

WHEN Hector Dangerfield, the Rabbit Man, recovered full consciousness, he was plodding northward in the general direction of his own flat. His fists were clinched with painful tightness. His mouth was wide open. He was stepping very high. He heard himself stuttering, incoherently:

"She loves me! She *loves* me! She kissed me—right on the mouth! Put her arms around me and hugged me too! Called me a dear! She kissed me! She loves me!"

The rabbit was transfigured into a love-bird. His pulses hammered in his sunken temples. His blood throbbed and swirled through his meager body. He felt twenty, not thirty-eight—an invigorated giant, not a thin-chested wage-slave exhausted at a hard day's end.

Steadying his racing brain, he forced himself to go over the whole incredible scene and the scenes that had led up to it. Yes, there could be no doubt that this wonder-woman loved him. To his simple code, her embrace could not possibly mean anything else. She loved him—him, the drab, meek drudge whom the boys at the office had so mercilessly nicknamed the Rabbit Man! The rapture of the gods roared through his soul.

But suddenly he remembered that Manhattan is not Olympus, and that the loves of the prehistoric deities are known by far uglier names in the twentieth century.

"She's—she's the boss' wife!" he told himself dazedly. "It'd—why, it'd be a sin! That's right—a sin. It wasn't her fault, poor kid! She was just kind of carried away, like the girls in books. But—but I've got to save her—and myself too. I *got* to. And Sadie, too! My Lord! What in blazes is there about me, anyhow, that makes 'em all love me?"

He was more than wontedly tender to Sadie that evening. And her mildly arid kiss stung him like a white-hot brand. Covertly, he had wiped his mouth before she kissed him. He explained his late homecoming and his need of early departure from home on the morrow, by rush of extra work in Brewster's absence.

Then, all night long, he lay very still, his eyes wide open, listening to Sadie's unsilenced breathing, and fighting out within his own mind the Armageddon battle that most men must wage at least once in their wedded lives.

That battle, as a rule, is for the strong, the magnetic, the good-to-look-at—not for rabbit men. Yet the victory—when there is a victory—is none the less glorious to the one than to the other. And as gray dawn trickled in at the bedroom's airshaft window, victory came to Hector Dangerfield—a victory as pure, as dazzling, as self-renunciatory as to Galahad of old.

The Rabbit Man bent over, his eyes wet, and kissed the mouth-ajar of his slumbering wife. Very softly he kissed her, very remorsefully.

Then, his Armageddon won, he fell asleep.

Please don't laugh at him. He had *won*—where Launcelot, Tristan, Antony and a dozen more of your favorite heroes have most signally lost. Rabbit Man or superman, the sad triumph is the same—the barren, heartbreaking, empty, divine triumph!

PROMPTLY at seven-forty-five Hector was waiting at the outer door of the Brewster offices. And one minute later Mona joined him there, carrying a satchel. She lacked her wonted color and vivacity. Her lustrous eyes were heavy—well-nigh as heavy as his own. He noted her aspect, and he thought he understood.

Almost without a word of greeting, the two went down to the vault. Hector plied the combination. The outer grating and then the gray steel door swung sullenly open. He stood aside, holding the heavy portal in place, while the woman passed in.

Ten minutes later she emerged. Her pallor was gone. Once more the gay light danced in her eyes, and her bright color surged flauntingly back.

Refusing his help with the bag, she ran up the steps, leaving him to close the gates. At the top step, she was waiting for him.

"Thank you, a million times!" she said, still clinging to the bag with her right hand while she held out her left to him. "And you *are* a dear!"

The Rabbit Man drew a deep breath. The moment had come—the moment for the dread consummation of which he had battled so valiantly all night long.

"No, Mrs. Brewster," he denied, speaking loudly and hoarsely, "I am not a dear. And you mustn't call me one—because it isn't right. I know that, now. It's—it's wicked. You didn't stop to think of that, of course. I know you didn't. You didn't think. You're pretty young yet. So I have to be sane for us both."

A queer gurgling note, as of stark amazement, broke in on his hastily stammered speech. But he raced on, not daring to look at her as he spoke.

"I know you care," he said. "And—I'm afraid *I* care too. But we both got to get over it—because it's wrong. And it isn't square to the boss or to Sadie. They trust us, you see. Why, Sadie thinks I'm the best man ever born. And I don't doubt but what of course Mr. Brewster thinks just the same of you. And we can't go back on 'em. We *can't.* It wouldn't be square. It's—it's got to be good-by, Mrs. Brewster..... It seems funny for me to be still calling you Mrs. Brewster, don't it, after what's happened? But I don't know your first name. And anyhow, I got no right to call you by it if I did..... Yes, it's got to be good-by, right here and now. I can't call to see you any more. And you'd best not stop at my desk to see *me,* either. It's the only safe way to—"

A trill of laughter that swelled through the whole tier of offices broke in on his passionate self-renunciation. In amazement he looked at Mona. Her head thrown back, she was giving vent to peals of untrammeled mirth, her body shaken by a spasm of ridicule.

"Poor thing!" exclaimed Hector, perturbed. "You're all hysterical! Don't take it like that!

"Oh, stop! *Stop!*" she panted, exhausted. "You'll be the death of me, you babbling idiot! Did you actually think—"

Laughter again drowned her words—laughter that all at once came to a hideously jarring halt. The vivid color ebbed from her face, leaving it gray and stricken. Clutching the satchel in both hands, she was staring in blank horror past the blanker face of the Rabbit Man.

Hector turned to see what had so stricken the youth and merriment from her eyes. Walking toward them from the front entrance of the offices was John Brewster.

EVEN as Hector turned, Brewster caught sight of the two. He stopped and stared with quick intentness from one to the other. Then, slowly, head lowered like an attacking dog's, he moved forward.

Mona, in dire terror, slipped the bag behind her. She stood quaking, one corner of her mouth twisted oddly downward, revealing a flash of eyetooth between the full red lips.

"Good morning, Mr. Brewster," said Hector. "We didn't expect you back till to-morrow."

"I came back a day early," answered Brewster, "—on a hunch. It's lucky I did."

He did not look at Hector as he spoke, but at Mona; and he continued to advance until he towered bulkily above the cowering woman.

"I stopped at the apartment on my way downtown," went on

Brewster, his words grating harshly between his shut teeth. "I missed you there by five minutes. But I got the note you left me. That was your game, eh? To make a clean-up and go off this morning with Cutter? Soul-mate stuff, eh? That note'll read nicely, in court. I was afraid you'd made the clean-up yesterday, but I came down here on the chance. Give me that bag!"

He fairly spat the command at her. She quivered and shrank farther away from him, against the stairway wall.

"Give me that bag!" he reiterated, reaching toward the satchel. "Give it to me, or I'll take it."

"Look here, Mr. Brewster!" put in Hector, tremulous yet unflinching. "That's hardly the way to speak to a lady, even when she's your wife. Now—"

"Shut up, you!" snarled Brewster. "I'll have plenty of time for you, later."

WITH a sudden motion he gripped the satchel and at one savage wrench tore it away from his wife's grasp. She cried out and snatched for it, but he thrust her aside and opened the bag.

Dumping its contents on the nearest desk-top, he brooded a moment over them with half-shut, apprais-ing eyes.

Hector, furious at his employer's rough-ness toward Mona, had taken a shaky step in his direction, with some vague idea of thrashing

as much of the big man as he could reach. But now, catching sight of the loot poured out on the desk, he stopped, gaping.

"H'm!" came a nasal growl from Brewster. "A very neat haul, for an amateur: the jewelry I'm holding as collateral for Mrs. Sutherland; your own jewelry, of course—you can take that and get out; that block of bonds Tim Crowley is trading against—negotiable, all of 'em; my mother's pearl necklace; and the three sheafs of bills for this week's pay-roll! You didn't overlook very much in my compartment, did you?"

"Well!" shrilled the woman in a gust of vicious fury, "what are you going to do? What are you going to do about it? Don't stand there snorting and sneering! What are you going to do? Send me to prison?"

"Prison?" Brewster laughed drearily. "No. Why should I? I've no grudge against the prisons. I'm going to punish you more than that! I'm going to—"

"Make me go back home and live with you?" she mocked, raging.

"No," he denied grimly, "not that. I said I was going to punish *you*—not myself. I'm going to do the thing that'll punish you worst and longest. Your note said you were sick of me, because I'm so gross and material and money-grubbing.

You said you love Cutter, because he's your soul-mate. Well, there's no worse punishment on earth or in hell than for two soul-mates to be condemned to live together. Here's your own jewelry. Take it and get out."

Her head high, the woman took the proffered case of jewels and turned to go. Hector timidly accosted her.

"Mrs. Brewster," he faltered, "I don't understand anything of this, but it looks like you're in trouble. If you want a nice home to shelter you while you look around a bit, my flat's open to you. Sadie will be glad to help you—"

"For heaven's sake," snapped the woman, "stop blithering and let me get by! If it hadn't been for your keeping me here, maundering idiotic rot, I might have gotten safe away before he caught me. Move aside!"

Hector shrank away from her rage-inflamed glare. She sped past him with the swinging, goddesslike tread he had so often admired. He looked wistfully and amazedly after her. He was beginning to understand. But even yet he couldn't believe. It didn't make sense. She was—

BREWSTER'S harsh voice recalled him to himself.

"And it was you who let her into the vault, you rabbit-faced goop!" the boss was thundering. "What d'you do a bone-head thing like that for? What right had you to go and—"

"She—she was your wife," stammered Hector. "She said she wanted her jewelry to wear to a party. And probably she did."

"What right had you to let—"

"She was your wife," said Hector with more firmness. "Sadie,— that's my wife, —Sadie and I have our savings-bank money in a joint account. I supposed all married folks did. It was your office. Why wouldn't your own wife have a perfect right to—"

"You quadruple, gooseberry-eyed idiot!" roared the exasperated Brewster. "If you had enough sense to be crazy, you'd be in an asylum. I—"

"Mr. Brewster!" spoke up Hector, horror at his newborn knowledge of womankind driving all lesser considerations from him and turning his mild temper into a total loss. "Mr. Brewster, no man can call me a rabbit or—or a gooseberry any longer, and get away with it.

I'm through being bullied! Get that? I'm *through!* And I'm through working for a man who can bully me. I resign. Understand? I *resign!* G'by!"

He strode away, his brain afire. This woman—this woman he had deemed so wonderful—she had fooled him. She had played him for a sucker, pretending to love him and all that. She was a thief! Yes, and she was wicked in other ways too—ways he had read about.

Hector Dangerfield was very thoroughly and very suddenly cured of his one craving to stray from the narrow path, into the primrose-strewn byways. And with the shock of his cure came a wave of remorse at his shameful if brief mental infidelity to Sadie.

Sadie! How sweet and dear and gentle and wholly good Sadie was! And how his heart now went out to her in an agony of love! You'd never catch Sadie kissing helpless strangers and calling them dear, or robbing her husband's vaults. Sadie was the real thing.

He had treated her abominably—in his own thoughts, at least. And now, by his moment of insane rebellion,—by the maniac wrath of a tortured rabbit,—he had thrown away the job that meant food and home to her!

HECTOR had almost reached the farthermost door. His feet began to lag. But they did not lag soon enough to suit John Brewster, who had stood thunderstruck at the revolt of his hitherto spineless serf. Through his own mental tumult, Brewster was beginning to remember that, while wives are plentiful, perfect cashiers are few.

"Hey, there!" he called almost civilly—so nearly civilly that Hector kept on in his retreat, thinking the boss must be speaking to some one else.

"Hey, there!" called Brewster again, as with perturbation he saw his most valuable employee's hand reach for the knob of the outer door. "Come back here, Dangerfield! I didn't mean to rile you. Make allowances, can't you, for the nerves of a man who's just lost a wife—even if she was a wife he'd been trying to lose for five years! It was a jolt!"

Hector paused in doubting astonishment. Brewster mistook his dull aspect for stubbornness, and he said soothingly:

"Don't say resign, son! You'll have sixty a week after this. I've been meaning to raise it for a long time. Let bygones be bygones..... Where are you going *now?*" he added peevishly as Hector sheered off from the door and scuttled toward the telephone-booths.

"I'm going to call up the wife and tell her about my raise, of course," prattled the Rabbit Man over his shoulder.

"It's worth it!" muttered Brewster resignedly to himself as he slouched into his private office. "He's the best cashier we ever had. I couldn't let him go. Besides, he'd 'a' blabbed all over the Street about how easy it is to lift collateral from my vault. And he'd 'a' gotten me the big laugh by telling how she tried to clean me out. Sixty a week is cheap, to keep his rabbit-mouth shut. And he's a good man—in his cage."

"*Sadie!*" almost screamed Hector into the receiver, "I've got another raise! We're boosted to *sixty!* No, no, not fifty—*sixty!* Get that? Now chase out, like a darling, and get a pair of seats for a show—a *real* show. This calls for a regular he-celebration. I tell you they can't keep a good man down. And—and Sadie, I forgot to say I love you, Sadie! You're a perfectly dandy girl!"

Caritas

THE scheme was very simple indeed. The Sentinel Film Corporation fathered it. It had no mother. Maguire, vice president of the Sentinel, not only had evolved the idea but had named it. He called it the Caritas Chain. Vague memories of a term and a half at evening high school, eighteen years earlier, apprised Maguire that *caritas* was Latin for charity. He explained this to Zigler, president and sole visible stockholder of the Sentinel.

Zigler's scholastic education had gone without high-school trimmings, having been interrupted when, at twelve, he went to work as handy boy in his cousin's one-room garment factory. From that moment he had become a self-made man, who bowed before his maker, and who had scant patience with folk fashioned along more showy and less practical lines.

Nevertheless, at this proof of his subordinate's classical lore the great man was secretly impressed. Higher education, though useless for oneself, was a pretty thing to buy, along with the more practical services of a good colleague. Besides, now that Zigler came to say the two words over, one after the other, *caritas* really did sound a good deal like charity.

Zigler was certain Latin must be a mighty easy language to learn—if, like himself, the student chanced to note its strong likeness to English. Zigler even nourished vagrom plans for spending an entire week's evenings—sometime—with a really good tutor, and mastering it, root and branch. It would be a handy tongue to speak in the office— with Maguire—when he did not want a stenographer or an actor or an exhibitor to know what he was saying.

Young Chris Lane, Maguire's sixty-dollar-a-week protégé in the Sentinel's publicity department, was almost as strongly impressed as was his overlord at the vice president's easy familiarity with Latin—until he went to the public library and asked for a lexicon, wherewith to verify the translation.

Lane always verified things. Not that he was suspicious, but because, for five years before coming to the Sentinel, he had been a newspaper reporter, assigned to police headquarters.

Yes; until he looked up *caritas* in the lexicon, Lane was almost as much impressed with Maguire's erudition as Zigler had been. After he read the translation he was infinitely more impressed. For, according to the brand of Latin dictionary on view at the library, *caritas* did not mean "charity" at all; it meant "high price." Which was an inspired definition for the Sentinel's Caritas Chain, originated and laid out by Maguire.

A series, or chain, of summer resorts was to be visited by a squad of three Sentinel employees between May and October. During the winter the squad's activities were to be shifted to such places as Palm Beach, Pass Christian, Asheville, and the like.

At each resort the richest class of temporary sojourners were to be approached by the Sentinel's spokesman with the following proposition:

In return for contributions amounting to $2974—"exactly the price of manufacture," and so on—the Sentinel was to make a two-reel picture, which would give splendid roles to the contributors and their wives and children.

This picture was to be shown at the local Casino or Country Club, at five dollars a ticket, the proceeds to be devoted to whatsoever charity the colony might choose. The film was then to be destroyed, lest it fall into unworthy hands, and lest the rabble later be allowed to gaze on Society at Play.

The Sentinel, it was to be explained to "prospects," had been growing wealthy through the public's appreciation of its peerless pictures. The Sentinel, therefore, wished to show its appreciation to the public by helping along the holy cause of charity. Wherefore, the Caritas scheme. The Sentinel had whittled down the price of production to the thinnest wedge, the net result being the aforesaid $2974.

This, it was to be explained, would pay—and just pay—the salaries and traveling expenses of the squad, the cost of films and of developing, and such other heavy charges as must attend the venture. Reimbursed for that amount, the Sentinel had no desire to profit further. The rest was charity—or *caritas,* if you prefer.

"'Tis pleasant, sure, to see one's name in print."

And there is positive magic in seeing one's face in films. Thus, there was a strong human-nature tug to the Caritas project, as to everything Maguire undertook to put across.

The difference between the Sentinel's avowed aims and the Sentinel's real hopes in the deal chanced to be the precise difference between charity and *caritas.*

The actual cost of making each two-reel picture in the Caritas Chain would average seven hundred dollars.

Actors, costumes, jewelry, props, settings, exteriors and interiors alike—in short, all adjuncts—would eagerly be supplied by the people who should appear in the picture. The Sentinel's total outlay, thus, would consist of the cost of film and development, and of three employees' salaries, which must be paid anyway.

The plan was simple. It was beautiful! It would net the Sentinel much advertising and $2274 at every resort where the three earnest workers should spend ten days on the making of a picture.

Whether or not the picture would be of a sort alluring enough to draw a fifteen-cent audience at a public theater was no concern of anybody's. It would assuredly draw a five-dollars-a-head local crowd. The performers would see to that. The acting might be terrible; but it would probably be of as good an order as anyone in the select audience could achieve. And the worse the acting, the happier would be those spectators who had not been asked to take part in the charitable work. The trio of Sentinel men picked out to tour the resorts were Regan, the second director; Blake, the camera man; and Chris Lane.

Lane protested loudly and long when Maguire told him of the assignment.

"I don't know anything about the Society crowd," he declared. "I don't speak their language. I'd probably crab the whole thing the minute I opened my head. Besides, you said you were going to send along a lightning scenario writer. Why can't he do my end of the job there, whatever my end of it is to be? Why can't he?"

"He's going to, Chris," replied Maguire, with the encouraging smile of a dentist to the man whose tooth he is about to pull. "He's going to. The same chap is to go to the places, in advance, to put up our proposition to these people, and write the scenarios to fit their especial talent, and to swing whatever publicity the resort newspapers will give the Sentinel. Same man for all three jobs."

"There ain't no sech animal!" scoffed Chris.

"There is!" asserted Maguire with that same tenderly encouraging smile. "He is Chris Lane."

Presently, out of the tumult of explosively disjointed protest babblings with which the frantic Chris assailed his chief emerged the half-tearful statement that Lane had never in all his twenty-seven years written a motion-picture scenario, and had not even the remotest idea how to devise a plot. Chris also repeated several times that he had no skill or experience in handling people of the type he was to meet at exclusive summer places. But the bulk of his emotion surged about his ignorance of plot building.

Maguire heard him out, the encouraging smile shining ever upon the sufferer. When Chris was exhausted and was certain his appeal had melted every heart within earshot, Maguire once more took up the tale.

"As for getting on with that crowd," he said unctuously, "I picked you out for the whole thing just on that account. You've got presence, son—presence! That's what you've got—presence! It's a rare gift, let me tell you. And it carries a man far, especially among the people you'll meet at those places. At that, the proposition's so easy," he went on with exalted assurance—"so easy, a tongue-tied mental defective with red hair couldn't fall down on it. I've written out your whole line of talk. All you've got to do is memorize it. Those plutocrats and their plutocrines are due to go into raptures over starring in movies, and having their houses and grounds and clothes and diamonds pictured. That's nature! It's nothing for ten of them to put up two hundred and ninety-seven dollars apiece for such a chance."

"But I never—"

"I've made out a list of gilt-edged 'prospects' for you to tackle too," cooed Maguire. "As soon as you land one resort the news will travel.

And at the rest it will be like selecting monocles for a blind man. We're starting you at Haverham because the boss knows a fellow there who'll put up the first two hundred and ninety-seven dollars and talk some of the Country Club crowd into chipping in. He's a man who travels in the right set. And he's under some kind of obligation to the boss—I don't know what. But he is. See? Chris, the whole road has been steamrolled and carpeted for you. Why, it's—"

"I tell you," vehemently persisted Lane, ignoring his chief's honeyed words and clinging miserably to his one trump—"I tell you I never made up a plot in my life. I don't know how. Why, I can't even make up stories to tell to my sister's kids. I just have to revamp Red Riding-Hood or Cinderella for them, with another set of names, when they ask me for a new one. In a million years I couldn't—"

"Good boy!" applauded Maguire. "You've hit the very thing we have in mind. Gee, but you've got a headpiece of your own! That's exactly what you're to do at—"

"*What's* what I'm to do?" asked Chris in sulky suspicion.

"Why, just what you do for your sister's kids," beamingly explained Maguire. "We've fixed up a bunch of six of Pieters' old scenarios, and six reading synopses to go with them. We picked them out of fifty because they lend themselves best to society stuff, and because they're the easiest ones to shift round so as to fit any peculiarities or specialties of the people who are to act in them."

"But I don't—"

"Oh, yes, you do, old man!" playfully contradicted Maguire. "Here's the idea: You go to Haverham, we'll say, with those six scenarios in your grip. You get the crowd interested in the Caritas Chain and get them to raise the $2974. The boss suggested three thousand dollars; but I showed him it would look more like figuring to actual expenses if we didn't make it a round number. Then you ask what kind of picture they want. Tell 'em they can have any kind. That's in the blank contract anyhow. It looks as if we suspected them of intelligence. Sort of compliment, you know.

"Well, not a mother's son or daughter there will have a ghost of a plot. So the minute they begin to look foolish it's your cue to offer to grind out a scenario for them. They'll jump at it. Then sketch one of your six plots to them. Do it offhand—as if it had just popped into your mind. They'll think you're a genius. If they don't like the first plot—but they will—spring the second on them. Then, when they are agreed on one, tell them you'll write the scenario of it that very night, and that you'll have it ready for the director so they can begin rehearsing next morning.

"Regan will take care of the rest of it. Just give him the Pieters scenario and turn him loose among them. We've been coaching Regan all week so he'll talk to them as if they were humans. It means his job. He's in front of a phonograph three hours a day, practicing how to talk civil. You'd never know it was Regan, to hear him. He's working up a nice smile, too, with his shaving mirror, every morning. So that's settled! Now—"

It was not settled. Not until after another thirty minutes of steadily losing warfare did Chris Lane surrender. Next day he set out for Haverham.

To live without hope is to live without fear. To be fearless is often closely akin to being invincible. Chris entered upon his money-raising campaign at Haverham with not one vestige of hope. He stated his business with no great enthusiasm, but with no trepidation. He unconsciously gave the impression of offering Haverham the one golden chance of its life, and of caring not at all whether or not Haverham might have the intelligence to take advantage of that chance.

To his dull amaze he found almost no difficulty in interesting a group of men in his scheme—especially after Zigler's local beneficiary had paved the way. The needful $2974 was subscribed by thirty people in a single evening, and the contract was signed. Chris telegraphed for Regan and the camera man to come on.

Next morning Lane was summoned to the Country Club to discuss further steps in the campaign. There he found gathered in a veranda wing fully half a hundred men and women, ranging in age from eighteen to sixty.

These were the lucky people chosen by the finance committee to appear in the picture. If the choice had been made to the accompaniment of a running fight that had left the ground behind it high-piled with dead hopes and mangled feelings, this was no knowledge or concern of Lane's.

The thirty stockholders had chosen as they or their womankind deemed wise; and the result of that choice was assembled—collectively—awaiting instructions.

Chris Lane faced the heterogeneous crowd and began his prepared speech, quickly recalling the salient points in the six plots he had memorized, and trying to decide which of the sextet would best fit this scratch aggregation.

"Ladies and gentlemen," he said, mechanically focusing his gaze on the least impersonal pair of eyes in his audience and selecting those of a thin girl in khaki, "I understand you have been picked out by the committee to act in this picture. The Sentinel Film Corporation's best director and star camera man will be here on the noon train. Work on the picture can begin first thing to-morrow morning. Nothing remains but to decide on a story and draw up a cast. Your committee will distribute the parts as they see fit.

"Of course the Sentinel could offer you the use of any of its many successes; but the president thought you would prefer a brand-new picture. Now if you care to invent such a picture for yourselves our contract permits you to do so. But as that would mean a good deal of thankless work for you I can save you the trouble. This happens at present to be my business—to supply picture plots and scenarios. Shall I outline an idea for a rattling good picture—an idea that has just occurred to me? It seems to fit in unusually well with the scenery hereabouts and with the personalities of—"

"No, thank you!"

It was the thin girl in khaki who broke in on his glib address. And now Chris realized that he had expected, from the first, some such interruption. He had not known why he expected it. He did not now know. But he understood at last that it was not friendliness he had read in the thin girl's eyes. It was an eager self-interest.

"I beg your pardon," he faltered; stilted diction and rapid delivery alike deserting him.

He noted that he alone seemed surprised at the girl's words. To the others the interruption seemed something they had awaited with due stolidity.

"No, thank you!" repeated the thin girl. "You won't have to make up a synopsis for us. Not even to turn a synopsis into a scenario. We're going to use mine. You know the contract says we may."

Lane did not answer. He gazed, round-eyed and helpless, at her. Then he glanced about the group. A little shabby-faced man in white—Marcus Derrick, who had subscribed the colony's maximum sum of five hundred dollars to the Caritas Fund—cleared his voice and said:

"Yes, Mr. Lane; the committee has kindly agreed to use my daughter's synopsis. I understand there are certain—certain technical matters about such things that she may need your help on. Perhaps you'd better go over them with her at—at her leisure."

He subsided behind his cigar. "Very good," assented Chris meekly.

"I'm going across to the Casino," said the thin girl. "If you'll walk there with me I'll tell you the story of the picture. Then I can send the script over to your hotel when I get home."

"By 'script,' " explained Derrick, "my daughter refers to the manuscript of her motion-picture synopsis."

"I see," answered Lane; a shade less meekly now, as he grew hot at the thought that Derrick had not even bothered to introduce him, and that the girl did not seem to consider such formality needful in making the professional acquaintance of a man of Lane's class.

The thin damsel detached herself from the compact group and moved down to the driveway below, carelessly nodding to Chris to follow. As the sulky youth obeyed, Derrick called over the veranda rail to his daughter:

"While you're at the Casino, Gracia, you might as well telegraph to Van to come on for the rehearsals. You remember what a help he was when you got up the Masque of Beauty last year."

"All right," answered Gracia over her shoulder as Chris fell into step beside her. "Good idea! Thanks."

"You know, Miss Derrick," ventured Chris, turning her father's suggestion over in his mind, "the company is sending its star director out here. Regan is the very best man in his line. And if he has one flaw it's his dislike of interference. Your friend Van really won't be needed to help—"

"I know," responded the girl. "I know. Everybody knows—except my father. Mr. Vansittart would only tangle things up, as he did when we gave our Masque. Something tells me I'll be so busy I'll forget to telegraph."

Chris looked at her in faint new interest. In spite of her thinness and the fact that she had greeted him somewhat as though he were a plumber's assistant, he began to like her just a very little. Also, he liked the long mannish stride that enabled him so easily to keep step with her.

And her eyes were good. They reminded him of those of a dog he had owned when he was a kid; not the solemn and professionally loyal type of dog, but a highly independent, own-your-own-soul pup, alive with ideas and gifted with a weird sense of humor.

"Listen, Miss Derrick," said Lane with a new courage. "Are you sure you wouldn't rather we'd use this plot of mine and save yours for some bigger time? There's a splendid market for original plots, you know; and—"

"Mine has been to market," she supplemented. "And it has squealed Wee-wee-wee! all the way home; in fact, it's been to nine markets. Nobody wants it. But perhaps when it makes a hit here, at Haverham, some manager will buy other plots of mine. That's why I wheedled dad into subscribing so much for the Caritas Fund. I made him do it on condition the committee would use my picture."

"I see," said Chris, liking her a grain more.

Then, after they had covered another fifty yards Casinoward, he asked:

"How did you happen to write it? Not that it's any of my business; but I thought—"

"I wrote it as a short story first; ever so long ago—nearly two years," she informed him. "But nobody seemed to care about printing it; so I wrote it as a play. And you'd be amazed to know how many managers didn't want it. One evening some of us went to the motion pictures over at the village. I had never been to them before; and it occurred to me right away that my story or play would make a splendid picture. I could see it at every step. So I bought a book that told how to turn a story into a scenario. And I did it. Since then I've sent it to ever so many places; but it always came back to me. Let me tell you a funny thing: I sent it to the Sentinel, among others. And it was returned. Isn't it queer that the Sentinel should be producing it after all?"

"Yes," he agreed with charming frankness; "it certainly is."

Nevertheless, when they reached the Casino and Gracia went to the news stall in search of a magazine she wanted, Lane stole a minute to send this telegram to Maguire:

Haverham crowd insists on using scenario by local talent. Contract permits it. What shall I do?

Gracia was waiting for him on the Casino balcony when he came out. She had seated herself boyishly on the rail. And she nodded him to a chair. After which she drove straight to the business at hand.

"I call my picture Salvation," she began.

"Salvation!" echoed the wondering Chris. "Then it's—it's a religious story—a sort of—of—"

"No," she denied; "it isn't. I wanted to call it Regeneration. But that title's been used on a story or a play, or something; so I looked up my book of synonyms. And I picked out Salvation. The hero is a crook; but he is a crook only because he hasn't had any chance. He is well born and well educated, though; and he—"

"I thought you said he hadn't had any chance?" involuntarily objected Lane.

"I mean no moral chance," said Gracia a little impatiently. "No one has taken any interest in him, and he has been led into evil ways. Neal Cantrell is to play the part. He'll do it very terribly, of course. But the Cantrells paid four hundred dollars; so he—"

"Naturally," replied Chris with understanding and with a morbid anticipation of seeing the completed picture.

"And your hero is a gentleman crook? Go on."

"Not a gentleman," she corrected; "just well bred. He falls in love with a factory girl, and for her sake he resolves to reform. It is a war, you see, between holy love and the craving for crime."

"Psychology stuff," assented Chris. "I understand. You—you play the girl, I suppose?"

The tan of her cheeks took on the shadow of a flush. Her eyes lost for a second their lazy assurance.

"I want to," she admitted. "So does Hilda Crewe. So do six other girls. They're all prettier than I. They'd all look better on the screen. But—well, it really isn't vanity that makes me want to play it. It's because I've created the character and I know how it ought to be played. The others don't. Not that that matters, I suppose. Let's get on with the plot.

"She lives with her married sister," continued Gracia. "The sister is married to a detective. The detective has sworn to catch the hero—like Javert in Les Misérables, you know."

"I know," said Chris—who did not.

"Well," went on Gracia, "there is a dance at a hotel in the city where they live."

"In the city?" muttered Chris, starting. "But—"

"The detective is sent there to protect the jewelry of the guests," she went on, unheeding. "Detectives are hired to do that in real life."

"I know," said Chris; "but I thought the scenes were all to be up here, round—"

"And," added Gracia, "the heroine and her married sister are there too."

"At the dance?"

"No; of course not! They are in a room upstairs. Their flat in the tenement is being redecorated, and they are at the hotel while it's being done—they and the sister's three-year-old child."

"Oh!" said Chris, with explosive interest. "I see."

"The hero learns about the dance and he goes to the hotel to rob," said Gracia. "Then the hotel catches fire. All the guests rush out, screaming. The hero sees his chance to run from room to room, stealing the money and jewelry, and so on, that the occupants have left in their haste. He collects a big suitcaseful of it. Then, as he passes through a fourth-floor room on his way to a fire-escape he hears a cry. It's the heroine's sister's three-year-old child, who has been left behind. Each of the sisters has thought the child was with the other. The hero can't get down the fire escape through the flames with his plunder and with the child too."

"No," babbled the dazed Chris. "He can't."

"He must make his choice," continued Gracia, eager with the bliss of creation. "It is the final battle of good and evil for possession of his soul. At last he sighs. And he throws away the suitcase of money and jewelry and rescues the child. He carries the child down through the flames while the crowds in the street cheer and weep. When he gets to the bottom of the fire escape he is nearly dead with pain and suffocation and fatigue.

"The detective—whose own child the hero has just saved, you know—is there, waiting for him. The hero is too weak to escape. He surrenders. The detective pretends not to know who he is and lets him go to where the heroine is waiting for him with open arms—just as the burning hotel collapses into a smoking ruin. Do you like it? And do you think Purified by Fire would be a better title?"

"Yes," said Chris vaguely.

His thoughts had sped miles beyond the recital, and now had plunged him into a slough of obstacles, neck-high. He was beginning to lose mental coherence.

"I'm glad you like it," said Gracia, less familiarly now that the zest was fading. "And you think the title—"

"Miss Derrick," blurted the unhappy Lane, beginning at the very middle of his miserable computations, "the contract calls for a two-reel picture. The plot you've outlined couldn't possibly be run off in less than—"

"Oh yes, it could!" she assured him. "You'll see that when I send the script over to you. At first I had it in seven reels. But last night I spent hours and hours in cutting it down to two. The first reel describes the life of the riverside tenement district and explains the characters. The second is taken up with the dance and the fire. There are only seventy-six scenes in all, and fifty-one captions. It can be played, I should think, in about half an hour or so."

"But"—protested Chris—"but—but—How about the locations,

and all that, Miss Derrick? The cost of the burning hotel—even if the exterior is only a painted front—will be more than a thousand dollars; a lot more. And the front will have to be practicable if the leading man is to come down its fire escape. Why, three thousand is more like it! And the riverside tenements—well, of course we can use a back drop for them and for the river. But—"

"No, we can't," she contradicted, "because the first scene is on an excursion boat, coming up the river. The heroine is on it—she and her sister. They see the detective in a police-patrol boat chasing the hero. The hero is in a naphtha launch. The patrol boat is gaining. The hero runs the launch alongside the excursion boat and jumps aboard the lower deck. The heroine takes pity on him and hides him. That is how they first meet. We shall have to go to New York or some other river city to take those scenes, I'm afraid, because the only river anywhere near Haverham is the Pequannock and that's only about as wide as this balcony. You could wade across it. Besides, they've neglected to build a city behind it for a background. And we—"

"Miss Derrick," cried Lane, in black despair, "a picture such as you're describing couldn't be made, in the way you want it done, for five thousand dollars!"

"So much as that?" she asked, surprised. "Why, my father and I worked out the expenses on paper and we figured it all under forty-five hundred. But you are in the business; so you know best. It's too bad it costs so much. But it's for charity!"

Chris rose groggily to his feet. For the first time he realized that he had brought to this Caritas assignment a subconscious craving to make good; and here he was letting the company into a net loss of several thousand dollars! The company that gave him his bread! The company to which he had grown to feel almost the same absurd filial loyalty he once had lavished upon his newspaper!

That this tragedy was caused by no fault of his and was quite beyond his control comforted him not at all. Five years of reporting had ground into Lane's soul the fact that results and not intentions count, and that the mere ethical question of fault is of interest to no one except the faultee.

He had been sent out by Maguire to make good on Maguire's most cherished scheme; a scheme that was to solidify Maguire still further with Zigler. Maguire had trusted Lane, had backed him, had staked all on Chris' fitness for the task.

And here, at the very first link in the Caritas Chain, the expenses were to exceed the profits by several hundred per cent! Moreover, would this not be a precedent for unrecognized geniuses and geniusettes at the Chain's future resorts? All because one thin girl in khaki—

"I'm glad you like it so much," Gracia was saying. "I'm going home now. I'll send the script across at once. Oh, what fun"—she went on, as if to herself rather than to the man—"what fun it must be—will be—to see one's own picture produced! Even here, where everybody knows dad bought the chance for me!"

"Yes!" mumbled Chris, his thoughts everywhere at once.

"I suppose"—she said with an odd childishness, and hesitating as she started to go—"I suppose it must be the wonderfulest thing in the world to read one's own printed book or to see one's produced play or motion picture, and to know it was accepted because it was so good—because it was too good to reject—too good not to be given to the whole world! It makes my silly little triumph look horribly small."

"I doubt if seven thousand dollars would cover it," announced Chris, coming to earth as the wistful-noted voice ceased.

"I'm so sorry!" she said, stiffening. "But then, as dad says, the contract doesn't set any limit on the price of production. And it's for charity. I'll have the script at your hotel before lunchtime."

She went away, walking with that boyishly swingy stride Chris had admired. But he did not watch her go. Before she had rounded the corner Lane was exhuming a sheaf of letters and papers from his inner coat pocket. From the mass he separated a slip of paper and pored over it with haggard eagerness. It was one of the blank contract forms.

No; there was not a line, a phrase or a word in the whole simple document that limited the price or the authorship. The contract assumed $2974 as the cost; but only so far as concerned such details as the photographing, the developing and the employees' salaries. It also guaranteed all expenses. And it did not circumscribe those expenses.

So certain had Maguire been that his "prospects" would rejoice in the chance of exploiting their own homes and clothes and jewels that it had not occurred to him to insert such a precautionary clause.

Thus, the Sentinel was bound by its own agreement to produce a two-reel picture, which the party of the second part might select. The six sample plots abounded in ballroom scenes, mansion exteriors, country-club backgrounds, and the like. Two of them contained golf matches, and one the climax of a tennis tournament.

"We might have known!" Chris fumed inwardly as he trudged back to the hotel. "We might have known! A tenement crowd would have wanted a picture all cluttered up with dukes and duchesses, and open-faced shirts, and a Comedy of Manners. So, naturally this silk-stocking bunch would clamor for slum stuff and for stunts. Those river scenes! Three boats to charter and a billion extra people! Why, the street crowd at that fire can't cost less than five hundred—even if we work trick-camera duplicates! And the lead will have to get an acrobat to double for him in the fire-escape act! And a hotel interior, and transportation to New York and back for the Haverham actors in the river scenes! And—"

He groaned and gave up computing. At the hotel he found a tele-gram (collect) from Maguire in answer to his own. It read:

"Let them use their own plot if they want to. Why shouldn't they? It's one to the good for us. Carry your own weight boy and don't waste the Sentinel's money and my time by wiring me about every measly detail that comes up."

Lane went to the telephone booth and called the Sentinel on long distance—only to learn from the vice president's stenographer that Maguire and Zigler had left the office ten minutes earlier on a three-days motor trip to some location or other, the address of which the stenographer did not know.

Put a timid child in water up to his neck, and his feet will cling nervously to the bottom. Throw him into ten feet of water, and Nature—whose real name is Necessity—will make him swim, unless he is of the type that is born to drown.

The departure of his chiefs for places unknown cut the bottom clean from under Chris Lane's feet. Whereat, his bemused brain all at once became steady and began to work far above form; for he did not belong to the drowning breed.

To all intents and purposes he was now the Sentinel Film Corpo-ration. At least, he was sole guardian of the Sentinel's imperiled inter-ests in Haverham. And those interests just now seemed due to receive a black eye from a blow that threatened to mar the prestige not only of Lane himself but of Maguire, the boss who had sent him thither.

This Caritas Chain was the joy of Maguire's heart. Its failure—and so costly a failure—at Haverham would hurt him badly with Zigler. It would inevitably lead the president to veto any extension of the scheme to other resorts. On Chris Lane depended everything.

At this point in Chris' meditations the script of Salvation was handed to him by a messenger. Chris did not so much as bother to unroll it. His mind was too busily racing. Within another half hour the race was won.

The director and the camera man were due to arrive on the noon train. Chris left word at the hotel desk that he would be back in an hour. Then he asked the way to the Derrick cottage.

He found Gracia reading in a hammock as he climbed the thirty-room cottage's porch steps. She was alone; and she looked politely astonished at sight of him. Chris resented the look and the girl behind it.

"Miss Derrick," he began, before she could speak, "I've done a rather nervy thing, and I don't know whether you'll approve. But—didn't you say something about wishing you could see a picture of your own that had been accepted on its merits? Didn't you? Well, anyhow, it seemed to me, afterward, you had. That plot you told me this morning now—it's far-and-away too big and too unique to be wasted on one private exhibition. So I phoned the office about it. I called up on long distance."

"You did!" she exclaimed, evidently puzzled at his rapid-fire harangue. "But why?"

"Just for the reason I've given you," he said. "The idea seemed too big to be wasted like this. Well, the office agrees with me. Miss Derrick"—portentously—"I'm authorized to offer you three hundred dollars cash for your Salvation picture. That's a hundred-and-fifty a reel—about double our regular rates. But it's worth the extra cash and we want to cinch it. Will you let the Sentinel have it for that? Will you? It's a top offer."

The girl was staring at him open-mouthed, stupefied; her lean face was pallid under its tan. Gradually the pallor gave way to a bricky red. The vagueness left her big eyes, to be replaced by a glow that made her almost beautiful. The supreme emotion of a writer's life was upon her. It was her Moment.

Chris dared not look longer at her. He did not know why. Eyes lowered, he hurried on:

"You see, Miss Derrick, we can give this thing the swellest kind of production—Cliff Herford and Madeline Burt for the leads, and all. I know the money part of it doesn't mean much to you. Still, it's something to know, as a beginner, that you're getting double the rates paid to most professionals. And if you like you can help direct the production. How about it?"

Another agonizingly endless ten seconds crawled by before the shivering Gracia found her tongue. Then, red and trembling, she made answer—almost shouting the staccato words: "Yes! Yes!! Oh, yes!!!"

"Good!" approved Chris, trying to steady his own voice. "Here's a memorandum I've scratched off as the company's local representative. We can sign it now, if you like. A regular contract will be sent to you later on. I'll give you a check for the three hundred to-day if you don't care to wait. How does this strike you?"

Pulling out a sheet of hotel note paper he read aloud:

"It is hereby agreed and covenanted that the Sentinel Film Corporation, by payment of three hundred dollars cash to Gracia Derrick, shall become and does become the sole owner of all motion-picture rights to and in a certain literary composition at present entitled Salvation, of which the aforesaid Gracia Derrick is author."

Gracia listened to his gobblelike reading of the ill-worded agreement as though to heavenly music.

"We can both

sign—here, at the bottom," said Chris.

"Oh, it can't be true!" breathed the girl. "It can't!! And after they rejected it once!"

"That was done by some chucklehead in the outer office, I suppose," Chris explained. "Such a swad of manuscripts come in all the time, the readers don't half do their work. But someone's due to be fired for letting this slip through our fingers."

"But at first you didn't seem to be much interested in it," she protested—"I mean when I told you the story."

"I wanted the office to confirm my snap judgment," said Chris. "It wouldn't have been fair for me to enthuse and hold out hopes, and then have to tell you afterward that the office—"

"Come into the library," she interrupted, ashake with excitement. "We can sign this right away. And then I can phone dad about it and—But what are we to do for a plot for the Caritas Fund?" she broke off in pathetic dismay. "I forgot all about—"

"Don't worry over that," Chris reassured her. "We'll use the plot I had in mind this morning. You people won't object?"

"Object?" she echoed rapturously. "Object? I—oh, come into the library! I want to sign this before I wake up. How soon do you suppose the Sentinel will produce it?"

"The first Saturday evening after doomsday!" returned Lane cheerily; but he said it in the depths of his own tumultuous soul. Aloud he answered: "I can't tell to the exact day; but we'll use all the speed on it we can—under the circumstances. You see—"

He stopped. She was bending over a writing table and affixing a sprawly signature to the memorandum.

"Three hundred dollars from two-nine-seven-four," he figured in silent rapture; "that leaves the Sentinel still nineteen hundred and seventy-four dollars to the good on Haverham, even after the seven hundred dollars for expenses comes out! I'll be the white-haired boy of the Sentinel office. And we'll doctor that contract form of Maguire's before I strike another resort. No more unlimited-price productions or local literary talent or—"

His thread of exultant thought frayed and snapped. He found he was watching the girl's long fingers as she guided the pen. Her hand was quivering as if she had palsy. Two blots already marred the paper.

Gracia looked up at Lane, her face deep-flushed, her lips working. And she laughed—a gleeful little laugh that had a choke in it.

"I'm so ashamed!" she apologized tremulously, handing him the memorandum. "It's—it's silly of me. I never felt this way before. But it isn't quite like anything else—is it? To think of a great concern like the Sentinel putting my work ahead of professionals'! It may even mean a career for me. I've written lots of stories—ever since I was little. Everybody laughed at me for doing it. They didn't understand. But you understand—don't you?—because you are in it yourself. Some of my other stories might make good pictures too."

The careless impersonality was gone from her manner. So was her former air of talking to someone from a lower world, which Chris had found so jarring to his self-esteem. Now it was craftsman calling to craftsman, artist to fellow artist, equal to congenial equal. And the new color and the eye glow had done wonderful things to the girl's brown face.

"I haven't thanked you," she said presently. "It was ungrateful not to—after all the trouble you've taken. It was fine of you. I shan't forget it—ever."

Chris, vaguely ashamed, gargled forth some banal disclaimer.

"You see," she continued, with a deepening of that new note of confidential intimacy which was beginning to grate upon the man's heart, "always I've been wanting to do something worth while, or be something worth while. I'm not pretty. And I'm not very popular. There was nothing I could do to make myself stand out from the rest—nothing except write. And that didn't get me anywhere—till just now. So perhaps you can see what all this means to me. It's—it's a career. Isn't it? There's nothing now that won't be possible."

For no reason that he could explain, Chris' mind whizzed back to the first of his newspaper stories which had seen the light. It had been written on the third day of his service as a reporter, six years earlier. It had dealt with the fortunes and misfortunes of a mouse that had invaded a full Subway car. He had scribbled the story to three-quarter-column length. And a murderous copyreader had hewn it down to a stick and a half. But the thrill had not been cut from it—the thrill of creation and of the knowledge that half a million people might read what he had written; the thrill of knowing that he had at last been initi-

ated in due and ancient form into the Degree of Public Entertainers.

"And perhaps"—the girl was saying—"perhaps Salvation will do a little good too. It may help to reform someone. Is that foolish? We writers have a tremendous responsibility, haven't we? I never thought of that before. But we have. I—What are you doing?" She broke off, her voice scaling an octave to a shrill protest that was almost a shriek.

Her anguished dismay was thoroughly justified; for Chris Lane was performing the most criminally idiotic act of his life.

Slowly, and as though each motion of the fingers were keen torment, he was tearing the memorandum across and across.

After that first wild protest the girl stood dumb, moveless, sallow with uncomprehending horror.

Chris no longer felt the need to avoid her eyes—now that there was nothing in their scared depths which a normal man's memory would care to hoard. He began to speak—lifelessly, in a toneless dead voice.

"I've torn this up," he said, "because I'm a fool. It would have gotten the Sentinel out of a rotten scrape; and me too. I'd have been praised—maybe raised—for putting it over. That's why I'm a fool for tearing it."

The girl did not answer, did not move.

"You see," continued Lane in the same flatly lifeless voice, "your picture was rejected by the Sentinel and the rest because it wasn't what they could use. You had us in a tight corner to-day when you insisted on our producing it for the Caritas. It would have cost so much it would have eaten all our profits and some four thousand dollars besides. And we are in this thing for profit, not for loss. Look up the word *caritas* sometime.

"I tried to save the day by getting rid of your picture for three hundred. It was a good idea of mine. And it was good business too, and legitimate. But—I guess I'm a rotten business man all right, and a dub besides; for I don't know, even yet, why I tore this up — except it was because I'm a fool, just as I said—and that's no reason. I'll take this script of yours back to the hotel with me and I'll turn it over to the director. Then I'll send in my resignation to the Sentinel. I'm best off in a cage somewhere, or else working for myself—anywhere where I can't crab my employers' interests the way I've done now."

She had not moved. The empty eyes in her blank face were still upturned toward him, her thin body gawky in its tense pose.

"Good-by!" said Lane, cramming the hated script into his pocket and clumping out.

He went to the station to meet his two associates on their arrival, and thus get the worst over at once. It would be almost a relief to have Regan swear whole-heartedly at him. But he found the train from New York had been delayed by a washout and would not reach Haverham for two hours. So Chris went drearily back to his hotel.

His senses were still gripped by the merciful numbness that is said to follow the impact of a high-power bullet. The fever of the wound had not set in. Stolidly and circumstantially he told himself for the fifth time what he had done. And he tried for the fiftieth time to tell himself why. But he could not. If she had been pretty—if she had been magnetic—even if she had honored him at the beginning by treating him as an equal, instead of bearing herself as she might have done toward a clerk across a white-goods counter—

Bit by bit—far off and nebulous at first—wriggled toward Lane's consciousness a feeling of shame at his betrayal of the Sentinel's trust. And this led him to a recollection of what his next step must be.

Accordingly he went into the writing room and tried to draw up his letter of resignation.

When the story should get about there would be scant hope of another motion-picture job for the double incompetent. Chris knew that; and the knowledge began to fester. Consciousness was creeping back to the numbed centers—sickeningly painful consciousness.

He had just finished and wastebasketed his fourth draft of the resignation letter when a bell hop brought him a note.

The envelope was square and stiff and very white, and rough to the touch. Its flap bore a hideous raised device in dark green. The address was penned in a sprawly hand, none too firm. Chris ripped open the envelope, aware of a dully hot dislike toward the writer. And he read:

"Dear Mr. Lane:

"Please send back my script by the bearer. I have decided not to use it for our Caritas picture.

"I have telephoned to the committee's chairman that we shall use a plot you are at work on, instead. Any plot at all.

"Does that clear things up? For you, I mean? But of course it does.

"I don't know yet whether I think you are splendid or abominable or—or just what you said you were. For a little while I didn't care to find out which. I never wanted to see you again.

"Perhaps you don't know what it means to have one's vanity extracted—without gas.

"But—well, I have another story that I think ought to make a perfectly wonderful picture; two others, in fact. Would you like to call to-morrow morning and see whether you agree with me?

"To-morrow morning—not to-day. I'm only human, you know—not a saint. And I honestly don't think I could be civil to you—just yet. I don't think any patient greets a surgeon dentist very cordially the next minute after the tooth is out. Do you?

"GRACIA DERRICK."

Long and longer Chris Lane scanned the sprawly lines, reading them over and over and over. He was roused from his trance by the bell hop at his shoulder, who said boredly for the third time:

"Man's waiting for an answer, sir."

Chris transferred his owl gaze from the note to the bell hop. For an instant he did not speak. Then, with intense conviction, he announced to the startled youth:

"Now I know why I did it. I'm dead sure. And I believe I knew why all along! The dandy, *good* kid!"

Pretty Baby

SHE was just five feet one in her French heels; as no outsider had seen her without these heels, her net height was a matter of doubt. For the rest, she had a little bit of a face with blue eyes two sizes too large for it, a tumbled aureole of fluffy corn-silk hair, a Dresden shepherdess figure, and cream-of-roses complexion.

The hair and the complexion were indigenous, whatever less gifted women might say. And the big eyes used to do entrancingly queer things, seemingly of their own accord. Taken all in all, Peggy Ferris was preëminently the one woman in all New York's six million population for whom the inspired phrase "Pretty Baby" might have been coined.

Her husband, Wade Ferris, called her "Pretty Baby" far oftener than he called her Peggy. Indeed, it is odd that entire strangers did not hail her in the same endearing fashion, on the principle that makes folk stop to squeal baby-talk at nurse-accompanied pink-and-gold-and-white infants in the street. Peggy was that sort of girl.

On the theory that fluffy hair denotes a fluffy brain—or more likely on no principle at all—Wade Ferris treated his wife as though she were six rather than twenty-six. Sometimes Peggy adored this. Sometimes she hated it.

When grim and hideous Tragedy—in the shape of a cut finger or a candy-headache or a rained-on hat—stalked into her life, it was heavenly to be gathered up in a pair of big arms and held close to a big chest and to be comforted and told how lovely she was and to be called Pretty Baby.

But when she wanted to talk politics or take an active interest in

Wade's business affairs (as her favorite feminine uplift author told her she should), it was humiliating to be laughed at and Pretty Babied and treated otherwise as though she were a mental incompetent.

Do you get the idea?

Peggy Ferris, like many an older and uglier woman, wanted merely to be an intermittent Pretty Baby. In the intervals she wanted to be a blend of Mrs. Good Deeds and the Three Learned Vestals of Greece. At such times, Wade's treatment of her aroused much the same mad resentment as might fill the breast of a Supreme Court judge were his bench officers to present him with a Kiddie Kar labeled "For a Good Child."

Of course, the fault was all Wade's. He ought to have known by instinct when to Pretty Baby his wife and when to listen in wondering reverence to her theories on life's problems. But then, if Wade had had the sense to do that, life would have held no problems for him. His superhuman wits would have solved them one after another, as fast as they came along.

LEON KIRBY, of all the men Peggy knew, had the intelligence to see beneath the airy surface down into the wonder-depths of her soul and there to read the latent strength and wisdom that were the *real* Peggy. She knew he could do this—because Leon had told her so himself. This confession at once set him apart from all other men and on a pedestal of his own. He was henceforth that rarest of men—the man who understands. Incidentally, he was Wade Ferris' best friend—at least, Wade was Leon Kirby's best friend. Perhaps this amounts to the same thing, perhaps not.

The climax came one day when Peggy chanced to read a magazine story which thrilled her. Most stories thrilled Peggy, whether they were stupid or stirring. She achieved this thrill by the simple mental process of putting herself in every story-heroine's place.

The yarn that thrilled her on this day and led to the climax dealt with a woman who was not content to be a mere chattel and butterfly, but who taught herself all the details of her husband's business. When that business was at its shakiest, the husband fell ill. On his recovery he went back to the office, expecting to face ruin. And lo! his splendid wife had not only carried his business safely through the financial storm but had started it on an era of unequaled prosperity.

"*I* could do that!" declared Peggy, addressing a fluffily exquisite girl in her mirror. "I *could!*"

She was still aflame with the idea when Wade came home. The woman in the story had gleaned her business knowledge by tactful questioning. Scarce was dinner ended when Peggy's tactful questioning began.

"Wade," she said earnestly as she held the match to her husband's after-dinner cigar, "how much money have you made to-day?"

"Why?" he asked. "Are the bills very terrible?"

"No," she frowned, amazed at his denseness. "I just asked because I wanted—"

"Oh. I guess I've made enough money to-day for anything *you* want, Pretty Baby," he reassured her. "And if I didn't make enough to-day, we'll use some of the money I made on other days. What is it and how much?"

"Will you *never* understand me?" demanded Peggy. "I'm not hinting for a present, and I haven't even overdrawn my month's allowance—at least," she added, spurred on by truth, "not enough to worry about. But a husband and wife are business partners. And I want to know more about my partner's business. How much did you earn to-day?"

A chuckle of real delight from Wade showed that the dull-brained fellow thought she had said something funny. Peggy stamped her foot. At once Wade grew very grave indeed.

"Well," he said, making tedious calculations on his finger-tips, "let's see. Just how much *did* I make? Of course, I can't be certain, down to the last penny. But I'll do my best. As nearly as I can remember, I made, to-day, about one hundred and eleven thousand, eleven hundred and eleven dollars and eleven cents."

"Whew!" she exclaimed. "Isn't that gorgeous!"

"A fair average day," he admitted.

"I should think so!" she declared.

Then, remembering she was there to learn and not to applaud, she resumed, in keen businesslike alertness:

"How did you earn it? Tell me exactly."

"Well," replied Wade, pondering more deeply than ever, "I had just reached the office when a poor old woman came in. She wanted to buy some bonds. All the money she had in the world was eleven cents. So I sold her that amount of Union Pacific—at nine A. M. quotations. It was quite a tidy block of bonds. And she went away very happy. I—"

"But Wade," expostulated Peggy, "I didn't think any bonds were so—"

"That was how I earned the eleven cents," proceeded Wade. "Then in came a man who wanted to make a safe purchase in real estate. It just happened I had secured an option on a fine corner lot, situated midway between New York and Jersey City. I sold it to him, spot cash, for eleven hundred and eleven dollars. He is going to build a submarine there, I believe. That accounts for eleven hundred and eleven dollars and eleven cents. Next I—"

"Wade," she said, perplexed, "I didn't even know there was any land between New York and Jersey City. And what would he want to build a—"

"I'm afraid I can't answer your question if you keep on interrupting," answered her husband in solemn reproof. "Next I found a blank check lying in the gutter, when I went out to lunch. It was signed with John D. Rockefeller's name. I suppose he dropped it there and didn't think it was worth picking up. But I took the trouble to pick it up. Every little bit helps, you know. I filled in the amount for one hundred and eleven thousand dollars and cashed it. That makes up the—"

"Wade Ferris!" cried Peggy in a gust of anger, "I don't believe one word you say. You're making fun of me!"

"Heaven forbid!" he disclaimed fervently. "I was just—"

"You were just treating me as if I were a child who had asked you to tell me a story!" she accused. "Oh, I *hate* you!"

He laughed aloud in pure glee at her kittenlike fury.

"Pretty Baby!" he shouted. "Oh, Pretty Baby! You're delicious!"

HE caught her fluffy head between his hands and kissed the tip of her up-tilted nose. Peggy tore free from him, white with wrath.

"You brute!" she stormed. "You treat me as if I were a baby! You seem to think I'm a fool, who isn't fit to be talked to seriously. Here I try to show an interest in your work and be a real helpmeet to you.

And you—oh, *stop* laughing in that asinine way! *Stop* it!" Her voice choked with tears. At this change, Wade choked back his laughter and was all contrition.

"Oh, Baby!" he soothed her. "Pretty Baby! I didn't mean to tease you. Honestly, I didn't. But it was so funny to hear you trying to be a grown-up business woman. Don't you bother your fly-away head over stupid business, kid. I'll attend to that end of the partnership. All *you* have to do is to be pretty and have a good time. That's your share of the firm's work."

"That's no partnership!" she flamed. "That is the way women live in a harem."

"There are worse ways of living," he told her. "I never heard or read of a harem wife's being discontented—unless she happened to be in love with some other man. Then her gentle husband generally ties her in a sack and throws her into the Bosporus. That's the only real advantage American women have over Turkish. There's a law, here, against tying them in sacks. Instead, they—"

"Oh, what's the use talking to you!" wailed Peggy. "You simply won't take me seriously! Why can't you let me share your business troubles and your office cares and be a real wife like—like women in stories? I'm sick of being a doll. Can't you see that?"

He laughed again, very kindly yet very annoyingly, and tried to stroke her hair. She pulled away.

"I've asked for bread, and you've given me a stone!" she sputtered. "Most women would be glad enough to spend your money without caring to know anything about the business that earned it. Most of them would yawn their silly heads off if you even tried to talk business to them. You ought to be grateful for a wife who is able to discuss serious things with you. All you want is to pet me and play I'm a baby. I'm not. I'm a woman—as much a woman as *Nora*, in 'A Doll's House.' Be careful you don't drive me to follow her example!"

"Let's see," mused Wade. "What *was* her example, anyhow? She was 'Pretty Baby' too, as well as I remember—till her husband caught her forging a check or something. And then, when he forgave her, didn't she say he was a stranger to her and pass out into the night? The only time I saw the play, it was so exciting that I slept through the middle part of it. So I'm not quite sure. But—"

"There are other ways to show a husband he doesn't understand his wife than passing out into the night," said Peggy darkly.

Now, here, Wade should have begged her, frantically, to tell him just what she meant by such a strange speech. Instead, he took it as a joke. Before she could press the point, he got to his feet and looked at his watch.

"There's a governors' meeting at the Bond Club at nine," said he. "I must be off. Don't bother to sit up for me, in case I'm delayed. By-by, kid."

"I'm not a kid!" she snapped. "And some day I'll show you I'm not! You wait and see!"

"You look like an Angora kitten, when you frown," he commented approvingly. "I'd like to tie a pink satin bow around your neck and—"

"Oh, I *do* hate you!" she exclaimed. "I—"

He cut short her invective by picking her up bodily, kissing her several times and setting her down again. While she was in midair she tried ragingly to kick his shins. But she only tangled her toes in her petticoat-edge and tore a yard of its lace.

WHEN Wade was gone, Peggy allowed herself the luxury of a good cry. She felt desolate—miserable, horribly ill-used and misunderstood. She had tried so hard to make Wade treat her as a wife should be treated! And his affectionate tolerance drove her frantic.

Out of the ruck of emotions gradually crystallized one resolve: Wade thought she was a child. She would show him she was a woman—not only a woman, but as shrewdly capable and businesslike as the woman whose story she had that day read.

When she should at last have proven herself a true financier and a business success,— but not until then,— she would go to Wade with proofs of her prowess. And then, wouldn't he be ashamed of himself for using the detestable name "Pretty Baby" to such a paragon?

All of which, in a way, was a line of thought parallel to that of the spanked boy who vows to run away to sea and to return to his awed and remorseful parents in later years as a highly successful pirate or trust-magnate or something. But it was also something more than that. Peggy Ferris' father had, in his day, been one of the most astute men in his own branch of finance; so had her grandfather. And in her hour of stress heredity was stirring and snarling and shoving.

How she was to win this great business triumph of hers Peggy did not at all know. But her allowance was ample, and she had money of her own besides, left her by her father. So the question of capital did not worry her. All that remained was to figure out a wise way to invest that capital. She could lay her pretty fingers on six or seven thousand dollars at a week's notice. But what could she do with it, to win freedom from the Pretty Baby yoke?

PEGGY was still revolving the puzzle in her angry mind when Leon Kirby's name was brought in. Leon Kirby himself followed. At a glance he saw his hostess' look of trouble. And he mentally attuned himself to it. But before he could make any of the conversational leads that suggested themselves to his ready mind, Peggy scattered all his ideas by asking abruptly:

"What business did you do to-day?"

"I—I don't understand," he stammered.

"You don't need to," said Peggy. "It is a test. I have asked the same question once before this evening. I want to see if all men give the same answer to such a question. If it is impertinent of me to ask it—"

"Nothing you can ask is impertinent, dear lady," Kirby interposed. "My affairs are yours—so far as you'll consent to make them so."

He had a queer intuitive sense concerning women, had Kirby. And this intuition now led him to answer her question categorically and with truth.

"I got to the office at nine," he said.

"I looked over my mail and dictated answers to some letters in it. Then I went to court. The case of Rogers *vs.* Kellogg was on the calendar for to-day. Our firm represents the Rogers interests, you know. But the hearing was adjourned. So I went back to the office. I spent the rest of the morning trying to straighten out the affairs of one of our women clients—a woman who thought she would go into business awhile ago. She rented and fitted up a bijou little lunch-room and tea-room. Then, just as she was ready to open it, her mother died in Italy, and she dumped the whole transaction onto our hands while she took the first boat for Naples. Her mother leaves so much money that the tea-room project is abandoned, and we have to close it out. Then I—"

"Wait!" broke in Peggy excitedly. She had at first listened with placid joy to his recital. It was as balm to her scratched spirit, after Wade's scoffing. But at the tale of the tea-room, inspiration smote her.

"Wait!" she commanded. "Tell me more about the tea-room. Where is it?"

Wondering, he obeyed. In equal wonder he answered a volley of questions that trod close on one another's heels, all of them anent the tea-room. By the time the last question was answered, Peggy Ferris' inspiration had hardened into resolution.

"I can afford that," she said at last.

"Afford what?" asked the puzzled Kirby.

"The tea-room, of course," said Peggy, "or the lunch-room, or whatever you choose to call it. And there is money in such places, if they are run rightly."

"What on earth are you talking about?" he queried. "I don't under—"

"About the tea-room you're trying to get rid of, of course," she replied. "What else should I be talking about? There are all sorts of money in that kind of place. I know there are."

"But—"

"All sorts of money," she reiterated, "if it's run rightly. I know, because I know how little money there is in such a place when it's run the wrong way."

"I don't—"

"But *I* do. Girls who want careers and haven't sense enough to stay at home start tea-rooms. So do sad-souled widows with need of making a living. They wheedle their friends into going to eat there. In that way they convert perfectly good friends into dyspeptic and steadily dwindling customers. They fit up the place like an *art nouveau* nightmare, and they serve weak tea and dry cake and burnt toast and criminal preserves. They sell the stuff at prices that would stagger Rothschild; and on the side they peddle horrible gift-shop stuff. Then they wonder why they go broke. Now, I'm going to do just the opposite thing. I'm—"

"But do you really mean you're going to—"

"To open a place where people will go because everything to eat and drink is better than they can find it anywhere else. People don't mind paying big prices. All they mind is paying such prices for stuff they wouldn't feed to a relation-in-law. Will you arrange it all for me, Leon? And—oh, I forgot to tell you—Wade isn't to know a thing about it, not till it is a bonanza. Promise not to tell him."

"But why should you—"

"Never mind why—perhaps because I don't need to, perhaps because I do. Won't you let it go at that—and help me?"

"Help you!" he cried. "I ask nothing better in life than to help you, Peggy. But it's so unnecessary—such a queer thing to do. Why do—"

"So *that's* settled!" she announced. "And now for details. I've thought up the name already. I'm going to call it 'The Hide-away.' That ought to appeal to spooning couples and to all kinds of people. And I'm going to have nooks and sheltered corners and alcoves in it, for the tables to hide away in. You said there's a yard too, didn't you? I'll put tables there in summer, with umbrella awnings. And—"

"Listen to me, Peggy!" exclaimed Kirby. "Something has happened—something you've not told me, something that's driving you to this experiment. It isn't like you, to branch out like this. Are— forgive me for asking—are you leaving Wade?"

"Leaving Wade?" she echoed. "Why do you ask such a thing?"

"Because," he said, mistaking her amazement for evasion, "because sometimes I've fancied you weren't happy with Wade. He's a grand old chap, Wade is. But he's—well, you've told me yourself that he doesn't understand your deeper self."

"He doesn't," said Peggy grimly.

"I knew it!" said Kirby in triumph. "And you *are* leaving him! Peggy, dear, you're not going to throw yourself away on keeping a tea-room. You are going to find happiness at last—the happiness that comes to a woman from a man who is her soul-mate. Sweetheart, you must know what you are to me. I—"

"I never stopped to think or to care what I might or might not be to you," returned Peggy very pleasantly indeed. "Not because I'm a saint,—I'm not,—but because you don't interest me at all—not in that way. And you've called me Peggy three times, this last five minutes. My memory is pretty fair, but I can't remember ever asking you to call me that. And now"—without even so much as a pause for breath—"sha'n't we go on with our plans for the tea-room? My old colored mammy is a wonderful cook. I think I'll put her in charge of the kitchen. And I'll have my waitresses wear Colonial costumes."

THE HIDE-AWAY TEA-ROOM hid itself away in a side-street off Broadway, just opposite the stage-entrance of the Olympia Theater. But it did not hide away so successfully as to prevent more and more people from finding it, as the first months of its existence crept on. It was a delightful nook, tucked off as it was in a handy backwater of the city's current. The soft-shaded lights, the quaintly dainty furnishings, the secluded table-nooks—all had a distinct charm of their own.

But New Yorkers do not care to feed upon mere charm, and at the Hide-away they were not forced to. The food was delicious—almost good enough to warrant its somewhat steep prices.

Actresses and chorus-girls from the Olympia, across the street, took to running over to the Hide-away for lunch, during rehearsals and on matinee days. Sometimes they were alone—in which case they ate frugally. Oftener they were with men—and then their orders were gratifyingly lavish. Men and women, too, from business offices near by, began to drop in for lunch or for tea.

Peggy herself superintended everything, usually remaining at the Hideaway from ten in the morning until after five. To her guests— chiefly to the swarm of theatrical girls—she chose to be known as Madame Aimée. By luck, none of her acquaintances chanced to see her there—none, at least, except Leon Kirby. Leon dropped in at least once a day. He had much perseverance.

There were a hundred business details wherein he could be of great use to her, in the management of the Hide-away. For, ardent and resourceful as she was, in the enterprise, she was woefully lacking in the matter of practical training. Yet through all his love for her Kirby was amazed at her natural aptitude for business and at her quickness in grasping its essentials.

Which brings our story to a day when Peggy emerged from the Hideaway's kitchen at about one P. M. and stood at the service door of the little restaurant to survey the battle-field.

Here, twice or thrice a day, Peggy was wont to stand, inspecting her guests and inwardly thrilling at their ever-increasing numbers.

To-day, as Peggy's big eyes slowly swept the tables, she noted with pride that only one of them was empty.

Even as Peggy stood there, a man and a girl came into the room. A Colonial-clad head waitress piloted them through the soft half-light to the vacant table. As they walked thither, the man's back was toward Peggy. She noted something familiar about it. As was her custom when anyone who might know her came into the Hide-away, Peggy shrank back a step into the shadows of the passageway that led to the kitchen. The man at down, facing the passageway.

And then Peggy knew that she had all along known he was Wade Ferris.

SHE put her hands behind her, palms flat against the wall. And she stared, wide-eyed. She was not doing any thinking at all. Then she looked at the girl.

The girl was as tiny as herself, and evidently was some years younger. Also she was indisputably pretty; and she had a disgusting way of looking up, through veiled eyes, at Wade as if he were a demigod. To think any sane man should he fooled by such a trick! Yet Wade was patently delighted by it.

Peggy waylaid the waitress who bore the errant couple's lunch-order to the kitchen. Snatching the slip from its bearer, she glanced over it.

"If he's ordered cocktails or—or anything at all to drink," she told herself with chill ferocity, "I won't let them have it! I—oh, dear! I wish Leon were here to tell me if I've a legal right to send for a policeman and have them thrown out."

Yearningly Peggy revolved this tempting scheme. Then, with a sigh of reluctance, she abandoned it. She was by no means certain the trespass law could be stretched to cover the case. Moreover, a guest-ejecting policeman would not add to the cozy tranquillity of the Hide-away. She read the order Wade had scribbled:

"Two half-cantaloupes, two portions of broiled chicken, candied sweet potatoes, tomato surprise, French pancakes with jelly, fruit salad, iced coffee with two extra orders of cream, fresh strawberry ice-cream, bonbons."

That was all. Nothing to drink but the cream-ridden iced coffee—not even a liqueur! Peggy's artistic soul shuddered as she read the awesomely messy and oversweet combination.

"He—he doesn't even know how to order a luncheon!" she mused accusingly. "One would think he were ordering for a kindergarten child. It's just a gastronomic way of saying 'Pretty Baby!'"

AT this point word came in hot haste that a waitress had fainted in the kitchen. By the time Peggy had revived her and had straightened out the panicky confusion among the other waitresses and returned to her point of vantage, Wade and his convoy were passing out into the street.

But they left behind them a heartbreak which took the form of wholesome wrath. All afternoon Peggy nursed her rage. And as the hours went on, it waxed hotter and fiercer. Wade had petted and babied her, from the day they had become engaged. He had sworn to her, over and over, with needless vehemence, that she had spoiled him for every other woman. He had even ignored tacit invitations, from

girl friends of hers, to flirt ever so mildly with them.

And all the time he had—he had—Why, no wonder he wouldn't flirt with her chums! As well expect an absinthe-swigger to dally with chocolate ice-cream soda or with sarsaparilla!

After a day with this creature and with others like her, he had shamelessly come home to his lawful wife and had soothed his diseased conscience by calling her Pretty Baby!

Pretty Baby, forsooth! That was all he considered her. And she had been so happy and proud in the hope that she could one day convince him she was a successful business woman! She, whom he neglected for girls who ate sickeningly sugary luncheons!

In the rebound, Peggy's thoughts flew to Leon Kirby. In a lightning-flare of inspiration she saw the difference between the two men. She had given Wade everything. And Wade had not only treated her as a child but had deceived her. She had given Kirby nothing. And Kirby not only saw how wise and womanly and competent she was, but he choked back his all-consuming love, lest it offend or annoy her. Why, Leon Kirby was of the stuff whereof Round-Table knights had once been made!

The comparison—goaded on by anger—brought its inevitable sequel. Wade had broken her heart. And it was not on the free list to break Peggy's heart—as Wade should speedily learn. Leon Kirby adored her. Better, still, he understood her. He regarded her as a superwoman, to be revered—not as a child, to be babied. He alone understood her. And the girl's resolve was taken—the illogical, resentful, furious feminine resolve that is responsible for more marriages, more divorces and more remarriages than any one other cause.

AT five o'clock Leon Kirby sauntered into the tea-room—and into the hands of Fate.

It was a very alert, set-lipped, bright-eyed Peggy Ferris who met him almost without a word and led him to the little cubby-hole she used for an office.

"Leon," she said, businesslike and brisk, "five months ago you said you loved me. Was it true or did you say it to make conversation?"

"Does the priest kneel before the Host, to flex his knee-muscles or to worship his God?" replied Kirby, hope surging wildly in his heart and well-nigh strangling him.

"Good!" she assented in that same impersonal and quick manner. "I asked, because I wanted to make sure. I *am* sure. I *was* sure. But I didn't want to make any more mistakes. I made my first mistake when I married Wade Ferris. I made my second mistake when I let him hoodwink me. I didn't want to make a third mistake, now that I am leaving him."

"Leaving him!" gasped Kirby. "*Leaving* him? Do you mean it?"

"It isn't my idea of a joke," she reproved. "Of course I mean it. I am going to divorce him. Please don't ask questions. I don't want to talk about it, any more than I can help, just yet. But I'll need your help in getting my divorce. And when I have gotten it—well, if you still care for me—"

"Still care!" he echoed. "Peggy, you're all this world to me—and heaven and hell besides. '*If* I still care!' Why—"

"You're none of those things to me," she told him with numbing frankness. "But at least you'll understand me. And that will be sweet, after—after—"

"I'll *make* you love me!" he prophesied, his face alight. "Love like mine *can't* go unanswered."

He caught her hands and looked down into her flushed face with stark worship.

So infinitely pretty and appealing and childlike was she that Kirby lost hold of his careful repression. With a cry of rapture he seized her in his arms, burying his face in the fragrant wonder of her hair and murmuring ecstatically, over and over again:

"Oh, Pretty Baby! *Pretty* Baby!"

A pliant if unresponsive woman had yielded to his embrace. A wildcat in dainty human form ripped free from it. Wheeling about and smoothing her tumbled hair, Peggy crossed the room to the hook where hung her hat and jacket. She skewered the hat viciously into place on her head.

Amazed, but still unaware that he had thrown away his chances with both hands, Kirby eagerly followed her across the office. Peggy whirled on her suitor, menacing him with a hat-pin. Simultaneously, she began to talk.

BEFORE she went home Peggy took a fast four-mile walk. And during that walk she did the hardest thinking of her whole life. The net result of all that hour's cogitation was summed up in the last two sentences she had spoken to Kirby:

"If I've got to be cursed with 'Pretty Baby,' I'd rather be called it by a man I love than by a man I don't. And if Wade is a married man making love to a single woman, is he any worse than you—a single man who is making love to a married woman?"

Peggy did not reach home until dinner-time. Wade was waiting for her. Before she could say one of the thirty scathing speeches she had rehearsed, he began:

"I tried for a solid half-hour to get you on the phone, this noon. Dear old Rumrill came into the office, trailing that fool kid daughter of his. She's on a vacation from the Morristown convent. He was called out to Chicago in a rush. So he wanted me to take her to lunch and put her on the Morristown train. I tried to get you to come along, to ease the agony. But you were out. She steered me to a measly little joint where some other convent-girls go when they're in town. And she ordered a lunch that would make a sugar factory look like a salt mine. Ugh!"

"A measly little joint?" quavered Peggy.

But Wade Ferris did not hear.

"I've had enough sweets to last me a century, and enough baby talk to last me a lifetime. You used to kick because I babied you. Well, sit down and we'll talk high finance and politics. It'll be a relief. And it'll get the sticky sweet taste out of my memory. Compared with that babbling kid, you are a monument of dry wisdom."

"I don't want to be a monument of dry wisdom," pouted Peggy, her soul athrob with joyous reaction as she nestled against him. "And what's more, I won't be a monument of dry wisdom. I—I want to—to be—Pretty Baby!"

The Wildcat

WHEN Cassius Wyble came down from his mountains to the 2000-population metropolis of Clayburg on his half-yearly trip for supplies he thought the old custom of Muster Day had been revived.

No fewer than eleven men in khaki were lounging round the station platform or sitting on the steps of the North America general store. Enlistment posters, too, flared from windows and walls.

These posters—except for their pretty pictures—meant nothing at all to Cash Wyble. For, as with his parents and grandparents, his knowledge of the written or printed word was purely a matter of hearsay.

Yet the sight of the eleven men in newfangled uniform—so like in color to his own butternut homespuns—interested Cash.

"What's all the boys doin'—togged up thataway?" he demanded of the North America's proprietor. "Waitin' for the band?"

"Waiting to be shipped to Camp Lee," answered the local merchant prince; adding, as Cash's burnt-leather face grew blanker: "Camp Lee, down in V'ginia, you know. Training camp for the war."

"War?" queried Cash, preparing to grin, at prospect of a joke. "What war?"

"What war?" echoed the dumfounded storekeeper. "Why, *the* war, of course! Where in blazes have you been keeping yourself?"

"I been up home, where I b'long," said Cash sulkily. "What with the hawgs, an' crops an' skins an' sich, a busy man's got no time traipsin' off to the city every minute. Twice a year does me pretty nice. An' now s'pose you tell me what war you're blattin' about."

The storekeeper told him. He told him in the simplest possible language. Yet half—and more than half—of the explanation went miles above the listening mountaineer's head. Cash gathered, however, that the United States was fighting Germany.

Germany he knew by repute for a country or a town on the far side of the world. Some of its citizens had even invaded his West Virginia mountains, where their odd diction and porcelain pipes roused much derision among the cultured hillfolk.

"Germany?" mused Cash when the narrative was ended. "We're to war with Germany, hey? Sakes, but I wisht I'd knowed that yesterday! A couple of Germans went right past my shack. I could 'a' shot 'em as easy as toad pie."

The North America's proprietor valued Cash Wyble's sparse trade, as he valued that of other mountaineers who made Clayburg their semiannual port of call. If on Cash's report these rustics should begin a guerilla warfare upon their German neighbors, more of them would presently be lodged in jail than the North America could well afford to spare from its meager customer list.

Wherefore the proprietor did some more explaining. Knowing the mountaineer brain, he made no effort to point out the difference between armed Germans and non-combatants. He merely said that the Government had threatened to lock up any West Virginian who should kill a German—this side of Europe. It was a new law, he continued, and one that the revenue officers were bent on enforcing.

Cash sighed and reluctantly bade farewell to an alluring dream that had begun to shape itself in his simple brain—a dream of "laying out" in cliff-top brush, waiting with true elephant patience until a German neighbor should stroll, unsuspecting, along the trail below and should move slowly within range of the antique Wyble rifle.

It was a sweet fantasy, and hard to banish. For Cash certainly could shoot. There was scarce a man in the Cumberlands or the Appalachians who could outshoot him. Shooting and a native knack at moonshining were Cash's only real accomplishments. Whether stalking a shy old stag or potting a revenue officer on the sky line, the man's aim was uncannily true. In a region of born marksmen his skill stood forth supreme.

He felt not the remotest hatred for any of these local Germans. In an impersonal way he rather liked one or two of them. Yet, if the law had really been off—

The zest of the man hunt tingled pleasantly in the marksman's blood. And he resented this unfair new revenue ruling, which permit-

ted and even encouraged the killing of Germans in Europe and yet
ordained a closed season on them in West Virginia. Still, there was no
sense in a busy man's risking jail or a fine by indulging his sporting
tastes. So Cash tried to forget the temptation, and proceeded to the
more material task of trafficking for his next half year's supplies.

A few months later the draft caught Cash Wyble and carried him
away in its swirling flood, depositing him in due time, with a quantity
of similar mountaineer flotsam, in the training mill of Camp Lee.

No half-grown wildcat dragged by the scruff of the neck from the
sanctuary of its tree hole was ever one-tenth so ragingly indignant as
was Cash at his impressment into his country's service. Born and bred
of fellow illiterates in the wildest corner of the Cumberland Range,
thirty-two miles from the nearest railroad, he knew nothing and
cared less about the affairs of the world that lay beyond the circling
blue mountain walls.

To Cash all persons who lived outside that circle were "Foreigners," even if their habitat was the adjoining county of his own state.

He had heard of England and of France and of Europe, in much
the same vague fashion as he had heard of Germany. He knew the
name of the President of the United States; of the governor of West
Virginia; of the mayor of Clayburg. Also of the political party whose
ticket his father had always voted, and which Cash, in consequence,
voted. He knew there had been a Civil War and—from pictures and
from paternal description—he knew the types of uniforms each side
had worn. The foregoing facts comprised his total knowledge of
American politics and of world history.

As to the causes and the occasion and the stakes of the present
war he had not an inkling. Nor could the explanations of slightly
better-informed recruits make the matter much clearer to him. It
most certainly roused no trace of enthusiasm or of patriotism in his
indignant breast. All he knew or was interested in was that he had
been forced to leave his shack and his straggly mountain-side farm
and his hidden moonshine still, at the very worst possible season for
leaving any of them.

He had been coerced into riding innumerable miles to a foreigner
state that seemed all bottomland, and there was herded with more
men than he had known were on earth. He had been dressed in an

amazing suit; made to wear socks and underclothes for the first time in his life; and daily put through a series of physical evolutions whose import was a sealed book to him. In all weathers, too, he must wear shoes.

Like the aforesaid caught wildcat Cash Wyble rebelled at every inch of the way. For his first two months of captivity he spent more time in the guardhouse than out of it. On his first day at camp he tried to thrash a lieutenant who was lining up a rawly shambling company and who spoke with unwelcomed sharpness to the mountaineer. Scarce had Cash atoned for this crime when he succeeded in giving a very creditable thrashing to a sergeant who was teaching his squad the mysteries of 'bout face.

Hearing that the near-by city of Petersburg was larger than Clayburg—which he knew to be the biggest metropolis in America—Cash set out to nail the lie by a personal inspection of Petersburg. He neglected to apply for leave, so was held up by the first sentinel he met.

Cash explained very politely his reason for quitting camp. But the pig-headed sentinel still refused to let him pass. Two minutes later a fast-summoned corporal and two men were using all their strength to pry Wyble loose from the luckless sentry. And again the guardhouse had Cash as a transient and blasphemous guest.

He was learning much more of kitchen-police work than of guard mount. At the latter task he was a failure. The first night he was assigned to beat pacing, the relief found him restfully snoring, on his back, his rifle stuck up in front of him by means of its bayonet thrust into the ground. Cash had seen no good reason why he should walk to and fro for hours when there was nothing exciting to watch for and when he had been awake since early morning. Therefore he had gone to sleep. And his subsequent guardhouse stay filled him with uncomprehending fury.

The salute, too, struck him as the height of absurdity—as a bit of tomfoolery in which he would have no part. Not that he was exclusive, but what was the use of touching one's forelock to some officer one had never before met? He was willing to nod pleasantly and even to say "Howdy, Cap?" when his company captain passed by him for the first time in the morning. But he saw no use in repeating that or any other form of salutation when the same captain chanced to meet him a bare fifteen minutes later.

Cash Wyble's case was not in any way unique among Camp Lee's thirty thousand new soldiers. Hundreds of mountaineers were in still worse mental plight. And the tact as well as the skill of their officers was strained well-nigh to the breaking point in shaping the amorphous backwoods rabble into trim soldiers.

Not all members of the mountain draft were so fiercely resentful as was Cash. But many others of them were like unbroken colts. The strange frequency of washing and of shaving, and the wearing of underclothes were their chief puzzles.

The company captain labored with Cash again and again, pointing out the need of neat cleanliness, of promptitude, of vigilance; trying to make him understand that a salute is not a sign of servility; seeking to imbue him with the spirit of patriotism and of discipline. But to Cash the whole thing was infinitely worse and more bewildering than had been the six months he had once spent in Clayburg jail for mayhem.

Three things alone mitigated his misery at Camp Lee: The first was the shooting; the second was his monthly pay—which represented more real money than he ever had had in his pocket at any one time; the third was the food—amazing in its abundance and luxurious variety, to the always-hungry mountaineer.

But presently the target shooting palled. As soon as he had mastered carefully the intricacies of the queer new rifle they gave him, the hours at the range were no more inspiring to him than would be, to Paderewski, the eternal playing of the scale of C with one finger.

To Cash the target shooting was child's play. Once he grasped the rules as to sights and elevations and became used to the feel of the army rifle, the rest was drearily simple.

He could outshoot practically every man at Camp Lee. This gave him no pride. He made himself popular with men who complimented him on it by assuring them modestly that he outshot them not because he was such a dead shot but because they shot so badly.

The headiest colt in time will learn the lesson of the breaking pen. And Cash Wyble gradually became a soldier. At least he learned the arm and the drill and the regulations and how to keep out of the guardhouse—except just after pay day; and his lank figure took on a certain military spruceness. But under the surface he was still Cash

Wyble. He behaved, because there was no incentive at the camp that made disobedience worth while.

Then after an endless winter came the journey to the seaboard and the embarkation for France; and the awesome sight of a tossing gray ocean a hundred times wider and rougher than Clayburg River in freshet time. Followed a week of agonized terror, mingled with an acute longing to die. Then ensued a week of calm water, during which one might refill the oft-emptied inner man.

A few days later Cash was bumping along a newly repaired French railway in a car whose announced capacity was forty men or eight horses. And thence to billet in a half-wrecked village, where his regiment was drilled and redrilled in the things they had toiled so hard at Camp Lee to master, and in much that was novel to the men.

Cash next came to a halt in a network of trenches overlooking a stretch of country that had been tortured into hideousness—a region that looked like a Doré nightmare. It was a waste of hillocks and gullies and shell holes and blasted big trees and frayed copses and split bowlders and seared vegetation. When Cash heard it was called No Man's Land he was not surprised. He well understood why no man—not even an ignorant foreigner—cared to buy such a tract.

He was far more interested in hearing that a tangle of trenches, somewhat like his regiment's own, lay three miles northeastward, at the limit of No Man's Land, and that those trenches were infested with Germans.

Germans were the people Cash Wyble had come all the way to France to kill. And once more the thrill of the man hunt swept pleasantly through his blood. He had no desire to risk prison. So he had made very certain by repeated inquiry that this particular section of France was in Europe; and that no part of it was within the boundaries or the jurisdiction of the sovereign state of West Virginia. Here, therefore, the law was off on Germans, and he could not get into the slightest trouble with the hated revenue officers by shooting as many of the foe as he could go out and find.

Cash enjoyed the picture he conjured up—a picture of a whole bevy of Germans seated at ease in a trench, smoking porcelain pipes and conversing with one another in comically broken English; of himself stealing toward them, and from the shelter of one of those hillock bowlders opening a mortal fire on the unsuspecting foreigners.

It was a quaint thought, and one that Cash loved to play with.

Also it had an advantage that most of Cash's vivid mind pictures had not. For, in part, it came true.

The Germans, on the thither side of No Man's Land, seemed bent on jarring the repose and wrenching the nerve of their lately arrived Yankee neighbors. Not only were those veteran official entertainers, Minnie and Bertha, and their equally vocal artillery sisters called into service for the purpose, but a dense swarm of snipers were also impressed into the task.

Now this especial reach of No Man's Land was a veritable snipers' paradise. There was cover—plenty of it—everywhere. A hundred sharpshooters of any scouting prowess at all could deploy at will amid the tumble of bowlders and knolls and twisted tree trunks and battered foliage and craters.

The long spell of wet weather had precluded the burning away of undergrowth. There were tree tops and hill summits whence a splendid shot could be taken at unwary Americans in the lower front-line trenches and along the rising ground at the rear of the Yankee lines. Yes, it was a stretch of ground laid out for the joy of snipers. And the German sharpshooters took due advantage of this bit of luck. The whine of a high-power bullet was certain to follow the momentary exposure of any portion of khaki anatomy above or behind the parapets. And in disgustingly many instances the bullet did not whine in vain. All of which kept the newcomers from getting any excess joy out of trench life.

To mitigate the annoyance there was a call for volunteer sharpshooters to scout cautiously through No Man's Land and seek to render the boche sniping a less safe and exhilarating sport than thus far it had been. The job was full of peril, of course. For there was a more than even chance of the Yankee snipers' being sniped by the rival sharpshooters, who were better acquainted with the ground.

Yet at the first call there was a clamorous throng of volunteers. Many of these volunteers admitted under pressure that they knew nothing of scout work and that they had not so much as qualified in marksmanship. But they craved a chance at the boche. And grouchily did they resent the swift weeding-out process that left their services uncalled for.

Cash Wyble was the first man accepted for the dangerous detail. And for the first time since the draft had caught him his burnt-leather face expanded into a grin that could not have been wider unless his flaring ears had been set back.

With two days' rations and a goodly store of cartridges he fared forth that night into No Man's Land. Dawn was not yet fully gray when the first crack of his rifle was wafted back to the trenches.

Then the artillery firing, which was part of the day's work, set in. And its racket drowned the noise of any shooting that Cash might be at.

Forty-eight hours passed. At dawn of the third day Cash came back to camp. He was tired and horribly thirsty; but his lantern-jawed visage was one unmarred mask of bliss.

"Twelve," he reported tersely to his captain. "At least," he continued in greater detail, "twelve that I'm dead sure of. Nice big ones, too, some of 'em."

"Nice big ones!" repeated the captain in admiring disgust. "You talk as if you'd been after wild turkeys!"

"A heap better'n wild-turkey shootin'!" grinned Cash. "An' I got twelve that I'm sure of. There was one, though, I couldn't get. A he-one, at that. He's sure some German, that feller! He's as crafty as they make 'em. I couldn't ever come up to him or get a line on him. I'll bet I throwed away thutty ca'tridges on jes' that one Dutchy. An' by an' by he found out what I was arter. Then there was fun, Cap! Him and I did have one fine shootin' match! But I was as good at hidin' as he was. And there couldn't neither one of us seem to git 'tother. Most of the rest of 'em was as easy to git as a settin' hen. But not him. I'd 'a' laid out there longer for a crack at him but I couldn't find no water. If there'd been a spring or a water seep anywheres there I'd 'a' stayed till doomsday but what I'd 'a' got him. Soon's I fill up with some water I'm goin' back arter him. He's well wuth it. I'll bet that cuss don't weigh an ounce under two hundred pound."

Cash's smug joy in his exploit and his keen anticipation of a return trip were dashed by the captain's reminder that war is not a hunting jaunt; and that Wyble must return to his loathed trench duties until such time as it should seem wise to those above him to send him forth again.

Cash could not make head or tail out of such a command. After months of grinding routine he had at last found a form of recreation that not only dulled his sharply constant homesickness but that made up for all he had gone through. And now he was told he could go forth on such delightful excursions only when he might chance to be sent!

Red wrath boiled hot in the soul of Cash Wyble. Experience had taught him the costly folly of venting such rage on a commissioned officer. So he hunted up Top Sergeant Mahan of his own company and laid his griefs before that patient veteran.

Top Sergeant Mahan—formerly of the Regular Army—listened with true sympathy to the complaint; and listened with open enthusiasm to the tale of the two days of forest skulking. But he could offer no help in the matter of returning to the *battue*.

"The cap'n was right," declared Mahan. "They wanted to throw a little lesson into those boche snipers and make them ease up on their heckling. And you gave them a man's-size dose of their own physic. There's not one sniper out there to-day, to ten who were on deck three days ago. You've done your job. And you've done it good and plenty. But it's done—for a while anyhow. You weren't brought over here to spend your time in prowling around No Man's Land on a still hunt for stray Germans. That isn't Uncle Sam's way. Don't go grouching over it, man! You'll be remembered, all right. And if they get pesky again you'll be the first one sent out to abate them. You can count on it. Till then, go ahead with your regular work and forget the sniper job."

"But, Sarge!" pleaded Cash, "you don't git the idee. You don't git it at all. Those Germans will be shyer'n scat, now that I've flushed 'em. An' the longer the news has a chance to git round among 'em, the shyer they're due to git. Why, even if I was to go out thar straight off it ain't likely I'd be able to pot one where I potted three before. It's the same diff'rence as it is between the first flushin' of a wild-turkey bunch an' the second. An' if I've got to wait long there'll be no downin' *any* of 'em. Tell that to the Cap. Make him see if he wants them cusses he better let me git 'em while they're still gittable."

In vain did Top Sergeant Mahan go over and over the same ground, trying to make Cash see that the company captain and those above him were not out for a record in the matter of ambushed Germans.

Wyble had struck one idea he could understand, and he would not give it up.

"But, Sarge," he urged desperately, "I'm no durn good here foolin' around with drill an' relief an' diggin' an' all that. Any mudback can do them things if you folks is sot on havin' 'em done. But there ain't another man in all this outfit who can shoot like I can; or has the knack of 'layin' out'; or of stalkin'. Pop got the trick of it from gran'ther. An' gran'ther got it off th' Injuns in th' old days. If you folks is out to git Germans I'm the feller to git 'em fer you. Nice big ones. If you're here jes' to play sojer, any poor fool c'n play it fer you as good as me."

"I've just told you," began the sergeant, "that we—"

"'Nuther thing!" suggested Cash brightly. "These Germans must have villages somewe'res. All folks do. Even Injuns. Some place where they live when they ain't on the warpath. Get leave an' rations an' ca'tridges for me—for a week, or maybe two—an' I'll gar'ntee to scout till I find one of them villages. The Dutchies won't be expectin' me. An' I c'n likely pot a whole mess of 'em before they c'n git to cover.

"Say!" he went on eagerly, a bit of general information flashing into his memory. "Did you know Germans was a kind of Confed'? The fightin' Germans, I mean. Well, they are. The hull twelve I got was dressed in gray Confed' uniform, same as pop used to wear. I got his old uniform to home. Lord, but pop would sure lay into me if he knowed I was pepperin' his old side partners like that! I'd figgered that all Germans was dressed like the ones back home. But they've got reg'lar uniforms. Confed' uniforms, at that. I wonder does our gin'ral know about it?"

Again the long-suffering Mahan tried to set him right; this time as to the wide divergence between the gray-backed troops of Ludendorff and the Confederacy's gallant soldiers. But Cash merely nodded cryptically, as always he did when he thought his foreigner fellow soldiers were trying to take advantage of his supposed ignorance. And he swung back to the theme nearest his heart.

"Now about that snipin' business," he pursued, "even if the Cap don't want too many of 'em shot up, he sure won't be so cantankerous as to keep me from tryin' to git that thirteenth feller! I mean the one that kep' blazin' at me whiles I kep' blazin' at him; an' the both of us too cute to show an inch of target to t'other or stay in the same patch of cover after we'd fired. That Dutchy sure c'n scout grand! He's a born woodsman. An' you-all don't want it to be said the Germans has got a better sniper than what we've got, do you? Well, that's jes' what will be said by everyone in this yer county unless you let me down him. Come on, Sarge! Let me go back arter him! I been thinkin' up a trick gran'ther got off'n th' Injuns. It oughter land him sure. Let me go try! I b'lieve that feller can't weigh an ounce less'n two-twenty. Leave me have one more go arter him; and I'll bring him in to prove it!"

Top Sergeant Mahan's patience stopped fraying, and ripped from end to end.

"You seem to think this war is a cross between a mountain feud and a deer hunt!" he growled. "Isn't there any way of hammering through your ivory mine that we aren't here to pick off unsuspecting Germans and make a tally of the kill? And we aren't here to brag about the size of the men we shoot either. We're here, you and I, to obey orders and do our work. You'll get plenty of shooting before you go home again, don't worry. Only you'll do it the way you're told to. After all the time you've spent in the hoosgow since you joined, I should think you'd know that."

But Cash Wyble did not know it. He said so—loudly, offensively, blasphemously. He said many things—things that in any other army than his own would have landed him against a blank wall facing a firing squad. Then he slouched off by himself to grumble.

As far as Cash Wyble was concerned the war was a failure—a total failure. The one bright spot in its workaday monotony was blurred for him by the orders of his stupid superiors. In his vivid imagination that elusive German sniper gradually attained a weight not far from three hundred pounds.

In sour silence Cash sulked through the rest of the day's routine. In his heart boiled black rebellion. He had learned his soldier trade, back at Camp Lee, because it had been very strongly impressed upon him that he would go to jail if he did not. For the same reason he had not tried to desert. He had all the true mountaineer horror for prison. He had toned down his native temper and stubbornness because failure to do so always landed him in the guardhouse—a place that, to his mind, was almost as terrible as jail.

But out here in the wilderness there were no jails. At least Cash had seen none. And he had it on the authority of Top Sergeant Mahan himself that this part of France was not within the legal jurisdiction of West Virginia—the only region, as far as Cash actually knew, where men are put in prison for their misdeeds. Hence the rules governing Camp Lee could not be supposed to obtain out here. All of which comforted Cash not a little.

To him "patriotism" was a word as meaningless as was "discipline." The law of force he recognized—the law that had hog-tied him and flung him into the Army. But the higher law which makes men risk their all, right blithely, that their country and civilization may triumph—this was as much a mystery to Cash Wyble as to any army mule.

Just now he detested the country that had dragged him away from his lean shack and forbade him to disport himself as he chose in No Man's Land. He hated his country; he hated his Army; he hated his regiment. Most of all he loathed his captain and Top Sergeant Mahan.

At Camp Lee he had learned to comport himself more or less like a civilized recruit because there was no breach of discipline worth the penalty of the guardhouse. Out here it was different.

That night Private Cassius Wyble got hold of two other men's emergency rations, a bountiful supply of water and a stuffing pocketful of cartridges. With these and his adored rifle he eluded the sentries—a ridiculously easy feat for so skilled a woodsman—and went over the top and on into No Man's Land.

By daylight he had trailed and potted a German sniper.

By sunrise he had located the man against whom he had sworn his strategy feud—the German who had put him on his mettle two days before.

Cash did not see his foe. And when from the edge of a rock he fired at a puff of smoke in a clump of trees no resultant body came tumbling earthward. And thirty seconds later a bullet from quite another part of the clump spatted hotly against the rock edge five inches from his head.

Cash smiled beatifically. He recognized the tactics of his former opponent. And once more the merry game was on.

To make perfectly certain of his rival's identity Cash wiggled low in the undergrowth until he came to a jut of rock about seven feet long

and two feet high. Lying at full length behind this low barrier, and parallel to it, Cash put his hat on the toe of his boot and cautiously lifted his foot until the hat's sugar-loaf crown protruded a few inches above the top of the rock.

On the instant, from the tree clump, snapped the report of a rifle. The bullet, ignoring the hat, nicked the rock comb precisely above Cash's upturned face. He nodded approval, for it told him that his enemy was not only a good forest fighter but that he recognized the same skill in Wyble.

Thus began two days of delightful pastime for the exiled mountaineer. Thus, too, began a series of offensive and defensive maneuvers worthy of Natty Bumppo and Old Sleuth combined.

It was not until Cash abandoned the hunt long enough to find and shoot another German sniper and appropriate the latter's uniform that he was able, under cover of dusk, to get near enough to the tree clump for a fair sight of his antagonist. At which juncture a snap shot from the hip ended the duel.

Cash's initial thrill of triumph, even then, was dampened. For the sniper—to whom by this time he had credited the size of Goliath at the very least—proved to be a wizened little fellow, not much more than five feet tall.

Still Cash had won. He had outgeneraled a mighty clever sharp-shooter. He had gotten what he came out for, and two other snipers, besides. It was not a bad bag. As there was nothing else to stay there for, and as his water was gone, as well as nearly all his cartridges, Cash shouldered his rifle and plodded wearily back to camp for a night's rest.

There to his amazed indignation he was not received as a hero, even when he sought to recount his successful adventures. Instead, he was arrested at once on a charge of technical desertion, and was lodged in the local substitute for a regular guardhouse.

Bewildered wrath smothered him. What had he done, to be arrested again? True, he had left camp without leave. But had he not atoned for this peccadillo fiftyfold by the results of his absence? Had he not killed three men whose business it was to shoot Americans? Had he not killed the very best sniper the Germans could hope to possess?

Yet, they had not promoted him. They had not so much as thanked him. Instead, they had stuck him here in the hoosgow. And Mahan had said something about a court-martial.

It was black ingratitude! That was what it was. That and more. Such people did not deserve to have the services of a real fighter like himself.

Which started another train of thought.

Apparently—except on special occasions—the Americans did not send men out into the wilderness to take pot shots at the lurking foe. And apparently that was just what the Germans always did. He had full proof, indeed, of the German custom. For had he not found a number of the graybacks thus happily engaged? Not for one occasion only, but as a regular thing?

Yes, the Germans had sense enough to appreciate a good fighter when they had one. And they knew how to make use of him in a way to afford innocent pleasure to himself and much harm to the enemy. That was the ideal life for a soldier—"laying out" and sniping the foe. Not kitchen-police work and endless drill and digging holes and taking baths. Sniping was the job for a he-man, if one had to be away from home at all. And in the German ranks alone was such happy employment to be found.

When Cash calmly and definitely made up his mind to desert to the Germans he was troubled by no scruples at all. Even the dread of the mysterious court-martial added little weight to his decision. The deed seemed to him not a whit worse than was the leaving of one farmer's employ, back home, to take service with another who offered more congenial work.

Wherefore he deserted.

It was not at all difficult for him to escape from the elementary cell in which he was confined. It was a mere matter of strategy and luck. So was his escape to No Man's Land.

Unteroffizier Otto Schrabstaetter an hour later conducted to his company commander a lanky and leather-faced man in khaki uniform who had accosted a sentry with the pacific plea that he be sworn in as a member of the German Army.

The sentry did not know English; nor did Unteroffizier Otto Schrabstaetter. And though Cash addressed them both in a very fair imitation of the guttural English he had heard used by the West Virginia Germans—and which he fondly believed to be pure German—they did not understand a word of his plea. So he was taken to the captain, a man who had lived for five years in New York.

With the Unteroffizier at his side and with two armed soldiers just behind him Cash confronted the captain, and under the latter's volley of barked questions told his story. Ten minutes afterward he was repeating the same tale to a flint-faced man with a fox-brush mustache—Colonel von Scheurer, commander of the regiment that held that section of the first-line trench.

A little to Cash's aggrieved surprise, neither the captain nor the colonel seemed interested in his prowess as a sharpshooter or in his ill-treatment at the hands of his own Army. Instead, they asked an interminable series of questions that seemed to have no bearing at all on his case.

They wanted, for instance, to know the name of his regiment; its quota of men; how long they had been in France; what sea route they had taken in crossing the ocean; from what port they had sailed; and the approximate size of the convoy. They wanted to know what regiments lay to either side of Cash's in the American trenches; how many men per month America was sending overseas and where they usually landed. They wanted to know a thousand things more, of the same general nature.

Cash saw no reason why he should not satisfy their silly curiosity. And he proceeded to do so to the best of his ability. But as he did not know so much as the name of the port whence he had shipped to France, and as the rest of his tactical knowledge was on the same plane, the fast-barked queries presently took on a tone of exasperation.

This did not bother Cash. He was doing his best. If these people did not like his answers that was no affair of his. He was here to fight, not to talk. His attention wandered.

Presently he interrupted the colonel's most searching questions to ask: "You-all don't happen to be the Kaiser, do you? I s'pose not though. I'll bet that old Kaiser must weigh—"

A thundered oath brought him back to the subject in hand, and the cross-questioning went on. But all the queries elicited nothing more than a mass of misinformation, delivered with such palpable genuineness of purpose that even Colonel von Scheurer could not doubt the man's good faith.

And at last the two officers began to have a very fair estimate of the mountaineer's character and of the reasons that had brought him thither.

Still it was the colonel's mission in life to suspect—to take nothing for granted. And after all, this yokel and his queer story were no more bizarre than was many a spy trick played by Germany upon her foes. Spies were bound to be good actors. And this lantern-jawed fellow might possibly be a character actor of high ability. Colonel von Scheurer sat for a moment in silence, peering up at Cash from beneath a thatch of stiff-haired brows. Then he ordered the captain and the others to leave the dugout.

Alone with Wyble the colonel still maintained his pose of majestic surveillance.

Then with no warning he spat forth the question: *"Wer bist du?"*

Not the best character actor unhung could have simulated the owlish ignorance in Cash's face. Not the shrewdest spy could have had time to mask a knowledge of German. And, as Colonel von Scheurer well knew, no spy who did not understand German would have been sent to enlist in the German Army.

The colonel at once was satisfied that the newcomer was not a spy. Yet to make doubly certain of the recruit's willingness to serve against his own country Von Scheurer sought another test. Pulling toward him a scratch pad he picked up a pencil from the table before him and proceeded to make a rapid sketch. When the sketch was complete he detached the top sheet and showed it to Cash. On it was drawn a rough likeness of the American flag.

"What is that?" he demanded.

"Old Glory," answered Cash after a leisurely survey of the picture; adding in friendly patronage: "And not bad drawed, at that."

"It is the United States flag," pursued the colonel, "as you say. It is the national emblem of the country where you were born; the country you are renouncing, to become a subject of the All Highest."

"Meanin' Gawd?" asked Cash.

He wanted to be sure of every step. While he did not at all know the meaning of "renounce," yet his attendance at mountain camp-meeting revivals had given him a possible inkling as to what "All Highest" meant.

"What?" inquired the puzzled colonel, not catching his drift.

"The 'All Highest' is Gawd, ain't it?" said Cash.

"It is His Imperial Majesty, the Kaiser," sharply retorted the scandalized colonel.

"Oh!" exclaimed Cash, much interested. "I see. In Wes' V'ginny we call Him 'Gawd.' An' over in this neck of the woods your Dutch name for Him is 'Kaiser.' What a ninny I am! I'd allers had the idee the Kaiser was jes' a man, with somethin' the same sort of job as Pres'dent Wilson's. But —"

"This picture represents the flag of the United States," resumed the impatient Von Scheurer, waiving the subject of theology for the point in hand. "You have renounced it. You have declared your wish to fight against it. Prove that. Prove it by tearing that sketch in two—and spitting upon it!"

"Hold on!" interposed Cash, speaking with tolerant kindness as to a somewhat stupid child. "Hold on, Cap! You got me wrong. Or maybe I didn't make it so very clear. I didn't ever say I wanted to fight Old Glory. All I said I wanted to do was to fight that crowd of smart Alecks over yonder who jail me all the time an' won't let me fight in my own way. I've got nothin' agin th' old flag. Why, that 'ere's the flag I was borned under! Me an' pop an' gran'ther an' the hull b'ilin' of us—as fur back as there was any 'Merica, I reckon. I don't go 'round wavin' it none. That ain't my way. But I sure ain't goin' to tear it up. And I most gawdamighty sure ain't goin' to spit on it. I —"

He checked himself. Not that he had no more to say, but because to his astonishment he found he was beginning to lose his temper. This phenomenon halted his speech and turned his wondering thoughts inward.

Cash could not understand his own strange surge of choler. He had not been aware of any special interest in the American flag. A little bunting representation of the Stars and Stripes—now faded close to whiteness—hung on the wall of his shack at home, where his grandmother, a rabid Unionist, had hung it nearly sixty years earlier, when West Virginia had refused to join the Confederacy. Every day of his life Cash had seen it there; had seen without noting or caring.

Camp Lee, too, had been ablaze with American flags. And after he had learned the rules as to the flag salute Cash had never given the banners a second thought. The regimental flags, too, here in France, had seemed to him but a natural part of the Army's equipment, and no more to be venerated than the twin bars on his captain's tunic.

Thus he could not in the very least account for the fiery flare of rebellion that gripped him at this ramrodlike Prussian's command to defile the emblem. Yet grip him it did. And it held him there, quivering and purple, the strange emotion waxing more and more overpoweringly potent at each passing fraction of a second. Dumb and shaking he glowered down at the amused colonel.

Von Scheurer watched him placidly for a few moments; then with a short laugh he advanced the test. Reaching for the sheet of paper whereon he had sketched the flag the colonel held it lightly between the fingers of his outstretched hands.

"It is really a very simple thing to do," he said carelessly, yet keeping a covert watch upon the mountaineer. "And it is a thing that every loyal German subject should rejoice to do. All I required was that you first tear the emblem in two and then spit upon it—as I do now."

But the colonel did not suit action to words. As his fingers tightened on the sheet of paper the dugout echoed to a low snarl that would have done credit to a Cumberland catamount.

And with the snarl six feet of lean and wiry bulk shot through the air across the narrow table that separated Cash from the colonel.

Von Scheurer with admirable presence of mind snatched his pistol from its temporary resting place in his lap. With the speed of the wind he seized the weapon. But with the speed of the whirlwind Cash Wyble was upon him, his clawlike fingers deep in the colonel's full throat, his hundred and sixty pounds of bone and gristle smiting Von Scheurer on chest and shoulder.

Cash had literally risen in air and pounced on the Prussian. Under the impact Von Scheurer's chair collapsed. Both men shot to earth, the colonel undermost and the pistol flying unheeded from his grasp. Over, too, went the table, and the electric light upon it. And the dugout was in pitch blackness.

There in the dark Cash Wyble deliriously tackled his prey, making queer and hideous little worrying sounds now and then far down in his throat, like a dog that mangles its meat.

And there the sentry from the earthen passageway found them when he rushed in with an electric torch, and followed by a rabble of fellow soldiers.

Cash at sound of the running footsteps jumped to his feet. The man he had attacked was lying very still, in a crumpled and yet sprawling heap—in a posture never designed by Nature.

With one wild sweep of his windmill arms Cash grabbed up the sheet of paper on which Von Scheurer had made his life's last sketch. With a simultaneous sweep he knocked the glass-bulbed torch from the sentinel, just as a rifle or two were centering their aim toward him; and, head down, he tore into the group of men who blocked the dugout entrance.

Cash had a faintly conscious sense of dashing down one passage-way and up another, following by forestry instinct the course he had noted when he was led into the colonel's presence.

He collided with a sentinel; he butted another from his flying path. He heard yells and shots—especially shots. Once something hit him on the shoulder, whirling him half round without breaking his stride. Again something hot whipped him across the cheek. And at last he was out, under the foggy stars, with excited Germans firing in his general direction and loosing off star shells.

Again instinct and scout skill came to the rescue as he plunged into a bramble thicket and wriggled through long grass on his heaving stomach.

An hour before dawn Cash Wyble was led before his sleepy and

unloving company commander. The returned wanderer was caked with dirt and blood. His face was scored by briers. Across one cheek ran the red wale of a bullet. A very creditable flesh wound adorned his left shoulder. His clothes were in ribbons.

Before the captain could frame the first of a thousand scathing words Cash broke out pantingly: "Stick me in the hoosgow if you're a mind to, Cap! Stick me there for life. Or wish me onto a kitchen-police job forever! I'm not kickin'. It's comin' to me, all right, arter what I done.

"I git the drift of the hull thing now. I'm onter what it means. It—it means Old Glory! It means—*this!*"

He stuck out one muddy hand wherein was clutched a wad of scratch-pad paper.

Then the company commander did a thing that stamped him as a genius. Instead of administering the planned rebuke and following it by sending the wretch to the guardhouse he began to ask questions.

"What do you make of it all?" dazedly queried the captain of Top Sergeant Mahan when Cash had been taken to the trench hospital to have his shoulder dressed.

"Well, sir," reported Mahan meditatively, "for one thing, I take it, we've got a new soldier in the company. A soldier, not a varmint. For another thing, I take it, Uncle Sam's got a new American on his list of nephews. And—and, unless I'm wrong, Kaiser Bill is short one crackajack sniper and one perfectly good Prussian colonel too. War's a funny thing, sir."

Forsaking All Others—

SECRET SERVICE—there's a thrill in the name! And there are a dozen keen thrills in this dramatic story of a daring venture.

RICK DEVENS was a lawyer, in private life. But "for the period of the war," he was a valued member of Uncle Sam's intelligence department.

He did not wear a uniform and strut around the lobbies of Washington hotels with a grim air of mystery. He dressed, as a rule, in quiet but decidedly good taste, and was as inconspicuous as a well-set-up man in the middle thirties can expect to be.

Eileen, his wife (whom he brought to Washington with him and with whom, after seven years of married life, he was ridiculously in love), knew in a general way that Rick was at the Capital on Government work. But she was content with his explanation that it was of a legal nature. Eileen was always "content with his explanations"—which may have accounted for the couple's ideal happiness and for the generally utter truthfulness of Rick's rare "explanations."

Gladly he would have told his wife the exact nature of his warwork and would have discussed every phase of it with her. But the departmental rules forbade this. So, with a nominal job in one of the legal bureaus, Rick was toiling hard as an actual member of the intelligence department. And no one outside of that department knew it. For the most part he was at Washington. But business sometimes led him on sudden trips of greater or less duration, far afield.

For example: The U. S. cruiser *Oakland* was making a short cruise in southern waters, in the first weeks of the war. The navy, just then, was rife with rumors of disloyal seamen, some of them active German propagandists, if not spies and workers of sabotage.

Word filtered to the quarter-deck of the *Oakland* that a newly joined oiler was causing some annoyance below by his continual grouchiness and by complaints which barely escaped the category of "mutinous language." Moreover, he seemed the ringleader of others who had shown signs of disaffection. There was not enough evidence to warrant action on the part of the ship's commander; but the oiler was thenceforth watched.

When the *Oakland* touched at Colon, she was boarded by a squad of Isthmian police, headed by a United States secret-service official. This official at once marched up to the oiler, saluted and stood awaiting orders. The oiler pointed in turn to four members of the crew.

"Those are all," he said tersely. "Take them along. The rest are loyal."

Then Rick Devens accompanied the police and their prisoners ashore, went to a hotel where he discarded his oiler-garb and took a Turkish bath. After which, he caught the first States-bound liner.

That was but one of his war-exploits. And there had been others far more dramatic. But for the most part, he was on duty at Washington, where he and Eileen had taken a tiny apartment that cost them three times as much as would a home of double the size in New York.

ONE morning early in 1918, Rick was summoned to the presence of his immediate superior, in the intelligence department—a man, by the way, who was supposed to be in the Capital to look after the interests of a khaki-supply contract, and who merrily instigated profiteering rumors against himself.

"We've got her!" announced Rick's chief, as Devens came into the private office.

He did not need to amplify his statement to the extent of saying whom he had "got." For Devens understood at once.

During the last six months, the intelligence department had been aware of a "leak" through which certain matters of the utmost secret import had sped directly from the White House to Wilhelmstrasse. Bit by bit, the list of suspects had been eliminated; and at last it became evident that the elusive news-getter was a woman. There, for a while, the gleanable information had rested; nor could it be extended.

Wherefore, Rick's instant grasp of his chief's exclamation, "We've got her!"

"Good!" said Devens. "Who is she?"

"There's Bannard's report," answered the other, shoving a typed sheet toward Rick. "Look over it. It tells the whole thing—how he got on her track and how he cinched it."

Rick glanced keenly down the close-typed page, nodding professional approval here and there. Once, he whistled aloud, murmuring:

"Mrs. Vivian Lorris! The last woman on earth I'd have thought of! I've met her once or twice. Stunning looker and crazy about admiration, too. But I took her for a silly butterfly. She—"

HIS voice trailed off as he continued to read. As he finished his perusal, Devens' brows puckered in chagrin.

"You said we'd 'got' her," he complained. "This report shows she's the woman we are looking for, all right. It shows it past all moral doubt. But it doesn't give any actual proof. Not an atom of proof that can arrest her or even deport her. Not even enough to interrupt her work. We don't seem to have 'got' her, at all."

"I meant we know now who she is," amended his chief. "The rest will be easy."

"Oh!" commented Rick, doubtfully. "Will it? I can't see how. She must be as clever as they make 'em. She isn't likely to—"

"No?" interrupted his superior. "Well, we think otherwise. Read Bannard's report again; and then take a look at the files. You'll find that, four times, she has got word through to Germany by men who were loyal to Uncle Sam—by men who were fools over her. She found they were to be sent across by the Government, in one capacity or another. And she coaxed them into taking along perfectly innocent letters, addressed to her sick mother in Lucerne. The letters had a better chance of delivery, she told them, if they were mailed in Paris, than here. And so they had. And a better chance of getting to the Wilhelmstrasse agent at Lucerne without rousing any suspicion.

Then—"

"Yes, yes!" agreed Rick, impatiently. "I know all that. But unless we can get hold of such a letter before it goes, and can get it decoded by one of our experts, I don't see how—"

"That's just what we're going to do," said the chief.

"You mean you're going to find out who carries the next letter and have him searched?" queried Devens.

The chief laughed, in high derision.

"Not quite," he scoffed. "In the first place, we can't very well search everyone who has met Mrs. Lorris. And we can't find out, by advertising, the names of the men to whom she expects to give such letters. She isn't the kind to let us get a hint at the identity of the letter-bearers—not in time for us to stop and search them. No, we've thought up a quicker and better way than that, a sure way, too. That's why I say 'we've got her.' We'll have the proof, and Mrs. Lorris along with it, inside of another month."

He paused for a moment. Then, as if with entire change of subject, he went on:

"We are going to send you to France next month, Devens."

"To France?" echoed Rick, in glad excitement. "You mean you're going to let me see real service, at last? I don't ask for a commission. I'll be happy enough to go as a buck private. When—"

"Hold on!" his superior stopped him. "You're on the wrong track. You're too useful to us to be wasted on the firing-line. No, you're to go over to Paris on work for the legal bureaus."

THE light of expectancy died out of Rick Devens' face.

"Oh!" he growled, grievously disappointed.

"Your trip isn't to be a secret," went on the chief. "Blab about it, all you want. I'll see there is a line or two in the papers about it, too. Even to the approximate date of sailing."

Rick listened to this with no interest at all.

"Meantime," resumed his superior, "I have a nice easy assignment for you, to keep you awake till you go. I want you to start in, as soon as you can, cultivating Mrs. Vivian Lorris' acquaintance. I want you to fall in love with her, as soon as you decorously can. In short, I want you to make a fool of yourself over her. Do you begin to get the idea? I don't see how you can miss it. You'll be one of the fools who fall under her spell. You are going across, in a month, to Paris on an unimportant 'outsider's' mission. And you're to allow her to give you the next letter she sends to that poor sick old mother of hers at Lucerne. I'll see she gets material enough to put into the letter, before then. That'll make it the easier for us to decode, when you turn it over to us."

Rick did not answer, but sat staring owlishly at his chief and turning over in his dazed mind the assignment he had just received. Presently he frowned and started from his daze.

"I don't want the job!" he declared bluntly.

His chief raised incredulous eyebrows, then said, with some stiffness:

"I don't suppose any of us are in this game because we 'want' our jobs. It's no personal joy to me, for instance, to read the sneers about my being a profiteer—even if I do start the yarns myself. Nor to be snubbed by a lot of decent people who think I'm here to skin Uncle Sam on a khaki-contract. But I go ahead with my stunt because it's got to be done, and because I'm of more use here than toting a gun or wearing gilt things on my shoulders. It's the same with you, and with others of us, higher and lower. We're here because this is the best way we can serve. Of course, if I'm mistaken—"

"You don't quite get me," replied Devens, uncomfortably. "It isn't that I stick at hard jobs. Perhaps my record proves I don't. It's only that I don't relish the idea of making love to a woman who isn't my wife, and of making fake love to any woman at all. And I don't like to wage war on a woman, either, or feel I'm the cause of her arrest. That's what I mean by saying I—"

"Perhaps you'd rather have the sweet knowledge that you've helped Germany, and maybe cost the lives of thousands of Americans, by your squeamishness in dodging the assignment?" suggested his superior. "For that's what it amounts to. You know some of the things that have happened already, from that woman's letters getting through to Wilhelmstrasse. Until we can get the proof to jail her, she's more dangerous to this country than a whole fleet of submarines, and a ton of bombs besides. This isn't the time for upstage talk, Devens; or for squeamishness, either. It's the time for every mother's son of us to do the thing we can do best. If we don't, we may live to see Prussian regiments marching up Pennsylvania Avenue. Will you do this, or won't you? It's within the square and angle of your work for the United States. You're not 'waging war on a woman.' You're waging it on Wilhelmstrasse. If this Lorris woman has sunk to betraying her adopted country and to making a living by sending Americans to their death, then it's time to forget she's a woman, and to think of her as you'd think of a she-rattlesnake or a rabid she-dog. Will you take the job?"

"YOU'RE right," gloomily assented Rick. "You're dead right. But I hate the assignment, just the same. Why in blazes don't you give it to Bannard? He's worked up the case, in fine shape, so far. Why can't—"

"Use your wits, man!" exhorted the chief. "Conjure up a picture of old Bannard. Do you honestly think any woman, outside of a blind asylum, would fall for him? Can you figure Bannard making love? No, we've gone over every man we can trust for such work. And you're the only one who can handle it. It isn't *my* decision. I'm just passing the order on to you from headquarters. Here's a thing that's got to be done—a menace to our ships and our men that has got to be cleared away. You seem to be the only man who has a chance of succeeding at it. It isn't nice work. I admit that. But will you do it?"

"Yes," said Devens heavily, after a scowling pause. "I will. And I ought to be kicked for doing it. But—I ought to be shot for refusing to do it. So there you are."

"Good!" was the chief's curt approval. "Go to it! We leave all the details to your own judgment. Take that copy of Bannard's report along with you, for reference. Well?" he added inquiringly, as Rick, pocketing the report, still hesitated.

"Well," said Devens, none too easily, "there's only one stipulation I must make. And I think you people will see the force of it. I must tell my wife about the assignment. And—"

"*What?*" fairly roared the other.

"I say, I must let my wife know about it," continued Devens. "I can vouch for her secrecy. So no harm will be done. You're a married man, yourself. You can't help seeing what it would do to my domestic life and to my reputation and to my wife's happiness if I were to start in making violent and open love to another woman—especially to a woman she knows and likes. Why, it would break my wife's heart to have me do such a thing, unless she understood I was doing it for the country she loves. Even so, I'm afraid she—"

But by this time his superior had so far recovered from his momentary stark amazement as to find voice. He broke in, angrily:

"Neither this country nor this department is interested in your domestic affairs! Certainly not to the extent of letting you risk the safety of a great mission like this by confiding it to a woman, even if she's your wife and you trust her. It can't be told to her. Get that fact into your brain and keep it there."

DEVENS flushed darkly, and half arose to his feet. His face was working. The chief waved him back to his chair and spoke more conciliatingly.

"Look here," said he. "I mean no slight or offense to Mrs. Devens—none at all. It isn't personal. We'll take it for granted she would stand for what you are to do, and that she wouldn't breathe a word of it to anyone. Well, then: You say she knows Mrs. Lorris and likes her. If she knew you are doing this for the Government, she would sit back complacently, we'll say, and let you go ahead. And as a good American, she'd shun Mrs. Lorris as a spy. Now, is all that the conduct of a jealous wife? Mrs. Lorris is no fool. She knows you have some sort of departmental job in Washington. When you begin to cultivate her, and your wife begins to shun her—won't she guess what's up? And won't we lose our last chance of nabbing her? She'll find a new way of getting her reports to Wilhelmstrasse, and we'll never catch her. You must have the sense to see all this. Haven't you?"

For a few seconds, Rick said nothing. The other man was covertly watching him, troubled, eager. At last, his voice hard and lifeless, Devens made answer, speaking more to himself than to his hearer.

"Life's such a lot bigger than the people who live it!" he began, in tired reflection. "I've always bragged that the way to duty is as clear as day, no matter how badly every other road is clogged. But it isn't. It is anything but clear. It—"

"I fail to see—"

"On the face of it," went on Rick, unheeding the interruption, "it's a straight proposition. A spy is sending messages to Germany—messages that mean fearful losses to the United States. There seems to be a chance for me to put an end to that spy's activity, and to save the lives, perhaps, of countless brave men. I seem to be the only available person for the job. So much for that. I—"

"Quite right," assented the other. "That's the situation. So—"

"ON the other hand," pursued Devens, in the same heavily ruminative undertone, "to do all this, I must kill my wife's glorious faith in me. I must shame her, in the eyes of the people we know. I must smash her heart, by making her think I have lost my love for her and that I love another woman. That may seem a very little thing to you and to most other practical men! But to me it is about the biggest thing in the world. This may sound maudlin and melodramatic to you. But—"

"It does," said his chief, crossly. "And it—"

"There's one thing more," added Rick, "—a thing many men remember too seldom, I think. When I married, I took a mighty solemn and binding oath at the altar, as every man does. I forget the exact language of the whole marriage vow; but it contains one clause that runs something like this: *'And forsaking all others, cleave only unto her!'* That's an oath; and the man who breaks it is committing perjury, as I should be committing it, if I turned my back on Eileen and made ardent love to Mrs. Lorris."

"You seem to forget that you've taken a pretty solemn oath to your country, too," observed the other. "Do you put your wife above the United States? Do you put her happiness, and your loyalty to her, ahead of—"

"Yes," was the sullen reply. "I do! What man doesn't—if he loves his wife, as I love mine? That's where women are different from men. And it's lucky for patriotism that they are. When the country calls, every true woman sends her husband or her son or even her father, out to fight for the flag—to risk death, for the Right. And it is splendid for them to do it. But men would lack the patriotic unselfishness to do the same thing—just as *I* lack the selfish patriotism to break my marriage oath and to make my wife go through the fire of grief and shame, by taking this assignment you offer me. I suppose it means my resignation here and the loss of all future chance to serve my country in the most efficient way I can serve. But I count the cost, and I'm ready to pay. That's all, I think."

HE got up and walked lifelessly to the door. The chief, peering at him from under beetling brows, let Rick turn the knob and open the portal before seeking to stay him. Then he said, as Devens was passing out:

"I want you to take twenty-four hours to think this over, before you turn in your resignation. You're hot under the collar just now. And you need time for some of these crazy theories of yours to simmer down. Report here, this time to-morrow."

Rick nodded and went out. He was sick and miserable. Never till now had he realized all his departmental work meant to him, nor how its loss would pain him.

He loved his country. He knew, without conceit, that he had done splendid service for the United States during the war, even though the authorities had vetoed his wish to serve in the field and had kept him at the far more perilous and difficult task of an intelligence department secret agent.

And now it was over! Not only that, but he had just refused an assignment which would have been of more benefit to Uncle Sam than all the rest of Devens' achievements put together.

The sense of failure began to sting Devens to wholesome anger; and with wrath came a fierce yearning to tackle the problem from some angle which would not involve his wife's happiness. Common sense told him there was no such angle. But common sense never yet was able to quench angry determination.

In his own office, he drew Bannard's report from his inner pocket and fell to studying its succinct phrases, over and over.

He was interrupted in this fruitless task by the swinging open of the office door. The breath of violets wafted in with the gush of outer air. Rick jumped up, joyously, to greet his wife as she hurried across the little cubbyhole room toward him.

Very dainty, very lovely was Eileen Devens; her face was flushed with fast walking, and her Irish eyes rivaled the azure of the great bunch of violets at her belt. Never had she seemed so priceless, so exquisite, to her husband, as now when he had just thrown away his career for her.

"I called you up," she was saying; "but you were out. So I stopped by, to leave word for you. Mrs. Lorris is getting up a little impromptu luncheon at the New Willard, to-day, as a good-by for Nels Amilon. He's just got a recall, for a bigger place in his national Legation—at Paris, I think it is. Anyhow, he leaves Washington late this afternoon and sails to-morrow. It's very sudden. He didn't know definitely till this morning. And Mrs. Lorris is recruiting a dozen people, by phone, for the send-off luncheon. She wants us to come. You can get away, can't you? *Please* do! Her luncheons are so jolly!"

"I'm sorry," said Rick, in a voice he tried to make steady. "I'd like to, ever so much, sweetheart. But I'm swamped with a batch of rush work that will keep me hustling, with both hands, for the next four hours. Don't look so blue about it! It can't be helped. And it's so important that I'll have to ask you to run along and let me get back to it, now. I'm sorry. Good luck!"

AS soon as he could get his wife out of the room, Rick went back to the report he had been reading when she came in. But now his whole aspect had changed. The despairing glum anger had given place to an almost hysterical eagerness.

At once he found what he sought, in Bannard's statement of the Lorris case. The name of Nels Amilon—military attaché of a neutral legation at Washington—figured prominently in the report, as that of the newest and most favored of Mrs. Vivian Lorris' squadron of admirers.

"It's a chance!" mumbled Devens. "A chance! One chance in three, perhaps! No—a better chance than that! He's been making a fool of himself about her. He's going back to Europe. He's not specially clever—just the sort she uses for her messengers. And it's two months since she has had a chance to send word, that way, to Germany. It's a cinch she'll send a message by him:—a 'letter to her poor old invalid mother at Lucerne!' It's—it's worth the risk!"

More calmly, Rick began to map out his plan. Amilon was a member of a foreign legation—a neutral legation, at that. Hence, his luggage could not be searched. Most assuredly his sacred person could not. He was inviolate. Mrs. Lorris could not possibly have chosen a safer or more sacrosanct messenger.

On the other hand, if an agent of the United States should seek to violate the sanctity of Amilon's official position, it must lead to all sorts of ugly international complications, at a time when every neutral nation had to be treated as considerately as a box of dynamite.

For a long time, Rick sat moveless, his eyes closed. At length he nodded and drew a long breath.

"It may mean a jail-term to me," he muttered, half aloud. "But it won't involve Uncle Sam. And Eileen, being a woman, will forgive me a lot more easily than if she thought I was making love to Mrs. Lorris."

NELS AMILON, tall, rawboned and ruggedly blond, came briskly into his dismantled suite of rooms at the Rawdon. He had had a delightful day. His merry luncheon at the New Willard had been followed by a charming tête-à-tête call at Mrs. Lorris' apartment—a call he had prolonged to so late an hour that he would now barely have time to change into service uniform, superintend the packing of the only trunk that had not already been sent on and drive to the station to catch the seven o'clock train for New York.

Amilon felt a certain complacently sentimental pang over parting from Mrs. Lorris at the very climax of this siege to her heart. And her shyly given first kiss was glowingly warm on his lips. But he was headed for promotion. And at worst, his absence from her was but a matter of a year or so. Perhaps, even sooner than that, he might hope to return to Washington. In the meantime—

The military attaché's sunny reverie faded. He had come to a halt in the center of his living-room. The one remaining trunk stood open, on the floor. He had hoped to find it neatly packed, with only space enough left to include his dress uniform, which he was about to discard for the service uniform lying across a convenient chair.

Instead, the open lid of the trunk revealed a sadly mussed-up array of clothing. Nor was his valet anywhere in evidence. The fellow had had orders to wait for his master, after seeing to the disposal of the bulk of the luggage.

In his place slouched a mangy-looking roustabout, tousled of hair, slack of jaw, and clad in soiled jumper and canvas overalls and brogans.

"What the deuce are *you* doing here? sharply demanded Amilon, as the roustabout came out from an inner room of the suite and stood grinning sheepishly at him.

"I'm waitin' to take that trunk of yourn," said the man. "I was to clear away any baggage you'd left. And the trunk's all I can find. Is it ready to go?

"Hmph!" commented Amilon, in strong disfavor, wondering how so trim a house as the Rawdon could employ so disreputable a porter. "All right. But the trunk's not ready. Where's my man?"

"I dunno," answered the porter.

And he told the truth. Amilon's valet was even now somewhere on the way to Richmond, in response to an urgent telephonic summons, received by him an hour earlier and purporting to come from his employer.

AMILON glowered for an instant. Then he looked more intently than before at his trunk. On this closer glance, he saw its contents not only were tumbled but had very recently been ransacked. Indeed, their searcher had evidently been so long engaged at his task that he had not had time to rearrange the topsy-turvy articles before Amilon's sudden return.

The military attache scowled. And he stared accusingly at the porter. Then he stalked toward the wall-telephone.

He was between the outer door and the man whom he suspected. Moreover, he was half a head taller and fifteen pounds heavier than the shambling figure in jumper and overalls. Therefore, with fine contempt for any resistance the puny creature might be inclined to make, he turned his back on the porter and put the receiver to his ear.

It did not remain there long enough for him to enter into conversation with the desk downstairs.

For, on the moment, a sinewy arm locked itself around Amilon's throat from behind. A knee was jabbed agonizingly into the small of his back. The muscular weight of one hundred sixty pounds was thrown into a sharp tug of the arm and a correspondingly sharp thrust of the knee.

Nels Amilon's big body shot backward, with express-train momentum, his spine threatening to crack, and his windpipe shut off. To the floor he thudded, with a shock whose noise was broken by the thickness of the rug on which he landed. By the time he touched ground, his further mental and physical processes were suspended by a short-arm jolt on his jaw. His lanky form relaxed and composed itself to coma.

Rick Devens reached the telephone in one stride.

"Never mind!" he called to the inquiring operator, at the far end of the wire. "I wanted a number. But I can't remember it. Sorry to have bothered you."

HE hung up the receiver and hurried back to his victim. Deftly, hastily, thoroughly, he went through Amilon's pockets. Every letter, every paper, and both of the man's pocketbooks, he confiscated. There was no time to sort them out in search of the letter he wanted. He stuffed his booty into the pockets of his overalls.

Amilon began to stir, spasmodically; and to gobble, deep in his throat, like a distressed turkey. Rick annexed the man's watch and a handful of bills from his wallet. Then he turned and let himself noiselessly out of the suite.

Along the corridor floor, to the right, he strewed the watch and money, that they might seem to have been dropped by the thief in his panic-flight. Then, going swiftly down the corridor,—to the left, he let himself into a room he had that day rented for a week.

He reached the door of this room, unobserved, just as a loud yell from Amilon's suite proved that the attaché had come to his senses and was seeking to rouse the hue-and-cry after his despoiler.

Rick's first action, on going into his own room, was to divest himself of his outer garments and brogans and to drop them down the dim-lit air-shaft. Then he dressed himself in his own clothes and washed away certain cleverly applied touches of paint from his face. Not until he had combed his tousled hair and once more stood forth in his own well-groomed character, did he set to work on the sheaf of envelopes he had seized.

For three minutes, he searched the heterogeneous mass of correspondence. Then he cut the linings of the two pocketbooks. After which, he slumped despondently into the nearest chair.

He had found nothing which could possibly be construed as a

letter from Mrs. Vivian Lorris, or from any other woman!

The ruse had failed. Either Mrs. Lorris had given Amilon no letter to smuggle to Europe; or else the letter had gone into a trunk already sent to the station.

Or else—

BUT Rick was positive he had given the suite and the trunk a thorough search; also that he had not overlooked any possible hiding-place on Amilon's person where a letter could be stowed away. Yet, as a super-forlorn hope, he prepared to return to the lion's den.

Down the hallway he went, following the sound. For a decided commotion was waging around the suite's door. Chambermaids, guests, bellboys, a clerk, the manager and the house detective were in one confused huddle in the hall and in the living-room of the suite. The center of the turmoil was a tall and wabbly man in uniform who was explaining for the ninth time that he had been set upon by three men dressed as hotel porters, overpowered after a hot fight and robbed.

Two or three employees were trying to console him by holding forth bits of treasure-trove they had picked up along the hallway, in the shape of a gold repeater and various scattered wads of money.

"Clear out of here, all, of you!" presently shouted the manager, above the babel. "Captain Amilon, if you will let me help you down to my office, I'll send for some brandy and for a doctor to examine your hurts. Then you can make out a full statement to my stenographer, for the police. This way, please!"

Rick furtively beckoned the house detective to one side. The detective was a former Government secret-service man; and at once recognized Devens.

"Craig," whispered Rick, "I want you to fix it so I can be alone in that suite for five minutes, when the others have gone. Can you do it? It's official business."

UNDER the manager's exhortations, the crowd in the hall was dispersing. Most of its members were following Amilon, whom the manager was assisting to the near-by elevator. Craig ushered Devens, unnoted, into the suite, unlocking its outer door with his pass-key and departing as the door closed behind Rick.

Five minutes more of the most rigidly painstaking search failed to disclose any trace of a letter.

"It's all off!" he growled at last. "I've made a fool of myself. And to-morrow I'll have to turn in my resignation. Just because Mrs. Lorris didn't give Amilon any letter to take across, and because the man who wrote the marriage service put in that line about 'forsaking all others!' "

He dusted off his hands and prepared to put on his coat which he had discarded during the search. Just then a very light and cautious tap sounded on the outer door. Still in his shirt-sleeves, Rick opened the door, prepared to find Craig waiting on the threshold to ask officiously if he could be of any help.

But the house detective was not there. The person who had knocked was a wooden-faced and middle-aged woman in neat black.

"Well?" inquired Devens, none too courteously.

The woman looked him over; then looked at the trunk, just behind him—the trunk whose nearest end bore in legible red lettering the name and rank of Captain Nels Amilon.

The sight of the trunk, and of the shirt-sleeved and perspiring Rick, who had apparently been busily packing it, seemed to explain much to the woman.

Her first aspect of doubt was cleared away.

"Captain Amilon's man?" she asked, in a low voice. "Good! He said I was to give it to you, if he had not come back yet. He said he had left word with you. I was to come straight up here, without stopping at the desk. And—"

"Eh?" asked Rick sulkily and with no special show of interest, as he caught sight of a thin envelope she was taking from the breast of her dress. "Then you're Mrs. Lorris' maid, are you? Yes? The Captain has been waiting for this letter, pretty near an hour. He had to go on, awhile ago. He told me to stay till it got here. You're late. You might have made us miss our train."

"It could not be ready, sooner," said the woman. "There were things to be added at the last minute, as Madame explained to the Captain this afternoon."

"I see," grumbled Rick ungraciously, as he took the proffered envelope. "All right."

HE turned back to the trunk. The woman softly departed. Rick gave her sixty seconds wherein to leave the corridor before bolting out of the suite, himself, and down the servants' stairway.

"You see," he explained confidentially to his chief, next day (as they finished a reading of the decoded letter which stopped up the most persistent Governmental "leak" of the war), "you see, a man doesn't have to be altogether worthless in a job like this—even if he's so old-fashioned as to live up to that 'forsaking all others' clause of his contract. Just the same, I'm mushy enough to wish it had been a man, and not a woman, that I've helped to nab. My one consolation is that Uncle Sam doesn't shoot women-spies. The worst he'll do to Mrs. Lorris is to intern her, comfortably, till the war's over, and then let her loose. But next time, give me some nice easy job,—like breaking up a nest of homicidal maniacs,—won't you? I deserve some such soft berth, after what I've been through."

The Dented Halo

WHEN Aroline Lippitt's mother died and left her rich, it was too late. And this was Aroline's first clear thought, when the first numbness had passed.

The Lippitts had been stodgy pillars of the stodgier up-State town of Dulham for a dreary number of years. Aroline's home life had been a choice blend of that endured by all the exemplary people in all the Sabbath-school library books she had ever read. There was everything in it, except what a normal young girl could desire. Food and clothing, both solidly healthful; a solidly ugly home and a solidly ugly social circle; a terrifically praise-worthy example in the lives of her parents: these were Aroline's earthly portion, up to the age of sixteen.

Then the same street-car collision which killed her father left her mother a bedridden cripple. And for a full quarter-century thereafter, Aroline was self-chained to the invalid's bedside. She did everything for her doomed mother. And she had no time nor incentive for anything else. Youth and young womanhood slipped wistfully by; unnoted by the girl, who was losing them without once having tasted either.

When Aroline was forty-one, her mother died. After which came the days of closed blinds and of tiptoeing feet and the ashamed thrill of interest in the adjusting of unfamiliar crape-folds; the blurred days of strange leisure and of dearth of object.

From it all emerged Aroline Lippitt in her forty-second year, with nothing to do and with nearly eleven thousand dollars a year to do it with. From it, too, emerged a new Aroline Lippitt—a woman who, for the first time in her life, had a chance to think about herself.

Since childhood, she had been taught that selfishness is a mortal sin. And it was a sin she had had no opportunity to commit. But now there was no one and nothing but herself to think about. Wherefore, without at all realizing what she was doing, Aroline gradually began to readjust herself and to take account of stock. Whereupon, she learned a number of interesting and sad things.

She learned, for example, that youth is a season of glory, and that youth was no longer hers. She learned (from the new brand of books she now read and from watching the couples who loitered past the house in the soft May twilight and from the snatches of laughter and music that floated across from less rigid homes) that there are such things as romance and love and—above all—a good time.

TIED to the bedside of an invalid who daily waxed more exacting, forced to read aloud, daily, for hours, from such sterling works as Baxter's "Saints' Rest," Thomas-à-Kempis' "Imitation of Christ," the sermons of the Reverend Jonathan Edwards, and "The Philosophy of the Infinite," she had been blinded to any other phase of life than that of sacrifice and hodden-gray duty.

Now, from curiosity, she took to reading magazines and such books as allured her by their jackets and titles. She knew she was doing wrong in preferring Rupert Hughes to Jonathan Edwards. But, to her own surprise, she didn't care whether it was wrong or not. She began to read newspapers, too. And she quickened at the things they told her.

On the verge of forty-two, Aroline Lippitt was beginning to waken. The wholly unspent reservoirs of youth had not yet dried up in her spirit; and they clamored for exit. Guiltily, yet as if to magic melodies, Aroline listened to their clamor. And, brazenly, she began to pore over fashion-plates.

These mighty changes did not occur in a day or even in six months. Nor were they unattended by many a qualm of conscience and by homesick yearnings for her safe old-time slavery. But hourly they gained ground.

It became necessary at last to "talk it out" with some one. But, except for her pastor and a very few of her mother's cronies, she had no intimates in whom to confide. And most assuredly none of these could understand or fail to be shocked. Aroline took to that final refuge of the non-communicate, the pen. Deliberately, shamelessly, she wrote out a brief statement of her own case. Having written this, she read it three times, to herself, slowly and aloud. After which, tearing the confession into tiny fragments, she burned the handful of scraps in the hideous old living-room Franklin stove. This is what she had written:

"I shall be forty-two next month. There are nineteen small wrinkles in my face; and there are thirty-seven white hairs (that I can count) in my head. I have been kissed four times that I can remember: once by my father, when I won the attendance-record prize at Sunday-school; three times, in all, by my mother.

"I saw a delivery man kiss a servant girl, in the area-way of the house just across the street, last evening. He kissed her more times than I could count. And she put her arms close about his neck, as if she were a very little child. It was not wicked. It was not vulgar. It was very beautiful and wonderful. It made me cry. I don't know why.

"I don't think I am a fool. For I have sense enough to know that I am a middle-aged woman and that no man would ever want to kiss me. But I can remember how fluffy my hair used to be, before I was too busy to bother with it. And I had a pretty color, too—as pretty as that servant girl's. Twenty-five years ago, some man might have been willing to kiss me like that, even though no man ever will, now. Yes, I think that is what made me cry.

"I missed all that, and I never knew I was missing it. I missed a lot of other things, too, that seem to me much more worth while. I missed the filmy soft dresses and the sweet hats and things that other girls wear. I missed the dancing and the laughing and the fun.

"It doesn't make me cry to remember how I missed those things, because it isn't really too late for any of them—for a *little* of all of them, anyhow. It is an awful thing to say, I suppose. But I've paid for my right to a good time. And I am going to have it. I say, *I am going to have it!* I mean that.

"If it is wrong to do what I am going to do, then let the Recording Angel be fair enough to subtract from the sin all the things I did for Mother and all the things I was never able to do for myself. I don't believe the remainder is going to be big enough to count much against me. If it is, let it!

"I say I'm going to have *one* good time. And I've figured the whole thing out. I am not going to have it here, at Dulham. I owe too much to our family name and to the people who were fond of Father and Mother and to the people at the church who seem so glad that I am carrying on Mother's interest in missions and in the Ladies' Guild. No, I can't have it here. I am not going to dent my local halo. But I'm going to have it, just the same. *I am!*

"And when it is all over, I shall come back here and go on with the things that are expected of me. But, then, when I hear people laugh or see them in pretty clothes or when I listen to dance music, I won't feel a lump in my throat. I'll just smile to myself and whisper: *'I know all about that, too!'* "

CALMLY and with iron purpose, Miss Aroline Lippitt went ahead with her sinful plans. And one day she departed from Dulham,—a grim little wisp of a figure in her styleless black, and lugging an elderly straw suitcase.

Six hours later, the same grim little wisp of a figure walked sturdily up to the garish desk at the St. Crœsus Hotel in New York and demanded a suite of two rooms and a bath.

This was not a haphazard jaunt. Its every step had been laid out with shrewd care, by the aid of newspapers, novels, magazine stories, a library book entitled "The Paris of America," a score of fashion journals and countless advertising sheets. Yes, Miss Aroline Lippitt was ready.

Going to her suite, she discarded the mourning garb she had worn from Dulham and replaced it with a less somber if equally unprepossessing dark blue traveling-suit she had bought surreptitiously at the Dulham department-store—this and a *tricorne* hat of sorts, purchased from the same place.

Thus arrayed, Miss Lippitt's reflection in the pier-glass seemed all but fairylike in its flippancy, by comparison with her everyday self. Solemnly, Aroline laid the discarded black bombazine on the floor. Solemnly, she walked to and fro upon its unlovely surface, a jounce of happy vindictiveness punctuating each stride. Then, remembering the thing must look presentable enough to be worn back to Dulham, she picked it up, gave it a perfunctory shake and hung it in a far corner of the closet.

This rite achieved, Aroline fared forth from the hotel and

summoned a taxicab. From a slip of close-penciled paper she read to the meter bandit the first of a series of names. It was the name of a Fifth Avenue shop, which had been favorably mentioned in its own newspaper advertisements, a shop which sold ready-to-wear garments of astounding gorgeousness, at a price far more astounding.

From shop to shop swept Aroline Lippitt. She knew pretty well what she wanted. And where she found need to change her ideas, her decisions were Napoleonic in swiftness. After the shops were duly ravaged, she betook herself to the hairdresser whose ad appeared oftenest in her surreptitiously bought New York papers. There, in the hands of coiffeur and facial masseur and manicure, she passed a delirious two hours.

DUSK was beginning to glimmer as Aroline departed from the hairdresser's. The visitor's nails were pink mirrors. Her massaged face glowed and flushed and itched. Her hair was arranged in a manner whose frivolity should have made her mother turn in her grave as madly as any squirrel in a wheel-cage. Another glance at her memorandum gave her the address of a much advertised dispensary of afternoon tea. And this address she confided to her taxi-driver.

The tea-room was lighted only by little pink bulbs, heavily shaded, one on each of the widely scattered wicker tables. In the rosy gloom sat folk, invariably two to a table, heads close together, hands usually interclasped with more or less furtiveness. Pussy-footed waiters glided down the dim aisles between tables, bearing many and picturesque liquids—and, once in a great while, tea.

The frank intimacy of the place warmed Miss Lippitt's heart. The loneliness of twilight in a strange city departed from her. Life all at once became charming again. She chose almost the only vacant table, and ordered a pot of English breakfast tea, with buttered toast.

Meantime, a steady stream of treasures flowed from various Fifth Avenue shops to the St. Crœsus Hotel and was convoyed duly to Miss Aroline Lippitt's suite. An incomplete list of the parcels' contents would have inventoried much as follows:

One triple-pelt white-fox scarf with head (chosen from a dozen others because of the friendly grin of the especial fox's furry little face).

One afternoon dress of sapphire-blue satin and Georgette crêpe with Oriental trimmings.

One large sapphire-blue satin hat. One small hat of shirred white maline, with wreath of tiny white ostrich tips. Aroline had hesitated long between these two hats, deciding at last in favor of the latter and then, to quell an agony of indecision, buying the former, too.

One floating white lace veil, suitable to go with either of the foregoing hats. Three pairs of long white kid gloves—bought in defiance of the clerk's hint that chamoisette or silk would be more comfortable.

One pair of incredibly high champagne-colored kid boots with stockings to match, and at a Monte Cristo price. One pair of pink kid and one pair of white kid evening slippers, with stockings to match.

One pink-flowered silk evening frock, rimmed with tulle. One white satin ditto, strung with mother-of-pearl sequins. One pale blue crêpe-de-chine negligee smothered in coffee-colored lace.

One long "Oriental neck-chain;" one pink tourmaline shirtwaist ring, with brooch to match. Much costly lingerie (mostly decked with Philippine embroidery, highly recommended in the ads) and quantities of flesh-colored garments of an intimate nature and made of crêpe-de-chine. One panne velvet evening wrap. One shepherd's plaid street-dress. One large and noncommittal trunk wherein to bear her clandestine purchases back to Dulham— there to lie unseen and unsuspected in the severely reputable attic of the Lippitt house.

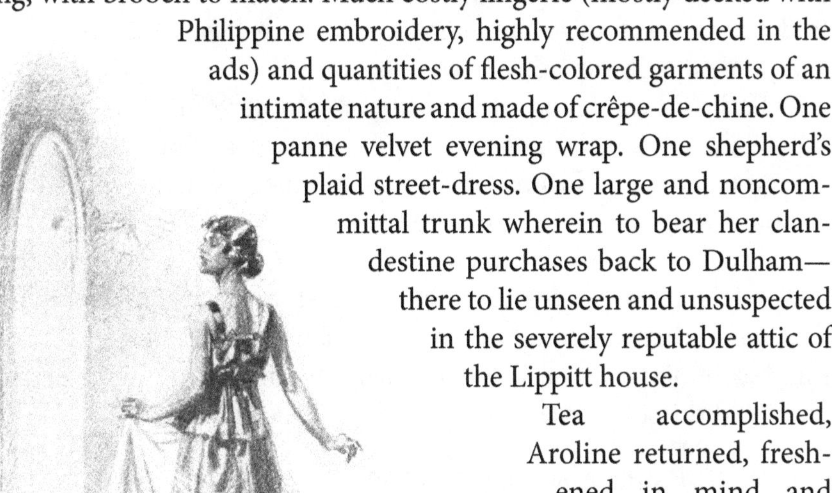

Tea accomplished, Aroline returned, freshened in mind and body, to the St. Crœsus and spent a solid hour of bliss on the rug in her bedroom, inspecting and re-inspecting the pile of new-bought belongings.

Back at home, the frugal household of her parents' time could have been run for the best part of a year on what Aroline had spent today in less than five hours. Realizing this, she rejoiced mightily in her sin and marveled at her own glad lack of conscience.

Then, robing herself in the white satin evening frock, she gloated on her reflection in the glass. At least, she continued to gloat until she got a full look at the lowness of the neck and pictured herself facing collective New York in such array. But a clever draping of the big white-fox scarf appeased all but outraged propriety.

Aroline was not at all puzzled as to the dinner she should order, for she had memorized a menu from a modern society novel. But, so flustered was she at the waiter's statement that she could not have Romanoff caviar, owing to war-conditions, that she wholly forgot to order the dry martini cocktail she had included in her dinner-memorizing. She did not recall the omission until the meal was half finished. And then—as a brief mental review of her fiction-mentors told her—it was far too late for such a prefatory beverage. Aroline was sorry. She much wanted to taste a cocktail.

She heard a man at an opposite table order one. Aroline kept a covert and curious lookout for the drink's arrival. She was surprised to find it served in so small a glass. She somehow had imagined that cocktails were served in dinner tumblers.

But when the man at the opposite table ordered and drank three cocktails in fast succession, she understood that fashion merely demanded they be served in little glasses, without circumscribing the number of glasses. She wondered why the man had not saved time and sated thirst by ordering all three cocktails at once.

DINNER over, Miss Lippitt put on her panne velvet wrap and went to the theater for the first time in her life. A month beforehand she had picked out from the theatrical notes the popular musical comedy which should usher her into the new world of theater-goers.

The next three hours were charged with astonishment of the most intense sort. From her reading of Shakespeare, Aroline sought to follow and to analyze the plot of the show. Failing, she laid the failure to her own stupidity and gave herself up to the joy of the rackety music and the eternal kaleidoscope of color. Some of the costumes made her gasp. Some of them heightened the effect of the masseur's work on her cheeks. Many of the jokes meant nothing to her. One or two of them she was quite certain she had misunderstood. And she blamed her own mind for imagining meanings which could not possibly exist at so public and respectable a performance.

Then came the drive to the cabaret roof she had chosen as a wind-up to her first evening in New York. The day had been the most glorious in all her starved life. Her clothes caressed her. Their rich beauty was a benediction. The bustle and flare of Broadway stirred her to the hungry soul. She leaned back luxuriously in the bumpy taxi and drew a long happy breath, redolent of the vehicle's moldily wet leather.

"This is heaven!" she announced to the cross-section of her flushed face visible in the cracked slice of mirror. "And the best part is that I've still got a whole celestial month of it. To-morrow, I'm going to begin my dancing-lessons. Oh, it's worth having been cooped up for forty-two years just to be free like this! And it's worth being cooped up for the rest of my life just to remember this, too!"

Aroline had read of the much-advertised difficulty of getting tables at popular cabarets. Also of the best way to get such a table. A dollar bill, slipped adroitly to the head waiter, made the fat potentate her slave and won her a table that almost under-hung the stage itself. Not only did the inspired bribe win her a table of honor; but it brought no less than two waiters dancing around her, waving menus and wine-cards and order pads, as though to drive away an invisible swarm of flies from her sacred head.

Quick mental rehearsal brought back to Aroline the details of a correct after-theater supper. And in a firm voice, she gave her order. This time, she was resolved not to forget the all-important item of cocktails. So she prefaced the supper mandate by saying sweetly:

"And you may bring me, first of all, three nice dry Martini cocktails, please."

A vague memory of the watery condition of her afternoon's cup of tea prompted Aroline to add the earnest injunction:

"And please make them extra strong, waiter."

The waiter stolidly marked a hieroglyph on the blank, then proffered the wine card. Aroline waved it politely aside. She did not desire liquor in any form. From childhood she had heard of the evils of

intemperance. And she did not intend to sully her good time by the sin of wine-bibbing.

Oddly enough, she did not include cocktails in the list of alcoholic drinks. Her knowledge of cocktails was based solely on the few society novels she had read. In such novels, a meal was always begun by cocktails. The hero of the story—yes, and the heroine, too—almost invariably sipped them.

Aroline supposed them to be some form of herbal bitters or similar medicated appetizer, such as her mother had often taken at the doctor's bidding. That they were groupable under the head of "non-temperate," was unsuspected by the elderly child, whose sole knowledge of the world had been gleaned from six months of chance literature.

A MAN, sitting alone and morbid at the next table, heard the queer order and stared in open interest at the woman who had given it. Puzzled, he tried to reconcile the command with the prim little voice that uttered it. And presently he was trying to reconcile the garish evening apparel with the prim little creature who was wearing it.

Aroline felt his gaze on her and instinctively looked up from her study of a much-undressed mermaid waltzing with a lobster, on the menu's margin. The man was young,—well under thirty,—and he seemed unhappy or perhaps cross. This much Aroline gathered before she dropped her coy glance to a renewed study of mermaid and lobster.

A minute later, she saw two other men stop at the cross youth's table, in passing, and shake hands with him. One of them addressed him as "Dick."

Just then the waiter placed three cocktails in front  of Aroline. And she promptly centered her interest on the drinks. She lifted the first glass to her lips, as nearly as possible in the manner of the man whom she had noted at dinner that evening. She remembered that he had swigged his first cocktail in a single gulp and had drunk the two others in more leisurely manner. Such, apparently, was the custom.

Aroline swallowed her cocktail, with creditable speed. It stung and burned as it darted down her throat. It brought tears to her eyes. And it tasted vile.

Yet it tasted no worse than had the anchovies which the waiter, at dinner, had persuaded her to take in place of the non-procurable Romanoff caviar. Nor did it taste as bad as had the brine-bitter olives in the *salmis*. It was probably an acquired taste, this liking for cock-tails. And Aroline set out to acquire it, by raising the second glass and forcing herself to swallow little mouthfuls of its contents.

This glass was even worse than the first. Aroline basely gave up her effort to acquire the taste, and she set down the glass half full. She was here for a good time, not for self-torture. Next, she caught the gaze of the cross and lonely man at the next table, still fixed quizzically upon her. She was frowning at the bitter cough-medicine flavor of the cock-tail. She feared lest the man might think she was frowning at him. To relieve him of such dread, she smiled reassuringly at him. He did not smile in reply but for some reason, actually seemed distressed. Also, he seemed just a little indistinct.

In fact, everybody seemed a bit indistinct and more than a bit undulant. The man at the next table was rather less indistinct than was anyone else. And he was glowering at her so funnily!

He certainly was funny—the funniest man she had ever seen; a trillion times funnier than the comedian at the show she had just quitted! Yet the comedian had been funny, too. And at memory of his antics, Miss Aroline Lippitt began to laugh.

All at once her merry face went grave, not to say panic-stricken. She put up a wandering and inquiring hand to her mouth. To the blurred touch, her mouth felt as usual. But she knew better than to trust to mere sense of touch. Something had happened! She wanted to tell some one about it—to get expert advice.

SHE rose to her feet, on the dreamily swaying floor, and took a cautious step to the next table—the table from which the cross-faced youth stared at her.

"Oh, Dick!" she exclaimed, her voice low-pitched, but vibrant with bewildered fright, "Oh, Dick, my *teeth* are so large!"

"That's all right," the man reassured her, rising and coming close to her side, as if to ward off the view of other guests, "It's all right. Don't worry. Better sit down and drink a glass of ice water; and then—"

"But Dick!" she interposed, speaking with eager tensity, "You don't understand. My teeth have been growing, ever since I got here. They're so *big!* I don't see how I manage to get my mouth shut. I—"

"Come!" broke in the

man, speaking with an authority so sharp that Aroline was tempted to cry. "Come! Take my arm. And try not to talk. So!"

Dazedly, Aroline Lippitt thrust her hand into the crook of the out-thrust arm. The man piloted her, skillfully and without attracting notice, to the outer door. When Aroline's head was clear enough to grasp another fact, she and her escort were standing beside a taxicab in the street below; and he was asking her for the third time:

"Where do you live?"

"One-forty-six Avon Place," she responded, perplexed at the question.

The man stared glumly at the taxi-driver.

"Must be in the Bronx," volunteered the latter. "Or maybe in Brooklyn. Most all the streets in them places has different names. Just like the towns out in Joisey an'—"

"Do you live in Brooklyn?" queried the cross youth.

"Of course not," replied Aroline, with some asperity—the more so because the chilly night air was playing odd pranks on her powers of thought. "I live in Dulham. One-forty-six Avon—"

"Oh, you're just visiting New York, then?" pursued the man. "Where are you stopping?"

"At the hotel, of course," snapped Aroline, beginning to resent these impertinent questions and yearning absurdly to go to sleep.

"What hotel?" persisted the man.

But now a strain of native wariness came to Aroline's aid. She had heard of polite and craftily inquisitive strangers waylaying people in New York. And she was on her guard. Not one word could be extracted from her thenceforth.

The man gave an address to the chauffeur, hoisted the numbed Aroline into the taxicab and climbed in beside her. By the time she had taken her seat, Aroline sank into a refreshing doze.

In a woefully short time, she was aroused from a dream of wading waist-deep through billows of Fifth Avenue raiment. The man was shaking her shoulder, deferentially, yet insistently.

"Come!" he said. He seemed always to be saying "Come!"

BLINKINGLY, Aroline let him lead her out of the cab and up the steps of a grimy apartment-house on an uninspiring uptown street.

An elevator stranded the two adventurers outside a slablike and unmarked door, whose bell the man rang,

A girl answered the summons. She struck the half-wakened Aroline as being decidedly pretty and winsome and not a little unhappy. Indeed, any woman (and no man) would have known the girl had been crying.

At sight of the cross young man, her face went scarlet and her eyes soft and glowing. But only for the space of an instant. Then an ugly hardness leaped into the soft eyes and the tender mouth-corners.

"This is a real surprise, Dick," said the girl, her voice coming stiffly from somewhere in the region of her upper front teeth. "Or perhaps I was mistaken in thinking you said you would never set foot here again? In either case, a call at twelve o'clock is just a—a—"

She stopped short, catching sight of Miss Aroline Lippitt, who had shrunk instinctively behind her escort. Dick paid no heed to the frosty greeting. Leading Aroline by the arm, he passed the staring girl and went into the apartment hallway. Once inside, he released the gradually awakening Aroline and addressed their hostess.

"There wasn't anything else to do," he said abruptly, "I dropped in at the Idiocy Roof to-night, to—to forget things. This lady was at the next table. She drank some cocktails. A blind man could see she wasn't used to them. They got her. I was afraid she'd grow noisy or weepy and get herself locked up, or something. She couldn't remember where she is staying in town. She isn't the kind to be turned over to the police. Something had to be done with her, till she could come to herself. I couldn't take her to the club. And there isn't any woman here but you I know well enough to take her to. So I brought her to you. That's all. You'll look after her, won't you?"

The girl was paying less heed to his explanation than to the unhappy woman who stood so dazed before her in the packing-box hallway. The rumpled gayety of the sequin-strung evening-frock, contrasting with the gentle bewilderment of the wearer's face, was a problem she could not solve.

Under the inspection, Aroline shivered a little and made as though to rally her dormant powers of speech. The shiver loosened the coil of white-fox fur around her lower neck, exposing about three square inches of honest and bony chest. With a jerky gesture and an apprehensive glance at the man, Miss Aroline made haste to rearrange the fur.

The girl nodded.

"All right, Dick," she said, in sudden decision. "I'll look after her. It—it was like you to bring her to me. I'm glad you did. Good night."

DICK made no reply. He walked glumly to the door and let himself out. At the departure of her knight, Aroline Lippitt roused herself, with a start, and took a step after him. The girl interposed. Speaking much more gently than in the man's presence, she said:

"Don't be frightened. You're all right. And now I am going to put you to bed. We can talk in the morning."

This girl, for all her gentleness, was speaking with authority. And the confused and sleepy refugee was not sorry to let some one else do her thinking for her. Meekly she suffered herself to be undressed and ensconced among the covers of a bed which, patently, served by daylight as a couch. The day had been long and fearfully fatiguing. The hour was incredibly late for the early-retiring Aroline. The remaining fumes of the cocktails were lulling her to inertia. Presently she was in a dead sleep.

It was nine o'clock in the morning when she was waked by the girl, who stood beside her with a cup of excessively strong black coffee. This pick-me-up she forced pleasantly upon the bemused Aroline. Its potency cleared away the sleep-mists and an incipient headache along with them. Also, it brought back memory.

"I'm so sorry,—so ashamed of myself, to have made you all this bother!" exclaimed Aroline. "I can't think what could have ailed me. I suppose it was the wonderful day I'd had. That and the theater and all the strange food. I was feeling first-rate. And then, all of a sudden, I got queer and far-away. And—wasn't it grand of that gentleman to be so nice and look after me? His mother must be proud to have a son like him!"

She paused; for into the girl's gently amused eyes sprang that same hard and unfriendly look which Dick's advent had evoked, the night before. Misreading the look, Aroline thought her hostess was jealous that all the praise should be Dick's. And she hastened on:

"It's *you,* though, who I ought to be gratefullest to. And I am. To think of your taking in a perfect stranger, like me, and caring for me as if I was your own mother! Oh, I don't know what to say!"

YET she managed to say it. Under the girl's tactful questioning, the whole crazy story came quickly to light, in all its laughable details. But somehow the girl did not laugh. And she kept Aroline from feeling overmuch the pangs of new-wakened propriety.

She sought to make the poor old reveler think her outing had been not only legitimate but praiseworthy. She even gave vehement approval to every shamefacedly confessed item of Aroline's purchases. And she forbore to horrify her guest by telling her of the effect of cocktails on the human brain. She went further. Under Aroline's civil counter-questioning, she told a few sketchy facts about herself.

Her name, it seemed, was Phyllis Bayne. She was a Smith College graduate and she had come to New York to study singing. And now, after a gruelling three-year apprenticeship, she at last had her chance. She had received the offer of an engagement to sing soprano roles with the Apollo Standard Opera Company.

Of course, for a year or so, she must content herself with secondary parts, and with understudy work. But it was a chance—a splendid chance. She would have been a fool not to jump at it. Nobody who really had Phyllis' welfare at heart could doubt that. No one who was not selfish and hidebound and disgustedly old-fashioned would be unkind enough to oppose so golden a scheme. It would be as vile as to clip the soaring pinions of an eagle.

And as for turning her back on the shining chance and settling smugly down to hum-drum matrimony—well, what did Miss Lippitt think of any purely hypothetical man who would suggest such a thing?

Aroline listened, as to a gorgeous fairy-tale. She had read of Melba, of Sembrich, of Galli-Curci. And here, before her very eyes, sat and orated a woman who was due to rival them, one day. Aroline had not read of the Apollo Standard Opera Company. But she had read of the Metropolitan. And doubtless the two were on a par.

Yet, through Phyllis' pæan of laudation at her own chance, the listener found herself noting a subnote of defiance—a subnote which, once or twice, threatened to merge into tears. This, at first, she could not at all understand.

"Oh," sighed Aroline, as Phyllis came to a stop, "what a proud and happy woman you must be! To think of everything you've risen to! And how proud and happy Mr.—Mr.—the gentleman who brought me here—must be, to have such a gifted young friend!"

THEN she saw, tardily, that she had somehow said the wrong thing at the right time. Phyllis' eager face went flint-hard.

"Dick Mercer," she said, coldly, "is too self-centered to appreciate my good fortune. He has behaved abominably about it. I don't care to say any more."

Now Aroline was tenfold sure she had said the wrong thing. Yet her lately neglected conscience would not let her heed the warning-signal. She remembered Dick Mercer's behavior toward herself. She recalled, with a shudder, that, but for him, she might now be in a charity hospital or even in a police station. And Phyllis' denunciation brought back to her the desperately miserable aspect of his face.

Being a woman, and having taken so rigid a course, of late, in novel-reading, she began to understand.

"Miss Bayne," she said timidly, "you've been so good to me that I hate to say anything to rile you. But Mr. Mercer was good to me, too—ever so good. I wasn't a darling girl, like you, I was a silly old woman, and ugly, besides. And he came to my help. And then he didn't even stay here long enough for me to thank him. That's why I don't feel I've got the right to let you go on thinking he's selfish and unkind or—or hidebound (whatever that means). He's not. Honestly, he isn't. He—"

"I'd rather not discuss Mr. Mercer; if you please," put in Phyllis, icily.

Aroline did not want to discuss him, either. Phyllis' tone fairly withered her courage. Yet, because gratitude to both man and girl was welling high in her heart and because she began to have a very fair insight into the situation, the frightened woman girt herself in the heroism of a cornered rabbit and plunged ahead with her theme.

"I wouldn't blame you a mite, Miss Bayne," she said, tremulously, "if you ordered me out of here, for keeping on nagging at you. But I wouldn't stop blaming myself, ever, if I didn't keep on. I never read a novel in my life till this last year. And since then I've been trying to make up for it. So they're more real to me than if I'd been reading them for years. And the thing in most every one of them that makes me mad is the way the lovers keep on misunderstanding each other and being at cross-purposes, clear up to the very last chapter. Sometimes, I want to holler at them: 'You poor ninnies, you're just shutting your two eyes and running away from your own happiness! Three words, from anybody with a grain of sense, would set you straight again!' That's what I feel like saying to those storybook folks, Miss Bayne. And of course I don't ever get a chance to. I have to sit back and watch them break their hearts."

SHE hesitated. Phyllis, looking indifferent, was humming to herself. Aroline went on, with a fresh hold of desperation upon her shrinking courage:

"Don't be too much offended at me, will you, just because I can't keep my foolish mouth shut, the first time I find any real-life folks in the same mess as those storybook lovers I've been telling you about? In the books, it gener'lly comes out all right in the last chapter. But I guess the last chapter, in life, isn't always like that. Is it? Or else the last chapter comes too late to be of much use—like an anchor, after the ship is wrecked. Just as the last chapter—with all the money and the liberty and everything—came, to me, too late to be of any use except to let me play the idiot yesterday. Miss Bayne, I'd just hate to go back home to Dulham, thinking the last chapter was going to come to you, too late—like it came to me! I'd hate, a lot worse, to remember that I didn't even bother to try to make it come any sooner to you."

"I'm sorry to have made you so upset over my affairs," said Phyllis, trying to be indignant, but failing to mark anything beyond her guest's pitiful air of resolution. "I ought not to have burdened you with them. Though why you should imagine there is any love between Dick Mercer and—"

"I don't imagine it," returned Aroline. "I know it, being a woman—even if I'm not very much of a woman, perhaps. Didn't I see your face, when you caught sight of him last night? And didn't I hear how his voice sounded when he spoke to you? I was pretty sick and dizzy, and more interested in myself than in anybody else, just then. But I've been remembering, ever since you began to tell me these things about your career and hinting about his wanting you to marry him, instead, and settle down.

"A career must be a grand thing. But if it bars out marrying and a home—and—and children—and love—Well, at forty-two you'll have the mem'ry of lights and applause and money and bo'quets and such, just as I have the mem'ry of Mother and all I was able to do, to make her sickness easier. But when it's all over, one mem'ry is more or less like another, I take it. You can't live on them, be they grand or petty. And when it's all over, you won't be so very different from what I am now. Will you? And you'll be astonished to see how soon the time will pass and it'll be over. Then it's what you've saved that'll count, not what's happened to you. If you've saved nothing but money and fame, I don't believe it'll mean much—Just as my money, and my name among the neighbors for being decent to Mother, don't make up to me for what I've missed. If you've saved love and a husband and a home with real children in it, that investment will last you and keep you rich all through the rest of your days, if you live to be a hundred. I'm—I'm talking like a preacher, aren't I? I never gabbled so much before. It must sound silly."

"No," answered Phyllis, gently. "It doesn't. And I appreciate your interest in us. But you don't understand—"

"Maybe not," assented Aroline. "Most likely I don't. If two sane folks don't know their own business, a blabby old woman isn't likely to be able to teach it to them. Only,"—with a little sigh,—"it would have been just beautiful if I could have gone back home, knowing that everything was coming out all right in the last chapter. And now I've got to go back, remembering the poor stricken way that splendid boy looked, when he was sitting there all alone at his table, and the way you're looking, right now. It—it must be wonderful to be able to make anybody stop looking unhappy! Almost as wonderful as having a home with a husband and babies in it. I—I hope it isn't brazen of me to speak like that, about a husband and—and everything—that I never had. But it seems to me that an engagement to sing lullabies to a body's own cuddly children would be a billion times beautifuller than an engagement to sing soprano in all the standard opera companies in the world."

The stark wistfulness in her eyes and the unrealized pathos of yearning in her tone—infinitely more than the banal preachment's mere words—were doing unaccountable things to the hearer's throat and eyes. The arguments themselves held nothing striking; nor were they as eloquent and frenzied as Dick's own. But behind them Phyllis read with merciless vividness the woman's own empty life, in all its sterile yearnings for what had been denied her. To Aroline, she knew, the last chapter had come, before one really interesting word of the story had been written. The rest, throughout the years to come, must be mere gray epilogue—such an epilogue as must follow the far more brilliant life-story Phyllis was preparing for herself.

A shrinking from the far-off phantom of empty loneliness gripped the girl. For the first time in her twenty-four years, it was given her to see the grisly vision which appears often and oftener to most of her elders— the vision of Youth dead and of Loneliness born, Loneliness which is no longer made bearable by Youth and by Youth's twin-sister, Hope.

A FEW hours later, a perspiring expressman deposited at the door of Phyllis' flat a large and serviceable trunk, quite heavy, and accompanied by a letter. Phyllis, with Dick Mercer looking over her

shoulder, read the letter, It ran:

"I figured I'd been robbed of two birthrights: a good time and romance. I gave romance up, as too dead to resurrect. But I came to New York for the good time. I've had it. And, thanks to you, I've had the romance, too—something I never dared hope to have in this world, or in the next, either. I'm starting for home. I'm taking back the good time I came for. And I'm taking back romance, besides,—your romance,—to make Dulham rose-colored for me.

"I've read about brides having trousseaus. And I am begging you not to be angry at me for making bold to send you one. It is new. I bought it all, yesterday. And it's a gloriously sweet trousseau. I was going to hide the trunk away in our attic. But just think of what our minister would say (he's my executor) if he should come across it when he rummages through my effects!

"It must be wonderful to be young. I haven't been old long enough to get used to age. And I've never been young. But in just one single day, I've had a good time and romance—thanks to you two. How many younger women can beat that record?"

Branded

IF Helen Ward numbered five hundred men in her here-and-there acquaintance, it was fairly safe to catalogue the thousand in this order:

One hundred of them were either in love with her or else waited but the spark of hope to make them so. Three hundred and ninety-nine of the remainder liked her better than almost any other girl they knew; and the wedded contingent among them wished furtively that their wives could make a personal study of her. (Helen was the kind of girl one marries.)

This accounts for all of the five hundred—with a single exception. That exception was Jim Ross. And Jim Ross neither loved Helen nor so much as liked her. He detested her. He hated her more consistently than ever in his morose career he had been able to hate anyone else.

He had begun disliking her on general principles. Perhaps on the same theory that made the Athenians banish Aristides, because they were tired of hearing him called "the Just." As a born and bred and expert lawyer, Jim invariably refused to take anything for granted. Hearing Helen's praises sung in a myriad different keys, he had sought to verify or confute the praise. And, naturally, he had ended by confuting it. To him, Helen Ward was a butterfly—a female drone in life's hive. She served no good end. And she did not put herself out to be cringingly agreeable to his important self.

Not until Helen's engagement to Ross's younger brother, Walton, was made known did Jim sweep from impersonal dislike for her into active and resentful hatred. He told himself that it was because Walt was throwing himself away on such a girl. He told many people so. No one but his own timid little wife could have proved otherwise. And Marcia Ross was too much in chronic terror of her aggressive husband to criticize him—even to herself.

Jim Ross had dreamed a dream. From his standpoint, it had been a beautiful dream. Because it had been about money. He had married Marcia two months before the death of her supposedly ultra-rich father. The father had died all but insolvent. And the blow had come close to breaking Jim's pure heart. He had never been able quite to forgive Marcia for her sire's poverty. True, he needed no more money than he and his brother had inherited at their parents' death, and he was making a good livelihood at the law. But that a man of his acumen should have saddled himself with a penniless bride was an endless grief to him.

Then into his ken and his guardianship recently had flapped a flat-chested and dish-faced damsel who, in her own right, possessed something like two million dollars. And Jim, straightway, had enlisted Marcia's feeble aid in throwing the heiress and Walt together at all times and places. Walt had rewarded this brotherly effort by engaging himself to Helen Ward—a girl with barely enough money to dress on. And just as the two-million maiden had begun to show a keen interest in Walt's society, too!

Still, Jim did not give up all hope. An engagement is not a marriage. Much may happen between the merging of those two blissful states. So he fought on.

Jim Ross used to say the chief difference between a night at Mrs. Greaves's country house and a night in a cell was that in jail there are no servants to tip.

It was Jim Ross's pleasing way to say a thing like that. It was on a par with his wonted view of life, and of those who sought to make it pleasant for him and for Marcia.

Mrs. Greaves, of course, heard of his sneer at her house-parties. And it vexed her not at all. She did not so much as bother to stop inviting Jim to Restmere. Her parties were too jolly and worth-while to be hurt by Jim's slurs or even by his presence.

"Some one has to ask the poor man somewhere," she used to say. "Everyone else has stopped inviting him. So now it's more exclusive to have him as a guest than not to. Besides, there's his poor wife. I like Marcia. I'd like her better if I didn't have to be sorry for her."

The "jail" resemblance at Restmere, to which Ross referred, was the quaint dormitory system: Restmere, two hundred years earlier, had been built with a view to the entertaining of hordes of guests.

Wherefore, on either side of the rambling house was a huge room, some fifty by a hundred feet. And along the sides of these two rooms were airy little alcoves—to hold a bed, a chair, and a dresser.

The alcoves all connected with the main dormitory-room, which was blended lounge and assembly-hall.

In Colonial days (when men and women used to sit at opposite sides of a church and so forth), the eastern dormitory had been set apart for women guests and the western for men. And, ever since, the odd old custom had been kept up. Such of the Greaves guests as did not like the arrangement were not forced to accept the hostess's invitation. But few of them objected. Even Jim Ross, despite his comparison between his alcove bedroom and a cell, continued, unprotesting, to occupy such a "cell" whenever he was asked to Restmere.

One of these rare invitations came to him and to his wife a fortnight after Jim heard of the engagement of his brother and Helen Ward. It was a week-end party for which Mrs. Greaves sent forth a dozen invitations, and for which she received, at once, precisely twelve acceptances.

Besides the Jim Rosses and Helen Ward, the guest-list included Jim's law partner, Barry Cahill—a hard-headed and taciturn man, who was one of the few living mortals whereof Jim wholly approved—and, naturally, Jim's aforesaid younger brother, Walton.

Jim and Mrs. Jim arrived at the Greaves home late on Saturday afternoon. They were the last guests to reach Restmere. They found their fellow revelers all assembled in the wide entrance-hall at tea. On a fat sofa-pillow at the hostess's feet sat a tiny cross-legged figure in kimono and obi, plucking daintily away at a samisen's strings and crooning sweet little queer songs in a queer little sweet voice. The other guests, teacups in hand, were grouped interestedly round the singer.

To Jim, the scene's central figure was puzzling. To Marcia, his wife, there was nothing perplexing about it. Mrs. Ross gained her few glimpses of social pleasure by going to various people's houses while her husband was at his office. And several times before she had met this mite of a Japanese woman.

Cherry San, as she chose to call herself, was a society fad that year, and was coining a fortune as a drawing-room entertainer. From house to house she was bidden, at fabulous sums, to sing in costume and to tattoo. One of the recurrent tattoo crazes was at its height. And many a New York woman was willing to pay insane prices for the privilege of having her white flesh disfigured by one of Cherry San's minutely small artistic designs.

Mrs. Greaves had summoned the Jap to Restmere for the amusement of her week-end guests. And the pleasure with which her songs were now received and encored proved the experiment a success. Cherry San, to-day, sang sometimes in Japanese, sometimes in English.

"And now for the tattooing—*please!*" called Helen Ward, as the singer at last laid aside her samisen and got to her feet.

"Please *not!*" begged Cherry San, flexing her little yellow hands. "Not yet. Unless you wish very bad art in tattooing please! When I play for so long, my fingers get what you call cramp and stiff. If I use the needles before my fingers have an hour to rest them then my hand wiggles, and I spoil my art. After dinner, by gracious leave, yes?"

"After dinner, then," assented Mrs. Greaves. "But it will have to be very soon after dinner. I'm asking twenty or thirty neighborhood people over for a dance this evening. And you know how it is in the country. People begin drifting in the minute they finish their own dinners. I want you all to come out and look at my new Italian garden before you dress. If you've finished tea, suppose we go now."

The guests followed her through the wide doorway out to the veranda and across the lawn. Walton Ross, to his brother's disgust, maneuvered not only for a place at Helen Ward's side in the irregular procession but also managed to detach her from the bulk of the party. Jim was glumly relieved to see Barry Cahill leave the rest and join the two lovers. Oblivious of Walton's lack of enthusiasm, Cahill proceeded to monopolize as much of Helen's attention as he could.

This unusual expansion on the part of his taciturn partner surprised Jim almost as much as it pleased him. He turned to his wife, who, as usual, was pattering along meekly at his side. "Look there, Marcia," he grunted joyfully, under his breath: "See Cahill trying to cut Walt out? I hope to the Lord he succeeds! She doesn't seem to object, either. See? I wonder if there's a chance—"

"But Jim," timidly protested his wife, "it would make poor Walt so unhappy if—"

"'Unhappy!'" snorted Jim, in the tone that always wilted his scared wife into silence. "'Unhappy?' It makes a man unhappy to have his vaccination take. But it saves him from smallpox. Not a chance, though, I suppose. Walt's got twice the money Cahill will ever have. The Ward girl knows which side her bread's buttered on. Still—" He grunted again, and fell silent.

Dinner was late. And, as usual on the first night of a house-party, it was a long-continued meal. When the women trooped out of the dining-room into the broad hall, they found Cherry San standing patiently beside a table on which was arrayed her tattoo-kit.

They flocked round her—Helen Ward most interested of all the six. The Jap answered their idle questions as best she could, the while taking out and arranging on the table her divers jars of tattooing fluid and her case of assorted needles. From the bottom of the kit she produced a roll of thin Japanese vellum on which were printed a host of colored designs.

The women were still looking over this chart when the men joined them and augmented the group round Cherry San. Jim Ross, whose dinner was already beginning to disagree with him, viewed the gay-hued vellum with no favor at all. Presently he broke upon the lively chatter by thrusting out a thick finger and tapping with disapproval one of the charted designs.

"Rare Japanese art, hey?" he scoffed jarringly. "That pattern, for one, is startlingly new and Oriental! A heart transfixed by an arrow! Was Saint Valentine a Samurai?"

"No," calmly intervened Helen Ward. "Tradition says he was the patron saint of thieves—and lawyers."

"But Mr. James Ross is right," shyly affirmed the tattooer, unvexed by the man's rudeness and not comprehending Helen's rebuke of it. "He is right as to the bad taste of that design. It is not art. It is not new. It is not even ancient. It has a—what you call a savor—of the sailor-man and the dock-worker. Not of the social world. It is bad art. I do not like to have it with my good designs. Yet I must. For some folk—lovers and the like—prefer it to—well, to this exquisite and blooming branch of flowering peach blossoms or this best-of-all rainbow-moth. You see—"

Her exposition was interrupted. The first earful of dance guests

was at the door. With a sigh of an artist whose work is temporarily shelved for less worthy matters, Cherry San proceeded to efface herself from the foreground.

Jim Ross was not in the least interested in the new arrivals, since he did not dance and did not care to talk. He stood where he was as the others gradually moved away. And, aimlessly, he began to play with the tattoo-kit. He picked up one or two of the shining needles, examining their ice-bright points, dipping them inquisitively into one or another of the open jars of liquid pigment, and smearing the resultant ink drops on a bit of paper to sample their colors.

Tiring, presently, of this tame sport, Jim left the table and stood for a while in a doorway, watching the dancers. Watching people dance is, for a non-dancer, perhaps the stupidest way to spend an evening. But Jim was not bored. For he fell to following the progress of Helen Ward.

She was dancing with Walton when Jim first caught sight of her in the swirl. But, five minutes later, he saw her fox-trotting with Barry Cahill. And life, for Jim, began to resume its charm. He caught her dancing with Cahill a second time a little later. He studied the swaying couples as though they represented an abstrusely fascinating law case.

Jim shifted his observation base to a black-shadowed niche of the veranda close to one of the open windows. He had noticed that couple after couple came to the window from time to time to cool off. The niche was a fine natural vantage-point. For example:

In another half-hour, Helen and Walton paused there, between dances. They were talking animatedly. And at once Jim was able to verify an aged proverb as to the kind of things listeners are likely to hear about themselves.

"Dear, I tell you he hates me!" Helen was saying, her guarded voice barely reaching the listener. "Honestly, he does. And you know it. Why, he looks at me as if I were a blend of the kaiser and the man who invented the income tax! I don't know why. For I always tried to be nice to him—just for your sake and poor Marcia's—as long as he'd let me. I suppose it's because you had the bad taste to ask me to marry you."

"Nonsense!" laughed Walton. "You're all wrong about old Jim. He dislikes most people on general principles. It's his nature. I suppose it's partly because his law work has shown him such a lot of the seamy side. But when he knows you better, he'll be dead sure to fall in love with you. Nobody could help it. Don't bother your glorious self about Jim."

"I don't," Helen assured him. "If I did, I'd get to wondering all sorts of horrible things about family traits. And then, perhaps, I'd begin looking at you the way he looks at me—Walt—do something for me?"

"Anything!" he promised.

"Dance with Marcia," she commanded. "The poor little thing is sitting over there, trying to smile and look festive. And, all the time, she is afraid Jim will appear from somewhere and scold her or glower at her. I know she is. He's so jealous she dare not dance with any other man, I suppose, for fear of a row with him. But you're her brother-in-law. So Jim can't be very jealous of *you*."

Walton Ross laughed indulgently.

"All right!" he agreed. "Only, you're wrong about Jim, sweetheart. If he's jealous of Marcia, it's only because he loves her. I guess that's one of the manifestations of love—in some chaps. I'd be as jealous as the very deuce—if you ever gave me cause."

"Marcia never gave him cause to be jealous," denied Helen. "You know that as well as I do. She worships him. And he bullies her to death. As for *your* being jealous—why, you wouldn't know how to be. And I love you for not knowing how. Now run along to Marcia," she ended abruptly.

The obedient Walton took his departure, leaving her standing there, half shielded by the window-curtain. Jim Ross fought back a yearning to shake his fist at the girl and to bellow forth a retort to her frank opinion of him. He hated her tenfold more than ever. His moody eyes followed Walton's course through the room toward the corner where Marcia was sitting alone, a deprecatory little smile on her face.

Then, all at once, Jim's muscles stiffened. A man had hurried up to Helen Ward, and was bending close to her as he said something in so low a voice that Ross could not catch the words. The man was Barry Cahill.

Jim leaned perilously far forward and strained his ears. He heard the words: "Italian garden," in Barry's rumbling voice. He saw Helen step forward at Cahill's side as if to leave the room. Then he saw Mrs. Greaves bearing down on her, with a new-arrived man in tow. And he heard Helen whisper to her escort a word that sounded like, "Later."

Jim Ross stayed not upon the order of his going. He sped from the veranda and across the lawn to a cypress-lined pathway leading to the patch of greensward which Mrs. Greaves had recently converted into a formal Italian garden.

The night was moonlit, with an occasional spring cloud blowing over the soft glow and shading it. There was plenty of illumination, whereby Jim could find his way to the evergreen-surrounded

Italian garden, and could choose a good listening-post there.

In the garden's center was a lily-pool bordered with flowering iris. At one side of this was a carven stone bench—an ideal seat for spooning couples. Set deep in the shrubbery, twenty feet farther on and facing the house, was a second stone seat. To this second seat repaired Jim Ross.

Lounging upon it, half sitting, half lying, he was concealed from any but the keenest sight, and, in that position, his head would not show on the sky-line above the clipped evergreens. He commanded a full view, not only of the opposite bench in the open but of the broad path itself and of the distant veranda and front doorway.

As a strategic position for eavesdropping, it could not have been improved on. Luck, assuredly, was with the solicitous elder brother this night! All he need do was to remain there until Helen and Cahill should keep their moonlight tryst in the garden.

Then it ought to be the simplest thing in the world to collect evidence enough to convince Walton of his sweetheart's unworthiness. A single kiss—nay, even the suffering of Cahill's arm to steal about her waist—an unconsidered love-word from her—Jim knew Walton would take his word for what he had seen and heard. Jim was truthful. And Walton knew it.

All that remained was to get indisputable evidence—evidence to which, if need be, Jim could swear. And Ross waited, grimly triumphant, for the furnishers of that evidence to come in sight.

The evening wore on. The dance-music reached Jim fitfully through the stillness. Now and again a woman in white and a man in black would stray across his vision, as some couple chose to stroll on the moonlit lawn instead of dancing in a hot room. At sight of these occasional promenaders, Ross would invariably crouch lower, in keen expectation. But none of them came so far afield as the Italian garden.

Once, between dances, he heard Cherry San's reedy-sweet voice singing to the tinkle of her samisen. And, diverted by the haunting melody, he recognized an air from the "Chinese Child's Day." He even made out a fragment of the quaintly accented words:

> Many things I sing—
> Of the cherry blossoms blooming in the spring,
> Of the bird that is homeward winging,
> Of the temple-bell a-swinging—
> You can almost hear it ringing.

Then, one after another, the cars that had brought the dance-guests came whirring up the drive to the veranda. And voices and laughter from departing neighbors told that the dance was at an end. After the last car had gone, several of the house-guests stood chatting on the veranda for a few minutes.

One by one they went back into the house, bound for bed. Jim, by the glow of the veranda lamps, could recognize some of them as they passed in through the double doorway. He discovered his wife and Walton and a few others as they moved indoors.

Then the veranda lights were switched off, and he heard the front doors closed. The shaded windows of the two huge dormitories gleamed into vision against the house's dark background. And still Jim Ross stayed at his post.

He had staked everything on those two scraps of overheard talk: "Italian garden," and "Later." They meant—if they meant anything—a secret moonlight rendezvous in the garden at the first free moment.

And, with the dumb stubbornness which had won him so many cases, Jim Ross was staying on. But Jim had had a hard week. The silence and the coolness and his half-reclining posture—all had wooed him to drowsiness.

He never knew whether he slept a minute or a half-hour. But, suddenly, he started up, blinking and bewildered—awakened from his doze by the uncontrolled sobbing of a woman not twenty feet away from him.

Dazed, not yet realizing where he was nor why he was there, Jim looked about him in the elusive moonlight.

Directly in front of him, and on the far side of the lily-pool, stood a woman and a man. They were close-locked in each other's arms. The woman's head was on the man's breast, and she was weeping. Her back was toward Ross.

The man, however, was facing him. And, as he raised his head for an instant, Jim saw him distinctly. It was Barry Cahill.

Jim Ross was always slow to collect his senses on awakening. And now he stared in owlish dullness at the couple, wondering where he was and what was happening. Only subconsciously did his mind focus on the scene before him.

Cahill was murmuring to the woman in his arms, and was seeking to soothe her hysterical grief. Jim heard her cry out brokenly, her voice sob-strangled past all recognition:

"Oh, I can't stand it any longer! I *can't!* He—"

And, at that point, Jim Ross remembered why he himself had come hither. His furtive task was accomplished. He had succeeded beyond his wildest hopes.

Here, in Barry Cahill's arms, wept Helen Ward! And she was bewailing her lot!

Presumably her lot in being engaged to Walton Ross! Jim had evidence aplenty for the breaking of the engagement.

A thrill of triumph swept away the last of the sleep-mists from Ross's brain. He was himself again—vigilant, crafty, eager. And he comprehended that one move alone remained to make his victory complete. He must see Helen Ward's face, that he might be able to swear it was she he had found in Cahill's arms.

All intent on this final proof, he jumped to his feet. As though by a signal, a cloud, whose feathery edges had been dimming the moon's full glare, swirled its dark center athwart the face of the orb. Jim's leap from the shrubbery brought the two lovers spinning round to confront him. Then, in almost the same motion, they wheeled and fled at top speed up the path toward the house.

In Ross's mind was a fierce chagrin. Thanks to the dim light, he had not yet seen Helen's face. It had been a whitish blur. He could not swear to her identity, morally certain of it as he was. Losing control of himself, as he saw his prey escaping, he roared after the fugitives:

"Take your time, Miss Ward! There's no hurry!"

As he spoke, he hurled his body forward in pursuit. But the others had gained too good a start for him to overtake them. As he ran, the moon shook off its grimy cloud and shone out again in dazzling radiance.

By the gleam, Ross could see the lovers gain the veranda steps. The man held open the front door for his companion. As she glided into the house, he stooped and kissed her. Then he slammed shut the door behind her and dashed round the veranda to the side entrance of the men's dormitory.

Jim Ross paid no heed to his vanishing law partner. He was after Helen, not Cahill. Feverishly he craved to catch her before she could traverse the long hall and reach the entrance to the women's dormitory. Up the low steps he sprang and across the deep veranda. As he flung open the front door, he saw a gleam of white showing triangular against the outer panel near the floor. And his heart gave a savage throb of joy.

For Cahill, in his loverly haste to close the door on his *inamorata*, had shut it a fraction of a second too soon. And the hem of her fluffy skirt had been caught between portal and jamb. She was a prisoner!

Jim, with one hand, swung wide the door. With the other, he made a lunging clutch at the newly freed white figure which fled before him. His outflung fingers closed round a cold little wrist just as the front door blew shut behind him.

In the pitch-black hallway the woman fought mutely to free herself. Jim thrust his unused hand into his waistcoat pocket in search of his match-box. It was not there. He did not know where to look elsewhere for matches to give him the brief glimpse he needed of his wriggling captive's face. Nor did he know the location of the light-switch.

There was something of the noiselessly desperate trapped beast in the woman's wild struggles to free herself. Panting sobs punctuated her writhings as she sought to tear away her wrist from the pursuer's sweating grip. So violently did she tug that, at one moment, Jim Ross all but lost his balance. He threw out his other hand to steady himself.

Down came his waving hand on a corner of the hall table. And something pricked him so sharply as to wring a grunt of pain from his twisting lips. His palm had come into contact with one of the tattoo-needles he had left strewn there. The pain bred a clever inspiration.

Bracing himself, and tightening his left hand's hold on the dumb prisoner's wrist, he picked up the needle with his right hand and groped for the nearest jar of pigment. Into this jar he plunged the needle to the full depth.

Brandishing the suffused point of steel, he turned back to the woman.

"Miss Ward," he said coolly, "light isn't the only way of identifying people. A tattoo-mark will serve just as well."

Pulling her hand nearer to him, he drove the needle into the soft flesh just where the palm joins the wrist.

Three times he jabbed the needle into the shrinking wrist—deep, slanting, ragged jabs. He had no time for a fourth stab.

Whimpering with agony and fright, the woman struck out in blind horror with her other fist. The random blow smote Jim Ross heavily across the bridge of the nose.

Anguish at the impact added to the surprise of the attack.

Instinctively, Jim slackened his hold on the branded wrist. And the prisoner took quick advantage of her chance.

Next morning, Jim Ross was the first man to enter the hall, where the guests always assembled for breakfast. One by one, the other men joined him there. But not a woman appeared. Even Helen Ward—a notoriously early riser—had not yet come from the dormitory. Jim waited her advent with quiet anticipation. As he waited, he strolled over to Walton.

"Walt," he said cryptically, "when the women come in, watch for one with a smudge or a sore or a bunch of scratches on the inside of her right wrist. Look sharp for it. And then remember I told you about it beforehand."

"What's the main idea?" asked Walton, puzzled.

Before Jim could reply, Mrs. Greaves came into the hall full of apologies for her own lateness and with word that the other women would be with them in a minute or so. Jim Ross did not hear a syllable of her salutation. His eyes were glued to her outstretched wrist as she shook hands with Walton.

His glance focused on a saffron smudge nestling in the crease between wrist and palm. And his jaw drooped in crass amaze.

It was not Helen Ward, then—it was this stately, gracious, lofty-souled hostess, this ideal wife and mother whom he had seen clinging so adoringly to Barry Cahill, there in the moonlit garden, when all her guests were supposedly in their dormitories!

A closer covert look at the hostess's wrist, as she shook hands with a man still nearer to him, revealed to Jim that the supposed smudge was a cleverly wrought bit of tattooing. On a space no larger than a girl's little finger nail was pricked a tiny saffron heart transfixed by a rosy arrow.

A second woman was coming into the hall from the dormitory—a buxom and noisy damsel named Polly Armytage. She was nursing her right hand in the cupped palm of the left, and looking down solicitously at her wrist as if it hurt her.

As Miss Armytage brushed past Jim, in her progress toward Mrs. Greaves, he saw that the wrist which she was so worriedly scanning bore, in its juncture-crease, an arrow-transfixed heart of the same size

and hue as the hostess's. And his head began to swim.

A moment afterward, Helen Ward entered. Glowing with youth and health, she gave the impression of a sweep of mountain air in a hot room. Walton Ross hurried across to greet her. Jim, moving like a sleep-walker, tagged at his brother's heels. And, by so doing, he saw something that escaped Walton's loverly gaze. Walton was looking into his sweetheart's laughing eyes. Jim was studying the wrist of the hand she had extended to his brother. And on that wrist he discerned a replica of the heart and arrow.

The three remaining women came in together. Jim Ross, hypnotized, ambled across the long hall to greet them—an act of effusive courtesy that astonished them all, especially his own wondering wife, who was last of the trio. On all three right wrists—even on Marcia's—he saw the tiny saffron heart and its pink arrow.

With a warning scowl, he stayed Marcia's further progress into the hall. Calling her away from the rest, Jim pointed dramatically to his frightened wife's wrist. Growling the words from deep down in his throat, he demanded:

"What's the meaning of this? What's the meaning of it? Speak up!"

"Please, Jim," she protested, shrinking back from her vehement spouse; "please! People are looking. Please don't growl like that, dear, or glower at me so, when everyone is here. And it—it frightens me to—"

"I'll speak and look as I choose!" he cut in, too angry to heed her almost tearful plea. "Tell me what all you women mean by tattooing yourselves like that! *Tell* me!"

"Oh!" quavered Marcia. "The hearts on our wrists? I—I didn't know you'd mind. Last evening, you seemed so interested in the pictures, and—"

"Tell me!" he interrupted harshly.

"Why," she faltered, trying not to cry as his accusing glare summoned her to answer, "why, there's nothing much to tell. Cherry San did it. This morning. That's what made us late. We—we thought it would be a lark and—and a pretty souvenir of this visit—if—if we all six had the same little design put on our wrists. We—I didn't think you'd mind, Jim. Honestly—"

"Who suggested the idea?" demanded Jim, his legal instincts abristle. "Whose idea was it for you all to be tattooed with the same design—and in the same spot? Hey? Whose?"

"Why—why—I think—that is—why, it was Helen Ward," replied Marcia. "She suggested it only for—for a lark, Jim," pleaded the unhappy woman. "She didn't mean any harm. Oh, please don't let it make you dislike her any more than you do! She's a dear. And—"

"She's a—" began Jim hotly, only to be cut short by the signal for breakfast.

As the guests trooped into the sunny breakfast-room, Jim found chance to whisper to Marcia:

"Did you happen to notice Miss Ward's wrist before it was tattooed—or while it was being done? Did you?"

"Why," bleated Marcia, "I didn't. I was so—"

"Yes," grunted Jim. "You always are."

Sullenly he sat down to breakfast. As he made pretense of eating, he gave grudging tribute to Helen Ward's alert wit. Yes; he bowed in glum resignation to her genius. Humbly, if ungraciously, he realized that she had beaten him.

Yet, even the cleverest witnesses may be swept off their feet by sudden attack. Jim's court-room experience had taught him that. And it had taught him how best to make such attack. Wherefore, as they arose from the table, he succeeded in drawing Helen Ward to one side in a niche of the veranda.

"Miss Ward," he began abruptly, "I stood here, last evening, while the dance was going on. I heard Barry Cahill arrange to go to the Italian garden with you. Something interfered, and you said you'd go later. He—"

"You heard remarkably well, Mr. Ross—for an eavesdropper," she made answer, her level gaze steadily upon his. "But even the most accomplished eavesdropper can't hear everything. Mr. Cahill brought me a message from Walt, whom I had sent to dance with Marcia. Walt wanted me to save him the next dance, so he could sit it out in the Italian garden. Just then, Mrs. Greaves brought up a man to dance with me. So I sent word to Walt that we must wait till later. As a matter of fact, we didn't go there at all. There were so many—"

"Pardon me," Jim broke in on her glib recital. "You did go there. Two hours later. Not with Walt. With Barry. You were—"

"Mr. Ross," was the sweet reply, "I have learned—when I am anywhere near you—to establish a continuous alibi. I was in the house or on the veranda—as plenty of people can prove—till after the last dance-guests went away. Then I went to the dormitory. Mrs. Greaves and Marcia and Polly Armytage went there at the same time. Any of the three can so testify. I was there until an hour ago. We didn't go to bed till three o'clock. Marcia and I sat and talked till then. My presence, every minute, can be accounted for by competent witnesses, you see. Now, if the cross-examination is quite ended—"

She finished the sentence by moving away to where Walton Ross was emerging from the hall in search of her.

Jim stared dully after the daintily stepping girl. In his heart of hearts, he knew this pat series of alibis had been framed by her in anticipation of just such a charge as he had been about to make. She had rattled it off with an ease that spelled rehearsal.

More than ever he was convinced of her guilt. But he was finally thoroughly convinced that she had beaten him—and could continue to beat him—at every turn. With a sigh of genuine misery, he surrendered.

At the doorway, fifty feet distant, Mrs. Greaves was saying goodby to Cherry San. Jim was not near enough to have heard their parting words, had he cared to. Which was rather a pity. For those words were worth his hearing.

"We all thank you so much!" Mrs. Greaves finished her valedictory. "Your songs were charming. So was your tattoo-work. It—"

"No, no!" disclaimed Cherry San, her smilingly upturned face clouding. "Not the tattoo-work, *madame!* Not that! That was very bad—very hasty—very poor. And no true artist would use that foolish heart-arrow design. But what could I do?"—with a despairing outspread of the yellow little fingers. "What else was there to do? There was no other design that was shaped right to hide those three hideous slanting marks on Mrs. Ross's wrist!"

Stefansson's Was Not the Story of a Dash — But of Leisurely Sojourn Whose Achievement Won for Him a Full Right to the Title, A Citizen of the Ice. —Photo by Paul Thompson, New York City

A Citizen of the Ice

SOMETHING more than a century ago a ship was blown far off its course by a tropical gale, and then was becalmed. During the hurricane the water tanks had sprung a leak.

Far out of sight of land, in unknown South American waters, the crew was dying of thirst.

A distress signal was hoisted from the masthead.

Even when a breeze at last sprang up the thirst-scourged seamen had scant strength left to man the yards. Only the captain's authority, backed by the captain's pistol, held some of them back from trying to swig sea water.

Then a sail was sighted. As soon as the newcomer was within hailing distance a multiple cry was wafted to it from a score of parched throats:

"Water! We're dying of thirst!"

Back came the laugh-punctuated reply:

"Dip in and drink, you poor lubbers! You're in the mouth of the Amazon."

The story stops there. But the picture remains of a band of men furious that their lofty heroics had been thrown away and that their martyrdom had been not only futile but idiotic.

A companion picture may well show the feelings of the scientific world when a big-boned young Scandinavian strolled back from the hostile Far North a year or so ago and announced in effect:

"The whole throng of Polar explorers, from Hendrik Hudson down, have suffered tortures or lost their lives in the Arctic because they wouldn't take the trouble to be comfortable there. I've lived up in the ice world for nearly five years. I never missed a square meal. I never froze a toe. I ate heartily and I slept warm. I'm fifteen pounds heavier than when I left civilization. Anyone can do the same thing.

It isn't a matter of magic or even of genius, but of simple common sense."

This was the message brought back by Vilhjalmur Stefansson to a world that had long mourned him as dead—a world which may or may not profit by his ridiculously easy solution of the age-old riddle of the north.

The Arctic Made Safe

AS LONG ago as 1906 he found the germ of his theory while he was wintering with an Eskimo tribe on the Mackenzie Delta. There he not only studied the methods whereby the natives supported life in a supposedly barren region, but he proved to his own satisfaction that the food and fuel which would keep an Eskimo fat and comfortable would do as much for a white man.

Coming home he proceeded to work out his beliefs with mathematical accuracy, testing each of them, learning wherein they differed from long-accepted ideas, and why they were practical.

When he had his formula completed he announced it, and went north to put it into effect. Returning, successful, he took a far more daring step. He declared that he was going to live for a certain length of time in a region which presumably could not support human life. Not on land, but on the hard surface of the Arctic seas. He told in detail how he was going to do it.

When at the end of a very few months he did not reappear people began to ask questions. On learning how little equipment he had carried with him into the unknown—barely one small sledful of clothes, apparatus, weapons, and so on—the men of science made grave calculations as to how long he and his companions could have kept alive, under the best conditions, on such a supply.

As a result of their expert figuring they agreed that the rash and luckless young adventurer must have died, and the rash absentee was given up definitely for dead. This in spite of the fact that Stefansson had outlined his every move beforehand and had said he would remain in the Arctic for a stated period.

At the end of the allotted time he reappeared, having lived up to his schedule in every detail.

This is not to be a windy recital of Vilhjalmur Stefansson's explorations in the north, but the tale of a discovery more important to the world at large than that of the Pole. Stefansson made the Arctic safe for all future explorers who will trouble to profit by his example.

His was not the story of a dash—with death running close behind the rearmost sledge pole—but of a leisurely sojourn whose achievement won for him a full right to the title, A Citizen of the Ice.

Explorers from the first had regarded the north as the implacable foe of the white man; a lifeless bourn where Nature fought with her direst weapons to repel human intrusion; where cold and hunger waited ever to seize their prey; where only a mountain of food and fuel could fight off the enemy; and where such food and fuel were almost impossible of transportation and quite impossible to renew.

Men, heavy-laden with stores, made frantic dashes into the Polar regions, in dread lest they might not be able to escape before those supplies should be gone. As a diver makes every effort to reach surface before his anguished lungs shall force him to draw another breath; as a fireman rushes into the burning house on his rescue mission and then seeks to get out again before the beams shall fall—so explorers made swift forays into the north, and did all in their power to make

An Arctic Relief Ship Frozen in the Ice

the journey as brief as might be.

The Bogy of the North

THE accounts of their deeds spread throughout the world, and with those accounts was born the deep-instilled belief that the north would not support human life. This in spite of the fact that the Arctic is strewn with Eskimos, who live wholly off the country and who thrive thereby.

So Arctic exploration took its place among the most hazardous pursuits known to adventure. Its exponents died in the frozen wilds and were remembered as martyrs. Or they reached home after incredible hardships and were honored as life-risking heroes. Then along came Stefansson and turned the solid beliefs of centuries upside down.

Part of his theory can be told much more effectively in his own words than in any of mine. He said to me, not long ago:

"The state of mind has everything to do with it. And the human mind from the first has been set in the firm belief that the north was no place for civilized man. The climate of France, for instance, was always invigorating and healthful. It developed a hardy and manly race, even in the early days of Rome. Yet innumerable Roman writers declared solemnly that so northerly a land was fit only for savages. Tacitus—perhaps the wisest of them all—warned his readers that France's climate produced a sterile soil, and that the combination of the two was such that its people could never hope to reach a high development or expect more advanced races to migrate thither.

"And so the bogy of the north ran through all the ages. In the Franco-British treaty of 1763, the French diplomats thought they were doing a mighty clever thing when they cajoled Great Britain into giving France, among other things, the little southern island of Guadeloupe in exchange for the whole Dominion of Canada.

"Man probably began his career as a subtropical animal. Until clothes and fire enabled him to drift northward he doubtless looked on the north with terror. And the tradition has come down, almost intact, to our own day.

"People who went to the Arctic made the journey in heroic mood, their souls attuned to the meeting of fearsome obstacles. They expected to elude death by the narrowest of margins, or to perish as martyrs to the glorious cause of human advancement.

"As the majority of mankind—even of heroes—prefer life to martyrdom, and as the zeal for exploration continued to urge men to Arctic travel the thing presently reduced itself to a mathematical system.

"Ice-resisting ships carried the expeditions as far north as any vessel could go. Then the provisions and fuel were transported the rest of the way, either on men's backs or in dog-drawn sleds. It was all worked out like a sum in arithmetic. The explorer computed beforehand how much food, to the ounce, each man and each dog was to eat daily; how much fuel was needed for warmth and cookery; what burden each man or dog could carry, and how far."

Lessons from the Eskimos

"In some cases the calculations went further. After all the dog food had been eaten a certain number of the sled dogs could be kept alive and on the job by the flesh of the other sled dogs; and if need be the last dogs were to be eaten by the men of the party.

"We used to read with thrills of horror how Richardson and his handful of surviving comrades struggled southward through the ice fields and fell greedily upon the bones and the scraps of leather which they found in deserted Indian camps on their way toward Great Slave Lake. It did not seem to occur to them or to their biographers that these men might just as well have secured and eaten the living animals from which such leather and bones had been obtained by the Indians. They were better armed for hunting than were the savages, and the game was plentiful and easy to shoot.

"The two ships of Sir John Franklin's last expedition were ice-caught near the north coast of Canada, between Victoria and King William Islands, in a splendid hunting country. For two years the expedition was stranded there. Its members saw the Eskimos, all round them, living in comfort. They saw how the Eskimos shot bears and harpooned seals.

"But the white men profited by none of these object lessons. When their cargo of supplies was nearly exhausted they deserted the ships and set out over the ice—dragging heavy and useless boats along with them—in the hope of reaching some settlement to the south. They carried all the food they could.

"And they began to die of starvation almost within sight of the abandoned ships!

"They perished, every one of them—more than a hundred men in all. They perished from hunger and cold in the same stretch of country in which hundreds of Eskimos were living and bringing up families and taking care of their aged and infirm and enjoying every needful comfort. The white men had good guns and steel knives as against the Eskimos' bows and arrows and stone knives. Yet they were not able to kill game to keep them alive.

"Perhaps their European stomachs revolted at the thought of gorging seal meat—which, by the way, is excellent fare—but assuredly it would have been preferable to the cannibalism to which the Franklin refugees were driven.

"In a nutshell, the fact remained that more than one hundred stalwart Europeans suffered themselves to starve to death in a land where thousands of natives were waxing fat.

"Then came Dr. John Rae's expedition in that very same region. Rae was sent out to find what had become of Franklin. He had camped with the Indians in various parts of Canada, and had thus forgotten his inbred schooling as to the fearsomeness of the Arctic winters and the barrenness of the north.

"Rae wintered near the spot where the last of the Franklin crew had died of hunger. He and twenty companions had made ready for the ordeal by killing plenty of caribou and other game and by gathering vast heaps of 'andromeda tetragonia,' a resinous variety of heather which makes fine fuel. The whole party wintered safely and pleasantly, without the loss of a man and without an hour's privation.

"They might have fared still better and have spared themselves much useless work if they had chanced to know the value of seal oil for fuel. But they sustained life with entire ease at the same place where the Franklin expedition's unfortunates had starved and frozen.

"Doctor Rae made a full report of all this, but it attracted practically no attention. The news that he had wintered snugly—where the traditional explorer would have gone through heroic sufferings to a glorious death—did nothing to alter popular or scientific opinion as to the horrors of the north. He had solved the Arctic problem so far as he had attempted it. But his example had no effect on those who came after him. They continued to attack the north in the same heroically desperate frame of mind—and to suffer and die.

"Peary ushered in a saner period. Like Rae he made use of native food supplies, and he employed Eskimos to hunt and fish for him. Yet, as he tells us in his book, The North Pole, it was his principle to carry along on sledges enough food and fuel to take him to his destination and back again.

"Nansen acted on this same plan. But his transportation system was not equal to Peary's. His plan included the killing of dog after dog as the sledges became lighter from the consumption of food, and of feeding these slain animals to the other dogs to keep up the latters' drawing strength. He found, after he reached the walrus grounds off Franz-Joseph-Land—where one bullet can secure tons of food and of fuel fat—that an exclusive diet of fresh meat is sufficient and healthful.

"I tried to profit by the various lessons taught by Rae and Nansen and the rest. I proved during my first winter with the Eskimos that I could live and thrive on seal meat or on fish; that salt and bread and vegetables are not necessary to human health; that seal oil will keep any house warm in the iciest weather; that the building of the ideal Eskimo snowhouse is not—as explorers have gravely affirmed—a mystic art which no white man can master.

Life on Arctic Seas

"In short, I reached the conclusion that a white man could live anywhere in the Arctic for an indefinite time by following the simple methods of the Eskimos, and that he could do so with ease and to the improvement of his health.

"I had noted that people who explored in the south always came back with their health impaired, and that those who explored the north always returned with their health improved. And I was eager to put my theories into practice."

It was in 1907 that Stefansson made known his belief that "on the mainland of North America and probably on the Arctic islands a white man, equipped with implements that could be hauled on one dog sledge, could live indefinitely and travel anywhere without support from ships or provision depots."

He persuaded influential scientists that he was correct. The result was a scientific expedition, four and a half years long, on the north coast of Canada, the north coast of Alaska and in Victoria Island.

The success of this venture proved, past doubt, the correctness of Stefansson's forecast. He had made the Arctic safe for exploration and had destroyed the bogy of the north so far as land travel is concerned.

But the sea remained to conquer.

The bulk of the far north is made up of ice-covered ocean. Thousands of miles of white expanse stretch out beyond the land; vast areas of seamed and fissured ice of varying thicknesses, according to the presence or absence of currents underneath, which had been looked on as the veritable abomination of desolation.

Stefansson now announced that the Arctic seas would support human life as readily as would the Arctic islands

or mainlands. To prove it he intended to strike out over this trackless expanse, with a few comrades and with a single sled of six dogs. He planned to stay there for years, far from any land, and to do so in the same comfort as on shore.

He set forth his scheme in detail. Nobody thought he was in earnest. It sounded like press-agent talk or the vapidest boasting. Even some of the men who consented to make the perilous experiment with him thought he did not intend to do a tithe of what he proposed.

After detailing his plan and the probable length of his proposed absence he vanished into the north.

"Why didn't you tie the lunatic and bring him back with you?" demanded a famous explorer of one of the men whom Stefansson had sent home before making the final departure for the ice country. "Why did you let him commit suicide?"

No word came from the absentee. Not even to the most optimistic of us did it occur that he could possibly be alive. And we mourned for a he-man, a man we had liked and honored, a man whose calm faith in himself had for once outrun his saner judgment.

We fell to comparing his outfit with Peary's on the latter's final triumphant dash for the Pole.

Peary's ice-fighting ship, under command of Captain Bob Bartlett—fearless adventurer and loyal lieutenant to his adored chief— carried the Pole's discoverer to the farthest point where its blunt nose could make headway against the ever-thickening ice. Then began the freighting of supplies northward by relays of dog teams.

When the most northerly bit of stable land was reached, at Cape Columbia, there was still about five hundred miles of ice between Peary and the Pole.

For that five-hundred-mile dash Peary pressed into service 139 dogs, 19 sledges and 24 men. His oft-spoken slogan was "Food, food, and more food!" Therefore everything but food—on which the party's lives might depend—was shaved down to the lowest possible degree, to make way for the needful provisions.

A Contrast in Arctic Equipment

The twenty-four men had but one rifle among them, and the barrel of that was sawed off to lighten the weapon's weight. There was just one pair of field glasses in the whole party. There was no bedding and there was practically no spare clothing. The men slept in their day clothes.

The nineteen sledges were piled with food—and with little else. Even the supply of fuel was cut down to a minimum. This tiny quantity of fuel was so apportioned as to allow barely enough for cooking, and to keep the snow houses at an average temperature of something like ten degrees above zero.

Food rations were portioned out with rigid care—two pounds daily per man and one pound per dog. As fast as sleds were emptied they were sent back.

All this meant tremendous labor, great hardship and the loss of about sixty per cent of the overworked and hungry dogs. By means of it Peary reached the Pole, every mile of the dash representing toil and privation.

By contrast to this scientifically worked-out journey of the world's most successful explorer let us glance at the outfit Stefansson took along for an infinitely longer stay on the surface of the frozen Arctic seas.

Peary had gone on the assumption that he must travel over ice which could yield him neither food nor fuel. Stefansson assumed that the seemingly hostile ice would yield him both. Stefansson was the first white man to realize that on polar ice he was really "in the mouth of the Amazon."

As they carried neither food nor fuel Stefansson and his few men needed only a single sled and six dogs. They were going to live off the country—or rather off the sea—so they went strong on ammunition and arms. Each man had a rifle, and there was a spare rifle besides. Each man had enough warm clothing to last him for two years or more, and had several pairs of stout boots.

Besides this there were hunting gear of divers sorts, cooking pots, a stove that would burn blubber, a tent, a tarpaulin for turning the sled into a raft, scientific instruments, photographic equipment, writing materials, ample bedding, and so on.

All this outfit was packed with ease on the light sled without making too heavy a load for the dogs.

Out into the unknown fared the man whose friends were presently to give him up for dead. And during all the endless months of his disappearance from the world the most thrilling and agonizing adventure undergone by his party was when one of them slipped on the ice and sprained an ankle.

For the rest, the expedition was living on the fat of the land— or, more literally, the fat of the sea. Seals were abundant and easy to shoot. Their flesh was palatable. Their blubber made excellent fuel. As a variant on this diet there was an occasional polar bear to be shot as he blundered past the camp on his usual winter hunt for seals.

After the first month or so the party no longer missed the salt and vegetables that once had seemed so needful a part of everyday diet. They enjoyed seal meat, and ate ravenously of it. Nor did the lack of variety interfere either with health or with appetite. The freshness of the meat—especially when it was underdone—prevented scurvy, that worst scourge of the explorer who must live on canned foods.

When the weather was warm—at zero or above—the men slept in their tent, for snow houses have a lamentable habit of leaking and dripping, from interior heat, when the mercury is above zero. In colder weather—anywhere from ten to sixty below zero—they would build a true Eskimo snow hut. The building of this type of house was once supposed to be impossible for white men. Stefansson and three of his followers became so adept at the job that they could erect such an igloo inside of fifty minutes.

The seal-fat stove speedily warmed the tent or snow house to a temperature of anywhere from sixty to seventy degrees Fahrenheit. This, and the bedding brought along, enabled the party to undress and go regularly to bed every night. No one who has learned the difference in explorer comfort between sleeping in day garments and in chang- ing them for night clothes will need to be told the added benefit to health and to spirits gained by this.

The explorer of tradition sat chattering in his furs before his soli- tary spark of fuel, and with numbed and mittened fingers scribbled half-decipherable pencilings in his diary. Stefansson, in shirt sleeves and slippers, wrote his diary with a fountain pen. He was as pleasantly warm and well fed when he wrote it as though he were in his own study—in ante-coal-conservation days.

Nor did the dark months of the winter affect his spirits and those of his men. Even when at noonday the outdoor light was barely strong enough for the reading of very large print they knew none of the weather blues which attack so many people in civilized climes during a week of rain or of gray clouds.

Stefansson cannot be made to see that months of dark or of twilight are depressing. He pooh-poohs the notion as bred of literature—claiming that poets once sang of the gloomy effect of darkness and that all the reading public has since accepted the dictum as true. To back his statement of the nondreariness of the Arctic night he points to the chronic cheeriness of the Eskimos and to the fact that he and his followers felt no inclination to mope.

Indeed, the only result of the months-long nights upon him has been to bring him back to the haunts of men with a strong preference for dusk rather than for sunlight, and for autumn rather than for spring or summer.

By way of sport, as well as to collect the needed supplies for light and warmth and provender, he improved on the native tricks for seal catching. Still working by precise calculation, he experimented until he proved that a seal cannot see more than three hundred yards ahead of it. Also that a man moving or lying on the ice will readily be mistaken by it for a fellow seal, especially if he be broadside-on to his intended prey.

Working on this hypothesis Stefansson promptly reduced the task of seal killing to a science. Creeping broadside-on toward the seals as they lay on the ice at the edge of their breathing holes, he was able to get within seventy yards of them before firing.

A Dead Seal May be Tricky

This close-quarters work was essential, for it was necessary to hoard ammunition. It was necessary, moreover, to plant the bullet in the brain of the victim and in no other part of the anatomy. A shot in the heart would kill with the same precision—but not before a quiver of the stricken brute would send its body sliding down the slippery slope of ice into the depths of the breathing hole and forever out of reach of the hunter.

A ball in the brain caused instant and motionless death, leaving the seal in the same spot as when it was struck, and causing no pain. This was but one of Stefansson's several methods of sealing. It gave him an unfailing abundance of fresh meat—and blubber.

The problem of drinking water was solved as easily as had been that of diet, and in the same way. Stefansson's first winter among the Eskimos had not only taught him that exclusive seal or fish fare would sustain life and health, but also that there is nothing more erroneous than the old superstition that the eating of snow to allay thirst is harmful.

One day, by reason of a blizzard, none of the men could go out to replenish a nearly empty larder. On that day the dogs were put on rations. The humans were not. With this single twenty-four-hour exception neither men nor dogs were confined to rations throughout the whole sojourn. They had all they chose to eat, and at any time they chose to eat it.

The dietary which put fifteen pounds on Stefansson's spare frame did as much in its way for his companions and his sled animals. On the journey back to civilization the party stopped for a day or two at an Eskimo village. There one of the dogs caught distemper from some stray curs and died. A second dog choked to death trying to swallow a greased rag. With the exception of these two casualties the same dogs lasted Stefansson five years—a contrast to Peary's loss of sixty per cent of his sled dogs in a few weeks!

The only perils of the long and unromantically comfortable sojourn were the semioccasional areas of ice whose underlying current was sluggish. Here the ice had frozen too thickly to permit of seal hunting. But the signs of such areas were soon as plain to Stefansson as are those of a near-by desert to land travelers, and he learned to skirt them.

"There was nothing hazardous or exciting about what we did," Stefansson told me.

"We simply used common sense. We knew we were in no danger. So we didn't worry ourselves sick.

"An American going to England would not load himself up with tons of ham and flour and eggs for his stay there. He would take along a letter of credit and then buy his ham and flour and eggs when he got over there.

"Our letters of credit were our rifles and ammunition.

"We figured that our cartridges averaged thirty to the pound, and that every pound of ammunition averaged us a ton of meat—and fuel. Speaking of fuel, our predecessors had not been able to heat their snow houses to any point of comfort because they were on fuel rations, and on the scantiest fuel rations at that.

"We were always so certain we could get the next seal in the same easy way we had got the last one that we were never on fuel or food rations, and we always burned enough oil to keep our houses or tents as warm as we wanted them.

"It was high time for someone to destroy the fear of the Arctic, because unless the conquest of the north by common sense had come soon its conquest by mechanics would have forestalled us.

"When the Wright brothers' first successful airship made its trial flight, at Kitty Hawk, years ago, when Count Zeppelin made his first practical dirigible I think every one of us realized that it must be only a matter of time before the supposedly inaccessible spots of the earth—from the peak of Mount Everest to the geographic Pole—could be reached with ease by the air route.

"That time is surely coming. It may be at hand. The airship has crossed and recrossed the Atlantic. Soon it will cross the Poles.

"But in the meanwhile I have shown how the Arctic regions may be conquered by normal means.

"Our discovery has opened to humanity a new and rich expanse of country, a vast region whose resources are not yet tapped, and which in time will provide countless forms of wealth and industry and food supply.

"If the old and tediously difficult and danger-fraught systems of Arctic exploration are to persist in spite of what we have shown—then it will be because exploration is not a serious profession, but a mere form of sport, like fly-fishing or fox-hunting, where the main consideration is not the actual catching of the game but the catching of it in the approved sportsmanlike way."

The Laugh

THIS is a fight story. There is a woman in it too. But she was not the prize of the contest. Nor—just as he was about to be knocked out—did the clean-limbed young hero's glazing eyes meet her inspiriting glance, firing him with a berserk ardor which won the battle and the world's championship.

It seems a pity to depart in such Bolshevistic fashion from the best established traditions of ring fiction. But probably no woman was ever the prize of a professional bout.

There seems to be more glamorous lure in a 65-35 split of the gate money than in the smile of beauty, when pugilists pull on the five-ounce gloves and begin to massage their shoe soles with resin.

And, most assuredly, the clean-limbed young hero who would allow his eyes to stray through the audience in search of a loved face, at a critical moment of the fight, would presently waken from a dream to see the unloving faces of his seconds bending over him.

Some Thackeray of the ringside has computed that there are precisely nine cardinal qualities in the make-up of a successful pugilist and that the lack of any one of those nine traits will bar him conclusively from high rank in his calling. The first and foremost of the nine requisites is that he must be a fighter.

And that is why Boob Guthrie was doomed and gated and side-tracked from the very start.

Boob had the speed, the eye, the hands, the instinct, the punch, the build. And there was no smear of cowardice in his heart. But he was not a fighter.

To be a fighter, in squared-circle parlance, means much more than having the mere ability and nerve to fight. It means the possession of a wild-beast streak—a streak which makes a man seek to hammer his foe to a pulp by every method that can get past the referee; that makes him fight with double ferocity when his opponent begins to weaken, and to reach a climax of relentless savagery when that opponent sways, helpless.

The average man will fight for all there is in him, so long as he himself is in peril or while the chances are even. But only the chosen few are void of that blend of imagination and good-fellowship that we call mercy. When their foe reels blindly and gaspingly, too weak to raise his swollen arms to guard his hanging jaw, they revolt at the idea of tearing in murderously and finishing the contest which no longer is a contest.

Boob Guthrie had not enough imagination to make him cringe at the idea of receiving a beating. But he had enough of it to keep him from any desire to inflict one. Wherefore the big, good-natured, shy chap won speedily his prefix of "Boob"—the only title he was to acquire in the ring.

He was assistant mechanic at Leder's All-Car Garage down at the foot of Union Street, where the street forms a T with the River Road; and he was making fairly good money. By another year he expected to be chief mechanic, and two years more promised to find him with the experience and the cash to start a little garage of his own—up Wyckoff way, where they were working on the new State Road.

In the meantime he was working and saving. In the evenings he was wont to stroll down to the Steel Works yards, where the young men used to box and throw the sledge and run barefoot hundred-yard dashes.

From the first the shabby and flabby old set of eight-ounce gloves attracted Guthrie. He put them on at every chance he could find, and these chances were many. For the Steel Works men, after hammering hot metal all day, used to revel in hammering one another in friendly fashion all evening.

Guthrie was a natural boxer. He had swiftness, snap, a genius for gauging distances; and he had various other qualities that so appealed to Baldy Snaith—a veteran third-rate pugilist in the Steel Works night shift—that the old man singled him out for a series of private lessons between shifts.

Then Leder died. His brother-in-law took over the All-Car Garage, hiring a working force of his own selection, and Guthrie was out of a job. The season was slack. No other local garage wanted an extra mechanic.

When Guthrie went down to the Steel Works that evening he was hailed by Baldy Snaith. The old man was chatting with a rat-faced little chap whose left ear looked like a pale cabbage rose and who wore very wonderful clothes.

"Here's the boy I was talking to you about," Baldy told the stranger as Guthrie came up. "Guth, shake hands with Mr. John E. Vedder. You've most likely heard of him oftener as Spider Vedder. Him and me was in the game the same time. He got up to be a manager, with a string of fighters of his own. I went t'other way. All in the day's chores. Spider is manager for Kid Scaasi, the new light-heavyweight champ. He's got him training for his fight with Kangaroo Brookins; up to the old Ryerson place on the River Road."

Guthrie looked with mild interest at the little man of the gaudy attire and cauliflower ear and ratlike glance. Vedder returned the look, his sharp gaze running over the other's body as might a butcher's over that of a steer offered for sale.

The manager's view took in the deep chest and wide-arching shoulders, the compact girth, the light-built thighs, the leanly power-ful legs, the coolness of the level eyes. He nodded noncommittally at Snaith, who proceeded with his oration.

"Mr. Vedder's traveling light on this training work of Scaasi's," said he. "He ain't a man to let a swarm of hangers-on gobble up a fight's profits beforehand and then bawl him out for not slipping fat bonuses to 'em afterward. He's traveling light, like I said, to save expenses. And now he's run into bad luck; first week of the training. Scaasi's second sparring partner broke a jaw this morning—in—in a kind of an acci-dent. And Mr. Vedder don't want to send all the way to town and pay out a lot of cash to get a feller to take his place—not if he can find some good, rugged local boy hereabouts who'd like to pick up a little easy coin by taking the job. That's what he come down here to see me about. And I was thinking if you—"

"You're on!" decided Guthrie with much haste.

Here was a momentary solution of his fiscal stress. Here, too, was a chance to get real money for the sort of work he loved to do. He accepted the offer enthusiastically. Nor did his enthusiasm die wholly away when he learned the wage and the full list of the duties that went with the position.

Thus did Guthrie find himself domiciled in the official family of Kid Scaasi, light-heavyweight champion of America, at the latter's ramshackle training quarters, a mile or so from town. Thus, too, did he proceed to qualify for his inspired nickname of "Boob."

The cognomen was welded to Guthrie during a try-out bout with one of Scaasi's entourage, the first afternoon of his engagement. The champion—a ganglingly wiry six footer with an incredible reach—bade Guthrie put on the gloves with one of the training-camp roustabouts, who was a husky of earlier days; whom much mixed ale had robbed of wind and speed, but who was handy as a masseur and general utility man, and who could still make a passable showing for a light round or two.

"Go into him!" was Vedder's curt order to Guthrie. "Don't play with him! Wade in! Show what you're like in action! Time!"

Then the manager joined Scaasi on a bench in one corner of the barn gymnasium and prepared to study the new man's possibilities. Presently from the faces of champion and manager the look of bored noninterest vanished. They hunched forward on their rickety bench to watch the go.

Guthrie was obeying orders. He was not playing with his man. He was wading in. Most of the roustabout's vicious attacks he blocked or side-stepped with little effort. Such blows as reached him did not seem to have any effect on him at all. Almost at once he checked the other's bull rush and took the aggressive. In a whirlwind attack he drove the roustabout to cover, sending him reeling across the ring at will, twice flooring him.

Scaasi and Vedder looked on with growing enthusiasm. This garage hand was a find—a comer. He was inexperienced, of course, in actual ring methods. He showed the earmarks of a beginner. But he had the goods. He was a natural boxer. He was as strong as a bear. He could take punishment. He could inflict it.

Vedder eyed him as an impresario might gaze on the possessor of a Caruso voice. Here, forsooth, was a right-promising man to add to his string; a fellow who could be sewed up on a long-term contract that might well mean a fortune to such a manager as himself.

The roustabout was tiring. Guthrie's attack had worn him down. Guthrie's shower of body blows had done queer things to the booze-indurated system. The roustabout was sick dizzy, all in. He sought feebly to clinch. Guthrie threw him off and rushed.

Champion and manager leaned farther forward. The moment had come. The three minutes of the round were long past too. But Vedder, who held the watch, made no mention of that. He and Scaasi were tense and gloating. Now was coming the supreme instant of the show—the slaughter time.

Their roustabout dared not "lay down." His tenuous job hung by a thread. He knew it. Without turning to look he could visualize the expressions on the two watchers' faces. He knew what he had to expect, and he braced himself for the avalanche attack that would leave him crumpled and smashed in a corner of the ring. His face was quivering and ghastly. But he kept to his lurching feet. The rat trap was open. The terrier was let loose at the squealing rodent. Scaasi sucked his under lip.

Then—nothing happened!

The roustabout in dumb wonder saw Guthrie halt midway in his final rush, lower his arms and step to one side, turning to Vedder for criticism of his manner of work.

He got no criticism. He got howls—howls from two sets of leathern lungs. Scaasi and Vedder, both on their feet now, were jumping and gesticulating.

"Go in!" Scaasi was screeching, his lips dripping and twisting. "Go in, you boob! Finish him! What's the matter with you? You had him licked! One more punch would—"

"I know," replied Guthrie calmly, albeit a bit puzzled and speaking above the dual din of blasphemous inquiry. "I know I had him licked. That's why I stopped."

His amazing statement froze the profanity stiff in the mouths of his hearers. In sheer bewilderment they stood gaping at him. In the experience of neither of them had such a reason before been given for failure to land the knock-out punch. It drove from them all power of speech. For a moment the gymnasium stillness was broken only by the heavingly sobbing breaths of the beaten roustabout.

Vedder and Scaasi found their tongues—both at the same time—

and silence did not descend upon the gymnasium again for nearly ten minutes.

During that period the champion and his manager alternated in telling Guthrie with charming frankness their opinion of him. At least they alternated at times. At other times they cursed in unison, and occasionally in close harmony as well.

When the session was ended for lack of breath and vocabulary, Guthrie knew just exactly where he stood with his new employers—and why—and the title of "Boob" was his, past all competition. It was the mildest of the seven thousand names they called him. Perhaps that is why it stuck, for stick it did. From that hour to his training camp fellows he was never anything but Boob.

Furious disgust had mastered the two professionals as they watched the blowing up of the most promising boxer they had seen in years.

Guthrie had everything. Before he had been in action two minutes they had seen that. And in a trice it was as though he had nothing. He was not a fighter. Cool mercilessness toward a helpless foe was not his. And without it he was worthless in the ring. Small wonder his audience vented its disappointment in cloud-burst words.

"Here!" snarled Scaasi at last. "Gimme the gloves! You've missed seeing one knock-out, Spider, but here's one you won't miss!"

He strode to the center of the floor, wrestling with the gloves the grinning Vedder handed him and motioning Guthrie to come up for the bout.

Out of the welter of abuse and ridicule the dazed Guthrie gathered that he was to spar a round with his employer. Well, that was what he had hired for, and he thrilled a little at the prospect. Except for the poor roustabout and old Baldy Snaith, he had never had on the gloves with a professional—and never, in his brief career, with a man who could make him extend himself.

Gladly he welcomed the experience; welcomed it with all the zest of a true athlete, resolving to do his level best and thus to atone for the bad impression he had made.

He did it.

Scaasi came at him in true whirlwind fashion, yet not letting the gust of anger interfere with his wonted coolness. Guthrie side-stepped

the rush, though with difficulty, and he was able to land a very creditable left in the meridian of his antagonist's countenance as he did so.
It was a jarring, spectacular blow. One of the handlers was so tactless
as to snicker.

That changed Kid Scaasi's wrath to a deadly calm. In he bored,
again and then again. Almost always Guthrie managed to meet his
attack with a more or less effective counter, or else to elude it. For the
bulk of the three minutes the seminovice was able to hold his own,
after a fashion, against the professional. True, he received a blow or
two that jolted him. But he felt he was landing at least one for every
two he took, and the knowledge lent new power to his work.

His judgment of distance, too, was proving useful. He believed
he was learning to gauge the champion's reach. Many another foe of
Scaasi's had formed the same idea—and had paid for the illusion. For
while the champion was working—and working hard—he was waiting
the suitable moment before bringing that phenomenal reach of his into
play. Just before the end of the first round he judged the time to be ripe.

He was chagrined that he had not been able to score a knock-out
against this amateur without resorting to the best of his ring tricks,
and chagrin lent vigor to the ruse when at length he did employ it.

Twice in succession he led clumsily for Guthrie's jaw. Guthrie by the merest backward move of his head avoided both blows. Each time he countered with some success, once to the wind and once to the face. Scaasi seemed to be tiring. For he was slow in defense and awkward in attack.

A third time from the same distance the champion essayed the same blow. This time, in launching his own counter, Guthrie scarce troubled to pull back his menaced jaw from the futile assault.

Two minutes later he opened his listless eyes, to find himself lying on a mattress in a room that whirled about him in circles. The bruised-faced roustabout was pouring water from a pail over the victim's dizzy head. In another corner of the gymnasium Scaasi and Vedder were chatting unconcernedly, their backs to him, their good humor entirely restored.

They were deciding that, though the Boob would never make a fighter, he was a first-rate sparring partner—especially at the price—and that it would be well to keep him on.

"It was that left of his!" the roustabout was mumbling hoarsely to the blinking Guthrie as he swabbed the water afresh over the face of his new associate. "He's always got three inches more of it than anyone thinks he's got. I'd 'a' gave you the tip if there'd been time. Look out for him, Boob! He's got it in for you. He don't like you. That ain't the last time you'll connect up with a knockout from him."

So began Guthrie's career as a sparring partner. So, too, in one-half hour he acquired his first knock-out and his first nickname.

Doolan, the roustabout, had been right in his mumbled warning as to the champion's feelings toward the Boob. Scaasi most assuredly had got it in for the luckless Guthrie. From the outset he took a grinding dislike to his new sparring partner and strove laboriously to make the latter's life a horror.

If there was any extra and distasteful chore to do round the training quarters the Boob was detailed to do it. If Scaasi chanced to be in an unusually villainous temper it was the Boob who must put on the gloves with him. And at such times the champion threw himself into the bout with a ferocious ardor that more than once led to a knock-out.

In Scaasi's equally frequent spells of high good humor the Boob was the inevitable butt of his elephantine wit and of his merriest and most homicidal practical jokes.

In all his mild life Guthrie had never known what actual and active hatred was, but he was learning. Into his nonrevengeful soul was creeping the germ of a right hearty and wholesome hate for this bully of his.

Again and again he was minded to throw over his job, but he stuck to it. For one thing, he was getting his board and lodging for nothing and a pittance of cash besides—cash which was swelling the fund needed for the buying of his garage, and which he augmented now and then by doing odd motor jobs in the evenings for Leder's successor at the All-Car Garage.

But the money aspect of the case alone could not have kept him in the Scaasi camp. Something else was holding him there; something he did not analyze in conscious form. This bully was tormenting him. To run away would be to confess himself whipped. The idea went against the grain with Guthrie. Every time he thought of leaving it barred his departure.

There was another advantage, the Boob realized, in staying where he was. Scaasi was one of the best men in his profession. He was a ring Napoleon, crafty and brilliant. At his weight of one hundred and seventy-two pounds he was supreme. He had never been beaten. And now, tiring of the anomalous light-heavyweight class, he was planning a climb toward the regular heavyweight championship. Bob Fitzsimmons and other immortals no heavier than Scaasi had scaled to that height, and Scaasi saw no good reason for not following in their illustrious footsteps.

His coming fight with Kangaroo Brookins, the Australian light-heavyweight champion, would clear away the last formidable man in his class. A victory in that battle would force the world's present heavyweight champion to heed Scaasi's challenge. Wherefore, to this coming fight, as to a last all-important stepping-stone, Scaasi was bending his best efforts.

Guthrie, knowing all this, knew also that he himself was receiving rare—if painful—education in the art of fighting. He was receiving it from a master. That master might hate him, but the Boob was receiving the education none the less, and he profited by it in every way he could.

In his rapid, daily bouts with Scaasi he fell to studying his employer; to studying his every move and the ring reasons for that move. When the other sparring partner was taking his turn with the gloves Guthrie watched the bout in all its phases, and profited by what he saw. Mentally he dissected Scaasi's work to learn its causes and its results—and he learned them.

He learned, for example, the secret of that extra three inches of reach; and he grew to know by infallible instinct just when and how it was going to be brought into play. Revolving the maneuver in his own mind he wrought over it until he learned to block—or otherwise balk—the once-certain knock-out blow. Practicing privately with Doolan, he perfected his theories.

He did more. If he was a glutton for punishment, he was also a glutton for work. Never was he too tired or too busy to duplicate in his own person every day all the details of Scaasi's rigorous and scientific regime of training. Meantime he was boxing regularly with the champion, and each bout was a lesson—a lesson whose principles he absorbed with avidity.

As a result the erstwhile novice was blossoming into a formidable boxer. His mighty body was becoming like whalebone and tempered steel. He was hardened to a point where murderous punishment no longer bothered him.

Not that he was becoming a fighter—that he would never be. His new education did not suffice to give him the tiger heart of the successful pugilist. Even yet he could not watch, without wincing, the occasional bouts between Scaasi and the helpless Doolan; bouts which always resulted in the agonized collapse of the roustabout. These bouts were becoming more and more frequent as Guthrie learned to avoid knockouts. Scaasi in his ugly fits felt the need of having some victim to slug to senselessness; and nowadays the lot fell to Doolan.

An item of interest gleaned by the Boob was Scaasi's worship of money, an adoration shared by his manager. Niggardliness was a second nature to him. By the hour, in leisure time, he would pore over his bank book or seek to scale down his slender training expenses. His chief reasons for deciding to go into the regular heavyweight class were that the big money lay there and that he had almost exhausted such revenue as remained in his present class.

It was their joint yearning for anything in the shape of a coin that led Scaasi and Vedder to plan an open-house afternoon at the training camp three days before the fight with the Australian. In other words, to throw open the training quarters to the public for an hour in the afternoon—at fifty cents a head—and to permit this much-favored public to see Scaasi at work with the skipping rope, the handball, the punching bag; and, as a climax, to let it see him box two rounds apiece with each of his sparring partners.

The plan was good enough, but the townsfolks' reception of it was not. Ticket sales lagged. Fifty cents was a lot of money in hard times for people to pay for the privilege of watching a thin man skip rope or spat a handball or swat an inoffensive bag or spar tame rounds with tamer employees.

So again Scaasi and Vedder went into executive session and next day the rumor crept about town that the sparring bouts were not to be at all tame—in fact, that a genuine knock-out was promised.

This put a new turn to the whole affair. And on the appointed afternoon several hundred boys and men, with a goodly sprinkling of wholly respectable—if silly—women and girls, filed through the impromptu wicket into the grounds of the old Ryerson place.

The number had been increased by a last-minute whisper that the promised knock-out victim was to be their fellow townsman, young Guthrie. No one in the crowd had any dislike for the Boob. Indeed, they did not yet know that he was a Boob, and his repute had been augmented by news that he was sparring partner to a champion prize fighter. But if anyone must be knocked senseless it is far more interesting to see that mishap befall somebody one knows than a total stranger. And the word brought a goodly addition to the pile of fifty-cent pieces.

The onlookers watched apathetically as Scaasi went through an uninspired imitation of his various bits of daily training routine. But the bovine faces brightened as Scaasi stepped into one corner of an improvised ring and Guthrie took his place in the opposite corner.

Doolan rang a bell and the bout began.

The first round was fast and exciting. Here in the presence of his old friends Guthrie strove to do his very best. It was pleasant, after all these weeks of bullying and jeers, to box for people who knew and liked him. For their sakes he put up the liveliest bout he could, and a mighty lively bout it was. Scaasi was forced to work his hardest to keep on even terms with his opponent.

So ended the first round amid a hum of approval from the audience. After a minute's rest the second began. Here again Guthrie kept his antagonist busy, and the blows began to grow heavier and less airily scientific. The local constable fidgeted, and hoped the town council might not hear of the affair. For to his unsophisticated eyes it was beginning to look much like a real fight.

Guthrie countered a left lead with a swing. Scaasi sought to block the blow. But much of its force broke through his tardy guard and landed flush on his face. To Guthrie the glove seemed to go too high to do any damage. But under its impact Scaasi's knees knocked together and his wide shoulders sagged. His arms dropped almost to his sides. In an instant he had lost his splendid pose of power and was reeling like a stage drunkard. He stumbled forward.

Guthrie, stung by his foe's plight, threw out his own arms instinctively to steady the falling champion. As he did so he heard a bellow of stark warning from Doolan. Then he saw Scaasi's limp body tense itself. But he saw and heard too late. Before he could grasp the meaning of the change—before instinct could make him fall on guard—he felt himself double like a jackknife under the force of a blow between chest and wind.

With his seemingly groping right foot thrust forward, Scaasi had shot his left fist out in a shoulder-swinging, cross-body blow that carried not only all his strength with it but the set of his hundred and seventy-two pounds as well. His gloved fist crashed into Guthrie's unguarded front.

At the parting of the ribs there is a spot about the size of a silver dollar. It is a nerve center known to old-time fighters as "the mark" and to science as "the solar plexus." The right kind of blow, delivered there with sufficient force, has the same effect on the body as might

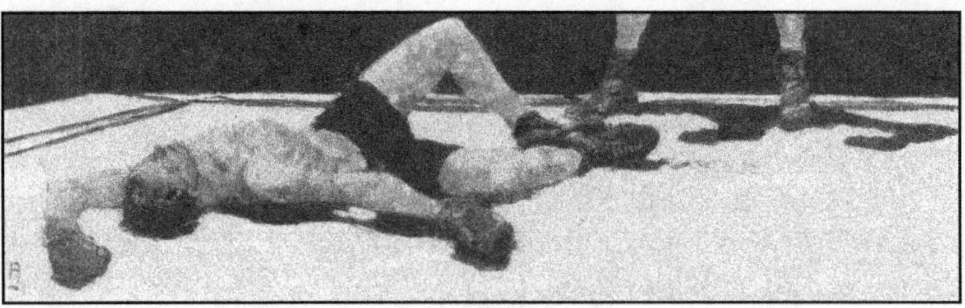

the sudden taking out of the backbone. The brain remains hideously clear, but the rest of the system is as impotent as is a new-born babe's.

Such a blow in 1897 transferred the world's heavyweight championship from Corbett to Fitzsimmons. Such a blow in the gymnasium of Kid Scaasi sent Guthrie to the floor, on his back, writhing spasmodically, not one of his muscles under control, his mind wide awake but powerless to control the remainder of him.

There he lay while Vedder rattled off the count of ten and while a mutter of displeased astonishment ran through the onlookers.

"See that, ladies and gentlemen?" declaimed Scaasi, standing over the anguished man and haranguing the spectators. "You've all heard tell of the yellow streak, and now you're seeing it. You see this feller's eyes are wide open. He isn't knocked out. He's as fit as any of you, but he's had enough. That's what's called laying down, ladies and gentlemen. I promised you a genuine knock-out to-day. I done my best to keep my word, but the Boob beat me to it. How can I knock out a feller who won't stand up to be hit?"

Delicately he applied his toe to the Boob's quivering ribs, exhorting him the while to rise and play the white man. His throat muscles paralyzed, Guthrie could only snarl in weak fury.

A woman laughed. It was a nasty laugh. It pierced the crowd's looser volume of chuckles and mutterings as a solitary mosquito's whine pierces all the other sounds of a summer night.

It was the laugh of a fool—heartless, shallow, cachinnatory—and it went through Guthrie's soul like the breath of hell. It was the crowning touch to the last and dirtiest of all Kid Scaasi's myriad practical jokes upon him. It caught the crowd, serving as the keynote and incentive to the wholesale guffaw that broke out from all quarters at sound of it. That laugh was to sting and scorch Boob Guthrie's inner ear for many a long day and for many a longer night.

Doolan and one of the other handlers, at a nod from Scaasi, lifted him from the floor and carried him into the next room. When he could stand unsupported he gathered his few belongings and slunk out of the training camp by the rear exit, catching the first train from town.

Four mornings later Guthrie read in a newspaper that Kid Scaasi had put the Australian light-heavyweight champion to sleep in the eleventh round and that he had issued a challenge to the heavyweight champion of the world—a challenge he and his manager were now considering.

The same newspaper said that Kid Scaasi was about to fill in the time until the arrival of a reply to his challenge by making a theatrical athletic tour of the Middle West.

Guthrie had heard Scaasi and Vedder discuss this tour and its details a score of times. That day the Boob made a flying visit to his home town to draw a slice of his savings out of the local bank. Then he disappeared. No one missed him.

The chief feature of Kid Scaasi's tour was an old one, even in those days. He and a sparring partner boxed an exhibition round or two nightly, as star act of the Jersey Lilies' Burlesque Show, and the champion gave brief samples of his prowess as a bag puncher. The ultimate swat of the bag, by scheduled arrangement, always snapped the frayed sash cord and sent the leather spheroid soaring out into the audience. But all this grand-stand work was a mere by-product of the tour's real aim.

When the show was to open at any mining or mill town the advance man plastered the place with announcements that Kid Scaasi, light-heavyweight champion of the world, would pay the sum of two hundred dollars cold cash to any local fighter who could stand against him for four consecutive rounds.

This hackneyed offer, by the way, was the salvation of many such tours. It always filled the theater to the doors at extra prices. And almost never in the history of four-round offers has there been any need to pay the promised prize money. Most mining or factory communities at that time had at least one man who had so often trounced his fellow laborers that he had acquired delusions of grandeur. While he did not necessarily regard himself as championship timber, yet he and his admirers were cheerily certain he could keep his feet for four rounds against any living scrapper. And the lure was passing strong.

To whale the head off a fellow miner or mill hand is a strangely different thing from pitting oneself against a professional pugilist—as these local paladins were forever finding out, long before the conclusion of the fourth round. Yet in the very next town the bait would be grabbed for just as eagerly the following night.

The touring champion played safe. Two hundred dollars was not enough inducement to bring any able fighter to the hick town to dispute the offer. Yet, to make certain, Scaasi inserted in his challenges the word "nonprofessional."

The Jersey Lilies' Show opened in Pitvale, the ten-thousand-population hub of the region's coal fields. Pitvale for a week had been placarded with the champion's sensational offer. A goodly group of grimy and muscle-bound miners had quarreled and fought and trained for the honor of competing for the golden two-hundred-dollar guerdon. The opera house was choked with sweating and jostling men.

At the close of the tepidly obscene performance the stage was cleared. The advertisement-spotted curtain rose on a roped arena with Kid Scaasi reclining gracefully on a stool, R. U. E. To the footlights strode Vedder, gloriously attired. While stage hands laid a runway from the apron to the foot of the orchestra's middle aisle, Spider proclaimed:

"Ladies and gentlemen of Pitvale: You have all heard of the champion's generous offer to the athaletes of your beautiful city. Kid Scaasi will now take on any gentleman in the audience for a four-round go. If the aforesaid gentleman can last four rounds against the champion—straight Mark's of Queensb'ry rules—we will forfeit to him the sum of two hundred dollars cash. In case you doubt our good faith, I'll say we have posted the money with a fellow citizen of your own—Mr. Mark Speyer, sporting editor of your Chronicle noospaper—who has kindly consented to ref'ree the bout and to turn over the cash to the man who can last out. Vol'nteers may now step up on the stage. First come, first served. Ladies and gentlemen, I thank you."

Before the last sentence was half spoken a big fellow in sweater and baggy trousers and sneakers had already left his front-row seat and was ascending the runway in two jumps. So quickly had he moved that he was on the stage before the first of the local aspirants had had time to stand up.

Crossing at once to where the sporting editor stood, he said loudly enough to be heard all over the house:

"I am a nonprofessional. I am a garage hand. Here is an affidavit from the mayor of my city to prove it. And I'm first to take up the challenge."

He was stripping off his thick sweater as he spoke and kicking his legs free of the encumbering trousers. Now he stood out in white jersey and trunks—and in such perfect condition as to cause a grunt of surprise from the referee.

At first sound of Boob Guthrie's voice both Vedder and Scaasi had wheeled about and stared with mouths ajar. Then they looked dully at each other. After which Vedder trotted across to where his principal sat and the two jabbered together in excited undertones. The referee glanced at them in wonder as the colloquy grew extended. The crowd shuffled its feet. One or two galleryites began to whistle. Boob Guthrie grinned sweetly and lolled back on his stool.

"If you were four-flushing on that cash offer," he called over to Scaasi, "say so! Don't keep us in the air all night."

The gallery applauded and added sentiments of its own. Someone in a box yelled: "Fake!"

The undertone that ran and grumbled through the whole house brought to an abrupt close the hot discussion between Scaasi and his manager.

"We gotta go through with it!" declared Vedder, hoisting his principal to his feet. "They're li'ble to wreck the place if we don't. That sporting editor is cor'spondent for a bunch of met'pol'tan papers, he tells me. He'll smear the story all through 'em. You gotta do it, Kid. And for the love of the Lord, *get him!* You gotta!"

With a conciliating wave of the hand Vedder stilled the rising tumult in the house and announced that the champion would be very glad to meet the unknown.

The crowd settled down to the treat, and the bout began.

Scaasi wasted no time in fancy boxing or in trying to show up his mild-faced adversary. There was no shadow of doubt in the champion's mind that he himself was by far the better man of the two. In a finish fight, or even in ten rounds, he would have been willing to stake his worldly fortune and hopes on the outcome. But there is as much difference between a four-round go and a ten-round fight as between the first three innings of a ball game and the whole game.

The champion knew himself for the better man. But he was far from certain that he could pound the Boob to senselessness within the brief time allowed for the task—and two hundred precious dollars hung on that dubious result, which had been the theme of his whispered talk with Vedder.

With all his wiry strength, with all his wild-beast ferocity, with all his ring generalship and craft, Scaasi tore into the Boob. Guthrie, for the most part, stayed on the defensive. Not a move, not a ruse of his enemy but was familiar to him by long and costly study. He foresaw the efforts to draw him out, to catch him within the scope of that deceptive reach, to lead him into trap after trap. To Guthrie it was all old stuff. Not in vain had he followed for weeks the champion's every mental and physical maneuver in the ring. The experience was standing loyally by him.

The Boob made no effort to force the fighting. He was well content to last out the required four rounds. Now and again he found himself enacting his old role of chopping block. But his condition and his new-learned skill enabled him to bear up under any assault he could not block.

The audience was howling with bliss. The referee was looking perplexed. Once, between rounds, he took another furtive glance at the affidavit Guthrie had handed him. This unknown was holding his own against the redoubtable Kid Scaasi in a way that promised to keep him on his feet for at least four rounds, in which case the referee foresaw a sporting-news item worth telegraphing to all the papers in his string.

At the beginning of the fourth round Scaasi purposely ran into a right-hand body blow of Guthrie's. The champion swayed on his heels and lurched forward as if half stunned. The Boob, smiling in pure joy, took advantage of his foe's mock distress to land a half hook on the other's jaw and to dance away safely out of reach before the indignant Scaasi could realize that the same trick could not be played, even upon the Boob, in two successive bouts.

Then, throwing boxing to the winds, Scaasi roughed it, striving frantically to save his two hundred dollars in the less than three minutes left to him for such salvage. Guthrie covered up under the hurricane and outrode it.

He was still fighting on steady feet when the bell ended the final round. Without a word to Scaasi, who stamped blasphemously back to his corner and to his manager, Guthrie took off his gloves and stepped up to the referee. The latter, still staring quizzically at him, counted out into his palm ten withered twenty-dollar bills, and asked:

"You say you're a garage helper—where did you learn to box like that?"

"Oh," replied the Boob vacuously, "that wasn't such a much. Three or four of us back home gets to playing with the gloves sometimes of an evening. I'm not anywheres near the best of the bunch back there. But I sized up this Scaasi lad to-night and I figgered he wasn't such a much either, so I took a chance. Why, some of the boys at the garage could have licked that four-flusher in two rounds. Thanks for the cash, mister. Good night!"

The gist of this modest speech was telegraphed duly to various metropolitan newspapers an hour later; as part of the vivid tale of an untrained garage helper who had had no trouble at all in staying with the much-vaunted Kid Scaasi for four fast rounds.

The world's heavyweight champion, reading the account next morning, telephoned his manager on long distance and disgustedly bade him send a curt refusal to Scaasi's challenge.

"Say that I ain't in this game for easy exercise," he exhorted the manager. "Tell 'em after folks have read that piece in the papers, a fight between me and Scaasi wouldn't fill a telephone booth at ten cents admission. He's a chunk of cammumbear. Tell 'em that, too, if you c'n get anybody to spell out the word for you."

Spider Vedder that same morning read the Pitvale Chronicle's story of the bout as he and Scaasi waited in the hotel lobby for train time. Indeed, he and Scaasi read it together, helping each other over the longer words. For, though the millennium of higher education has approached to the point where the average prize fighter nowadays can sign his own "signed statements" for the press, the road of perusal is still a bumpy one to many of the craft.

They were just finishing the reading when Boob Guthrie strolled into the lobby and came over to where they sat.

"Well?" said the Boob.

Both men looked up, at the pleasantly voiced salutation. Scaasi went purple and scrambled wrathfully to his feet. Vedder intervened to avert a row. They had had quite enough publicity in Pitvale.

"What the blue hell do you want?" he snapped at the intruder.

"Clear out of—"

"I don't want anything," was the gentle retort. "But I thought maybe you might. If you don't I won't butt in on you—not till your show hits the next stop. Then you'll see me on the stage when you call for local volunteers. And at the next stop after that—and at the next. Those are the only three where your offer is posted so far and where your cash is put up with the sporting editors. By-by!"

Unconcernedly he moved away. Scaasi in black rage made as though to rush at him.

Vedder, blessed with an infinitely closer approach to mentality than was his principal, thrust the latter sharply back into his chair and pattered off at full speed in the wake of the departing Boob. He caught up with Guthrie in the doorway.

"Say, look-a here!" sputtered Vedder in a tone he sought to make friendly. "What was that crack you sprung just now about trailing us and crabbing our show? You'd never go doing such a dirty trick as all that, old scout?"

"Mr. Vedder," said Guthrie, halting and beaming down on the wiggling little man, "I'm the last chap in the world to do a dirty trick to anybody. Least of all to a fine pal—like the Kid. I'm just after a pokeful of easy cash—that's all. And this seems a comfortable way of coining it. I've taken the bother to look up your dates. That's why I'm here. That's why I'll be at the next place—and the next and the next. By that time you'll have to pull down your offer or lose two hundred dollars a night. Without that four-round bout your show will be a frost and you know it—after the way I've showed your champ up and the way I'm going to keep on doing it at the next three towns. He won't be able to get a sailor dance-hall purse for a fight by that time."

"Say!" quavered Vedder, green and sweating. "You—you say all you're after is easy cash. Ain't there—ain't there some way you and me can fix this thing? Ain't there? Say, be a good feller and lissen now! Let's talk this over."

A half hour later Vedder rejoined his scowling principal. The little manager was actually grinning. As they set forth for the station he opened his soul on the theme closest to it.

"Well," he chuckled, "I got it all fixed. It's a cinch! He's dead easy— the Boob—like all cheap grafters is. Here's the notion: This rotten noospaper yarn is due to go all over the country. And it's due to do pretty near as much for the Boob as the same kind of a yarn did for Jack Munro, the time Jeff boxed all comers, out to Butte; and Munro happened to knock the big feller down. That put Munro on the sporting map, even if he didn't stay there long. And—"

"Stop drooling about Jeff and get to us!" exhorted Scaasi. "Where do I come in on—"

"I'm getting to that. It seems there's to be a big athaletic carn'val down to Merleburg, only about three miles from the Boob's home town. It's to be next month. The Boob's sore at the way you showed him up that day at the training camp. He wants his home folks to know he ain't a dead one. He wants me to fix it up for you and him to box six rounds at that carn'val, so—"

"No!" stormed Scaasi. "What d'ye take me for? There's no money in carn'vals. And I won't go six rounds with the Boob. If it was ten, now—"

"Hold on!" soothed Vedder. "You don't get the drift of it. The Boob's willing to have you put him out, but he don't want it done till the last round, so the home folks can see he ain't a one-round dub. He says it's no disgrace to be knocked out clean in six rounds by a champ like you. But he's sore on the way you made his neighbors think he was a quitter that day. He wants that wiped out. He'll lay down peaceful in the sixth round. And he wants five hundred dollars for doing it. If we won't fall for that he swears he'll foller the show and—"

"Five hundred dollars!" shouted Scaasi. "You're crazy!"

"I'm so crazy," assented Vedder, "that the check I'll give him, just before him and you go into the ring, will be drawn on the Pine City Second National. We've got a balance of nine dollars and sixty-five cents in there. He didn't hold out for a certified check. Most likely he never heard of one. He—"

"But even at that," protested Scaasi, "I can't see why I—"

"I'm doing the seeing for this outfit," was the calm reply. "You've got a black eye because the Boob lasted four rounds with you. Well, I'll change that black eye to a gold mine. Here's the idea: The story is going to be sent out that you got dead drunk here and couldn't keep wide enough awake to stop an amachoor that boxed with you. The amachoor is so swelled up that he wants a six-round go with you. You take him on for that at the carn'val and you put him out. That cleans the slate and shows you was drunk when you met him here, and it leaves you with as big a rep as ever. Get it now? And for a bout like that we ought to be able to make mighty soft terms with the carn'val c'mittee."

Bit by bit the gist of the scheme dribbled through Scaasi's brainpan. He smote his manager on the shoulder at last in high approval.

"And you say I'm s'posed to give him just a love tap when the time comes for him to go out?" he asked. "Well, Spider, when that signal comes and he leaves his jaw open for the tap, the Boob is sure due to think the Chicago Limited has tapped him. By the time he wakes up that nine dollars and sixty-five cents of yours will have rolled up five hundred dollars in compound int'rest. Write to them carn'val folks to-day!"

For five lively and spectacular rounds the Scaasi-Guthrie bout had danced along. The carnival throng was enthralled by the snap and dash of it. The cliques of sporting men, who had been drawn thither by news of the match, were eying the Boob with wondering interest. From the first minute in the ring it had been apparent to them and to the correspondents that this was no untrained garage helper. There was something behind the whole affair that piqued their curiosity.

Guthrie was fighting gamely and well. If he was not the peer of his adversary, at least he was making Scaasi do his best. Once or twice in the earlier rounds the initiated thought they saw openings whereof the tigerlike Scaasi might have availed himself and did not. But, knowing what the champion had at stake, they acquitted him of stalling.

Then the two came up for the sixth and last round. They met in the ring's center. For a minute or more they were at it in hammer-and-tongs fashion at close quarters. Then for an instant they sparred. Then—loudly, resonantly, clarionlike—Vedder at the ringside blew his nose.

Obedient to the signal, Guthrie waded awkwardly to the attack, his guard low. There was a glint in Scaasi's half-shut eyes as he blocked the Boob's loose swing and countered with his right for the jaw.

Into that lightning-swift punch went every atom of the champion's strength and hate. He braced his whole body for its delivery. No longer needing to look out for guard or counter, he smote as though he were attacking a punching bag.

But Boob Guthrie's jaw was not there when the right lead whizzed toward it. The Boob's head had bent suddenly forward and to the right, impelled by a similar motion of his entire frame—a motion whose supreme force centered in the piston drive of his left fist.

Scaasi's wet glove grazed Guthrie's darting head. Guthrie's left fist found its goal in the champion's purposely unguarded solar plexus.

Scaasi was moving forward at the time from the momentum of his own wasted blow and he helped thus by thirty per cent the impetus of his opponent's onslaught.

Kid Scaasi, light-heavyweight champion of the world, sat down in midring. This he did with much suddenness. Then, more slowly, he fell prone on one side. Twisting, purely through reflex action of his palsied muscles, he rolled over presently to the other side. His eyes were wide open—so was his mouth. A glare of ludicrous horror was frozen on his distorted face.

The referee, with the steadiness of clock ticks, was counting him out. The frenzied Vedder was scampering along the narrow outer edge of the ring, trying to fling a sponge of ammonia upon his principal's nostrils.

Then came the count of ten and with it a roar from the spectators.

With one upraised hand Boob Guthrie checked the racket. With the other he shoved back Vedder from the effort to lift Scaasi to his feet.

"This isn't a knockout!" yelled the Boob into the milling mass of uplifted faces. "You saw I didn't hit him hard enough to smash a fly. You saw he didn't even try to block me. Look at him! He's wide awake. He just lay down. Don't blame him, friends! A man can't help being yellow if he's built that way.

"And now," he added, a sudden quiver making his big voice scale a half octave as he glowered across to where a group of flashily attired women sat—"and now laugh, some of you! Laugh! I've got that much coming to me!"

One inquisitive reporter, out of many of his guild who had sought Guthrie from the moment he jumped down from the ring, found him three hours later emerging from the doorway of the All-Car Garage, where once he had worked.

"Well, Big Fellow," hailed the newspaper man, "where have you been hiding yourself? You're a celebrity now. There are no less than three managers on your trail at this minute. The ring—"

"Ring nothing!" scoffed the Boob joyously. "I've got a job! The man who runs this garage has promised me a third interest in it for the cash I've saved—I'm not counting a five-hundred-dollar check I've just mailed back to Vedder—and for the trade he says my name'll bring it after my stunt at the carnival. Say, old man, steer those managers off if you get a chance, won't you—unless they want some first-class motor repairing done?"

But as he turned back into the garage there was a little sick twinge at the Boob's heart through all his new joy. He had chanced to recall for the fiftieth time the anguish in Kid Scaasi's eyes as the champion lay writhing on the floor of the ring.

And the memory made Guthrie keenly unhappy. You see, he was not a fighter. He could never have been made into a fighter—except perhaps for a brief space, and by the nasty laugh of a woman whose face he never saw. Now that his bill was paid, he was just a Boob again.

The Lotus Eater

Part I

ENOCH ARDEN went to sea. He was shipwrecked on a desert isle. His friends mourned him as dead. When, at last, he was rescued and came home, he found Mrs. Enoch had taken to herself a brand-new husband, with whose loving aid she was amassing a brand-new family. Whereat, Enoch forbore to jar her domestic bliss by news of his presence, and crawled off into a corner and died.

All of which is set forth in the published poetical works of Alfred, Lord Tennyson—bound in blue and gold, with center-rules dividing the small-type pages into two inadequate columns each, and with messy mid-Victorian illustrations strewn through the volume.

It is beautifully easy for a man to make mighty sacrifices and to obliterate his own life-happiness for the sake of sparing his loved ones a single pang—as long as that man chances to have his sole existence in a book of poetry, as had Enoch Arden. But in real life, the throbbingly potent personal equation has a queer way of standing poetry ideals on their heads in a snowdrift. For example, there was Madge Barret's husband.

Madge Barret was one of the women whom God made. Everybody believed that. Two men knew it—past all doubt. These two men, Dirck Vane and Philip Carson, were chums. They had been chums from boyhood. They continued to be chums until both of them fell in love with Madge Barret.

Thus the "triangle" was formed. But it disintegrated in less than six months, when Madge's engagement to Dirck Vane was announced.

Carson, at news of the betrothal, broke his life-habit of sobriety in one epoch-making debauch. Then he went to the Kentucky mountains, where he invested such capital and such shreds of enthusiasm as he could scrape together in a search for oil-properties.

He throve at his new venture. Perhaps because he did not care whether he prospered or starved. Perhaps because Fortune, having broken his mainspring, sought to atone for the deed by gilding his case. In any event, he did well. And his luck was as Dead Sea apples between his teeth.

To the normal man—in spite of the ravings of poet and fictionist—sweethearts have one trait in common with ferryboats: If you miss one of them, you can usually get the next. The heart will writhe; so will the vanity. But the world is full of women.

The missing of a run-after ferry-boat will cause profanity and despondency, and a yearning to slay the man who slammed the gate in one's face. But presently one calms down, and waits in unconscious philosophy for the next boat, which is certain to come to the slip sooner or later. And at the day's end, the general result is much the same as though one had caught the boat he wanted. The rivers are full of ferry-boats.

Philip Carson was not a normal man, perhaps. Certainly he was not normal where Madge Barret was concerned. He was a quiet, unemotional fellow—on the surface—altogether unlike his chum, Vane. And Madge Barret was the first woman he had loved. And she was destined to be the last and the only. There are many "one-man" dogs. There are some "one-man" women. There are a very few "one-woman" men. Phil Carson was such a man.

Wherefore, when Madge married his chum, Carson's heart died in great pain. And he buried himself in the desolate places of the South, that he might be beyond the ken of the man who had been as a twin brother to him, and the girl who had been his very soul. Which withdraws Philip Carson from our story for a term of years—and brings us back to Madge and Dirck.

The new-wed pair were gloriously happy. To the bride her splendid husband was the First Man. To Dirck, his wonder-wife was the First Woman—who counted. And life was a continuous honeymoon dream for the two.

Dirck had all the money he needed—almost as much money as he wanted. And his desultory law business gave him much leisure time. This surplus time and money the couple invested in a lazy honeymoon journey that lasted for six months, beginning at the church portals in New York and ending amid the tepid breezes of the South Pacific.

They
had been
idling   in
Lower   Cali-
fornia   when
the whim came to
Madge to tour the
Pacific islands in the
same deliciously lazy way
they had been loafing through
the West. It was a Jack London
book—a book they had been reading
aloud together—that gave her the idea. A week
later, she and Dirck were waving a jolly farewell to
the California coast from the afterdeck of the stodgy little tourist-
steamship Malaiti.

It was a dreamy paradise of a voyage—amid white-beached and green-palm islets, and over a sea that seemed to drowse in its own balmy loveliness. For a solid month, Madge and Dirck reveled in it.

Then, on a cloudless and windless midnight, the Malaiti crashed into a submerged derelict.

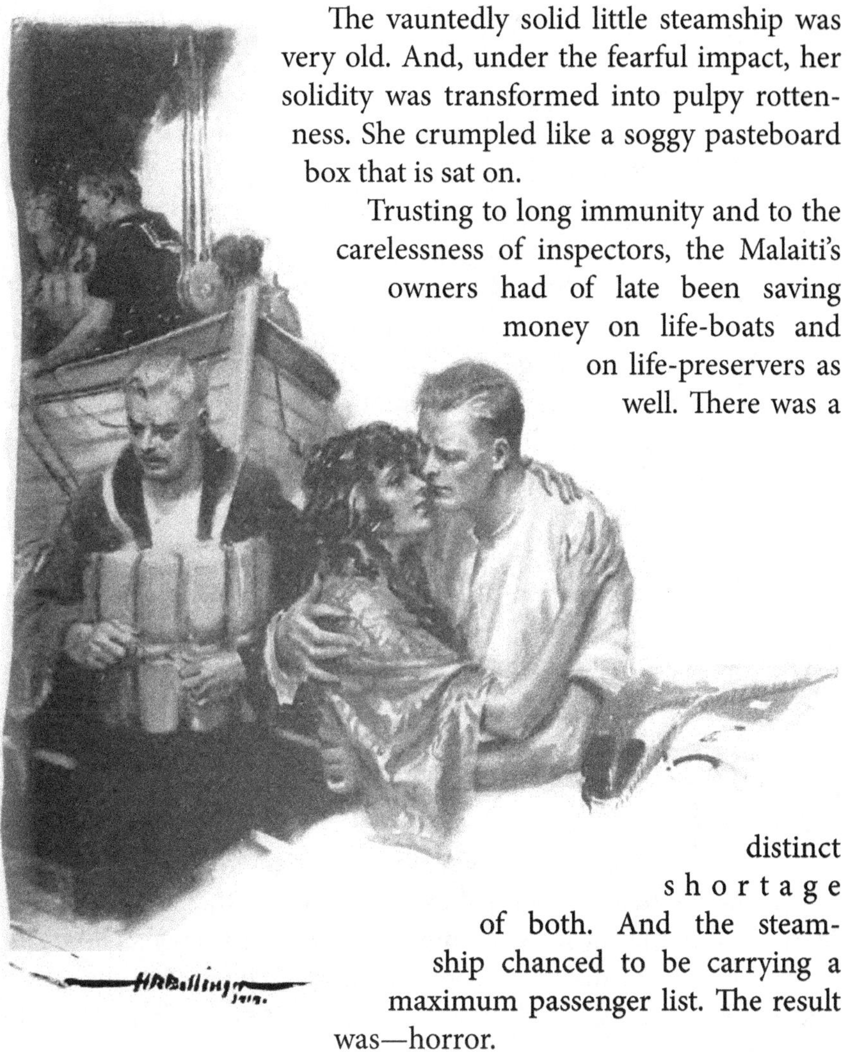

The vauntedly solid little steamship was very old. And, under the fearful impact, her solidity was transformed into pulpy rottenness. She crumpled like a soggy pasteboard box that is sat on.

Trusting to long immunity and to the carelessness of inspectors, the Malaiti's owners had of late been saving money on life-boats and on life-preservers as well. There was a distinct shortage of both. And the steamship chanced to be carrying a maximum passenger list. The result was—horror.

The captain kept his head. His crew stood by the iron discipline he had long since hammered into them. So he and his officers wrought unhandicapped, save by the aforesaid double shortage, and by the fact that the ship was going to pieces with incredible quickness.

Women and children were marshaled. The boats were lowered without mishap, and were manned and provisioned.

So busy were the officers in this task, and so filled with grim joy at finding that a careful packing would afford place in the boats for every child and woman; that they did not pause to scan the erstwhile peaceful horizon. Which is why they did not take note of a lively little tropical typhoon until the swirling gale was all but upon them. Not that it would have made any difference either way. As the last squad of women was brought forward to be lowered into the final boat, Madge ducked under the waving arm of the first officer and rushed back to the huddle of men passengers in the waist of the sinking ship.

Running up to Vane, the girl wife flung both arms tightly round his neck and clung to him in a frenzy of adoration.

She did not cry. There was no panic in her sweet voice or in her softly level eyes. In both gaze and tone there was nothing but love— utter love, which, at this supreme moment, drove out all such lesser emotions as fear or selfishness.

"Dear heart," she was saying, oblivious of those around them, "is it true that there is room for only the women and the babies in those boats?"

Dirck nodded, holding her closer. Then he made shift to lie right gallantly.

"After you people have gotten off," he said, "we men are going to take to the rafts. They aren't quite as comfortable as the boats, perhaps, but they are even safer. And they will hold us all. We're only a few miles from land. We'll all meet there before daylight. You're not to worry, dear."

It was a good lie. There were no rafts on the Malaiti. Dirck knew that from his many desultory examinations of the ship. He hoped Madge did not know it. And, though she had just heard a chattering seaman bewailing that the vessel was raftless, she did homage to the brave lie by seeming to believe it and to glean comfort from its recital. Then,

"Dirck," she went on, her soft arms tightening a little round his neck, "it's been a heavenly six months. I didn't know any people could be as happy as we've been. If we live on twenty years or more, I'll get to be stout and gray and ugly. Life will be humdrum. We'll settle down into a dull middle-aged couple, with youth and romance and our divine insanity all gone, and our honeymoon days buried under the dust of workaday years. I wish—honestly I do, beloved!— I wish we could go to sleep *now*, while we are still in the glory of it all, before the world and the years spoil it. I wish we could end it together, while it is still so stainless and beautiful and dear. *Can't* we, Dirck?"

The man was shivering, though neither from cold nor fright. He looked down into the eyes upraised to his troubled gaze; eyes as fearless as a little child's and abrim with deathless love for him.

"I wish we could, too, sweetheart," he muttered; "I wish it with all my soul. But we've got to play the game as God deals us the cards to play it. I love you, so—I—"

The last boat had received its last passenger, except one. The captain caught sight of Madge clinging to her husband, fifty feet away from where the bobbing life-boat waited to cast off. At a sharp word from him, two sailors came running to where the close-embracing lovers stood on the reeling deck.

"Good-by, dear!" whispered Dirck, as he noted their hasty approach. "Kiss me good-by. It—"

"No!" cried Madge, her voice ringing out above the welter, as defiantly as a silver bugle's. "No! I am going to stay with you! Did you really think I'd go like this and leave you? Don't you suppose I understand? It won't be death—it'll be heaven—if we face it together. We—"

The foremost sailor's hand was on her shoulder. Dirck Vane drew her away from the man's grasp, swung her from her feet high into his own arms, and rushed his lips to hers. Then, before she could free herself or guess his intent, Dirck was running along the deck, carrying her as lightly as though she were a baby and pinioning her arms in one of his.

He reached the rail and lowered his wife to the men below, who were waiting impatiently to receive her. Not until she felt herself held out bodily over the rail did Madge realize what her husband was doing. Then she cried out in frantic protest, and sought to catch at his relinquishing arms. But already the sailors were lowering her into the boat.

"Dirck!" she wailed. "*Dirck!* Take me back to you! I won't—"

The first breath of the typhoon caught her words and drove them into her throat. She fought with helpless vehemence against the men who were settling her in the bottom of the boat. She caught a moment's glimpse of her husband's face, looking down at her from the buckling rail, far above. As the light-flicker illumined it, it seemed to her the face of a god.

Then the typhoon smote the sleepily rolling waters. And the boat wallowed away into a blinding smother of darkness.

When Madge Vane landed at San Francisco, five weeks later, from the tramp steamship which had picked up the foundering life-boat, she learned that only one boat besides her own had escaped the typhoon and that the Malaiti had gone to fragments in sight of this second boat-load's occupants.

Not a man aboard the ship but had been sucked under by the vessel's sinking. In such a sea, the stoutest swimmer could not have lived three minutes. The Malaiti had strayed far off the usual trade-routes in the leisurely pleasure-jaunt. No ships had reported the saving of any male passengers or the picking-up of so much as a stick of wreckage.

A score of vessels had rushed to the spot at news of the disaster. That was all the good they did. There was not room for the most chimeric scrap of hope.

And, as soon as she was definitely assured of this, Madge let her nerves go. Followed a two-month siege of what old-time doctors used to call "brain fever."

When youth and vitality dragged the unwilling woman out of the Shadow Valley, she went back to New York to piece together the broken fragments of life. Her heart was broken by the loss of her god-husband. But her body was still vibrant with girlish strength. And she lived.

Even in the medieval romance, the Elaines and Ladies of Shalott and other heroines who die of broken hearts are depicted in the very beginning as pallid and fragile damsels. A golf-playing, horseback-loving twentieth-century girl like Madge Vane may break her heart as thoroughly as ever did Elaine. But life claims its own. And life has a queer way of keeping on—especially when one wants it to stop. Which accounts for the fact that the world is still populated.

Madge not only lived but gained back her loveliness and her buoyant health—both sorely against her own will. And in time—as was but normal—the world caught her up into its current once more. Little by little, so subtly that she did not observe the change, she slipped from her heart-broken isolation and into her former groove of life.

It was not that she had forgotten Dirck or that she ceased to grieve for him. Always the memory of her husband was alive at the back of her thoughts. Often—but seldomer as the years moved on at a less and less dragging pace—the vision of him would arise, unbidden before her, with an agonizing vividness.

Sometimes, through no summoning, his face would reappear, startlingly distinct, to her closed eyes—his face as she had seen it for that fleeting instant when he had leaned over the rail above her, with all his soul in his eyes in wordless farewell. And, at such times, she was fain to bite her lips in an effort to force back the cry of stark anguish which sprang from her heart.

Yet, being only mortal, and a decidedly healthy mortal, she saw this vision less often and less vividly as the years wore on. And everyday life joined in a conspiracy with Time to blur the past and to make the present seem worth while. She had been twenty years old when she lost her husband. At twenty, there are few miracles which time and environment cannot achieve.

Three years after the Malaiti wreck, Philip Carson came back to New York.

He had aged a bit down there in the mountain silences, and he had grown taciturn. Loneliness and heart-atrophy and ceaselessly grinding work had taken their toll of him. In compensation, they had made him rich.

Carson had not returned to Manhattan for the fun of spending his new wealth or even of taking up his old life. He had come back because he had read of the Malaiti disaster and of his chum's death. He knew Madge was free. And his dead heart came to life again with racking birth-pains.

Yet Phil was a wise man, and tactful withal. He did not spoil his possible chances by rushing to Madge the moment he learned she was a widow. He did not know women half as well as did Vane. But he knew one woman—as a devotee knows his saint—because that one woman was his all.

He knew how utterly Madge had given herself to the blond young giant she had married. And he knew that not all the buoyancy of youth and all the much advertised healing of Time could teach her to look at another man—yet.

So for three endless years he waited, keeping in touch with the stricken girl through the medium of common friends whom he lured into correspondence with him. And not until a careless phrase in one such correspondent's letters told him that Madge had finally discarded black for lavender did Carson wind up his affairs in Kentucky and set his face toward New York.

Madge was unaffectedly glad to see her old friend—the man whom Dirck had loved as a brother. It seemed a sort of bond with the beautiful past. Eagerly she welcomed Phil into her lonely life.

Followed several months of cautious campaigning, wherein Carson was helped by such powerful allies as Midge's own desolate longing for soul-companionship and by nature and by youth. In time, the combination was strong enough to triumph over the gradually fading image of Dirck Vane.

When Philip dared lay his heart at her feet, all the careful preliminaries seemed to have gone for naught. She was shocked that he should think a love like hers could be given a second time. She was disappointed in his lack of loyalty to his chum's memory.

Philip made quiet answer:

"The living have *some* rights, too, dear girl, as well as the dead." And he continued the siege.

Dismayingly soon, Madge's sense of shock died away. She was amazed at her own inability to keep the past as vividly in her mind as the present. She turned to Carson for explanation. And presently she found it.

A little more than three and a half years after the loss of the Malaiti, Madge and Carson were married. And (the ghost of Dirck being laid tenderly to rest) they were very happy in their new-found love.

When the Malaiti went down, Dirck Vane and half the other men who crowded the starboard rail sprang far outward into the swirl of the typhoon-whipped sea. Most of these were caught in the suction and were pulled far under water, where their bodies thrashed impotently in the subsurface whirlpool until flesh and soul were torn asunder.

Dirck was caught by an eccentric eddy which spun him far outboard and sent him colliding, with a breath-expelling shock, against a huge floating hatch—a hatch that had become entangled with some of the cordage of a spar.

With the last vestige of his mighty athletic strength, the man crawled upon the hatch and twisted an end of the cordage about his body. Then he fainted.

When he came sickly back to consciousness, the typhoon had vanished. So had any trace of the ship or of its possible survivors. So had the night. Dawn was butting its way up from the ocean-edge, revealing a trackless and unflawed wilderness of sea.

Dirck climbed higher on his uncouth craft and, taking off his shirt, rigged up a sorry imitation of a distress-signal. This done, he settled back to the full sensations of a sick-headache and a raw throat.

Presently he began to notice things. He observed, for instance, that the spar was making certain progress instead of lying awash of the waves. It had evidently been caught in one of the mysteriously swift and narrow currents which lace the seas round the Polynesian group. And a stiff breeze was not only easing the heat of the new-born sun but was aiding the current to propel the wallowing spar. Yes; the man was not stationary. He was traveling, and at a perceptible pace—a pace which remained steady throughout the whole torturingly hot tropic day and on through the night.

The next dawn waked him from a few hours of feverish sleep to a sensation that his spar was no longer moving forward. It was not moving at all, even to the slap of the rollers. It was as solidly motionless as any rock.

Dirck opened his bleared eyes and lifted his head to study this phenomenon. And he felt a surge of new life as he discovered the cause. The spar had run aground on a sand spit which rose barely to the surface of the windless sea. The spit formed the outer wall of a lagoon perhaps a half-mile wide, at whose far side Dirck could see the snowy beach and the black-green verdure of a low-lying island.

Clad as he was, and not stopping to test the chances of walking to land along the curve of the sand spit, Vane rolled into the lagoon and struck out through the milk-warm water toward the beach. Easy as was the swim, it told heavily upon his shocked and thirst-parched system. He was hardly able to buffet his way to shore and to crawl, crablike, up the white beach to the nearest patch of shade.

There he lay until a scrap of strength came back to him. After which, he scrambled to his feet, his crazy thirst scourging him on in search of fresh water. He noted a rough trail through the trees and underbrush, and followed it into the woods. A quarter-mile farther on, the trail widened into a well-trodden clearing, in whose center bubbled a spring that had been hollowed artificially to a basin-depth of a foot or two.

Vane flung himself prone on the ground at the side of the spring and plunged his face deep into the icy water. He sucked up pints of it, in great, noisy gulps like those of a thirsty horse.

Dirck Vane had lived. He had loved. He had known all the wild joys which youth gives to a strong man. Yet, in his twenty-eight years, he had never felt such all-encompassing ecstasy as gripped and thrilled him now as he drew in huge mouthfuls of the ice-chill fresh water which seemed to percolate to every atom of his parched body and to start the blood coursing anew through his exhausted frame. He drank and drank until his surfeited stomach refused to hold more.

Then, getting to his feet, he stared about him in dull animal contentment. And, not ten yards away, his idly roving gaze lighted on a wattle-plaited basket with perhaps a dozen ripe bananas and other fruits lying in its bottom.

Now, in his normal senses, Dirck Vane would long since have taken alarm. The trail from the beach would have told him the island was inhabited. The artificial hollowing of the spring would have confirmed the knowledge. The presence of this fruit, still fresh and unspotted, would have warned him that the island was not only populated but that some person, or people, had been at this very spot within a few hours. Also, he would have recalled that, while some of the Polynesian islands are inhabited by friendly and gentle folk, others are the homes of murderous savages and even of cannibals.

But always in moments of physical stress the body assumes command and usurps completely the throne of the mind. (Did ever anyone with an ulcerated tooth try to make love or to write a sonnet?)

Dirck worshiped his young wife. Yet, during his deliriously happy minutes at the spring, his body's drink-rapture had driven Madge temporarily from his mind—along with everything else that was as not directly concerned with the slaking of his horror-thirst.

So, now, the only message the fruit brought to him was a realization that he had not eaten for thirty-six hours. He fell upon the basket and wolfed the bulk of its contents. Then, after another long draft from the spring, he stretched himself on the ground for a few minutes' rest before continuing to explore his new surroundings.

And again the body claimed its own. The man fell at once into a sleep of utter fatigue. For ten hours he lay there like one dead, while shrewdly kind old Mother Nature made good the ravages of exposure and famine in his powerful physique and renewed his drained vitality.

The afternoon sun was slanting through the palms when Dirck Vane awoke. For an instant, he did not open his eyes, but lay drowsily content. In the vague recesses of his memory, he had a feeling of some recent mishap—a mishap which was now past, and which had left behind it an indolent reaction of comfort and of well-being.

He knew, too, that some one was looking down on him. And a faint smile crossed his face. Without bothering to lift his closed lids, he knew who the gazer was. Thus, a hundred times had Madge looked down on him as he slept. Presently she would stoop and kiss him. Then his drowsy arms would creep round her slim young body, and he would draw her down to him, as always he had done. She—

But the expected kiss did not press his waiting lips. Sleepily, Dirck wondered why. And he opened his tired eyes to find out. Above him stood a girl—honey-gold of skin, rounded and soft of gracious outline, clad in a single woven garment, her feet and ankles and arms and bosom bare. With lustrous dark eyes she was staring at the prostrate man, her pretty face alight with wondering interest.

Then, bit by bit, the stupidly blinking Vane remembered.

With a groan that shook him to the very soul, he rolled over on the ground and buried his face in his hands, while waves of hideous memory surged over him and buffeted his soul to agonized breathlessness.

Presently, through the hell of his revulsion, he felt a trailingly magnetic touch on his heaving shoulder. He started up. Beside him the native girl was kneeling, her big eyes alight with pitying sorrow. So might a thoroughbred dog look upon the grieving master he loves. The sweet sympathy, wordless and magnetic as her touch on his arm, was as balm to Dirck's bruised heart.

As he stood—miserable, irresolute, bewildered—eying her thus, she rose from her knees. Her warm hand slipped down his arm until her fingers found and imprisoned his. With her other hand she pointed through the tree-gap, where the trail continued its landward way from the clearing. A thin reek of smoke was curling up beyond the farthest vistas of the trail, betokening hut or village. And it was toward this that the girl was pointing.

Looking again up into the man's haggard face, she clasped his fingers the tighter and put her free hand on his shoulder once more. Gently she drew him toward the trail. Apathetic and dazed, he suffered himself to be led.

The trail opened into a clearing, in whose center was strewn a ragged cluster of huts. At the hail of Dirck's conductress, these huts poured forth a half-hundred natives, who ran forward in eager curiosity to greet the stranger.

In the straggling throng, women predominated—tall, deep-breasted women, soft of eye and of outline.

Four years, to a President of the United States, doubtless flits past on electrified wings. To a convict or to an engaged couple, the same

space of time is said to lose its wings and to plod along on leaden feet. To Dirck Vane, on his lotus-island in the South Pacific, the next four years were as a dream—sometimes seeming to endure forever, sometimes to pass in a blur.

Without books, without any but physical work, without ideals or a future or ambitions, without companions of his own world, his first mad rebellion against fate had gradually smoldered to ashes. In its place had come a bovine content—the content of one who knows he is cut off forever from those he loves and from his past, and who subconsciously learns to adapt himself to his enforced surroundings.

After he had once drifted into this state of mind, life ceased to be a torture and resumed its sway in a manner far from unpleasant.

The island was in one of the inner swirls of the Polynesian vortex, far out of trade-routes and practically inaccessible to ships by reason of the scarce-submerged sand-bars and shoals which strewed its encircling waters for many miles out to sea.

Not within the memory of the oldest inhabitant had a white-man ship touched there. Which perhaps accounted for the friendly simplicity of the natives and for their hospitable greeting of the first white man whom most of them had ever seen.

In former times—so Dirck gathered, as he picked up the hang of their crude language—the island had been well populated and had carried on a certain amount of trade with other isles of its group. Then a pestilence, which seemed to have been smallpox, had ravaged it, cutting down the population to one-tenth its earlier numbers.

The malady had been carried thence, by native traders, to other islands, where it had wrought havoc. And, because of this pestilence, the natives of all surrounding islands had shunned the place and had put a tabu upon both itself and its remaining inhabitants. It had thereafter been a hermit isle, sparse-populated, its canoes forbidden to touch at any other island.

And, to restock the land, the chief had decreed a return to the long-abandoned custom of polygamy.

Dirck Vane, one morning four years after the wreck of the Malaiti, was sitting at the forest-edge, lazily mending a broken paddle in preparation for a day's fishing in the lagoon. On the beach in front of him lay his native canoe. Three furlongs back along the forest belt's trail stood his hut, where his gold-skinned native "head wife" was busy with her few primitive household tasks. In the hut-yard, her three cream-hued babies were playing. Elsewhere, in more distant huts, were Vane's three "subsidiary wives" and their respective broods of cream-colored off-spring.

On Dirck's once-alert face had long since settled an aspect of drowsy calm. True, the memory of Madge was still uncomfortably poignant in his heart. But he remembered her, and mourned for her as though she had been long dead.

He knew he should never again set eyes on her. He had an odd feeling of certainty that she had escaped the wreck and that she had reached home in safety. He did not know why he was so sure of this. But he never for a moment doubted it.

The knowledge did nothing to lessen his own realization of loss. He could never get to her. To him, she was dead. Thus he had turned his back on the beautiful past, lest he go insane with fruitless yearning. And he had set his face resolutely to the placid future, here in Lotus Land. With time, this had been easy to do.

This morning, after an hour's fumbling at his labor of paddle-splicing, he finished the job and laid aside the mended implement. Carelessly his eyes swept the sea as he got up and made ready for his fishing-trip.

Of a sudden, he leaped high in air, with a great shout of amaze.

There, cautiously skirting the sand spit's outer fringe, a half-mile to seaward, a small schooner was creeping along. It was the first civilized craft Dirck had beheld in four endless years. The sight carried him in a rush out of his bovine calm.

Wholly without conscious volition, he found himself bounding toward his canoe, then running waist-deep into the lagoon to launch it, and paddling with maniac speed across to where the white-winged schooner was drifting along the farther rim of the sand spit.

The sight of this link with the outer world had set him ablaze. He did not stop to tell himself that here was a chance to return to Madge and to home and to his career—the one chance of a lifetime. But he felt it all, without analyzing it. And it lent incredible power to the sweep of his paddle.

He grounded on the sand spit at the lagoon-rim. Leaping into the water, he snatched up his canoe, swung it above his head, and bore it to the seaward edge of the spit, relaunched it, and paddled madly out to intercept the all-but-becalmed schooner.

In native garb—or garblessness—and tanned as dark as an Arab, he came alongside and hailed the little knot of men who had been watching amusedly the fevered struggles of this supposed Polynesian to overtake them.

The first of several American faces Dirck's eager glance encountered was that of the man who had chartered this schooner for a prowling exploration-tour of the island-group—Ford Manchester, writer and explorer and world-wanderer.

"White men!" yelled Dirck deliriously, as he climbed up the schooner's side and thrust back two officious *kanakas* who would have barred his sacrilegious progress. "White men, for God's love, take me *home!*"

Part II

IT was nearly half an hour later, down in Ford Manchester's tiny cabin, as he was dressing himself in a set of the explorer's garments, that Dirck first remembered his native wives and his little swarm of cream-skinned youngsters. Until then, the dizzy excitement of seeing a familiar face, of receiving a white-man welcome, of speaking again in his own language, of knowing he was home-bound—all these had been sufficient to crowd from Vane's mind every lesser thought.

But now, with recollection, came a wrenching twinge—a twinge of remorse, not of sorrow. He knew his island spouses would grieve bitterly and noisily for their vanished white lord. But he knew, too, that among natives, as among animals, grief is a short-lived guest. Presently his mates would console themselves with husbands of their own color and race.

As for his roly-poly babies—well, their mothers loved them far too dearly to let them suffer in any way. And there was a comfortable livelihood for all on the sparsely populated island. He could have taken none of these children nor any of his wives to civilization with him. For their own sakes, even more than for his own, it had been kinder to leave them behind.

And again Dirck's thoughts turned forward in ecstasy toward home.

Two months later, Dirck Vane set foot in San Francisco. Borrowing enough money from Manchester to outfit himself and to pay his way East, he took the first available train for New York.

Vane did not telegraph to Madge. He did not know how a telegram could reach her. She might still be living in New York. She might be in the suburbs or even in some other city.

She had been an only child. And her father's death, a year before her marriage, had left her without near relatives. The average New Yorker does not occupy the same house or flat for four years in succession. Dirck thus did not know to what friend he could apply for accurate news of her. It seemed quicker and simpler to go directly to New York and there pursue the quest in person. Which he proceeded to do.

He was so lucky as to strike a clue before he had been in Manhattan for three minutes. As he walked out of the Grand Central Station, it occurred to him to consult a telephone-directory. Entering the nearest drug store, he pored excitedly over the bethumbed gray volume he found hanging beside the brown 'phone-booth.

The book contained several "Vanes," but no "Mrs. Dirck Vane" or "Mrs. M. Vane."

Next, Dirck bethought himself of his old-time chum, Phil Carson. True, Phil had gone to Kentucky on some sort of wild-goose chase after oil or coal or something. But there was a chance he might have come back again before now. And Vane turned from the V's to the C's. There, readily enough, he found Carson's name and address. The latter was on Park Avenue, near Seventieth Street.

Dirck raised his brows as he read the address. Either Park Avenue real-estate values had deteriorated in the past few years or else Phil had struck it rich out there in Kentucky. In any case, it would be great to see the dear old chap again. And there was even an off-chance that Phil could tell him something of Madge's whereabouts. If only for the sake of his old friendship with her husband. Carson must have kept some sort of track of Madge.

As a hastily summoned taxi whizzed Dirck northward through the early dusk toward Carson's home, the returned wanderer for the first time found his elation giving place to a nervous terror. With the goal in sight, he grew sick with fear.

Suppose his glorious girl wife had not escaped the wreck after all? Suppose she had escaped only to grieve herself to death over her husband's fate or to succumb to the hardships of that voyage in the wabbly life-boat? Suppose— The man's wildly joyous anticipation was fast turning to a shuddering dread.

The taxi drew up at the curb of a mountainous apartment-house. Dirck forced his trembling legs to a semblance of steadiness as he made his way indoors and found the elevator. Unwilling to bear the delay of waiting to be announced, he stepped into the car and said sharply, if quaveringly, to the sable elevator-boy,

"Mr. Carson's apartment."

The youth wavered, glancing toward the hall telephone. Dirck thrust a five-dollar bill into his hand. Up shot the car. The lad even gave a good measure for the tip by announcing that Mr. Carson had come in a bare three minutes earlier.

A dapper Jap admitted Vane to the apartment and ushered him into a dark-furnished living room. Dirck forbore to send in his name to his chum, looking forward with a childish eagerness to surprising Phil. So he merely told the Jap to say that a school-days' friend had called.

As the servant went to deliver the message, Dirck employed the brief interval in fighting for self-mastery and in seeking to steel his overwrought nerves to bear any tidings Phil might give him of Madge. Subconsciously, he noted the severe elegance of the room and its proclamation of wealth blended with perfect taste. He had no mind for speculating on these things. In his heart, two questions were shouting themselves over and over:

Is Madge alive? Where is she?

The heavy door-curtains parted and Philip Carson came into the room. Time had dealt kindly with him. Dirck, through all his own perturbation, could see that. Phil was stouter than of old. His face had lost the ascetic sternness that had once underlain its features, and it was mellowly genial. Visage and figure, as well as costume, spoke of happy prosperity.

Disregarding everything else, Dirck strode stumblingly up to the politely inquisitive Phil, panting:

"Is Madge alive? *Is* she? For God's sake, man, *tell* me!"

At sound of Vane's voice, and as the light from the hallway fell clearly athwart the visitor's contorted face, Philip Carson stiffened all over like a man who receives an electric shock. His ruddy cheeks went green-gray. A light sweat beaded his forehead. His jaw dropped. His eyes bulged grotesquely. He swayed and caught at the curtains for support.

Noticing none of this, and with his mind centered on one supreme object, Dirck seized his host by the coat and shook him convulsively.

"Is Madge alive?" he croaked, his throat sanded with dread. *"Is* she? Is she alive? Is she all right? *Tell me!"*

Philip Carson nodded. His gray lips shaped themselves into a noiseless, "Yes."

Dirck sank back into a chair, weak with blissful reaction. For a moment, so tremendous was his relief, he could not speak. Carson stood blinking down at him, as wordless as he. It was Dirck who first recovered voice and motive power.

"Thank God!" he gasped, his lips not yet wholly firm. "Oh, thank *God!* Forgive me for howling at you, old man, and for shaking you. But I've been through a hell of fear. I— Why, you look as if you'd seen a ghost! I didn't know it'd break you up so to meet me like this. I ought to have sent up my name. But I was in too much of a rush to find out about Madge. Where is she? You're dead sure she's all right?"

"Where have you been?" demanded Carson dazedly.

They were the first words he had spoken. They seemed to be jerked from his writhing lips in spite of himself. This latter query to a friend risen from the dead struck upon Dirck's suddenly relieved senses as most ludicrous. He laughed hysterically and made equally hysteric reply:

"I? Oh, I've been on the South Sea island where I was stranded when the Malaiti sank. A native girl took pity on me. Then, a couple of months ago, Ford Manchester happened along in a schooner. And—"

"Why did you come back?" flamed Carson, in a sudden gust of rage that shook him out of his wonted sane calm. "Why are you here? You died! You have been dead four years! You—"

"Phil!" broke in the astonished Vane. "Why, Phil, old chap, what sort of greeting is this for a friend who has come home as I have?"

Carson's incredible reception of him had checked the reactive hysteria in Vane and had startled him into his normal self. He could not understand—could not believe—that his boyhood chum really felt the abhorrence for him which so plainly showed in Phil's words and look. Coldly, speaking with slow effort, the host said:

"Your death was reported. It was verified to a certainty. The insurance companies made full payment. Your estate was administered. Your wife mourned you sincerely and deeply. For more than three years she was faithful to your memory. Then—"

"What do you mean?" demanded Vane, stung to new fear by Carson's hint. "Faithful to my memory for more than three years? What then? Speak up! What are you driving at? What—"

"Six months ago," went on the laboredly slow voice, "Madge did me the honor to marry me."

Dirck leaped to his feet, his mouth wide open, meaningless words seeking to shape themselves from between his twisting lips. His fists were clenched until the knuckles shone bone-white and the nails bit deep into his sweating palms. Then he slumped back into his chair.

"Tell me," he whispered.

"I came back to New York a year ago," pursued Carson, still forcing his speech to slow precision. "I met her again. She was just beginning to go around to places once more. I had always loved her. I left the East because she married you. I never loved any other woman. That was why I went into the wilderness to live. When I read of your death, I still stayed there in the mountains. For I knew how she had cared for you. And I knew she would have no thought yet for any other man. But I knew, too, that she was young and that a few years may do much. So I waited until I heard she had put off mourning. Then I came back. She still thought her heart was dead. But gradually I taught her to—to care. And at last she married me. That is all—all—except that we have been happy and that she has proved she really loves me. Why—"

"I see," interrupted Vane, dimly wondering at his own unnatural coolness. "I see. And now that I have come back, what do you mean to do?"

" 'Do?' " echoed Carson. " *'Do?'* "

"Yes," said Dirck. "She is my wife, you know. I can't pretend to be glad to hear how she has consoled herself, or to say I'll be as idiotically rapturous over our reunion as if—as if you had stayed in Kentucky. But she is my wife. And I love her more than anything and everything else. And I am going to take her back. I am going to take her back, because life would be death without her. What do you mean to do, Phil?"

For a moment, Carson glared at him dazedly, in visible effort to marshal his shattered faculties. Then he made answer:

"She is not your wife. You were adjudged dead. Legally dead. My marriage to Madge was lawful. She is my wife. If you think I am going to be a cross between a fool and a martyr and turn her over to you and smash my one chance of life-happiness—well, you're wrong. She is my wife. And I'm going to hold her. She—"

"If you are hinting that I ought to follow Enoch Arden's sheep-like example and go away quietly and leave Madge to you," replied Dirck, fighting hard for self-mastery, "I can tell you you're wasting your time. Madge married me because she loved me. When we were in the wreck, she refused to leave me and save herself. She did it out of no false heroism, but because she loved me so much that life would not be worth while without me. I saved her in spite of herself. I saved her because I loved her too unselfishly to let her die with me. The minute I could get away from that island-hell, I raced across the world to get back to her. Man, do you think for a minute that I'm going to give her up—after all that? No. We belong to each other, she and I—We *belong.* God gave her to me. By a miracle, God gave her back to me. We—"

"You speak of the island as a 'hell,' " retorted Carson. "Yet just now you said something about a native girl who 'took pity on you.' Your relations with that girl—or with some other—or *others*—were they snowily platonic? Did you spend those four years in holy celibacy, mourning the loss of Madge? Did you?"

"I spent the four years mourning for Madge—as I should have mourned her forever if death had parted us in the natural way," Vane defended himself. "As to my morals—which had nothing to do with my heart or my memories—I lived as any other hot-blooded giant of my age would have lived under the same circumstances."

"Then you—"

"If Madge had died four years ago, would you have expected me to go unmated for the rest of my days? Would you have thought less of me for taking up what was left of life?"

"I—" began Carson, but Vane drove on:

"You say you went to Kentucky because you loved Madge. That was nearly five years ago. Do you mean to tell me that up to the past six months there was no woman of any kind in your life? If there was or if there was not is no concern of mine. And it is no concern of yours how I spent my own years of exile. I have come back here for my wife."

"For *my* wife," sharply corrected Philip. "For the wife that is worth fighting for to the death. You can't honestly expect me to—"

"She knew us both in the old days," cut in Dirck. "And she chose me. That is the answer. We both had our chance. And she chose *me*."

"Yes," assented Carson, wincing as at a whip-slash; "she chose you. Do you imagine I've forgotten that? Do you imagine it hasn't been before my mind, night and day, for five years? You were the first man in her life. 1 think that always gives a man a mysterious hold on a woman's heart and on her thoughts."

"It does," affirmed Dirck eagerly; "it— "

"With a man, of course, it's all different," continued Philip. "There are apt to be any number of women in his life, in one capacity or another, before he marries. As there were in yours. But, to a woman, the husband of her youth always has a subtle claim that no later man can efface. I grant all that."

"Then—"

"But Madge was a child—not yet twenty—when she married you," insisted Carson. "Between twenty and twenty-five a woman's nature develops and changes and matures more than a man's does between twenty and thirty. The man a girl would gladly have married at twenty, she would not look at when she is twenty-five. Any woman will tell you that. Well, you are the man Madge fell in love with as a girl of nineteen. *I* am the man her maturer mind and heart chose, out of all the world, five years later. She won't throw over the glorious present for the immature past. I know her too well to believe that."

"She is my wife," repeated Vane doggedly. "I won her, once, against you. And I am going to win her again."

"You won a half-developed, romantic girl," scoffed Phil. "The same powers that won her then would have no lure for a grown woman. Dirck, for heaven's sake, do the decent thing! If Madge knows you've come to life, it will make her hideously miserable. It will cloud all her future. She has mourned you; and she is healed at last from the wound of your death, and she is happy. Are you cur enough to torture her a second time?"

"'Torture her?'" echoed Dirck. "No! To make up to her for the torture she and I have gone through, I'm going to tell her the whole truth. I am going to tell her of my mate on the island. Yes; and of the other native women and kids, too. I'm going to make a clean breast of it. She is no fool. She'll understand that it was as though we had been separated by death—that I had no hope of seeing her again—and that my body lived on while my heart died. If I can forgive her for taking another husband, she can surely forgive me for—"

"We are jabbering like two fools," interrupted Carson. "Since you won't get out and leave her to her happiness, there is only one thing to do. The choice doesn't rest with us. It rests with Madge—and with nobody else. She will have to be the final arbiter, no matter how loudly we prate of our 'rights.' Nobody has any 'rights' over a woman nowadays except that woman herself. We both love Madge too well to want her to do anything but the one thing that will make her happiest. The choice is with her."

"Yes," sullenly agreed Vane; "the choice is with her. Let her choose. Where is she?"

Carson glanced at his watch.

"She told me this morning she was going to a matinee," he said, "and to tea, somewhere, afterward. She ought to be at home in half an hour or less, I should think. When she comes back, I'll put the case to her fairly and without bias, though I'd rather be shot than make her so wretched. And I'll 'phone you her decision at once, if you'll tell me where you are staying."

"I am staying *here*," returned Dirck imperturbably, "till Madge comes home."

"But—"

"I've waited four years for a sight of her," added Vane, "and I'm not going to leave here and sit smugly in some hotel till it pleases you to discuss the thing with her and to make your plea and then send me word. I'm going to stay here till—"

He broke off short in his speech as the sound of the closing front door of the apartment was followed by a swiftly soft tread down the hallway toward the room where they sat. The light footstep awoke memory-throbs in Dirck's brain and set his pulses to hammering.

Both men sprang to their feet and faced the curtains which shut off the room from view of the hall. Carson and Vane alike were ghastly pallid and aquiver. Their bodies were tensely set; their mouths were white gashes.

"Are you in there, Phil?" They heard a gay query, whose tone did unaccountable things to Dirck Vane's throat-muscles.

"Yes," Carson made grating reply; "come in!"

To Vane, he growled,

"Now let her choose!"

"Yes!" breathed Dirck chokingly. "Let her—choose!"

The curtains were swept apart and a woman entered the room.

The years had been kind to Madge. She was still, in outward aspect, the wonder-girl whom Dirck had won. There was a strength, a sign manual of experience, a depth of developed character in her flower-face which had not been there of old. But, apart from that, Dirck's first rapt glance could detect no change.

Straight up to Carson the woman hurried in glad greeting. Then she halted her wifely progress at sight of the room's other occupant.

For a second, she scanned Dirck's face—at first with hospitable curiosity, then with a blaze of recognition.

The two men stood motionless. Madge flashed a wide-eyed glance from one to the other.

"Dirck!" she babbled, her flower-face ash-gray and haggard, all the youth and buoyancy stricken from it in that one stark moment of shock. *"Dirck!"*

She swayed a little, and Vane took an instinctive step to steady her. But Carson moved between them. Mastering himself as best he could, Phil spoke. His voice was flat and shaky, and deep in his eyes smoldered a fire of pain. Yet he made shift to keep a semblance of his

wonted quiet manner.

"Madge," he said, "Dirck was washed ashore on a South Sea island. No ship touched there for more than four years. Then he was able to get passage home—to you. That is all."

Still Madge did not speak, nor did she seem to hear. After that first impulsive cry, she had stood stonelike, her eyes wide and staring as she gazed expressionlessly at the returned wanderer.

To a casual onlooker, Dirck Vane, just then, was marvelous good to gaze upon. Far more so than when his size and his graceful athletic strength had first caught Madge Barret's fancy. The four years of active outdoor life and perfect health had given to him an added depth of chest and semblance of physical power, had imparted to his carriage and bearing a certain Panlike freedom. Not even the stress of the moment could take from his countenance the glow of the open or mar his half-savage good looks.

By contrast, Philip Carson seemed almost puny, despite his well-knit body and his excellence of grooming. The pallor of cities was on Carson's cheek. The soft flesh of cities was blurring his compact physique. The life of cities and the brain-work of a successful man had put lines into his face—whereas the four-year existence of a healthy animal had left Dirck's visage as unlined as a child's.

The two men were about of an age. Yet Vane looked the younger by a decade. Dirck's hastily bought ready-made clothes draped his magnificent figure as they might have draped a Canova gladiator's. By comparison, Carson's suit—a costly artistic triumph of an inspired Fifth Avenue tailor—made its wearer look merely smug.

But Madge seemed to note nothing below the eyes of the man who had come back to her from the dead. Long and wildly she stared into those eyes. Then, as with a painful effort, she shifted her gaze to Carson. And again it was the eyes alone she looked into.

So, for a space, stood the three, wordless, fighting for calm. As Madge's wide eyes lost some of their turmoil of bewilderment, Carson spoke once more.

"Dirck was cast away on an island, in the South Seas," he said over again, to his wife. "It was not until after four years that he could get away. He took the first ship home—to you."

He seemed as one trying to teach a lesson to a stupid child. And this time, he saw, by Madge's eyes, that she understood. Vane, listening, gave mute credit to his rival for stating the case with such bald brevity and for abstaining from any details of the island life.

"We must face it, sweetheart," went on Phil, his strained voice softening. "I'd spare you from it if I could. But you must see I can't. It's got to be faced—and by you. The decision rests with you—and with you alone. Dirck and I have agreed on that. We—"

"Dirck!" panted the woman, finding words in a rush. "Dirck! You were drowned! All the men left on the ship were drowned! You were drowned, and—" She checked herself, as if realizing the absurdity of her babbled words. And again she turned to Carson, this time with her brow furrowed in utter perplexity. "What—what does it mean?" she murmured confusedly.

But Vane, watching, saw that the trance of complete stupor was slowly lifting. And, before Philip could answer her, he interposed.

"Dear, for years I've been looking forward to this—looking forward to it as a life-sufferer might look toward heaven. Haven't you anything to say to me, except—"

A swirl of dark red swept away the ashy pallor from Madge's face. And, with the color, came the tears. She took an uncertain step toward Dirck, hesitated, turned half-way toward Carson, then collapsed in the nearest chair, sobbing with the abandon of a little child.

Awkwardly, Philip Carson went over to her and stretched forth one hand to lay it on her heaving shoulder. Then, by main force, he checked himself. He was playing fair—although the effort drove beads of sweat to his forehead.

"Madge," said Vane, "Carson is right. It is up to you—and to you alone—to make the choice. I think we have reached the crisis in the storm when conventionality and morals and public opinion and even duty can be thrown overboard as excess luggage, and when you can let your heart do all the talking. It is up to you to choose—not from duty or from any other motive but your own inclination—to choose which of us you want for your husband. The other one will get out quietly, and with no fuss. I know I can vouch for that. Do you want me—or do you want Phil?"

"Wait!" intervened Carson, as the woman shuddered a little and buried her tear-streaked face deeper in her quivering hands. "Wait till to-morrow before you decide, Madge. We will both leave here—Vane and I. We will leave you to fight it out for yourself. You are too upset now to make calm decision on a point that involves all your future. You must have time to quiet down and to think it all out—alone—and to decide once and for all. It isn't fair to you, or to us, to let you decide now. Take the night to think it over. To-morrow afternoon, at three, Vane and I will come back here. Then, if you're ready, you can tell us what you have decided. If you aren't ready then, we will wait until you are. You're not to be hurried or influenced in any way. God knows," he broke off, "I'd save you the anguish of it all if I could! But nobody can go through this thing for you but yourself. Come, Dirck."

He moved toward the door, laying his hand imperatively on Vane's shoulder.

But Dirck shook off the clasp and went back to where the weeping woman cowered.

"One minute," he urged, waving Carson aside and bending over Madge. "Phil is behaving in this like a white man. And I can't do less than he's doing. While you're making up your mind, Madge—if you haven't already made it up—there's something you've got to take into consideration. On the island, down there, I had no hope of seeing you again. I was as a dead man in another world, but with the same smashingly vital body I had always had. You know enough of human nature by this time—you knew enough of *me*—to know a he man in such circumstances has mighty little in common with Saint Anthony or Galahad or any other of those ice-blooded old-timers. I—"

"Dirck," remonstrated Carson, as Madge lifted her face from her hands, "surely there's no need of going into all that now. Madge has had enough to endure for one day. Come!"

But Vane would not have it so. In the same urge of fair play toward his rival, he continued:

"There were women in my life down there. In my life—not in my heart. Women—and—and children. It is right for you to know. If you are the Madge I remember, I believe you will understand and forgive—

just as I understand and forgive your taking another husband, not only into your life but into your heart—after you lost me. We both have something to forget. Perhaps neither one has the right to cast stones at the other. If we begin again, you and I, it must be with a clean slate. That is all," Vane ended, forestalling an interruption from Madge. "I'm ready, Carson. We'll be back at three to-morrow."

Side by side, the two men left the room. Springing to her feet, Madge ran after them. But, at the curtained doorway, she halted. Panting, fighting back her hysteria, she stood there, clinging for support to the heavy curtains as the outer door of the apartment closed softly behind Vane and Carson.

There she stood, statuelike, immobile, expressionless, her heart and soul too much engrossed to permit of any outward show of the tumult seething within her.

From the instant she had entered the room and had beheld the two men, her decision had been made—had been irrevocably made. Through the shock and surge, that fact had been fixed, unshakable, in her mind. She knew where lay her love, her life, her future. Had not the men forced her to delay the expression of her verdict, she would have voiced it loudly, triumphantly, while they were still with her.

For better or for worse, she had seen, in a flash of revelation, that there was but one man on earth for her; and to that man she was ready to cleave forever. All the time and reflection imaginable would never be able to move her decision.

Yet Madge was not wholly sorry that they had insisted on giving her twenty hours to think it over. The time would be none too long for her to marshal her nerves and emotions to the calmness needful for facing the two men who loved her above all the world, and to one of whom she must lay waste the whole future. She was half glad, for the respite.

Dawn, next day, found Madge hollow-eyed from sleeplessness, yet with a great peace possessing her. Bravely she awaited the ordeal. With a joy that was all but pain, she looked forward to the giving of herself forever to the man of her choice—to proving to him that he and he alone was her lord and mate.

She went furtively to a chest of drawers in her own room. With a haste that may have hinted at guilt or may have been mere eagerness, she opened a lower drawer. Removing a shimmering top layer of tissue-paper, she peeped at a mass of queer, filmy little clothes neatly piled there. After which, she slammed shut the drawer and ran from the room.

The stroke of three brought Philip Carson to the apartment. Nervously, Phil glanced about him for his antagonist. Before he could speak, the Jap brought in to Madge a letter which had just been delivered by messenger.

Both Madge and Carson recognized on the envelope Dirck Vane's strong, loose handwriting. By tacit impulse, as the woman tore open the letter, she motioned Phil to look over it with her. Together, they read:

"No; I am not crazy; and I am not a yellow dog. Or perhaps I'm both. In any case, I am running away. And once more I am 'dead.' Only, this time, there will be no resurrection—on the hither side of the grave. I give you my word for that. I have just had a talk with my lawyer and wound up my affairs.

"It is hard to explain so that it will sound sane and logical. But I owe it to you to try. And I can do it best by giving the facts as briefly as possible in their order.

"I left you, last night, with every intent of coming back at three this afternoon to learn my fate. At the moment, that seemed the most important thing in the world to me. It was the thing I had been keyed up to for more than four years—the thing that had been an all-encompassing obsession to me from the instant I set eyes on Manchester's schooner till I stood face to face with you. It had blinded and deafened me to everything else.

"Then, as I left your apartment last evening, the reaction set in. I had found the goal. The verdict was 'past' me. There was nothing to do but to wait for it. The tension had snapped. I had eyes and ears and mind once more for what was going on around me. I felt like a man who has just come out of delirium. And I began to notice things.

"I left Carson, and I turned west, instinctively, toward Broadway.

I had no special objective—except to get something to eat and find a hotel room for the night. As I said, I was at liberty, for the first time, to notice what was going on around me. The first thing that struck me was the raspingly growling roar that is the voice of Manhattan. You New Yorkers grow so used to it you never hear it. But if you had been living four years on an island where silence rules supreme, that roar would be torture to your ear-drums and to your nerves—as, all at once, it was to mine.

"I wonder, too, if you know how New York smells,—how any big city smells? Probably you don't. City-dwellers don't. I never did till last night. Four years of clean sea and clean sand and clean jungle may have sharpened my nostrils. They probably have. Certainly they showed me the contrast between my 'cleaner, greener land,' and the mingled stench of gasoline and asphalt and stables and garbage and sachet and sweat and stale cooked food—and other things which go to make up the blended scent of Broadway.

"It fairly turned me ill—that and the horrible ceaseless roar of the city. And a queer wave of homesickness came rushing over me— homesickness for the island at that twilight hour, when the dusk would be all deep lavender and heliotrope, and crowded with stars such as you Northern people never see.

"And the ocean would be rolling sleepily along the white beach or crisping against the reef outside the lagoon, and some night-bird in the jungle would be starting its mate-song. And the girls would be weaving *leis* by the fire, and the babies would be calling little sleepy bits of nonsense to each other from their night-mats. And if I were out late in my boat, there would be soft dark eyes scanning the water for me, and I'd hear scraps of laughter or love-calls as my canoe slithered its prow into the beach-sand.

"Yes—that all came over me with a rush. It turned me dizzy. I couldn't believe it at first. But it was true.

"*I was homesick!*

"I tried to tell myself my terrible ordeal of exile was over and that I was among mine own people again, and that, next day, I'd be holding in my arms the woman I had crossed the world to find. (For I've never doubted what your verdict would be, whatever Phil may think, or whatever you may have made him think, or whatever you think

that you yourself think.)

"I conjured up all these thoughts. But it was no good. I was homesick. Wretchedly homesick. Homesick for the island I had so often prayed to be rescued from. Four years will do much—even in civilization. And in the South Seas, it can weld stronger chains than can a lifetime here.

"I started to cross Broadway. A filthy, gas-reeking taxi-cab spun past me, hitting me a glancing blow that bowled me over and sent me sprawling on my face in the gutter. (I could have rolled over and over, the full length of my island, without getting one-tenth as much dirt and offal on me as I got in that tumble against the Broadway curb.)

"Two kind strangers lifted me to my feet and dusted me off before the usual crowd could collect. I was grateful to them—until I found that one of the two Good Samaritans had got my watch and stick-pin. On the island, a man can leave all his worldly wealth piled up on the beach for a year, and then come back and find it intact. Down there, a helping hand comes from the stirring of a helping heart, not from a craving for graft.

"The taxi knockdown didn't do anything worse than bruise me. And neither of the Good Samaritans had had time to locate my cash. But both incidents rubbed in the homesickness a hundredfold. You people in cities don't even dream of your own perils; you are so used to them. On the island, if any creature should rush along the trails, upsetting or killing everything that gets in its way—as your swarms of taxis and other motor-cars do—the natives would band together and destroy it as a public menace to life and happiness. And a man who would rob an injured stranger would be hounded from every hut.

"I went into a restaurant to eat. The food was spiced and seasoned as the Lord never meant food to be. My long-cleansed palate told me some of it was putrid, and my four-year-normal stomach told me that more of it was as indigestible as carpet-tacks.

"Women in the restaurant were jabbering at the top of their lungs like a covey of jungle peacocks before a rain-storm. They were dressed in clothes that cramped them and made them misshapen, and in feathers and jewelry as silly as nose-rings. They were paint-smeared. Their eyebrows were shaved into silly half-moons. (In my day, women left the use of razors to men.)

"They were flattering fat men with jaundiced faces and bald heads and great swinging paunches. Flattering them, because such men can give them the jewels and cars that clean-limbed and level-eyed younger men can't afford to.

"And I thought of the island—where a man's strength and youth and virility count as wealth, and where paunchy old men are sneered at as lazy and gluttonous and useless, and are denied the right to wear the red flower behind the ear.

"To get my mind off such thoughts, I went to a musical comedy. If an island woman should display her shape to public view with the leering wantonness of the show-girls I saw there, or should dare to speak such lines as did some of the women principals in that show, she would be slit down the nose and driven from the village.

"Down there, women lead moral lives. If those lives are not in accord with Puritan morals, neither are they in accord with the

Broadway lure.

"It was the show, I think, more than the stuffy and rackety hotel room that clinched a resolution you may term insane—but which I know to be the sanest thing in my third-rate life. The thought of spending the rest of my days in such surroundings of noise and smell and lust and danger and artificial glitter—it was all too much for me.

"The island was calling me. Its call was growing stronger and stronger every hour. I could shut my eyes and see the fire-blue lagoon and the white beach and the waving palms. I could hear the joyous calling of the children—my children, strong and straight and clean—and the laughter of girls and the whisper of the wind in the jungle and the sob of the flood-tide on the reef. And it was all calling. Calling to me, who am, by rights, a part of it.

"I thought the thing out—there in the hotel room for whose nightly use I was paying enough to support an island family in luxury for a year. I forced myself to call up your face and to remember how I loved you. (I still love you. I shall always love you, my wife.)

"But it was no use. We had lived in a different world for four years—four of the most formative years of our lives. And I knew I could never hope to silence that fearfully luring call of the island, or to settle down to the false life I left behind me so long ago.

"My clothes—the boardlike yoke of a collar that gripped my throat, and the stiff shoes that tortured my free feet, and the clogging folds of useless cloth on legs and arms—fidgeted me till I could have torn them to shreds. And to think I would have to wear such things forever!

"Why go further into the matter? By this time, you understand. Or else you would not understand if I should write on for a century. In either case, it doesn't matter.

"I am running away!

"I am going to catch an afternoon train that will take me to San Francisco. The moment I get there, I am going to the water-front and charter a schooner to take me home.

"Yes—*home!* To the only home that can henceforth seem like anything but a prison to me. Luckily, I had jotted down the latitude and longitude of the island when Ford Manchester gave them to me. I did it then out of sheer sentimentality. But I thank God I happened to do it. For it is the key to home.

"And some morning, soon, with the dawn tide, I shall sail for the island. By the time this scribbled letter reaches you, I shall be well on my way West.

"You were happy with Carson before I came back from the dead. Be happy with him again. And forget the ne'er-do-well who butted momentarily into the smugness of your well-ordered hothouse life.

"Or, if ever you think of me, let it be as you thought before you knew I was still alive. Nature made me an animal. Four years of life according to nature scraped off my twenty-eight years of veneer. (It would do the same thing for more men than you may realize.)

"So, good-by. This time, for always. For the rest— Oh, it will be well with me in my Lotus Land! I'm going *home!*"

Albert Payson Terhune's 1883-84 journey through the Holy Land provided background for several of his works, including *Syria from the Saddle*, the Najib stories (published in the 1910s and 20s in Popular Magazine and collected as a book in 1925), and "The 'Tip' of the Rocket" in the present volume.

Photo courtesy of Sanctum Archives.

Appendix A

Publication information
for the stories
in this book

The Beat that Failed

Lippincott's Magazine, November 1900

The Seal of Silence

Lippincott's Magazine, January 1902
Front text:
Author of "Syria from the Saddle," "Columbia Stories," etc.

She and the Monster

Argosy, October 1908
Front text:
A thrilling fight that was won by an aim which went wide of the mark.

A Bridegroom's Dilemma

Argosy, September 1909
Front text:
A honeymoon advent in Paris that was marked by a frightful experience in connection with a trip to the bank for money.

A Jersey Knight Errant

Argosy, November 1910
Front text:
The Applause that Came Not After a Clever Ruse in Connection with the Chase After a Stray Peacock.
Edits: The period at the end of the following first line was changed to a colon:
Vanity slumped six points. I repeated dully.
"A peacock?"

The Watcher in the Hall

Top-Notch, July 1 1911
Front text:
What a world of human interest is the many-storied apartment house in a big town—New York, for example! It is the stage of this remarkable drama. While picturing with a truthful and entertaining touch the life of one of those huge

combination homes, the author unfolds a tale which, you will agree, is a decidedly live wire all the way.

(A COMPLETE NOVEL)

Note: The original story had two Chapter XIs. This error has been retained in this book.

Note: The correct chemical formula for sulfuric acid is H_2SO_4.

The Montclair Flurry

Top-Notch, January 15 1912

Front text:

New Jersey Tale of a Vanishing Art Treasure...

(A COMPLETE NOVEL)

Edits: The following sentence was punctuated thus:

"That man," declaimed Alstyne hoarsely, "is Walt Whitson?"

The question mark was changed to an exclamation mark (because one *never* "declaims" interrogatively).

The Girl Who Couldn't Go Wrong

Smart Set, July 1913

When Man Meets Man

Top-Notch, January 1, 1914

Front text:

Tale of the Northwest Mounted Police.

(COMPLETE IN THIS ISSUE)

Illustrator not credited, but opening-page illustration is initialed.

An Inside Scoop

Popular, August 10, 1914

Illustrator not credited.

An earlier version of this story appeared in Lippincott's, November 1900, under the title, The Beat that Failed. Authors would sometimes rework stories from earlier in their careers. Editors might have been aware of specific instances or not, and might have approved or not. Certainly, many pulp fiction editors reprinted earlier-run stories, sometimes identifying them as reprints, sometimes not.

The Editor, for better or worse, decided to include the two versions in the same volume.

The Tale of the Taxi-Meter

Green Book, January 1915

Illustrations by Charles Dean Cornwell.

Front text:

A SHORT STORY THAT MAY GIVE YOU A MENTAL JOLT
Author of "Whose Wife?" etc.

Original captions:

Page 179: The three—who had drunk just enough to make them obstinately jolly—were already sitting in a huddled row on the steps

181: She was tall, statuesquely full of figure, as dark as a Spaniard.

188: "Talk on," adjured Craddock. "It's refreshing to find a sweet bud of innocence, like yourself, in this wicked world. There, there! I didn't mean to get your back up by joking about it. And you know I'm interested."

The Man Who Went Wrong

Blue Book, May 1915

Spot illustration not credited.

Front text:

He began life as a white man and suddenly became a cur; and his wife—but read for yourself this vivid, dramatic and unusual story.

Author of "At $32 Per," "His Wife's Sister

Clarissa-Out-of-a-Book

Red Book, July 1915

Illustrated by J. H. Gardner-Soper

Front text:

A summer-time story, just as different from anything else Mr. Terhune has written as a story could be.

End text:

"In His Wife's Name," which is in some ways the best of the many excellent stories Mr. Terhune has written for The Red Book Magazine, will be in the August issue, on the news-stands July 23rd.

Original captions:

Pages 212-213: He stared dully. The girl with her wide, fearless blue eyes, and the cat with its sleepy yellow orbs, stared back at him.

223: "Up with your hands, young man. Up with 'em!"

Edits: The word "ginham" was changed to "gingham."

The Greater Radiance

Blue Book, September 1915

Illustrator not credited.

Front text:

Mr. Terhune has a peculiar knack of making something vitally new out of an old theme. This story of an artist and his wife and his model is one of this writer's best.

Author of "Whose Wife?" "A Post-marital Engagement," etc.

From the "Tip" of the Rocket

Adventure, October 1915

Illustrator not credited, but illustration is signed.

Front text:

Author of "The Treasure Jar."

The Welcher

Blue Book, May 1916

Front text:

He rescued her from starvation when he found her staring in at a restaurant window, and then—she proved a "welcher." . . . . One of Mr. Terhune's most impressive stories.

Author of "The Years of the Locust," "A Return to Youth—and Trouble," etc.

End text:

Another vivid story by Albert Payson Terhune will appear in an early issue of THE BLUE BOOK MAGAZINE.

The Songbird

Green Book, April 1917

Front text:

HER SINGING WAS A TRAGIC CACOPHONY—AND IT WAS ONLY AFTER HE HAD MARRIED HER THAT HE FOUND THIS OUT

The opening page title had an asterisk after it, referring to the following footnote at the bottom of the first column:

*"The 101st Man," by Albert Payson Terhune, was advertised last month for publication in this issue, but it has been found necessary to postpone publication of that story and to substitute "The Songbird" in its place.

The Rabbit Man

Red Book, May, 1917

Illustrated by Robert A. Graef

Original captions:

Page 299: "So you're cashier now, Mr. Dangerfield? I'm ever so glad! I hated old Hinkle. He was so stuffy and grouchy and—"

304-305: "You're a dear!" she cried in sudden fervor. Before the utterly dumfounded man could guess her intent, she had thrown both arms around his neck and kissed him on the mouth!

308: "H'm!" came a nasal growl from Brewster. "A very neat haul: the jewelry I'm holding for Mrs. Sutherland; your own jewelry; that block of bonds Tim Crowley is trading against; my mother's pearl necklace; and the three sheafs of bills for this week's pay-roll!"

309: "Well!" shrilled the woman in a gust of vicious fury, "what are you going to do? What are you going to do about it? Don't stand there snorting and sneering! What are you going to do? Send me to prison?" "Prison?" Brewster laughed drearily. "No. Why should I? I've no grudge against the prisons."

Caritas

Saturday Evening Post, December 15, 1917
Illustrations by Fanny Munsell
Original captions:
Page 322: "Not a Gentleman," She Corrected; "Just Well Bred. "He Falls in Love With a Factory Girl, and for Her Sake He Resolves to Reform"
329: But at First You Didn't Seem to be Much Interested in It. I Mean When I Told You the Story
332: "And Perhaps," the Girl Was Saying, "it May Help to Reform Someone. Is That Foolish? We Writers Have a Tremendous Responsibility, Haven't We?"

Pretty Baby

Green Book, August 1918
Illustration by Robert A. Graef
Original captions:
Page 340: "Oh, I do hate you!" she exclaimed. "I—" He cut short her invective by picking her up bodily, kissing her several times and setting her down again.
346-347: Peggy stared, wide-eyed. ...The girl was indisputably pretty; and she had a disgusting way of looking up, through veiled eyes, at Wade as if he were a demigod. To think any sane man should be fooled by such a trick!
350: "I don't want to be a monument of dry wisdom," pouted Peggy.

The Wildcat

Saturday Evening Post, October 19 1918
Illustrations by Clark Fay
Original captions:
Page 363: By Sunrise He Had Located the German Who Had Put Him on His Mettle Two Days Before.
365: So He Was Taken to the Captain, a Man Who Had Lived for Five Years in New York.
370: And at Last He Was Out, Under the Foggy Stars, With Excited Germans Firing in His General Direction and Loosing Off Star Shells.

Forsaking All Others

Blue Book, April 1919
Illustrator not credited, but illustration is signed (looks like "Gavin Hall").
Front text:

SECRET SERVICE—there's a thrill in the name! And there are a dozen keen thrills in this dramatic story of a daring venture.

The Dented Halo
Green Book, April 1919
Illustrations by William Oberhardt
Original captions:
Page 393: Robing herself in the white evening frock, Aro1ine gloated on her reflection in the glass.
396: "And you may bring me, first of all, three nice dry martini cocktails, please."
398: "Oh, Dick!" she exclaimed. "Oh, Dick, my teeth are so large!"
End text:
"Tidy Emotions," another of Mr. Terhune's dramatic stories, will appear in an early issue.

Branded
Cosmopolitan, July 1919
Illustrated by H. R. Ballinger
Front text:
If you can guess the ending of Mr. Terhune's fascinating story before you can come to it, you are cleverer and keener than Jim Ross—and he was clever and keen enough to be a successful lawyer.
Original captions:
Page 413: Presently he broke upon the lively chatter by thrusting out a thick finger and tapping with disapproval one of the charted designs. "Real Japanese art, hey?" he scoffed jarringly. "That pattern, for one, is startlingly new and Oriental! A heart transfixed by an arrow! Was Saint Valentine a Samurai?"
416: Jim leaned perilously forward and strained his ears! He heard the words: "Italian garden," in Barry's rumbling voice.
418: Cahill was murmuring to the woman in his arms, and was seeking to soothe her hysterical grief
422: A moment afterward, Helen Ward entered. Glowing with health and youth, she gave the impression of a sweep of mountain air in a hot room.
Edits: The word umprotesting was changed to unprotesting.

A Citizen of the Ice
Saturday Evening Post, August 23 1919
Captions accompany photos in this book.

The Laugh
Saturday Evening Post, August 23 1919
Illustrated by Harvey Dunn

Original captions:

Page 447: Scaasi's Wrath Changed to a Deadly Calm. In He bored, Again and Then Again.

452: There He Lay While Vedder Rattled Off the Count of Ten and a Mutter Ran Through the Onlookers

463: "This Isn't a Knock-Out! He Just Lay Down. A Man Can't Help Being Yellow if He's Built That Way"

The Lotus-Eater

Part I: Cosmopolitan, September and October, 1919

Illustrated by H. R. Balinger

September installment:

Front text:

YOU know the story of Enoch Arden. Do you think the man of 1919 would do as Enoch did? Apply the question to the men of your acquaintance as you follow the story in this gripping short novel.

THE author of this story is one of the "writing Terhunes." He is the son of Edward Payson Terhune and Marion Harland, a brother of Virginia Terhune Van de Water and Christine Terhune Herrick. Stories as vital and heart-touching as this are his specialty. They will appear frequently in Cosmopolitan.

Original captions:

Pages 466-467: "Dear heart," she was saying, oblivious of those around her, "is it true that there is room for only the women and the babies in those boats?"

472: She was disappointed in his lack of loyalty to his chum's memory. Philip made quiet answer: "The living have some rights, too, dear girl, as well as the dead"

477: She clasped his fingers the tighter and put her free hand on his shoulder once more. Gently she drew him toward the trail. Apathetic and dazed, he suffered himself to be led

479: The memory of Madge was still uncomfortably poignant in his heart

End text:

Dirck is going home—to find his wife married to another man. What will happen then? Mr. Terhune tells in **October Cosmopolitan.**

October installment:

Front text: This is the story of a modern Enoch Arden.

Dirck Vane and his bride were on the happiest of happy honeymoons when their ship was wrecked on the South Seas. The bride was rescued, but Vane was given up for lost. She returned to New York and, after the edge of her sufferings wore off, married Philip Carson, a former suitor and friend of Vane's. The newly married couple were extremely happy—until in walked Vane.

This is the situation presented by Mr. Terhune in the first part of this story last month. This month, he presents the solution as it worked out in this case.

Is that the way it would have worked out with any three people you know?

Original captions:

Page 489: "Yes!" breathed Dirck chokingly. "Let her—choose!" The curtains were swept apart and a woman entered the room. The years had been kind to Madge. She was still, in outward aspect, the wonder-girl whom Dirck had won

492-493: "That is all," Vane ended, forestalling an interruption from Madge. "I'm ready, Carson. We'll be back at three to-morrow." Side by side, the two men left the room.

496: "I couldn't believe it at first. But it was true. *I was homesick!*"

Edits: The word "furture" was corrected to be "future."

The word "envelop" near the end was corrected to be "envelope."

General Notes

The contraction **won't** in several stories was spelled without an apostrophe. This seems to have been the convention of the time, not limited to one magazine title.

The word **ain't** was also used without an apostrophe (very odd, as a word like sha'n't was used with both).

The apostrophe was inserted in both, for this book.

In the source material, the opening line of a new chapter often starts with a drop cap. When that first line is dialogue, many magazines also dropped the opening quotation mark. The Publisher simply does not like that, so in this book, such lines start with an opening quotation mark.

Several longer stories were broken up into chapters, headed by Roman numerals. For at least one, the opening was not headed by a Roman numeral I in the source, so it was not included here.

Appendix B

Terhune Letters

The following letters were purchased at auction, at the Windy City Pulp and Paper show in 2005.

"Davis" was Robert H. Davis, an editor Terhune worked with for many years.

> "Sunnybank"
> Pompton Lakes
> New Jersey
> July 2 6
> 191_
>
> Dear Davis;
>
> Mr. W. H. Wright, editor of "The Smart Set," sent for me today, to order a series of "Raegan" stories for that Magazine.
>
> I told him I had just sold you one Raegan story ("When the Gate Was Left Open"). He wants to get it for his series, and wants me to ask if you will sell it back to him, or to me; for the price you paid; — $35. He says he'd like to have all the "Raegan" stories for "Smart Set" and not have the character in any other magazine during the series' run.
>
> I have already written two Raegan stories [The first one has been printed] for him and am beginning a third.
>
> Drop me a line, if you have time, letting me know whether the foregoing proposition suits you or not.
>
> Sincerely
>
> Terhune

August
Fourteenth
1923

ALBERT PAYSON TERHUNE
SUNNYBANK
POMPTON LAKES
NEW JERSEY

Dear Davis;

In case you don't want to wade clear through the enclosed letter (which please let me have again), its gist is that there is a small offer for the picture rights to my Argosy serial,"In The Name Of The King"; and a conjecture that you people may be approached in such a way as to part with those rights for a moderate sum.

The letter has been answered with a blanket exhortation to go to it.

Now I am a simple soul,as you may recall. I promised my dying greatgrandmother two things as I bade her farewell. One was that I'd never weld women and booze into the same nocturnal exploit. The other was that I would try to become a wholesale money collector.

In view of the second promise I am unleashing the tribe of Weir upon you. I hope they can soften your heart to the extent of letting me get at least the price of a few cases of Scotch out of the wreckage of my serial.

Some day when you are busy I shall blow into your office. I haven't a damn thing to sell you; and,if I had,it probably wouldn't be worth your buying. But I'd like to sit around for half an hour and waste your time and listen to you talk; for you talk rather brilliantly when one isn't working for you. Also it will be fun to count the number of phone calls in that half hour.

As ever,

The Flood Fighters

A novel first serialized in Country
Gentleman magazine in 1920,
published under a pseudonym and
not reprinted until now.
By Albert Payson Terhune

In Treason's Track

A novel of the
American Revolution
by Albert Payson Terhune

The Woman Tamers

Six essays on
heart-breakers of history
by Albert Payson Terhune

The White Way

A tale of New York's Broadway
by Albert Payson Terhune

An Albert Payson Terhune Reader III

26 stories by Terhune from pulp magazines of the 1910s and 20s,
featuring all original illustrations
by Albert Payson Terhune

Cheddar Cheese
a novel by Francis Lynde

Books are available from the major bookstores online,
as print books and as e-books.

Human Interest Stuff
a comic book adaptation
of an Albert Payson Terhune story
written by Rodney Schroeter
illustrated by William Messner-Loebs
published by the
Wisconsin Writers Association

Contact the Silver Creek Press for details